Support a neighborhood Author!

I grew up just down the street on Harvey Ave and this is my debut novel!

Seeking reviews on Amazon for anyone willing.

Cheers!

# SOMEWHERE

# Somewhere

## RYAN FREERKSEN

Copyright © 2024 Ryan Freerksen
Illustrations and Cover Art Copyright © 2024 Ryan Freerksen

All rights reserved.

No part of this publication may be reproduced, distributed, or transmitted in any form or by any means, including photocopying, recording, or other electronic or mechanical methods, without the prior written permission of the publisher, except as permitted by U.S. copyright law.

ISBN: 979-8-9903807-0-7 (Paperback)
ISBN: 979-8-9903807-1-4 (Hardcover)
ISBN: 979-8-9903807-2-1 (eBook)

Library of Congress Control Number: 2024906834

The story, all names, characters, and incidents portrayed in this production are fictitious. No identification with actual persons (living or deceased), places, buildings, and products is intended or should be inferred.

Book Cover Art by Anna Freerksen
Illustrations by Ryan Freerksen

First published in Bolingbrook, Illinois in 2024

Dedicated to the worst boss I have ever had (you know who you are) for giving me such intentionally menial tasks that my mind wandered and these characters were born.

To my sister, for being the first to read my manuscript and giving me endless, often hilarious feedback, and to my wife, for believing I could do this long before I believed it myself.

# CONTENTS

CHEERS FROM BEYOND – 1
PROLOGUE: SOMEWHERE, 1936 – 2
CHAPTER 1: A CAPTAIN AND HIS SHIP – 10
CHAPTER 2: THE BIOLOGY PROFESSOR – 15
CHAPTER 3: BROTHERS – 21
CHAPTER 4: FIVE HOURS – 27
CHAPTER 5: AT THE DOCKS – 31
CHAPTER 6: SOMEONE ELSE'S LIFE – 38
CHAPTER 7: ANOMALY – 48
CHAPTER 8: MORA – 58
CHAPTER 9: WELCOME TO THE KINGDOM – 71
CHAPTER 10: THE ILLUSION – 82
CHAPTER 11: SWALLOWED UP BY THE WORLD – 87
CHAPTER 12: UNTAPPED, UNTAMED FURY – 96
CHAPTER 13: DEFIANCE – 101
CHAPTER 14: CONSEQUENCES – 111
CHAPTER 15: THE LAWS OF THE LAND – 117
CHAPTER 16: MIDNIGHT IN THE TEMPLE – 126
CHAPTER 17: STACKING THE DECK – 140
CHAPTER 18: AN UNLIKELY ALLY – 153
CHAPTER 19: THE HILLSIDE – 158
CHAPTER 20: MYSTERIES AND LEGENDS – 166
CHAPTER 21: HISTORY LESSON – 171
CHAPTER 22: THE TEMPLE GATES – 177
CHAPTER 23: ASSAULT ON KING MORA – 182
CHAPTER 24: ASCEND – 201
CHAPTER 25: ORIGINS OF A MONSTER – 214
CHAPTER 26: THE PERILS OF PASSION – 224
CHAPTER 27: THE LONG ROAD BACK – 230
CHAPTER 28: POWER – 234
CHAPTER 29: THE EYES OF THE PEOPLE – 240
CHAPTER 30: THE SCATTERED PIECES OF A PUZZLE – 251

# CONTENTS

CHAPTER 31: QUALITY OF A LEADER – 257
CHAPTER 32: MAY I PRESENT YOUR KING – 261
CHAPTER 33: A CHALLENGE – 272
CHAPTER 34: TRAITOR – 281
CHAPTER 35: SECRET MEETING – 290
CHAPTER 36: IN THE SHADOWS – 296
CHAPTER 37: AMONG THE PEOPLE – 306
CHAPTER 38: PAST LIVES – 313
CHAPTER 39: FRACTURE – 320
CHAPTER 40: TIMES OF CHANGE – 332
CHAPTER 41: SOMETHING TO FIGHT FOR – 340
CHAPTER 42: FUTURE AND PAST – 344
CHAPTER 43: BORDER SKIRMISH – 350
CHAPTER 44: THE LIFE AND DEATH OF HENRY FINE – 357
CHAPTER 45: THE MAN WHO SHOULD NOT BE – 362
CHAPTER 46: THE WEST – 369
CHAPTER 47: THE WINDOW – 379
CHAPTER 48: FLIGHT FROM THE TEMPLE – 394
CHAPTER 49: THE PRISONER – 406
CHAPTER 50: MOVES AND COUNTERMOVES – 413
CHAPTER 51: WESTERN DOMINION – 422
CHAPTER 52: THE DOOR – 433
CHAPTER 53: THE KING OF THE PAST – 446
CHAPTER 54: THE NEUTRAL TERRITORY – 459
CHAPTER 55: THIS IS HISTORY – 474
CHAPTER 56: STREETS OF RED – 482
CHAPTER 57: ALEC – 503
CHAPTER 58: CYRUS – 505
CHAPTER 59: SUNDOWN – 507
CHAPTER 60: REBIRTH – 523

*"Every story ever written down is biased. The truth is twisted and warped by the writer. Not always intentionally, to be certain, but it is an inescapable truth. When a person sits down to write a story, be it a fiction, a historical account, or a journal entry, make no mistake, it is from the point of view of the writer. And point of view is ninety percent of a story. This is especially dangerous in historical writings, as the reader often does not realize that the story is biased. While facts may be presented exactly as they occurred, intention is lost. Or perhaps it is more accurate to say only one side's intentions are presented. Allow me to give an example in the form of a tale: A father and his son are trekking through a forest. The father loves his son and would do anything to protect him. The pair is set upon by a hungry lion. It bears down on the boy, who shrieks and clings to his father's leg for protection. The father summons all of his strength and takes on the vicious creature, miraculously landing a killing blow to its head with a stone. In this tale the lion is the antagonist and the hero prevailed by protecting his son. Allow me to tell one more tale: A mother lion lies with her cubs in the forest. She loves her cubs and would do anything to protect them. She feels the vibration of approaching footsteps and her cubs panic. They cry and cower in fear, looking wide-eyed to their mother for protection. The mother lion summons all of her strength and, baring her teeth, lunges out of hiding to meet their attacker. Same story, different point of view. Point of view is ninety percent of a story. I am pressing on this point because if my journals are ever recovered, they will tell a story, and I believe it is a story worth telling. True to the point that I have been incessantly making, this story will be from a certain point of view... but it will not be <u>my</u> point of view. It is clear to me that I will die here. My greatest hope, without much faith, is that my words will somehow make it back one day. I am a historian, but I do not want to go down in history as the spinner of a false yarn, especially one as important as this. There is truth within my endless pages, but also monstrous bias. I implore you to keep that in mind as you read.*
*Cheers from beyond... "*

Entry from the Journal of Dr. Henry Fine
Undated

# PROLOGUE

**Somewhere, 1936**

Lightning tore across the sky in a burning, vibrant crackle that briefly illuminated the mismatched, rustic homes of a small town before the heavy, drenching sheets of rain reclaimed the street from view. The gale had become a roaring inferno of noise, hammering against the thatched roof of Celia's small, cramped lodging that she had lived in her entire life. A newcomer may have worried about the integrity of the structure, especially as a gust of wind pummeled its side with renewed vigor, but things were built to last in Westtown.

As water began to pool at her feet in the open doorway, Celia decided she could delay no more and would have to make a run for it, storm or no. She tightened her heavy, woven hood around her head, tucked her chin low and sprinted out into the rain, wrenching the door shut behind her as she went. She ran down the cobbled stone road, her splashing boot falls casting damp echoes around the narrow corridor. The incessant downpour thrummed off her cloak as she turned down one windy street after another, uncomfortably aware that eyes were likely watching her from behind the dimly lit slits in the windows of every home she passed. Celia herself was welcome to go where she pleased in this town, but the same could not be said for one of the people she was heading to meet, at least not in the strictest sense. There likely wouldn't be any trouble, but one never knew.

As she rounded another corner, a sharp noise carried on the wind caused Celia to slow her run, inclining her head towards the sky to listen. She told herself it may have been her imagination, and even started to believe it, when it rang out again. It was unmistakable this time and came from the next street over; a scream. This was followed by panicked voices, some sort of a struggle, and then a bone-chilling screech. The screech would have registered as quite foreign to an outsider, and indeed it had rendered Celia immobile with fear, but she was no outsider and the noise was all too familiar. One or both of the King's loyal creatures were on the prowl, and it seemed they had just claimed a victim.

Celia gathered her courage, forcefully reminding herself that the creatures did not attack without cause and continued forward. Choosing to keep clear of the main thoroughfare, she ducked through an alleyway and picked up her pace, keen to put as much distance between herself and the scream as possible. When she emerged on the next street down, however, her heart caught in her chest and she paused once again. Rainwater was draining towards her through the gaps in the mismatched flagstones of the road, but up ahead a darkness was tinting the flow. It was quite colorless in the oppressive night air, appearing black and haunting as it trickled, but there was no doubt in Celia's mind that its true color was crimson. She apprehensively allowed her gaze to track ahead until her eyes found what she knew they would, a body. It was a man, lying on his side in the middle of the walkway, dark blood pooled around him. She could not see what types of wounds he had sustained, but she could guess.

Celia approached him slowly, avoiding his unseeing gaze as it stared blankly at the opposite wall. She breathed a silent sigh of relief upon confirmation that she did not recognize the man. It felt wrong to simply leave him where he had fallen, but she had lingered too long already, and there was nothing that could be done for him. She stepped cautiously around his crumpled form, walked several paces, then broke into a run. It was against her better judgement and every ounce of her logical brain warned her against it, but it felt entirely out of her control. She almost thought she could hear footsteps chasing after her but she didn't dare look back. She whipped around another corner, then another, and another until the familiar heavy oak door finally swam into view. She reached out to the worn, copper handle and heaved it open, stepping finally out of the rain and into the dank, dimly lit room.

    Suddenly bathed in the warm glow of torchlight, she winced slightly and ran her hands over her sopping wet face, flicking droplets of water onto the weathered floor. Celia was a young woman in her mid-thirties; her dark, shoulder-length hair clinging to her neck in the rain. She was quite pretty, although there was something in her eyes that only comes from having seen too much. That tired, slightly worn look was a trait shared by most who lived in this town.

    The tavern was small with multiple torches lining the walls, each splashing its warm glow to a small area and leaving the rest of the room in spindly cast shadows. It wasn't difficult to spot her two friends; they were the only patrons in the place apart from Horace, who was passed out in his usual spot. Celia made her way to her friends at a worn, knobby table in the far corner. They both glanced up as way of greeting, Garen giving her a forced smile, the sort that never reached his eyes. They met here the same time each week, making pleasantries rather unnecessary.

    "You alright?" Garen asked.

    "Nothing a drink can't fix," replied Celia.

    Tytus pushed a drink towards her, barely looking up from his own. She had a passing thought of telling them about the body she had encountered in the road, but decided against it. They would only say that she should be used to it by now, but it was the sort of thing she would never get used to. Garen must have noticed the insincerity in her voice, however, because he reached out and placed his hand gently over hers, inadvertently preventing her from seizing her drink.

    "I know things seem bad right now, but they've been bad before. Our people have always made it through."

Celia pulled her hand away and brought her drink to her lips, then pausing. She replied, "But things are worse than they've ever been, do you disagree?"

Garen considered this a moment before answering, "Kinda."

Tytus, appearing to awake from his stupor, chimed in, saying, "The King thinks we're on the right track. We just have to stay the course."

"*Your* king, not *the* King," answered Garen. "That madman is not my king."

Tytus offered his agreement with a slight nod of his head, but it was more of a non-committal wobble. Celia knew it was a difficult topic for him. He served as one of the temple guards so was privy to more of the goings on of the King. Their previous leader had ruled with the same iron fist, and Tytus had served him just as loyally. But that was before the Kingdom was split in half.

Not content with letting the conversation die, Garen pushed, "All I'm saying is that *my* king has shown there is a different way of doing things, I don't understand why your people can't grasp that."

Unable to ignore the conversation any longer, Tytus responded, "It's not that simple Garen. Yes there's a different way of doing things and I'm not here to say which is right, but splitting the Kingdom in half? That's never been done in our documented history and it sets a dangerous precedent." Garen started to jump in but Tytus talked over him, "And if you want proof that it solves nothing, just look at how arbitrary the kingdom borders have been drawn. It's nothing more than petty disagreements between the two kings."

Celia narrowed her eyes slightly. There was something different in the way Tytus argued for his new king. He had always been a loyal soldier, but there was a new brand of fervor that flavored his resolve. Was it true belief?

"These aren't petty disagreements though," Celia insisted, slightly worried to hear his reply. "Tytus, you and I manage okay here but not everyone does. Garen's right, his king fights for his people, ours does not."

Tytus shook his head, "I think their interests are more aligned than you want to admit. Think about it, who is it that really benefits from splitting the Kingdom?"

"Oh come on, they're complete opposites," Celia scoffed. "Believe me, I wish our new kings could find a middle ground, I know it's the people who end up suffering. All I can say is it's hard to find middle ground when you have nothing in common."

"Nothing in common?" Tytus looked surprised, then understanding washed over his prematurely lined face. "Have you not heard the rumors?"

Celia glanced sideways at Garen, who responded, "I've heard a lot of rumors about the kings, that doesn't mean..."

Tytus cut him off, "Believe me, this one's true."

Garen thought about this a moment, then shook his head, saying, "Incredible."

Tytus shrugged and lifted his drink, "Power can change people. It can bring out the best in someone...it can bring out the worst in them...it shows who a person really is."

Garen locked eyes with Celia across the table, making the slightest of eye rolls. "Poetic," he said dryly.

Tytus looked up from his drink again, realizing that his lofty psychoanalysis was not being taken seriously. A smile broke across his face and he leaned back in his chair. "Hey, it's for better minds than ours to sort out. Until real change comes, here we are." Raising his mug into the air he smiled, and in a sarcastic, mock tone said, "To the Kingdom."

At that moment, the door to the tavern slammed open, spraying rainwater across the stone floor. They all looked with alarm at the entryway, expecting perhaps one of the locals who had drunk too much. Celia's breath caught in her throat when she saw the unmistakable silhouette of an officer of the King. She instantly put her hands flat on the table and looked down intently at the drink in front of her. Tytus and Garen had already done the same. The tavern had gone entirely silent save the howling wind and pummeling rain outside the open door.

From the entryway came a female voice, "Well don't let me break up the fun," it sneered.

Celia tried to control her breathing while staring down at the table. She had to stay calm, and say nothing if possible.

"My friends and I were just in the area," came the voice again, and then Celia heard it; the soft clicking of talons on stone. Her heart began to pound in her chest, and she heard a familiar cackling hiss.

She could hear the woman start walking slowly into the tavern, running her hand along the empty tables as she went. "We simply thought we'd stop in for a drink, especially when we heard one of our friends from the East was in town." Celia could see Garen's hands tense up on the table across from her. She squeezed her eyes closed, trying to calm herself down.

It sounded like the woman had reached Horace's table, who she highly doubted had regained consciousness. Celia opened her eyes and dared a sideways glance in the direction of the woman. She was indeed at Horace's table, with her head tilted to the side, studying Horace's unconscious, drooling face. Celia was squinting at the back of the woman's head, hoping for a better look at her when a scaly, talon-tipped foot stepped down heavily on the tavern floor right beside her chair. Celia bowed her head again quickly and slammed her eyes shut; she could hear the rattling, hissing breath a foot away from her neck.

"It's just curious," the woman said as she approached their table, "with *everything* you have in your Kingdom, that you would need to come west for a drink."

Celia could feel wiry, quill-like feathers brush against her cheek, and hear the soft, crackling inhale as it smelled her. She couldn't move. She was at once too terrified to move and terrified she would move inadvertently and alarm the creature.

The woman had reached their table. She pulled the fourth, unoccupied chair out and sat down between Celia and Garen. "Don't mind if I join, do you?"

"I just came for a drink," Garen mumbled softly.

"Of course, of course," the woman said in a false, overly understanding tone. "The King welcomes visitors. But you have to understand not everyone who crosses our boarders is just here for our ale."

Horace made a grunting sound from the other side of the tavern and Celia could hear the clacking footsteps leave her side and move off in his direction. She allowed herself a deep breath but did not take her eyes off her mug on the table.

"So is it the company?" the woman questioned. Celia felt the woman's fingertips brush against her cheek but didn't dare look up. "Are our people just that much more charming than yours? She is a pretty one, I'll give you that."

Garen finally spoke up again, "I'll leave... if that's what you want. I can head back."

"Not without taking something with you first," the woman responded quickly. "We have something we'd like you to bring to your king."

"I don't know the King," Garen replied.

"This will be your icebreaker then. You see, not everyone who comes from your kingdom is here for the drinks and the company. Did you know your king sent a traitor across our boarders?"

"I... I did not."

Celia jumped as the woman slammed something down in the middle of the table with a loud thud. She could hear an alarmed hiss from across the room.

"Finish your drinks," the woman said, "take your time, you are welcome here. But when you leave, you will take this with you, and present it to your king *personally*."

"Do you have a message you want me to relay," Garen asked, his voice sounding a little stronger now.

The woman placed her hand on the object in the center of the table, "This is the message."

Celia allowed her eyes to drift up from her mug and saw a small canvas package tied with a makeshift bow made of rope. A shiver ran up her spine when she saw a small amount of deep brownish-red blood beginning to soak through one end of the fabric.

The woman stood up from their table. "Enjoy your drinks," she said, and Celia felt her hand glide along her shoulder, "It's a beautiful evening."

With that she turned, and her footsteps echoed through the damp tavern as she moved towards the door and out into the still pounding rain outside. Celia could hear the clicking of talons run to catch up with her, followed by the heavy wooden door slamming closed, and then silence.

Celia finally looked up from the table, slowly at first, and scanned the room. Other than the wet footprints covering the floor and the water gathered around the door, it was as if nothing had happened. Horace still slept at his table, the tavern owner had gone back to cleaning behind the bar, and the rain outside continued to pour. Celia glanced over at Garen, trying with some difficulty to avoid looking at the bloody canvas package on the table, then at Tytus, who had been silent since his interrupted toast.

Garen looked back at her with a gentle nod, his eyes saying clearly what they were all thinking; they should be used to this by now. He picked up his mug, raised it into the air, and with a defeated shake of his head, said dryly, "To the Kingdom."

# CHAPTER ONE

## A CAPTAIN AND HIS SHIP

### Atlantic Ocean off the Coast of New York, 1935

The sun beat down harshly onto the bald head of Captain Robert Froescher. Angry red splotches were beginning to form from prolonged exposure, but he preferred it out here to in his cabin. The sense of freedom he felt standing in the warm breeze while gazing out over the endless blue horizon was something he could never quite replicate while on land. He would begin to feel stir-crazy whenever he was between trips and longed to get back out on the ocean. Robert Froescher was an immense man with an equally immense moustache; stubble lining his cheeks all the way down his neck. He had a disheveled, slightly unkempt appearance, but out here on the water with his ship sprawling out in front of him, he felt like a king. And indeed he enjoyed a deep and loyal respect from his crew, a contrast to his status on land where he blended in with the rest of the captains who shipped cargo between Europe and New York.

Robert was happy to have New York behind him for now, he never enjoyed his time there. He supposed it was just like any other city, but he found it especially dirty and offensive. He spent most of his time near port when he was between trips, and the loud bustling docks and strange smells would wear on him. The atmosphere never used to bother him so much, but as he settled into middle-age, he found that he'd largely lost his appetite for city life. Not to say that his shipping vessel was immaculate by any means. The decks were cluttered, the crew was noisy, white clusters of salt buildup coated almost everything, and yet it was home to Robert.

A gull screeched loudly overhead and brought Robert back to the present. He looked up at the bird and watched it fighting with another gull over a fish. The two twisted and rolled through the air, chattering and snapping at each other, before landing on a nearby rock formation stabbing vertically from the water. Now that he noticed it, there were actually several rocks approaching the right side of the ship. They would pass with plenty of clearance, but it was unusual to find that sort of thing this far out. Robert pulled his weathered, yellowing compass from his pocket and glanced down at it. This was more habit than anything else; the crew had noted that he often studied his compass without reason. Perhaps it was a nervous tick. Either way, they were still headed due east. Robert scanned the horizon, looking for a small land mass that might explain the rocks. There was nothing as far as the eye could see. Robert shrugged; the rocks were passing the right side of the ship now, so in a matter of minutes they'd be long past.

Robert leaned back heavily on the rusted railing again and took a deep breath of the Atlantic salt air. He often found himself in this very spot, and sometimes the occasional crew member would join him. He glanced hopefully behind himself to see if anyone was approaching, but there was no one. Sometimes he did crave the quiet time alone with his thoughts, but at this particular moment he wouldn't turn down some company. It was approaching midday, maybe he would make his way down to the main deck. Robert pushed himself upright from the railing and stretched his back with a grunt. Just then a vibrating shutter reverberated through the metal floor and forced him to grip the railing again to steady himself.

It was over as quickly as it had started, but he had never felt anything like that on his ship before; or any ship for that matter. He turned quickly to head below and ascertain what had happened when an even more forceful shutter caused him to lose his footing entirely and fall to his knees. A deep, extremely loud groaning came from the depths of the ship. This time the vibrations did not cease and the noise was becoming deafening. Robert clutched the railing tightly and with significant effort wrenched himself off the floor. His knees screamed in pain but he planted his feet firmly and managed to get back to a standing position. He looked around himself in all directions, searching for other objects he could use for balance to get himself down below. He reached into his pocket and clutched his compass again with one hand. What could cause this? He knew they couldn't have hit something because he would have felt the impact. It had to be something mechanical with the ship.

Robert made a decisive choice and released his hold on the railing, propelling himself towards some metal piping near the stairs that led to the main deck. He wobbled unsteadily and outstretched his hand towards the pipe, still ten feet from him. Unable to control his trajectory at this point he threw himself forward; seven feet to go. Five feet. With his hand inches from the pipe, Robert began to close his fingers when the entire ship lurched violently to the side, slamming him shoulder first onto the metal floor. He began to slide backwards towards the rear of the ship, scrambling in vain to find any object to grip with his outstretched hands. He smashed to a halt in a crumpled heap, stopped by the wall behind him. It was only after he had stopped moving that he realized the entire ship was being pulled backwards and to the right. The metal frame was screeching under the pressure and the drag from the back of the ship was causing the water beneath to roil and crash around the sides. Robert could feel an intense pain around his teeth that extended up into his sinuses and behind his eyes. It was as if some invisible force were trying to pull his face out through the back of his head. He howled in pain as the pressure intensified, certain that his head was going to explode. And then with an ear-splitting crunch, an impact on the rear side of the ship brought it to a sudden halt. The pull from behind his eyes did not stop, however, and he was being pressed up against the rear wall by something. The entire ship was making the most horrible sounds of groaning and shrieking metal and Robert could see in front of him the metal railings he had been leaning on before were beginning to actually bend. The tops began to twist inwards creating a surreal, dizzying optical illusion. He closed his eyes tight and snatched his compass from the floor next to him, certain this was the end. His mind raced as he thought of everything he wished he could have done in life, but dying aboard his ship out on the ocean was how he always wanted to go. He only wished he could have had someone with him. He didn't think anyone deserved to die alone.

Although was this the end? He felt like his mind was beginning to clear a bit. In fact, the pain in his head was beginning to lessen as well. He opened his eyes and saw that the railings, although now warped and twisted like an abstract painting, had stopped bending. The grinding metal sounds all around the ship were beginning to lessen and he could hear the panicked yells of the crew from below. Robert cautiously leaned forward away from the wall and found that the intense pull towards it had lessened greatly. His head was left with a dull pain and his gums were throbbing, but whatever had happened seemed to have passed. He looked down at his hand, pale white from clutching the compass so tightly. He relinquished his grip and let it fall to the floor next to him. He was happy to see the glass was still intact; it hadn't broken. Or had it? His compass now showed north as being directly behind him. He had to get his bearings; the ship must have gotten turned around during the turmoil. For the second time Robert heaved himself to his feet, this time feeling bruises beginning to form along his side, and looked out at the rest of the ship and the ocean beyond. The ship was tilted to the side a bit and had smashed into one of the rock outcroppings he had seen them pass. Every railing and outer wall he could see was hideously bent towards the back of the ship; but the ship itself was still facing roughly the same direction they had been headed, east, which meant north was off to their left, certainly not behind them.

Robert stumbled towards his captain's quarters, still dizzy from the headache that had now settled behind his eyes. He realized he probably shouldn't be moving around just yet after the beating he took, but he ignored the throbbing pains and continued. As he approached the door to his quarters, he saw a couple of his crew members ahead, evidently having come looking for him after the chaos. They said something to him, probably asking if he was okay, but he wasn't paying attention. Robert shoved past them rather roughly and staggered into his quarters. The room was in shambles with everything, including his desk, having been shoved to one side. He ran into the side of the table with more force than he had intended and slammed his hands down flat to steady himself, his crewmen right behind him. Robert looked down at the worn, wooden tabletop and the mounted compass on top of it. The needle was not moving or wavering in the slightest; it too said that north was unquestionably directly behind the ship.

# CHAPTER TWO

# THE BIOLOGY PROFESSOR

Dr. Alec Dorn sat hunched over his small mahogany desk in his tiny, wood-paneled office, one of his student's papers laid out in front of him, taking up the very last empty space left on its surface. The paper he was grading was dreadful, and not just by college standards. Alec doubted a sixth-grade teacher would pass this paper, much less a college professor. But he was used to this level of commitment from his students. He had no illusions about it; his class was a blow-off class, the kind you took to simply pad your schedule. Alec himself had always had a fascination with Biology, but every year new students would arrive thinking they could pass simply by knowing their animals.

Alec rolled his eyes at seeing how much red pen he had used on this paper. He was far from a stickler and had always viewed himself as the fun young professor, although he had to admit he was finding it harder and harder to connect with his students. At thirty-seven years old, he felt like he was barely out of college himself, although when he actually counted the years, it told another story. His desire to be liked by his students had put him in a difficult position with the other professors a few times over the years. He often felt like he wasn't respected by his peers the way he should be. He did have a PhD after all, and despite his sometimes reckless spirit, he did take education and continuing knowledge very seriously.

"Knock knock," came a voice from the doorway. Alec looked up to see Diana, a professor friend of his, poking her head sideways through the barely head-sized gap in the open door. Boxes of books and papers had made opening the door more than a couple feet impossible in recent years.

"Hey," Alec greeted her, but she just continued to stare at him, a smile creeping across her face before transforming slowly into a broad grin. "What?" Alec asked. Diana just continued to grin at him. "What?" Alec asked again, trying to keep a straight face and feign confusion, although the hint of a smile at the edge of his lips threatened to give him away. "Ya know, I'm very busy here, Diana. I've got this paper in front of me, and it's a real masterpiece, so if you don't mind…"

"I heard you had a fun class yesterday," Diana said finally in a playful, singsong voice.

Alec slammed his pen down on the desk in mock outrage, but a smile finally broke on his face. "That was blown entirely out of proportion, there's barely even a story to tell."

"So it is true!" Diana's eyes lit up and she squeezed half her torso further through the door, knocking over a box of papers in the process. "I thought maybe the students were exaggerating! Where did you even get a Lemur?"

"First of all it was a Macaque, and second, I'm not getting into it," Alec retorted. "We are professors at a university, professionals; it was simply a learning exercise and I will not dignify these unfounded rumors with a response," he said, doing his best to act offended.

"Of course, you're right," she came back. "My apologies, *Professor*…but you're not denying that it got out of your classroom then?"

Alec picked up his pen and threw it at the doorway. Diana ducked out of the way and started laughing uncontrollably. "Okay, okay, it's not that funny," Alec said, finally allowing himself to laugh too. "You shouldn't joke though, I've heard the Dean's not amused, I could be in some trouble." Diana didn't stop, though, and Alec just shook his head and laughed too in spite of himself. "Alright, is there something you wanted?" he asked.

Regaining control of herself, Diana responded, "We doing lunch today?"

"I can't," Alec replied, "I've got a thing."

"Fine, be that way," Diana said playfully, "then walk me to my next class at least." When Alec hesitated, she pushed, "Come on Professor, you could use a break."

So Alec, with considerable effort, slid his way out from behind his desk and squeezed through the partially open door and out into the hallway. They walked through the bustling corridors of the college, talking easily as they went. Conversations with Diana were always easy. They had both started at the college years ago right around the same time, and they had been close ever since. Despite some persistent rumors, they were friends only, nothing more. Not to say there wasn't an attraction between them, but Alec always considered their general playfulness and occasional flirting as fairly innocent.

Diana was talking now about one of her classes and describing a debate that had stemmed from her lecture today. They exited the dimly lit building into the blinding sunlight and cut across the fairly small campus, heading towards her lecture hall on the opposite side. As they approached the partially enclosed outdoor corridors of the red brick building, Alec noticed one of the other professors talking to a young, bespectacled man in a suit he didn't recognize, and to his alarm the professor looked his way and pointed right at him. The man in the suit started walking towards them, a confident, authoritative quality in his stride. Diana stopped talking mid-sentence when she noticed him approaching. The man held out his hand to shake, even as he was still ten feet away, walking fast.

"Dr. Dorn," he called out, not a question but a statement. Diana glanced sideways at Alec as the man stopped in front of them and grasped his hand roughly. "Lieutenant Allen," he introduced himself.

Diana raised her eyebrow at Alec and said, "Okay, well that's my cue to leave. Young minds to shape and all that, *Dr. Dorn*, we'll talk later." She walked off towards the lecture hall, but turned around once she was out of view of Lieutenant Allen and teasingly mouthed to Alec, "You're in trouble." She grinned at him once more, spun on her heel and continued on towards class.

The Lieutenant was still shaking his hand vigorously, and Alec decided it had gone on far past what he was comfortable with. He loosened his grip in what he thought was a clear sign that he was done with the handshake, but Lieutenant Allen did not seem to take the hint. Leaving Alec no choice, he awkwardly pried his hand free and asked, "So what can I help you with?"

At first the Lieutenant was extremely resistant to giving any explanation as to why he was looking for Alec, insisting that they drive somewhere together to meet with his commanding officer. After Alec refused to leave campus without further information, the two went back and forth deciding on a place to speak within the college grounds. Trying his best to avoid explaining why his office was not an option, Alec finally suggested one of the unused classrooms at the far side of campus.

As the Lieutenant got himself seated, fidgeting with his jacket to make sure it sat just right, Alec studied him and decided this was not a man who was in charge of anything. He likely didn't know much about why he was here, but rather was given specific instructions to carry out, and he was trying his best to do just that. His authoritative walk and demeanor seemed to be overcompensation for his bubbling uncertainty.

"Okay, so," Lieutenant Allen started finally, his inexperience becoming far more apparent now that he was tasked with more than simply introducing himself. "General Raleigh was hoping to speak to you himself, but why don't I brief you here and then, if you're agreeable to it, we can go and see him?"

"That sounds fine," Alec answered, anxious to hear what they could possibly want with him.

"Yesterday, a cargo ship crossing the Atlantic bound for England was nearly capsized," the Lieutenant began. "The circumstances surrounding the near disaster were… unusual."

"Unusual?" Alec repeated back.

"That's right," the Lieutenant answered slowly, seeming to gain some confidence upon realizing he had a captive audience. "You see, according to the captain, the ship was dragged backwards violently by an, as of yet, unknown force before becoming lodged on a small land mass."

Alec took a moment to process what he'd just been told, and more excitingly, the implications of them coming to a biology professor for guidance. If it were an animal that dragged a cargo ship, it would have had to be massive. Now desperate for more information, Alec asked, "So were there any markings left on the sides of the ship?"

"No, we don't believe so," Lieutenant Allen answered. "We haven't gotten a team out to the wreck yet, that's why we came to you."

Alec's mind was racing deliriously. He had no idea how they had found out about him, but the fact that they clearly considered him a leading expert in the field of biology was incredibly exciting. The recognition he had been longing for his entire life could finally be within reach. "So what sort of clues do you have?" Alec asked, trying unsuccessfully to contain his excitement. "Did the captain see something in the water?"

"I don't believe so," the Lieutenant said, pulling a few crumpled pieces of paper out of his jacket pocket and flipping through them. "Not according to the report."

Alec couldn't help his thoughts racing ahead. Would he be able to put together his own team? Would he be leading the team, or just a part of it? He had to slow himself down though, one question at a time. "So did the crew hear something in the water then? I mean, how do you know it was a life form?"

Still riffling through his papers as if looking for additional answers, Allen said, "We, uh, we don't believe it was a life form."

Alec was confused. "Then why do you need a biologist?" he asked.

Lieutenant Allen, now turning each of his papers over, desperate for clarification, stuttered, "Uh, umm, are you not a theoretical physicist?"

Alec's disappointment was instant and crippling. He should have known. "No, I'm not," he said finally, a dull ache weighing on his stomach. "You're looking for my brother."

"Your brother?" Allen asked, now turning a deep shade of red as the realization of his mistake dawned on him. "I... I don't understand how I could have..."

"Dr. Cyrus Dorn," Alec said, now wanting more than anything for this conversation to end. "That's who you're looking for, he's also a professor at this university."

Allen, looking increasingly uncomfortable, stammered, "Well I'm terribly sorry... not sure... I just asked if someone could point me in the direction of Dr. Dorn...I never thought to..."

"It's fine," Alec finally said, deciding to put him out of his misery. "You can find him in Building A next to the administration building, Room 108, that's his office."

Lieutenant Allen hurried out of the room as fast as he could after getting directions, mumbling apologies as he went. He had lost a bit of his confident stride as he left, looking more like a lost first year than the important military man Alec had first seen walking across campus. Alec shook his head. He shouldn't be so disappointed; of course they had been looking for his brother. Cyrus was a well-respected man, and now it sounded like he would be asked to lead this mysterious expedition. Alec thought back on the minimal details the Lieutenant had given him about the shipwreck. Even if it wasn't an animal, he was curious what had happened. He was due to meet his brother for drinks this evening, maybe he'd ask him about it then. What sort of force could pull a cargo ship backwards in the middle of the ocean?

**CHAPTER THREE**

# BROTHERS

An ear-piercing shriek rang out across the campus grounds. Alec glanced up in the direction of the commotion and saw a group of students standing in the grass, one of the girls being lifted onto the shoulders of one of the guys. She screamed and laughed in delight, playfully punching at him to let her down. Alec continued on across the courtyard and out onto the main street. He kept his head down, as he usually did; entirely consumed by his own thoughts. At the moment, his mind wandered to that shipwreck. Even though he now knew it had not been an animal that attacked the ship, he couldn't shake the image of an enormous, long dormant sea creature from the deepest depths of the ocean resurfacing from the ancient past. He dreamt of himself leading a team out to investigate, maybe getting swept into one of those adventures you read about in stories. And returning here victorious, having discovered, and of course conquered, a brand-new species. He smiled to himself, thinking of the notoriety it would bring him, and how he'd be a celebrity in his field, and indeed the world.

"There he is!" came a booming, jovial voice, pulling Alec out of his fantasy world. He had arrived outside the pub, and Dr. Cyrus Dorn stood up from the patio table he had been sharing with his wife, beaming from ear to ear and holding out his arms to hug his brother. Alec smiled and met him for his usual, full-armed embrace, feeling Cyrus's hand hammer into his back several times before releasing him. Even though the two saw each other on campus all the time, Cyrus had always been a hugger, and had a way of making people feel like he was genuinely excited to see them. At thirty-nine years old, Cyrus Dorn was two years older than Alec, and about half a foot taller. Where Alec could be introverted and quiet around people he didn't know, Cyrus was charming and gregarious; the sort of person everyone felt an instant bond with. While Alec had a quintessential care-free-professor look with stubble up to his cheekbones and slightly unkempt hair, Cyrus was clean-cut and clean-shaven. His wife Cynthia, now stepping forward to hug Alec herself, was equally well put-together, and often surprised people when they learned she had a rather adventurous spirit. Her long, perfectly straightened hair and upper-scale outfit masked her wanderlust well, but she accompanied Cyrus on nearly all of his expeditions in the field. She kissed Alec on the cheek and smiled brightly, asking how he was doing.

As the three of them sat down at the outdoor table, Cyrus flagged the waitress and ordered a round of drinks. "We're celebrating," he exclaimed. "Alec, I have some exciting news!"

Alec briefly debated whether he should feign ignorance or not, but decided against it, simply responding with, "Yeah, I heard."

Cyrus shook his head and said, "The Lieutenant mentioned he came to you first by mistake, what a dumb shit. A waste of your time, you're a busy guy and accommodated your schedule for him; the least he could do was make sure he had the right family member."

Alec could tell Cyrus was overstating his outrage to make the situation less awkward, but he appreciated the gesture. In the end he just shrugged it off and insisted it wasn't a big deal.

As their drinks were delivered, Cyrus said, "Now, before we get into all that... the macaque incident..." Alec threw his hands up and began to defend himself, but Cyrus cut him off, "I've taken care of it, don't worry. I spoke to the Dean and he agreed it was simply a training exercise that got out of hand."

Unlike his mock outrage when Diana had brought it up, Alec did not like having to explain himself to Cyrus. "It didn't *get out of hand*, a student came through the door late and it ran out into the hallway. We wouldn't even be having this conversation if Professor Melner hadn't panicked when he saw it."

"Alec, Alec, I'm on your side," Cyrus soothed in what Alec felt was a fairly condescending tone. "All I'm saying is I've taken care of it. I convinced the Dean that disciplinary action is not required."

Cynthia jumped in, "Leave him alone Cy, he doesn't need a lecture."

"I'm not lecturing him, I'm just letting him know I've taken care of it. And I know he's gonna be more careful next time, so…"

"Cy, stop," Cynthia said, more forcefully this time. "He's not your kid brother on campus, he's your peer."

Alec was beginning to lose his temper now; he could feel his anger boiling to the surface. The last thing he needed was Cyrus coming to his rescue and he did not need Cynthia speaking for him. He was about to say just that when Cyrus conceded, "You're right, I'm sorry." Cynthia caught eyes with Alec and winked at him, clearly under the impression she had just done him a favor by leaping to his defense. He knew her heart was in the right place so he shouldn't be frustrated with her. In general, they had a very close relationship, and she was someone he always knew he could count on.

"Okay so moving on to more important things," Cyrus finally said, breaking the silence and clapping his hands together, "we're getting food, right?"

Cynthia said she wasn't staying for dinner because she had to 'get things ready', and mentioned as she was getting up that the two brothers had a lot to talk about. "Cy, I'll see you at home, and Alec, I'll see you tomorrow." She left before Alec could ask why they would be seeing each other tomorrow; they didn't have any plans that he could think of.

"So," Alec questioned once they were alone, "let's hear about this expedition of yours."

Cyrus's eyes brightened and a smile crept across his face. Lowering his voice in dramatic fashion, he said, "Alec, this could be huge."

Knowing that Cyrus was not one to fantasize when it came to science, Alec's interest was piqued. "Why, what happened to the ship?"

The smile spread across Cyrus's face revealing his completely unchecked excitement. He leaned in close and said, "I don't know." The smile never left his face. "I *don't* know. And that's what makes it so damn exciting."

"So it wasn't an animal, could it have been some sort of current? Or maybe…"

"No no no," Cyrus interjected, "you're oversimplifying it. I believe we're in truly uncharted territory here. General Raleigh said the entire ship's crew felt an immense force pulling them backwards. This could fly in the face of everything that's been theorized to date about gravity and general relativity."

"Don't you think you're getting carried away just a little bit?" Alec cautioned. "You haven't even seen the site yet. Maybe you should wait until you get there."

"Until *we* get there," Cyrus corrected, his eyes still glowing with enthusiasm and anticipation. "I need you with me out there."

Alec balked, "Out of the question. You don't need me; we've already established they don't need a biologist for this. Besides, I can't get the time off, I have class."

"You're coming," Cyrus insisted excitedly. "I've already spoken to the Dean; he's agreed to get your class covered…"

"Why do you do that?" Alec interrupted, annoyed once again by Cyrus's insistence on fighting his battles for him. "I didn't ask you to talk to the Dean for me, and I haven't agreed to come."

Cyrus grasped Alec's wrists from across the table and leaned in again. "Alec, I need you out there. This could be the most significant scientific discovery of our time, and I want you to be a part of it with me." Cyrus's eyes never left Alec's; his gaze piercing and unblinking. "This could be our time. Think of the fame, the notoriety… the glory."

Alec smiled in spite of himself. "You don't even know what's out there," he began. "There may be nothing to discover but more ocean."

"Maybe," Cyrus allowed, but the smile refused to leave his face. "I don't believe that's true though. I believe something happened out there on the Atlantic that is beyond our understanding of the known universe. And I believe that you and I are going to be the first ones to discover what that was… together."

Alec considered his brother's proposal, allowing everything he had said to wash over him. He would be crazy to turn down an opportunity like this. Maybe Cyrus was getting carried away a bit, but it was nearly impossible not to get drawn in by his excitement. At long last Alec sighed and responded, "Okay when do we leave?"

Cyrus pulled a watch from his jacket pocket, glanced down at it and exclaimed, "In ten hours."

"Ten hours!?" Alec nearly shouted in disbelief.

"Ten hours," repeated Cyrus. "So you're going to get home, get packed, and meet us on the docks at five-thirty tomorrow morning. It's a day and a half journey by ship to get us to the site. We will have a small team with us, who they are selecting, but you and I are in charge."

"And Cynthia's coming too I take it?" Alec asked, now understanding why she said she would see him tomorrow. That had been fairly presumptuous of her; she must have known that Cyrus could talk him into anything.

"Of course," Cyrus confirmed, "she's packing now."

The rest of the evening went by in a blur of excited theories and far-fetched scenarios. It was after nine before Alec realized how late it had gotten. Agreeing it was time to head out, Cyrus looked around for the waitress to pay.

"I think we pay inside," Alec said, reaching into his pocket. "But I've got it, don't worry."

"No no, I've got it," insisted Cyrus. "When we are rich and famous, you can get the next one."

Pulling out his money, Alec responded, "It's done, don't worry about it."

A grin crept across Cyrus's face, and before Alec had time to react, his brother had leapt from the table and sprinted towards the door. Alec raced after him, dodging between tables and nearly barreling into a surprised-looking couple exiting the pub. Cyrus ducked through the door and pulled it shut behind him, Alec on the other side attempting to wrench the handle open. Once the door latched, Alec could see his brother through the glass turn to the cashier to pay.

Pulling the door open and stepping in to stand next to his brother in defeat, Alec quipped, "Aren't you supposed to be a respected Professor?"

Cyrus just grinned at him and said, "What's life without a little fun and excitement."

## CHAPTER FOUR

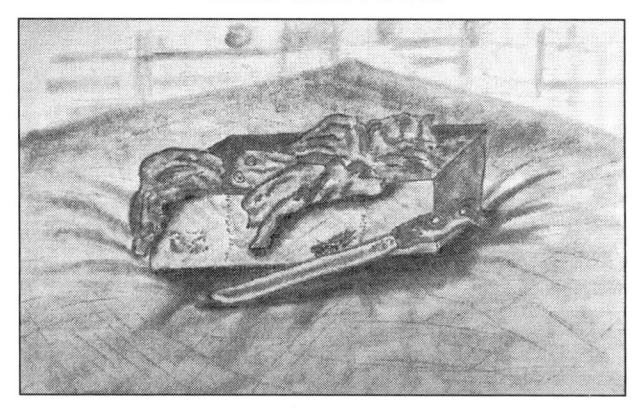

# FIVE HOURS

Alec's suitcase lay open on the bed, various clothing items and supplies spilling out of it and strewn about the room. Diana sat in the corner, a beer in hand, asking Alec for the third time to repeat exactly what his brother had told him.

"He's just convinced it's going to be huge," Alec explained again. "He says he doesn't know what to expect, but he thinks it will be a significant discovery."

"But what makes him think that?" Diana pressed. "I don't understand how he's jumped to that conclusion."

Alec just shrugged, concentrating more on deciding what he needed for the journey then the conversation. He assumed all of their time would be spent on the ship, but what if their findings led them to land? He rifled through his closet, tossing the occasional shirt out. He found a compass in a box near the back that he had entirely forgotten he owned. In the same box he came across an extremely well-made steel machete. Cyrus had brought it back for him from one of his expeditions in South America. He picked it up, debating if there were any reason he could possibly need it, apart from the idea that a machete seemed like something an expedition leader would bring.

"So are you excited?" Diana asked. "Nervous? Gotta say, I never pegged you as the expedition leader type."

"Thanks for the vote of confidence," Alec responded dryly. "I'm not fooling myself, this is Cyrus's trip, I'm just a guest on it."

"Ooo what if you find yourself up against some sort of huge sea monster!" she joked, likely trying to veer the conversation away from the direction it was headed.

Alec laughed to himself, "I had the same thought, actually."

"Better make sure you pack your spear then, so you can take it down," she said sarcastically.

Alec rolled his eyes, "I'm sure I must have one lying around here somewhere."

Looking at the clock he realized it was nearly midnight, which meant he was going to be getting very little, if any, sleep before he had to be at the docks. He had decided he was excited for the expedition after all, even if he did not like the way Cyrus had went about 'inviting' him. Alec had never been on an exploratory mission like this. Now that he thought about it, he had never been on any type of trip that could be considered a *mission*. Cyrus was the real adventurer, mostly for work, but his longtime fascination with maps and cartography meant that he wanted to see the world. He was an important mind in the scientific community, and he enjoyed plenty of preferential treatment from the Dean and the rest of the university staff.

Alec, on the other hand, always seemed to be in second place. It was as though the year and a half gap between the two being born was all the head start that Cyrus needed, and Alec was hopeless to catch up. Not that Alec was without accomplishment, far from it. He had a prestigious degree and was teaching what he loved, but he had a deep-seated longing to be recognized amongst his peers. It often seemed as though Diana were the only one who didn't view Alec as the 'lesser' Dorn brother.

"So what do you know about the rest of the team?" Diana asked as she rummaged through a day pack he had filled with supplies, apparently oblivious to the fact that someone might view this as an invasion of privacy.

"Umm, not much really," Alec admitted, pulling the pack away from her. "Obviously Cynthia's coming."

"Oh that's good," Diana said. Alec had confided in her once that it seemed his and Cyrus's relationship was sometimes better when Cynthia was around. Not that they weren't close in general, as far as siblings go. Alec felt they had a very strong relationship, and he owed a lot to his brother. Cyrus was the one who pushed him to get his degree and helped him through school. Cyrus got him the job at the university. Cyrus's words of recommendation had led to many of Alec's research grants. Cyrus always seemed to be there to make sure he didn't fail. The only problem was it sometimes left Alec feeling like he couldn't adequately accomplish things based on his own merits. It left him longing to stand on his own two feet for something.

"Don't you have to be at the dock in less than five hours?" Cynthia asked, realizing for herself how late it had gotten.

"Exactly," replied Alec, not appreciating the reminder when the pressure was already starting to get to him. "So why don't you wander on home, I'm just finishing up here anyways," he lied.

"Fine, you want me to head out, I will," Diana sighed, standing up and heading for the door.

Alec smiled and shook his head, walking to the door to let her out.

"Have fun out there, be safe," Diana said in a rare moment of sincerity between the two. "I know you're anxious to prove yourself, just take things slow."

"I'll only be gone a few days," Alec reminded her. "No time to get into any trouble, I promise."

Alec watched her as she strolled out into the cool night air, waving over her shoulder as she went. He was suddenly overcome with a strange feeling, as if he had forgotten to tell her something; or perhaps wanted to tell her something. He shrugged, whatever it was, he was sure it could wait a few days until he returned. It was probably just nerves about the upcoming trip anyways. He looked up at the night sky and the various constellations he could make out. He reflected on how it was the same night sky no matter where you were in the world. Indeed, many of the stars he was looking at right now were long dead and burnt out; their light simply taking many thousands of years to reach earth. But from down here, you would never know, everything looked peaceful. There was something oddly comforting about that.

Alec took a deep breath of fresh air before turning to head back inside and finish packing. To think, tomorrow at this time he'd be in the middle of the ocean, well on his way to that perplexing shipwreck.

# CHAPTER FIVE

## AT THE DOCKS

Alec arrived at the docks at five in the morning after a restless night of anticipation. The blue, pre-dawn light was barely starting to illuminate the sky out over the black, roiling ocean. The massive expedition ship's hulking silhouette swayed back and forth, creaking against the wooden railings of the dock. It didn't appear that anyone else from the team had arrived yet, but the boardwalks were far from empty. Apart from a few deckhands rushing about preparing the ship for departure, a dozen or so rough looking workers in between jobs at sea were milling around off to the right, every one of them with a beer in hand, almost all of them very clearly drunk.

Alec approached the ship, dragging his unwieldy bags behind him, but found the gangway to get aboard roped off. A crewman piling large, heavy-looking crates noticed him and exclaimed rather harshly, "Not ready yet. Drop your stuff, we'll get it on board."

Alec paused, wondering why no one else was around this close to departure. "Where should I go?" he asked, trying to sound more self-assured than he was actually feeling.

"Don't care," the man said, continuing to pile crates. "Just stay out of the way."

Alec stood considering the man for a moment, but it was clear the conversation was over. He dropped his bags into a pile where he stood and turned to walk towards the railing, looking out over the water. The cool breeze and salty mist coming off the ocean was strangely calming. Staring out over the vast expanse of deep blues and inky blacks, his mind wandered to the shipwreck, waiting for them out there somewhere. What else waited for them out there?

A bottle smashed off to his right and he glanced briefly in the direction of the drunk crewmen. A few of them were talking to each other, but many sat by themselves; one man was actually slumped over asleep, a beer bottle still clutched in his hand. The men would find themselves here after their contract aboard a vessel ended. They would mill around on the docks until work opened up, then head out to sea again. Most did not have a home to go to, at least not in this port. Their clothes were worn down and faded from the salt air and harsh sun out on the ocean, and many of them had large beards and wild, unwashed hair; except for one. Standing apart from the rest of the crowd, a woman leaned against the chain railings with her arm casually draped over the side and a beer bottle in her hand. She was staring directly at Alec. The woman was gorgeous with shoulder-length dirty blonde hair and piercing green eyes, which at the moment were unwavering, but she did have a rugged, slightly wild look. Alec awkwardly tried to look away from her, but her eyes stayed focused on him.

"Hey," she called out, her gaze never leaving Alec's face. Alec looked around to see if she were talking to someone else, although her intense stare made it pretty clear she was talking to him. "Yeah you," she called again, taking a sip of her beer. "Come here."

Alec didn't know what to make of her, and didn't like the idea of approaching the rough-looking dock workers. Although in fairness, she did not share the same rough appearance that they did. She seemed out of place with her faded green cargo pants and beige canvas jacket; a bright red undershirt beneath standing in sharp contrast to the neutral tones of the rest of her outfit.

"Come here," she called again, still not moving from her casual lean against the dock railings. Alec walked forward slowly, his uncertainty painfully obvious. As he stopped a few paces from her, she pointed her beer bottle at the ship and asked, "You going out on that?"

Unsure how much he should tell her, or indeed if he should talk to her at all, Alec replied with a simple nod of his head.

The woman smiled in amusement at his hesitation and asked, "So where are you going?"

"I'm part of an investigative team," he replied.

"Oh ho, fancy," she retorted. Alec wasn't sure if she were being genuine or not. "What's your name?" she asked. When Alec hesitated, she pushed, "What, you don't wanna tell me?"

Someone bumped into Alec from the side, throwing him off balance. He stumbled sideways and turned to see a particularly rough, and particularly drunk, dock worker staggering towards him. The man said something to him, but his speech was so slurred Alec couldn't make it out.

"Excuse me?" Alec asked, alarmed as the man reached out and grasped his arm.

"Hey, leave him alone," the woman yelled, finally standing up from the railing and walking forward. The man didn't even glance in her direction but continued to grab at Alec's jacket before finding a pocket and trying to reach his hand inside. Alec tried to back up but the man held tightly onto his arm. The woman arrived and attempted to force herself between the two; grabbing the man's wrist to pull it out of Alec's pocket. "I said shove off," she yelled.

The man turned to her, finally seeming to realize there was another person near him. He released his hold on Alec and turned his attention instead towards the woman, reaching out at her. Faster than Alec could blink, the woman lashed out with her fist, connecting squarely with the man's lower jaw. A loud crunch echoed out across the dock and the man smashed down onto the ground, coming to rest face-down in a heap on the wood flooring.

Alec watched the events unfold in horror and started to back away in anticipation of the man getting up again ready to fight. But the man did not move, and a closer look showed that he was unconscious. The woman shook spilled beer off her hand in annoyance and came to stand next to Alec. "So what did you say your name was?" she asked again, as if nothing had happened.

"I... I... Uh..." Alec stammered. "I'm Alec...I mean...Dr. Dorn."

The woman smiled in amusement again and said, "I'm Nel."

"It's uh... nice to meet you," Alec replied, unsure how to carry on a conversation after what just happened. "Are you okay?" he asked, although he realized it was a stupid question as soon as it left his mouth.

Nel smiled, a disarming, almost innocent smile, and responded, "I'm fine." She put her arm around Alec's shoulder and leaned against him in the same way an old friend would. "I like you Alec," she said, and shook her head laughing to herself. Alec had no idea what to do. On the one hand, the woman was beautiful and he did not hate the attention from her. On the other hand, she seemed to be a street person and she had just knocked a man unconscious right in front of him.

Blinding yellow headlights pierced the pale morning haze as a car rounded the corner and turned in towards the docks to park. Alec felt immense relief as he saw his brother's tall form step out of the car, followed closely by Cynthia. Cyrus looked his way questioningly as Lieutenant Allen bustled behind him to retrieve their bags from the back.

"You alright, Alec?" Cyrus called out as he approached, understandably confused to find his brother with a strange woman's arm wrapped around him.

Cyrus looked as though he were about to introduce himself when Lieutenant Allen appeared at his side and exclaimed, "Ah, I see you two have already met." He also shot a judgmental glance at the bottle in Nel's hand.

Alec turned to look at Nel in confusion, who straightened up and polished off the rest of her beer. "Well you had me waiting long enough, I had to pass the time somehow."

"You're part of the expedition?" Alec stammered in disbelief.

Lieutenant Allen, with a hint of disapproval in his voice, jumped in and said, "Dr. Dorn, meet your field equipment tech Nelida Yore."

Nel winked at Alec, then slapped him on the back and said, "I knew I liked you." She then walked on towards the ship, calling back, "so we heading out or what? We won't find adventure hanging around the docks." She jumped over the rope blocking the gangway, tossed her empty bottle over the side into the water, and made her way through the door to the ship.

Cyrus looked to the Lieutenant for approval, who raised his eyebrows and said, "I suppose it's time to board."

*****

The expedition ship was massive, although they discovered their quarters were very small and cramped. Alec didn't mind, though, he was excited to get underway. Once he had stowed his personal items next to his tiny bed, he made his way out to the main deck. The faint blue glow over the horizon had given way to the yellows and golds of sunrise. The crew was busy getting the last of the supplies stowed before they headed out to sea. Clanging and shouting rang out all around him as people bustled back and forth preparing the ship. Through the general barking of orders and yelling from the workers, Alec started to hear the raised voices of two people clearly in a heated argument. Even before they rounded the corner, Alec recognized one of the voices as his brother's. Who would he be arguing with already? As they came into view, Alec saw Cyrus gesturing wildly to a tall, muscular man with a squared jaw and a full head of dark, impeccably combed hair.

The man shouted, "Pushing forward blindly without a plan is how people get hurt. But since you're so bull headed that you refuse to see past your own ambition, that will be on you!"

"You can't accomplish anything in this world without risk," Cyrus yelled back. "We're explorers, and if you aren't prepared to put it all on the line to discover something new then you're on the wrong ship!"

"My God, you're delusional as well as irresponsible. We're not *exploring* anything! This is a well-traveled shipping line! What are you expecting to find out there?"

Cyrus looked like he wanted to take a swing at the man. "At least my mind is open. Evidently you're just here for the free ride. Well understand one thing, I'm in charge while you're on this ship so you will damn well respect me while you're here. Aside from that, stay the hell out of my way and we'll be good."

Cyrus turned and started to walk away but the man called out after him, "What rock did they dig you out from under? I guess you're what passes for an expert on such short notice." Cyrus walked back and squared himself up directly in front of the man, looking as though he wanted to fight. The man, holding his ground, continued, "And no, I don't have to respect you."

Cyrus tensed up and clenched his fist tightly. Alec thought there may actually be a fight, but then Cyrus stepped back with a smirk, nodding his head as if to say, 'this isn't over.' He then turned and strode off, without so much as a glance at Alec. The man shook his head in disbelief and walked towards Alec, saying, "What a condescending blowhard. Can you believe that guy?"

Alec didn't know how to respond. He didn't want to get involved, especially since 'condescending blowhard' could easily be an accurate description of Cyrus, but this man clearly didn't know they were brothers. The man stopped right beside Alec and turned to watch the bustle of the crew with him, then extended his hand sideways and introduced himself, "Jack Viana."

Alec grasped his hand and shook it. Jack had an aggressive, bone-crunching handshake. "That's quite a grip you've got there, Jack," he said, before admitting, "I'm Alec... Alec Dorn."

"Dorn?" Jack questioned with a raise of his eyebrow. "So, are you two...?"

"They're brothers," came a familiar voice from behind them. They turned to see Nelida Yore approaching, a big smile on her face. Evidently she was enjoying the drama. "Don't worry though," she continued, "I've already got a feel for Alec, he's one of the good ones."

"Is that right?" Jack said skeptically, while Nelida pushed between the two men, draping her arms around both of their shoulders.

"We're all going to be close, I can feel it," she said. "I'm glad I have two capable guys to watch my back out there."

Alec was embarrassed to realize he felt a pang of jealousy at Nel's affection towards Jack. Which he knew was absurd of course; they had just met and he didn't know her at all. But there was something about her, some slightly dangerous quality that drew him in. Suddenly Alec felt the floor beneath him begin to vibrate, signaling the engines kicking into action. Ever so subtly, the horizon beyond the ship began to rotate as they turned towards the open ocean.

Nel turned to Alec and Jack with raised eyebrows and a beaming grin, her eyes alight with anticipation, and said dramatically, "We're off!"

**CHAPTER SIX**

## SOMEONE ELSE'S LIFE

The sun was out in full force, twinkling and dancing off the vibrant cobalt waves as the expedition ship pushed on to the east. The majority of the day had passed without incident, the steady, rhythmic drumming of the engine making the hours bleed together. Alec stood leaning over the side railing watching the bottlenose dolphins leap in and out of the frothy wake coming off the ship. His thoughts drifted once again to the shipwreck that waited out there beyond the horizon. Cyrus had spent most of the day harassing various crew members and pushing his authority on anyone who stood still too long. Alec found it best to stay away from him entirely for the time being. Jack Viana had proven to be more than able to hold his own against Cyrus. Being the first mate on the ship, Jack felt his own authority trumped Cyrus's, and of course Cyrus felt the exact opposite. From what the rest of the crew could tell, it was a bit of a grey area.

Nel had been staying mostly to herself so far, observing the chest-pounding and ensuing arguments with visible amusement. She seemed to be quick to laugh and quite opinionated if pushed, but she carried herself with such palpable confidence that no one wanted to bother her. She had a habit of winking at Alec every time she passed by him; something he was sure she did to everyone, but he liked either way.

Lieutenant Allen had joined them on the expedition and seemed thoroughly out of his element away from the city. If he had come across as bumbling and inexperienced at the university, out here on an actual voyage he seemed entirely incompetent. There were times he seemed mystified as to how he ended up out on the ocean in the first place. No one, including and especially Lieutenant Allen himself, seemed to know what his role or function was on the ship. It was technically a military expedition so perhaps he was along to make sure they had a physical presence in the field, but he had made a point to stay out of all decision-making.

The captain was rarely ever seen, leaving it to Jack to interact with the rest of the crew. He was an older man and seemed to be grooming Jack to take his place; grooming him by essentially letting him do the job.

There was one other scientist on board; a small, excitable man named Dalton Sydney. When Alec first met him, he talked at length of his work studying ocean currents and the relationship between the tides and the moon. Alec had to admit that most of the technical aspects went pretty far over his head, but that didn't stop Dalton from ranting on for a half-hour more. By noon, everyone on the ship had been cornered by one of Dalton's scientific ramblings at some point or another. People had started taking extra precautions to ensure they didn't get trapped alone with him, but he always found a victim in the end. Only Nel seemed impervious to his lectures. The one time she found herself prey to a particularly enthusiastic talk about tidal waves in Japan, she simply put her hand on his shoulder and said, "Dalton, I love you, but I don't understand a word you're saying," and walked away.

Then there was Cynthia, who seemed to be struggling to find a balance between supporting her husband and not alienating herself from the rest of the crew. Cyrus seemed to be looking to her for support, but she knew how he could be and was trying to stay neutral.

In general, Alec preferred it away from the rest of the team, alone with his thoughts. That sort of alone time would likely be hard to find in the coming days, but at the moment it was peaceful. No sooner had the thought crossed his mind than footsteps signaled someone approaching. Alec felt guilty for immediately hoping it was not Cyrus, but he didn't think he had the energy for him right now. He was surprised when it turned out to be Cynthia, who had not talked to him much since they got underway.

"Mind if I join you?" she asked, leaning on the railing next to him without waiting for a response. "So… a week on a ship out in the middle of nowhere with Cyrus in charge… what were we thinking?"

Alec laughed aloud, happy to hear her finally say something critical of him. "Yeah, we really didn't think this through, did we?" he replied with a smile.

"There's got to be a brig on this ship somewhere, right? Maybe we can lock him in there for a couple days," she joked.

"We may not even have to," Alec responded, shaking his head with a chuckle. "I'm pretty sure most of the crew is planning a mutiny at this point."

Cynthia smiled, looking out over the ocean; her long hair blowing in the breeze. "He needs you here, though, you know that, right?"

Alec shook his head dismissively. "No he doesn't. No one needs me here. I'm a biologist; by very definition my not-so-narrow field of study is *life*. But I'm fairly certain it wasn't a life form that pulled that ship."

"We don't know what we'll find out there, but that's not what I'm talking about. You're his support, Alec. Do you know, when he first heard of this expedition, you were the one he couldn't wait to talk to about it."

"That's what you're here for," Alec replied, half rolling his eyes at the thought of Cyrus needing him.

"I may be his wife but you're his brother," Cynthia insisted. "The bond between the two of you is something I can never replace. Look, I've known you a long time Alec, longer than I've known Cyrus even…"

"You think I don't know that," Alec cut in, his mood darkening by the second. "Let's not dredge up the past." When Cynthia didn't respond, he continued, "I can't be there to support him if he's pushing everyone away. I'm sorry, I love him, but he can be such an arrogant ass in situations like this. It's no wonder the crew hasn't warmed up to him, he's done nothing but push them around and scream that he's in charge.

Maybe he should try including them in his plans for tomorrow instead of just barking orders."

"You're right, of course," Cynthia agreed, nodding her head. "He's planning a sort of 'mission briefing' tonight after dinner. Maybe you should suggest he take a more collaborative approach."

"I'm not suggesting anything to him," Alec responded, a little harsher than he intended. When Cynthia seemed taken aback by his refusal, he continued, "I'm sorry, I'm just trying to stay out of his way. This is his expedition, and he can lead it however he wants."

Cynthia looked as though she wanted to say something more but ended up turning and walking away. He probably shouldn't have been so short with her. She hadn't done anything wrong; neither had Cyrus for that matter, at least not to him.

\*\*\*\*\*

After dinner, Cyrus had everyone gather in the mess hall for his 'mission briefing.' The mood was tense among the rest of the crew and there were audible grumblings as everyone waited for the presentation to start. Jack sat front and center, as if preparing to heckle a performer. Dalton sat right next to him, but in contrast seemed excited and ready to begin. Nel sat in the back corner, one of her feet propped up on a second chair, and Alec sat with Cynthia, preparing for the inevitable trainwreck to unfold. No other crew members had elected to join, although they were likely going to be staying with the ship no matter what they found out there. Lieutenant Allen was nowhere to be seen; Alec wouldn't have doubted if he had gotten lost somewhere on the ship.

"Okay everyone," Cyrus began, his voice booming with authority and purpose. "Let's get started. I wanted to make sure we had an opportunity to discuss as a group what the plan is for tomorrow when we arrive at the site and what I'm expecting from all of you."

Alec closed his eyes at hearing that last piece, knowing it was only going to further ruffle everyone's feathers.

"First let's start with our purpose out there," Cyrus continued. "All we know right now is that two days ago a cargo ship encountered something during its voyage to England. My understanding is that the ship has crashed about a day's journey east of here. Evidently a rescue team has already been dispatched ahead of us and will be retrieving the crew. I've been told that all injuries were minor. Our job, however, is to find out what happened to the ship in the first place. The captain described an immense force pulling the ship backwards, against the current, and theoretically against the laws of physics."

Alec could feel the group as a whole collectively rolling their eyes at the overly dramatic proposition. He was certain Jack would have something to say against the statement, but it was Dalton Sydney who spoke up first. "Here's the thing," he began, as he so often did, "the laws of physics are fairly rigid and unyielding. Now I'm open-minded enough to entertain what you're saying, but there are infinite alternate possibilities we should be looking into first."

"I agree with you," Cyrus responded quickly, attempting to cut off Dalton's rebuttal before it had a chance to snowball. "We don't know what's out there, and it could be anything. But it's our job to find out. We're explorers, and the Atlantic is our frontier…"

"I'm going to have to stop you right there," Jack cut in, "I'd like to remind everyone that this is a shipping line we're on, used hundreds of times a year. Hell, I've been out this way countless times. I don't know what we'll find but I can assure you all, we are not explorers. There's nothing out here but ocean, and well-travelled ocean at that."

Cynthia finally spoke up in a calming, collected voice, "Thank you Jack, everything you say may be true. But what everyone can agree on is that we don't know. And if our job is to find out what happened to that ship, we need to keep our minds open… all of us do."

"Well, speaking for myself my mind is plenty open," Nel called from the back, "so maybe we can table this discussion of what we may or may not find and talk about our actual plan for tomorrow."

Cyrus looked frustrated at being cut off but Alec nodded at him, confirming that her point was a valid one. With a sigh, he began again, "Okay for tomorrow, we're taking out two small dinghies. I want Jack, Cynthia, and Lieutenant Allen in one, and myself, Alec, Dalton, and Nelida in the other." He then looked directly at Jack and said, "Jack, when you're on that dinghy Cynthia is in charge. We will be off the ship and out in the field, and I expect you to stay in line while we're out there."

Alec expected an explosive response from Jack, but to his surprise he simply threw up his hands and acknowledged, "You're in charge in the field." Cyrus nodded in satisfaction, until Jack added, "And when something goes wrong out there, I'll make sure they know who was in charge."

Cyrus had turned a bright shade of red and was clenching his jaw, likely to stop himself from yelling. Instead of blowing up, he leaned in towards Jack and said quietly, "If you don't want to come tomorrow, just say the word. I do not need you. And I'm sure there is a deck around here for you to mop."

Now Jack was clenching his jaw; in fact his entire body had tensed up, but he didn't say a word. Cyrus straightened himself up to address the room as a whole again, which had gone awkwardly silent. Dalton was looking down at his hands nervously; Nel was grinning in the corner.

"So, two teams," Cyrus continued, "I want to inspect the exterior of the ship first, then make our way on board. When we're in the water I want the dinghies in close proximity to each other. Always within earshot. Any questions?"

Alec got the feeling Cyrus had originally intended for a longer explanation, but his rhythm had been thrown off by the backtalk from the crew. When no one said anything, Cyrus concluded with, "Okay, then get some rest, we'll be arriving at the site about midday tomorrow." With that, he turned and left the room, leaving everyone in confused silence at his abrupt departure.

Alec glanced sideways at Cynthia, whose head was down. She turned to him and nodded, "That could have gone better." The rest of the room began to stand up and shuffle around. No one was talking.

Finally, the silence was broken by Nel and her characteristic bluntness, "Anyone want a drink?"

"Yeah, I don't think there's a bar on this ship Nel," Jack replied dryly as he headed for the door.

She flung her arm around Jack and said, "You underestimate me, I came prepared."

As Nel and Jack walked out the door with Dalton bouncing behind them excitedly, Cynthia turned to Alec and whispered that she was going to talk to Cyrus. Alec nodded and watched her leave, but remained in his chair. He thought maybe he'd head up to the deck and watch the night sky. He wouldn't be able to sleep yet.

"Hey Doc," came a voice from the door. Alec looked up to see Nel leaning back in the doorway, a large bottle of some brownish liquor in her hand. She shook it and said, "We're gonna need some help finishing this."

And so Alec found himself sitting on the floor of the ship deck looking out over the deep black ocean, passing a substantial bottle of whiskey back and forth between Jack Viana, Nelida Yore, and Dalton Sydney; the strangest foursome he had ever been a part of.

Jack was laughing uncontrollably while trying unsuccessfully to tell a story about a previous voyage. It occurred to Alec that he had not seen him smile before now. Even Dalton had shared a story that was not science related and lasted an appropriate amount of time. They came to find out that Jack and Nel had been on voyages together before, although hadn't spent much time with one another. They seemed close from Alec's perspective, but he was starting to realize that was just Nel's way with people. It wasn't just that she was overly friendly, she seemed to enjoy testing the boundaries of a stranger's personal space.

"Okay Alec," Jack exclaimed, shoving the bottle towards him. "I think I know everything worth knowing about your brother at this point, what's your story?"

Dalton laughed, and Nel jokingly cut in, "Hey, that's *Doctor Dorn* to you, Jack."

Jack smiled, but pushed, "No seriously, though, you and your brother seem like polar opposites to me. What's the deal?"

Nel and Dalton were both looking expectantly at Alec too, so he took a swig of whiskey and asked, "Well, what is it you want to know about me? I'm a professor of biology at Dane University in upstate New York. Cyrus works there as well. I don't get out in the field much and…" He paused for a moment, debating if he should finish his thought aloud or not, before finally saying, "and I don't think I really have any place on this voyage." He took a big sip of whiskey and pushed the bottle into Dalton's hand.

The group was quiet for a moment before Jack finally asked, "In what way?"

"Yeah, none of us *belong* anywhere," Nel chimed in, "that's why we're here. We make our own way."

Alec shook his head, "you're not understanding me, my brother brought me along. I'm only here because he wanted me here, not because of what I can offer. He's the expedition leader, which leaves no place for me."

Dalton, who had been quietly listening throughout the entire conversation, finally said, "That's the wrong way to look at this." When he realized everyone's focus was actually trained on him for once, he continued, "you're on this expedition now. It doesn't matter where you came from or how you got here, you're here now. You're a part of it. We're all players in this story now, and any one of us can change the narrative at any given time. We don't know the parts we'll play, but if you spend your whole life searching for your place in the world, you'll exclude yourself from everywhere you think you don't belong." He paused, looked straight into Alec's eyes, and said, "you make your own place in this world."

Everyone was silent, contemplating Dalton's unexpected philosophical offering. Even Nel wasn't smiling, nodding slowly in approval with a far-off look in her eyes. Alec had to admit there was something that made a lot of sense in Dalton's statement, and for the briefest of moments, he felt emboldened by it.

Jack reached over and pulled the whiskey bottle out of Dalton's hand. "I like that," he said to Dalton, nodding his head thoughtfully, "I like that."

He went to take a drink from the bottle but Nel snatched it out of his hand before it had reached his lips. She raised it into the air and said, "To making your own place in this world." Everyone nodded and mumbled their agreement, before she added, "even if you have to take it by force."

Everyone laughed, Jack even cheered in approval. The bottle got passed around again and the night continued on with more stories, more laughter, and a lot of drinking.

Alec wasn't sure what time it was when Jack finally announced that he was heading to bed, but it must have been late because the moon was shining brightly from high in the sky, surrounded by a sea of stars more vibrant than he'd ever witnessed before. Dalton followed soon after, mumbling something that was either badly slurred due to the drinking or in fact a foreign language. As his footsteps faded away down below, Alec and Nel were left alone in silence with just the steady rolling of the ocean and the rhythmic soft clanging of metal on metal as a far-off pulley banged against the ship frame in the breeze. Alec had to admit he was enjoying himself. Never before had he felt so removed from his comfort zone, but Dalton was right, it was his own self-made walls that were preventing him from appreciating this adventure they were on. He was out in the middle of the Atlantic sharing a bottle of whiskey with a beautiful woman he didn't know while watching the reflection of the night sky dance and flicker off the ocean waves. He felt as though he were living someone else's life. Someone bolder.

Nel, taking the bottle from Alec, asked in a low voice barely above a whisper, "What are you thinking about right now, Doc?" She was sitting right beside him, leaning slightly against his shoulder, her head resting on the piping behind them.

He paused a moment before responding. "Just thinking about how vast the ocean is," he lied.

Nel turned to look at him, taking another long drink of whiskey as she studied his face. "You're a good guy Alec," she said finally. "Can I tell you something?"

"Ummm, sure," Alec responded uncertainly. He had no idea what she was going to say, but he was acutely aware that the dynamic was beginning to feel a lot more intimate.

Still looking him in the eyes, she said, "You're a good guy but I think there's more to you than that. I think you have this image in your head of the kind of person you are, and the kind of person you're supposed to be. But I don't think that's you. I think that's who people have told you you are, and you've believed them. But you don't have to." She had not broken eye contact with him, something he found extremely disarming. "I look forward to meeting the real you," she whispered, before turning back to look out at the ocean.

Alec was taken aback. He did not know how to respond. If he were being honest with himself, that was not the direction he thought the conversation was heading. He stammered, trying to find the right words.

Nel looked sideways at him again and smiled. "You don't have to respond. That's kind of the point. You don't have to do anything you don't want to." She leaned her head sideways, bringing it to rest on his shoulder and closed her eyes, the faintest hint of a smile on her lips.

Alec studied her face for a moment before looking out over the dark horizon again. Yes, he thought to himself, this was definitely someone else's life.

**CHAPTER SEVEN**

# ANOMALY

Alec got a late start the next morning, nursing a headache and feeling especially dizzy after spending the night on the swaying, rocking ship. Once he made his way out to the deck, however, it seemed pretty clear he had not missed much by sleeping in. Jack and Cyrus had already gotten into an argument about the plans for the day, Dalton was talking Cynthia's ear off about lunar cycles, Nel sat hunched in the shade, and the ship pushed ever onwards to the east.

After spending the night drinking and bonding with Nel, Jack, and Dalton, Alec noticed they now seemed to share some unspoken bond; with Jack nodding and smiling every time he passed by and Dalton acting as though they had known each other for years. Even Nel, who had already been overly friendly, seemed to be watching him a little more closely. A few different times he had noticed her studying him from her seat in the shadows, as if she were trying to figure him out. She always smiled and looked away when they locked eyes, but it made him wonder what she was thinking.

As noon approached, Alec thought he might join Nel in the shade but was intercepted by Cyrus, who had said very little to him since they boarded. Cyrus looked fairly anxious, as though he were losing some of his confidence about the voyage. He patted Alec's shoulder and the two started walking down the deck, away from the rest of the crew.

"You seem to be getting along well with the team," Cyrus said, trying hard to make the statement sound light and casual.

"They're a good group of people," Alec answered with a nod, "you should really give them a chance."

Cyrus shot Alec a look and grumbled, "It's not that simple. Every team has its growing pains but when you have a mouthy bastard like Jack, it becomes a toxin in the group."

"Jack may not be the problem," Alec mumbled softly.

Cyrus looked sideways at him with raised eyebrows, shook his head and said, "Look, I'm glad you're getting along with them, I really am. I know it can be hard for you." Alec wondered if that was an intentional jab at him or his brother trying to be comforting. Cyrus continued, "I really need you on my side out here, though. You may not understand this, but in order to be an effective leader you can't let your people second guess your decisions."

Alec stopped walking mid-stride and turned to his brother. "See, it's statements like that right there, that's the problem." Cyrus looked surprised, but Alec had had enough of his brother talking down to him. Rather pleased with the look of confusion on Cyrus's face, Alec continued, "I mean, do you hear yourself when you talk? You will never be an effective leader with this condescending, combative attitude."

Alec thought he must have been emboldened by the conversations of the night before because he had never confronted his brother like that before. And Cyrus looked positively shocked, as if he had assumed Alec would always be on his side without question. When he didn't respond back, Alec continued again, "If you want your people to be loyal to you, you have to listen to them. I mean really listen to them. And understand that maybe, just maybe, they might have ideas worth listening to. Jack's not your enemy, he's just someone with differing views than you. Try treating him with some respect and he could be a useful asset to you."

Cyrus looked completely dumbfounded. Alec couldn't tell if he was hurt or enraged. It seemed as though he had simply been stunned into silence. Maybe Alec had been too harsh on him. Cyrus probably hadn't meant anything by his statement. After a few moments of silence, Alec lowered his voice and said, "I'm sorry, I'm not saying you're a bad leader. I was just trying to remind you to take it easy out here. I shouldn't have said all that."

Cyrus blinked several times and finally replied, "No no, don't apologize. I get it."

Now it was Alec's turn to be shocked. He had never seen his brother admit to his own faults before. Maybe all Cyrus needed was a stern reminder to keep his attitude in check. "I'm glad," Alec said, softening his voice significantly, "and look, I didn't mean to come at you so aggressively, I wasn't trying to hurt you."

"No, I get it," Cyrus repeated again. "I'm glad you said something. I shouldn't have expected you to understand what it takes to be a leader."

Alec felt like he'd just been slapped across the face. "Cy, I didn't mean…"

"Save it," Cyrus spat back. "You can feel how you want about it, but the fact is they came to me to lead this expedition, not you. *If* I want your advice, I'll find you. Until then, listen and do as you're told."

Cyrus turned on his heel and strode away at a brisk pace, leaving Alec staring after him in disbelief. He was going to call to him but excited yelling from the front of the ship drew his attention. Several crew members were running across the deck and Dalton, leaning out over the front railing, turned around and shouted, "We're here!" Alec started walking towards him, with Cyrus racing past to see for himself.

As he approached the front railing, Alec could see several small Navy ships in the water, and on the turbulent ocean ahead the giant remnants of the crashed cargo ship's ruined frame came into view. It was quite a bit larger than their ship, but was tilted precariously to one side. It did not sway much in the water, despite the waves crashing against its side, and as Alec's gaze reached the exposed hull, he could see why. The metal was smashed and bent against a rock outcropping so forcefully the rock appeared to actually be embedded in the side of the ship. And it wasn't just the hull that was damaged. Every railing, beam, handle, and foothold was horrifically warped and twisted. The entire frame looked as though it had been melted. Not melted, Alec decided; it was more like it had been pulled. Like every appendage sticking off the ship had been pulled backwards by an energy with enough power to bend metal. And those materials that could not bend appeared to have broken off entirely, like a wooden ladder off the back that now only included three rungs ending in a splintered mess of shrapnel. Strangely, there did not appear to be any debris in the water. Maybe the Navy ships had cleaned it up already?

As Alec glanced down the line of onlookers staring off the back of the ship, many had their mouths hung open in confusion and awe. Dalton was shaking his head as if he simply could not comprehend what he was seeing. Nel and Jack both looked thoroughly confused. And Alec agreed, what he was seeing did not make any logical sense. There was nothing in the known world that could have done this to the heavy metal frame of a cargo ship. He couldn't help thinking that Cyrus had been right; this defied the laws of physics as they were currently understood.

Cyrus, who had been in a visibly angry mood just seconds before, grinned in spite of himself and turned to the team. "Alright, gear up everyone! I want to be out on the water in five!"

The excitement from the team was palpable. For the first time since embarking, no one was arguing or bickering, in fact no one was even talking. They boarded the dinghies in silent anticipation and paddled out onto the rough ocean waters. The shipwreck loomed directly ahead, positively towering over them from down on the surface of the Atlantic. Collapsible ladders had been rolled down the sides of the ship at several places; one was in use as the Navy worked on evacuating some of the crew. The majority of the hull seemed to be intact, with the exception of the one side being impaled on the rock. There did not seem to be any other signs of damage.

A Navy crewman was at the base of one of the ladders, waiting to help them climb aboard. Alec found the swaying, unsteady ladder climb rather nerve-wracking, but no one else was complaining so he clenched his teeth and pushed his fear aside. The worst part was climbing over the bent top railing and onto the deck, but his anxiety faded once he had his feet planted on a level, steady surface once again. Once the entire team had boarded, they made their way down the ship, Alec running his hand along the warped railings. There was something incredibly eerie about the twisted structures surrounding them, accentuated by the relative lack of crew and ghostly silence. He had never been on board a ship without the general hustle and bustle of the deck-hands and men at work. There was a palpable sense of dread in the air that hung heavy, an almost indescribable feeling that something bad had happened, even though they now knew all crew had survived the ordeal with only minor injuries. In fact the event, whatever it had been, seemed to be entirely over. Whatever had pulled on these railings, and the rest of the ship, didn't seem to be pulling anymore.

The team approached a group of Navy men ahead, standing around a robust man with a giant walrus moustache. They all turned as the team approached, and one of the officers called out, "Dr. Dorn?"

Cyrus, leading the team, extended his hand and introduced himself, without bothering to do the same for the rest of the crew.

The officer put his hand on the large man's shoulder and said, "This is Captain Froescher. He's ready to brief you on any details from the incident you might have questions on."

"It's good to meet you, Captain Froescher," Cyrus exclaimed, flashing his most winning smile. "The details of your ordeal have been rather hazy as they've been described to me. Why don't you start from the beginning and tell us what happened."

So Captain Froescher launched into a long-winded telling of how he felt the deck of the ship shutter and vibrate violently before being pulled backwards without perceptible cause. He had witnessed the metal handrails bending right in front of him and described a horrible pressure behind his eyes as his entire body had been pressed against a solid wall behind him. As it turned out, Captain Froescher had a proclivity for telling long stories, and was drawing out each moment of his tale as though he were reciting a Shakespearean monologue. Dalton, of all people, appeared to lose interest first, and turned to look out at the horizon behind the ship.

"And then there's this," the captain said dramatically, producing from his pocket an old-looking compass. "Notice anything strange about it?"

The team all leaned in over the compass, except for Dalton who was evidently distracted by the horizon. Alec saw the problem right away, and so did a few other members of the team, but that didn't stop Captain Froescher from theatrically explaining. "This compass is no longer pointing north. It's pointing in the direction the ship was pulled, and so is the mounted compass in my quarters."

Cyrus studied the compass with a look Alec had not seen on his face before. Was it confusion? Concern? Jack reached out and brushed his finger along its surface. "Can I see that?" he asked.

"Dr. Dorn," came Dalton's voice from the railing. Had he finally decided the captain's story was worth his time? But Dalton wasn't looking at the group. He was still staring intently out at the ocean. "Dr. Dorn!" he said, more forcefully this time. "You need to see this."

The team rushed to the railing and looked out at the horizon. But there was nothing there; just endless blue water, a few rock outcroppings breaking the surface of the waves, and three or four seagulls flying low searching for fish. Alec turned to Dalton, trying to deduce exactly what he was so fixated on, and saw that his eyes seemed to be trained on the flying gulls. Alec looked back at the birds, but they didn't seem to be doing anything out of the ordinary. One was chirping and cawing from above while several others skimmed the surface of the water. Even from a biologist's perspective, this behavior was not that exciting to watch. One gull dove down and, with a small splash, plucked a fish out of the waves. It glided a couple of feet above the roiling ocean, flapped its wings gently, then vanished.

Alec blinked in confusion. Where had it gone? Had he lost track of it? He scanned the area quickly but there was no sign of the bird anywhere. Had he not been watching them so closely, he never would have noticed, but he was certain it had been there just a moment before, and now it wasn't. There were now only three gulls circling the nearby rocks. There had been four before, right? He couldn't be sure. He was beginning to second-guess what he had seen. But then, in the blink of an eye, a second bird vanished from view. This time he was positive; nothing had stopped it or hit it or interfered with it in any way. It was flying one moment, then it was simply gone the next.

Alec turned to the team for confirmation of what he was witnessing. Cyrus looked pale white with his mouth ever so slightly open. In a soft, almost hypnotized voice, he muttered, "Get to the boats." Then, seeming to come out of his perplexed stupor, he turned to the team and almost yelled, "To the boats, now!"

The team scrambled down the hanging ladders off the side of the ship and piled into the two dinghies as fast as they could move. The boat with Cyrus, Alec, Dalton, and Nel was pushing off towards the rock formations before Jack, Cynthia, and Lieutenant Allen had even reached their own. But Alec could tell Cyrus was not prepared to wait on anyone. The choppy water tossed them about as they approached the rocks, making it especially difficult to pinpoint exactly where the birds had been disappearing from. Cyrus scanned the horizon frantically, looking for any clue, anything out of the ordinary. Jack's voice called out from behind them. Cyrus paid it absolutely no attention but Alec turned to see him waving and gesturing. Their dinghy was still about thirty feet behind them, and falling still further behind.

"Cyrus, stop!" Jack called out, still without a reaction from Cyrus. "We need to think this through!"

Alec was beginning to see Jack's point, they had no idea what they were barreling into, and they were already breaking his rule of keeping the dinghies close. "Cy, slow down," Alec urged, trying to keep his voice steady, but Cyrus was only looking forward with a fiery intensity. Jack was still calling his name from behind, but his voice was starting to be drowned out by the increasing intensity of the waves. Their boat was beginning to tilt violently from one side to another, threatening to dump them all into the dark, foaming ocean. They were also getting dangerously close to the rock outcroppings, but they had very little control of the boat at this point.

"Mind those rocks!" Dalton shouted out, but Cyrus was still frantically scanning the area. Alec realized this was probably very near where he had seen the gull vanish, but there was nothing around them. Cyrus's searching was becoming more and more desperate until he finally stood up in the swaying boat, craning his neck for a better vantage point of the area. Alec noticed there were no more birds flying around. He was trying to figure out if they had also vanished or simply flown away when a wave crashed against the side of the dinghy, tilting it so dramatically that water poured in over the edge. Everyone managed to hold on as the boat righted itself except for Cyrus, who fell backwards over the side and into the water; at least he would have fallen into the water had they not been so near one of the rock outcroppings.

Alec saw Cyrus's head smash against the rock structure with an audible crack. His body went instantly limp before he crumpled into the ocean and was sucked below the bubbling surface. The panic was immediate as everyone scrambled to the edges of the boat looking for him to resurface.

"Somebody grab him!" Cynthia yelled from the other boat, still fifteen feet behind them. Alec had no idea what to do, not trusting his own swimming abilities in such rough waters. Dalton looked entirely beside himself with fear, grasping the side of the dinghy with white-knuckled hands, and Nel was clutching her forehead, which was bleeding profusely from beneath her hand.

While Alec was completely frozen with shock at the ensuing chaos, Jack leapt into action, launching himself from the other boat into the white-capped surf. He dove below the crashing waves, his head reappearing only briefly to get his bearings before vanishing again. Alec scanned the water in panic, cursing himself for his inaction. Another wave sent the boat careening into the side of the rocks, splintering the wood paneling and allowing the cold Atlantic water to rush in. Alec tried to grab hold of the rock to steady the boat but algae growth had made it slippery and he lost his grip.

After what felt like an eternity, Jack finally resurfaced supporting Cyrus over one shoulder, who appeared to be unconscious and bleeding badly from the back of the head. Jack yelled out for help but the boat was taking in water fast and could no longer hold their weight. Nel looked like she was now blinded by the blood seeping into her eyes as she kept pressure on her forehead. Their only hope would be the other boat, but it was never going to get to them before they sank. Alec's side of the dinghy was now halfway underwater, soaking him up to his waist. Another wave broke over the siding, forcing the boat completely below the surface, leaving Alec, Dalton, and Nel treading water where it had been moments before.

White, foaming waves pounded over their heads, making it impossible to even tell which direction the other boat was. Alec could barely catch a breath between each violent swell. His ears were filling with water as his head was dunked again and again. The pressure in his ears was building, along with an even more intense pressure behind his eyes. His whole head felt as though it were filling up with water, and a slowly building pain in his teeth made it feel like they were about to be ripped from his mouth. Alec yelled out in pain, struggling to keep his head above the surface of the crushing ocean. As he reached out with his hands to fight the sucking waves, he realized his fingers were being contorted inwards; forced into clenched fists. His entire body was seizing up, each of his joints curling in on themselves. He kicked frantically, fighting with everything he had to keep his head above water. He was certain his skull was about to explode from the pressure, which was now forcing his jaw to clench shut. An extremely loud ringing in his ears made it impossible to tell where anyone or anything was around him, but he was certain he was about to die. The muscles in his legs were now beginning to seize up too and that was the only thing stopping him from sinking like a stone to the bottom of the Atlantic.

Alec reached out blindly with his clenched hand in a last desperate attempt to find something, anything, to keep himself above water. To his surprise he felt his fist grind against something hard and rough. He reached out with his other hand and it too felt a large, flat surface. He forced his fingers open as much as he possibly could to find a grip on the unknown mass before he was dragged away again, but strangely, he felt like he was being pulled towards it. His body pressed into his arms and his chest hammered into the large object, knocking the wind out of him. Alec gasped for breath, inhaled deeply, and choked when he sucked in what felt like sand and dirt. He began coughing uncontrollably and realized that the large object he had run into seemed to be solid ground. He could feel rocks and pebbles beneath his hands now, but no water.

He sputtered and gasped, spitting out ocean water all the while, but he could not get his bearings straight. It seemed as though he were on his hands and knees now, on flat ground. And it was not just flat ground, it also felt like dry ground. The rushing noises in his ears were beginning to lessen and the pressure behind his eyes was slowly going away. As the ringing subsided, he could hear others around him coughing and groaning, but no more waves. He couldn't hear water of any kind; in its place he could hear birds chirping, and what sounded like a gentle breeze blowing at the trees.

# CHAPTER EIGHT

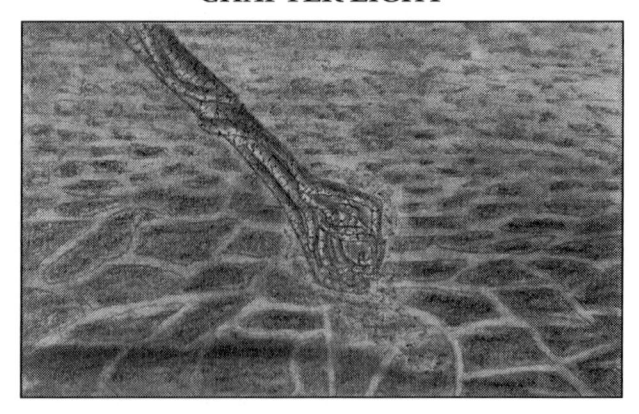

# MORA

Alec opened his eyes slowly and winced as harsh sunlight flooded his vision. He forced them open, barely able to see anything as they adjusted. There was definitely solid ground beneath him. The ground looked peculiar though. Directly in front of his face was what looked like a reddish piece of translucent bark that had been burnt around the edges. Alec gave it a flick with his finger and it bounced away. Actually, the entire ground looked odd, seeming to be made up of dark, burnt sand and stone with deep ribbons of glowing embers beneath creating a crackling, fractured pattern, like mud when it's dried in the sun. The ground looked like it should be hot, but it wasn't.

Alec raised his head to look around and discovered the cracked, glowing ground extended out in front of him a few hundred feet, pushing up against a line of trees that looked to be the edge of a forest. He did not understand. He had just been in the water, surrounded by nothing but ocean. Where was he? Had he hit his head possibly? Or had he died and this was heaven... or hell? He shook the thought from his head and suddenly remembered he had heard other people behind him. He spun around to see Jack, Cyrus, Nel, and Dalton all gazing around with the same confused, uncomprehending looks he was sure he had. The first thing he noted was that Cyrus was awake, although he looked pretty out of it. Nel had a fairly superficial cut on her forehead that nevertheless was covering half her face in blood. She must have hit it on the side of the boat during the chaos. Jack and Dalton looked okay apart from being soaked and confused.

There was debris lying all around them; pieces of splintered wood, metal nuts and bolts, even a pair of eyeglasses, but there was no sign of the other dinghy. The forest surrounded the illuminated orange and burnt black field completely, but the Atlantic was nowhere to be seen. Alec wanted to say something; he felt like he should say something, but he did not know what to say. Any words he could use would not describe the total and complete bafflement he was feeling at the current moment. It seemed useless to even talk at all because it was so far beyond his understanding. It was as though he were in a fog; a hazy cloud that he could not think his way out of. Like his brain was going in slow motion and was hopeless to catch up to reality.

Jack Viana spoke first, but instead of voicing the obvious question, he turned to Cyrus and muttered threateningly, "What did you do?"

Cyrus just stammered as he looked around at the surrounding field, his eyes wide and unblinking. Alec moved clumsily towards Nel and attempted to examine her cut forehead but she flinched as he reached for her and pulled away, stating defensively, "I'm fine Doc." He wasn't even sure why he had tried to look at her wound, he just felt like he should be doing something. Looking after an injured person made sense to him. Nothing else did. A familiar cawing sound made everyone look up. High in the sky above them were three seagulls, circling around each other and chattering back and forth. There was something oddly comforting about that sight.

There was another sound as well. Alec tilted his head to listen and realized with a start that it was footsteps, *running* footsteps! Everyone looked around wildly for the source of the noise, expecting perhaps to see Cynthia or Lieutenant Allen. At the far end of the field Alec finally identified the source; four people were running out of the forest from a narrow foot-trail he had not seen before. It was immediately evident these were not people from their ship. The first thing he noticed was their wardrobes, which looked almost like armor from this distance.

And they were each carrying something. Alec squinted and realized they were each carrying a sword. It was as if four knights of old had just run out of the past and into present day. The closer they got, however, the less they looked like knights from the past. Their *'armor'* actually seemed to be made of leathers and cloths, cut and colored in a way that was clearly meant to look like the middle-ages. And their *'swords'* were not actually swords in the strictest sense, but rather large machetes that appeared to be rusting through.

Despite their strange appearance, they were approaching very fast, and they were armed. The group's dumbfounded silence suddenly gave way to panic as they realized they had nowhere to go and nothing to defend themselves with if the newcomers turned out to be hostile. Dalton quickly darted to the back of the group, apparently with no intention of standing his ground. Cyrus got unsteadily to his feet and gingerly touched the back of his head, but Jack and Nel strode to the front of the group ready to confront the approaching foursome. Alec, emboldened by the bravery of his newfound allies, walked to stand next to them but Nel held out her arm, almost protectively, keeping him behind her.

The *knights* slowed their approach about ten feet from the group, the one in front planting his feet and pointing his battered weapon at them. He opened his mouth and called out to them in a deep, commanding voice, "He is coming! Bow for your king."

Alec glanced sideways at the rest of the team. Nel stood expressionless with one eye half closed from blood caked over it, and Jack had his eyebrows raised in a confused scowl. No one made any move to bow, not even Dalton.

Jack called back to them, "Hello there! We seem to have lost our way; can you tell us where we are?"

Alec felt 'lost our way' was putting it mildly, but he credited Jack for keeping a level head. Looking back at the lead knight, however, he had not reacted at all. He still had his machete pointed at them and the same stony-faced glare. "You are outsiders here, and you will bow for your king."

Alec observed that these people did not seem surprised or confused about seeing them. On the contrary, the way they said 'outsiders' gave him the distinct impression they were not the first 'outsiders' they had come across.

Cyrus gave a nervous laugh and boldly responded, "What king? Are you the King?" When the man did not respond, Cyrus continued, "We need to speak to whoever's in charge. And until that happens, we are not bowing to anyone."

The knight never changed his expression, but lowered his machete and strode towards them, the other three following closely behind.

"Hey, hey, hey," Jack exclaimed, backing up and putting his hands in the air. "We're not looking for trouble, we just want answers."

The knights were fanning out to flank their group from the sides, and the lead knight approached Cyrus head on. In one swift motion, the entire team had their legs kicked out from beneath them. Alec's shoulders were forced to the ground roughly and he saw Dalton fall next to him with an audible whimper. Cyrus and Jack were still trying to talk their way out of the situation, even from lying face down on the ground, but they were receiving no responses from the men. Alec was terrified any moment he would feel the touch of cold metal on the back of his neck, but the knights just stood over them, holding them down.

An unearthly shriek echoed out from across the field so loudly Alec flinched from where he lay. Despite all the confusion, he was sure of one thing; he had never heard a noise like that in his life. He began to feel the ground vibrating beneath him and heard what sounded like wheels rattling against the earth. He risked what he intended to be a quick glance in the direction of the sound but once he saw what was approaching, he could not look away.

A man was standing upright being pulled on what appeared to be an ornate wooden chariot, its two large wheels bouncing erratically on the uneven terrain. But it wasn't the chariot, or the man riding it, that made Alec's mouth hang open; it was what was pulling them. Dragging the vehicle were two of the most bizarre and horrifying creatures he had ever seen. They each stood about five feet tall and looked like some sort of bird; but unlike any bird he had ever heard of. They had long, wiry muscular legs ending in three-toed scaly feet with sickeningly long and sharp black talons. Their torsos were feathered with what appeared to be quills running along their backs, and strange, leathery little arms that looked to have membrane connecting them to the bodies, almost like a bat's wings. Their necks were long and feathered like an ostrich, ending in a small head with a pointy, hooked beak. Their faces had horrifically huge, venomous-yellow eyes with dark slits for pupils and pebbly skin surrounding the sockets. Off the backs of their skulls were crowns of splayed, black quill-like feathers, giving the entire creature an angular, spiny appearance. The two animals were making clicking, chittering noises as they ran; their busy heads darting back and forth as they pulled the bouncing chariot.

  Alec moved to back up as they approached but was held down by one of the knight's hands on his back. The creatures stopped on their own within a couple feet of the group, with the chariot rocking to a halt behind them. One of the bird-like animals peered down at Alec with the meanest, most cunning eyes he'd ever looked into, but made no move to attack. From the chariot behind, a heavy foot stepped down and strode over to stand above them. "No, no, no, what is this?" came what sounded like a gravely concerned voice. "We've talked about this; these are our guests, and who knows, maybe our future people. This is no way to treat them." The voice sounded somehow harsh and kind at the same time. "Let them up, please, let them up right now." Alec felt the hand removed from his back and he pulled himself to his knees, looking up at the man looming over them. He looked to be in his mid-forties with shoulder-length dark hair that was starting to turn grey along the sides. He had a kind, smiling face, but his eyes were piercing and cold. He wore a dark, somewhat tattered travelling cloak but a fairly modern looking combat boot stuck out the bottom. A strange pendant that looked like a bronze clawed foot holding an orb the size of a marble hung from his neck to complete the bizarre ensemble.

  "My friends, please, stand," he urged them, offering his hand to Cyrus, who was nearest to him. Alec made a point to step back a pace as he righted himself, attempting to put as much distance as possible between himself and the birds. "Don't worry my friend," the man said, putting a reassuring hand on Alec's shoulder. "They only do as I say." Alec still could not take his eyes off them. This was a creature entirely unknown to science, and wildly unlike any animal he was aware of. "So, you must have questions," the man said, addressing the team as a whole, "fire away, fire away, I'm here to help."

The entire group seemed too alarmed and perplexed to speak up. No one knew what to make of the man, not to mention his horrifying pets. Cyrus finally broke the silence, asking the obvious, "Where are we?"

The man squinted his eyes shut and exclaimed "Oh no, no, starting with an impossible question right out of the gate." He walked over to Cyrus and said, "I like it, and I like you, but you're getting ahead of yourself here. Please, please, please, something easier." The group exchanged confused glances, and the man continued, "How 'bout introductions. We don't even know each other yet." He walked over to the chariot and pulled out two identical, five-foot long scepters, which were rough and rustic in appearance and sharpened into points on the bottoms. They looked like twisted, blackened bark but from within, visible between the grooves in the wood, shone a red, transparent material. It reminded Alec of ruby. The man walked back towards the group with a scepter in each hand and said, "I am King Mora, and this..." he pointed one of the scepters at the cracked, glowing earth and it glowed more vibrantly, "is sacred ground." Not only was the orange ash-like substance below the ground pulsating more brightly, but the red within the scepter had started to glow as well. "These are the sacred Fire Fields of Mon Tah," the King exclaimed.

Alec sensed trouble coming, and apparently Jack did as well because he quickly responded, "We sincerely apologize, we didn't know. We did not mean any disrespect."

The King looked at Jack, then began to laugh. "I'm joking with you!" The King shouted in delight. "Don't worry, don't worry, not everything around here is sacred, I assure you. No such place as Mon Tah!" He continued his echoing, belly laugh, while the team shifted uncomfortably and each forced a smile. "No, no, here's what you need to know," he continued jovially, pointing back the way he had come, "that trail leads to the Temple, it's sort of the center of my Kingdom, you can find me there if you ever have any problems. If you go off to the southwest, you'll find town; you can all find a place to stay there. These are our

Fire Fields, as I've mentioned, and behind you to the east is the rest of the Kingdom; more rural but a decent population lives there."

The King looked at the team as though he had likely covered any questions they might have. Nel eventually spoke up, "So, *King* Mora," she began with what Alec thought was far too sarcastic-sounding fealty. "We were on a small boat, a part of an expedition ship. We were in the water one second and the next..." She trailed off, possibly realizing how crazy it sounded. It struck Alec that it was the first time one of them had acknowledged out loud what had happened to them. It made it all uncomfortably real, as if admitting what they'd experienced suddenly made it necessary to find an explanation.

King Mora was nodding his head understandingly, not appearing surprised in the slightest by the circumstances of their arrival. "Every year more come. Some were in the water when they arrived, some were on a ship; one poor bastard was returning home from war. The fact is the world is a vast and mysterious place, and people get swallowed up by it all the time. The good news is my Kingdom is a place of welcoming. Follow a few simple rules and you can make a life here."

"Make a life here?" Dalton balked.

Cyrus, shaking his head, said, "No we need to get back. I have a wife waiting for me. In fact, she was out on the water with us..."

"You won't be seeing her again," the King responded without the slightest hint of compassion or sympathy. "I don't know how else I can explain this to you, you're here now. And we are being very welcoming. Give it a try, you may find you like it here."

"That's not the point," Jack retorted aggressively. "We can't stay here; we don't belong here. We don't even know where *here* is."

The King looked momentarily angry by Jack's outburst, but then a broad smile overtook his face and he said gently, "My friends, I understand. You must be weary from your journey, and I'm certain you want to relax after the ordeal you've been through. I can have someone set you up in your new homes..."

"No, stop," Cyrus snapped, "You're not listening to us; we are not staying here."

The King's expression darkened, the smile finally leaving his face entirely. "You have just broken one of the very few rules I have here; you will not disrespect me... ever."

The group went silent. Having been caught up by his strange appearance and demeanor, they had forgotten that this was a man they knew absolutely nothing about, and as he locked eyes with each member of the team, Alec had one thought; this man is dangerous. The two bird-like creatures appeared suddenly agitated, each taking on a more threatening stance even while still being tethered to the chariot. Their eyes were sharp and searching, scanning the group before them while making rattling, hissing sounds.

"Oh now look what you've done," the King said, much softer and less aggressively then he had been a second before. He approached one of the creatures and stroked it gently on the neck. "You've upset my friends here," he continued, turning and whispering to them soothingly, "it's okay my darlings, calm down."

The team stared in cowed silence. To everyone's surprise, it was Dalton who finally spoke up; trying a lighter approach to release the tension. "That is a hell of a bond you have with those animals," he exclaimed in what Alec felt was convincing enthusiasm. "The mutual trust on display there is just staggering."

The King looked up at Dalton, studying his face with his unreadable eyes. Alec began to worry Dalton had somehow offended him further, until he finally broke into a smile again and declared excitedly, "They're incredible creatures." He walked back towards the group beaming once again and said, "please forgive my rudeness; they get upset when I get upset."

Alec patted Dalton on the back for course correcting the situation with his quick thinking, but to his regret, the King seemed to notice the gesture. He was now pacing his way through the group, dragging the two scepters along the blackened earth as he went. "The truth is, I would help you leave if I could. It's not my rules keeping you here. You've found yourselves in a place entirely apart from the world you know. The good news, as I've tried to explain to you, is that we welcome outsiders. I'm going to direct you to a man named Ydoro in town, he's sort of our welcoming committee for newcomers. He can help get you settled." He paused and looked around at the team smiling expectantly, as though he were waiting for a thank you. No one spoke. Alec's mind felt like it was moving in slow motion again, struggling to make sense of everything. He noticed the smile momentarily flicker from the King's face as he looked back at them.

"Have you ever seen ground like this before?" the King asked, indicating the glowing orange ash illuminating from beneath the cracked, burnt-looking stone and sand. "We call it frozen fire. Quite safe to come in contact with... but given the right touch..." He upended one of the scepters in his hand and held the twisted root of a top within a few inches of the ground. The ground beneath pulsated brightly and a trail of glowing particles of ash floated into the air and created a strange, spiraling orbit around the staff head. "It's not so harmless anymore," the King continued, watching for their reactions. "It's a good thing we're friends, eh?" He brought the head of the scepter back up into the air and the glowing embers followed it, continuing to orbit briefly before burning out and vanishing. An enormous, warm-looking smile suddenly broke across his face again and he exclaimed exuberantly, "I'm just so happy you're here! Are you happy to be here?"

The group exchanged uncomfortable glances before mumbling their agreement that they were indeed happy. There was a strange, child-like quality about the King. Alec could not tell if the continuous, sudden mood swings between threatening and welcoming were an act or not. One thing was becoming increasingly clear, however; they needed to tread lightly around this man. "I like you, all of you," the King said, still beaming as he looked around the group. "Especially you," he said, pointing at Dalton. "What's your name?"

Dalton looked taken aback and responded, "Uh, thank you. I'm Dr. Dalton Sydney."

"Dalton," the King repeated. "Mr. Dalton. You know why I like you Mr. Dalton? You know just the right way to talk to someone to make them happy. You know the exact right words to make someone do what you want."

Dalton furrowed his brow in confusion but before he could respond, the King lashed out with frightening speed and thrust one of the spear-tipped scepters straight into his neck. The group gasped in horror as Dalton clutched at the scepter, trying to stem the blood spurting from the wound. The King raised his foot and kicked Dalton squarely in the chest, sending him careening backwards and coming to rest directly in front of the two awaiting creatures. With a piercing screech and lightning speed, one of the birds struck out with its sharp beak and long neck, the same way a snake would bite a victim, nearly severing Dalton's neck clean in half with one snap.

The field instantly became a frenzy of chaos as the team shouted and screamed, with Jack rushing towards Dalton and the creatures, even though it was very clearly too late. The nearest creature hooked its talon-tipped foot into Dalton's abdomen and hissed threateningly as Jack approached, and the King began to laugh.

"Relax," the King called out. "I was just making a point, you understand."

Nel made a move towards the King but Cyrus got there first, punching him hard in the lower jaw. The King staggered backwards and Cyrus punched him again, this time hitting him in the cheek. The King went down onto one knee, his head bowed in pain, but before Cyrus could advance further, the King raked both scepter heads across the ground creating a fiery storm of glowing ash in their wake. In one swift motion, King Mora whipped the scepters to point forward towards Cyrus, sending brilliant streams of burning sand and rock directly into his face. Cyrus howled out in pain and fell to his knees, clutching the right side of his cheek.

Shocking even himself, Alec charged headlong towards the King, aiming to tackle him entirely off his feet and wrestle one of the weapons from him. The King saw him coming, however, and in a quick sweeping motion, shot a blast of the red-hot embers into his shoulder and chest. The burning, searing pain was instant and excruciating and the force was strong enough to launch him backwards off his feet. He landed on his back with his eyes pressed shut from the agony, but he opened them again quickly when he realized his upper shirt sleeve was on fire. He batted at the budding flames frantically and was able to put them out fast, leaving a large, scorched hole in his shirt and burnt fabric melted into an angry red wound.

"Everybody calm down!" King Mora shouted. "I'm disappointed in all of you. I had higher hopes for you."

Alec struggled to turn onto his side, unable to stand after being thrown backwards. The four knights had not made a move during the struggle, standing silently on all sides of the group. Jack was knelt down near Dalton's motionless legs, having somehow wrenched the body from the hissing creatures. Cyrus was still on the ground with one hand pressed over his right cheek and eye; charred red skin showing from beneath. Nel was the only team member left standing, and she was facing the King with her jaw set and her eyes unblinking with hatred. King Mora looked at her with cold, calculating eyes and said, "I'm going to need that bow from you now." She remained planted where she stood, and Alec was certain he was about to see her killed as well. The King studied her, then lowered the scepter heads towards the glowing ground threateningly and said with a grin, "You gonna make a move, beautiful?"

Nel, without breaking eye contact, finally responded in a steady voice, "Oh, I'll be coming for you," and then slowly lowered herself to one knee in a respectful bow.

The smile returned to King Mora's face instantly and he announced happily, "I knew this was going to work out, I just knew it!" He was positively beaming again and strode towards his chariot with a spring in his step. "Go find Ydoro," he repeated, "He can get you settled. And please please please don't leave your friend just lying here in my Fire Fields," he said, referring to Dalton's lifeless body. "I don't want to have to worry about running him over next time I'm passing through." He mounted his chariot and, with a casual salute of his hand, said, "Til our paths cross again…"

The chariot jerked into motion as the creatures pulled forward with relative ease. The King never whipped them or gave any visible signal for them to start walking; it seemed they just knew. As they rattled off the way they had come, King Mora leaned off the back of his chariot and called back to them, "I'm so glad you've come! It's a madhouse around here!" He turned away and continued calling out in a singsong voice, "A madhouse. A madhouse." The guards quickly dispersed as well, running after the chariot, which had reached the tree line and disappeared up the trail.

The fractured team stood in silence; every one of their heads hung in defeat. How could this have happened? An hour earlier, they had been arriving at the shipwreck; the mood alight with anticipation and curiosity. Now the group was broken. They were in a strange new world run by a madman, they had no idea what had become of Cynthia or Lieutenant Allen, and Dalton Sydney's bloodied body lay on the ground in front of them. Alec felt like he should be reacting in some way; with sadness, or rage, or hopelessness; instead he just felt numb. He knew all of those feelings were there, but his brain was pushing them to his subconscious. Everything he had witnessed was simply too much to comprehend with emotion in the mix. Dalton had been his friend, though, and he deserved better.

"I want to bury him," Alec finally said, breaking the heavy silence.

The group nodded in agreement, and Cyrus responded in a low, subdued voice, "Absolutely. Why don't you and Nel find a spot beneath the trees and look for branches to start digging. Jack and I can take care of the body."

An hour ago, the idea of Jack and Cyrus doing anything together willingly would have been out of the question. Now, Jack nodded silently and stepped forward. Nel and Alec began walking towards the edge of the Fire Fields, staying away from the path the King had taken. Alec looked sideways at Nel and finally asked, "Are you okay?"

When she did not respond, Alec reached out a hand to place on her shoulder, but she recoiled at the gesture.

"Stop," she said harshly. "Look, I get it. You're looking for emotional support after what we just saw. I feel it too. But we can't lose ourselves to grief and misery right now. We cannot." She stopped walking and turned to him, putting a hand on each of his shoulders. "We were weak. And that animal took advantage of us because we were weak." There was a burning fire in her eyes that both impressed Alec and frightened him a bit. "We will not be weak the next time we see him. Do you understand?"

Alec just nodded and Nel continued walking. Maybe she was right and they should be thinking about what to do the next time they saw the King; but right now Alec felt nothing but sorrow, and he needed to bury his friend.

## CHAPTER NINE

# WELCOME TO THE KINGDOM

Cyrus gently ran his fingers along his temple, tracing the edges of the raw, charred burn that covered almost half his face. His right eye was swollen shut but he had hope that the eyeball was undamaged because he was able to move it around beneath the lid. He could not worry about his own injuries right now, however, the team needed someone to lead them, and if he were being honest with himself, he was no longer sure he was the person for the job.

Burying Dalton had been one of the harder things he had ever had to do. They had dug at the ground for hours using sticks and rocks and their bare hands. It was absurd that he would take it this hard when he had only known the man for forty-eight hours, but the hole they all felt in the team was so real. Cyrus also felt responsible for the safety of the team, and it was his own bullheadedness that had strayed them off course. No one had said a word the entire time they were digging, but once the dirt was put into place and a large stone was set to mark the spot, it seemed only right that something should be said. When no one spoke up, Cyrus stepped forward, but his words failed him and all he was able to mutter was, "I'm sorry Dalton."

After the burial, the team had walked back to the area where they had first found themselves; it was easy to find because of the collection of debris surrounding it. Despite spending a full hour examining everything, from the ground to the air to every bit of shattered wood, they could find nothing unusual about it. There was simply no explanation for how they had been transported here from the middle of the Atlantic Ocean. After debating for quite a while, it was decided that their best move for the time being was to walk into town and find this man named Ydoro. None of them liked the idea of following any of the King's directions, but out in the middle of the open fields, they were very exposed. Nel had made the argument for pushing further into the surrounding forest and setting up camp there, but Jack pointed out that they did not know the area and the King was likely to discover them.

So they found themselves walking through the forest along a trail that seemed to lead in the direction the King had pointed. The forest felt subtly different from any forest he had been in before. He could not quite put his finger on it, but there was something distinctly *unfamiliar* about it. Alec had even spotted a bird that he was unable to identify. He said it looked similar to a Resplendent Quetzal, but the markings and coloration were not quite right. At first, they thought they could use the brilliant green bird to narrow down where they were in the world, with the sighting pointing towards Central America, but Alec insisted it was a different species entirely, and one he had never heard of before. Alec had been very quiet since their arrival, but he absolutely refused to have a personal conversation with Cyrus. Cyrus did not blame him, but he felt it was his duty as the older brother to make sure he was okay. His pushing so far had only succeeded in aggravating Alec further, however. He also worried about Cynthia. He kept telling himself that more than likely her and Lieutenant Allen's boat had remained on the ocean, and they were safely back on the ship by now, but he could not be sure. Being unable to piece together exactly what happened in their final moments on the ocean, there was precious little he could be sure of. Alec was still willing to speak to him about their current situation, so the two had been debating back and forth about what they knew and tossing wild theories around as they walked, with Nel and Jack occasionally chiming in.

"So, a portal to another world?" Jack was asking skeptically, "is that what we're thinking now? Is that even remotely possible?"

"You saw those creatures," Alec answered, shaking his head. "I don't think we can put anything off the table at this juncture. And you saw what the King could do with those staffs. He called it *frozen fire*, but I don't know of any element that behaves like that, do you?"

"So if we're thinking we got pulled through... something," Jack continued slowly, trying to piece his thoughts together as he spoke, "and that's how we arrived here, that means we're assuming the same thing also happened to the seagulls we were watching."

"Yes exactly," Alec responded, "didn't you see them flying above the Fire Fields? Now I can't be certain they were the same ones, but..."

"Okay so that means it was that same force that pulled the cargo ship? Why didn't it get pulled through like we did?"

"Because of the rocks," Cyrus suggested. "The ship was being pulled, forcefully enough to bend metal it turns out, but it got caught on those rocks."

"Okay but that's very different than what we experienced," Jack persisted, "I mean, they were pulled by a force strong enough to warp their ship, but we didn't feel anything unusual until we were within a few feet of... it. The force you're talking about... we would have been pulled off the ship."

Everyone quietly considered this. He had a point, whatever that initial force was that pulled the ship, it was not the same as what they felt; or it had substantially lessened.

"And why didn't the other dinghy get pulled through after us?" Nel posited. "They should've been right on top of us, they couldn't have been more than fifteen feet behind. If all of these events were caused by the same anomaly, then why did it lose so much strength between pulling the ship backwards and us going through, and why did it close right behind us?"

The group was mystified into silence once again. They could theorize all they wanted but the truth was they did not have enough information to come up with an answer. They were all starting to realize that.

"What we can all agree on is that we need to find a way to get back through," Cyrus said finally. "We didn't find any answers in that field, but if we're heading towards a town, that should mean more people. Maybe one of them can help us. The way the King kept talking about 'outsiders' sounded like we weren't the first."

"And what are we doing about the King?" Alec asked as though he were waiting for the topic to be brought up. "That can't be ignored."

Cyrus was not following. "What do you mean exactly? What is it you want to do about the King?"

"Well, are you just content to let him get away with this?" Alec asked in a tone thick with accusation.

"My goal, my *only* goal, is to get the rest of the team out of here safely," Cyrus countered. "We can't be thinking about getting even right now. I wish something could be done, I really do, and if we come across him again, we will have to take action, but we've got nothing. Look at us, we have nothing but the clothes on our backs. We don't even have our bags or any supplies."

"That's not entirely true," Alec stated, and for the first time, Cyrus noticed that Alec had a small hiking pack slung over his shoulder.

"Where did you get that?" Cyrus asked in surprise. "Was that always with you?"

"Yeah, I had it with on the boat, it got dumped into the water when we sank but it showed up in the Fire Fields with us."

"Tell me you have something useful in there," Cyrus said excitedly as the group stopped walking and Alec dropped the bag from his shoulder. He opened the drawstring top and dumped out the contents onto the forest floor. The majority of the supplies were unhelpful; an extra shirt, an extra pair of socks, but more interesting was a medium-sized machete of very high quality and a compass. Cyrus snatched the compass up as soon as he saw it, expecting it to provide answers, or at the very least more questions. But as he examined it, he frowned in disappointment. It was behaving exactly as a compass should behave. It was not spinning in a circle, it was not flipping between opposite poles, it was not even pointing the wrong direction; it was pointing north, and as near as Cyrus could tell by the position of the sun, it was exactly right. He was not sure what he had been expecting, but in a place as unusual as this, he was surprised that, according to a compass, there was absolutely nothing unusual about it.

The group packed up the bag and started walking again, sharing theories or concerns as they came to mind. It was late afternoon by the time the edge of the forest came into view, and beyond that was a rustic little town full of bustling people. It seemed entirely out of place to them after everything they had seen. Despite all the questions and mysteries they had been presented with, despite the general alien nature of everything around them, here was an actual functioning village with people going about their daily routines without a care in the world.

People were arguing and talking in the streets, many of them seemed to be carrying crops or pulling wagons full of them. A woman walked past leading a steer on a tether; was it his imagination or did the steer look a little odd? It almost seemed to have slightly longer legs than normal. None of the people stopped what they were doing as the team approached; indeed, they did not receive a single glance in their direction, although Alec was yelled at to get out of the way as a rough looking man pulling a wagon pushed his way through. The area had the look of a marketplace, with a few small stands set up along the rough stone walls of the surrounding structures. None of the buildings were more than one story and there did not seem to be electricity of any kind. Peering in through the open windows, Cyrus could see torches lining many of the walls. The main road in front of them was wide and comprised of dirt and dust, creating a yellowish-orange fog as it was kicked into the air by the town occupants. The narrower roads leading away from the common area looked to be made of stone and had a winding quality that reminded Cyrus of rural towns he had visited in South America. The town appeared to be fairly large with streets snaking away in all directions and the right side sloping upwards. Dwellings dotted the green hillside and at the very top, overlooking everything else, stood a strange looking fortress. It was not quite a castle, although great lengths seemed to have been made to make it look like one. For one thing, it was not nearly as big or as grand as a legitimate castle; for another there was something very utilitarian about its appearance. It did not have any of the historic charm one would expect from an ancient castle. In fact, it seemed devoid of character altogether; it was simply bleak and foreboding looking.

An elderly woman with a wagon walked in front of them and Cyrus tapped her shoulder and asked, "Excuse me, Miss, can you tell us where we can find Ydoro?"

The woman looked extremely perturbed at being interrupted mid-stride but once she laid eyes on them, her demeanor softened a bit. She looked them up and down and responded, "Yeah, he's in the far building there," gesturing to the opposite side of the square. She glanced at them one more time with a strange look in her eyes, and said, "Welcome to the Kingdom," and shuffled on her way.

The group made their way through the swirling dust in the streets to the building they had been directed towards. They found themselves looking at a heavy wooden door with a brass knocker carved in the shape of a strange-looking serpent. Cyrus knocked uncertainly and the door was almost immediately flung open by a small man in heavy grey robes that were fraying along the edges.

"Welcome to the Kingdom!" the man exclaimed, smiling from ear to ear. He had a strange accent that none of them could place. It could almost be British except his words were more clipped, and the inflection was not quite right. It seemed like a mix of accents, actually. "Come on in, come on in," the man said, stepping aside to admit them. He was a young man; Cyrus would guess early thirties, with dark, wild hair and a trimmed beard. "First day here, eh?" the man asked as they stepped inside. "Well, I am Ydoro, and it's my job to get you settled and acquainted to our lifestyle here." The place was small with tapestries hung over almost every inch of wall. He had a wooden desk in the far corner of the room with one chair, and a door next to it led off into another room obscured from view. "So you knew to come here, that must mean you've met our king?" Ydoro asked. The group exchanged awkward glances but said nothing. "Great man, great man," Ydoro chimed as he shut the door behind them. "Our last king was manipulative and cruel. He turned communities against each other. Then King Mora came and put an end to the chaos. He introduced law and order back into our streets." Cyrus thought this was a pretty obvious and scripted plug for the King, but stayed quiet. "So, we have housing for you. Several units up the street, all together of course, but you'll get to know your neighbors as well."

Based on his seemingly pleasant demeanor, Cyrus decided to test the waters with one of his many burning questions. "So Ydoro, what is this place?"

Ydoro looked at him in confusion, but the smile stayed in place. "It's the Kingdom," he replied as if the answer were obvious.

"Yes but what Kingdom? Does it have a name?" Cyrus pushed.

Ydoro just laughed and replied congenially, "It doesn't have a name. It's the unnamed Kingdom." He had now busied himself rifling through papers on his desk.

Hoping he was not pushing his luck with Ydoro's friendly nature, Cyrus continued, "Where did all of these people come from, though? I mean, where are you from?"

"Well, I'm from here," Ydoro replied in that strange accent. "I was born here."

"Okay but not everyone was, right?" Cyrus insisted, finally seeing an opening to ask the questions he really wanted to ask. "We're not from here obviously, and you don't seem surprised to see us."

Ydoro looked him in the eyes and smiled, but his smile was becoming less sincere with every question. "The world is a mysterious place," he offered, "but you're here now, and I think you'll be very happy. Eventually you'll be expected to work and earn your keep, but don't worry; we'll give you some time to get adjusted first."

"We're not staying," Alec said firmly.

Cyrus worried how Ydoro would take that statement, but his good-natured smile never left his face. "Oh," he replied in friendly amusement, "well why don't you give it some time. I think you'll feel differently soon. Now how 'bout I show you to your new homes."

*****

They walked through the streets with Ydoro in the lead, pointing out various landmarks and places of interest. He confirmed what everyone already suspected; that the fortress on the hill off to the north was where the King lived. He called it the Temple. He told them the King rarely came through town, but would occasionally show up to settle a dispute. They were each given a small amount of money to start off, but it was explained to them that money was rarely used. Rather, most transactions were handled in trade. The money itself was comprised of coins, all the same looking. There did not appear to be any differing bills or amounts, and the coins were crude and rough looking, almost as if odd bits of scrap metal had been pressed with the Kingdom insignia. Indeed, many of the coins appeared to be made of different metals entirely, but Ydoro explained they were all worth the same.

Try as Ydoro might to present the place as their exciting new home, the team barely listened to his welcome tour; all of them still struggling to comprehend the reality of their situation. Every one of them only wanted to talk about one thing, getting home, but it seemed that both Ydoro and the King staunchly refused to discuss it, or even acknowledge that this new place was foreign to them. Cyrus felt as though he were walking through a dream.

After leading them up a narrow stone street away from the dusty square, Ydoro stopped outside a series of doors in a row, all cut into the side of the same stone building. There was one for each of them, and they proved to be very small, individual living quarters with nothing more than a narrow cot, a small wooden dresser, and a tiny bedside table.

"This is where I leave you for now," Ydoro exclaimed as the sun slowly began to set. "I know you will have more questions and need more direction in the coming days; you know where to find me now. Welcome to the Kingdom, we're so happy to have you." He bowed his head with a flourish of his robes, then turned and strode away down the winding street.

The group watched him leave with even more questions than when they had first arrived. Ydoro seemed friendly enough but the way he avoided any talk of where they had come from or how they could get back was frightening. It was as though everyone thought by ignoring the team's obvious desire to leave, they might forget they had been transported here by a freak occurrence. Cyrus had no intention of being drawn in by Ydoro's false friendliness and strange welcome tour. The locals could spin it in whichever way they wanted; the truth was they seemed to be prisoners here.

With Ydoro out of sight, Cyrus turned to the team with raised eyebrows and Nel immediately stated, "I'm not staying here."

"Okay I understand that," Cyrus responded in what he hoped was a level, calming voice, "but it'll be getting dark soon and we don't know where we are. Tomorrow we can get our bearings but for now, we need to stick together. And this place offers us shelter."

"Absolutely not," Nel said, shaking her head, "Have you forgotten what happened to Dalton? These people are animals, and we need to get as far away from them as possible."

"Nel, Cyrus is right," Jack insisted, "we can't accomplish anything once night falls, and we'll be exposed."

"We're already exposed!" Nel nearly shouted, "You really think we're safe here? Sorry, but I'm not staying."

Nel turned to walk away down the street while everyone in the group called after her. Alec ran to catch up and pulled her aside, whispering something in her ear. The two talked back and forth out of earshot of Cyrus and Jack, who watched, waiting to see if they would need to run after Nel. Even though Cyrus agreed that no one and nothing should be trusted, he could not imagine their odds improving by wandering the surrounding forest in the dark. Alec finally said something to Nel that caused her to nod in agreement and reluctantly walk back to rejoin the group. "I'm holding you to that," Nel said to Alec as she walked to her quarters and slammed the door shut.

"What did you say to her?" Cyrus asked Alec.

"I made her a promise," Alec answered vaguely, "so now what?"

Cyrus, Jack, and Alec talked through the sunset and into the night, sitting on the ground of the open stone street with their backs against the building. They discussed everything from the peculiarity of the town to their plans for leaving it. The sun had long been down by the time Cyrus realized the team had not had anything to eat or drink since the expedition ship. Ydoro had made no mention of where they could find such things, but it was not something that could wait, especially considering the way they had been exerting themselves. Cyrus also saw a potential opportunity to appease the group just a bit, and hopefully reestablish their precarious bond. He decided to walk back into the main town square and look for an open shop, or at the very least some water, and Alec elected to join him. Jack offered to stay behind in case Nel resurfaced and needed anything.

Alec and Cyrus walked in silence most of the way to town, finding it difficult to navigate in the moonlight. With the tension between them palpable, Cyrus finally whispered, "Look, Alec, I know you don't wanna talk, but what I said to you on the boat…"

"Cy, I'm not in the mood," Alec quickly shut him down. "You had the chance to have this conversation with me and you chose to pull rank, so now I don't want to hear it."

"You're right, and I'm sorry," Cyrus offered, "I shouldn't have said that. I was frustrated that I couldn't get the team to listen to me…"

"And look where it got us," Alec cut him off, "we followed you as our leader, but you refused to listen when we were in danger. Out on the dinghies, why didn't you stop when we said to?" When Cyrus did not respond, Alec pushed, "It's not a rhetorical question, I want to know; why didn't you listen to us?"

Cyrus was not used to Alec being so confrontational and was wondering what had changed. He stammered and answered, "I… I don't know. I just got too caught up in the thought of discovering something new. We were so close…"

"Well congratulations, you've discovered something new," Alec retorted venomously. "Is it everything you'd hoped for?"

"I'm sorry," Cyrus said again, "I really am, I know it's my fault we're here…"

"Then it's also your fault that Dalton's dead," Alec snapped, and walked ahead, putting an end to the conversation. Cyrus was not used to admitting his faults, but the guilt he felt was gnawing at him. Alec was right, if he had been able to work better with his team, things would have played out differently.

They arrived in the previously bustling town square to find it deserted. All of the shops and stands were closed up, and other than a few windows with dim torchlight trickling out, there were no signs of life anywhere. Not feeling confident in knocking on random doors, they decided to walk back to Ydoro's place and have him point them in the right direction. They approached the wood door with the serpent knocker and rapped on it several times. From within, they heard the sounds of a chair dragging against the floor and a loud cough, but no one answered. Cyrus shrugged at Alec and tested the door, which proved to be unlocked. He peered inside and called, "Ydoro?"

"We're closed!" yelled a slurred voice he did not recognize, "come back tomorrow!"

Cyrus would have obeyed had he not caught sight of the man sitting in the dark of the room. The man was slumped over the table with a bottle spilled out in front of him. He locked eyes with Cyrus and even in the dim, flickering light from a single torch on the opposite wall, he recognized the man as Ydoro; but he looked nothing like the guide they had encountered earlier. He was dressed in modern clothing, with modern shoes; even his wild, untamed hair was slicked back into a more contemporary look.

At first, it appeared Ydoro did not know who they were, but then recognition crept into his eyes, and he muttered, "Ah shit."

Cyrus realized with a start that the reason he did not recognize Ydoro's voice at first was that the bizarre accent was gone. He spoke now as if he were from the states; combined with his appearance he would not have been out of place at the New York docks they had shipped out from yesterday.

Ydoro attempted to force another winning smile, but it fell from his face almost instantly. He hung his head in defeat and muttered, "Hell, I don't have the energy for the act right now, I just found out my friend was killed."

**CHAPTER TEN**

# THE ILLUSION

Cyrus let himself into the dimly lit room with Alec following closely, and closed the heavy door behind them. His first thought was to wonder if this was all some sort of twisted game. The Ydoro sitting before them now was nothing like the strange, welcoming guide who had led them around town earlier. It seemed as though his entire appearance and demeanor was a lie, not to mention his accent.

"What the hell is this?" Cyrus demanded in anger.

"You're not supposed to see this," Ydoro mumbled, attempting in vain to use the table to push himself into a standing position.

"So what is this, all an act?" Alec yelled even more aggressively than Cyrus had. As Ydoro stammered, Alec seized him by the shirt collar and wrenched him to his feet threateningly. "My friend died here, is this all a game?"

"No, no, please, let me explain," Ydoro insisted, "it's not me, it's the King." Alec slammed his fist into the wall behind Ydoro's head, still holding onto his collar with the other. Cyrus stepped forward in alarm at his brother's outburst of anger, worried he would have to intervene. "Please," Ydoro begged, trying to shield his face, "I'll tell you anything you wanna know. It's the King, King Mora. I'm a prisoner of his, we all are."

Alec released his grip and Ydoro staggered sideways, crashing against the table to steady himself.

"No more games," Cyrus threatened, "What is this place? Where are we?"

"I don't know!" Ydoro cried, "I was fifteen when I came here, and we never figured out how."

"Who's we?" Cyrus demanded.

"My father and I, and a handful of crewmen," Ydoro answered, trying to position the table between himself and Alec. "We arrived here just like you did; a lot of us have."

"Then why the act?" Alec pressed, moving the table aside as he pursued Ydoro across the room. "Why the tattered robes? Why the accent?"

"It's how the King wants it," Ydoro insisted, "He wants to rule over a Kingdom of peasants; he wants to be a god among the locals here. If you've met him then you know what he can do. I was told my part was to play the quirky, welcoming local. So that's what I do."

Cyrus shook his head in disbelief. "So the whole town is made up? Everyone's just acting?"

"No, no," Ydoro said, "Many of the people here are locals. They were born and raised here. What I told you about the last king wasn't a lie, they've always had a king ruling over them. But as a culture, they're a very passive people. And that has been seen by many outsiders as an opportunity for power."

Alec finally let up on his threatening pursuit around the room and Cyrus contemplated everything Ydoro had told them in silence.

"I'm sorry," Ydoro finally said, "everyone figures it out eventually, I just couldn't keep up the charade right now, I found out this evening that…"

"Do you mean to say that the King is an outsider too?" Alec interrupted him. "You said that outsiders see this place as an opportunity for power, does that mean the King is an outsider?"

Ydoro silently nodded his head and leaned back against the wall. "I *think* he came here a couple years after I did. He was ruthless even then, but the unchecked power he's gained has driven him mad."

"Then where did he gain the power to throw fire?" Cyrus demanded, gently touching his burned face.

Ydoro slid down the wall to sit on the stone floor, shook his head and said, "The King doesn't have any power, it's all an illusion to keep his subjects in fear. It's the scepters he has; the minerals inside them react with the sand in the Fire Fields. I don't claim to know what the chemical makeup is, but it's not magic…"

"It's science," Cyrus muttered, finishing Ydoro's sentence for himself. He made his way to the chair by the wall and eased himself into it. He was beginning to feel dizzy. "But we're talking about elements that don't exist in our world," Cyrus began slowly. "So are you saying…?"

"It's still our world, near as I can tell," Ydoro answered, gazing up at the ceiling as though he could see the night sky beyond, "It's just a little… off."

The mood had changed dramatically in the room. Ydoro sat broken and hunkered against the wall, and the fight had gone out of both Alec and Cyrus. It was clearly pointless attacking the man before them, who was evidently as much a victim as they were.

"How long have you been here?" Cyrus asked softly, almost afraid to hear the answer.

Ydoro thought about it briefly and responded, "Twenty-one years. Hell, when you put it that way. I talk about our world, but I've been *here* more of my life than out *there*. I was helping my father on a fishing vessel. And I never went out with him, but I begged and begged to go, until my mother finally agreed to let me." Ydoro had a far off look in his eyes, making Cyrus think he likely had not processed these memories in a long time. "He didn't last too long here, my father. Got sick, passed within a year. My friend who died today, he came over with me. Looked out for me after my father died."

"What happened to him, your friend?" Cyrus asked.

"Not quite sure," Ydoro responded, "his wife said he headed to the Temple yesterday afternoon but never returned. Everyone around here knows what that means."

"Why would the King want him dead?" Alec questioned.

"It could be anything; maybe he said something to upset him, maybe he was late on a crop delivery, or maybe it was just that the King's birds were hungry. It's a way of life around here."

Alec crouched down at the mention of the birds, bringing himself eye to eye with Ydoro, still leaning against the wall. "What are those birds?"

Ydoro shrugged and said, "If you're looking for their technical classification, I can't help you. We call them Neodactyls."

"Neodactyls?" Alec questioned skeptically. "Why do you call them that?"

"Well, there's this prehistoric animal with wings called a Pterodactyl, I suppose that's where the name came from," Ydoro explained with relative disinterest.

Alec responded with a short laugh and a nod but did not let Ydoro or Cyrus in on the joke. "Okay, but how does the King control them?"

Ydoro had started shaking his head before Alec had even finished his question. "We don't know, but they have been passed down from king to king, and their loyalty along with them."

Cyrus furrowed his brow in confusion. If these kings were all unrelated and had taken the Kingdom by force from their predecessors, how would a couple of animals know to switch loyalty?

"The scepters have always remained with the king as well," Ydoro continued, "dating back decades from what I understand. All a leader has to do is make an appearance with those creatures at their side and make a display with those scepters and they own the people. Who's going to stand up to that?"

Cyrus just shook his head. He did not know if this wealth of new information made their situation better or worse. There was certainly something comforting in knowing they were not alone in this strange land. However, it came with an unsettling realization that sat like a stone in Cyrus's stomach; not one of them had ever found a way out of this place.

Cyrus had so many more questions his head felt like it would burst. His mind could not seem to sort through everything he wanted to know, and what he ended up asking was not pressing or critical to their survival in any way, but rather a curiosity as something occurred to him.

"You say you're from the states with your father, right? Your name's not Ydoro, is it?"

Ydoro looked up at him with defeat in his eyes and answered softly, "No, it's not. But my old name is long lost."

## CHAPTER ELEVEN

# SWALLOWED UP BY THE WORLD

Any one of the team who had hoped a good night's sleep would make them feel better awoke disappointed. On the contrary, Cyrus opened his eyes to see the drab stone ceiling of his new living quarters and shuttered at the thought of facing the new day. Their first afternoon in this new world had felt surreal and dizzying; a feeling that was only amplified by the terrible events of the day and the loss of one of their own. The second day, however, had dawned with the crushing realization that they were stuck in this place indefinitely, and were in very real danger. Even the death of Dalton, which had left them all feeling initially numb, was now filling Cyrus with a bubbling anger that concerned him. He was not worried for himself, but he knew Alec was taking it particularly hard, and he was not confident in his brother's ability to control those feelings. He stopped himself from exploring that train of thought. It was exactly that sort of protective attitude that Alec was misinterpreting as arrogance; and it was very important that they remain strong together.

Cyrus and Alec had decided that Ydoro's revelations of the night before could not wait until morning, so had woken Jack and Nel to share with them. It was a long night of heated discussions and debates, and the mood this morning was one of hopelessness. No matter which way they looked at it, the simple fact was that no one had ever found a way out of this place. It seemed that everyone at some point eventually gave up on the world they knew and settled into life in this new one. The fact that Cyrus could look around at the busy village and not be able to identify which people were born here and which were brought here scared the hell out of him. These outsiders had truly and irretrievably been swallowed up by this strange world and they no longer felt or acted like prisoners; this was home to them now. Ydoro had mentioned being a prisoner of King Mora, certainly, but not of this place. It seemed he hardly remembered the world he had come from.

Jack was proving to be a more analytical mind than Cyrus had expected upon hearing about Ydoro's explanations. As Alec and Cyrus had sat and filled him in, he asked a question or two, but mostly just absorbed everything. Nel was another story. While she had been amused and observant on the ship, she now seemed to carry a burning fury everywhere she went. It seemed she was internalizing everything instead of voicing her frustration or anger. She seldom said anything to reveal her feelings, but her face and body language betrayed her unyielding appearance. She would more readily talk to Alec than anyone else, and he seemed to gain strength by feeling needed. The two of them would regularly split off as the group walked through town and converse in heated whispering.

Ydoro had by the next day slipped back into his strange, phony accent and wardrobe, but when they were alone behind closed doors, he would drop the act. He did not seem ashamed by his drunken reveal of the night prior, rather he explained that the façade only lasted so long for newcomers before they learned the truth. The 'eccentric local' act was really only for the benefit of the King, but since one could never be sure if they were in the presence of a true loyalist or not, Ydoro had simply adopted the performance as his lifestyle. Cyrus was surprised to learn that King Mora did in fact have plenty of devoted supporters in town. Some people truly bought into his charming persona while others simply did not have a problem being ruled over with an iron fist. Comparatively, Ydoro described the King before Mora overthrew him, a man named King Irias, as a leader many regarded as much worse. Evidently

King Irias had ruled for decades without being challenged because he turned many of the commoners against each other. He truly was born in this place and was adamant that no outsider should have any authority in it. Under his rule, outsiders could choose to stay in the rural settlements to the east with very few luxuries and the majority of their crops taken as 'donations' to the West, or they could try to make it on their own. Very few who had gone off on their own over the years were ever heard from again. As for Mora, reports were foggy on exactly where he had come from and when. Some people swore he was a local all along who had finally become fed up with the hierarchy of the Kingdom while others, Ydoro included, were convinced he was an outsider who refused to be beaten into submission. What everyone did agree on was that about fifteen years ago he had stormed the Temple and taken it for himself, killing King Irias in the process. As Ydoro had explained the night before, the locals were a very passive people and would not generally second-guess a takeover of that nature. Indeed, even the King's guards stayed out of the 'disagreement', respecting the leadership of whomever came out victorious. While this notion seemed unbelievable to Cyrus, Ydoro assured him it was the way of the local culture.

Ydoro was now leading them through the dense forest towards an overlook that the King requested all newcomers see. Apparently it showed the vastness of the Kingdom and what surrounded them. Ydoro had already told them, however, that what surrounded them was nothing but water. Perhaps the King wanted outsiders to see this to show that there was no hope of escape. The trek was strenuous and entirely uphill. Ydoro was in his tattered robes again, but at least out away from the townsfolk he used his regular accent. Cyrus spent more time taking in his surroundings than the previous day's hike, and while something felt strange about the forest, there was also something familiar about it. It was a temperate rainforest so a bit cooler than he was used to from his travels in Central and South America, but the foliage was quite dense and there seemed to be an abundance of freshwater falls scattered throughout.

Jack asked, "So is there anyone living out here away from the towns? Or is that it?"

"You wouldn't want to live out here," Ydoro replied ominously. "These jungles are home to some real monsters. We're okay now, but I wouldn't be caught out here at night if I could help it."

Alec snorted, "It can't be worse than living in town under Mora's thumb."

"Town's not so bad," Ydoro insisted. "I understand your grievances with the King, but we hardly ever see him. He likes to make an impression, especially if a rather large group of newcomers arrives. I guess he thinks it will keep them in line; but I can pretty much guarantee you won't have another run-in with him. It's all just a big show."

Nel, who had been silent all morning, said, "That *big show* robbed a man of his life. He can't assume we would let that go."

Ydoro considered that thoughtfully before replying, "I don't think he assumes that. I think he just knows that you can't do anything about it."

An ear-splitting scream echoed throughout the forest causing everyone to jump. Cyrus immediately started scanning the dense foliage for the source of the voice. It had definitely been a woman's voice, was it possible that it was…?

Cyrus tore off into the jungle with Ydoro yelling something after him. Cyrus did not care, though. If there was even the slimmest chance that his wife was out there somewhere, he had to find her. He heard the scream again, confirming he was heading in the right direction. Even if it was not Cynthia, someone was clearly in need of help. The scream rang out again, from the west. He course-corrected and continued barreling through the branches, nearly losing his footing more than once. He was close now. It was strange that he kept hearing near identical screams that lasted about the same amount of time. One would expect the inflection to change if someone was in trouble.

Cyrus skidded to a halt on the dried leaves beneath his feet as he heard another scream, this time very near him. He held his breath listening for any sign of movement. A rustling in the trees above caused him to look up with a start. There were about ten large, brownish bats above his head in the overhanging branches, gliding from tree to tree. He shook his head and began to scan the ground, looking for footprints or signs of a struggle. Another shrill scream echoed throughout the forest, extremely close, but this time he was certain it came from directly above him. He looked back up at the bats, and as he watched them dancing around the branches, one opened its mouth and let out a long, high-pitched screech. It sounded so much like a woman screaming, but it wasn't. The sound had perhaps been distorted a bit as it echoed off the rolling hills because now hearing them so close, Cyrus did not think it sounded nearly as human as he originally thought. There was a more guttural quality to it from this close range that was lost from a greater distance.

Cyrus took a deep breath and nodded his head in embarrassment. Of course it had not been Cynthia, he was being foolish, and reckless. Another scream pierced the air from above. Watching the bats, he noted how odd they looked. They were large with bristly hair along their backs and heads, and their snouts were grossly elongated, similar to a Flying Fox but hugely exaggerated. Running footsteps finally announced the arrival of the rest of his party, with Ydoro crashing through the foliage and stopping short as he spotted Cyrus.

Glancing up at the animals in the trees, Ydoro said, "I see you've discovered our Shrieking Bats."

"Shrieking Bats, huh?" Cyrus responded sheepishly. "Got that right."

Alec was shaking his head while staring up at the animals with wide-eyed fascination. "I've never seen bats like these, what are they?"

"I think you'll find there are a lot of *curiosities* in these forests," Ydoro responded. "This is not any jungle you know."

Another screech rang out and Alec nearly tripped over a branch because he would not take his eyes off the bats. Realizing his interest, Ydoro offered, "Did you want a better look at them?"

As it turned out, the Shrieking Bats nested in a nearby hollow, and as the team discovered upon their approach, they were not afraid of people in the slightest. Ydoro walked within two feet of several hanging, sleeping bats and crouched down in front of them, and they did not move at all. Alec hesitated initially, then approached quietly and knelt beside Ydoro. Cyrus peered over their shoulders, only mildly interested given their current situation. The nearest bat opened its eyes briefly, revealing pale-yellow, almost white eyes with small, round irises in the center. It yawned, showing a row of sharp, hooked teeth running the length of its elongated mouth, but then faded back to sleep, unbothered by the audience.

Alec started whispering questions about the bats to Ydoro, and Cyrus began to get annoyed. He was sure he would find this much more fascinating had they not just yesterday arrived in a seemingly new world, but it bothered him that Alec was acting as though nothing had happened. Finally fed up, Cyrus said, "Alec, you about done here? This isn't a damn field trip."

Alec rolled his eyes as he stood up, "This is a brand-new species. Do you get that?"

"I do," Cyrus answered, "but maybe this isn't the time to be playing biologist."

Alec looked like he was going to say something else, but eventually just shook his head and responded, "I am a biologist," before shoving past Cyrus and heading back the way they had come. Nel put her hand on Alec's shoulder as he approached her, a gesture of sympathy and understanding. Was what he said really so bad, Cyrus wondered. He had not meant anything offensive by it; he had just been frustrated when it seemed Alec was not treating their predicament with appropriate weight. And the fact that Nel was rushing to comfort him clearly meant she was on his side. It made him realize he had not had a real conversation with Nel since they met. He did not know her at all.

The rest of the hike to the top of the hill passed uneventfully. The team was fairly quiet, asking Ydoro the odd question as they came up. The view from the top was indeed quite a sight. Cyrus could see off in all directions, and it was immediately clear they were surrounded by water. Across the valley in front of them, they could see the hilltop with the King's Temple perched on its peak, overlooking the town they had walked from. To its right was dense forest until a faintly glowing orange clearing revealed the Fire Fields from the day before. Beyond that was more forest and their first look at the second town to the east, although it was barely a town. There appeared to be a small village square in the middle but extending beyond that everything became spaced out very quickly. Cyrus could see dwellings similar to their own new homes, but they appeared to be freestanding along dirt roads that all led out towards crop fields in every direction but west. The Western town had crop fields surrounding it as well but comparatively, Cyrus could see why the King described this as the more rural town. Everything else, as far as the eye could see, was dense rainforest, culminating in blue shorelines all around.

"So what body of water is that?" Jack asked.

Ydoro shrugged and responded, "We have no way of knowing. What I can tell you is that it is salt water." It was remarkable; if Cyrus did not know better it could very easily be the Atlantic he was gazing at.

"Well thanks for this, Ydoro," Nel said sarcastically while staring out over the vista, "this is damn pretty."

"Look, the King wanted you brought here to prove the hopelessness of your situation," Ydoro explained, "but it doesn't have to be that. Things aren't so bad here. People do make a life for themselves in this place. It is what you make of it."

Nel grinned and said, "Bold words coming from a man in peasant robes and a fake accent."

Ydoro just nodded his head and responded, "Okay, well rest here everyone. We head back down in twenty."

The team split up with everyone ambling around the hillside in mild curiosity of their surroundings. Cyrus took the opportunity to approach Nel, who was sitting herself down beneath a large tree. She looked surprised as she saw him walking towards her, raising her eyebrows with a bemused smile on her face.

"What can I do for you, boss?" she said with the subtle hint of an attitude.

"It just seems to me that we haven't really gotten to know each other," Cyrus said as he took a seat beside her. "I thought maybe it was time we changed that."

"Uh oh, so you're here to charm me into submission with your perfect smile and your well-polished people skills? Try Jack, I'm not interested."

"Ouch," Cyrus responded with a smile, "no I'm serious, though. I think it's important to work together as a team, and in order to do that…"

"Look, Doc," Nel interrupted him, "I get it, but you're just not my kinda people, and I'm pretty sure I'm not yours. You like to have things a certain way and be in control at all times. That doesn't work for me."

"You've been talking to Alec," Cyrus said with a nod of understanding. "I'm really not that bad, I promise. Alec and I just have a complicated relationship."

"It's not complicated," Nel said with a laugh. She had a way of keeping the conversation light while still making sure her words stung. "You're just used to Alec living in your shadow, but guess what; you've now proven to be a shit-poor leader. Maybe it's Alec's turn."

"I agree I've made some mistakes…" Cyrus began.

Nel leaned towards him, still smiling, and said in a low voice, "Ya wanna know a secret, Doc? Even before you royally screwed up and got us stranded here, I still thought you were the lesser of the two Dorn brothers." She leaned in still further and whispered in his ear, "This is Alec's story now. Why don't you sit this one out? We don't need you anymore." She smiled again and leaned back against the tree. "You may find you like playing second fiddle, who knows," she exclaimed loud enough for Jack, who was walking nearby, to hear. She winked at him and shut her eyes as if she were going to nap, a self-satisfied smirk on her lips.

Cyrus stood up, somewhat baffled at Nel's hostility towards him, and walked away in Jack's direction. It was beginning to seem he had no allies out here, including his own brother.

"Give her time," Jack said as Cyrus walked past. "We're all coping in our own way."

Cyrus paused, surprised at Jack's supportive words. He was under the impression they despised each other. "You don't blame me for being here?" Cyrus questioned.

"Eh, you've got a lot of character defects," Jack responded with a laugh. "You and I may never see eye to eye, but getting us stuck here?"

Jack shook his head, "That wasn't you. Whatever happened to us, it would've happened whether you, or I, or anybody had been in charge."

Still surprised at Jack's kindness, Cyrus blinked and responded, "Well…. thanks."

Jack smiled and clapped Cyrus on the shoulder. "It doesn't make us friends or anything," he said, and began to walk off.

"Hey," Cyrus called after him. "Thanks for saving my life."

Jack just laughed and nodded his head. "Anytime," he finally said before turning and walking away.

Cyrus stood contemplating the two conversations he just had, neither of which had gone the way he had expected. Perhaps he was not so alone out here after all.

**CHAPTER TWELVE**

# UNTAPPED, UNTAMED FURY

Alec was seething. It had now been two weeks since they had become trapped on this inexplicable island surrounded largely by people who had given up, but he refused to lose sight of the real enemy. They had not seen King Mora since he had murdered Dalton in the Fire Fields, but Ydoro had just relayed a message from the King that they were expected to begin working this week. In this Kingdom, you did not work for money, you worked to earn a place in society. Alec did not have a problem with the idea taken by itself, but he had no interest in having a place in *this* society. It seemed to him that this society functioned by design to imprison outsiders that it had caught in its web. The idea of having them start working now was to force them into a routine, and to force them to accept this world as their own.

Alec was finding it difficult to bring Jack and Cyrus around to his way of thinking, but Nel was determined to get out from under the King's thumb. Several times, Alec had brought her back from the brink of impending self-destruction by assuring her they would take action. It was just a matter of finding the right time; and that right time would be determined by Jack and Cyrus in the end. Something would need to push them into action, and Alec was certain that was coming. He just had to make sure they did not get too comfortable here, and that was exactly the purpose of assigning them work. Alec had never been much of a fighter, nor one for confrontation in general, but right now he wanted to fight. He had been meek and mild his whole life and he had nothing to show for it. He had always been a cautious person, in contrast to his brother, who was far bolder and more adventurous. Even as kids, Cyrus would want to find new shortcuts home from school, tiptoe along the line of possible danger, and test the limits of the rules imposed on him. Alec was always too much in his own head. He always wanted to be brave and carefree, but his logical nature would stop him from being spontaneous. He was meticulous and worked hard in life to be successful, but now that his success was being stripped away, he could feel something inside himself changing. Dalton's words from weeks back had stuck with him; this adventure was as much his as anyone else's, and it was up to him to decide the role he wanted to play. Even though the adventure had turned into a nightmare, or perhaps because it had, Alec recognized the truth in his statement. He was not content to play a peasant for the rest of his life, he deserved better than that.

Alec had been pacing his small living quarters for the last twenty minutes, silently raging at the news Cyrus had dumped on him. What really upset him was not the fact that the King was demanding they start working but the fact that Cyrus was ready to go along with it. He had thought for sure this would be the moment Jack and Cyrus would agree to take a stand. Finally unable to contain his anger any longer, Alec stormed out onto the dark street and knocked on Nel's door.

"Hey there neighbor," Nel greeted him with dry sarcasm as she opened the door.

Striding into her room without waiting for an invitation, Alec fumed, "Did Jack talk to you?"

"Yeah, he just left," Nel responded in a surprisingly mild-mannered voice, "and before you start, because I can tell you're in the throes of some sort of tantrum right now…"

"Don't make light of this," Alec barked. "You shouldn't be so calm. This is a big deal, and Cyrus and Jack are just gonna roll over and die here…"

"Alec stop," Nel said more forcefully. "Think about it a sec. This might not be a bad thing. We can use this."

Alec had no intention of allowing his slowly building tirade to lose momentum, but the fact that Nel was so calm and collected piqued his interest. "I... how so?"

"Well the King is ordering you to start working, right? All of us, we have to start earning our keep here."

"He's trying to force us to lose all hope of leaving, and Cyrus and Jack..."

"Are planning to obey, I know," Nel interjected, "but do *you* plan to start working?"

"Absolutely not," Alec stated resolutely.

"Neither do I," Nel responded, "and my guess is our refusal will get a response from the King."

Alec considered this a moment. "You want to use the King's reaction to coax Jack and Cyrus into action."

"Your brother's a pompous shit but he would never let anything happen to you. If Mora makes a move against you, Cyrus will grow a backbone."

"Okay... but what if we aren't able to defend ourselves from Mora?" Alec questioned, only now thinking about the danger in picking a fight with a man like that.

"What have we been talking about the last two weeks?" Nel demanded, beginning to lose her patience. "You promised me we would bring the fight to him. That means we have to take a stand at some point, and yeah, it's gonna be dangerous, but a second ago you were all amped up and ready to go." Alec looked down sheepishly and Nel studied his face. "Oh what, now that it's you personally provoking the King, it's too dangerous?" When Alec did not respond, Nel snapped, "Fine, I'll do it myself, but I thought you were stronger than this. I thought you were finally starting to stand on your own."

"That's not what I meant," Alec said quickly. "I won't let you stand up to him yourself, of course you can count on me. We just need to think it through. I mean, after Dalton..."

Nel stepped in towards him and put her hand on his arm. Her entire demeanor had softened significantly, and she was now looking at him with an almost innocent, yet piercing gaze. "I won't let anything happen to you," she whispered softly, "you're my only friend out here."

Alec stared into her eyes, somehow captivated by her as he always seemed to be. "Can I ask you something?" he said softly. "That day on the ship, after we'd spent the night drinking with Jack and Dalton, you were sitting in the shadows watching me. What were you thinking?"

Alec expected her to deny it, but to his surprise Nel put her hand on his chest and said, "I was thinking I saw a fire in you. Some untapped, untamed fury. A power even you didn't know you had."

Alec was drawn in by her steady gaze, but then shook his head and smiled, beginning to turn away. That didn't sound like him. Nel brought her hand up to his cheek, commanding his attention again. "It's in there, I can see it," she insisted without breaking eye contact. Her face was very close to his own now. "Let go of the mild-mannered scientist and allow your real self to come out."

Nel somehow had a way of making him feel stronger than he thought he could be. He looked into her eyes and nodded with what he hoped was visible confidence. "I… I can do that." He wished he hadn't stammered; that did not sound as strong as he had intended.

Nel smiled and leaned in even closer, her face only inches from his. "Don't worry, I'll help you," she whispered. She stared into his eyes for another second, then abruptly patted his cheek, winked, and turned away. Alec blinked in confusion as she walked to the other side of the room and sat against the bedside table. "The trouble will be we need Ydoro's help," she said more loudly now, seeming to ignore the moment they had just shared.

Alec shook his head and said, "I don't get you."

"What?" she questioned innocently with a smile. "If we're standing up to the King, we've got a fight coming. Ydoro knows the King, he knows the area, and he knows the people and their customs. We need him."

Evidently Nel had no intention of addressing what had just happened between them. Had he just imagined it? Not knowing what to say, he elected to drop it and replied, "You're right, that's the only way this works. His friend was just killed by the King, I'm sure we can use that..." Alec stopped himself mid-sentence. When had he become so callous? He was not going to use the man's grief as a tool to manipulate him. That was not the sort of man Alec Dorn was.

But Nel was nodding fervently in agreement. "I don't think it'll be hard to bring him around. He's obviously very malleable or he wouldn't be working as Mora's greeter for fifteen years."

"Well, I don't think it's his fault," Alec started, feeling guilty for his previous train of thought. "I don't think he had a choice."

"That's exactly my point, no one has ever given him a better choice. That's what we're gonna do."

"What's our plan exactly?" Alec asked. "I mean, what's our end goal?"

"I don't care about this Kingdom or this world," Nel spat. "We're not from here so I don't give a damn what happens to it. But I want to look Mora in the eyes while he takes his last breath. That's my only goal."

Alec just stared back at her without responding. He was secretly wondering if he were up for this. Their conversation was interrupted by a sharp knock on the door.

Nel walked towards the door but turned to Alec before she opened it and whispered, "Not a word to Cyrus or Jack. They have to make the decision on their own." Alec nodded his understanding and Nel opened the door. To both of their surprise, there was no one there. Nel stepped out into the cool night air and looked down the road for someone. There was no one in sight but they both heard the crunch of paper beneath her foot as she stepped.

They looked down together and Nel bent to pick up a single piece of yellowed parchment. Nel turned it over in her hand and Alec leaned in to read it. Scrawled across the paper in messy block letters was a single sentence: "HE CAN HEAR YOU."

## CHAPTER THIRTEEN

# DEFIANCE

J ack Viana looked sideways at Cyrus as they walked towards the edge of town. Cyrus was looking up at the sky as they followed Ydoro onto one of the many small dirt paths that led into the surrounding forests. Jack was trying to decide if he had misjudged the man, who he had now known for several weeks. Everything about Cyrus used to bother him, right down to his perfectly manicured appearance and arrogant gaze. The man he studied now, however, was run down and weakened, perhaps even softened by this place. He now had the beginnings of a rugged-looking beard, and his clothes were tattered and dirty from use. He also sported a fairly substantial facial wound. The burn was mostly healed by now and his eye was able to fully open again, but the skin had a strangely charred appearance, different from the melted look of a typical burn. It seemed likely he would have a scar there forever.

It was not just his appearance that had changed, however. He was recently more thoughtful and level-headed than Jack realized he could be, and while he had entirely given up on being the team leader, he always seemed to be putting the wellness of the group first. By contrast, when Ydoro had strongly suggested they all meet their respective 'bosses' before they began work the following day, Alec and Nelida were the ones who had refused. Ydoro's proposal made sense to Jack, even if he did not like the idea of resigning to a daily routine in this place. He was not sure exactly what sort of work they would be doing, but it was apparent that nearly everyone worked hard labor, with the exception of those with specialized crafts. It did not matter to Jack; he had been working on shipping lines since he was twelve and knew the meaning of a hard day's work. He was still young but already first mate on a ship thanks to his work ethic, and he was likely to replace the captain when he retired in a few years. Rather he *would* be in line to replace the captain, if he ever got back there.

Unlike Cyrus who had a wife he was desperate to get back to, Jack did not have anyone waiting for him back home. He had always been friendly and quick to laugh, which tended to give people the impression he was more sociable than he really was. Deep down he often felt more like a loner, which made it easier for him to pour his life into working at sea. With minimal personal relationships and a non-existent social life, it was no wonder he was such a hard worker; and his first impression of Cyrus Dorn was that everything had been handed to him.

The three men hiked through the forest for half an hour towards the far west side of the Kingdom, which Jack knew from the overlook Ydoro had shown them weeks before was comprised of mostly crop fields. They were not meant to start work until tomorrow, but Jack was happy at the very least to be shown how to get there. It was somewhat baffling to him that Alec and Nel refused to join them. They had muttered some half-formed excuse, but Jack was certain it was a simple case of them being stubborn. He understood the urge to not conform to this new society they had been forced into, but it was also wise to pick your battles. Jack was not planning to give up on leaving this place, but they did not have many options right now. Another reason Jack was anxious to meet his new work team was to hear from more locals and try to understand this place a little better. The last few weeks had not given them many opportunities to interact with other people from town, but working alongside them outside seemed like the perfect place to bond with them. What he wanted to know more than anything was how an entire culture could be so passive as to allow an outsider a position of power over them. If it happened as Ydoro said, Mora simply assassinated the previous king and took his place; but how could an entire community of people be okay with that sort of power grab? Jack could not make sense of it, but perhaps talking to the locals would help him understand; and what Alec and Nel failed to grasp was that you needed to understand the rules before you could break them.

The path narrowed ahead, and then opened into a vast clearing with neatly lined rows of crops extending all the way down the sloping hills to the royal blue ocean beyond. On the hillsides above them were what looked to be a series of caves, and dozens of people were scattered throughout, tending crops, hammering at rocks, pushing carts, transporting tools. The hillside was positively bustling with people hard at work, but what caught Jack's attention the most was the comradery he was witnessing. People were talking with one another and laughing; they seemed to be enjoying their day. He was struck once again with the realization that these people did not feel trapped here.

"Ydoro!" a tall, wiry man with a balding head called out. He approached them with an air of importance, carrying a heavy-looking mesh sack over one shoulder.

"New workers, they start with you tomorrow," Ydoro explained with his bizarre, and fake, accent.

The man just nodded and glanced around at the fields, sweat dripping off his temple. "Alright, well welcome," he mumbled in a half-interested voice. "The work's not all that difficult; I can show you what you'll be doing tomorrow. Meet the crew and all that. But basically this is where the bulk of our food comes from; that and fish. So we tend to these fields every day…"

"Tannus!" a voice yelled from off to their left, interrupting his speech. Jack turned to see a woman he would have pegged in her early twenties approaching fast from the higher hills. She was small and petite but the muscle definition in her arms showed her strength. "Not that one," she called out, pointing. "I want that one for my team." Was she pointing at Jack?

Jack turned to look at the man, apparently his name was Tannus, who shrugged and said, "He's all yours."

"Great," the woman responded brightly, finally reaching them and slapping Jack on the back. "You don't mind, do you?" she asked Jack. "I mean, Tannus is competent and all, but I just rescued you from a hell of a boring speech."

"Something else you need?" Tannus asked grumpily.

"Nope, I'm good," the woman replied with a smile, grasping Jack's upper arm and wrenching him away from the group. He turned to look back at Ydoro, who nodded his approval and waved him along. Cyrus looked confused, as if unsure if he should follow, but Ydoro held him back and Tannus began his welcome speech from the beginning. Jack turned away and continued following the mysterious woman up the hillside towards the caves above.

"I am sorry you won't be working with your friend," the woman said as they made their way uphill.

"He's not my friend," Jack replied, his calves burning with each step.

"Hmm, complicated, I like it," she said, somehow covering twice as much ground as Jack even though his legs were quite a bit longer. "So you new here?"

"Uh, yeah, I guess so. A few weeks now," Jack replied, still surprised by everyone's flippant reaction to their arrival. "Have you been here long?"

"All my life," the woman answered, still not breaking stride. "I'm Annica, by the way."

Jack, who was now trying his hardest not to wheeze between words, answered quickly, "Jack."

"Well glad to have you here, Jack. We'll be working up in the caves."

Jack slipped on some loose rocks but caught himself with his hands. He quickly righted himself before Annica could notice and asked, "So why did you want me on your team?"

"I didn't want you, I wanted your muscles," Annica replied bluntly. "It's hard work in the caves, I need strong people." When Jack did not immediately respond, she looked over her shoulder at him and added, "Don't worry, I'm sure you have other good qualities, too."

Jack was now breathing heavily and loudly, no longer able to hide his exhaustion, when a man passed them on the right, heading downhill with a cart filled with large stones. The man was holding onto the handles and leaning back at an alarming angle, using his weight to prevent the cart from careening downhill too fast. "Those are going to the southern end," Annica called to the man, who grunted in acknowledgement but did not slow down. Jack thought of the incredible amount of strength it must take to support that cart full of rocks in the way he was. "They're building a new set of homes at the southern end of town," Annica explained, although Jack had not been all that curious where the man was taking the rocks.

"Alright relax, we're here," she said, arriving at the mouth of one of the caves and sitting down on a stone ledge. Jack dropped himself next to her, trying to catch his breath. Annica just smiled and acknowledged, "The climb takes some getting used to."

Jack looked back the way they had come and didn't feel so embarrassed for struggling anymore; they had climbed quite a long ways. Ydoro, Cyrus, and Tannus were still visible in the valley, but the distance to the caves was much greater than it had looked from below. There appeared to be a whole network of caves in the higher part of the hills, and the majority of them had teams filtering in and out of them. Jack noticed the entrance to one cave was blocked off by an enormous piece of wood that was propped up by a single, strategically placed wooden brace.

"So what's your story Jack?" Annica asked, looking at him with mild amusement.

"My story?" Jack replied. "Well, I was working on a ship, jumped overboard, somehow ended up here. You have an explanation for that?"

"No," she answered, "but you're not the first."

"I want to know your story," Jack insisted. "You say you've been here your whole life, so you were born here?"

"That's right," Annica said, laughing at his curiosity. "So were my parents, and so were theirs."

"So you've never known the real world?" Jack asked in astonishment.

Annica made a face and said, "This is the real world, Jack. I think that's the hardest thing for newcomers to understand, but to all of us, this is the world. It's all relative."

Jack nodded in agreement, "Fair enough, but aren't you curious what else is out there? If people continue to come here from another world, doesn't that make you wonder?"

"Wonder what?" Annica asked. "When you were out working on that ship, did you think about other worlds besides your own?"

"Well no," Jack answered, "but our world didn't have a portal leading to another one."

Annica shrugged and responded, "Apparently it did."

She had a point. Jack decided to go out on a limb and try to pivot the conversation. "So, where I come from, we don't have a king."

Annica studied him as if she were trying to assess his line of thinking. "So I've heard," she answered slowly. "King Mora brought peace to us when we were at our weakest."

"So I've heard," Jack repeated cautiously. He debated whether to continue or not, but eventually said, "and I would believe that, except the man I met... let's just say he didn't seem all that peaceful."

Annica's eyes narrowed a bit. "Is that right?"

"It is," Jack replied, not taking his eyes off her. He was remembering Ydoro's warnings that the King had plenty of loyal supporters amongst the population. "Perhaps I'm wrong," Jack offered.

"Perhaps," Annica said, watching him.

They were entering dangerous territory. If Annica was loyal to Mora and he kept pushing his luck by speaking ill of the King, the price could be high. Attempting to lighten the mood a bit, Jack mentioned, "Now I heard that King Mora wasn't originally from here, just like us. Is that true?" He hoped his question sounded like excited curiosity rather than a slight against the King.

"No, that's not true," Annica answered. "I know that's a legend that some of the older generations like to pass around, but King Mora was born here."

"Did you know him? Back then?"

"Before my time," Annica smiled, "but there are stories about him growing up on the streets in town, and finally confronting King Irias."

"How did he beat him?" Jack asked.

"They say King Mora convinced Irias to fight him one on one, without his birds. Irias had become old, and his undoing ended up being his refusal to accept that. King Mora was younger and stronger."

It occurred to Jack that every time one of the locals presented him with a history lesson, the events were never witnessed first-hand. The stories often began with 'people say' and tended to be vague and generalized. Perhaps that accounted for the discrepancies, or in this case the total disagreement, in how events transpired.

Making a conscious effort to push the conversation just one more time, hoping to judge Annica's response, Jack finally said, "And no one has ever attempted to overthrow Mora in the same way?"

Annica's eyes became alight with intensity, but what was she thinking? Was she angry? Was she thinking she had just uncovered a traitor?

She opened her mouth to respond when a deep crashing rumble caused them both to whip around; people were shouting and running out the entrance to one of the adjoining caves where a rockslide had been loosened by one of the workers. Annica jumped up and ran towards the ensuing chaos. As the last of the rocks came smashing out the opening of the cave, a large man with a beard launched himself out ahead of them and, showing a surprising amount of agility for such a stout person, rolled sideways onto the safety of the grassy hill. As the rocks rolled to a halt, the bearded man let out a belly laugh from his back where he had landed.

"Is that everyone? Is everyone out?" Annica yelled frantically.

"I was the last one," the bearded man confirmed, still laughing.

"I'm glad you think it's so funny, Cain," Annica said disapprovingly. She then kicked him hard in the side and said, "Now get up, help your team clean this up."

Cain rolled over, still laughing, and heaved himself to his feet. "Nah, I'm taking a break. Almost got killed, I'm taking five."

Annica just rolled her eyes and walked back towards Jack. The rest of the men who had run out of the collapsing cave went back to work moving rocks. "This is the fun you get to join tomorrow," she said. "Don't worry; we haven't lost anyone in several years."

Jack was unsure if this was a joke or not. "Is that what happened to that one?" Jack asked, pointing to the cave with the spindly brace in front of it.

Annica glanced back at the boarded-up entrance and responded, "Yeah, something like that. Why don't you head back down and rejoin Ydoro. We start bright and early tomorrow morning." Jack nodded and thanked her for her time. He began to walk back down the hill when she called out, "And Jack…" He turned to look at her. "Be careful."

Was that general advice? Or a warning? There was still an intensity in her eyes that he could not read. He continued down the hill trying to figure out whose side Annica was on; all the while with her staring after him. Jack wasn't sure he liked Annica. She had a disarming appearance, and seemed nice enough on the surface, but Jack could easily see her being a zealot; a blind follower of the King.

\*\*\*\*\*

The sun had nearly set by the time they approached town again. There had not been much talk on the way back. Jack was still contemplating Annica and her team, while Cyrus was likely just dreading the physical labor of the following day. Jack still found himself wondering where Mora had come from; was he an outsider as Ydoro said, or was he born here as Annica insisted? He would probably never know for certain, and it did not matter much anyways, but he was curious all the same.

"I thought you said not to be out here after dark?" Cyrus asked, looking around at the dense forest.

"We're nearly back," Ydoro replied, now speaking in his real accent once again. A scream overhead announced a Shrieking Bat flying by and caused Jack and Cyrus to jump, but Ydoro did not react at all. He really did act entirely at home in this place, and Jack was reminded that this was the only home he had known for his entire adult life.

"Do you ever dream of getting out of here?" Jack asked. "I mean, back to where you came from, where we come from."

Ydoro replied simply without ever looking back at him, "I used to."

They exited the forest into the familiarity of town and Ydoro split off, heading back towards town square and his own living quarters. The town was dark now, as it always was once the sun went down, other than the occasional splash of light from a torch. After several weeks, they were familiar enough with the small network of windy streets to find their way.

Jack looked sideways at Cyrus and asked, "So how was the rest of your time with Tannus?"

"God, that guy is a wet blanket," Cyrus responded with a laugh. "He droned on for probably fifteen minutes after you left, explaining every type of grain and crop they grow."

Jack smiled and quipped, "You'd think after being sucked through a portal to another world we'd at least get away from bad bosses."

Cyrus laughed aloud and started telling a story about an old professor of his, but Jack slowed as their living quarters came into view and he realized with a start that something was wrong. Every one of their four doors was wide open, but no lights were on inside. Where were Nel and Alec? Cyrus stopped his story mid-sentence as he saw the open doorways ahead.

The darkness was crushing and impenetrable, making it impossible to see anything inside the buildings, but Jack approached the entrance to his own room cautiously, squinting to see. He had a lantern hanging on the nearest wall; he just needed to feel around and find it. Jack stopped in the frame of the doorway and began to run his hand along the inside wall. The darkness was claustrophobic and played tricks on the mind. Through the blackness, he thought he saw something in his room catch the light, but then it was gone. He was just imagining things; he just needed to get his hand on that lantern. He took a step further inside and his hand brushed past a wooden peg on the wall. The lantern should be just after that peg. Jack thought he heard a sound from inside his room, almost like a sharp intake of breath. He peered through the darkness and definitely saw something catch the light this time, something round. Was it moving? Then another round circle of light appeared. It was eyes!

Jack scrambled backwards and smashed into Cyrus in the doorway. Jack forced him backwards out the door and nearly tripped over his own feet trying to put distance between himself and the room. The eyes grew in size as they approached the doorway and the shape of an enormous, hooked beak came into view as it emerged into the moonlight. The Neodactyl stepped a scaly foot silently onto the street and bristled as it arched its neck. Jack could see its long, slender tongue raise as it opened its mouth in a nearly silent hiss.

Jack considered running, but realized it would be impossible to outrun this thing. He was completely frozen with fear, and judging by the lack of sound coming from behind him, so was Cyrus. Out of the door to the right of his own, Alec's door, the second Neodactyl appeared, silently stalking towards them. When it did not stop, Jack and Cyrus began backing away down the street, slowly at first, and picking up the pace when the thing did not slow down. They passed the dark open door to Cyrus's room and the first Neodactyl joined the pursuit. Jack nearly lost his footing as they reached Nel's doorway, but regained his balance.

A harsh voice from inside Nel's dark room called out, "That'll do."

Cyrus and Jack froze and the approaching Neodactyls stopped in their tracks, still not taking their enormous, unblinking yellow eyes off them. Jack stared into the dark room and a person came careening out of it, crashing to the ground in a heap. The person propped themselves onto their hands and knees and the moonlight revealed Alec's face.

King Mora came striding out of the black room, his dark robes flowing behind him and a machete in his right hand. He grasped Alec roughly by the hair and wrenched him to his knees, bringing the machete to rest along the side of his neck. King Mora looked at Jack and Cyrus with wide, dangerous eyes and said, "Let's have a talk."

## CHAPTER FOURTEEN

# CONSEQUENCES

Cyrus looked around wildly, his mind scrambling for any idea of what to do. King Mora's steel machete was already beginning to draw blood along Alec's upturned neck, threatening to cut it open at any moment. The inescapable truth was that King Mora had all the power right now and they were at his mercy to allow Alec to live. For the moment, he appeared to be okay. There were the beginnings of a bruise forming along his cheek where he had likely been hit, but his face did not show defeat, but rather defiance. There was no sign of Nel anywhere. The two Neodactyls prowled along the sides of the buildings and came to stand on either side of Jack and Cyrus; their necks retracted like springs ready to strike.

Cyrus, realizing the hopelessness of their situation, threw his hands up in the air and decided to feign ignorance, although he could guess what this was about. "What's going on here? How can we help you, King Mora?"

"I thought we were friends," Mora called out dangerously, "and I also thought I was very clear when we last spoke."

"Very clear," Cyrus answered, "what's the problem you have with my brother?"

Alec looked at Cyrus in disgust, apparently not agreeing with his handling of the situation. Mora pulled Alec's hair tighter in his fist and Alec winced. "I have very few rules around here, and I'm a man of my word," the King began. "The last time we met, you people insulted me, and you paid the price. But you think I enjoy killing?" Cyrus thought the truth was likely yes, but he kept his mouth shut. "There's an established order. A way we do things around here. Everyone knows the rules and they obey them. And since I'm a man of my word, when I say to follow the rules and I will treat you well, I expect everyone to listen. That's how I know you didn't listen when I explained you would be expected to work around here."

Cyrus glanced down at Alec, who looked away, refusing to meet his gaze. Cyrus knew Alec was angry about conforming to this new society, but the last time they had talked, it was agreed he would be starting tomorrow with the rest of them. Something must have changed. "I'm not sure where the miscommunication lies," Cyrus said with his most placating voice, "but I assure you we are all planning to begin work tomorrow as requested."

King Mora seemed slightly thrown by Cyrus's willingness to be so agreeable, but the hesitation did not last long. "You're the charmer, I get it. You always know what to say, but your brother here…" Mora lifted Alec's head further upwards and slid the machete lightly towards the center of his throat.

Cyrus began to panic and yelled out, "Isn't that right, Alec? You plan to work tomorrow, right? Tell him you plan to work tomorrow."

Alec opened his mouth to respond but Mora shook his head and sneered, "You can't save him Dr. Dorn. He's made his choice."

Cyrus was running out of ideas of what to do. He could not watch his brother die here. "It's not too late," he said desperately, "we can work something out, what do you want?"

The King smirked at him and replied, "I want you to watch this." He twisted the machete in his hand and looked into Cyrus's eyes. "The thing is, you could call for help right now; just start shouting at the top of your lungs, and no one would come to your rescue. Because you're in my Kingdom now."

The King bent over Alec and extended his arm across his body. Cyrus was frantic, and in a last desperate effort to save his brother, he decided to test Mora's theory. "FIRE! FIRE IN THE SQUARE!"

King Mora looked up at him and furrowed his brow; then smiled as people started peering out their windows and stepping out their doors. "You think I mind doing this with an audience?" the King laughed. "You can't save him. I've already told you, I always keep my word, and the people know that."

"I'm counting on it," Cyrus replied in a low voice. He then threw himself onto his knees and yelled, loud enough for the locals gathering in the street to hear, "Thank you so much my King! Thank you for showing my brother mercy! You are right, a strong ruler knows when to be firm and when to be lenient, and we thank you for giving us a second chance!"

King Mora's face twisted in anger and he moved to draw the machete across Alec's throat, but then he looked up at the curious group congregating around them and thought better of it. He scanned the crowd in fury, and the realization dawned on his face that he could not follow through with his execution without appearing as a true monster to his precious peasants. If what he claimed was true and he never betrayed his word, he had no choice but to let Alec go.

Cyrus smirked up at him, still from his knees, and said softly, "Your move."

King Mora looked murderous, but he shoved Alec harshly away from him, who crumpled in a heap in front of Cyrus. "I've spared his life because I recognize the value of a strong worker," Mora called out to the crowd. "And the last thing I want to do is deprive our fields of a strong pair of hands." Mora glanced down at Cyrus and his face betrayed the briefest flash of a grin. "I also must commend our newcomers; it is so generous of them to allow one of their own to come work in the Temple for me."

Cyrus put a protective hand over Alec, but Mora turned around and strode back into the darkness of the room behind him, emerging again with Nel unconscious in his arms. She had blood beneath her hairline and her arms and legs hung limp. Alec made a move to stand up but

Cyrus forced him back to the ground. Mora stood above them and whispered, "Don't play games with me again." He then whistled and one of his guards emerged from down the shadowy street and took Nel's limp form from him. Mora then made a clicking noise with his mouth and the Neodactyls ran silently to his side, one of them leaning close to Cyrus's face and hissing threateningly. A distant Shrieking Bat call distracted the creature briefly and it lifted its head to the sky in alarm. Mora reached out a hand and gently brushed the bristling feathers along its head and said to Cyrus, "You know where to find us."

The King turned and strode down the street, the Neodactyls close behind, followed by the guard carrying Nel. The locals shut their doors quickly as the King left, the street emptying as quickly as it had filled. Cyrus, Jack, and Alec were left on the dark stone road in silence, the only sounds the nearby calls of frogs and the distant, echoing screams of Shrieking Bats.

Alec made a move to stand up, but Cyrus put a comforting hand on his shoulder, urging him to take it easy.

"Get off of me!" Alec erupted, violently shaking Cyrus's hand away and staggering to his feet. "Enough waiting and seeing, enough trying to adapt, enough! We need a plan! I want to hear our plan to get her back and take that tyrannical freak out of power!"

Jack was glancing down the street nervously and Cyrus again attempted to quiet Alec. "Just listen to me, let's think about this."

"You didn't want to make a move because you thought Mora would leave us alone," Alec bellowed, "but now he's proven he won't! How many more of our team do we have to lose before you two will wake up?" Cyrus tried to reach out to him again but Alec shook him off. "If you won't help I'll storm the Temple myself, but I'm going up there!"

"Alec," Cyrus tried to interject but he was cut off again.

"These townspeople may be afraid of him but I'm not! He has no power other than those birds, and I'm going to show him…"

"Alec, stop!" Cyrus finally yelled with enough force to interrupt Alec's tirade. He leaned in towards Alec cautiously with his hands extended upwards, as if he were approaching a wild animal that could turn aggressive at any moment. He lowered his voice, barely above a whisper, and said, "Alec, I agree. We can't ignore him any longer."

Alec blinked in surprise at Cyrus's admission. "You agree?" Alec repeated skeptically.

"Of course," Jack chimed in with a low, mumbling voice. He was still watching down the road for signs of Mora's return. "Alec, we're not going to let him keep Nel. He's become a problem that can't be ignored, we agree with you."

"We just have to plan our next move," Cyrus whispered, "and right here in the middle of the street is not the place to do it. So please, come inside and we can talk this through."

Alec shook his head, finally looking a little more rational. "We can't talk inside. Mora heard us in there. Somehow he heard us." He pulled a scrap of paper from his pocket and handed it to Cyrus. Printed across it were four words, 'He can hear you.' "It was outside our door this afternoon. Somewhere out there we have a friend."

Jack was reading the note over, his lips forming each word as he processed it. "He must have locals listening in on us… and Ydoro put us in these rooms, that son of a bitch!"

"Now we don't know that he's involved," Cyrus reasoned. "He doesn't seem to have any true loyalty to the King."

"We don't know that," Alec hissed. "All we really know about him is that his entire persona is an act. That doesn't gain my trust, it just means he's a good liar. Maybe that was the plan to get close to us."

"He's not wrong," Jack said.

"Okay," Cyrus agreed, "it's possible, but we don't know. And the truth is…" He stopped briefly and looked both ways down the street, and then lowered his voice further. "The truth is if we are going to storm the Temple, we need someone who knows this world. Charging in there without knowing where we're going or what we'll encounter will only give him the advantage."

"He's right, Alec," Jack insisted. "I know this is emotional, for all of us. I care for Nel too, but we have to be smart. We're done waiting, I promise you, but we *have* to have a plan. Let us figure out our move, and we will be right by your side."

Alec looked sideways at Cyrus who nodded in agreement.

"I want him dead," Alec pressed as if trying to give them a reason to back out.

Cyrus did not like the idea, nor the side of Alec he was seeing, but he resigned, "If that's the move we have, he'll die. But this isn't about revenge, Alec. Our endgame is to remove a very real threat. Remember that."

Alec hesitated as if trying to find a flaw in his brother's logic, but he eventually nodded his head and reiterated, "No negotiating, no deals, no talking. We're *removing* him."

"You have my word," Cyrus agreed.

"Okay," Alec said, finally appeased. "We need a plan then."

Cyrus looked down the dark street once more and said softly, "We need to talk to Ydoro."

**CHAPTER FIFTEEN**

## THE LAWS OF THE LAND

"I want in," Ydoro exclaimed enthusiastically.

"In on what?" Cyrus asked, confused. They had just arrived at Ydoro's door and had told him nothing about their plans. It was late, the three of them had talked through options for about an hour on the street before deciding to come down here and wake Ydoro. If they were going to talk to him, it had to be now.

"This is a small town, news travels fast around here, especially to me. I heard about your encounter with King Mora in the street. He took your friend?"

"He did," Jack admitted hesitantly.

"So you're going after her, right?" Ydoro asked. "Am I wrong?"

The group exchanged glances, unsure of what to tell him. Finally, Alec stepped forward and said, "Here's the deal, Ydoro; how do we know we can trust you? We don't know you."

"You don't trust me? I've been your only ally here since you arrived."

"Why are you so eager to take on the King now?" Jack questioned, skeptically. "I mean, when we arrived, you were content playing your role as the welcoming committee, and had been for decades. What's different now?"

"Well I've been waiting for people like you," Ydoro insisted with wide eyes. "I couldn't exactly take on the King myself, that would be suicide!"

"So why isn't it suicide now?" Cyrus asked. "Even if we wanted to confront the King, it's us against his army."

"No no, the King doesn't have an army. It's just a handful of guards. And if you challenge Mora publicly, he'll want to face you head on. Believe me, he won't want his guards interfering."

"He would face all of us by himself?" Alec questioned in disbelief.

"Well, not by himself," Ydoro conceded. "He'll make it look like you have the advantage, make you believe it; trust me when I say you won't. You'll be walking into a trap."

"So what's our play then?" Jack asked.

Ydoro shrugged as if it were obvious and responded, "Make a trap for him first." He looked around the group, all of whose eyes were fixed on him, and continued, "Make him believe he has the upper hand. You make your challenge appear impulsive, but it won't be. He won't know you've already stacked the deck against him. Until it's too late."

Everyone considered this a moment before Alec asked, "How would that work?"

"Mora's dangerous," Ydoro conceded, "but the real threat inside that temple is not him."

Cyrus nodded, and his stomach lurched uncomfortably. "The Neodactyls."

The group as a whole shifted awkwardly. It was an obstacle that could not be ignored. As long as King Mora had control over those creatures, they had no hope of getting near him.

"The way I see it, you have three options," Ydoro said. "You kill them, which I don't know how you would do, you sever Mora's bond with them, which we don't know how to do, or you incapacitate them."

"Not easy to do I'm guessing," Jack said, leaning against the table and looking more defeated with each passing moment.

"Not easy," Ydoro agreed, "but the real problem is making sure Mora still believes he has the upper hand. He will never agree to a challenge if he realizes the Neodactyls are out of commission."

Thinking aloud, Cyrus said, "So we need to find a way to get them away from Mora once we're inside the Temple."

"We're getting ahead of ourselves here," Alec declared. He turned to Ydoro and said, "We still don't know if we can trust you."

Ydoro looked Alec right in the eyes and responded, "I don't think you have much choice."

Alec bristled and started towards Ydoro, who put his hands out in defense. Cyrus put an arm out in front of Alec's chest, holding him back. He was again startled at seeing this side of his brother. He had never been this bold, this aggressive before.

"Look, I can help you," Ydoro was insisting, still with his hands up at Alec. "I can help you, but you have to trust me. I've been inside that Temple, I know the King's weaknesses, and I know the laws of the land around here. Threaten me all you want but tell me, how are you possibly going to pull off this mutiny without me?"

"Why do we need to know the laws of the land?" Jack asked. When Ydoro looked at him with raised eyebrows, he continued, "Look, we want to trust you, but you have to give us a reason to. If what you're telling us is true, then we're all on the same side. So prove it."

Ydoro took a resigned breath and explained, "You need to understand how this culture works. Mora has turned this place into his own playland, but the people have let him do it. By and large they're okay being told what to do. That may be a foreign concept to you, but they like rules in place. Many of the locals don't like Mora, in fact you'll find quite a few who absolutely despise him, but in their minds, he's earned his spot as their leader."

"By killing their last king," Jack said.

"Precisely," Ydoro answered. "They don't do elections here or voting of any kind. You want power; you grab it, simple as that. Do you see where I'm going with this?"

"You're worried by removing Mora we're leaving a void that could be filled by someone even worse," Cyrus nodded.

"No," Ydoro said bluntly, "I'm saying if you remove the King, you'll be expected to rule in his place.

The room went silent. Cyrus looked over at Jack and Alec, whose brows were furrowed in confusion. Finally, Jack spoke up, "Wait, what?"

Cyrus shook his head, "This isn't our land, we don't want to rule it. We're not staying here."

Ydoro shrugged and said, "We can table the conversation for now, but you should understand what you're getting yourselves into."

Cyrus said, "Look, not to be overly frank, but we don't give a damn about this culture or their established order. They can do whatever they like once Mora's gone. For now, tell us how we can get to him."

"Well, to start with, you have to work tomorrow, all of you," Ydoro said, looking at Alec. "It's important because, at the moment, the King can't kill your friend after telling the public she was coming to work for him. He can't risk the image he's created, but if you give him a reason to harm her, like refusing to work after assuring him it was a misunderstanding... you get the idea. So work tomorrow, and talk to no one of your plans."

"Okay, fine," Alec agreed impatiently, "Then what?"

"If you confront the King outside the Temple, he will likely let you in... and once you're inside he will toy with you until he's bored, and the Neodactyls will tear you apart. I believe your best bet will be to confine them in a room inside the Temple; lock them away so they can't help him. I can only think of one way to do that... but you're not gonna like it."

"Yeah, what's that?" Cyrus asked apprehensively.

"Bait," Ydoro responded, "human bait to be specific."

The team grumbled and Cyrus said, "That's suicide. If someone gets locked in a room with those things, they're not coming back out."

"Agreed," Ydoro nodded, "which is why there's one specific room you will have to lead them to. It's at the far north end of the Temple. It has two doors, one that leads in from the main hallway, and another on the opposite wall. If you timed it right, someone could lead them in, escape through the other door and close it while someone else locks the first door."

"That's your plan?" Alec exclaimed in disbelief. "Lead them on a chase and hope you can outrun them in time? Forget it."

"I agree, that's way too risky," Jack said, "and if any one thing goes wrong, we all die."

"Not to mention we don't know if it would even work," Cyrus pointed out. "Mora has control over them, and since we don't understand the depth of that control, we can't count on them being drawn away from him."

"Maybe not," Ydoro said, "but they're predators. Whatever control the King has over them, their instincts are that of wild predators. Alec, this is your field, is that true?"

Alec thought a moment before replying uncertainly, "I would be inclined to agree. Animals can be trained into submission, but natural instinct is an incredibly powerful force to overcome. We of course don't know anything about *Neodactyls* but if you were dealing with trained lions for instance, even if they were impeccably trained to obey their master, I have no doubt we could lure them away if they were given the right incentive. The trouble becomes we don't know what sort of bond these creatures have with the King, but it can't be just training. Ydoro, you said yourself that they have passed from king to king. They may be trained, but how would they know to recognize the new king? It doesn't make sense."

"We'd have to test it first, then," Cyrus said. "Not human bait, though. We need to think of a different way to lure them away once we are in the Temple, and we need to test it on them ahead of time."

"I can't imagine the King letting us borrow them," Jack retorted dryly.

"There may be a way, though," Ydoro said.

A loud knock on the door made them all jump. Cyrus looked at the others in panic. Even Ydoro looked alarmed. It was the middle of the night, who would be calling at this hour?

"You need to leave, now!" Ydoro exclaimed in a frantic whisper. "Out the back, come on, now!"

The team scrambled towards the back room. In the chaos, Alec inadvertently bumped into the small bedside table, which slammed against the wall loudly.

"Ydoro," called a voice through the front door.

Ydoro rushed them all to the back room and pointed them towards a door in the rear. He turned back towards the main living area and whispered quickly over his shoulder, "Move quietly, get some distance, and then run like hell!"

"Ydoro, now!" the voice called through the front door again with a pounding knock.

Cyrus reached the back door first and grasped the handle firmly. He pushed against it but it seemed to be stuck.

"Coming!" Ydoro called to his mystery guest at the front door.

Cyrus could hear the handle of the front door being released. He took a step back and threw himself bodily into the back door with his shoulder. To his relief, the door flung open with a crash to the forest beyond. He took one step outside and froze when he heard the front door open and the man step inside. The whole team stopped moving instantly, afraid any noise they made would alert the caller in front now that they were inside. Cyrus swore under his breath and tilted his head, listening for an opportunity to run.

"Good evening," Ydoro's voice said from the front room. "What can I help you with?"

"Who's with you?" a voice asked.

"What? No one, I was just sleeping," Ydoro replied unconvincingly.

"A lot of noise in there for sleeping," the voice said.

"I... I... Okay fine, I was drinking. It's been a rough week. You startled me when you knocked. I was... it made me..."

"Get dressed," the voice cut him off, thankfully stopping Ydoro from improvising his excuse further. "The King wants to see you."

"What, now?" Ydoro asked in alarm.

"That's what he said."

It must have been one of Mora's guards. What would they want with Ydoro at this hour? Cyrus took another gentle step towards the forest, the moss growing on the ground muffling the sound well. He cautiously took another, and the team followed. He took a third step and a buried branch snagged loudly against some dead leaves. Cyrus froze again, wincing at the noise.

"Are you sure you're alone?" the guard asked from the front.

"I... of course. I may have left the door open back there, that's probably..."

"Ydoro, I don't care if you have someone with you. What you do at night isn't my concern; but I need to see who it is."

Cyrus knew they could not stay here much longer. The guard would be coming back any second to inspect. Instead of attempting to walk further into the forest and onto unknown terrain, he tried walking along the back of the building, hugging the wall as he went. Jack shook his head vigorously but Cyrus waved him along. He reluctantly followed and Alec crept along behind him. Looking forward, Cyrus could see the corner of the building. If they could get around to the side, they could wait until the guard left. He could no longer hear the voices from the front room. Was it because they had stopped talking or were they now out of earshot? Cyrus reached the corner and softly crept around it, breathing a sigh of relief as he did so. Jack tiptoed to the corner next, but at that moment Ydoro's voice rang out much closer than it had sounded before, saying, "You don't need to go back there. I assure you there's no one back here."

Jack rounded the corner louder than he had intended but Alec looked over his shoulder at the back door and realized he would not make it in time. He scanned the area in panic and at the last second threw himself behind a mid-sized tree just as Cyrus heard the guard step out into the forested rear of the building. Everyone held their breath. Cyrus could not see the guard around the corner, but he could see Alec pressed tightly against the tree; a tree that barely looked wide enough to conceal him. Alec's eyes were shut and he looked like he was silently mouthing curses.

"I told you there was no one back here," Ydoro's voice came from the rear door.

The guard did not respond and Cyrus could imagine him scanning the dark forest for signs of people. Jack looked at Cyrus and mouthed,

"We need to move," but Cyrus held up a finger for him to wait. He was listening for the right moment.

"There really is nothing back here," Ydoro insisted, "and if we're going to the Temple tonight, we should really get moving."

There was another few seconds of silence, no doubt because the guard was still searching the moonlit forest, and then the door slammed shut.

"Now!" Cyrus said loud enough for Alec to hear from behind the tree. He barreled forward along the side of the building towards the front street. They had maybe five seconds before the guard would reach the front door again. He tucked his head and exploded through a tangle of thick foliage, emerging on the main road with leaves flying around him. His feet caught on a root and he fell hard onto his palms, but he refused to break stride and launched himself back to his feet and down the road. He could hear heavy footsteps behind him, so he assumed the other two were following closely, but there was no time to turn around. Cyrus sprinted as fast as he could down the center of the square before lurching sideways and ducking behind another building and heading back towards the forest. Off the main road, he chanced a look behind him and verified that both Jack and Alec had made it with him. He faced forward again and careened through the trees, no longer concerned with how much noise they were making. He was not even confident they were heading the right direction to get 'home,' but the important thing was to get as much distance as possible between themselves and Ydoro's place. Cyrus was starting to feel a cramp in his side and his ankle was throbbing from when he tripped, but just a little bit farther. They came across a large, upturned tree and Cyrus crashed to a halt behind it, ducking into a crouch with Alec and Jack doing the same. The moment they stopped moving there was silence. Cyrus pressed his eyes shut and listened for any sign they were being followed. There was nothing. Cicadas and crickets chimed rhythmically and a toad croaked nearby, but that was it. No footsteps. No sounds of pursuit.

Cyrus exhaled in relief, collapsing onto his back to finally catch his breath.

"What the hell was that?" Alec asked, wheezing.

"Could they have heard us talking?" Jack asked, leaning against the tree in exhaustion. "Why would they come for Ydoro at this time of night?"

Cyrus stayed quiet, continuing to listen for footsteps: nothing. He was confident they had not been followed, but he could not be as confident that the guard had not spotted them running through the town square. There was no way of knowing if they had cut into the forest before the guard made it to the front door.

"What are you thinking, Cyrus?" Jack whispered.

Cyrus knew they were hoping for a plan, or at least some words of comfort, but he had none. After a pause, he admitted, "I don't know. We have no idea if Mora had people listening in on us or not, or if Ydoro is giving us up right now, or if that guard saw us running off."

Jack bowed his head and nodded grimly.

Cyrus pushed against the tree and brought himself to his feet, looking around to try to determine the direction back to their living quarters. "I think come sunrise, for better or worse, we'll have more answers."

## CHAPTER SIXTEEN

# MIDNIGHT IN THE TEMPLE

Nelida Yore opened her eyes slowly and breathed in the damp, musky smell of wet stone. Her cheek was pressed against a dirt covered rock floor; definitely indoors judging by the echoing drip of water rhythmically splashing into a nearby puddle. Her head was throbbing and she could not see anything in the oppressive darkness surrounding her. She lifted her head carefully and peered around before shutting her eyes again as she was overcome by dizziness. Nel winced and lightly touched her forehead. She felt dried blood beneath her fingers. What had happened to her? The last thing she remembered was talking to Alec in his room. Or was it her room? It was all so fuzzy.

She took a deep breath and forced herself to her feet, putting her hands out to steady herself in case she fell. She was seeing double of everything, but at least her eyes were adjusting to the darkness. There was an object in front of her with some sort of pattern on it. She squinted her eyes and focused intently on it, willing the two blurry images to become one. The edges of her vision slowly swam together to form a picture, and she realized she was staring at a wall of heavy iron vertical bars. She was in a cell. Nel swore aloud and quickly scanned her surroundings. She was alone in a small cell with no light, no bed, nothing of any kind. Three stone walls and a fourth made of bars. How had she gotten here? She thought back to her conversation with Alec. Had someone come to the door? No, someone had knocked but no one was there. They had left a note, that was it. A warning. Then what? She couldn't piece it together. She had a blurry image of two poisonous yellow eyes coming out of the darkness at her; and then nothing. So Mora must have taken her.

She lashed out violently at the bars and yelled out, "Mora, you son of a bitch! Where are you? Mora!"

"He can't hear you," answered a gentle, soothing voice. It sounded like it had come from down the dark hall, perhaps from a cell next to hers.

"Who's there?" Nel asked, a little more aggressively than she intended.

"A fellow inmate," the voice remarked, "and he can't hear you. Mora's living quarters are on the opposite side of the Temple."

"I'll make him hear me."

"You're welcome to try," the voice said, "although I have an easier way if you want to talk to the King."

"I don't want to talk to the King," Nel responded quickly, "I want to kill the King."

There was a pause. Eventually the voice answered, "Even better."

"So you got a way to help me do that?" Nel asked, losing her patience with this game. "I assume you want something in return for your help? Cut the crap, what is it?"

"Just your name," the voice responded, and an old, weathered hand with pale skin hanging off the bones reached around the corner from the adjoining cell and offered a handshake. "My name is Henry."

Nel blinked in confusion, then grasped the hand firmly in her own. "I'm Nel."

"Good to meet you, Nel," Henry said, "I haven't had a real conversation in years."

"Well I kept up my end of the deal," Nel said, sidestepping what was likely going to be an emotional tangent, "you said you have a way to get out of here?"

"I do," the voice responded.

"Then how come you haven't used it?" Nel asked.

"Because I'm over here," the voice said. "You have some luck on your side, that cell you're in is defective."

"Defective, huh?" Nel asked, unsure whether she trusted this mysterious Henry.

"It is," Henry insisted, "take a look at the right side of those bars, at the top where they meet the rocks."

Nel moved to the other side of the cell and examined the area he was describing. "Yeah, I see it."

"Give it a push," Henry said.

Nel pushed at the bars uncertainly but nothing happened. "I think you need to check your intel, Henry," she said in frustration.

"No, no, give it a real push," he responded, "at the top right corner."

Nel felt foolish pushing at these very solid-looking bars and wondered if she were somehow being tricked, but she rolled her eyes and gave the bars a forceful shove. To her surprise, a large chunk of rock where the iron had been drilled in separated from the main wall and the bars bowed outwards slightly. It was no wonder the defect had been overlooked; unless you put direct pressure on the bars from the inside, the rock wall would look entirely solid. If anyone checked the structural integrity of the bars themselves, they appeared solidly in place, permanently buried in the stone; it was the stone itself that was cracked.

"I told you," Henry said, hearing the crunch of the rock giving way.

The bars did not provide a lot of movement and pushing heavily on them only offered up a narrow gap at the top corner of the cell, but it would be enough for her to squeeze through. She grasped the bars firmly and pulled herself up by her arms, awkwardly feeding them through the small gap followed by her head and shoulders. Her legs kicked out behind her, unable to find anything solid to push against, but it didn't have to look pretty as long as she got out. With her head outside the cell, she glanced up and down the hallway, but the darkness was so complete she could barely see anything. At the end of the hall to the right there appeared to be very faint firelight trickling down a stairway. She kicked out again with her legs but could not contort herself enough to find the wall. Instead, she bent her arms at an uncomfortable angle and used them to shimmy her body up. She got her waist free but her hips became stuck. Nel laughed to herself, imagining how absurd she probably looked wedged between the metal bars and the stone wall. She tried to push on the bars again but they were not offering any more give.

"You okay over there?" Henry called out.

"Fantastic," Nel called back, sarcastically. She gripped the bars tight and pushed herself up with all of her strength. To her relief her hips scraped through and she was free, albeit with some freshly forming bruises. She fed her legs out through the gap carefully and, despite attempting to right herself, ended up pitching forward and slamming down hard onto the dusty floor of the hallway. She inhaled sharply trying to regain her breath, then rolled over onto her back and closed her eyes for a moment.

"You made it," Henry called victoriously.

Nel opened her eyes again and looked over in the direction of his cell. She could not make out any details, but she could see his form crouched against the bars. He looked frail even in silhouette. He must be old judging by the feel of his hand when she shook it. Nel stood up with some effort and looked at her cell with the bars bowed outwards. It would probably be smart to push them back into place, she thought to herself. If she did not succeed, she would not want the King or his guards knowing of the cell's weakness. She reached up and gave the bars a full-bodied push. They fell back into place easily and the rock attached to the end of the metal fit snugly back where it had cracked off from. The cell looked as secure as ever. She walked over to Henry's cell, still unable to see much detail. What she could make out was a small old man with stringy wisps of a white beard and a smiling, gaunt face. His pale appearance sent a shiver down her spine, but he had kind eyes.

"Thanks for that," Nel said, never one to overstate her gratitude. "So… is there anything I can do to help you out?" She really hoped he would say no, she had to get moving.

Henry shook his head and replied, "I'm too old to run. How 'bout this; if you do what you say you're gonna do, come back and get me afterwards."

"You've got a deal," Nel said with a smile. She turned abruptly and strode down the hallway towards the stairway with light coming down it. She wanted to get away from Henry before he got overly chatty. He seemed kind enough, but she knew dead-weight when she saw it. She would not be able to carry a weak old man with her for what she intended to do.

Nel reached the curving staircase and slowly crept up it. She was surprised there were no guards around. You would think at least one guard would be planted outside the cells. It was just further proof that Mora was no match for her. He was all show. He made a big production of everything, and the locals would cower and bend to his will, but not her. Nel had been on her own far too long to be intimidated by a self-made dictator. She had been on her own for so long, in fact, it was difficult to imagine a time when she had a family, but she did once. She had grown up in New Orleans; the middle of five girls all raised by their mother, an English teacher. Her mother had been very loving and caring, even as she struggled to support all of her kids. Their house had been a place of learning with books strewn about on every surface. By all accounts, her childhood had been a good one; but when she was thirteen her mother got sick and never recovered. It forced the two older sisters to grow up far too fast and they shouldered the responsibility of caring for the younger two. That left Nel in an uncomfortable middle ground where she was not quite old enough to be responsible for the fractured family, but not young enough to need as much help as the youngest two. It worked poorly for a little while, but she jumped quickly at the first opportunity for work and never looked back. It wasn't that she didn't care for her sisters, but there was something depressing about clutching to the shadow of what their family had once been.

Nel had reached the top of the stairs and there were still no guards. She really needed a weapon or her plan to kill the King would not get very far, although the thought of killing him with her bare hands was appealing. She would just have to improvise; she was good at that. Navigating this fortress would be the real trick. Knowing how Mora seemed to love the hierarchy he had created, it was a good bet his living quarters would be at the highest point of the building. If only she could find another staircase. She was walking down a hallway, still with no windows so she figured it must be underground. The walls were covered with tapestries; or at least they looked like tapestries until you examined them up close. They in fact seemed to be painted blankets and large pieces of cloth. Some of the designs on them were done quite well, but it was odd décor. It once again made her think that everything in this place felt like a poor imitation of the Middle Ages.

She finally came to another staircase and made her way up it, crouching down when she reached the top and saw an enormous, open entryway. There was a huge door on one wall maybe a hundred feet from her that must have been the main entrance, and one guard stood in front of it; although he appeared to be picking at his nails and did not even notice her head poking into the room. She looked around and spotted a smaller door at the far end of the room that led further into the Temple. That was where she wanted to go. She would have to think of a way to get rid of the guard. He was clearly distracted, but even so, she would not be able to cross the large room without him noticing. Perhaps she could draw him towards her with a noise and then take him out.

Before she could flesh her plan out, the front door opened with a loud echoing groan, revealing two people in the doorway. The guard turned to them and Nel saw her opportunity. Without thinking of the consequences of being caught, she vaulted herself off the stairs and ran as quietly as she could across the room. She could hear voices talking at the front door, so she assumed that meant they had not spotted her, but she did not turn around to find out. She reached the far door and slipped through, praying there was not anyone on the other side.

She breathed a sigh of relief when she found herself alone in the next room, but the room itself was bizarre. It was a giant open space with stone floors and a freestanding metal ladder in the very center that led straight up to an opening in the ceiling about a hundred feet above. What possible function could this room have? Then again nothing about this Temple seemed practical. She crossed the room slowly and peered up through the square opening in the ceiling above. Could that be where Mora lived? She decided it was unlikely. This room would be positioned near the center of the Temple; Mora would likely want windows to see out over his Kingdom.

She found another staircase and made her way up, then down more hallways and up more stairs. This place was like a maze, but almost entirely empty as she was discovering. The inside of the Temple was proving to be just as drab and utilitarian as the outside. She finally reached an area that had a slightly warmer feel; at least the torches were lit, and the floor was made of wood in this wing. Perhaps that meant she was getting closer. She rounded a corner and to her horror, a single guard turned and looked her right in the eyes. The guard's mouth opened in alarm. She was terrified he was about to yell for help, but he didn't. She stared at him, frozen with indecision. Should she flee? Could she best him even without a weapon? Why wasn't he attacking her? The guard turned to look down the empty hallway behind him, then looked back at Nel. His face remained unchanged, but his hand reached onto his belt and pulled a large knife from a sheath. She backed up a step, but he didn't approach her. Instead, he turned towards a doorway off to his left, holding the knife at his side, and dropped it. The knife hit the wooden floor with a soft thud, shaking vertically where it had struck. The guard never looked back in her direction again but continued through the door and out of sight, leaving the knife stuck in the floor where he had been standing.

Nel continued forward cautiously and peered through the door the guard had walked through. He was gone. Apparently the King had enemies everywhere. She bent down and tugged the knife from the wood flooring, turning it over in her hands and examining the blade. It would do just fine. She walked down the length of the hallway and around a corner. There was another staircase but this one was only six steps high and far less steep. It led gently into a finely decorated, carpeted room with windows along the far wall and several smaller rooms attached. There was a massive bed visible through one of the doorways and torchlight bathed the entire area in a warm, orange glow. If she were looking for further confirmation that these were the king's quarters, she found it in the far-left corner of the room. There was a curved, cushioned bench that formed a half-circle around what looked like a raised metal fire pit; except it wasn't regular fire within, it was *frozen fire*. Rocks and ash from the Fire Fields had been collected in the basin, and stuck into it vertically forming an 'X' were the King's scepters, glowing vibrantly. It reminded Nel of an altar of some kind.

Nel crept slowly from room to room, studying this glimpse into the mysterious King's private life. On the surface, it seemed Mora really did live the life of a medieval king. Where the rest of The Temple was dark and grey, these rooms were elegant and gold, and just as Nel suspected, the curved windows on the far wall offered sweeping views of the rolling island countryside. The town she had been taken from was visible way down in the valley below. It was still nighttime outside, she must not have been unconscious too long. She walked cautiously into one of the adjoining rooms that was more sparsely decorated, finding what seemed to be an enormous closet, or perhaps a storage room. There were neatly folded stacks of clothing covering most of the surrounding shelves, but other things as well. She noted several gold artifacts sitting in a forgotten pile, some sort of urn with a greenish sandy substance inside, and some extremely old looking machetes and knives in the corner. Nel ran her hand along the clothing piles while walking the perimeter of the room. Her fingers brushed something hard under one of the pieces of folded cloth. She carefully lifted the top layer and uncovered a heavily used black revolver with silver metal shining through from beneath the worn finish. She gasped and snatched it up instantly. She had learned to shoot long ago and knew her way around a handgun; but she was disappointed when she opened the chamber and discovered it was without bullets. Nel swore and began rifling through the other piles of clothes, but there was nothing there. She scanned the room quickly, searching for any spot Mora may have hidden them. Why would Mora even have a handgun? It seemed in sharp contrast to the man she had met. Perhaps he had taken it off another castaway like them. The bastard probably didn't even know how to use it.

No obvious hiding places stood out to her, so she shrugged, resigning to tearing the entire room apart; but she paused when she saw a neatly folded greenish-tan pile of clothing along the far wall. It wasn't the clothes that caught her eye but what looked like a gold coin carefully placed on top. It only gave her pause because the way it was placed indicated some sort of importance. It was too neatly separated from everything else not to have personal significance to the King. Nel started towards it but immediately stopped in her tracks when she heard something from the main room. She held her breath, listening for the noise again. It had sounded like a sniffing sound. She waited; her head cocked to one side, but the room was silent. Had she imagined it? Just when she decided she must have been hearing things, the sound came again and she whipped around this time, facing the open door that led out to the main living area. Through the doorway she could not see anyone, but much of the room was obscured from her position. Nel raised the knife the guard had left for her and tiptoed forward. She was still holding the useless revolver in the other hand, but she did not dare put it down for fear it would make a noise. It suddenly occurred to her that if the Neodactyls were out there, this pathetic little knife would not be enough to fend them off. It didn't matter; she was committed now. Even if those birds tore her apart, all she needed was one clean shot at the King. The moment she saw him, she would lunge forward and bury the knife in his heart. There would be no talking, no begging. She fully expected to die immediately afterwards, but that was okay.

She peeked around the corner towards the main entrance to the room: nothing. She slowly scanned the room looking for movement. The dancing torchlight played tricks with the shadows, but there was no one here. She finished her slow sweep, looking towards the altar with the scepters on it in the far corner, and her stomach dropped when she saw a person sitting on the bench in the shadows. It was a man, but not King Mora. Whoever it was, they were bent over their knees in a defeated posture, their long, wild hair obscuring their face. They wore a dark traveling cloak similar to Mora's, but had a large, unruly beard peeking out from beneath their downturned face. The man had not noticed her enter the room; he was too busy staring at his feet. He brought his hands up to his face and rubbed at his eyes, sniffing once again. Whoever the man was, he was crying. Nel looked around the room verifying there was no one else around. She watched him for another minute, weighing her options. Finally, she decided she didn't care who the man was, or what he was crying about. If he was in this room, he was clearly important to the King and therefore could be used as leverage.

She took a step towards him, her knife raised out in front of her, and then another step. She was still too far away to charge him; the trick would be to get as close as possible before alerting him of her presence. The thought had barely entered her mind when her foot came to rest on a loose floorboard and a soft creak broke the silence. The man's head snapped up and locked eyes with her. He had tears running along his face and an even bigger beard than she had originally noticed. His eyes looked dangerous and threatening, but strangely they softened as he looked at her. All of Nel's resolve had left her and she just stared at this broken shell of a man. She could still use him, but she was having second thoughts about hurting him. His long, greasy hair hung in sheets around his face, almost entirely obscuring a strange, reddish patch of skin along the side of his forehead. The man had still not said a word, but the way he was looking at her was unsettling. He looked confused, uncomprehending. She raised her knife a little higher, but her hand began to shake. His eyes looked familiar. A shiver ran down her spine and her legs began to weaken. She knew this man.

"Nel?" The man finally said.

Nel shook her head and her eyes began to water. She was in a dream; she had to be in a dream. "Cyrus?" Her voice was shaky.

Her eyes weren't tearing up out of sadness or anger or even fear; it was utter hopelessness. What she was seeing did not make sense, and it was suddenly apparent that they were up against something beyond their comprehension. The man she was staring at was not the Cyrus she knew. She had just seen him earlier today and he looked nothing like this. Cyrus was clean cut, albeit with a bit of a beard growing since they had arrived here; but his hair was still relatively short. The most apparent change in his appearance since they had arrived was the burn on the side of his face, an attribute that this Cyrus shared. Perhaps an even more pressing question than his altered looks was what was he doing in the Temple? How did he get into King Mora's room?

Nel was shaking her head in disbelief, and she seemed to be backing away, although she did not remember making a conscious decision to do so. She noticed that Cyrus was saying something to her, but he seemed far away. It felt like she was in someone else's body, watching these bizarre events unfold through a foggy lens.

"What?" Nel finally asked, still backing away from the man she was starting to realize could not possibly be Cyrus. Her knife was again raised towards him, although he was making no attempt to come after her.

"How are you here?" The man asked with wide eyes.

He sounded like Cyrus, but it could not be him. This was some sort of trickery.

The man finally stood up with his hands raised in a gesture of trust. It would not work. She would not let this person, this *thing*, come anywhere near her.

"Nel, don't," the man said, stepping towards her. "You know me, I'm on your side."

That settled it; this was not the real Cyrus. Nel shook her head and said with a shaky voice, "Sorry Doc, if it were really you, you'd know you were never on my side."

The man furrowed his brow and Nel spun on her heel and bolted towards the door behind her. She slammed hard into something solid and nearly fell backwards. It was a person. A man. She pushed against them in panic, but they grabbed her wrists with incredible strength. She looked up into the wild, piercing eyes of King Mora, who was grinning widely at her. She tried to twist the knife in her hand, but he flung it from her grip to the floor. He tried to wrap an arm around her neck, but she opened her mouth and bit down on his inner hand. He grunted in pain and threw her roughly to the ground. Exactly what she was hoping for. She scrambled forward and grasped the knife from the floor, spinning wildly and lashing out towards his legs. He backed up in alarm, but she kept swinging. She was too panicked to land a good blow; he was easily dodging her swipes. After another swing and a miss, Mora bent to grab her by the hair. Realizing her moment, Nel lunged upwards with the knife, burying it up to the hilt into his stomach. Mora howled out in pain and released her, clutching at his wound.

Nel clambered on her hands and knees, the bloody knife still gripped tight in her fist. She glanced in the direction of the strange altar where the scepters stood but was surprised to see the Cyrus imposter was no longer there. She scanned the room frantically, but he seemed to have vanished entirely. She stood up and wheeled around towards Mora again. To her horror, he was not keeled over and dying as she had expected. He was no longer pursuing her and seemed to be in a great deal of pain, but his hand was pressed against the side of his abdomen, not his stomach. He was bleeding freely from beneath his robes, but it seemed she had not landed the killing blow she had thought. Nel was at least satisfied to note the ever-present smirk had left his face. He was clearly weakened, either way, and that was the window she needed. She stepped towards him, knife outstretched, and Mora backed away from her in fear.

Nel forced a grin, attempting to hide her desperation, and said, "I told you I'd be coming for you."

She lunged forward, aiming straight for his chest, but a blur of quills and scales slammed into her, knocking her to her back. One of the King's birds had careened around him from the outside hallway and was now standing over her snarling and hissing. She turned her face away from its open, hooked beak and a scaly foot came to rest on her chest. She could feel the enormous talons catching against her shirt and knew that it could disembowel her with one kick of its leg. It bent its head even closer to hers and screeched menacingly, but she refused to look into its gigantic yellow eyes. She lay still, facing away from it, until she saw the second Neodactyl prowl into view. It seemed to be patrolling the room while the one on top of her held her prone. There was no escaping them, and no getting to the King. She released the knife from her hand and let it clatter to the floor.

"Smart move," Mora said, although he sounded shaken. "You know, I respect a true fighter, and you certainly are that. What do you think, is she worth keeping around, or should I just kill her now?"

Who was he talking to? The Neodactyls? But then a familiar voice with a fake accent replied from the hallway, "She could be a liability. Still, she's got spirit. She could be useful to you."

Nel knew they shouldn't have trusted Ydoro. She made a mental note to kill him next time she saw him.

"You're growing soft, Ydoro," The King said, "Or is there something you're not telling me?"

"I meant in the interest of leverage of course," Ydoro clarified. "You are a wise leader; the decision is yours."

"Of course it is," Mora said, "Guards!"

Footsteps signaled the approach of two guards from the hallway. Nel could not see them clearly from her position on the floor, but Mora bent over her and plucked the discarded knife from the floor.

He examined it while standing over her and asked, "Now where could you have gotten a knife. Not one of my own, was it from a guard?"

Nel did not respond.

Mora looked to one of the guards and asked, "Where's your knife?"

The guard unsheathed a similar dagger from his belt and responded, "Here, my King."

"And yours?" the King asked, turning to the second guard.

Nel craned her neck to see but could not get a good look at his face.

She heard the guard pat the sheath on his belt and say, "I... I don't seem to have it my King. I must have dropped it."

In a swift, almost casual motion, the King swept the knife along the guard's throat, releasing a spray of blood that caused the Neodactyl standing over Nel to hiss. The guard gasped and sputtered but the King had already turned away from him, addressing the second guard.

"Take our wandering guest back to her cell," Mora demanded. The first guard fell to his knees and gave several more futile gasps before smashing to the floor beside Nel. "Make sure she stays there this time."

The Neodactyl removed its foot from her chest and crept towards the dying guard instead. The second guard wrenched her to her feet roughly and she finally got a look at Ydoro, standing sheepishly behind Mora. Nel glared at him, but he averted his gaze.

Mora reached out and brushed her cheek gently. He was clearly trying his hardest to hide how much pain he was in. "Don't make me regret keeping you alive, beautiful," he said.

"You will," Nel promised, ignoring her better judgement.

The King smiled and nodded. "I like your spirit."

The guard pulled her away towards the door, but she looked back again at the open room, searching for the Cyrus lookalike.

"Wait," she said from the hallway. "Just tell me one thing; who was that man in your room earlier?"

The King looked at her in confusion.

"The man in your room," she repeated, "he was crying. Who was it?"

Mora just stared at her, and she could see in his eyes that he did not know what she was talking about.

"Forget it," she said, shaking her head. She enjoyed the feeling of knowing something Mora did not, even if she could not understand it herself. "I must have been seeing things."

The guard pulled at her arm and led her away down the hall. She smiled to herself as Mora stared after her; a searching, bewildered expression having settled on his face.

**CHAPTER SEVENTEEN**

## STACKING THE DECK

Jack brought the pickaxe down with a deafening crunch, splitting the rock clean in two. He wound his arms up and did it again, and again, and again. It wasn't bad work, but fairly mind-numbing. That left him free to think and plan and contemplate; although at this point, he was just going in circles without anyone to bounce ideas off of. They had eventually made their way home the night before, taking quite a while to navigate their way out of the dark forest after running from Ydoro's house. None of them slept that night, expecting a rap on their doors at any second announcing Mora's return to town. He never came. No one ever came. They did not hear from Ydoro the rest of the night after he was taken to the King's Temple, and no guards showed up again. When the sun rose announcing the new day, they took Ydoro's advice and went to work. Alec had been placed on the team working the fields with Cyrus, leaving Jack stuck in the caves by himself.

A loud laugh echoed from deeper in the cavern. Jack was not alone in the cave, but he was fairly certain all of his crewmates were avid supporters of the King. The large, bearded man, Cain, walked past him, slapping him on the shoulder as he went. Jack brought the pickaxe down hard again, picturing King Mora's grinning face as he did it. What he and Cyrus had promised Alec was true; they had to take a stand. Awaking this morning without Nel there made their situation feel crushingly real. They had to get her back, but they would need a better plan than Ydoro's proposal of using human bait to distract the Neodactyls. Even listening to his own thoughts sounded absurd. When did this become his reality? Weeks earlier, he had been living his life just like everyone else. Nothing outlandish or even particularly interesting ever happened to him. Now he was brainstorming ideas to storm the castle of a tyrant who ruled over a made-up land with made-up creatures with made-up names. Except they weren't made-up. Monsters were real, and this was his reality now.

Jack slammed the axe down again, his frustration fueling his power.

"Easy there, killer!" a voice called from outside the cave.

Jack looked up, wiping sweat from his brow, to see Annica approaching with a smile on her face.

"That rock do something to you?" she joked. "I can give it a talking to if you want."

Jack laughed and shook his head. "Just a hard spot is all. I thought it could use a little extra strength."

"In that case hand it over," Annica said, snatching the axe from his grip.

She wound up her arms and swung hard, smashing through the rock and sending debris flying into the air. She continued smashing at the rock and said, "Ya know, there is something satisfying about using your raw strength to destroy something. Good way to manage your anger too, I'll bet."

Jack nodded in agreement.

Annica took another swing and said, "So how are you settling in here?"

Another loaded question. Jack would have to really watch what he said around her. Ever since their first conversation he had been on her radar. He should not have pushed his questions so far; it gave him away.

"It's been okay," he finally answered, purposely keeping his response generic and simple.

"Everyone treating you alright?" she asked, still smashing at the rocks.

"Sure," Jack responded, and then thought better of giving such a noncommittal answer. "People have been very welcoming."

Annica stopped swinging and planted the pickaxe on the cave floor with a dull thud. "Have you always been this bad of a liar?"

Jack looked at her quizzically as if he did not understand her question.

"News travels fast around here. I heard the King took your friend last night. But you're telling me you don't feel any kinda way about that?"

Jack tried desperately to think of a way out of these questions. "She wasn't really my friend," he answered weakly.

Annica raised her eyebrows and nodded. "Alright. So either your far more callous and cold than I thought… or you're still lying to me."

She lifted the axe and pushed the handle into his chest. "Break's over," she said. "Ya know, I'm your friend right now, Jack. Don't make me into your enemy. You keep lying to me, that's exactly what I'll become."

Jack was saved from responding by Cain, who peered his head in through the mouth of the cave and announced there was a problem with a shipment going out. Cain seemed to be her right-hand man. The two of them stood in stark contrast to each other. Where Annica was short and thin, young and cute, Cain was large and rough in every way. He was not overly tall, but his robust and stocky build made him appear like a larger man, and his gut was at least three times the size of Jack's. He had that big, unkempt beard covering the lower half of his round face, and his hair of about the same length and color formed a sort of mane around his head.

Annica sighed and strode out after him, calling without bothering to turn around, "Think about it, Jack."

They were gone, and Jack was alone in the cave again. Annica was going to be a real problem, and the more Jack witnessed the comradery of the 'cave crew', the more it became apparent they thought and functioned as one. If Annica was an avid Mora supporter, that meant they all were.

*****

The rest of the day passed without incident. He had not been able to come up with any better ideas for confronting Mora, which made the day feel like a waste. He leaned his pickaxe against the cave wall and exited onto the green hillside, which was positively glowing in the harsh, late-afternoon light.

He started down the hill when Annica called out from behind him, "What's the hurry, Jack?"

Jack closed his eyes and cursed under his breath, but turned around with a smile on his face. "Just heading home for the night."

Annica was sitting reclined in the grass outside the mouth of a cave, surrounded by about ten of her crew, Cain included. They each had a drink in their hand and seemed to be in good spirits, chatting and joking with one another. Cain was doubled over on the hillside in the throes of a laughing fit.

"Why don't you come join us?" Annica called to Jack, holding up a bottle of clear amber liquid.

"I'm good, but thanks," Jack called back. He was already uncomfortable with how interested in him she seemed to be; no good could come from drinking with her in such a relaxed setting.

"C'mon, one drink," Annica pushed. The rest of the team was now looking his way as well, every one of them sizing him up. It was extremely uncomfortable, as though he were being studied for weaknesses. It only solidified what he already guessed; that this was a trap.

"I really have to get going," Jack insisted, "maybe next time."

Annica did not respond but rather just stared back at him, a falsely sweet smile on her face. No one on the team was laughing or talking to one another anymore. Even Cain had composed himself and was gazing in Jack's direction with an unreadable expression on his face.

Jack waved to them and turned to walk down the hill towards Alec and Cyrus, who he could see waiting at the edge of the forest down below. Halfway down the hill, Jack dared a glance back and was startled to find the entire crew still staring after him. What did they want? Were they hoping he would join them in their love for the King? That they could somehow convert him into a loyal Mora lackey?

He turned back around and joined Cyrus and Alec, his heart pounding in his chest and a sense of dread beginning to settle in his stomach. He was planning to tell them right away about everything that had transpired, but their faces were both glowing.

"What is it?" Jack asked, somewhat apprehensively since he had heard nothing but bad news since arriving here.

"Cy thought of a way to distract Mora's birds!" Alec whispered with barely contained excitement.

Jack looked to Cyrus who nodded. "It occurred to me last night when I was kneeling in the street. One of the Neodactyls moved in towards me but heard a Shrieking Bat call from the forest and got distracted. I think if Mora hadn't soothed it, it may have run off."

"You think we can use bats as a distraction?" Jack asked.

"We were able to approach them the other day with Ydoro," Alec insisted. "They're docile. They have no reason to fear people."

"Wait," Jack cut in, "you want to catch one?"

Alec smiled and responded, "We want to catch a few."

Cyrus put his hand on Jack's shoulder and guided him out of the grassy fields and into the cover of the forest. He pulled what appeared to be a canvas tarp from beneath his jacket and said, "Alec managed to swipe this from the worksite. It's a bag. And over here..." Cyrus led him deeper into the forest to an upturned tree trunk with long-dead roots creating a thicket of shadowy coverage. Nestled within the twisty maze was a decent sized wooden crate. "That should hold them," Cyrus announced, grinning.

Jack nodded, "I'm impressed. So you want to catch the bats with that bag while they sleep, then use the crate to hold them. I don't know, this plan sounds a little..."

"It'll work," Alec insisted. "Think of what Ydoro told us, if we challenge the King outside his gates, he'll let us in to face him, just to prove his power. But he's relying on his birds to get the upper hand. If we can get these bats into the Temple as a distraction, we can drive them away."

"That sounds risky," Jack warned. "I'm not saying it won't work, but there's a lot that can go wrong." Jack looked to Cyrus for support, but Cyrus looked down, almost sheepishly. Jack was pretty sure he understood. Alec was going to storm the Temple with or without them, just as he had said he would. Cyrus's only options were to let his brother go himself and likely die in the process, or help with his half-formed plan.

"Nel is in there right now, Jack," Alec reminded him. "I'm not waiting any longer. We're grabbing the Shrieking Bats tonight, and confronting Mora tomorrow at dawn."

Jack's eyes widened and he once again looked to Cyrus to be the voice of reason, but he once again stayed quiet. Alec was staring at him expectantly.

Jack sighed in defeat and said, "This is a bad idea, I just want to be on record about that."

Alec smiled and said, "Grab that crate, we're heading up towards the overlook now. If we can get there before sunset, I think our chances will be better. If they're anything like bats in our world, they'll be active once the sun begins to set."

*****

Alec spent most of the trek to the highlands trying to explain in many different ways why the plan would work. He explained it so many times, in fact, that Jack thought he likely knew it was impulsive and reckless, but he would not be swayed. In Jack's mind, even hearing the plan out loud sounded ludicrous. Relying on wild animals to execute an already precarious plan was foolish. On top of that, relying on anything Ydoro had told them was also a bad idea. They had no way of knowing if his assurances about the King accepting their challenge were genuine. It was entirely possible, even likely, that Ydoro was telling them only what Mora wanted them to hear. They could easily be walking into a massacre. The only positive that Jack could see was that Ydoro had not been told about the bats, or that they were confronting Mora tomorrow.

In fact, none of them had seen or heard from Ydoro since he was taken to the Temple by the guard the night before.

A deafening screech overhead announced their arrival to the hillside where the bats nested. Jack had to admit they would likely work well as a distraction. They were incredibly loud and moved extremely fast, darting from tree to tree. Most animals would react to them. His problem with Alec's plan was not the bats, but everything else. The group was gazing up at the trees where the large, fur-covered creatures glided gracefully, the late-afternoon sun illuminating the thin membranes of their wings. Each of their wingspans was probably two feet, making them fairly sizable animals.

Alec was already looking ahead to the alcove where the sleeping bats had been found before. Sure enough, there were many still in there, hanging upside down with their eyes closed, although some seemed to be starting to wake up. Jack looked up at the sky and noted the sun was definitely beginning to go down, casting long, deep shadows in the increasingly orange light. They would have to get to work quickly if they wanted the bats to stay put. The group approached the hollow, made up of several fallen trees up against a large, moss-covered boulder. It was not a very large area, with a vertical opening only a couple feet wide, although the bats could likely fly out the branch-covered top if they were alarmed. Jack counted twelve bats as they crept towards it, attempting to be as quiet as possible. He eased the crate down to the forest floor, wincing as it cracked a branch in the process, but the bats did not seem to mind. In fact, the bats only started to look their direction as Alec whispered to Cyrus to get the bag ready.

Suddenly the bats were becoming more restless, with many of them opening their eyes or beginning to crane their long necks in the direction of the team.

Alec held out his hand to stop them all from moving. Why were the animals suddenly concerned about them when last time their approach went almost entirely unnoticed?

"What's going on?" Jack whispered to Alec up ahead.

Alec looked to be searching his mind, his eyes darting around as if scanning his brain for an answer. He suddenly spoke up with a loud, normally articulated voice, "Everyone stop whispering." Jack would have thought the loud voice would have caused the bats to flee, but they had not. "Stop creeping around, stop whispering, just act normal." Jack looked back skeptically. He highly doubted the bats were bothered by them not 'acting normal'. Noting his reaction, Alec, in the same natural voice, insisted, "It may sound strange, but animals can perceive a threat based on body language. They know we're here; they've known we're around since we got to the hillside. They weren't bothered by us last time because we weren't sneaking around. We were just acting normally. By tiptoeing and whispering and moving slowly, we act like a predator would act, and it's making them nervous."

Jack looked over Alec's shoulder at the alcove and noticed the bats did indeed seem to be settling back down. Many of them were closing their eyes again or looking away. The group as a whole began to look less fidgety.

"Okay," Alec began again with a clear voice, "Cyrus, get the bag ready, and move forward with purpose. Not overly fast, but walk normally."

Cyrus looked uncomfortable. Jack could not blame him. Alec was essentially telling him to approach the nest with the perfect speed and intention. He took a deep breath and worked his hands into the opening of the canvas bag, then nodded resolutely and strode forward towards the alcove. He did not slow down as twigs cracked and leaves rustled beneath his feet, and Alec's theory proved true; the bats remained undisturbed.

Cyrus came to a halt directly in front of the alcove, only two feet from the nearest bat. He turned to Alec who nodded encouragingly. There was no way this could work. Jack was shaking his head to himself, certain something was about to go wrong. Cyrus fed his hands around the bag, using it as both a receptacle to grab the bat in and a shield in case it lunged at him. He moved the bag out slowly towards the nearest bat, which opened its eye slightly revealing a yellow-white orb and a tiny black pupil. Cyrus had the bag within a foot of the bat when he suddenly shoved his hands forward and grasped the hanging animal with the canvas. There was an immediate flurry of wings and screeching as Cyrus wrestled the bag around the bat, trapping it within. The resulting shrieks were deafening and the bag was shaking violently as it tried desperately to escape.

Alec darted forward to help his brother subdue the bag but ducked as a second bat careened out of the twisted cave and nearly hit him in the head. He looked in the direction of the nest and saw the entire colony was flapping and hissing furiously. Another bat released the branch it was hanging from and dove towards Alec, folding around his neck like it was made of liquid. Jack saw blood and knew Alec had been bitten, but his pounding and clawing at the creature was proving useless. The animal had flattened itself around the curve of his neck and shoulder so completely that Alec could not find a grip to tear it off. The thin membranes of the wings almost appeared to be suctioning onto his skin, all the while the animal's teeth were sunken into the side of his throat. Jack sprinted towards the chaos and tried to get his fingers beneath the bat's wings, but it was impossible. Every appendage was either flattened beneath its wings or had a hook in his flesh.

The rest of the bats were flying from the opening as well, and Cyrus was swinging the bag with the captured bat around his head like a madman, attempting to keep them off him. Jack reached for the bat on Alec's neck again but a second one smashed into his arm and wrapped itself around his sleeve. His shirt offered just enough protection that the bat was struggling to bite down on his skin, so Jack reached down for the nearest branch he could find and jammed it hard into the animal's back. The bat made a whelping sound and immediately released its hold, flying into the trees and screeching all the way. Jack turned to Alec, still spinning on the spot trying to loosen his attacker, and stabbed the stick into its back as well. It shrieked and let go of Alec, flapping towards Jack with its teeth gnashing together threateningly. Jack swiped out with the stick, more as a deterrent than with any real hope of hitting it. The motion worked and the bat gave one final hiss before flying into the trees with the rest of the colony.

Jack sighed in relief and looked to his team. Cyrus was still holding the bag with the single bat inside, which seemed to have settled down a bit, and Alec was holding his hand to a small puncture wound on his neck but otherwise looked okay. Their plan had not been a complete failure, but they had only succeeded in catching one of the animals. They would just have to hope that one would be enough.

They managed to get the captured bat into the crate without issue. The crate was not large, it could be carried, with some effort, by one person. It was little more than thin pieces of scrap wood nailed together, but it was enough to keep the bat contained. It seemed the bat had gone into a sort of passive state while inside the bag, perhaps as a defense mechanism, and it was barely moving now that it was inside the crate.

"Okay who the hell thought it was a good idea to catch these things?" Alec laughed, still holding his neck.

Jack was impressed to see Alec poking fun at himself. It showed the tiniest flicker of maturity, something Jack had come to realize was not one of Alec's strong suits.

"Hell, we got one at least," Jack offered. "How's your neck?"

Alec dabbed at the wound with his hand and checked for blood. With a shrug he responded, "Doesn't seem so bad."

"Nah, he's tough," Cyrus said, and clapped Alec on the back.

Cyrus was clearly trying hard to stay in his brother's good graces. Between his agreeing to Alec's reckless plans and his uncharacteristic declarations of support, it seemed he had really taken their criticisms to heart. The trouble was, Jack had begun to realize he trusted Cyrus's judgment a bit more than Alec's. Alec was proving to be far too emotional to make smart, informed decisions, and that worried Jack.

"So if we want to be outside the Temple by sunrise…" Alec began, but he was quickly shushed by Cyrus, whose eyes were suddenly wide and searching.

"What is it?" Jack whispered in alarm.

Cyrus was scanning the surrounding forest slowly. He finally whispered back, "I thought I heard something. Voices."

Jack listened, tilting his head from side to side, but all he could hear was the gentle breeze in the trees. Then he heard it; the clear sound of several voices in conversation, and they were approaching. Jack turned to the others frantically. They were entirely exposed out here.

"Grab the crate," Cyrus urged in a panicked whisper. Jack and Alec both reached for the wooden box but as soon as it was jostled, the bat within started hissing and flapping. They froze, but it was no use. The bat had become agitated again and let out several angry shrieks.

Jack spun around to look in the direction of the voices. He could not see them yet, but they were not far off. Everyone searched around desperately but they were out of options. They could either leave the crate behind and run for it or stay here and get caught. And how would they explain being out in the middle of the woods at dusk with a bat in a crate?

Suddenly Jack had an idea that was either incredibly brave or entirely foolish. He had no time to debate which one. He sprung into action, turning to Cyrus and Alec, he whispered, "Meet at the Temple, sunrise tomorrow!" He spun away from them, leaving their stunned faces staring after him, and broke into a run towards the approaching voices. As it turned out, he had made his snap decision in just the nick of time because he had barely rounded the first clump of bushes before he came face to face with six of the King's guards.

The guards all raised their mismatched weapons in alarm and shouted out at him to stop, which he did while feigning surprise.

"Oh thank God!" Jack exclaimed in mock relief. "I've been trying to find my way home for an hour! I got turned around, and really started to panic once the sun started to set!"

The guards exchanged amused looks and started to lower their weapons.

"You were coming from the western fields?" one guard asked.

"That's right," Jack answered. "I've made this trek enough times by now you'd think I'd know my way."

Jack knew Alec and Cyrus would be able to hear this conversation and he prayed they were using the time to clear off the path.

"Now wait a minute," one of the guards said, using his rusted machete as a pointer towards Jack. "Isn't he one of the new arrivals? The ones who have been giving the King trouble?"

Jack's heart caught in his chest. He began to shake his head in denial.

"That is him," another guard agreed. "I think it's his girlfriend we have locked up in the Temple."

Jack shook his head again, but the guards were already raising their weapons against him. "You must have me confused with someone else," Jack insisted. "I've been here for years."

The guards were not buying it, though. "We better take him to King Mora," one guard said to another. "Something doesn't seem right about this."

"Now wait a minute though," another guard said, "maybe that means the others are around here, too. How many were there?"

"Look, I'm telling you, I'm not new here," Jack pressed.

"I think it was two guys and the girl," a guard answered, ignoring him entirely.

"Are you sure there weren't three guys?" another asked.

"Where are your friends? Are they out here with you?" the nearest guard questioned.

"Who?" Jack played dumb.

"Okay, we can play it like that," the guard said, stepping forward. "We're going to take you to the Temple, get this sorted out. If the King doesn't know you, you'll be on your way in no time."

Jack was shaking his head but was running out of excuses. The guard took another step towards him. Jack put up his hands in a sign of defeat, then bolted to the right, attempting to sprint past the guards and lead them away from the area. He overestimated how quickly he could gain speed, however, and the guard blocked him easily with his machete outstretched.

"Hey now," the guard sneered, "I thought we had the wrong man?"

Jack raised his hands again and opened his mouth to respond when Cyrus barreled out of the underbrush to the right and slammed headlong into the side of the guard. The guard toppled sideways and crashed to the ground hard. Both Jack and the remaining five guards were frozen in shock. Cyrus snatched the fallen guard's machete from the ground and yelled, "Jack run!" before charging towards the group of guards with the machete raised over his head and a battle cry echoing from his lungs. The guards were so baffled by the sudden change in the situation that they scattered out of his way with terrified looks. Cyrus took his opportunity of having the path behind them cleared and ran straight past them, dropping the machete to his side and sprinting away through the forest. The guards scrambled as they realized their error and began to give chase.

The leading guard turned as he started to run after Cyrus and called to the two in the rear, "No, you two after that one!"

The two guards turned their attention to Jack, just as the fallen guard was swaying to his feet. Jack did not hesitate this time and ran off to the west, away from the path Cyrus had taken, and hopefully away from wherever Alec had found to hide with the crate.

**CHAPTER EIGHTEEN**

# AN UNLIKELY ALLY

The forest had gone silent around Alec Dorn. He allowed himself to breathe a little easier. It had been several minutes now since Cyrus had left him, whispering the same thing Jack had whispered before charging off: "Meet at the Temple tomorrow at sunrise." When Cyrus had realized Jack would need help, he ran off, leaving Alec alone with the sole prize from their impulsive mission; a Shrieking Bat in a crate.

Alec was surprised at how quickly Cyrus had run to Jack's defense when he did nothing to stop Mora from taking Nel. He found himself wondering if Cyrus would be so fast to rescue him if he were in trouble. Jack was supposed to be someone Cyrus couldn't stand, and yet it often felt in recent weeks that they were ganging up on Alec. Apparently his only true ally was currently rotting away in a cell. His blood had boiled when he overheard the guard mention 'Jack's girlfriend' locked up in the temple. He knew he should be grateful for the confirmation that Nel was still alive, but thinking of her locked up only fueled his urge to storm the Temple. The other two thought the plan was reckless and dangerous. Even Cyrus, who had gone along with convincing enthusiasm, did not actually agree that it was a good idea. Alec could see it in his eyes, hidden behind the false supportive smile. Perhaps it was reckless and perhaps they would die trying to overthrow Mora, but it somehow felt like the most important thing that Alec would ever do. Back in their world, Alec would never amount to more than he had already amounted to. He would never build a significant reputation. He would never gain the notoriety that he sorely deserved. He would never make it into the history books. But out here on this strange island in this strange world, the rules were different. He was someone else out here, or at least he could be. Nel believed he had a powerful personality, capable of shaping his destiny, hidden beneath the surface. Alec wasn't sure that was true, but the fact that Nel believed it made him feel strong. He wanted to be that person, definitely for himself, but also for her. He found himself caring quite a bit about what Nel thought of him.

Now, however, he was alone in the middle of the forest hiding with a captured bat. That did not feel important. It felt like he had been left behind while the leaders did the more courageous jobs. He shook the thought out of his head. That was not how it happened. Jack was trying to buy them time and Cyrus was trying to help Jack. This was all in order to execute Alec's plan after all. He cursed himself for not taking the initiative as they had. He was stuck here hiding because he had failed to act.

Alec eased himself into a standing position, peering around the thicket of dark leaves to make sure none of the guards had doubled back. He was alone. The orange glow from the setting sun was beginning to fade so he knew he didn't have much time before the forest would be very dark. It was already starting to take on the cool, bluish cast of evening. The question now was how to get the bat back to town and into his room without drawing attention to himself. Then tomorrow he would have to be at the Temple gates at sunrise. It was going to be a long night. He sighed, then reached down for the crate and wrenched it into his arms. The bat inside screamed and started flapping in aggravation, the calls echoing out through the forest. Alec began walking in the direction of town, staying just off the path in case more guards showed up. The crate was heavy and unwieldy and the bat moving around was not making it any easier. He regretted again not running off to distract the guards.  He thought he would prefer being chased by them than trekking through the night with this giant cage.

Alec's foot caught in a root and he stumbled forward, using the crate to brace his fall.  The bat screeched angrily and Alec swore aloud.  He reminded himself this would be worth it tomorrow.  Tomorrow he would finally have his chance to confront Mora and bring that tyrant down.  He fully intended to kill him, even though he was painfully aware he had never killed anyone before.  He didn't even really know how to kill someone and had not given much thought to how he would do it.  Alec had been in a fight once when he was in second grade, but that was about it.  The fight had started over some childish name-calling and had ended in a flurry of fists before a teacher broke it up.  The bigger story had been when his brother found out about the fight and wanted to break the other kid's nose.

Some birds off to his right began cawing and chattering in agitation.  Alec looked through the underbrush in apprehension, concerned that perhaps a predator was nearby.  He recalled Ydoro warning them to stay out of the forest after dark.  The animals they had encountered so far had been bizarre enough; he shuttered to think what the local carnivores looked like.  Alec picked up his pace as much as he could with the awkward crate pressed against his chest.  What if he could not get the bat back to his room?  And was it even wise to take it there, considering the guards were potentially already suspicious of the 'newcomers'?  His progress was painfully slow, and he would still have to lug it to the Temple before the sun came up tomorrow.  Alec stumbled again but this time his grip on the sides of the wooden crate failed and it careened away from him, bouncing and rolling into the bushes ahead.  Alec yelled out in frustration and clenched his fists in anger, wanting more than anything to punch something.

"Stop where you are," said a gravelly voice from behind him.

Alec froze, still on his knees on the forest floor.  He turned his head slowly around to find two more guards standing ten feet behind him.  They were studying him suspiciously, and Alec knew there was no story he could make up that could explain why he was out here at this late hour by himself.

"We heard there was some trouble in the area," one of the guards said. "Get up, we're taking you to the King."

Alec shook his head, but his mind was blank. He could not think of a single excuse to talk his way out of this.

"There you are!" came a different voice from behind the guards. They turned in unison to find Ydoro strolling down the forest path confidently, his dark travelling robes billowing in the evening breeze. He was looking straight at Alec and brushed past the guards without breaking stride. "Do you know how long I've been waiting for you?"

Alec stuttered in confusion, still unable to think of anything clever to say.

Ydoro grasped the collar of Alec's shirt and pulled him to his feet roughly. "It's nearly dark and there's still work to be done. If I catch you slacking off out here again there will be hell to pay." Ydoro looked into Alec's eyes and winked.

"This man's with you?" one of the guards asked.

"What does it look like?" Ydoro snapped. "Mandatory overtime, trouble with the new structure being built to the south. It seems our newest recruits still need some extra supervision." He turned to Alec again and yelled, "You'll work through the night if that's what it takes to get the job done right!"

"We received word of some trouble out in these woods," the guard said.

"Well, it's not us," Ydoro barked authoritatively. "Or would you like to march us up to the Temple and you can explain to King Mora why we won't have those new facilities done on time?"

"Not at all, sir," the guard replied quickly. "Please carry on, just let us know if you see anything unusual."

"Will do," Ydoro said dismissively, and he shoved Alec forward down the path and away from the guards. Alec looked down at the fallen crate, lying sideways in the shrubbery, just out of sight of the guards.

"Leave it," Ydoro whispered in his ear, guiding him forward forcefully. They rounded some trees and left the guards behind.

Alec turned and whispered, "I need that crate, I can't leave it."

"We'll come back for it," Ydoro assured him, "just give the guards a chance to leave. They won't follow this way."

They continued further down the path before Ydoro led him behind a particularly large tree and stopped. He listened to make sure they weren't being followed. Satisfied they were alone, he turned to Alec and asked, "Okay, what are you doing out here?"

"I... I was just on my way back from work and I got turned around..."

"Cut the shit," Ydoro said. "Do you have any idea what I just saved you from? The King is done playing games with you people. He's coming for you all, tomorrow."

"What do you mean?"

"I mean exactly what I said," Ydoro hissed. "I've been at the Temple, and Mora wants to bring you all in. Trust me when I say he's not bringing you there to talk. If you want to take a stand, this is your chance, your *only* chance."

Alec considered what he was saying. He still did not trust Ydoro, but his options were currently limited. He finally conceded and entrusted Ydoro with their plan, breaking down everything that had been discussed and what had happened to Cyrus and Jack.

Ydoro listened intently, never interrupting or even reacting. When Alec finished, Ydoro thought a moment before responding, "Well, it's not the worst plan I've ever heard. Either way, you're out of time, and I like your chances better if you storm the Temple rather than waiting to be brought in."

"Did you see Nel while you were there?" Alec asked.

"I did," Ydoro replied grimly. "She's holding her own, but Mora has lost his patience. Look, we're going to have to stay out here tonight. We need to grab that crate and hunker down 'til morning. If another guard finds us with that, I won't be able to talk our way out of it. Better to camp out 'til morning, then meet your friends at the Temple."

"I thought you said not to be out here after dark," Alec questioned.

"Well it's not my first choice," Ydoro admitted warily, "but the sun's nearly down, we're out of options."

**CHAPTER NINETEEN**

# THE HILLSIDE

Small birds screamed and flapped out of the way as Jack crashed through the underbrush and sprinted through the forest. He did not know where he was going, or even which direction he was headed, but the three guards were right on his tail. His only goal was to lead them away from Alec and the crate, which he had succeeded in doing, but now what? He had been running aimlessly through the forest for twenty minutes now and had not been able to lose them. Jack was in decent shape, but he would be hard pressed to keep up this speed for much longer. He would need to find somewhere to hide, but where? He did not know this area, and the guards were far too close.

One of the guards yelled out to him again but Jack ignored him and kept running. There was no way in hell he would stop, no matter what they said. If they caught him, he would be taken to the King. And any meeting with Mora at this juncture would almost certainly result in death. The group had proven to be a thorn in Mora's side since they had arrived here. The only reason he had not moved against them yet was because his people were watching the situation unfold. Without the people following him, Mora was nothing, and he knew it. It was painfully clear to Jack now, however, that they had just given him a reason to finish it. If they survived tonight, they had no choice but to move against the King tomorrow. It was too late to alter course now that the guards were after them. Word would get back that they had been up to something in the woods, and even if it wasn't clear what they were planning, it would be enough to condemn them. So the plan would have to move forward tomorrow. Jack had to lose these guards and he had to meet Cyrus and Alec at the Temple gates at sunrise.

Jack began to feel a sharp cramping in his right side, threatening to slow him down. He chanced a look back, but the guards were much too close to slow down. The nearest was roughly fifteen feet behind him with the other two closely following. Jack scanned the ground ahead, looking for any branch or rock he could use as a weapon. Nothing would be lethal enough. He would never be able to fight off three armed guards with a stick. He had long since left the network of trails, but he could see the last remnants of sunset radiating through the trees up ahead. It seemed to be some sort of clearing. Perhaps it would offer more options. Jack pushed the pain from his cramp to the back of his mind and ducked his head as he slammed through a thicket of bushes and into the clearing. He was higher than he had known, emerging near the middle of a sloping hillside. There was a deep valley below and steep terrain above ending in pointed, rocky peaks. This area was familiar. There were wheelbarrows and tools scattered amongst the rocks and in the grass, and a dark network of caves to his right. He had somehow looped back to the hills he had been working earlier today.

He continued running parallel to the hillside, not heading up or down, and scanned the area desperately for options. Echoing voices carried on the windy slopes and he realized the worksite was not quite empty. High on the hill above him sitting near the entrance to one of the caves, Annica, Cain, and the rest of their crew looked down at him in surprise, still with drinks in hand.

Shit, Jack thought. His cover was blown. He looked back again and the guards were gaining on him, their machetes raised. On the hillside above, the workers were scrambling into action, dropping their drinks and jumping to their feet. They were going to cut him off. He would have no choice but to run down into the valley. Annica was barking orders at Cain, who sprinted across the grassy hill with astounding speed.

He was running parallel to Jack some thirty feet above him on the hill, his beefy legs showing their strength. He was faster than Jack. But he did not run down the hill towards him. Instead, he barreled towards the boarded-up cave entrance and launched his full weight into the board supporting the wooden barrier. It crunched loudly, echoing throughout the valley, but did not give way. He stepped back and threw himself at the board again, this time running straight through it and causing the door to buckle outwards in an eruption of splintering wood. As the door smashed to the ground with an earth-shaking thud, dozens of enormous boulders came spiraling out of the entrance and careened down the hill. Jack was relieved to note that the rocks were going to miss him; he was already almost out of their path. But Cain was still watching them roll expectantly, and Jack realized the rocks were not meant for him.

The three guards realized too late what was happening and began to scramble in all directions, shouting out in alarm. Some ran downhill, some turned back the way they had come, but it was no use. Each of the boulders was about five feet wide and tumbling down the hillside with unstoppable momentum. Jack's legs shook and wobbled over the quaking earth and he winced when he heard the screaming behind him come to a sudden end with shocking finality.

He slowed his pace to a jog, breathing heavily and pressing his hand into the cramp in his side. He turned slowly around but he already knew there was no longer anyone pursuing him. The hillside had gone quiet as the last of the boulders reached the bottom of the valley far below and came to rest in the soft cradle of grass and dirt. There was deep red blood smeared into the grass of the sloping hillside and several indistinct masses that must have been the remains of the three guards. Jack took care to not focus on them too closely and instead brought his gaze up to Annica and Cain and the rest of his apparent rescuers.

Annica was staring down at him with her hands on her hips, surrounded by six of her crew members. "It seems I misjudged you, Jack," she called down to him. "I guess you're not one of Mora's spies after all."

Jack began walking uphill towards the group, still shaking his head in disbelief. "You're not with Mora?" Jack asked, still trying to catch his breath. "I don't understand."

"Why would you think we were loyal to the King?" Annica questioned, "We're the laborers."

Jack finally arrived at the cave entrance where the group stood and shook his head again. "I had you pegged as zealots. The way you talked, I thought…"

Annica laughed and responded, "How did you expect me to act with your prying questions? We've had problems in the past and learned to trust no one before we know them. People don't always tell you where their loyalty truly lies, but their actions will always speak."

Jack nodded his head in agreement, seeing her point. He had entered her crew with a mind to get answers; in the process, he must have come across as a spy trying to weed out potentially mutinous subjects for the King. "So you trust me now?" he asked, attempting to verify he was in no danger right now.

Annica paused a moment, then nodded. "If you've managed to bring the wrath of the King in the way it seems you have, you've earned my respect. Those guards wouldn't be after you unless you'd done something to upset the King."

"Actually, they chased me because they found my friends and I in the forest after sundown," Jack admitted, praying this would not cause her to rethink her trust in him.

Annica just smiled and responded, "Believe me, they weren't out there for no reason. You must be on the King's radar. Besides, you're on our side now after this," she indicated the bloodied hillside behind him. "If anyone asks, I'm saying this was your idea." Jack shuffled uncomfortably but Annica smiled at him. "Relax, Jack, we're all on the same team now." Noticing that he still looked uneasy, she said, "C'mon, let's see who we got," and she strode down the hillside.

Jack began to follow her before realizing she was referring to the crushed guards. He stopped halfway towards the bodies, not feeling particularly interested in seeing them up close, but Annica stepped right up to the closest one and, looking down at him, said, "Oh yeah, I remember this one, seen him on patrol a couple times." She shook her head and said, "Pity."

She walked over to the next bloody mass and looked down at him. "Shit!" she exclaimed and looked away.

"What is it?" Cain called out, jogging down the hillside towards Annica and the crushed body.

"It's Halan," she said, walking away towards the third body.

"Dammit," Cain said, looking at the body for himself.

"Who's Halan?" Jack asked the nearest crew member to him, a clean-shaven young man of maybe twenty-five.

"An old friend from town," the man replied. "Damn shame."

"I don't understand," Jack said. "He's the enemy though, right? He works for Mora, doesn't he?"

"He *did* work for Mora, yes," Annica called out, hiking back up the hill towards him. "That doesn't mean he was a bad guy. You'll find that plenty of the guards under the King's employ have no real loyalty to the King. It's just a job, like anything else."

"But he was chasing me," Jack said, "they all were."

"Of course they were, that's their job," Annica said, "but if you were king, they'd do the same for you, and the king after you, and the king after that."

Jack found himself struggling with the dynamics of this society again. "Why would they be enforcers for someone who they hate?"

"Is it so different where you come from?" Annica asked. "I assume you have a leader of some sort, yes?"

"Sure," Jack agreed, "we call him the President."

"Okay, and does this President have guards? Enforcers? People to spread his will?"

"Well sort of," Jack nodded, "but it's different. The President is elected by the people, and he doesn't necessarily get to spread his own will. It's about what the people want."

Annica scoffed as if the idea were unbelievably absurd. "Even so, people will always follow power, even if it's just the perception of power. That's just the way things are. So people like Halan, they might do things differently if they had their way, but enforcing the laws of the land doesn't make them bad people."

Jack nodded, sensing this could be a touchy subject and not wanting to fall out of her good graces so quickly. "So do you regret saving me, then? Would you have done something different had you known it was your friend chasing me?"

Annica shook her head, "If you're fighting against Mora, you are more important."

*****

Jack eventually decided to tell Annica and her crew the truth about what they had been up to out in the forest after sundown. It had not been his intention to tell them, even after they revealed their loyalties did not lie with the King, but as the evening turned to night and the darkening sky became alight with stars, it felt right. They had started a fire in the entrance of one of the caves and hunkered down away from the wind, talking into the night. It was a relief to talk to someone outside of their group about their plans. Admitting out loud that they were moving forward with an assault against the King was somehow freeing, but his relief soon turned to anxiety when he saw the skeptical looks on the crew's faces.

It was a dangerous, and perhaps reckless, plan but they were committed at this point. In fact, in order to back out now, he would have to abandon his friends who would be waiting for him tomorrow morning at the Temple gates. Friends? He had never considered his crew 'friends' before now. Were they his friends? They had been through so much at this point it was difficult not to have formed some sort of bond with them. It felt like a lifetime ago that he was arguing with Cyrus onboard the ship, or drinking with Alec and Nel… and Dalton. Dalton never got the chance to experience this world, not really. Mora had murdered him to prove a point. Thinking about him and what had happened to him only solidified Jack's resolve.

"I understand your desire for revenge, I really do," Annica assured him after hearing about Dalton's fate and Nel's capture.

"It's not revenge," Jack insisted. "It's taking a stand."

"Even so, it's a suicide mission," Annica said. She was looking at him with a strange expression on her face. Was it concern? More like pity. "If you think you can beat him on your own, then by all means. But know what you're facing."

"Are you offering your help?" Jack asked hopefully.

Annica shook her head. "Do you know why we're able to stay out here in the middle of the night with a roaring fire and not be bothered by the guards? Because we make the King believe our loyalty."

"In other words, you've sold your loyalty for the measly perks the King offers you," Jack said in poorly hidden disgust.

"Look, if we followed every idealist with a mind to overthrow the King, we wouldn't be here today," Annica replied. "We're not loyal to the King, he just thinks we are."

"What's the difference?" Jack scoffed. "If you fall in line behind him, then you're with him. It's not your declarations that define your loyalty, it's your actions."

Annica thought about his statement a moment, then replied, "I'm sorry you feel that way, Jack. And I don't blame you for thinking it, but you don't know how this world works."

"No, but I know how *my* world works," Jack responded, "and I know what history has proven about human nature."

Annica looked at him expectantly, clearly awaiting a finer point. Jack shook his head, realizing it was a losing argument. She had not seen the history of his world. She had not witnessed the rise and fall of empires and dictators; she had never seen the difference between a ruler and a leader.

"Look, Jack," Annica said slowly, that same look of pity in her eyes, "I think you're a good guy, and I know you think this plan is your only option, but it doesn't have to be. Things aren't so bad out here, you could join us, live a real life, let the next wanna-be king fight Mora someday."

Jack was quiet a long time before he responded. It was an appealing prospect, and these people did seem happy. But he didn't belong here, in these caves; on this island; in this world. "My friends are counting on me," he finally said. "I'm not abandoning them."

Annica just stared at him across the fire, the shadows dancing across her face and flickering on the cave walls. It dawned on Jack once again just how young she was. If they were back in the world he knew, she would probably be fresh out of college.

"It's suicide, Jack," she said softly. The pity in her eyes had turned to genuine sadness, but he heard defeat in her voice and knew she was done trying to talk him out of it.

Jack shrugged, a gesture entirely more confident than he was feeling. "I've never done anything of much importance in my life, maybe this is it."

**CHAPTER TWENTY**

# MYSTERIES AND LEGENDS

Thick, heavy droplets of rain splashed against the immense overhanging leaves of the forest, the noise causing a rhythmic, hollow tapping as the night wore on. It wasn't a full-blown rainstorm, at least not yet, but the cold water was only adding to the discomfort of the night. Alec was finding it extraordinarily awkward being trapped in this small alcove with Ydoro. The man sat on the leaf-covered ground across from him, his strange, foreign robes splayed out around him and one arm casually draped over the crate containing the restless shrieking bat. They had waited a good long while before chancing a walk back to the path where they had left the guards. The guards had gone, and the crate had remained where it had fallen; tipped on its side, cradled in a nest of brambles. With Ydoro's help, they had carried it off the path a ways and found a suitable hiding place to rest until morning. They had barely said another word to each other since settling in for the night. It wasn't out of distrust at this point. Ydoro knew too much anyways, if he was going to betray them, they couldn't stop him. Alec simply did not know what to talk to this man about. He had never been great at small talk to begin with. Even in his own world, Alec preferred the company of his few known and established friends, and always viewed getting to know new people as kind of a chore. He could remember a particularly horrible night about a year ago when Cyrus had pushed Alec into going to a faculty party with him. Alec had remained strong in his refusal until Cynthia convinced him it would be fun. He ended up spending the night standing near two other socially awkward professors with absolutely nothing to say while Cyrus and Cynthia drank and laughed the night away.

This was infinitely worse. What he wouldn't give for a drink right now. No sooner had the thought entered his mind than Ydoro reached into his cloak and pulled out a fairly large flask and took a swig. He held it out to Alec without a word, who took it from him and tried a sip. Whatever it was it burned his throat and instantly let a rush of cold air into his sinuses. He shook his head to clear it and took another sip.

He handed the flask back to Ydoro and said, "Why is it any situation feels more natural once you have a drink in your hand?"

Ydoro shrugged and responded, "It just means you're an alcoholic."

Had Ydoro just made a joke? Alec looked into his face, and Ydoro laughed. He wasn't sure he had seen Ydoro actually smile since their arrival here. Sure, he had worn that fake, 'gracious host' smile on his face the day they arrived, but that had proven to be phony. Alec felt like he had finally glimpsed the real man beneath the character he had created for himself.

"So, you said you were how old when you came here?" Alec asked.

"Fifteen," Ydoro responded darkly.

"And almost twenty years ago now you said?"

Ydoro nodded and took another drink.

"I can't imagine being here that long," Alec said shaking his head. "Did you ever try finding a way out?"

"Well at first," Ydoro admitted, "but that didn't last. Of course Irias was the king back then, so we had the freedom to investigate ways off this world. He was a different kind of monster. Cunning and manipulative man, his words were his greatest weapon. The amount of damage he did to this society is immeasurable. But you didn't see him riding around the island on a chariot killing citizens at will. He never had to lift a finger against anyone, he could always convince others to do it for him."

"So you did look for ways out of here, back then?"

"We did," Ydoro nodded. "My father was convinced the key was in the Fire Fields. That's where our group first landed as well."

"I knew we didn't look hard enough," Alec exclaimed, his mind already starting to spin wild theories again.

Ydoro shook his head with a look of pity in his eyes. "We searched. We searched for years. There's nothing out there. And not everyone who has arrived here showed up in the Fire Fields. One poor soul was first discovered wandering around the Temple. He didn't last long."

Alec hung his shoulders in defeat and grabbed the bottle of liquor from Ydoro. "There must be some pattern," he thought out loud, "some commonality."

Ydoro had a far off look in his eyes. Alec could tell he had not thought of these things in a long time. "There's a legend told by some of the locals," Ydoro began, "that says new arrivals come when the king has killed someone. That it's the god's way of punishing the king for his transgression."

Alec sighed. He was a scientist. Perhaps their arrival here was beyond the current understanding of science, but he wasn't going to put stock in old wives tales.

"Don't worry," Ydoro said, noticing Alec's raised eyebrows. "I don't believe it either."

"Out of curiosity," Alec asked, "did Mora kill someone before we arrived here?"

Ydoro paused, then responded, "Yeah, he did. And it was out in the Fire Fields."

The last sentence hung in the air for a minute. Alec certainly didn't believe in 'the gods', but he couldn't help feeling like he was missing something. There had to be a connection, a clue out there somewhere. But he didn't have enough pieces to put this puzzle together.

Alec shook his head to clear it, then took another swig of the strong liquor, probably defeating the purpose. "So do you think this plan of ours is going to work?"

Ydoro considered the question, then responded, "Anything's possible. I think it's a long shot, but crazier things have happened."

"Yeah, us being here is one of them," Alec said with a laugh.

Ydoro chuckled, again a first that Alec had seen, and snatched the bottle back. He took a long drink and said, "I'll probably be dead tomorrow so might as well enjoy life while I can." He raised the bottle to Alec and said, "To our last day on earth… so to speak."

Alec smiled and took a drink himself. Ydoro was getting more gregarious as the night went on; he was probably feeling the liquor. Even so, Alec felt like he was finally seeing the real man behind the mask.

"Hell, it'll likely be a bad death too," Ydoro continued. "Being torn apart by Neodactyls would be at the bottom of my list of ways to go."

Alec was silent a moment, then finally responded, "You know 'dactyl' means finger, right?"

"Huh?" Ydoro grunted between swigs from the flask.

"Pterodactyl translates to 'Wing Finger' due to the elongated fourth digit on their hands," Alec explained, "so *Neodactyl* technically means 'New Finger.'"

Ydoro brought the flask down from his lips and furrowed his brow, then he burst into laughter. It was a full, belly laugh, the sort Alec had not heard in a long time. Ydoro held out the flask to keep from spilling, his entire body convulsing with fits of laughter. Alec started to laugh as well, slowly at first, but Ydoro's complete loss of control was infectious. Soon the two of them were wiping tears from their eyes, their voices reverberating out from the alcove and being lost in the steadily increasing rain.

"I guess that's what you get when there's no scientists around to name a new species," Ydoro exclaimed.

It was therapeutic to laugh. It felt normal, a feeling sorely missing from his life recently.

"So being torn apart by a *New Finger*, huh?" Ydoro said, finally regaining control of himself. He laughed and shook his head again. "I suppose I can live with that."

Alec stared into the face of the man sitting across from him; his eyes creased into squints from laughing, tears having formed around his eyelids. Despite his appearance, this was a man who was lost, just like himself. He didn't belong here any more than Alec or his brother did. It was just that time had erased so much of his past by now. Would this be Alec in twenty years?

"What's your real name, Ydoro?" Alec found himself asking. He couldn't help it; he had to know who this quirky, foreign-seeming man used to be.

"Ehh," Ydoro waved his hand dismissively. "It doesn't matter anymore. That person's long gone." His laughter had stopped and the smile threatened to leave his face. It seemed he preferred to just forget he ever lived a life before this place.

"It does matter," Alec insisted. "It's who you really are. Besides, if we're dying tomorrow anyways, what does it matter?"

Ydoro nodded and smiled again, but this time the smile wasn't genuine. His good humor had faded away again. He extended his hand to Alec and said, "Randall Evans."

"Randall Evans," Alec repeated. The name was so... normal. It didn't belong in a place like this. Alec was suddenly filled with hopelessness once again, although he wasn't entirely sure why. He grasped Randall's hand in his own and, shaking it firmly, said, "Alec Dorn, it's good to meet you Randall."

"Good to meet you," Randall/Ydoro responded with a half-smile, although a sadness had settled behind his eyes. He released Alec's hand and bowed his head from the falling rain.

## CHAPTER TWENTY-ONE

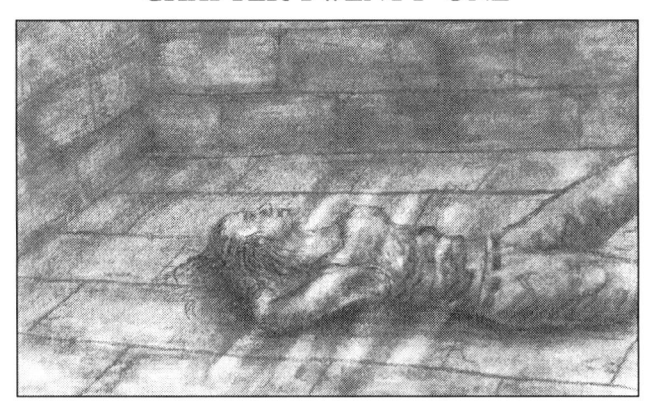

# HISTORY LESSON

Cyrus's bearded and burnt face swam in and out of her mind as she slept. There was no bed, so Nel had spent an uncomfortable and restless night curled up on the damp stone floor of her cell. They had not been able to figure out how she had escaped the first time, so she had the option to escape again if an opportunity presented itself, but right now she was biding her time. Seeing Cyrus hadn't been a dream, even though it felt like it now. She had seen him, talked to him. He had been sitting in the king's quarters, crying it looked like, but how? And why did he look so different? And where had he gone once Mora showed up? She had turned and run into Mora, and during the ensuing fight, she had lost sight of Cyrus. Mora had not seen him, that much was clear. It was clear not only because of his clueless expression when she had asked about him, but because Mora had visited her cell the following evening interrogating her on what she had seen. It seemed to infuriate Mora that something had happened within his own Temple, within his own room in fact, that he did not know about. He had threatened her with torture and death, he had tried being intimidating, he had tried being gentle, but she wouldn't give him anything. He clearly wasn't used to being denied what he wanted. What Nel found especially odd, however, was that in all of his demanding questions about what she had seen in his chambers, he never once asked how she had escaped from her cell.

Eventually Mora had left, promising pain and suffering the next day if she did not talk, and she had tried her best to sleep. He could torture her all he wanted, it brought her too much satisfaction knowing something Mora didn't. If only she understood what she had seen. She did not tell Henry, her cell-block neighbor, about her encounter. He seemed knowledgeable enough about some of the oddities of this place, but she didn't know him.

Nel could see barely a sliver of the night sky through a three-inch horizontal window at the top of the cell wall. It was still dark out; she wondered what time it was. She would guess it was nearly morning, but given how sporadically she had slept, it was impossible to gauge.

"You awake, Henry?" Nel asked quietly into the blackness.

"I'm here," Henry's soft voice replied. "Can't sleep?"

"On the stone floor? I don't know how you do it," Nel responded.

"You get used to it," he said.

"So are you from here, Henry?" Nel asked. She was only mildly curious, but at least talking to him helped pass the time.

"Hell no," came Henry's voice. "I'm from the real world, outside of Boston."

"Boston, eh? How did you end up here?"

"It's a long, sad story," Henry said. "I used to have a wife, and a kid... Benjamin. I was a history teacher, a professor. It's hard to imagine, but when I first came here, I thought I had discovered something special. I thought I had stumbled across the holy grail of discoveries. An entire world apart from our own, it was mesmerizing."

Nel thought he sounded like Cyrus a bit, at least how Cyrus used to sound when he talked about being explorers.

"My first thought when I came here was 'I have to document everything about this place,'" Henry continued. "I sketched, I took notes, I interviewed people... years went by and I amassed volumes and volumes of information on this place. I was recording their history for the first time."

"So what happened?" Nel asked.

"Well I'm sure you can piece it together from there," Henry responded. "Mora got wind of what I was doing and paid me a visit. He didn't take kindly to the way he was represented in my notes. I tried to argue that history is not biased, it's just the facts, but he wouldn't listen. He locked me up, and I haven't seen daylight since. All those years wasted..."

Henry trailed off, and Nel could picture him hunched in his cell, thinking back on his passions from a lifetime ago. "I'm sorry Henry," Nel finally said. "So why didn't he kill you? You're the only prisoner here, why keep you alive?" Nel realized this was a fairly blunt question considering he was obviously feeling reflective, but she was curious.

"Because I was wrong," Henry replied softly, "history is always biased, and it's always written by the victors."

"And Mora was the victor," Nel nodded her head in understanding.

"He wanted me to continue my work," Henry explained, "and tell their history... from his point of view."

Nel understood, and it made perfect sense from what she knew about Mora.

"See, Mora doesn't see himself as the villain," Henry continued, "few villains do. He thinks he brought law and order to this land. And assuming I die in this cell, that's the story history will tell. Everything is biased, everything ever written down, spoken, or thought is twisted and skewed based on the narrator. It's an inescapable truth, and something I accepted far too late."

Nel recognized plenty of truth in Henry's statement, but if she were able to succeed in killing Mora, then she would make sure history would tell things as they really happened. Or was that exactly the point? If she killed Mora and rewrote history, would that not be told from her own point of view? She rubbed her eyes and shook her head. She was far too tired for these sorts of thoughts.

"So what do you do around here when you can't sleep?" Nel asked, trying to change the subject. "Have you just been staring at the wall for years?"

"You a baseball fan?" Henry asked.

"Not in the least," Nel responded.

"Well I always was," Henry explained. "The Boston Red Sox, I grew up watching them, ever since I was a little kid. My Dad and I would go to game after game, every season."

Nel began to zone out as Henry started recounting his favorite players and favorite games. In her own world she couldn't care less about baseball, in this world it seemed especially pointless. Her mind wandered to escape plans, and not just how to escape her cell, that part was apparently easy, but how to take Mora down in the process. She still didn't think it had been a mistake seeking out Mora a couple nights back. It was true she hadn't succeeded, but she had more knowledge now. She had also injured him. While it had not been the killing blow she had hoped for, that stab wound to his side was no small injury. Next time she came face to face with Mora, he would not be able to overpower her so easily. She glanced up at the narrow window at the top of her cell and saw the dark sky beginning to turn a deep blue color. Dawn was just about here. She would not risk leaving her cell again during daylight, she was sure there would be more people around. That meant she would likely be getting another visit from Mora today, possibly with his promised pain and suffering, but he wouldn't get anything out of her.

Henry was still describing a baseball game he had seen as a kid, apparently unaware she was not listening to him. He was probably just happy to have someone to talk aloud to after all these years. Nel laid down on her back and put her hands behind her head. The sky outside was warming up fast, announcing the rising of the sun and the arrival of the new day.

"MORA!" A voice cut through the silent morning air, echoing through the stone dungeons from outside the Temple. Henry stopped his story and Nel lifted her head to hear.

The voice shouted out again, "MORA!"

It sounded like Alec's voice. Nel scrambled to her feet and craned her neck frantically towards the window at the top of the wall.

"COME OUT HERE MORA! COME OUT HERE AND FACE ME LIKE A MAN!"

Nel leapt up towards the window, gripping the crumbling rock ledge beneath it. Her arms were strong enough to lift her body, but the ledge offered very little surface to grip. She slipped off once and jumped up again, this time pulling her face up to the narrow opening. She cursed when she realized there was nothing to see but a couple shrubs at the base of the Temple wall and the sky beyond. She jumped back down and spun around, her mind racing. Alec was here, she was sure that was his voice. From the sound of it, he was planning to confront Mora. The trouble was, Alec wasn't a fighter. He had a strength to him for sure, but he would be no match against the King. This was her opportunity.

"Henry!" Nel called out. "That's my friend out there, I have to help him."

"Help him?" Henry questioned in exasperation. "It doesn't sound like your assassination attempt went well the first time."

"I'm going," she declared. "If I don't make it back..." she trailed off, unsure exactly what she wanted to say. "Well, I just hope you get out of here somehow."

She moved to the side of the cell, examining the area where the bars could be separated from the wall.

"Wait," Henry said. "I want you to succeed, I really do. There's a sand-like substance that Mora has, one of his loyalists in town makes it for him. It's some sort of dried-up plant that's ground with herbs..."

"Look Henry," Nel interrupted, throwing her weight against the iron bars and hearing the rock crunch free, "I have to go, I'm sorry."

"It's a compound," Henry pressed. "Whatever the mixture is, it'll knock you out like a blow to the head."

Nel paused. "It's some sort of toxin?"

"I don't know what it is, I don't pretend to understand it," Henry explained. "What I know is when you throw it towards someone's nose or mouth, they go down like a rock. It doesn't kill them, but they don't regain consciousness for maybe twenty minutes."

"I don't suppose you have some on hand?" Nel asked, wondering why Henry didn't mention this weapon before.

Henry chuckled, not treating the situation with the proper gravity. "No, but Mora will have some in his chambers, I guarantee it. It's a course, sandy substance that has a greenish tint to it. You'll know it when you see it."

Nel considered this a moment, then jumped up to slither her way through the newly made opening in the bars. She wasn't sure if she would be able to use Henry's advice; after all, she had no idea what Alec's plan was, or indeed if he had a plan at all, but it was something.

# CHAPTER TWENTY-TWO

## THE TEMPLE GATES

"MORA!" Alec shouted again, his voice bouncing around the high stone walls of the Temple and echoing through the valley and town below. He had been yelling for several minutes now, with guards occasionally peering over the wall above, then disappearing from sight. He had a dull, nagging concern that a well-aimed spear from above could end his mission before it started, but he was choosing to trust Ydoro's instincts that the King would not want to appear as a coward by not facing him in person.

Ydoro was hidden just beyond the trees with the Shrieking Bat, which they had transferred back into the canvas bag. Ydoro assured Alec that he would be storming the Temple with him as soon as the doors opened. Alec would not necessarily trust his loyalty, but Jack had arrived early this morning and was crouched right alongside him. Ydoro and Alec had made the journey to the Temple in the shadows of pre-dawn, long before the sun came up, and waited. It was just before sunrise that Jack had arrived as promised. He had hugged Alec, relieved they had both made it through the night, then questioned Ydoro and his motivations. After spending the night drinking and talking with Ydoro, Alec felt he had a better understanding of the man, and was possibly even coming to trust him. He would have to be watched, however, at least until Mora was overthrown.  It was with some concern that they watched the sun peek over the horizon, still with no sign of Cyrus.  He had not been seen or heard from since he barreled into the guards who were questioning Jack, then ran off into the forest, three guards in pursuit.  Alec was worried about him.  Any number of things could have happened in this place.  Alec, Jack, and Ydoro had waited, but once the sun was up, the plan was moving forward, with or without him.  If Ydoro was to be believed, they were out of time and Mora would be coming for them today.

It was Ydoro's idea that Alec show himself alone at the Temple entrance.  He said it was essential that Mora thought this was an impulsive, foolish act fueled by anger.  Alec tried not to contemplate whether that was in fact true or not.

"MORA!" Alec shouted again.  "STOP HIDING MORA! COME OUT HERE AND FACE ME!"  His voice was going hoarse, and he was dangerously close to losing his nerve.  The more he thought about it, now that he was in the moment, the stupider this plan seemed.  How would he possibly take on the King, in his own fortress, surrounded by his guards... and those creatures?

"Dr. Alec Dorn!" called a cheerful, lilting voice from the wall above.  King Mora's smiling face appeared over the stone ledge, his greasy hair looking especially disheveled.  He brushed it away from his eyes and took his time running his hands through it, flattening it down.  "I do apologize," he called down, "I'm not an early riser like some of us apparently."  He was wearing that same fake welcoming smile he had shown them when they had first arrived.  It made Alec wonder why he still bothered with the act.  Now that he had straightened his hair and adjusted the folds of his cloak, he said, "What can I help you with, my friend?  I would invite you in, but you seem to be... in a mood?"

Alec's eyes flicked sideways towards Ydoro, hidden in the brush.  He had been hoping he would not have to play games with Mora.  Ydoro nodded his encouragement.  Jack looked wary.

"Who have you got down there in the trees?" Mora called out.  When Alec did not immediately respond, he continued, "My friend, I know you wouldn't come here by yourself, so who's down there with you? I can see you looking at them."

So much for convincing Mora he was alone. Figuring there was no point hiding it now, Alec nodded to Jack. He also gave Ydoro a look he hoped he would understand; to stay hidden. Jack stood up and strode out into the clearing at the entrance of the Temple. Alec thought he was consciously trying to walk with an air of confidence.

"Jack Viana!" Mora called down as Jack stopped beside Alec and turned his face up to the King. "And where's the elder Dorn?" he asked, scanning the area below. "No Cyrus today?"

"Cyrus was killed, actually," Alec called up. He didn't know why he said it, and for all he knew it could be true, but it seemed like a good idea to keep as much of their plan from Mora as possible.

But Mora just grinned and replied, "You think there's anything happening in this Kingdom that I don't know about?" When Cyrus still did not appear, Mora shrugged and said, "Okay, he's dead if you say so," but he clearly didn't believe it. "So what can I help you with this morning, Alec?"

It was just like their first meeting; Mora was smiling warmly but his eyes told an entirely different story. Right now they looked positively maniacal, as though he were daring Alec to push him.

"I'm here for Nelida Yore," Alec declared.

Mora's eyes lit up and the smile on his face widened. It was clear this was exactly the demand he had been hoping for. "Well you lost her, as I already explained to you. Perhaps you need to understand how things work around here."

"I understand perfectly," Alec retorted. He was feeling bolder by the second watching Mora's twisted, arrogant face. "If you want something, you take it, simple as that."

Mora shrugged and said, "Actually yes."

Jack finally spoke up, "That's exactly how you came to rule, Irias had power and you reached out and took it for yourself."

If Jack had been hoping bringing up Irias would shake Mora, he was disappointed. Mora laughed and responded, "That's exactly right. Irias was weak, and the weak cannot rule."

Alec thought this might be his chance. "So if you were to be overpowered, man to man... I mean if someone were able to beat you... without your guards..."

Alec was losing his nerve again, but it didn't matter, because Mora just laughed and said, "No need to beat around the bush, Doctor. If you want to face me, my guards won't stop you."

Alec glanced sideways at Jack, and past him to Ydoro, still watching from the cover of the trees. This was exactly where Alec had wanted the conversation to go, but somehow he didn't think arriving there was his doing.

"Well hell, don't be timid now," Mora called out, "this is why you came here, right?" Alec didn't respond, so Mora continued, "Ya know, I'm pretty good with people but I can't quite figure you out. Are you the meek, mild-mannered scientist or are you the hot-tempered fighter with ambitions of power?"

Alec didn't see himself as either of those things necessarily, but if Mora was having trouble reading him, that was only a good thing.

"Perhaps the reason you're conflicted," Mora continued, "is you're still playing by the rules of your world. The rules of my world are very simple, if you want something, you better be strong enough to take it."

Alec knew that Mora was trying to push him into a conflict, which was exactly what Alec wanted, wasn't it? Then why was he hesitating now? Perhaps it was because Mora was taking the bait so readily. It seemed like this was exactly where Mora wanted this confrontation to lead.

Alec had still not responded to Mora, and Mora was now grinning ear to ear. "Why don't I simplify this for you further," Mora said in a horrifically delighted tone, "my guards won't stop you, and your challenge is accepted." The heavy wooden doors in front of them swung open and two guards stepped aside allowing them entry. "The Temple is open to you," Mora announced, "If you want me..." he leered at them and winked, "...come and get me." The psychotic grin still spread across his face and his eyes never leaving Alec's, he backed away from the towering wall and out of sight.

Alec looked to Jack, who appeared just as dumfounded as Alec felt. It was a trap, it had to be. Talking their way into the Temple had been far too easy. Should they abandon their plan at this point? Where would they go if they did? The island was not that big, Mora would find them, and somehow Alec knew this confrontation would not be forgiven.

## CHAPTER TWENTY-THREE

## ASSAULT ON KING MORA

Jack's heart began to hammer in his chest. His hands were shaking and the edges of his vision started to pulsate. He did not feel incapacitated, far from it. In fact, he felt more focused, more powerful than he had ever felt before. He imagined that was the adrenaline kicking in. This was a bad idea; there was no denying it. Even Alec, whose own plan it was, looked green and hesitant now. But Jack stared ahead at the open Temple gates with unwavering determination. Perhaps it was the smugness that Mora showed them. His confident, grinning face had looked down at them from the wall above, daring them to challenge him. And Jack wanted to face him now. Jack had been in fights before, and he was a big guy. Life at sea amongst the crewmen wasn't always the easiest. As a general group, the deckhands and workers were an assortment of society's misfits and not particularly well-known for their conflict resolution skills. Jack had learned to hold his own at a young age. The Neodactyls were an admittedly horrifying prospect to fight off, but they were only animals, and Jack had a machete that he had taken off one of the crushed guards from the hillside. It was tucked safely into his belt, hidden beneath his shirt. Alec also had one from the bag he had arrived with.

Ahead, the heavy wooden gates of the Temple stood wide open and two guards flanked the inside hall beyond. They were turned facing each other, evidently granting them passage. Jack really hoped Ydoro was right about the guards not interfering. He looked to Alec, standing beside him with his eyes wide and his jaw set but quivering slightly. Beyond him, Ydoro finally approached from the treeline, the canvas bag containing the Shrieking Bat slung over his shoulder. He looked up at the high wall above, confirming that Mora had not reappeared. Jack had to admit that it was a bold choice for Ydoro to move against the King after living under his shadow for so many years. Jack hoped that showed his confidence in their plan, although his shaky, hesitant demeanor said otherwise.

Ydoro positioned himself on Alec's left side and quickly scanned the surrounding forest. "Still no Cyrus," he noted, "but we're committed now."

Alec did not react at all to Ydoro's words. He was still staring straight ahead at the open doors. Jack put a reassuring hand on Alec's shoulder and said, "We're taking back our lives today."

Alec gave a single, strained nod and started forward. Jack and Ydoro looked at each other and followed suit. There truly was no turning back now, Jack thought. It seemed to take an eternity to reach the open doors, and as they passed through the entrance, Jack glanced at the guards to either side of them. One guard stood expressionless and staring; a true soldier doing his duty. The other had the same, statue-like stance, but as he caught Jack's eye, he winked. Jack smiled to himself; perhaps Ydoro really did know what he was talking about. They passed the guards and found themselves in a vast, open entrance room made of grey stone. Some ornate-looking carpets were spread across the floors and some odd furniture dotted the room, but overall, the area was cavernous and not particularly inviting. Without windows on any of the walls, the few scattered torches cast limited bouncing orange light into some areas, leaving others in deep, flickering shadow.

Jack noticed Alec's eyes darting from corner to corner, frantically scanning the area as though he expected Mora and his birds to jump out at any moment. That did not seem likely to Jack, however. Mora would probably want to make a show of it. They crossed the enormous entryway and walked through a door on the far wall that led into an equally enormous room that seemed to have no obvious function other than a free-standing metal ladder in the center that rose about a hundred feet to an opening in the ceiling and presumably a room above.

Jack looked quizzically to Ydoro, who said, "It leads to the roof and the battlements, where Mora was standing earlier."

"Strange design choice," Jack replied.

"It was added after Mora took power," Ydoro explained, "he's the one who added all of the 'embellishments' to make it look like a castle. He insisted on being able to look down at approaching visitors."

Jack rolled his eyes, but Alec remained silent. Jack was beginning to worry that Alec would not be able to keep his nerve. What would happen if Alec abandoned the plan?

"So this room we're using to trap the Neodactyls…" Jack began.

"It's in the upper levels," Ydoro confirmed, "near the king's quarters."

Jack paused, then asked, "Do you really think this will work?"

"The way we've planned it? No," Ydoro responded bluntly. When Jack looked surprised, he continued, "It doesn't mean we won't be successful. Stay adaptable, and stay sharp. He's only one man."

They reached a wide stone staircase and followed it up to the higher levels. Torches lit the dank, windowless hallways leaving black scorch marks on the rock walls they were affixed to. After several turns and several more staircases, it became apparent to Jack that this place was like a maze inside. The hallways were mostly narrow and claustrophobic, and with minimal decorations or landmarks it would be impossible for him to find his way back out alone. Ydoro clearly knew his way around, however, as he pressed forward with confidence.

They turned a corner to find themselves in a significantly warmer part of the Temple, with wooden floors and more space to breathe. They could also glimpse daylight streaming through into a room at the end of a long corridor ahead.

"The king's quarters," Ydoro answered Jack's unasked question. "but the room we want the bat to fly into is behind us."

They turned to look down the corridor in the opposite direction and saw a single door standing ajar at the very end.

"If we can get the Neodactyl's to follow the bat through that door, it leads to a wing of the Temple that is separate from the rest. That door is the only way in or out."

Jack contemplated their plan, trying to envision a scenario where it would actually work. He couldn't. He shook his head and said, "There's no way. Even if we got the bat to fly that way…" He trailed off, still shaking his head.

"I think it's possible," Ydoro insisted.

Alec shook his head and finally spoke for the first time since entering the Temple. "Won't work," he grunted. He still looked green.

"It's too late now," Ydoro said, "and remember what I told you yesterday, the King was coming for you today. You were out of time." He began walking away from the open door towards the king's quarters and continued, "It has to be from in there, it's a big enough space that if we release the bat down the hall from the far end…"

Ydoro was stopped mid-sentence as his head pitched backwards, blood flying from his mouth. A long red and black object had swung out from an open door to the right of the corridor and connected violently with his jaw. Ydoro slammed to the floor and King Mora sprung out into the hallway with one of his scepters in hand, crouching slightly like a cat ready to pounce. He looked down at the motionless Ydoro in front of him and made a tisking noise.

"I always knew you were weak," he said in disgust. Then he looked up at Alec and Jack and grinned. "You found your way in, I'm glad."

The canvas bag carrying the Shrieking Bat had fallen to the floor with Ydoro and was now moving slightly from the inside. Mora had not noticed, however. He straightened himself up and pointed his scepter at them like a sword. Jack noticed he made a strange face when he did it, as though it were somehow difficult for him.

"I do hope you didn't pin your entire plan on Ydoro," Mora taunted, "the poor man's not much of a fighter."

"And you are?" Jack retorted, braver than he felt. "You better be sure of it up here, away from your Fire Fields. Without that burning sand to launch around, all I see is a man with a stick." With that, Jack unsheathed the rusted machete from his belt and held it out in front of him.

Jack had hoped to see Mora's confidence waiver, but he just smiled more broadly. "Ya know, I'm going to be running out of cell space soon once Ydoro's down there, I suppose your friend Nelida's execution will have to be moved up."

Jack knew Mora was trying to goad them into doing something rash. Jack would not take the bait... but Alec did.

Silent for the entire exchange, Alec suddenly lunged forward and slashed his machete down towards Mora's face. Alec was incredibly fast, but Mora was faster. He parried Alec's blow with the scepter and grabbed ahold of his wrist, slamming his entire body into the stone wall. Mora wielded the scepter with frightening speed and precision, landing several shockingly violent blows before sending Alec careening backwards and onto his back at Jack's feet. The entire confrontation had lasted barely a couple seconds. Alec stood shakily to his feet again, his machete still in hand. Mora had not been bluffing; he was an incredibly strong fighter. In fact, it seemed to Jack that he possibly had some real training in his past.

Mora watched them with maniacal amusement and said, "Let me know when you're ready for round two." He lowered his scepter and continued, "In the meantime, let's see how fast you can run."

The words had barely left his mouth when both Neodactyls wheeled around the corner from the king's chambers and sprinted full speed down the corridor towards them. Their scaly feet hardly seemed to make a sound as they advanced; their heads barely moving on the ends of their bobbing necks as their yellow eyes zeroed in on their prey. Jack reached down and snatched the canvas bag from the ground but there was no time to do anything else. He scrambled around and fled down the hallway right behind Alec, who darted through a doorway to the left and into a small room with a wooden door on the far wall. Alec flung it open and ran down the staircase on the other side, jumping over the steps three at a time. Jack reached the staircase right behind Alec and turned to close the heavy door once he was through; too late. The nearest Neodactyl had reached the door and slammed its body halfway through. Jack kicked at the snapping creature and it hissed horribly, lashing out with its long neck. Jack recoiled as the horrifically sharp beak closed inches from his face, and released the door, bounding down the staircase towards Alec waiting at the bottom. He did not turn to see how close the creatures were following as they launched themselves down a corridor and turned down another, and another. Jack could see another heavy door ahead of them. They had to make it through the door with enough time to latch it behind them.

Alec barreled through ahead of him and fell out of sight. There must be another staircase leading down. Jack put on an extra burst of speed, but a high-pitched snarl told him the Neodactyl was right on his tail. Jack careened through the doorway and turned on his heel, slashing upwards wildly with his machete. To his amazement, the blade connected squarely with the approaching Neodactyl's exposed breast. There was a streak of deep red blood and flying feathers followed by an echoing guttural howl, but Jack had sacrificed his footing on the top step to land the blow and he pitched backwards, smashing off the wrought iron railings and catapulting down the stone staircase. He extended his leg to brace himself against the impact of the fast-approaching wooden wall at the bottom, but his foot splintered straight through the ancient, brittle boards. He scrambled to free his foot as Alec rushed forward to help him, wrenching his leg free with a forceful tug that shredded Jack's pant leg and sliced his calf painfully. Jack turned to see the injured Neodactyl at the top of the steps, visibly slowed by its wound but still approaching fast. Alec heaved Jack off the bottom step and into a small room beyond, then, to Jack's relief, slammed a heavy door shut behind them with a loud clang indicating it had latched.

There was silence in the room and the Neodactyls could be heard beyond the door, chittering and clicking before their fading footsteps announced their retreat back up the stairs and away down the corridor above. Jack took deep, rattling lungfuls of air, struggling to catch his breath. Alec had collapsed on the floor next to him attempting to slow his heart rate, and the Shrieking Bat within the bag flapped against the canvas furiously in agitation. Once his breathing had slowed and the red spots around his eyes had started to subside, Jack finally looked around the room they had found themselves in. It was a small, wooden room that looked sort of like a study that hadn't been used in years. There were cobwebs at the corners of the ceiling and covering the wooden furniture, which included an old desk, a single chair, and a small cot. Piled in different parts of the room were stacks and stacks of yellowed papers, and scattered throughout were notebooks and journals. Jack pushed himself off the floor and made his way to the desk, picking up a tattered old, leather-bound journal and peeling it open. Dust on the sides of the binding fell away and within was tiny, scribbled handwritten notes punctuated with the occasional sketch. Jack leafed through the book, pausing occasionally at a drawing of the town square, or one of the Temple they were in now. There were sketches of people too. They appeared to be locals based on their wardrobes and surroundings. Some of the people had entire pages dedicated to their portraits, some had names labeled at the bottom, but many didn't. Jack flipped further through the book and stopped at a journal entry labeled May 18th, 1922.

*There is something eerily familiar about this place. Perhaps not familiar, but certainly not as foreign as I first found it. There is real life here, a real society. I am consistently having to remind myself, even still after all this time, that these people have never known anything other than this world. They follow the King blindly because they have never known anything else. The King continues to watch me closely. The man is deranged and reminds me very much of the dictators of my world. The difference is that there are no other global powers to challenge him here.*

The entry went on for another two pages. Jack flipped back to the front cover and looked at the inside binding. In the same small handwriting was scrawled the name *Dr. Henry Fine.*
"Hey Jack, check this out," Alec said softly from a small table near the cot. Jack walked over and Alec handed him an old, folded piece of paper with the words *'For Benjamin'* written on the front. Jack unfolded the paper and read a handwritten note in the same handwriting as the journal.

# SOMEWHERE

*Benjamin,*

*By the time you read this, if you ever read this, I know I will be long gone. Even as I write this, I can conceive of no way this letter will ever find its way to you. I have found myself entirely lost from our world, the world I shared with you and your mother. The two of you have no doubt spent years wondering what became of me. I fear you will think I deliberately deserted you, but I have faith that you knew my character better than that. The truth is I have found myself in a strange land that seems entirely apart from our world, both in space and time. I was working in Sudan, just as I said in my last letter, until I traced an ancient burial site to a cave in the west. Myself and a guide trekked our way in, and then something happened to us. I felt blinding pressure in my head, and it felt as though I were being squeezed through a very small space. I cannot explain it. I realize this may be a little much for you to understand at your age, but perhaps some day you will want to know. Come to think of it, even as I write this, you are far older than I remember you. I am sorry I have not been there to watch you grow up. When I first arrived here, the prospect of finding this new, undiscovered world was intoxicating. And for a few years life was pretty good for me. Unfortunately my journey has taken a dark turn and the local ruler has locked me away. I am unable to continue my documentation of this world as I intended, and I fear my recordings of this place will be dramatically altered to serve King Mora's desires. He is keeping me alive for now, but I do wonder how long it will last. I suppose this letter is more for me than for you, since I have no way of getting it to you. But I hope you know that you and your mother have never been far from my mind, and here at the end I do regret ever leaving your side.*

*Your father, Henry*

Jack folded the letter up and handed it back to Alec, who replaced it where he had found it. There was rectangle of dust on the small table highlighting exactly where it had been sitting for so many years. Jack was silent for a minute. He felt strange, as though he had just read something he shouldn't have. This man Henry had evidently been locked away in this room years ago by Mora. He had been from their world it sounded like, and he had never escaped back to it.

"What do you think happened to him?" Alec asked, looking around the room.

Jack shrugged and responded, "I'm guessing he died eventually." For some reason he did not want to let on how much the letter had bothered him. "C'mon, let's keep moving. Don't forget, we're here for a reason."

Jack moved towards a second door on the far wall. It occurred to him the door might be locked if this was used as a cell at one point, but it opened easily with a loud creak. They proceeded down a narrow, damp corridor lined with several sets of bars along one wall. Jack crept forward slowly and peered around the wall into the first cell. He nearly jumped out of his skin when he saw a small, frail-looking old man looking back at him. Jack's heart started pounding and he moved down the hall to the next two cells looking for Nel. They were empty.

"She's not here," Jack announced as Alec looked hopefully after him.

"She *was* here," said the old man in a weak voice. "Pretty young woman, I'm assuming that's who you're looking for?"

Alec moved in close to the bars. "Where is she?"

"She was here," the old man said again, "she left when she heard you yelling at the gates."

"What do you mean she left?" Alec asked. "Who are you?"

"My name's Henry," the man said, "and your friend fled, I think she was trying to help you."

"Henry?" Alec repeated. "As in the Henry whose room we just walked through? With all the papers and journals?"

"Good lord is that still back there?" Henry said with a hollow laugh.

"We assumed you had died," Alec explained. "Based on your letter to your son..."

"Not yet," Henry said with a shrug, "but your friend's in real danger. I directed her towards the king's quarters..."

"Why would you do that?" Alec questioned.

Henry started explaining about some sort of weaponized powder, but Jack's attention was drawn to the staircase at the end of the corridor, leading up to the floor above. For a second, he had thought he heard something... a clicking.

"I know a bit about how the Kingdom works," Henry was explaining, while Alec, clutching the bars of his cell, was hanging on his every word. "If you do things just right, you could change this place... make it whatever you want..."

Jack strained to hear Henry's soft voice from the end of the hall but then he heard it again; a distinct clicking from the staircase around the corner.

"Alec," Jack whispered frantically, but Alec only half glanced in his direction, still listening intently to Henry.

The clicking happened again, this time followed by a soft but unmistakable hiss. A Neodactyl was coming down the staircase towards them, and it was approaching slowly... deliberately.

Jack turned and approached Alec, as quietly as he could manage, although every bone in his body told him to run. "Alec," Jack whispered again, grasping Alec's arm roughly and pulling him away from the still talking Henry. "They're here."

Judging by the look on Alec's face, he did not need further explanation of who 'they' were. Jack scanned the corridor frantically, looking for anything they could use to fend them off. They were trapped in here. There was one open cell they could barricade themselves in, but to what end? The only other option was to go back the way they had come, back through Henry's old writing cell and back up through the door they had fled through minutes earlier.

Alec was wide-eyed, backing slowly down the hallway away from the sounds of the approaching creatures. He then turned to Jack and whispered breathlessly, "The room we came through to get here, Henry's original room, we shut the door on the other side."

Jack nodded in agreement but didn't see the point of his statement. He did not need to be reminded they were trapped in here.

Alec forcefully spun Jack towards him and continued, "That room is closed from the other side, that means the door here is the only way in or out."

Then Jack understood. He looked down at the crumpled canvas bag hanging from his hand. The Shrieking Bat within seemed to have calmed down but was still moving around a bit. He looked down the corridor to the open door at the far end, leading into the room they had just come from. The hallway was narrow. If this didn't work, they would die. Jack could hear the clawed foot of one of the creatures reach the bottom of the staircase. It was just around the corner now. Jack bent himself low and backed quietly into the open cell next to Henry's. Alec followed and crouched next to him, evidently having trouble keeping his breathing quiet. Jack was poised low to the ground just inside the door of the cell, positioned as if he were about to begin a race. He clutched the canvas bag in his hand and closed his eyes, pleading silently that this would work. He could not see down the corridor in the direction of the approaching creature, so he listened, praying he would be able to tell when it had turned the corner. There was a soft, hollow dripping sound echoing off the walls and Alec's shallow breathing next to him was making it nearly impossible to listen. The clicking came again, this time much closer than before. A soft footstep padded against the wet stone, and then another. Was it in the hallway yet?

"Do it," Alec whispered in his ear. But Jack waited. He had to make sure the creature was in the hallway.

There was another footstep, and another. Jack fed his fingers silently into the opening of the bag.

There was one more footstep and Henry's raspy voice from behind the stone wall whispered, "Now."

Jack grasped the bottom of the bag and flipped it upwards violently with a whipping motion. The bat within erupted through the opening and flew into the corridor with a loud shriek. There was an alarmed screech from the hallway as the Neodactyl reacted to the sudden appearance of the bat. With a panicked fluttering of wings, the Shrieking Bat rocketed down the hallway towards the open door of Henry's old cell and two streaks of colored feathers announced the Neodactyls giving chase. Jack had been unsure until he saw them race past, but it was both of them.

Jack launched himself into the hallway and down the corridor after them. They had both entered the room and were snapping wildly at the circling Shrieking Bat, which was emitting alarmed, high pitch screams from the ceiling. One of the Neodactyls leapt onto the desk in the middle of the room and lunged upwards, crashing to the floor with an explosion of falling papers. The second Neodactyl suddenly cocked its head back towards the hallway and hissed in alarm when it saw Jack barreling towards it. It dug its taloned foot into the floorboards and propelled itself forward, but Jack had reached the heavy door and slammed his whole body into the wooden surface, smashing it shut with an echoing clang.

The chaos that sounded from within the room was instant and terrifying. Jack could hear smashing furniture and splintering wood, consistent crashes against the door and the furious snarling howls from the trapped creatures. Claws could be heard raking against the other side of the wood door and the shadows of movement danced against the stone floor from the half-inch crack at the bottom. But the door held.

Jack backed slowly away and allowed himself a brief sigh of relief. It had worked! Maybe not in the way they had planned, but the creatures were trapped. Jack stopped his progress when he felt something soft beneath his foot and realized he had backed into Alec, who was now standing in the hallway staring wide-eyed at the door and the otherworldly noises beyond. He finally locked eyes with Jack and gave a weak smile, as though he didn't dare believe they had actually succeeded.

"Incredible," Henry was saying from his cell. "Incredible!"

"Alec, we have to go," Jack said, refusing to allow himself to relax. "We have to take down Mora. If he finds out where those birds are locked up, we'll be back to square one."

Alec nodded in agreement, setting his jaw in defiance. "You're right," he said, his voice much less shaky than before, "We have to finish this, now."

Jack clapped him on the back, happy to see his resolve resurfacing. They started down towards the other end of the corridor, the snarls and screams still echoing from within the room behind them. Henry watched them as they passed his cell, nodding his encouragement.

"Good luck, my friends," Henry said in his soft voice.

"We'll come back for you when it's done," Alec promised with fiery certainty.

They turned the corner and proceeded cautiously up the curving staircase to the floor above. After following several hallways and another flight of stairs, they emerged back in the entry hall, to their mild surprise. Jack realized again he had very little understanding of the layout of this Temple. Without Ydoro guiding them anymore, it would be very easy to get turned around. He wondered briefly if Ydoro was okay, but he couldn't allow himself to get sidetracked right now. They crossed the huge entrance room into the adjoining room with the high ceiling and free-standing ladder. Should they go back up towards the king's quarters, the way they had come from? According to Henry, that was the direction Nel had headed.

"Okay I think I've let you come far enough," called a familiar, taunting voice.

Jack and Alec wheeled around to find King Mora striding into the cavernous room from a door along the side wall. He wore his usual gloating grin and held a rusted machete in one hand. He stopped fifteen feet from them and planted his feet, raising his arms away from his body in a show of mock benevolence.

"I hope you get it by now," Mora called out, "the house always wins."

It was a strange phrase coming from Mora, Jack thought. It seemed so modern.

"You can cut the act," Alec called back, "you have nothing without your birds."

Jack winced as he heard the words. He did not want Mora knowing that his creatures were incapacitated. But Mora just laughed in reaction to the statement.

"You think I put the entire fate of my Kingdom on the shoulders of two animals?" He shook his head, still laughing, then snapped his fingers.

Two guards walked out from the same door Mora had arrived through, and they were dragging a third person from under the arms. They knelt the person roughly at Mora's feet and even before he looked up, Jack knew who it was. Cyrus's face was bloodied and bruised, but his eyes still showed a fierce resolve. He looked angry rather than defeated. He shook his head as he looked at them, as though mad at himself for getting captured.

Alec started towards him, but Mora drew his machete and held it to Cyrus's throat in the same way he had done to Alec days earlier. "That's far enough Doc."

The two guards that had dragged Cyrus out receded back into the shadows along the wall but did not leave the room. For the first time since entering the Temple, Jack had no idea what to do. He had not planned for this. Mora and Cyrus were still fifteen feet from them, any attempt to charge them would be hopeless.

Jack dropped his own machete to the stone floor with a metallic clang, and Alec looked sideways at him, likely deciding if he should do the same.

"That's very kind of you Jack," Mora called, "but it's not going to save him, and it's certainly not going to save you. In fact, pick it back up, I want you armed."

Jack scanned the room, looking for any way out of this.

"Pick it back up Jack," Mora repeated in a lilting voice, and he pointed at the dropped weapon with his own machete.

There was no missing it this time, Mora had winced when he pointed. Something was hurting him. Jack, trying to keep his expression casual, scanned Mora's body, searching for wounds. Mora brought the machete back to rest against Cyrus's throat… and then Jack saw it: There was a small amount of blood seeping through Mora's shirt around his abdomen. It was barely visible beneath the drape of his cloak, but it was definitely there. Jack didn't know what sort of injury it was, but it was clearly bothering him, and if it was still seeping then it was fresh. Jack and Alec would not be able to do anything from this distance, it would have to be Cyrus. Jack had to get Cyrus to notice the wound.

"I said pick it up!" Mora yelled.

Jack bent and retrieved his machete from the floor, his mind racing.

"Better," Mora called, and he adjusted the machete along Cyrus's neck. "Now any last words to the great Cyrus Dorn?"

"You don't have to do this," Alec said.

Perfect, Jack thought. While Mora looked at Alec and laughed, Jack locked eyes with Cyrus. He fixed him with a piercing stare until he was sure Cyrus understood that he was trying to tell him something. While Mora continued taunting Alec, Jack moved his gaze from Cyrus to his own hand and waggled his fingers. He needed Cyrus to watch his hand. Cyrus stared at him. He didn't get it. Jack tried again, locking eyes with Cyrus, then moving his eyes down to his own hand and waggling his fingers. Cyrus gave an uncertain nod. Jack wasn't sure if Cyrus had understood.

Mora was in the middle of a speech to Alec, proclaiming how he was all-powerful.

"I have something to say," Jack called out, interrupting Mora mid-sentence. Mora looked taken aback, but grinned and nodded. Jack waggled his fingers again, and, to his relief, he noticed Cyrus watched his hand closely.

"I know you think you're all-powerful, Mora" Jack began, "but you're the king of nothing. You rule over a people who don't care who rules them. You don't rule the way you do to instill fear or beat your people into submission, you do it to make yourself feel strong." He waggled his fingers again and glanced meaningfully, and briefly, at Cyrus. "You may feel powerful, you may feel strong, but your strength is just an illusion. Here's the thing about strength; if you take a strong object and hit it in just the right way…" Jack gave his fingers one more waggle and then slowly but deliberately ran his hand along his abdomen, exactly in the spot where Mora was bleeding from. "…they crumble," Jack finished, and Cyrus's eyes widened in understanding.

Mora grinned back at him, but Cyrus had gotten the message. He spun around on his knees and hammered his fist directly into Mora's bleeding abdomen. Mora buckled and let out an echoing howl of pain, releasing his grip on Cyrus. Cyrus scrambled out of the way as Mora attempted to lunge after him but slammed to his hands and knees on the floor, blood dripping out of his newly opened wound.

Cyrus bolted to his feet and ran to meet Jack and Alec, who were both standing their ground, machetes raised towards Mora. Mora gasped a few rattling, wheezing breaths and slowly brought himself back to his feet, his hand pressed into his side which was now bright red with blood. He was hunched sideways a bit but seemed to be fighting through the pain.

Mora grinned and shook his head, but this time the grin seemed forced. "This didn't kill me before, it's not going to slow me down now," he said, indicating his wound. "But if you're feeling brave, let's see what you've got."

Jack considered him for a moment, then made a decision. He raised his machete and started towards Mora. If there was a time to beat him, this was it. Mora grinned and straightened up, holding his own machete out defensively.

"Stop!" came a female voice from behind him.

Jack whipped around along with Cyrus and Alec. Nel was walking towards them from the corridor leading deeper into the Temple. She had a machete in one hand and a small cloth pouch in the other.

"Nel!" Alec exclaimed.

Nel barely acknowledged Alec but strode towards Jack, holding up the cloth pouch.

"This is how we take him down," she said.

Mora grinned again. "You've been in my quarters again," he said. "Best be careful with that stuff."

"What is it?" Jack asked as Nel stopped at his side.

"It's supposed to knock him out," Nel explained. "Henry told me about it," she exclaimed at Mora, clearly hoping to needle him with the revelation.

Mora made an odd expression, as though he were surprised a fellow prisoner would reveal his secrets to her. Cyrus and Alec had walked up to join them, ready for a fight.

"Where's your cocky smile now?" Nel called to Mora, who was standing defensively but still seemed to be in a good deal of pain.

"I wouldn't worry about me," Mora answered, and he raised his hand and snapped his fingers again.

The two guards standing in the shadows of the wall stepped forward and unsheathed their own blades.

Jack took a step back. "I thought you were fighting us yourself," Jack said, though he felt foolish saying it.

Mora laughed and responded, "That's one of the perks of being the king." His eyes were glinting with a diabolical hunger. "I can change the rules."

Cyrus turned to Nel and whispered quietly, "How much of that stuff do you have?"

Nel shook her head, "I think it's only enough for one."

Mora looked to his guards and said, "Kill them all, bring me that powder."

It all happened incredibly fast. The two guards sprinted towards them at full speed, raising their machetes to attack. Jack stepped sideways as they swung, parrying a blow from the nearest guard. The entire room had erupted into sudden chaos. Cyrus and Alec had spun away from the group, engaging the second guard in a frenzy of swinging metal and fists. There were no rules in this sort of combat. It was not like the stylized swordplay seen in entertainment, and no one was trained enough to engage in a legitimate duel. This fight was brutal and violent and chaotic. Cyrus hammered his rusted machete into the guard's weapon, then smashed into him with his shoulder, and struck out with his fist. Nel was ducking left and right as the first guard swung furiously, clearly attempting to connect with her neck.

Jack lunged forward to help her but caught sight of movement to his right. He turned just in time to see Mora barreling full tilt towards him, his face twisted in psychotic fury. Jack managed to block his first swing with the machete but quickly began backing up in defense. After seeing how quickly Mora had dispatched Alec in the corridors above, Jack knew how well trained he was. Mora continued to advance towards Jack, who was now practically tripping over his own feet in an attempt to back away. He blocked two additional swings from Mora and ducked a third, but it was clear his abdominal injury was not going to

SOMEWHERE

slow him down, and Jack was absurdly outmatched. Mora hammered at Jack's machete with his own again and again, then thrust the handle up to connect with the side of Jack's head. Jack fell to the ground, his hands slamming onto the cold stone floor. The room was spinning from the blow, and he could feel blood dripping down the side of his face. Jack shook his head to try to clear his vision and saw Mora's combat boots standing in front of him. No doubt the King was about to strike down with his machete. Jack gripped his own weapon and thrust it upwards, hoping blindly to run it through Mora's stomach. The sound of scraping metal against metal told him that Mora had blocked the attack, although Jack was still too disoriented to see straight. He felt Mora's hand tighten around his wrist and then blinding pain around his cheek bone as Mora's fist smashed into his face. Jack staggered backwards and fell to the floor again, hearing his weapon clang from his grip. He was defeated already, and he had not managed to land a single blow.

"Jack!" called Nel's voice from across the room.

Jack shook his head to bring the spinning room back into focus and saw Nel, still ducking around the slashing guard, bouncing on her toes and holding something up in the air. The bag of powder! She wound up and launched the tiny bag past the attacking guard. Jack scrambled to his feet to catch it but Mora dove in front of him to intercept. It was clear the powder was the only weapon that concerned him. As Mora stretched out his hand to catch the falling bag, Jack launched himself forward, tackling Mora around the mid-section. Mora slammed to the floor hard, Jack right on top of him. The bag had glanced off his hand and fell to the ground five feet from them. Jack seized on the opportunity and stabbed his elbow down on Mora's injured abdomen. He yelled out in pain and Jack hit him across the face with his fist. He hit him again. And again. And again. Blood was pouring from Mora's nose now and spattering across the stone floor. Jack had to kill him, here and now. This man was evil, and he had to die.

Suddenly Jack felt pressure around his left ear and realized Mora had ahold of his hair. Mora tugged his head sideways and slammed his fist into Jack's cheek again. Stars erupted behind his eyes for the second time, and he stumbled backwards. Mora rolled himself over and lunged across the floor towards the fallen bag of powder. Jack reached to his left for his dropped machete and gripped it tightly. He raked it across the stone and propelled himself towards Mora, throwing all of his weight behind his weapon. Mora spun around and whipped his hand towards Jack; but it wasn't just his hand. He held the small bag open between his thumb and fingers and released the shimmery green contents directly into Jack's face.

Jack's nose and throat burned instantly as though he had just swallowed metal shavings. The edges of his vision began to cloud with a poisonous-looking yellow-green fog. The spots of firelight around the walls began to shine with a blinding intensity, and as Jack moved his head, streaks appeared across his field of vision. Something was happening to his body as well. It felt as though his arms were extending, drooping off his skeleton and piling onto the floor in shapeless heaps. Indeed, he could feel his knuckles scraping against the ground, but they no longer felt like knuckles. It was as though his every appendage was pooling beneath him, like he was dissolving. His vision was pulsating in and out of focus and he found his face very close to the stone floor. His arms were not drooping off his body after all, he had fallen.

No, he had to fight. He had to continue... what? It had been important... but he could no longer remember what he had been doing. Jack moved his foot beneath his body to support it. If he could only get himself standing again... but his foot was no longer there. It too felt as though it had melted away. He felt his body pitch forward and braced himself for the impact of the floor against his face... but the impact never came. He just fell straight over himself, head over heels, and spun downwards through nothingness in a dizzying, relentless circle.

## CHAPTER TWENTY-FOUR

# ASCEND

Cyrus could feel the skin open along his cheek as the guard's weapon slashed across it and his head whipped backwards from the impact. He brought his hand up to his face and felt warm blood trickling down through his fingers and onto his neck. He gripped his own weapon more tightly and swiped out wildly as the guard easily ducked out of the way. Alec was attempting to drive the guard backwards by continually hacking at him with his own machete, but the guard was blocking his every wild blow.

Cyrus heard Nel yell out but couldn't hear what she said. He glanced around quickly, surveying the enormous room behind him. Nel was quickly bouncing from toe to toe in a continual sort of dance as the second guard swung his blade powerfully from his shoulders over and over again. He appeared exhausted, Nel was quicker than him and tiring him out. Cyrus scanned further into the center of the room and saw a person on their hands and knees, struggling to stand. It was Jack and his eyes were rolled up into the back of his head. He crawled shakily forward and then collapsed onto his front. Was he dead? Cyrus had not seen what happened to him but realized in horror that King Mora was lifting his blade from the floor and beginning to stride towards them to join the melee. He was bleeding from the nose and mouth but otherwise seemed undamaged. There was no doubt in Cyrus's mind; Jack had been their strongest fighter, yet he had been dispatched so quickly.

Cyrus didn't know whether to continue helping Alec or turn his attention to Mora, but the decision was made for him when Mora suddenly broke into a run. Cyrus split off from Alec and the guard and raised his machete to fight the King... but then thought better of it. He ran sideways, hoping the King would follow, which he did. All he could think of was putting as much distance between himself and Mora as possible. His only hope would be to catch him off guard.

"Where are you going?" Mora called out with a laugh, still pursuing him across the huge room.

Cyrus reached the free-standing metal ladder in the center of the room and positioned it between himself and the charging king. The King laughed and swung his blade hard around the side of the ladder, hitting the side with a deafening clang. He knew he wouldn't hit Cyrus from that angle, he was toying with him, like a hunter trying to scare an animal out of a burrow. Behind Mora, Cyrus could see the exhausted guard attacking Nel, still swinging hard as she continually ducked out of the way. He was much slower now; he had tired himself out. He gave one more powerful swing, which Nel sidestepped, then thrust her own blade forward with all of her strength. The blade went straight through the guard with a wet sounding crunch. The guard made a gurgling noise and blood trickled out of his mouth.

Mora glanced over his shoulder at the noise and Cyrus, in a panic, jumped onto the rungs of the ladder and began to scramble up it. He wasn't trying to run away, he just needed to put some distance between himself and the King. He had to work out a plan before taking him on. Cyrus heard another ear-splitting clang from below and felt the ladder rungs vibrate beneath his hands.

Mora's laughter echoed throughout the room. Cyrus looked over his shoulder to the room below. Nel wrenched her machete free from the guard's belly and ran towards Alec and his opponent. Cyrus was glad she was going to help Alec, but that meant he was on his own. Mora was still laughing some ten feet below, but he sheathed his weapon on his belt and mounted the ladder himself. Cyrus stuffed his own weapon into his belt, turned, and began scrambling up the ladder faster. Glancing over his shoulder every few feet, Cyrus could easily tell how much more comfortable Mora was on this ladder than he was. Mora was practically swinging from each rung like some sort of deranged ape. He moved with such fluidity he would be catching Cyrus in no time. Cyrus sped up. It was a long way to the top. A very long way. His stomach was churning just thinking about how high up they were. All he could think of was getting through the opening in the ceiling above with enough time to get the jump on Mora. Cyrus glanced over his shoulder again and Mora was mere feet from him. He would never make it. He tried to stomp down on the rungs below where Mora's hands gripped them but, to his horror, Mora nearly grabbed his ankle in the process.

Nel and Alec, far below, had evidently beaten the second guard and were looking up at Mora and Cyrus, fifty feet above them now. They were shouting, their voices bouncing off the cavernous walls and ceiling, but Cyrus couldn't understand them. Nel mounted the ladder and began to climb, apparently hoping to catch Mora from below. But she would never make it in time. Cyrus pulled himself faster and higher up the ladder. He thought of unsheathing his machete and using it, but how? From this angle there was no way to engage him without falling. Cyrus looked up and saw the opening in the ceiling finally approaching. It was larger than it had looked from below, probably five feet squared. According to Ydoro, this led to the battlements above the outside gate. He was nearly there; another ten feet and he would be through.

With a lurch in his stomach, Cyrus felt a hand close around his ankle. He looked down into the twisted, grinning face of King Mora. Mora gave a hard tug and Cyrus nearly lost his grip on the metal rung he was clinging to. He tried to pull his leg free but Mora tugged at it again, harder this time. Cyrus's hands were sweating but he wouldn't let go. He couldn't. He reached down with one shaky hand and pulled his machete free from his belt. Holding the weapon in an extremely precarious, awkward grip, he swung down at Mora, praying to hit anything. He didn't. He adjusted his grip on the handle and swung down at him again, more deliberately this time. Mora released his grip on Cyrus's ankle and swiped out with his hand, grasping onto the rusted, dulled blade. He jerked the machete forcefully and it slipped straight out of Cyrus's hand. Mora flung the weapon out into the open air to their left and reached up for Cyrus's ankle again. Not this time, thought Cyrus. He had started up the ladder again with renewed vigor and was nearly at the top. Five feet away. Two feet. He gripped the upper lip of the squared hole in the ceiling and began to pull himself through it. He was vaguely aware of a group of guards standing back from the trapdoor, watching his ascent, evidently not having been given orders to attack.

Cyrus pulled his torso into the room above followed quickly by his legs, but Mora was right on his tail. He scrambled to move himself from Mora's reach, but Mora was already halfway through the trapdoor, pulling himself with his arms. He reached into his belt and unsheathed his machete. Cyrus hastily tried to retract his legs but Mora was faster. He lunged his upper body forward, sacrificing his footing on the ladder and stabbed his machete down into Cyrus's calf. Cyrus screamed. The white-hot pain coursed through his entire leg and travelled up his spine. He had never felt pain so intense. And the blade was still buried in his leg, twisting horribly under Mora's weight, who was using it as a handle to support his dangling legs still hanging out the trap door.

Mora looked straight into Cyrus's eyes, an animalistic rage burning behind them; and he was smirking. His lips were curving around the edges into a gloating smile, and he gave the handle of the blade a forceful twist. Cyrus howled in pain again and Mora moved to grab his other leg with his free hand. Cyrus wrenched his good leg away before Mora could grip it and kicked out at him. It had little effect and Mora reached out again. Cyrus retracted his leg again and kicked out hard. This time his boot heel connected powerfully with Mora's jaw. The impact forced Mora to release his hold on the machete handle and fall backwards. His body fell through the opening in the floor and he reached out to grasp the top rungs of the ladder to stop himself. His hand reached out and his fingers, centimeters away from the metal rung, closed around thin air. Cyrus could see the look on Mora's face change instantly, as though it were in slow motion. The ever-present grin on his face was replaced by a look of total incomprehension. He was free-falling, and for the first time since they had met him, he looked terrified. His eyes widened and his mouth opened in a scream of panic. His arms and legs were in a constant, frenzied motion, grasping out desperately at nothingness. He fell past Nel on the ladder, still looking up at Cyrus with an expression of utter disbelief. Cyrus watched as he grew smaller and smaller until, at long last, with a sickening, crunching splat, King Mora smacked into the stone floor far below and all of his flailing limbs came to an instant, permanent stop.

The enormous room was silent. Even from this high up, Cyrus could see blood beginning to pool around Mora's body, which was twisted and broken; his arms and legs splayed out beneath him at odd angles. Cyrus didn't know what to do. He just continued to stare dimly through the opening in the floor. Everything felt very surreal. Had he really just killed someone?

Nel, still twenty feet down on the ladder, looked up at Cyrus and gave a disbelieving smile. "Hell yeah, Doc," she called encouragingly. She clearly didn't think he had it in him. Neither did he, for that matter. He hadn't meant to kill him, not really. He had been prepared that Mora might have to die, in fact Alec had seemed insistent on it, but he had thought it would be different... cleaner somehow. This had been so sudden, so brutal. And he certainly hadn't expected that he would do it himself.

Far below, Alec walked over to the King's lifeless body and bent over it, as though checking for a pulse or something. Cyrus dimly realized how absurd that was given the look of the body, but his mind felt too hazy at the moment to question it.

"You okay, Doc?" Nel called up to him. To Cyrus's surprise, her concern actually seemed genuine. He nodded his head, but in truth he felt a bit queasy. "C'mon Doc, come on down."

Cyrus was mildly alarmed by a noise to his right, and he lifted his head to see four guards approaching the trapdoor slowly and glancing through it to their king's ruined body below. They didn't say a word. They hardly reacted at all, in fact. One of the guards finally turned his attention to Cyrus's injured leg, still with the machete buried in the calf. Cyrus had thoroughly forgotten about it, which was incredible because now that he remembered it, searing, unbearable pain coursed back through his body. The guard knelt on the ground beside Cyrus and one of the other guards cut a large strip of his own cloak off and handed it to the first.

"This is going to hurt," the guard said to Cyrus, looking him straight in the eyes. He then grasped the machete handle and wrenched it free of Cyrus's leg. The wound instantly began bleeding freely and Cyrus looked away, his stomach lurching uncomfortably. The guard began bandaging the wound with the strip of cloth and cinched it tightly. "You're going to have a hard time making it back down there," the guard warned Cyrus, "best take it slow."

Cyrus didn't have a choice; it was a slow process getting back down the ladder. With every step on his injured leg, he felt like he might pass out. But with the help of Nel below and the guards above, Cyrus found himself on the ground level of the cavernous room once again. He glanced uncomfortably down at Mora's motionless body and was slightly horrified to see his eyes still open, staring blankly up at the ceiling high above. He still wore an expression of shock and confusion.

The guards eased Cyrus to the floor where he prodded gently at his wounded leg. Nel rushed over to Jack, still lying face-down where he had fallen. She flipped him over and started checking his body for wounds.

"He's still breathing," Nel announced. "I can't find any injuries; I think it may have been that powder."

"If that's the case, it will wear off," one of the guards said, reaching down and lifting the small, now empty pouch from the floor and turning it over in his hands.

"Tytus, look at this," one of the other guards said, looking down at the body of the man Nel had stabbed. They apparently knew him well because they all bowed their heads in sorrow. The guard named Tytus knelt down and gently closed the man's eyes with his hand.

"So what does this mean?" Alec questioned, speaking up for the first time since Mora had fallen. Alec was acting strangely. He had not come to check on Cyrus once he was down from the ladder and he had not rushed to see if Jack was okay. It was Nel caring for the team.

The guards straightened up and one of them said, "The Kingdom is yours." Except he wasn't talking to Alec. He was looking straight into Cyrus's eyes when he said it.

Cyrus looked around thinking maybe the guard meant the group as a whole, but there was no question. His unwavering stare made it clear he was addressing only Cyrus.

Nel chuckled and shook her head. "This place…" she muttered in amusement, but Alec was looking at him with an intensity that was difficult to read.

Cyrus shook his head. "I don't want the Kingdom."

"But it's yours," another guard insisted.

"Look, however your people want to handle the king's replacement is fine," Cyrus began, "but I'm not… I don't want…"

"Well at least try the food before sending it back," Nel said. "Look, Doc," she leaned in close to Cyrus and put her hand on his shoulder, "I know we're not planning to stay here, but if we rule, it will make it that much easier to find our way out of this place."

Even with Nel leaning in close, the guards were definitely still able to hear the conversation. To Cyrus, it felt wrong to announce himself as the leader of these people only to leave them when the opportunity presented itself. They had lived under the merciless rule of King Mora for years, they deserved better than someone who would abandon them. But he could see Nel's point as well. His number one priority had to be getting back to Cynthia. Cyrus just nodded noncommittally. Alec was standing within earshot as well, listening to the conversation silently, but his eyes were not on their faces; he was staring at Nel's hand on Cyrus's shoulder.

Cyrus needed guidance, now more than ever. If he were being honest with himself, he no longer trusted the judgement of Nel or Alec. He had not allowed himself to admit that until now, but his brother had become unpredictable, and he did not like the way he was watching him now. Alec was running entirely on emotions since they came to this place, and it was making him reckless. It was his actions that had led Nel to being captured in the first place, and eventually led them here.

With a sinking feeling, he realized that Alec had gotten exactly what he wanted from the beginning.

"I need to talk to Ydoro," Cyrus finally announced. Ydoro had lived here a long time, he could guide Cyrus on what to do now that Mora was dead.

"He... he was with us," Alec said shakily, "but I'm not sure he made it."

"What happened to him?" one of the guards asked in alarm.

"When Mora sprung on us upstairs..." Alec began, but the guards immediately jumped into action.

"We'll find him," one of the guards called over his shoulder, already racing off towards the staircases through the next room, one of the other guards on his heels. "Tellas, you go to town and get the doctor for him," he shouted to the remaining guard, referring to Cyrus's injured leg. And then they were gone.

Alec, Nel, and Cyrus were left in the giant room on their own, aside from Jack's unconscious form on the ground next to them.

Nel wasted no time pressing Cyrus further now that they were alone. "Look, Doc, we have an opportunity here, that's all I'm saying. If we allow another ruler to take over, there's no guarantee they will be sympathetic to our cause. There's someone in the dungeons you'll want to meet, he's an old historian, from our world, and I think he spent a lot of his time here looking for a way back."

"There's someone from our world locked in the dungeons?" Cyrus asked.

"Think about it," Nel continued, "if you rule here, we're in charge. Everything is open to us. We can question the man in the dungeons, we can question anyone we want. Someone has to know how to escape this place."

Alec, who was still standing several feet away from them, said, "Are you sure you're ready to lead again? I thought you were done with that after getting us here?"

Cyrus blinked and shook his head in surprise.

"Alec," Nel chastised, the way she would to a child who had said something inappropriate, "you're not seeing the big picture here. It's not about leading, it's not about ruling, it's about us taking charge. If Cyrus is king, we have power. If someone else is king, then we have nothing."

Alec clearly did not like being told off in this way, but it seemed his newfound boldness did not yet extend to Nel. He remained silent until footsteps finally announced the return of the guards, and to Cyrus's relief, they were supporting a groggy but conscious Ydoro between them. Ydoro smiled weakly at them, a bandage wrapped tightly around his head with blood seeping through it.

"I have to apologize," Ydoro said as they approached, "I ended up being no help at all."

Cyrus got unsteadily to his feet and limped towards Ydoro. "From what I hear it sounds like you got us in here," Cyrus said, putting a reassuring hand on his shoulder, "you've proven yourself, my friend, how are you feeling?"

"He's a traitor!" Nel called out, "stay away from him, Doc."

She was approaching swiftly and Cyrus saw her hand reach down for the machete hanging from her belt. He put out his hands to try to intercept her, but he was unsteady from his throbbing leg and she easily brushed past him.

"Nelida," Ydoro began quickly, "I know you saw me with Mora that night, I couldn't... there was nothing..."

Nel raised her blade towards him but the two flanking guards both unsheathed their own blades and thrust them out in front of Ydoro, protecting him from harm.

Nel balked at them but stopped her advance. "What the hell do you think you're doing?" she demanded, "we just overthrew your king, according to your laws..."

"*He* defeated King Mora," one of the guards interrupted, pointing his machete towards Cyrus, "that doesn't make you anything. And Ydoro is under the protection of the people of this Kingdom. Unless I hear a direct order from the ruling king telling me otherwise, he will not be harmed."

Nel looked at Cyrus in exasperation and cocked her head towards Ydoro questioningly. "Well, *King Dorn*?"

Cyrus's head was beginning to spin. "No, leave him be," he finally said.

Nel threw her blade to the floor at Cyrus's feet. "This man was there the night Mora caught me," she insisted venomously. "He's not one of us, don't make that mistake, Doc."

"I had been summoned here by the King," Ydoro defended himself from between the guards, "He questioned me about all of you, I had to keep my act going. That's the only way I've survived here…"

"I know how you've survived here!" Nel yelled back, "by throwing everyone else to the wolves!"

"Nel, stop it!" Cyrus said forcefully.

"All of you stop it!" yelled a voice from the other side of the room.

Everyone turned to see two men approaching from the main entrance. One was the guard, Tellas, who had run into town, and the other was a massive, jowly older man with a pink face and a hobbling limp. He was carrying a leather bag in one hand and a carved walking stick in the other; shaking his head fervently as he approached.

"What the hell is this?" he called out. "Sit yourself down, all of you. On the floor. Right now!"

Cyrus had no idea what to make of the man. "I… I was just named king…" he began rather lamely, attempting to assert his apparent new authority.

"Good for you!" The enormous man barked, the fat on his neck swaying as he spoke, "*My King*, want to lose that leg?! Sit your ass down, now."

Cyrus did not know whether he was amused by this man or intimidated by him. He turned to Ydoro questioningly but saw that Ydoro had already sat on the floor in compliance.

"Down, down down," the large man commanded, finally reaching them and jabbing a stubby finger towards the floor. "C'mon, off that leg, right now."

Nel and Alec were both staring at the man, not knowing what to make of him. Cyrus finally lowered himself to the ground, easing his injured leg out in front of him.

"Yep, that's a mess," the man confirmed, looking down at his bleeding leg, "But I'm gonna have a look at Ydoro and your unconscious friend first."

The man knelt down beside Ydoro with a great wheeze and started unbandaging his head. "So you killed King Mora, huh?" The man asked matter-of-factly, apparently addressing Cyrus even though his eyes were scanning Ydoro's injured head. "Good! The man was deranged. Totally unfit to rule." His fingers were running along a gash in Ydoro's forehead. "So how 'bout you? Are you fit to rule?"

Cyrus had no idea how to respond. "Well I'm not deranged I don't think."

"Well that's a start," the man said gruffly. "I'm Dr. Garse. And if you keep fighting like this, we're going to be seeing a lot of each other."

"I... I don't plan to keep fighting," Cyrus responded. He felt like he was being scolded by the school nurse for fighting on the playground.

"Ydoro, you're on bedrest," Dr. Garse announced. "No excuses," he continued, stopping Ydoro who looked like he was about to argue. "You've had a serious head injury, this new king is gonna need you. You want to be useful? Then you rest. Starting now."

Dr. Garse heaved himself from the floor and lumbered his way over to Jack, who was still unconscious in the center of the room. He bent low and started examining him.

"Hmm, Powdered Dreamwood?" Dr. Garse muttered. It didn't seem he was asking anyone in particular. "Yeah this young man'll have a hell of a headache when he wakes, but he'll be okay. Get him to a bed."

Dr. Garse straightened himself up and started back towards Cyrus. "What the hell are you still doing here, Ydoro?" he suddenly demanded. "I told you, bedrest, now."

One of the guards helped Ydoro to his feet and started to guide him further into the Temple. "I'll be in the northern wing if you need me," Ydoro called to Cyrus over his shoulder as he was led away.

"Interesting man," Dr. Garse said as he knelt down beside Cyrus and began to unravel the piece of cloak around his leg. "He's well respected around here. Complete shit in a fight, apparently, but that's okay." Dr.

Garse laughed at his own joke and opened his bag, spilling medical supplies out onto the ground with a clatter.

"You're from the real world?" Cyrus asked as he saw the supplies strewn about the floor, which looked to be military first-aid equipment.

"You're *in* the real world," Dr. Garse grunted. "If you mean I'm from your world, no I'm not. My father was, near as I can tell."

"Near as you can tell?" Cyrus questioned. He winced as Dr. Garse rubbed some gritty substance on his wound.

"Near as I can tell," Dr. Garse repeated. "He used to talk about another world, back when I was a boy. Didn't sound much like your world though, if you ask me."

"Yeah, it's changed a lot in the last few decades," Cyrus agreed, "war will do that."

The doctor grunted in response and poured some sort of liquid over Cyrus's open wound, which reacted with the gritty substance and began foaming extremely painfully.

Cyrus bit his lip and clenched his fists tightly against the pain. "So your dad," Cyrus began again, trying to ignore the sizzling noises coming from his wound, "if he wasn't from around here, didn't he try to find a way back to where he came from?"

Dr. Garse shrugged and answered, "He had nothing to go back to. He was poor back home, no family, some medical skill, but that's about it. Here, he was an important man. Would you go back?"

"I have a wife," Cyrus responded darkly. He was beginning to notice a change in himself when he would think about Cynthia, waiting for him back home. Where he used to draw comfort and hope thinking about her and imagining their reunion, now he felt hopelessness and loss. It seemed more and more likely with each passing day that they would never find a way back to their world. No one ever had before, and people had spent their lives trying.

"You want some advice?" Dr. Garse asked, now wrapping a clean bandage around Cyrus's leg, which had stopped sizzling and was much less painful now, but felt strangely stiff, as though his skin was wrapped too tightly around the bone. "Well I'm giving you some anyways," Dr. Garse continued when Cyrus didn't respond. "Don't waste your life looking for an escape. Embrace where you are, make a future for yourself here." He then laughed as he finished wrapping the bandage and said, "Hell, your future is wide open, you can make anything you want of your life now. When was the last time you could say that?"

**CHAPTER TWENTY-FIVE**

# ORIGINS OF A MONSTER

Dr. Garse left shortly after, leaving Cyrus with instructions about cleaning his wound and directions to his home in town should he need anything else. Cyrus did not know how to feel about Dr. Garse but Alec seemed to like him a lot.

"He just tells it like it is," Alec insisted. "Yeah he's a bit gruff, but I like the points he was making."

"It sounded to me like his advice was to give up," Cyrus responded, using Nel as a crutch to stand himself up.

Cyrus was still finding it hard to believe what had transpired in the last hour. The plan to storm the Temple had seemed so incredibly foolish to him. He had only gone along with it to appease Alec, who was barely speaking to him at the time. Truth be told, it was miraculous that they had survived the assault on the King, much less come out victorious. Now Cyrus found himself in a strange position; where the guards, and presumably the entire Kingdom, now viewed him as their king. He did not want that. He had always been an outgoing personality, and people did tend to follow him because of his gregarious nature, but the journey that had led them to this world had left him shaken. How could he be a leader of a Kingdom if he could not even keep his own team of six safe?

Cyrus had instructed the guards, who had been staring at him expectantly, to move Jack up to one of the empty rooms and watch over him until he awoke. He wanted to rest himself and get off his throbbing leg, but Nel and Alec insisted he should meet the prisoner Henry first. Cyrus was intrigued to hear from a historian. Who else could offer such perspective into this alien world. He was shown the keys to the cells by one of the guards and hobbled down the winding stone staircase behind Alec and Nel. As they arrived in the dimly lit corridor with cell bars lining one side, the first thing he noticed was the scratching and snarled breathing coming from the closed door on the far side.

He turned to Alec and asked, "Is that…?"

"The Neodactyls," Alec confirmed with a nod. "Both of them. The plan actually worked."

Cyrus looked apprehensively at the wooden door, trying to convince himself of its strength. Nel and Alec walked halfway down the corridor and peered through the bars of one of the cells.

"Did I promise I'd be back for you or what?" Nel said with a smile.

A raspy, soft voice from inside the cell answered, "I can't believe it. So does this mean… is he really gone?"

As Nel confirmed that King Mora was truly dead, Cyrus limped forwards and looked into the dark cell to find a frail-looking, elderly man smiling at them.

"You ready to get out of there?" Alec asked the beaming man.

"I haven't seen the outside of this cell in over a decade," Henry said, shaking his head. "I won't even know what to do with myself."

"A man of your talents, we'll keep you busy," Nel said, and she held out her hand for Cyrus to give her the keys.

Cyrus handed them over and asked, "I hear you're a historian?"

"That's right," said the old man as the lock scraped open with a metal crunch.

The door swung ajar and Henry hobbled his way out into the corridor. "My research is down there," he said, pointing to the door at the end of the hall. "We'll have to get the room's current occupants out first of course," he joked as an echoing snarl bounced off the walls from behind the door.

"How long will it take them to starve?" Cyrus asked, thinking it would be far easier to let them die while locked away rather than attempting to kill them.

"Let them starve?" Alec asked in shock. "Hang on now, those creatures have been loyal to every king, that's what Ydoro said. So why not us?"

Cyrus gave a humorless laugh. "I'm not letting them free to find out. That never made much sense, anyways. How would an animal know who was currently ruling?"

"There's only one way to find out," Alec said with a shrug.

"Tell me you're not being serious," Nel said, looking sideways at Cyrus in concern.

"Why not?" Alec responded. "Ydoro told us they've always shared a bond with the ruling king. That's us now… sorry, that's *you* now," he corrected himself, nodding towards Cyrus.

"He's right," Henry chimed in, "they won't hurt you." He patted Alec on the back in support.

"We're not talking about this," Cyrus announced. "If I'm king, their supposed loyalty is to me. And I say we let them starve in there." He had not wanted to assert his authority over Alec, especially given how fragile their relationship had been recently, but someone had to be the voice of reason here. What Alec was suggesting was suicide. To his relief, Nel agreed.

"Alec, don't be a fool," Nel insisted. "Your brother's right, what the hell are you thinking?"

Alec looked at her with an expression of utter betrayal on his face. He shook his head as though he could not believe that she was not supporting him. He looked like he was thinking for a moment before he suddenly announced, "I'll show you."

Alec turned and strode towards the latched door. Nel yelled his name and reached out for him but Alec shoved her hand aside harshly. The narrow corridor suddenly erupted in shouting from Cyrus and Nel, but Alec ignored them, reaching the door and extending his hand towards the handle.

Cyrus began to rush towards Alec to stop him but he was already unlatching the door. He looked around wildly in panic, first positioning himself behind Henry, who had not moved, then rushing into Henry's open cell with Nel scrambling in behind him. Nel gripped the bars of the cell door, ready to slam it shut as soon as the creatures appeared. Cyrus craned his neck to see down the corridor as Alec opened the wooden door slowly.

The snarling and scraping noises stopped instantly. Cyrus couldn't see into the room, but the animals had not launched themselves at Alec as he had expected. There was quiet in the corridor aside from a faint hissing coming from beyond the open door. At long last, Cyrus could make out movement in the dark room and two shapes approached the hallway. Alec took several slow steps backwards and the two Neodactyls finally stalked into view. Their enormous yellow eyes were scanning the cell block like hunting predators, but they made no move to attack. Alec was breathing heavily and standing very rigid. Henry was still motionless in the center of the corridor, but the creatures were beginning to take notice of him. Their quills along their backs began to stand on end and their long necks began to recoil threateningly. Ever so slowly, Alec started to raise his hand towards the nearest Neodactyl. Cyrus winced as he helplessly watched. Alec slowly extended his fingers out and the very tips gently brushed against the colored plumage of the animal. It's back twitched in response but it did not move. Alec cautiously ran his fingers along the creature's neck feathers up to the back of the head. He stopped as his hand gently rested against the back of its skull. It hissed gently and cocked its head. Then, to Cyrus's amazement, the bristling feathers along the animal's back went down, its neck relaxed a bit, and its stance eased into a far less threatening position. Both Neodactyls took their eyes off Henry down the hallway and looked at Alec. They weren't looking at him like a predator would; they were docile.

Cyrus was shaking from head to toe. This was impossible. How could an animal possibly know that they had taken Mora's place? Nel slowly opened the door to the cell and cautiously walked into the firelit corridor, Cyrus following behind her. Both Neodactyls snarled in alarm at their appearance and moved forward threateningly. Cyrus approached them, still shaking uncontrollably, and extended a hand towards them, the way he would to a dog he was unsure about. The nearest Neodactyl's eyes widened menacingly, and it snapped out at him, narrowly missing his outstretched fingers. Cyrus recoiled in alarm and Alec put another calming hand on the back of its head. It relaxed again, but did not take its yellow eyes off Cyrus.

Cyrus backed up a few steps and said to Henry, "I don't understand. Why is it just him?"

Henry smiled and answered, "They always follow the king, and no one else."

"But... that's me," Cyrus replied, "I mean, not that I..." He trailed off. It seemed so trivial arguing about who the true king of this fake Kingdom was.

"It's true," Nel confirmed, "Cyrus killed Mora."

"Did he?" Henry looked surprised. "I don't know how that can be."

Cyrus looked at Alec, who was again looking at his brother with a strange expression on his face. Perhaps this was a good thing. Alec was clearly unhappy at the prospect of Cyrus ruling, and Cyrus did not want any part of it. It was all for show anyways, wasn't it? They had no intention of staying, they just needed to leverage their power to get back home.

"So what does this mean?" Nel asked, still keeping her distance from the Neodactyls.

Cyrus smiled to Alec and responded, "It must mean we were meant to co-rule."

Alec thought a moment, then smiled broadly. He nodded at Cyrus and said, "I can do that."

Alec's attitude improved significantly after that. Nel stayed mostly quiet for the remainder of the conversation. She seemed bothered by the entire situation, and toward Alec in particular. It was hard to blame her, Alec was proving to be increasingly reckless. In this instance, it had worked out for him, but things could have gone horribly different. Everyone was still keeping their distance from the Neodactyls except Alec, who seemed more and more at ease with them. It appeared the creatures had bonded with him instantly, though Cyrus could not understand why. Perhaps it was because they encountered Alec first. It must have been some sort of imprinting, the way birds imprint on the first creature they see when they are born. What Cyrus could not make sense of, however, was how they knew that Mora had died. Cyrus was finding it dizzying just thinking about it, and the pulsating pain in his leg wasn't helping.

Cyrus questioned Nel further about the mysterious powder that she had tried to use on King Mora, and that ended up being used on Jack. She explained that Henry had told her about it, and she had found it in the king's quarters. Everyone agreed that the king's quarters were worth further exploration, so they made their way up the many winding staircases, with Henry leading the way. Cyrus was finding all the stairs painfully difficult with his injured leg, however considering the severity of the wound, it was incredible he could even walk. Whatever Dr. Garse had put on his leg seemed to work well.

When the group arrived on the upper levels of the Temple, the Neodactyls split off and entered a room next to the king's quarters. They must have been trained to stay in there because a glance inside looked similar to a zoo habitat. Cyrus, Nel, Alec, and Henry continued down the hall and entered the king's quarters, a raised room with curving windows along the far wall, several smaller rooms, including a bedroom, off to the left, and a strange glowing altar in the corner with the king's scepters standing upright forming an X.

Cyrus began to limp further into the room but caught Nel's eye, who was looking at him with a funny expression.

"What is it?" Cyrus asked.

"You've never been in here before, right?" Nel asked softly.

It was a strange question, and something in her eyes made it clear she had a reason for asking that she wasn't sharing. "Of course not," Cyrus answered. "How would I have?"

Nel shook her head dismissively. "No reason, forget it." She strolled off towards one of the adjoining rooms before Cyrus could question her further.

Alec had made his way to the crossed scepters and the glowing embers below them, which proved to be frozen fire upon closer inspection. Alec lifted one out of the fire, which gave off a swirl of ash, and held it close, studying the strange weapon.

"I suppose you're splitting those up too?" Henry asked. He almost had a tone of disapproval in his voice.

Alec looked to Cyrus, then nodded and pressed the scepter out into his chest. "One for each king," he said, puffing out his chest in importance.

Cyrus took the scepter, which was far heavier than he had expected. He brought it close to his face, inspecting the material. It looked like ancient wood that had been burnt in a forest fire. But it wasn't wood. It had a stronger feel to it, even though the entire surface was cracked in a spider-web pattern, the way bark would sear off a tree. And while the twisted knot at the top appeared charred and blackened, a ruby-red glow inside, visible only in the deepest cracks of the crust, gave the weapon an unnatural feel. Indeed, Cyrus was confident this was an entirely foreign material he was holding.

"I'm not sure why we will need these," Cyrus confessed, leaning it against the wall.

"You'll want them," Henry insisted. "The people will more readily respond to you as their leader if you have them. These scepters have been carried by the king going back generations."

Cyrus nodded but continued exploring the perimeter of the room, leaving the scepter leaned against the wall. Alec stayed by the frozen fire altar, swinging his own scepter back and forth through the air as though fighting off imaginary foes. Cyrus walked through the door to the adjoining room Nel had gone through, which seemed to be a storage area. There were strange objects and trinkets covering the shelves along the walls, along with folded pieces of cloth, clothing, and weapons. Nel was examining some papers closely and Cyrus began to poke around a pile of dulled knives.

"Hey Doc," Nel said. Cyrus glanced in her direction and saw her eyes had not left the paper she was holding. She finally looked up at him and said, "You may wanna take a look at this."

Cyrus approached apprehensively and took the paper from her, which turned out to be a photograph. It had yellowed a bit with age and was beginning to curl around the edges, but the photo showed a group of about twenty American soldiers from the Great War. They were all clean cut and very young, staggered at various heights with the soldiers in the foreground kneeling in the dirt. They each held a rifle planted along their side and wore expressions of square-jawed defiance. Even as he scanned the young, fresh faces of the soldiers, he knew what he was going to find. And sure enough, kneeling in the very front row was a youthful, clean-shaven King Mora, dressed in a crisp uniform and showing the slightest hint of a smile. He looked far younger and far less wild, but there was no mistaking him.

"And there's this," Nel said quietly, handing Cyrus an old letter, sticking partway out of a worn-out envelope. Cyrus pulled the letter out and quickly scanned the loopy scrawl. It was a letter from a loved one, a wife it sounded like, whose husband was off fighting in the war. It was signed *Eleanor* at the bottom, and at the top it was addressed to *Jackson*. Cyrus turned the envelope over in his hand. The front was addressed to *Jackson Morany.*

Cyrus nodded his head in understanding. This answered several burning questions about King Mora, but for some reason it left Cyrus with sadness. Mora had been from their world after all, and a soldier in the war as it turned out. How had he ended up out here? What ever happened to Eleanor? He was loved at one point, at least by one person. Mora was a monster, there was no denying it, but he wasn't always. Something had changed him, made him the way he was; perhaps this place. He hadn't belonged here any more than they did.

Alec and Henry finally made their way into the room and began craning their necks to see what Cyrus was looking at. Cyrus handed the letter and photograph to Alec without a word and walked back out to the main living area. He could hear Alec reacting to the revelation and begin discussing with Nel in excitable tones, but Cyrus stopped listening. He stood by the great windows looking out over the sprawling Kingdom, bathed in golden sunlight as they approached midday. Why was this bothering him so much? Perhaps there were just too many parallels between Mora... *Jackson Morany*... and himself.

Nel walked out into the main living area, followed closely by Alec, still talking excitedly.

"Yeah, whatever you say, Alec," Nel replied in audible annoyance to whatever Alec was telling her.

"What is it?" Alec asked in confusion. He reached out for her wrist and turned her to face him. "What did I do?"

"What the hell was that stunt with those birds?" Nel demanded. "Are you totally out of your mind? You could have gotten us all killed."

"I didn't though," Alec insisted. "I knew that would work."

"No, you didn't," Nel shot back. "You had no idea what would happen, but you didn't care. You put all of us at risk."

Alec reached a hand up and brushed his thumb against her cheek in a confident show of affection. "I would never let anything happen to you."

Nel shoved his hand away in agitation.

"I came here to rescue you!" Alec barked in surprise.

Nel shook her head and yelled back, and soon the two were arguing back and forth in the middle of the king's chambers. Cyrus looked awkwardly at Henry, who was pretending not to notice the ensuing fight. Cyrus turned and let himself out of the room with Henry quietly following him. Alec and Nel's voices were still echoing off the walls as they turned down a side corridor and found a series of bedrooms that seemed unused. Jack was lying in the bed of one of them, still unconscious from the powder.

"Will he be waking up soon?" Cyrus asked Henry quietly. He was beginning to worry how permanent the damage would be.

"Soon," Henry confirmed. "Trust me, I've seen the effects before. Your friend will be fine."

Cyrus nodded, hoping he was right. "I suppose we have a lot to learn about this world. How this place works."

"You will," Henry assured him. "It's your Kingdom now, your people."

Cyrus looked at Henry. He was a small man. Maybe not always, but time had twisted and shrunken his body into the frail, weakened person he was now. He had wisps of practically translucent white hair that revealed much of the papery-thin scalp beneath, and a splotchy brown birthmark on one side of his forehead. He looked kind, but sad. Of course it was no mystery why, he had long lost any possibility of seeing his family again.

"You've been here a long time," Cyrus said. "I don't mean to bring up the pain of your past, but you must have tried to leave this place. When you first arrived here at least?"

"Of course," Henry said, nodding his head. "Although I'll be honest, when I first found this place, I wasn't desperate to leave. This was what I lived for; finding something, a part of history that had not yet been discovered. And here was an entire place that seemed apart from our own world. It was exhilarating, to be frank. It was a long time before it dawned on me that I may never see my family again. I had been working in Egypt for some time, so I was used to being apart from them." Henry trailed off a bit. "I suppose it never occurred to me that I was stuck here until it was too late."

"I can understand that," Cyrus said softly. "When I first heard about the anomaly, out there on the ocean, the possibilities running through my head were endless... but the possibility that something bad could actually happen to us never honestly crossed my mind. What is that? Is that vanity? Or just being a piss poor leader maybe."

Henry shrugged. "It's just being young I think. Young and headstrong in the face of discovery. That's no sin."

Cyrus laughed hollowly. "I'm not that young."

Henry smiled, the paper-thin skin wrinkling around his eyes. "It depends on the point of view I suppose."

## CHAPTER TWENTY-SIX

# THE PERILS OF PASSION

Alec took several long, deep breaths... then he struck the stone wall in frustration. Nel had stormed out on him a few minutes earlier, accusing him of being rash and endangering the lives of the team. If one of them had been hurt then she would have a point, but considering everything had gone exactly as he had hoped it would, she didn't have a leg to stand on. Alec wasn't the impulsive one anyways, that was Cyrus. Cyrus had always been headstrong, Alec was far more level-headed. Besides, hadn't it been Cyrus who had led them here in the first place? Nel's anger was clearly misplaced, but she was so stubborn Alec hadn't been able to calm her down.

Alec turned away from the enormous windows overlooking the Kingdom and looked down at the glowing 'embers' of frozen fire beneath the one remaining scepter standing upright in its base. Cyrus had left his own scepter leaning forgotten against the wall. Alec shook his head. It baffled him that his brother so casually set aside power of this magnitude. It was not just physical power that they had seized, although the scepters certainly offered that. They had also seized real power over this land and its people by overthrowing Mora. It was intoxicating, and it was making Alec feel invincible. Nel, however, was dampening his spirits. Alec had known what he was doing when he released the Neodactyls. He knew they wouldn't harm them. But how could he explain that to Nel?

"Knock knock," came a voice from the door.

Alec looked up to see his brother, looking as impressive as ever despite his injured leg and scarred face. Even beaten down and wounded, Cyrus somehow pulled off the rugged look. It bothered Alec.

"How'd it go with Nel?" Cyrus asked, limping his way into the room.

"Not well," Alec mumbled, turning away from him.

"You wanna talk about it?" Cyrus asked.

"That's not really what we do," Alec responded. He and his brother used to discuss women in their respective lives, but that was before Cynthia.

"It could be," Cyrus said with a shrug. "Don't worry, give her time and I'm sure she'll come around."

Alec wasn't sure if he found Cyrus's advice condescending or not, but before he could stop himself, he had started venting. "Why do I have to explain myself to her? Everyone's fine, I knew we would be. And now we have power, real power in this place. How can she have a problem with that?"

"Why do you care so much what she thinks of you?" Cyrus asked.

Alec glanced up at his brother, weighing how he wanted to respond. With a shrug, Alec finally said, "I don't know, she's… interesting."

Cyrus smiled and nodded his head. "Nel is a *lot* of personality for you."

"Well I'm not saying that," Alec quickly backtracked. "She's just someone I thought was on my side."

"She is," Cyrus replied. "Trust me, you two have developed a bond that none of us share with her. It's great."

Alec smiled in spite of his lingering doubt. He did have a bond with Nel.

"Not to mention you just stormed this Temple to save her," Cyrus continued. "If you do like her…"

"She's hard to read," Alec admitted. "Sometimes I think she could be interested in me, but other times… and now she's mad about me releasing the Neodactyls… I don't know."

225

"Yeah that wouldn't have been my first choice," Cyrus agreed, nodding. "It's hard to blame her for being upset. If that hadn't worked, none of us would be here right now."

"I knew it would work though," Alec insisted, "you wouldn't understand. I just knew it would work."

Cyrus shrugged. "I'm glad it did. Look, give her some time to cool off. You're still her closest ally out here."

Alec smiled again and said, "So you really think she'd go for me?"

Cyrus laughed and nodded his head. "I really do. And hell, it's not like she has a ton of choices around here."

Alec laughed too. "I may have some trouble finding a good spot for a first date."

"Hey, at least you've got plenty of scenic beauty," Cyrus responded. "Ya know, when Cynthia and I went out for the first time..."

"Don't do that," Alec interrupted him, the smile suddenly leaving his face.

"No, I was just saying..." Cyrus began again.

"I know, and I'm telling you, don't," Alec repeated. He absolutely refused to have a discussion about how Cyrus and Cynthia first started going out.

"Alec, it's been the better part of a decade..." Cyrus said.

"And you still don't get it," Alec snapped back hotly. He turned back to the window and continued, "Just let me be, alright?" His eyes fell on the forgotten scepter leaning against the wall. He snatched it up and turned to Cyrus again. "And take this damn thing with you. It's the weapon of a king, don't just leave it lying around."

Cyrus took the blackened staff and silently left the room.

Alec shook his head once he was alone again. Cyrus never had much sense when it came to others. For a moment they seemed to be having a healthy conversation. Now he was fighting with two people on his team.

Alec sunk to the floor in front of the altar with the remaining scepter stuck in place. He leaned against the cushioned bench partially surrounding the area and stared into the frozen fire, shimmering and dancing warmly. He reached out his hand and felt heat coming off of it. According to Ydoro, the minerals in the sand only glowed brightly and became hot when they were near the scepters. Some sort of chemical reaction apparently. This really was a different world.

Alec closed his eyes and leaned his head back. He rubbed his temples. A headache was beginning to set behind his eyes. He had slept very little out in the forest last night, perhaps that's what he needed to clear his head.

"You okay?" asked a woman's voice as he heard approaching footsteps.

Just what he needed, another fight with Nel.

Alec, continuing to rub the temples around his closed eyes, said, "Look, I'm not in the mood, okay?"

"Okay, that's fine," Nel responded. She sounded much calmer than before, much more supportive.

"I'm just going to get some sleep," Alec said. "We can talk more later."

Alec's heart caught in his chest as he felt her hand come to rest on his thigh. She ran her hand along his leg in an entirely too familiar way. He kept his eyes closed, not necessarily wanting her to stop. He finally said, "Ya know Nel, I can't quite figure you out."

"Nel?" The voice questioned. "I should hope not."

Alec instantly felt a shiver run up his spine. If this wasn't Nel, then who was this crouched beside him? He slowly opened his eyes, his heart beginning to hammer in his chest. A woman was on the ground next to him, blurry at first as his eyes adjusted. Then she came into focus and he found himself looking into the familiar blue eyes of Cynthia Dorn.

His lip began to quiver. The skin all over his body was tingling and crawling. How was she here?

"Cynthia?" he finally asked in disbelief. She looked the same as ever, albeit a little more dolled up. She had subtle hints of makeup around her eyes and seemed to be wearing lipstick.

Cynthia smiled warmly and responded, "Who else would it be?"

She looked entirely familiar in every way, and her eyes showed genuine kindness and compassion, but Alec felt nothing but terror. She leaned in and kissed him gently on the cheek.

He carefully pushed her hand away from him, shaking all the while. "I... how are you... I don't understand."

Cynthia's smile had now been replaced with a look of concern. Her brow furrowed and she said, "Are you okay? You look like you've seen a ghost."

She reached out to rest a supportive hand on his cheek but Alec flinched as though she had struck him. He had nowhere to move with the bench pressed against his back and he was beginning to feel trapped. He needed air. He recoiled to the side as she reached out for him again and began to crawl clumsily backwards around her.

"Alec, what's wrong?" Cynthia asked, now looking extremely worried.

Alec continued to scoot backwards away from her, shaking his head in confusion.

"Alec?" She reached out her hand again, but this time Alec jumped backwards, slamming his elbow into the hot altar holding the frozen fire and the scepter. The scepter swayed slightly but didn't fall. He glanced at the weapon, considering grabbing it in defense, then looked back to Cynthia. She was gone.

The alcove with the curved bench surrounding the altar was empty. Alec whipped his head from side to side, quickly scanning the rest of the room, but he was alone. He looked back to where she had been crouched just a second before. She had been right there.

"Cynthia?" he said hesitantly.

There was no answer. He slowly reached out his hand and ran it through the air where she had been. He felt nothing. She was totally gone.

Alec was now shaking uncontrollably, and his mind was reeling dizzily. What had just happened? She couldn't be here. And she was acting totally different towards him. Far too affectionate. She was acting the way she used to before she met Cyrus. But she looked like she did now, or rather how she had looked when he last saw her out on those dinghies in the ocean.

A terrible thought occurred to him. What if she had died out there? *Could* he have just seen a ghost? But if that were the case, where did it go?

He realized tears had formed around his eyes. He stood himself up and shook his head forcefully. Maybe he was seeing things. He was working on very little sleep after all. Maybe it had been a hallucination. He stumbled his way into the bedroom and collapsed on the bed. Yes, it had just been a hallucination, he thought to himself. Simply the result of lack of sleep. He shut his eyes and tried to forget what he had seen. Yes, definitely a hallucination.

Suddenly he sat bolt upright as a thought occurred to him. Alec jumped out of bed and practically ran into the storage room. He started frantically searching the shelves, tossing items to the floor as he went. There had to be one here somewhere. There had to be. He tore the room apart until he finally spotted a shiny, silver plate in a corner of the room. It would do. Alec rushed to grab it and held it out in front of his face. He stared into his reflection, looking pale and scared, and turned to see his right cheek. There on his skin, barely noticeable but unmistakable, was a small reddish-pink smudge. He touched it gently with a shaking finger. It was lipstick.

**CHAPTER TWENTY-SEVEN**

# THE LONG ROAD BACK

The fog was unyielding. It passed by his face like dense smoke, curling into white wisps and obscuring everything from view. He squinted his eyes into tiny slits, trying to will himself to see something, anything. What was he searching for? Now that he thought about it, he couldn't seem to remember. And where was he? He started to walk forward but found himself blocked by a white metal bar at waist level. Had that been there before? He reached out and touched it with his hands, it was cool and damp. It was a railing. He was standing on a ship. That certainly explained the fog. But why was he here?

"Jack!" Someone yelled from behind him. He whipped around. There was no one there, at least not close enough to see through the fog. It seemed someone was looking for Jack. Was Jack missing?

"Jack!" He shouted back.

A woman came running out of the fog towards him. He didn't know her, but she looked frantic. To his surprise she ran right up to him and grabbed his shoulders roughly.

"Jack!" She shouted straight at him. "Jack, there you are!"

He looked side to side. Apparently she was talking to him. Did he know this woman? She didn't seem familiar.

"Jack, it's time to go," she said.

"Is it?" He replied. Where were they going?

"Jack!" A gruff voice called from off to his side. He turned to see a large, muscular man approaching him. He looked to be around seventy and in great shape. He was beaming and clapped Jack on the back. "I hope you realize my plans for you. I won't be around forever, this will all be yours."

"Thanks," Jack responded dimly. He didn't know what this man was talking about, or who he was. He turned back towards the woman, but she was gone. How strange.

"So what d'ya say?" The man asked, and he held out his hand to shake.

Jack just smiled mildly and reached out for the man's hand. But the hand turned to smoke. Jack's hand closed around nothing. He looked up into the man's smiling face. He continued to smile even as he dissolved into thin air. Jack was alone once again. Something was not right. He started walking forward.

A bird screeched overhead and Jack looked up. There was nothing but stars, endless stars. How strange, Jack thought. He was certain it had just been daytime. And what had happened to the fog? Laughter broke out behind him and Jack spun around. There were four people all sitting on the deck of the ship, and they were laughing. As he approached, he heard pieces of their conversation.

"That's why we're here. We make our own way," a woman said.

Jack approached slowly. He did not want to interrupt but something was seriously wrong, and he couldn't figure out why he was here.

"We're all players in this story now," one of the people was saying, "and any one of us can change the narrative at any given time."

"Excuse me," Jack interrupted as he came to stand by the group. They all looked his way. Each one of them looked vaguely familiar, but he couldn't place them. "Can you tell me where we are?"

They all smiled at him warmly, almost with a hint of pity in their eyes. "We've lost our way," one of them responded.

"I should never have left the boat," another said, this one wearing glasses and a sad smile. His neck appeared to be covered in blood now.

Jack wanted to help him, but he seemed anchored to the spot. The man just shrugged and said, "I didn't make it."

"Who are you?" Jack finally asked.

"We're you," responded another.

A chill ran up Jack's spine but before he could ask another question he felt the ship shutter violently.

"Is that normal?" Jack asked apprehensively. The ship shook again and Jack fell to his knees. But the ground was soft, sort of like sand. But it glowed with an angry orange hue. It looked hot to the touch, but it wasn't. He looked up but the ship and the smiling group of people were both gone. In their place stood a man, a bizarre looking man in a black cloak. He was facing a woman, who was looking at him with a cold, fierce stare.

"Oh, I'll be coming for you," she said to the cloaked man. She then lowered herself to one knee in a respectful bow.

Jack looked back down at the glowing sand. It reminded him of something. He picked up a few grains of the orange sand and let them run through his fingers. They turned green before his eyes. A sickly green. It gave him a headache just looking at it. It didn't look like sand anymore, either. It was more like a powder. This powder had been important to him. He wasn't sure why, but it reminded him of... something.

Suddenly the powder rose up out of his hand and engulfed his face in a putrid green haze. Jack coughed violently. It burned his eyes and burned his throat. Jack shook his head back and forth trying to clear his mind. It was working. The haze began to clear and he saw a strange man's face pulsate in and out of focus. The man was very old, but did not look kind. He smiled at Jack but it was not a friendly smile. It was the most horrible smile Jack had ever seen. The man's face began to crack along the sides of his cheeks, as though the ever-spreading grin was tearing his fragile skin straight in half.

Jack tried to get away from the man but realized he was lying down. He seemed to be on a bed of some kind. Jack tried to push himself into a sitting position but the man put a hand onto his shoulder to keep him down.

"Woah woah woah, easy there," the man said. Jack looked into the old man's face again but it no longer looked threatening. In fact, the smile was kind, as were his eyes. "You've been through a lot, Jack," the man said soothingly. "You're going to be fine, just take it easy."

"Who are you?" Jack asked.

Another man approached over the old man's shoulder and looked down at Jack with a smile. Jack knew this man. His name was Cyrus.

"Welcome back my friend," Cyrus said. "Do you know where you are?"

Jack looked around wildly but did not recognize anything. He just shook his head.

"It's okay," Cyrus assured him. "We're in the Temple. It's ours now."

Jack's mind was beginning to clear. He thought back to the last thing he remembered. He had been fighting. And something had happened to him.

"Mora!" Jack finally said.

"He's gone," Cyrus said with a hint of a smile. "We have a lot to catch up on."

## CHAPTER TWENTY-EIGHT

# POWER

Nel climbed the stairs two at a time. She was fairly sure she was going in the right direction, but this place was such a maze she couldn't be certain. She had been aimlessly drifting around the Temple, contemplating her argument with Alec when the guard had approached her. She had been apprehensive at first; she still couldn't get used to the idea that the guards were loyal to them now. The guard, however, was only attempting to convey a message; that Jack was awake.

Truth be told she actually welcomed the disruption from her thoughts. She had just been starting to wonder if she had been too hard on Alec, and feelings of regret were something she avoided on principle. She had never been very good at admitting she was wrong, not that she was certain she *had* been wrong. Alec had put them all in danger, there was no doubt about that. However, she had to admit that this new-found courage he seemed to have tapped into was exactly what she had wanted from him. How could she blame him for finally being bold enough to make real decisions? Either way, she had no intention of telling him she was wrong. She had said what she said and that was the end of it. He could choose to get over it or not.

She reached the hallway leading towards the king's quarters. Good, she thought to herself, she was going in the right direction after all. She slowed herself as she proceeded down the hall and turned into the side corridor leading to Jack's room. She wasn't very good at seeing sick or injured people. There was a fragility about them that unsettled her. Perhaps it brought up uncomfortable memories of her mother when she was sick.

Nel peered slowly around the corner into Jack's room. He was alone, sitting in bed studying several papers in his hand. Nel recognized them as the letter and photograph from Mora's quarters.

"Good to have you back," Nel remarked as a way to announce her presence.

Jack looked up at her and smiled weakly. "Seems I missed quite a bit while I was out," he said.

Nel smiled and joked, "Nothing major." She proceeded into the room, still slightly uncomfortable watching Jack gingerly ease himself into an upright position.

"Cyrus filled me in," Jack said. "Mora's death, the Neodactyls… our new kings."

"I know what you're going to say," Nel responded, noting the hesitation in Jack's voice. "I know you don't get along with Cyrus, but Alec…"

"Actually that's not what bothers me," Jack interrupted. "But what are we doing here? We can't rule this place, we need to find a way out."

Nel laughed. "Now you sound like Cyrus." When Jack didn't seem amused, she continued, "Think of it this way, we're in charge now. That means we can scour this world for a way out, unimpeded by anyone. Hell, we make the rules now. We're kings and queens."

"No, there's two kings," Jack corrected her. "Where does that leave you and I?"

"Don't be like that, this is a good thing. We have freedom we didn't have before."

Jack thought a moment, then leaned in and softly asked, "Do you really think those two brothers can co-rule?"

Nel was surprised by his hesitancy. He seemed to be making a much bigger deal about it than needed. In a low voice, she said, "They're not really co-ruling. At least not for long. The real power lies with Alec. He has control of the Neodactyls, what tangible power does Cyrus have?"

"Cyrus has the support of the people," Jack retorted. "It sounds like the guards view him as the true king, and I'd be willing to bet the people in town will see things the same way. If you ask me, Cyrus is the one with the real power."

Nel opened her mouth to respond but couldn't think of anything clever to say. Jack had a point.

"Okay then," Nel finally answered, "then how do we change that?"

Jack hesitated before he responded, as though he were weighing each of his words extremely carefully. "Perhaps the real power is exactly where it needs to be."

"What do you mean?" Nel asked accusingly. "I don't think I'm understanding you."

"I think you are," Jack said carefully. He was talking very low and very calmly, like they were having the most commonplace conversation, but his eyes betrayed how important he viewed the situation.

Nel had known Jack for years, perhaps not very well, but they had gone out on expeditions together before. He always struck her as a very level-headed, no-nonsense sort of person. He had been lined up to become captain one day soon and she had looked forward to working under his command. But he was foolish if he thought Cyrus had, or would ever have, any real power. It disgusted her to think of him throwing his support behind a broken, has-been expedition leader like Cyrus Dorn. She had to admit, looking at the weakened, injured man propped feebly on the bed in front of her, she couldn't see a future captain anymore. It was sad, but this place had broken him down.

He was still looking her in the eyes, but understanding was starting to wash over his face. Nel didn't really feel like being around him right now. She broke away from his uncomfortable stare and began to turn towards the door.

"Take it easy, yeah?" she said.

Jack nodded morosely, still watching her with a strange look on his face. Was it regret? No, she thought to herself, it was disappointment.

Nel left him in his bed and walked down the hall towards the king's quarters, *Alec's quarters*. She hadn't thought she was ready to talk to Alec yet after their argument, but following her conversation with Jack, she felt compelled to be around someone who understood her.

She entered the room to find Alec holding one of the scepters over the frozen fire altar at the far side by the windows. He was waving the scepter in a circular motion, causing the strange ash to pulsate brightly and individual glowing granules to hover around the staff head in an orbiting rotation. It was the same thing they had seen Mora do in the Fire Fields when they had first arrived. Alec seemed frustrated and prodded the glowing ash with the scepter, releasing a tiny storm of embers over the wood floor. He stood upright and planted the scepter harshly back in place on the altar, then turned towards the windows shaking his head. Nel felt a pang of guilt seeing him in such distress. She knew it was caused by their argument.

He was facing out the windows, still unaware she had entered the room, so she approached slowly and placed a comforting hand on his back. To her surprise, he jumped in alarm and spun to look at her with confusion in his eyes.

"Hey, you alright?" Nel asked.

Alec seemed to relax slightly when he saw it was her, but began to pace away, causing her hand to fall from his back.

"I'm fine," Alec responded, though he was clearly bothered.

If he was looking for an apology, he could forget it, Nel thought. Perhaps she could at least explain her anger though. "Look, Alec," Nel began.

"Do you believe in ghosts?" Alec interrupted her.

"Ghosts?" Nel repeated. She was lost.

"Maybe not in the strictest sense of the word," he responded. He was still pacing, and Nel noticed his eyes were darting from side to side, as though trying to follow infinite fleeting thoughts. "An entity, maybe," he said, "but not quite… exact."

"Alec, what are you talking about?" Nel asked in concern.

"Do you think something could have happened to the other boat?" Alec asked her, finally meeting her eyes for the first time. "Out there on the ocean. We were ahead of the other dinghy by, what, twenty feet maybe? We passed by the anomaly and ended up here, but the other boat never came…"

Nel was having trouble following his line of thinking. He was talking about the day they had arrived here, but why? "What does it matter what happened to the other boat?" Nel asked.

"I was thinking of Cynthia," Alec admitted.

"Cynthia?" Nel said, "Cyrus's wife?"

"She wasn't always his wife," Alec responded. "Everyone likes to forget that, but they weren't always together."

"Why are we talking about Cynthia?" Nel asked.

Alec finally stopped pacing but refused to meet Nel's eyes again. "I met her first," he began. "It was years ago now, of course. But we were close. Not a couple maybe, at least not officially, but there was something between us. And Cyrus knew that."

Nel didn't know how to respond. Having conversations about passions of the heart wasn't exactly in her wheelhouse. But she felt for Alec, and it explained quite a bit about the Dorn sibling dynamic. Even so, Alec would have to find a different shoulder to cry on.

"Alec, I get it," Nel began, "and it's not surprising coming from your brother. He's a self-absorbed, pompous bastard who thinks everything in the world is his for the taking. But this is ancient history, right? So why now?"

Alec opened his mouth and paused, as though he were considering telling her something. Eventually he replied, "I just wonder how things would have turned out differently."

"What? If you were with her?" Nel asked. She shook her head. "Situations may change, but people remain the same. She'd still be the same. Cyrus would still be the same. And for better or worse, you'd still be the same too." When Alec just looked down in defeat, Nel felt a twinge of repulsion towards him. She continued, "You'd still be the same self-doubting, weak, inferior Dorn you are now." That finally got Alec to look up and balk in anger. "Until you do something about it," she finished.

"The Neodactyls are under *my* control, because *I* acted…"

"I'm not telling you to be reckless, I'm telling you to be a ruler," Nel snapped back. "That stunt with the birds? Yeah, it worked out for you, but it was a pale, obvious attempt to prove yourself. Someone with real power doesn't have to prove themselves. People respect them. People fear them." She moved in closer and hammered her fists into his chest, making him stand straighter. "That's the person I see in you, struggling every day to get out. What are you so afraid of? You're still acting like you live in Cyrus's shadow, but you have a new life now. Claim your power."

Alec was staring at her with a fiery intensity in his eyes now. His lips were curling slightly into the smallest hint of a smile. He nodded his head, and moved in to kiss her.

Nel wasn't surprised by his move, but she held up her hand to his mouth, stopping his advance. He looked stung that she had stopped him, but she gave him a look indicating she wasn't turning him down.

"Prove it," Nel said. "Prove you're the person I think you are."

Leaving Alec with a look of disappointment and confusion on his face, Nel turned and strode out of the room, saying as she went, "It's time to climb out of your brother's shadow. Let's meet the real Alec Dorn."

Nel could feel Alec watching after her as she went. Good, she thought to herself. Maybe that's exactly what he needed to become a real ruler.

## CHAPTER TWENTY-NINE

# THE EYES OF THE PEOPLE

Alec opened his eyes slowly and blinding white sunlight flooded his vision. He winced and blinked rapidly until the curving stone ceiling of the room came into focus. Sun beams played across the open air above him, catching the particles of dust and illuminating them in vibrant streaks of yellow. It was still strange waking up in the king's quarters, even after three days here. The Temple was theirs now, but it didn't feel that way. The guards around the Temple were respectful and accommodating, some of them even serving as virtual guides helping them navigate their new rule over the Kingdom. But the Temple felt foreign, even more so than the Kingdom itself at this point. It felt like they were in the home of the enemy.

Of course they weren't in the home of the enemy, Alec thought to himself as he turned over in his bed and sat upright. The enemy was dead, and the Kingdom and this Temple were theirs now. Alec stood up and stretched, the wooden floor feeling cool against his feet. He took a step away from the bed and stopped, raising his face towards the ceiling and slowing his breathing. If someone were to see him, they would likely think he was meditating, but in fact he was listening. Listening for any movement from the adjoining room. There was only silence. He slowly and quietly walked forward and peered ever so carefully around the corner into the main room that housed the frozen fire altar. His scepter stood in place atop of it and the frozen fire glowed and danced warmly below, but there was no other movement. Nothing was out of place and there was no one in the room. Alec exhaled deeply, though he wasn't sure if it was out of relief or disappointment. This had been his routine for the last three mornings, and every morning was the same; the room remained empty. It was reaching the point where Alec was starting to doubt what he had seen on his first day here. Perhaps that was natural for your mind to try to justify something it knew to be impossible. One could discount almost any experience as a hallucination or trick of the mind in order to escape the uncomfortable truth; that things were at play that were beyond understanding. Of course everything that had happened to them since they arrived in the Kingdom was beyond understanding, but this was different. He *had* seen Cynthia Dorn, talked to her even. She had approached him right here in this room. He knew it to be true, even as his mind tried to resist it.

He hadn't told anyone about his encounter. His mind also tried to justify why he was keeping it a secret. He told himself it was because the team would think he was crazy or that it would only strain everyone further. The truth was he kept it to himself because of the way Cynthia was acting towards him. It had seemed like Cynthia was *his* wife, not Cyrus's. It had felt right, but something was most definitely wrong. There was no way she could be here. And where had she gone? The one theory he kept coming back to was that something had happened to the other dinghy out on the ocean and she had died. Then again, she had left lipstick on his cheek where she had kissed him. A ghost couldn't do that, could it? That also would not explain why she was acting so different. His mind was beginning to spin again. This was the same rabbit hole his mind would get caught in every morning, and it was an endless circle.

Alec dressed, slipped his necklace around his neck, grabbed his scepter from the altar, and stepped out of his quarters into the long hallway leading away into the Temple. This was the hallway where they had first encountered Mora when they stormed the Temple. The same hallway where they had initially planned to trap the Neodactyls. It felt like forever ago, but it was just three days past. So much had changed since then.

No one seemed to be around and the only sounds were the faint shuffling and hissing from behind a door to his left. As he stopped walking just outside the closed door, the noises within ceased abruptly. Alec listened, then reached his hand out towards the handle. He was now quite confident the Neodactyls wouldn't hurt him, but every morning when he opened their door, he couldn't help but feel a slight pang of unease. They were animals, after all, and extremely dangerous ones.

Alec twisted the handle down and pulled the door open in a swift, assertive manner. The two Neodactyls within were ready for him and jumped forward aggressively, only breaking their mock-charge when they were a couple feet away. They stared up at him, sniffed in his direction, then relaxed. The quills along their backs slowly folded back down to rest within the lines of their sleek plumage. Their necks relaxed and their tail feathers drooped downwards. They were at ease. Alec was learning to read their body language. It wasn't dissimilar to other animals he had been around. The important thing with these creatures was that they smelled him. They were used to the rest of the guards in the Temple and rarely acted aggressively towards any of them. The only reason he had to keep them locked away in this room during the night was because they had not taken to Cyrus, Nel, or Jack yet. Alec supposed that made sense; the Neodactyls didn't know them yet.

Now that they were released from their room again without incident, Alec breathed more easily; he straightened himself up, adjusted his clothes a bit, tucked his necklace beneath his shirt, and strode forward importantly, the Neodactyls flanking his sides. He made his way down the winding maze of staircases and eventually emerged into the dining area. It was a fairly small room compared to the cavernous nature of the rest of the Temple. This room was very serviceable but plain, without making a statement. Alec chuckled to himself at the thought of Mora having company over for dinner. He supposed Mora always ate alone and that was why the room was so bare.

Jack and Cyrus were already seated at one of the run-down wooden tables, deep in a hushed discussion about something. Nel was nowhere to be seen. Some fruits and what looked like a slab of strange meat were in the center of the table. As they discovered on their first day in the Temple, there were in fact kitchen staff to prepare their meals, and they seemed to have taken no notice or interest in the change of rulers. They continued on with their jobs behind the scenes, the same way the Temple guards did. Both Jack and Cyrus looked up when Alec entered, and both shot an apprehensive glance at the Neodactyls. Alec lay a reassuring hand on each of the bird's backs, which had started to bristle slightly. They relaxed and left his side, stalking around the perimeter of the room.

"Morning Alec," Cyrus said with a vaguely judgmental glance at the scepter clutched in his hand.

"What's going on?" Alec asked as he came to sit beside them. He didn't like the way they had stopped their whispered talking as soon as he entered the room.

"Just trying to figure out our way forward," Cyrus answered unconvincingly.

Alec waited for him to elaborate but he didn't. "Well, it's good to see you up and about again Jack," Alec finally said to break the silence. Why did it feel like he was being excluded from something?

"Thanks," Jack answered. "Yeah, still a bit of a headache, but it's getting better."

At that moment, Nel walked into the room from the front of the Temple. Alec tried to think of something clever to say to her but didn't get the chance. Right on Nel's heels, Ydoro strode into the room with a big smile on his face. They hadn't seen him since he was injured during their assault on King Mora. Last they had heard, he had been told to rest by Dr. Garse.

"I have great news!" Ydoro exclaimed, taking a seat at the table and helping himself to some of the fruit. There were still traces of his fake accent, but it was clear he was trying to phase it out. Alec supposed it had become second nature to him after all those years.

"How are you feeling?" Cyrus asked.

"Like I've been reborn!" Ydoro said with a spark in his eyes that confirmed the truth of his statement. "I've been talking to people in town, from Easttown too actually, and they are quite enthusiastic about the change in leadership. Even Mora's supporters are reserving judgement on you. The story of how you took the Temple has spread like wildfire. Everything I've been hearing has been about your strength and how you rose up to fight after being persecuted by King Mora. In short, the pair of you have become legends overnight."

His last few words hung in the air for a moment. Alec couldn't help it; he was swelling with pride. These people had been put upon for years, decades even, and within a month of their arrival that was all changed. Alec smiled and nodded his head, but Cyrus looked uneasy. He smiled as well, but it was a nervous, uncertain smile.

"I'm... glad they're happy," Cyrus said, "but we're not heroes."

"Sure you are," Ydoro insisted, "in their eyes. You're their king now! Both of you!" Seeing that Cyrus was still not comfortable with the idea, he continued in a softer voice, "Look, you may not feel like the legends the townspeople perceive you as, but no one does behind closed doors. What matters is the impression they have of you. That's what makes you powerful."

Or weak, Alec thought to himself, but he didn't share it out loud. Perception was important, Ydoro was right. But it worked both ways. They could have power but still be weak if the people viewed them as such.

"So your reputation via word of mouth is strong," Ydoro continued, "but I think it's time to take the next step."

"Which is?" Cyrus asked apprehensively.

"Show yourselves," Ydoro answered in a tone that suggested he knew Cyrus wouldn't like it. "It's time you went out there and met the people."

Cyrus waved his hand dismissively. Jack looked thoughtful. Nel was nodding in agreement.

"Look, these are your people now," Ydoro insisted. "I did warn you about this. It didn't end with King Mora's death, these people need a leader."

Cyrus was still shaking his head. "We have more important things to do. I want to see the Fire Fields where we first arrived. Our top and only priority should be finding a way out of here."

"Cyrus," Jack said, still looking contemplative, "perhaps Ydoro's right, we may have overthrown the king, but we're not at the finish line yet. We need to solidify ourselves as the rulers before…"

"We don't have the time," Cyrus interrupted him, "we have better things to do then pose as a make-believe king to these people."

Until now, Alec couldn't quite figure out why Cyrus was so avidly against being a ruler to these people. After all, the Cyrus he'd always known relished the idea of being in charge. Many who knew him thought he was a natural leader. But there it was, plain as day; Cyrus didn't want to rule because he couldn't see how it gave him any real power. He viewed this Kingdom as *make-believe*, and thought of their newly acquired status as equally fantastical. He was wrong, of course. Real power was theirs for the taking, so long as they played the part.

Ydoro continued trying to sway Cyrus, and Cyrus continued to plant his heals more firmly, refusing to concede. Nel had been uncharacteristically quiet during the entire exchange. Alec looked over at her and was surprised to find her looking straight back at him. It was like she was waiting for him to do something. Alec raised his eyebrows, hoping she would speak up if she had something to say, but she stayed quiet and gave him a slow but deliberate nod.

"I'll go," Alec finally announced, bringing silence to the room. Nel's mouth curled into an approving smile. "I'll go meet the people."

Ydoro was looking at him, frowning thoughtfully, before nodding his head in agreement. Cyrus and Jack were both shrugging non-committally.

"Well okay then," Ydoro finally said, "I can work with that. I think if we walk up the main road, maybe address everyone from the center of…"

"Actually," Alec cut in, and he saw Nel's smile widen, "I had my own idea. What happened to Mora's chariot?"

*****

It took some time and talking to the Temple guards before the chariot was located and brought out to the main entrance hall. It was really nothing fancy once you saw it up close, but it was sturdy. It had large wheels with long, spindly spokes flanking the main platform, which was little more than a wooden stand with wrought iron handrails bordering the front three edges. How Mora or his predecessor managed to train the Neodactyls to pull the thing was anyone's guess, but it certainly made a statement. Alec's first view of Mora, riding out of the forest and across the Fire Fields pulled by those two otherworldly monsters was something he would not soon forget.

The Neodactyls were currently pacing around the chariot, sniffing and hissing quietly. They were familiar with it, and seemed to know what was going to be expected of them. However, when Alec moved to the front harnesses, the birds just stared at him expectantly. While he was becoming more comfortable with the creatures by the day, he still wasn't about to wrestle the leather harness and buckles around their necks without a clear invitation. He held the contraption in his hands hoping one of the Neodactyls would approach, but they didn't. It left him standing there awkwardly while Cyrus, Jack, Nel, and the guards watched expectantly. It was crucial that everyone felt he had a bond with these creatures, but right now he felt out of his element.

"If I may, my King?" said one of the guards softly, approaching him from the right. Alec tightened his grip on the harness in his hands. He felt it was important to do this himself. But the guard wasn't reaching for the harness. Instead, he leaned in close to Alec's ear and whispered, "King Mora would always make a clicking noise with his tongue." The guard demonstrated with an audible click, which caused both Neodactyls to cock their heads curiously, but they continued to look at Alec, as though awaiting instructions. Alec handed the guard his scepter to hold and, taking his advice, mimicked the click with his mouth. To his surprise, the nearest Neodactyl approached and placed itself directly beneath the harness in Alec's hand, as though it had been waiting.

Alec looked around at the group watching him and smiled at their astonished faces before lowering the leather straps over the Neodactyl's head and fastening it around its brightly-feathered breast. The second one was easy now that he knew the trick, and soon both birds were tethered securely to the chariot, shuffling slightly in place and hissing patiently.

With a slight weakness in his knees and his fists clenched to stop them from trembling, Alec approached the back of the chariot and stepped shakily onto the platform. He felt the base sink slightly as his weight pressed down onto the wheels, but it felt strong. The guard who had shown him how to click for the Neodactyls stepped forward with the scepter and held it up for him to grab. Alec wrapped his hand around the rough, cool material of the staff, and he felt strong. He looked over to Cyrus, who was actually smiling in spite of himself. He shook his head and shrugged his shoulders as if to say 'I hope you know what you're doing.'

He did know what he was doing. Two guards ahead of him were opening the front doors and standing aside, prepared to let him pass. Sunshine poured in through the entrance and pooled along the floor in glowing patches. It was easy to forget there was a whole world out there from the stuffy lower levels of the Temple. Everyone stared at him, waiting for him to depart, but first there was something he wanted to do.

He turned around and extended his hand out the back. "Nel," he said, "will you join me?"

Nel raised her eyebrows as though impressed by his confidence. She stepped forward, and though she did not take his offered hand, she did raise herself onto the platform and gripped the handrails tightly. Alec looked at her and she winked at him approvingly.

Alec looked forward again, a self-satisfied grin on his face, and whipped the straps gently but assertively. The Neodactyls, in almost perfect synchronization, sprung forward towards the open door, the chariot lurching after them. In barely a moment, they were out the door and nearly blinded by the burning sun of the day. The chariot picked up speed as they rolled across the clearing out front that sloped gradually but steadily downhill. They were at the end of the clearing in no time and reaching the treeline where a path entered the woods and presumably led towards the main town. So far, the Neodactyls hadn't required any direction, but he supposed any forceful pulls of the straps would do the trick. It was a bumpy ride, especially once they entered the forest path, but it was exhilarating at the same time. He watched the backs of the birds' heads, barely moving as their necks and backs contracted and pivoted from side to side as they ran. He looked back at Nel, who was clutching the rails and looking uneasy but excited at the same time.

As they continued down and out of the hills, the trees slowly became a little more sporadic, and Alec began to notice people peering out from the forest curiously. He could tell they didn't quite know what to make of him. How would Mora have addressed them? Probably ignored them entirely, Alec suspected. He had no intention of being anything like Mora, so he raised his hand slowly and waved to the onlookers. Some of them looked to one another in visible confusion, but smiles were starting to show on their faces. A few of them waved back, uncertain at first, but more enthusiastic as the chariot rumbled ever forward. As they neared the edge of town ahead, people were starting to run out towards the path, craning their necks to catch a glimpse of him. The excitement seemed to be spreading along the path ahead of them faster than they were actually moving. People were already waving wildly as they whipped around each corner. Off to their left, someone let out a cheer of support, and a few others began clapping. When they finally careened out of the forest and onto the winding stone streets of the main town, the quickly gathering crowd was ready for them and erupted in cheers and applause. People were running down side streets towards them, leaning out windows, rushing out doors, even scrambling along rooftops to be a part of the growing spectacle. Alec beamed and waved to the crowd as the chariot zoomed onward, trying his best to maintain sturdy footing with both of his hands off the railings. He felt Nel's hand on his waist and smiled more broadly. He lifted his scepter into the air and the crowd cheered even more loudly. He had no idea what he had done to garner this kind of support, but he had to admit he was enjoying it immensely. Perhaps after living under Mora's rule for so long, they were just excited to have a king who truly saw them.

Far too soon, the chariot had reached the opposite edge of town, but the Neodactyls didn't stop. They continued onto another path leading into the woods. This was the path they had taken on their first day here, and Alec knew exactly where it was leading. The people from town were clearly not done with him yet. Looking back over Nel's shoulder, he could see many people from the crowd were actually running after them, following the chariot wherever it was headed. This forest path was far more populated than the one leading to the Temple, and the palpable excitement from the people was only continuing to build. Alec looked back to Nel, who was watching him with a funny look on her face. He couldn't tell exactly what the look meant, but it was certainly an approving look.

Before long the chariot bounced its way to the end of the forest and out into the dazzling glow of the sun and the vibrant black and orange flicker of the Fire Fields. People were busy at work along the treeline but came running forward when the chariot made its appearance. The people from the main town following the path also came running out to join as well and soon a decent sized crowd had gathered, all clapping and yelling and waving their hands excitedly in the air. Alec raised his scepter once again, and then a thought occurred to him. He extended the scepter down towards the fiery blackened sand whizzing below them and a storm of glowing ashes started forming around the staff-head. The crowd quieted slightly and the people started looking a bit uneasy, but the clapping didn't cease. It occurred to Alec a bit too late that the townspeople's only experiences with the scepters were likely as weapons, but he was about to change that. Alec continued to rake the scepter head across the glowing ground before suddenly thrusting it up over his head, releasing a dazzling explosion of fiery sparks towards the sky. The ever-growing crowd erupted in applause and fresh cheers at the display, the beaming smiles returning to everyone's faces. He did it again, this time spinning the scepter in a circular motion creating a glowing shower of embers, much to the delight of the crowd. He raised his hand in the air again and the people as a whole waved back enthusiastically.

Alec was grinning ear to ear now, he couldn't help it. He felt loved. He felt respected. He felt *powerful*. He turned to look at Nel, who was also waving half-heartedly to the crowd, but her attention was directed towards Alec. She was smiling at him and nodding her head. Alec grinned back, then leaned in and kissed her. He didn't know what had come over him, but he felt truly alive for the first time in a long time. The kiss was short, not to mention bumpy due to the tilting and bouncing chariot, but she didn't stop him this time. She raised her eyebrow slightly, but smiled back at him. The crowd loved it. As soon as he had kissed her, the cheers had grown louder than ever. Alec turned back out to face them, an even bigger grin on his face now. He raised both his hands over his head, the scepter still clutched in one, then swept it across the ground once again and thrust it up towards the sky. A fresh explosion of sparks and ash burst into the air, once again met with deafening applause.

## CHAPTER THIRTY

## THE SCATTERED PIECES OF A PUZZLE

Cyrus had his head bowed and was nodding up and down in agreement.

"Alec can take all the joy rides he wants," Jack was saying, all the while pacing around the dining room. "But Cyrus is right, our time needs to be spent finding a way out of here. I mean, have we already given up on that?"

"I understand," Ydoro insisted, "but the area has been searched. No one has ever found a way back."

The one thing Cyrus kept thinking to himself was that they needed to backtrack. Perhaps it was unimportant how others from the past got here. Perhaps they needed to narrow their focus to their own journey here. He finally spoke up and said just that, but was met with skepticism.

"The trouble is no one came here in the same way, or from the same location, or even arrived in the same location," Ydoro answered, "I think we need to focus on figuring out what the common thread is between these arrivals."

"Fair enough," Cyrus said, "but in order to do that, we need to track our own journey."

Cyrus proceeded to break down their journey from the twisted and damaged cargo ship out on the ocean to their fateful ride out in the dinghies. He hammered his fist into his palm, willing himself to keep track of the order everything occurred in. Jack nodded in agreement as he went, filling in the blanks during the time Cyrus had been unconscious. It quickly became evident that it was impossible to track exactly what happened once they were in the water. They had been tossed around in every direction, trying with all their might not to drown. No one saw what happened in those moments.

"I just remember struggling in the water one minute, then feeling land beneath me," Jack explained, shaking his head, "and when I opened my eyes, I was out in the Fire Fields."

"Right," Cyrus concurred, nodding his head and refusing to be baffled into silence, "so something from *here*... pulled us from *there*. Are we in agreement on that?"

Jack and Ydoro both thought a moment, then both nodded in agreement.

"We're also assuming that whatever pulled *us* here was also what pulled the ship through the ocean." He stopped a moment to explain to Ydoro the shipwreck that had started their journey in the first place. He also explained their theory about the ship getting stuck on the rocks and preventing it from coming through the *portal* that they themselves had succumbed to. "So it was roughly three days before we arrived here that the ship nearly capsized out on the Atlantic. According to the captain, it was smooth sailing until the ship was violently pulled backwards due to some unseen and sudden force." Cyrus paused a second, gathering his thoughts before finally coming to his point. "So Ydoro, what happened *here* three days prior to our arrival?"

Jack nodded his head fervently and Ydoro closed his eyes as though trying to force himself to remember.

After a few moments of strained silence, Cyrus thought of something that could help jog his memory. "The night we arrived here, you said your friend had just died. So what happened three days before that?"

Ydoro opened his eyes again and Cyrus could see them darting back and forth as if he were trying to chase a string of thoughts. He finally nodded and started talking, very slowly at first as his mouth caught up with his mind. "There was a man… a man from Easttown…"

"A man?" Cyrus asked, his heart beginning to beat faster, "what man?"

"He had started causing trouble for King Mora," Ydoro answered. "It happens every so often; someone gets it in their head that they can overthrow the king, so they try… and fail."

"But we were different?" Jack asked.

"I don't know," Ydoro admitted, "there was just something different about you. Usually it's just a single instigator who has vastly overestimated their fighting abilities. This particular man thought he could challenge the King and win in hand-to-hand combat. He couldn't, and he died for it. I don't even remember his name…"

"Okay but what happened?" Cyrus pressed, "I mean specifically?"

"Well, the man had been causing problems for a while. When it finally came time to make his move, everyone advised against it. But he had been training up and thought he was ready. Mora was riding through the Fire Fields when the man confronted him. He had fashioned a spear, but you saw how Mora fights. The man didn't stand a chance."

"Did you see the fight?" Jack asked.

"Not personally, but I've talked to people who did. It wasn't a long duel. Mora blocked his attacks and impaled him with one of the scepters. No one was surprised."

There was a connection, though, Cyrus was sure of it. "That's not coincidence," he finally said. "That was the same day the anomaly appeared in our world. And the same place where we first showed up here. The Fire Fields must be the key…"

Ydoro was already shaking his head before Cyrus had finished his thought. "It's not *always* the Fire Fields, though. People have shown up all over the island over the years."

There was silence as they all considered this. Finally, Cyrus said, "Okay but there is a constant. If it's not the location, then what?"

"Well we know Mora's not the constant," Jack said thoughtfully, "he came from our world."

"If local legends are to be believed," Ydoro offered, "perhaps the constant is death. According to myth..."

Exactly what local myths had to say on the topic Cyrus did not hear due to a commotion at the entrance of the Temple. It seemed Alec and Nel had returned from their ride through town. Jack shot him an apprehensive glance before exiting the dining room and heading out towards the entrance chamber. Cyrus and Ydoro followed to find Alec dismounting the chariot and grinning broadly. He seemed to be in extremely high spirits and Nel was smiling as well. Alec gave the Neodactyls a pat before signaling for a nearby guard to untie them and roll the chariot away.

"You should've seen them! The people!" Alec exclaimed.

"You enjoyed yourself?" Ydoro asked, smiling at Alec's enthusiasm.

"There's real life out there!" Alec said, "I mean, these people have been oppressed for so long, you should have seen the looks on their faces when their new ruler came through town!"

"Don't you mean new *leader*?" Cyrus said before he could stop himself. Alec ignored him.

"We made it all the way down to the Fire Fields," Alec continued, "We were going to go farther but there was barely any point. *Everyone* was out there to see us. I don't think there's much to see in Easttown anyways."

"Well I wouldn't necessarily say that," Ydoro began, but Alec continued to talk over him.

"Those are good people out there, and they've been oppressed long enough," Alec was saying, still grinning.

"So, speaking of the Fire Fields," Cyrus interjected, "we were discussing the possibility they may have played a role in our coming here."

"Really?" said Alec, although he didn't sound remotely interested.

"Ydoro mentioned something intriguing..." Cyrus began, but Alec had already stopped listening. He was whispering something to Nel, who was smiling and nodding in agreement. "Do you not wanna hear this?" Cyrus finally said in annoyance.

Cyrus fully expected Alec to react in anger the moment the words had left his mouth. To his surprise, however, Alec simply turned to him and said, "Sorry, Cy, just enjoying the moment here. You should try it from time to time."

Cyrus raised his eyebrows. The rest of the room was silent with all eyes watching them. Was Alec purposely trying to bait him by being so dismissive? He finally shook his head and said, "I'll enjoy the moment when we're back home." He turned back towards Jack with the intention of continuing their earlier conversation without Alec.

"Right," Alec said, "when we're back home." There was something accusatory in his tone, although how a desire to escape this place was a crime was anyone's guess. "So tell me," Alec continued, "Ydoro's explained to us how this place works. We killed the last king; don't you think we inherit some responsibility to the people out there?"

Cyrus shrugged and responded, "They can appoint whoever they want as king once we're gone. Not seeing the problem here Alec."

"The people have already recognized a new ruler," Alec insisted, still in a tone far calmer and more level-headed than was characteristic of him. "This power we have can't just be given away."

"What power?" Cyrus snapped, unable to make his voice not sound condescending. "We have no power. It's all a facade. This place isn't real and neither is your sad, desperate grip on your first taste of authority."

Cyrus realized he shouldn't have said it, even before he had finished. It was harsh and demeaning, but he couldn't help it. Alec was acting like a child.

Alec's eyes flashed and his nostrils flared, but once again he did not lose his composure. He shook his head and responded slowly, "It's not that. In fact it's not about me at all." His voice continued to stay level, but every word was dripping with malice. "You're used to having authority, and in this place, where you have none..." Alec paused, and leaned in towards Cyrus with his voice barely above a whisper, "... it's finally showing how weak you truly are."

With that, Alec turned on his heel and strode out of the room. Unlike everyone else present, who were all staring down at the floor awkwardly, Nel grinned at Cyrus and turned to follow Alec out of the room. As she walked away, Nel called over her shoulder, "What did I tell you, Jack. Hope you picked the right side." And they were gone.

Silence hung in the air. Ydoro fidgeted with a loose thread on his robes and Jack had his eyes closed in an awkward grimace.

"What did she mean by that?" Cyrus demanded of Jack.

Jack opened his eyes and stared back at Cyrus. "I need to talk to you… I think we have a problem."

## CHAPTER THIRTY-ONE

# QUALITY OF A LEADER

Alec stormed down the hallway in a rage. It felt as though his brain were on fire. How dare Cyrus speak to him that way. Alec had managed to keep his composure during their exchange, but the effort had taken every ounce of energy he had. He could hear Nel running quickly behind him, struggling to keep up. It was possible she was speaking to him as well, he couldn't be sure. He was in no mood to talk. He clenched his fist tightly around the scepter in his hand. It made him feel strong, and he desperately needed that. As he passed by a torch anchored to the stone wall Alec suddenly swung out with the scepter, connecting with the glass and metal frame and sending smashed shards fifteen feet down the hall. He was almost to the king's quarters now and Nel was still bouncing after him.

"Alec!" She was practically shouting. "You did well! Really!"

Alec entered his quarters and strode over to the frozen fire altar, smashing the end of the scepter back into the base to make it stick. Burning ash sputtered across the floor. Alec picked the scepter up again and stabbed it back down violently into the metal urn. He did it again and again, sending a storm of glowing embers flying in every direction.

"Alec honestly, that was incredible!" Nel insisted. "Cyrus didn't even know what to say."

Henry came hobbling into the room at that moment, looking as feeble as ever.

"And where have you been?" Alec demanded of him.

Henry just chuckled mildly and responded, "It's a lot of stairs for an old man like me."

Ignoring him and turning back to Nel, Alec roared, "I just can't believe him! I'm not saying I don't want to leave, but we've been given a gift. A responsibility. How do we just turn our back on that?"

"If I may," Henry began softly. Alec shot him a menacing look, daring him to disagree. To his surprise, Henry continued, "I think you're right. The burden indeed falls to you to transition the Kingdom now that King Mora is gone."

Alec nodded, but then shook his head and said, "Obviously my brother doesn't feel the same."

"If I may be so bold, sir," Henry said respectfully, "it shows the quality of a leader to be willing to compromise, and you agreeing to share power with your brother does indeed show the quality of leader you are. But he doesn't deserve your generosity."

"Careful," Alec warned, "he is my brother either way, and I don't know you."

Henry put his hands up in a gesture of surrender but continued, "You are a natural ruler, he is not."

"He's right, Alec," Nel pressed. "This is the Alec Dorn that I saw buried deep down back on the ship. This is that *fire*! Don't try to bury it again. Become who you actually want to be."

"I don't *want* anything," Alec insisted, "I'm just trying to..."

"See that's the problem!" Nel cut him off. "You can't even admit what you really want! If you want more, then *be* more. Remember what Dalton said to you?"

Alec did remember, in fact he had thought about it a lot since they arrived here, but it didn't stop Nel from repeating it.

"He said you can choose who you want to be," Nel continued, "what part you want to play. And if you choose to be a leader, then you need to own it. Stop second-guessing your instincts."

Alec took a deep breath and nodded. She was right, they both were. What he felt out in town while they were on the chariot was unlike anything he had ever felt before. He had come back on such a high, only for Cyrus to try to tear him down again. Cyrus may be his brother, but he couldn't stand Alec feeling important.

"I do want to give you some advice, though," Nel continued.

Alec gave her a dangerous look. In the mood he was in right now, he couldn't stomach a lecture. "If you want me to trust my instincts and lead as a king, I don't need advice."

Alec knew his anger towards Nel was misplaced and fully expected her to bristle at his statement, but to his surprise she shook her head almost sympathetically and continued, "That's exactly the advice I want to give you. If you want to be taken seriously as a ruler, you have to keep your emotions in check."

Alec's nostrils flared and, with an irony that was not entirely lost on him, he felt a swell of burning emotion bubbling to the surface. Nel, however, continued talking before he could respond. "Throughout history, true rulers don't have to scream to everyone how powerful they are. They show their power by *displaying* power. They show strength with acts of strength. Stop getting drawn into these arguments with your brother. He's baiting you."

Alec opened and shut his mouth several times, trying and failing to find a retort to her statement.

"That's why you did so well just now when Cyrus tried to push you. You kept your composure, and your point stuck. Don't let your anger get the better of you now."

Alec hung his head slightly, then glanced sideways at Henry, who he was slightly embarrassed to remember was hearing this entire conversation. But Henry smiled reassuringly at him and said softly, "Oftentimes the strongest rulers are the ones you don't realize are ruling."

Alec looked back at Nel who smiled and winked at him. "Chin up, King Dorn. You just won your first toe-to-toe with your brother. Keep it up."

Alec didn't like the insinuation that he and his brother were at odds with each other, but perhaps their relationship was truly fractured. It felt more and more as though he were clinging to what their relationship once was and ignoring what it had become. Either way, looking into Nel's eyes was intoxicating and, as always, it made him feel stronger than ever.

# CHAPTER THIRTY-TWO

# MAY I PRESENT YOUR KING

How long had it been now? Cyrus strained his mind trying to map out exactly how long they had been on this island… in this world. Months, he would guess, but he couldn't be quite sure. Time seemed to behave strangely here. Perhaps it was just that their daily lives were so unrecognizably altered from what they had previously been that it was hard for him to chart. Things were better now, he supposed, when compared to how they first arrived. They no longer had to fear for their lives. There was no longer a madman lording over them spouting arbitrary rules and threatening violence. If he were being honest, though, the entire team had slipped into a sort of complacency in recent weeks that he did not think was healthy. They were actually getting used to the new world, as baffling as that may have seemed initially. Cyrus still spoke to Jack regularly about mounting an effort to escape back to their world, but those talks no longer felt urgent. Whereas originally it was an immediate and pressing goal, now it seemed their brainstorming sessions devolved too quickly into theoretical questions about what had happened to them and how it had been possible. They had made infuriatingly little headway, and he himself was just as much to blame. Somehow the idea that their predicament might be permanent had worked its tentacles into his brain and taken hold there, leaving him with a lingering, persistent sense of defeat.

Cyrus swung his legs out of bed and sat up in his small, stone room. Despite himself also being considered king along with Alec, he had allowed Alec to stay in the king's quarters. It seemed somehow more important to Alec, and Cyrus hadn't seen any issue with it at the time. He ran his hands through his hair and down the sides of his face, trying to force the weariness from his eyes. His hair was starting to grow a bit longer now, and his beard had mostly filled in. It was a strange feeling to him, as he had always felt a true scholar should be clean-shaven and well-polished. He had not worn a real beard a day in his life, not since his father had taught him how to shave as a young teen. Alec had always been a bit *rougher* looking, at least in Cyrus's eyes. He secretly felt that might have been one of the reasons that his perpetual reaching for success had always fallen just a bit short. Of course, if one were to ask Alec now, he would surely tell them he had found his true calling, a thought that caused Cyrus to roll his eyes and shake his head wearily. The other feature that still felt strange to Cyrus as he rubbed his eyes was the extensive scar that crept out from beneath his beard and covered a good deal of the right side of his face. The skin felt rough and leathery now that it had mostly healed, not smooth and shiny as tended to happen with normal burns. It no longer hurt him, but did leave a constant stiffness that he was still getting used to.

Cyrus shook his head, willing his thoughts to move on from his physical discomforts. This was exactly the complacency that was worrying him. When they had first arrived, seeing people who had once been from *their* world having so comfortably settled into a life in *this* world was unspeakably horrifying. Now that did not seem so impossible. Would time truly just erase all hope and desire to escape and leave them forever resigned to growing old in this place? Cyrus made a mental promise to not allow that to happen. Cynthia was out there somewhere waiting for him. At least he hoped she was. He still thought about Cynthia every day and dreamt of being reunited with her, but whenever he allowed his thoughts to linger on her for too long, his dreams inevitably turned to nightmares. The terrifying truth was that he did not have any clue what had happened to her or the other boat. The fact that the other dinghy did not follow them through whatever anomaly swallowed them bothered Cyrus more than anything else that had happened. Not only did that not fit with the team's admittedly weak theories, but it also meant his wife's whereabouts and safety were anyone's guess. Was she back home, organizing search parties to find them? Had it been long enough now that she'd had him declared dead? Had there been a funeral and service for them before everyone inevitably moved on with their daily lives? Or was she not back home at all? Was she... elsewhere?

Cyrus shook the thought from his head and stood up. This sort of dwelling on what may or may not have happened to the rest of the team was not productive. What would be productive was to find Jack and work out a real plan for exploring the island. It seemed ridiculous but they still had not made it back to the Fire Fields to explore the area where they had first arrived. Cyrus stood up and dressed, resolute to make this the day they started clawing their way back to the real world. Alec had been no help whatsoever when it came to escape. While he may have initially tolerated their theories and plans, now he had no appetite for them at all. It was clear that he felt more and more comfortable in the new world by the day. The Neodactyls were still inexplicably drawn to him and followed his every command and gesture. Cyrus had given up trying to figure out why, but it didn't make sense. Alec spent a lot of his time riding out into town on his chariot. He called it 'riding with the people', but Cyrus wasn't fooled. He was getting high off the love and admiration the locals were showering him with, but the baffling part was that Alec had done absolutely nothing for them. He would ride out, oftentimes with Nel at his side, wave to the people, create a light show with his scepter, and ride back. Were the people so scarred from Mora and Irias's previous torments that waving and smiling could pass as ruling? It didn't really matter to Cyrus, but Alec's complete lack of desire to leave was a little startling. Nel seemed to follow Alec around wherever he went. She generally didn't say much when they would talk as a group, but Cyrus had a sinking suspicion that she was whispering ideas in Alec's ear behind closed doors, causing a further rift in the group. Indeed, Jack had described a conversation between himself and Nel soon after they took over the Temple that chilled him. Evidently, Nel had proposed that she and Jack work towards helping Alec seize absolute control of the Kingdom by establishing himself as the one true king. Luckily, Jack had recognized the danger in her proposal and told Cyrus, who promptly questioned Alec about it. Alec denied any such conversations were taking place with him and laughed off the idea as ludicrous. It was a sticky situation for Cyrus, as he did not remotely care who was *ruling* this Kingdom, however Jack pointed out the danger they faced in allowing Alec's ego mixed with his increasingly abundant immaturity to go unchecked. For now, Cyrus had decided the solution was to uneasily wait and see.

He slowly made his way through the Temple and down the many winding staircases. He was mostly used to the Temple by now, although he still didn't know where many of the side passageways led. He was sure that Ydoro could explain what every room was for and where every hallway led but he was rarely seen in the Temple these days. He spent most of his time out in town, amongst the locals. Cyrus supposed that was a good thing. According to Ydoro, he was further solidifying the Kingdom under their control.

Cyrus emerged onto the main floor and crossed the gigantic, cavernous room with the ladder in the center of it. He looked up to the tiny rectangular hole at the top that led to the battlements. It seemed so long ago that he was dangling up there with Mora slashing at his heels with a machete. Cyrus turned through a door on the left and entered the dining area, which was empty. He pulled out a chair, intending to sit and eat while he waited for Jack to awake, but he was interrupted when a person walked through the door leading to the entrance hall.

"I'm sorry to disturb you my King," the guard said. As with all the guards, he wore crudely sewn leather and fabric garments that borrowed heavily from the look of medieval knights, and he carried a long machete on his belt. Cyrus was getting used to the guard's presence and could recognize most of them by sight, even if he didn't know their names.

"There are six people in front requesting to speak to the king," the guard continued. When Cyrus looked at him quizzically, he replied in a lower voice, "I believe they are from Easttown."

"Easttown?" Cyrus questioned, "Did they say what they want?"

"They did not, sir," the guard responded. "If you like I can find out. Or I can see if your brother…"

"No no," Cyrus replied, "I'll talk to them."

As the guard led Cyrus towards the front of the Temple, he reminded himself that he was supposed to be these people's king. He consciously stood up a little straighter and squared his shoulders. While he had no interest in ruling, he did not want to appear weak, and truth be told he was becoming increasingly uncomfortable with how Alec was handling certain situations. They passed through the door leading to the cavernous entrance hall and Cyrus got his first look at his guests. They stood fanned out in front of the main door, which stood open letting blinding beams of sunlight pour over their backs creating long, spindly shadows across the floor. The person in front was a short, thin young woman with a very pretty round face and unmistakable muscles on her bare arms. To her left stood a fairly round, bearded man who was built like a tank. Each one of the six had serious muscles wrapping around their arms and stood in a confident, almost threatening manner.

The guard escorting Cyrus cleared his throat and announced, "May I present your King, Cyrus Dorn."

The guard stopped his approach ten feet from the guests, clearly expecting Cyrus to do the same. Cyrus supposed a king would traditionally keep their distance from their subjects as a way of demonstrating the separation of power, but Cyrus approached the group all the same and offered his hand.

"Welcome," he said, shaking hands with each one of the group. The woman in front raised her eyebrows in surprised approval. "Welcome to the Temple," Cyrus continued, "please come in." He beckoned further into the entrance hall. His kindness towards them seemed to be working; the group as a whole was starting to relax its aggressive stance.

The woman in front nodded graciously and said in a respectful but confident voice, "Thank you my King, let me introduce myself…"

Cyrus opened his mouth to insist that she did not need to call him *my King*, but before the words had left his mouth, the woman looked over Cyrus's shoulder and a grin spread across her face. "Well, well, look at this!"

Cyrus turned to see Jack approach the group from behind him, a look of surprise on his face. "Annica!" Jack called out. "Cain!"

"Good to see you alive, Jack," Annica exclaimed, stepping forward and grasping Jack's hand, ramming her shoulder into his chest in a sort of halfway hug.

"You're Annica!" Cyrus exclaimed, finally remembering her face from their brief encounter and realizing who the group was. Of course he had heard all about the team Jack had been working with in the caves up on the hillside, not to mention the way they had rescued Jack in dramatic fashion. Jack's description of the way they had crushed his pursuing guard with boulders was something he would not soon forget.

"I'm going to go out on a limb and assume you're not coming back to work," Annica joked to Jack. Jack stammered a bit but Annica clapped him on the arm and assured him she was kidding. "News travels fast around the Kingdom," she continued. "We all had bets going on if you would come out of your assault alive or not."

"What sort of odds did I get?" Jack asked with a laugh.

Annica and most of the others lowered their heads sheepishly, but Cain beamed back at him. "You've made me a rich man, Jack," he announced jovially. "Or, at least I can pay for the next round of drinks."

The group stayed in the entrance hall for some time, talking and joking. They were intrigued to hear about the fall of King Mora and how the morning of the assault had played out. Annica reported that their victory at the Temple had reached legendary status amongst many of the locals. There were tales of them besting Mora in hand-to-hand combat. Some said Mora had been thrown from the battlements. One telling spoke of Alec Dorn striding into the Temple alone and stopping the Neodactyls mid-charge simply by raising his hand at them. Cyrus supposed some part of the truth was embedded in each of the stories, but suspected Ydoro had something to do with their fantastical embellishments.

It felt surprisingly normal to converse with people in such a light, casual way. While their surroundings and everything they talked about was entirely alien, Annica and her team made it feel like they were discussing the most commonplace events. Jack had clearly developed a bond with the team, something that was pleasantly surprising to Cyrus. There had been such a vast separation between themselves and the locals of the Kingdom since they arrived here, and that distance only widened once they overtook the Temple. These people seemed real. These people *were* real. For the first time, Cyrus felt like he was peeking behind the curtain and seeing what the people of the Kingdom were truly like.

As if reading his mind, Annica turned to Cyrus and said, "We actually came here today to talk to you, my King. We were hoping to present you with an opportunity."

Cyrus furrowed his brow. He suddenly felt like he was back home and a particularly tricky salesman was about to attempt selling him something. That turned out not to be the case.

"I don't mean to presume where your priorities lie," Annica began in her same confident voice, "but it seems to me this is an opportunity to start fresh. From what I can see, you have very little in common with your predecessor, so perhaps you would be open to a few suggestions."

Cyrus simultaneously felt impressed and railroaded by Annica's bold approach, however she paused at that moment and raised her eyebrows, as if asking permission to continue. It was a small gesture, but one that demonstrated enough respect that it disarmed him. Cyrus nodded his head in approval and Annica gave the slightest hint of a smile before continuing.

"You have the opportunity to bring Easttown into the fold. Truly bring us to the table, allow us to work together with the rest of the Kingdom. For too long Easttown has been sidelined as the manual labor pool to the rest of the Kingdom but enjoy very few of the rewards of the society."

Cyrus had not been expecting a simple request, but this seemed like a no-brainer. He didn't really understand the politics at work in the Kingdom, but it never made much sense to him that Easttown was kept so separate. If all Annica was requesting was uniting the people, there was no downside that he could see.

Noticing the agreeable look on Cyrus's face, Annica seemed to gain even more confidence, if that were possible. "It's not just about allowing us to have a say, you understand? It's about sharing resources. We come and work out here, mine for stone, build your houses, build your roads; but none of this work ever pays off for us in the East. Have you been to Easttown?... My King?" She added this last part hastily, as if suddenly realizing who she was addressing.

Cyrus wasn't offended, on the contrary he was coming to respect her more and more. "I have not," he answered her.

"It's not the same as the town you see below your fortress. It's run down, our roads are overgrown, our homes are crumbling. All of our work and resources are funneled into a part of the Kingdom we don't get to see or enjoy."

Cyrus nodded thoughtfully and Annica smiled, seemingly encouraged by his interest. "Begging your pardon, my King, but you live up here in a fortress entirely your own. Now, you've earned that and earned your place up here, you fought for it. But not the entire Kingdom gets to reap the benefits of their work. And I'll just say this one last thing as a gesture of trust; Easttown may not remain satisfied with their place on the food chain forever, it may be best to make reparations while they're still willing to listen."

This last statement was not meant as a threat, Cyrus knew that; but he winced all the same when she said it, because at that very moment, Alec had entered the hall from the right.

Alec strode in as impressively as he could manage; chest puffed out importantly, head held high, and the charred-looking scepter gripped firmly in his hand. He clearly had wanted to appear regal to their visitors, but his eyebrows raised as he caught the very last sentence of Annica's pitch. He had broken his stride momentarily but recovered quickly, closing the remaining distance between them with a few heavy, echoing footfalls.

"Have I missed something?" Alec questioned as Annica and her team turned, just noticing the new arrival. His scanning, slightly narrowed eyes were accusatorial and searching.

Annica smiled at who she must have deduced was the second king and extended her hand out to him. "Annica," she introduced herself, but her hand was left hanging in the air. A deafening silence permeated the hall as Alec observed Annica's offered hand with undisguised contempt. Realizing her mistake, Annica withdrew her hand and bowed her head slightly, "Apologies my King."

Alec turned his gaze to Cyrus and Jack, suspicion setting behind his eyes. "What's this I hear about Easttown?"

Annica answered, "I was simply mentioning to the King..."

"You are addressing your king right now," Alec cut her off.

"Alec," Cyrus began, intending to diffuse the situation and rescue Annica.

Annica raised her eyebrows at Alec's statement, and retorted, "I am addressing *one* of the king's right now."

Alec looked shocked that a commoner would talk to him in such a manner.

Annica continued, "I'm merely pointing out that I was under the impression I *was* talking to the king."

"You were talking to *one* king," Alec snarled, "This Kingdom has two."

Annica, refusing to be cowed into submission, replied calmly, "Well that's my point exactly. My understanding was that this Kingdom was ruled by two equal leaders, which affords your brother the ability to converse with me in your absence. If that's not the way your shared Kingdom works, then really you're not two equal rulers at all, you're merely two halves of a whole ruler."

Alec's eyes flashed dangerously but he kept his composure, something he was getting better at with each passing day. He sneered at her and said, "I hope that made you feel strong, because you may regret talking to me like that."

Annica looked back at him innocently, but her eyes betrayed her intentions. She was baiting him.

"Okay that's enough," Cyrus announced. Nothing productive could come from this interaction and Alec was beginning to look murderous.

Alec, who hadn't taken his eyes off Annica, said, "No I don't think that is enough. I think this *Easttowner* is struggling to understand the way things work in this Kingdom."

At that moment, as if on cue, the pair of Neodactyls slinked their way into the entrance room from behind Alec, hissing softly and snaking their heads back and forth in almost perfect unison. Annica's face betrayed a flicker of fear and Alec gave a self-satisfied smile.

Jack stepped forward and said loudly, "Alec, we said that's enough."

Alec rounded on Jack, his face twisted into an ugly caricature of fury. "*You* have absolutely no say in how I conduct myself."

Cyrus, surprising even himself, barked, "Stand down *now* Alec."

The words echoed powerfully throughout the cavernous room and hung in the air for what seemed like an eternity. Alec stared at Cyrus, the first time he had really locked eyes with him since entering the room. Cyrus didn't look remotely sympathetic or understanding. He had tried very hard since their arrival to avoid giving his brother direct orders and to allow him to discover his own strength, but that ended here. Cyrus continued to stare into Alec's bulging, hate-filled eyes and for the first time, he realized that he did not recognize the person who was staring back at him. It was a sobering thought.

At long last, Alec blinked and turned away from his brother, evidently backing down from the challenge. He whistled and the Neodactyls sprung to his side, chirping expectantly. Alec turned back to face Annica and her team, crossing his arms over his chest, indicating very clearly that, while he may have been leashed by his brother, the conversation with her group was most definitely over.

Annica nodded her understanding, but her cunning green eyes were still studying Alec, sizing him up. Cain had not moved throughout the entire exchange, but it was clear he was ready to jump to action at a moment's notice. The rest of her team looked similarly prepared. Annica nodded her head curtly at Alec, but it was far short of a bow. She then turned her attention to Cyrus and tilted her head down respectfully.

"My King," Annica said to Cyrus, "think on what I've said." She then turned to Jack, said his name with a wink, and turned to leave. The rest of her team preceded her out the door without a word, although Cain did give Jack a casual salute as he went.

An awkward silence hung in the air the moment Cyrus, Jack, and Alec were finally alone. Cyrus looked to Jack in exasperation, and Jack just shook his head in disbelief.

"Something to say?" Alec demanded. The Neodactyls both bristled at his raised voice.

Cyrus shook his head, "Plenty to say. What the hell was that?"

"What do you care what they think of us?" Alec retorted. "You would let her and her mob come in here with a list of demands and threats…"

"That's not what happened," Jack snapped at him. "You would know that if you would think before you acted."

Alec ignored him and shrugged his shoulders with a smirk.

"What's funny?" Cyrus demanded.

"You just have no idea what the people want. You're never out there; you never spend any time with the people but you act like you know them." Alec turned to walk away, the Neodactyls eagerly following him. "The Kingdom is thriving the way it is," Alec said as he went. "If you don't want to rule, why don't you stop pretending to."

In a few seconds he was gone, and Cyrus looked at Jack once again, who stared back with his mouth hanging partly open. Cyrus could almost see the half-formed words of shock trying and failing to leave his lips. Maybe there was nothing to say at all. But Cyrus would be haunted by what he saw when he looked into his brother's eyes for a long time to come.

## CHAPTER THIRTY-THREE

# A CHALLENGE

Where the hell was she? Alec prowled his quarters in the way he often did, feeling like a captive lion at the zoo. Once the king of the Jungle, the lion paced this way and that, powerless to alter its fate, damned to cycle through its own endless loop until its mind inevitably turned to mush. Or until a keeper made an error. The lion in the zoo enclosure looked docile, seemed resigned to its pathetic existence as an attraction, but never truly lost itself. If a keeper ever made a critical error and opened the wrong gate, or forgot to secure a part of the enclosure, they would pay the price. That's how Alec felt. He felt like seeing Cynthia in his quarters all those weeks ago was a peek at something he wasn't supposed to see. He felt like the keeper had made that critical error by allowing him to see her. Seeing her had given him hope and given him strength, but now she was gone again.

Truth be told, he did not feel hope and strength when she had first presented herself to him. He had been confused and scared. So what had changed his mind? Only in the deepest parts of his own consciousness would he concede those true feelings. In those lost, ignored parts of his subconscious, Alec couldn't help but feel this meant there was a Cynthia out there that was his and not Cyrus's. This, of course, begged the question of why he cared so much about that. He had a good thing going with Nel, and Cynthia was ancient history. And yet he felt this incessant draw, a hunger almost, to claim Cynthia as his own.

Of course, all of that was pointless to ponder about because she had not shown herself to him again, and yet he did feel a sort of presence in this room. The hair on the back of his neck often stood on end as though someone were watching him, or sometimes he would even hear a noise from the main room when he was asleep in bed. The first few times he thought maybe Cyrus was lurking around out there, but whenever he got up to investigate, the room was always silent and dark.

He wasn't sure why he never questioned his own sanity with regards to what he had seen. Perhaps it was the way this place was so alien to him that his perception of normal had been skewed. Or perhaps it was the fact that he had found lipstick pressed into his cheek that night, which offered his mind something to point to as proof that it had been real. The truth was he never questioned his sanity because Cynthia had *felt* real. She had felt *different* to be sure, but she had also felt real. He didn't think he could have conjured up something so believable in a dream or vision.

At that moment something caught his attention from outside his room and down the hall. There were faint voices drifting down into his quarters, but it was the sound of someone shushing someone else that piqued his interest. He couldn't be sure who the voices belonged to, but he thought he recognized one as Nel.

Alec began walking slowly and silently out the door leading into the hallway. He stopped short of actually tiptoeing because somehow it felt undignified for a king to be creeping around his own castle. Rather he convinced himself he was simply walking towards the hushed voices, but as quietly as possible. Halfway down the hallway he realized he had left his scepter behind, leaning against the wall of his quarters. These days it was strange for him to leave his room without it, but it was pointless to go back for it now. Approaching the whispering voices, he verified it was indeed Nel, and she sounded to be in a heated discussion with Jack.

"You don't know what you're talking about," Nel was insisting in an urgent sort of whisper. "In fact, as far as I'm concerned, you gave up your right to an opinion when you chose your side."

"It's not about sides," Jack growled back. "You'd know that if you weren't so close to the problem. But we're at a pivotal crossroads right now, and I fear if something doesn't change this trajectory soon, we'll all be powerless to the consequences."

It sounded like Nel was laughing, but it was a hollow, humorless laugh. "Jack you couldn't stand Cyrus before, and Alec was your friend. Don't you think he deserves your support?"

"No I don't," Jack replied bluntly. "You may not want to hear this about your new pet project, but Alec is unstable. And if Cyrus has any strength at all he will put a stop to Alec before he's able to do any irreparable damage."

"I'll worry about that if Cyrus ever finds any real strength," Nel shot back.

The shuffling of footsteps seemed to signal the end of the conversation and the approach of one or both parties, so Alec backed down the hall quickly and rounded the corner, headed back towards his quarters before they could see him. He was simultaneously filled with pride over Nel's loyalty and betrayal over Jack's words. Jack had been different since the boat, there was no doubt about that, but now it seemed clear he was entirely Cyrus's man. Alec thought back to their night on the deck of the ship, drinking and laughing together, and felt sickly, creeping disgust working its way up his throat from the pit of his stomach. It had felt then like he had found his people, but just like Cynthia before him, Jack had abandoned him for his brother.

As Alec entered his quarters, he felt the now familiar prickling sensation on the back of his neck. The room didn't make him uncomfortable, but he never felt quite alone. It was still a surprise, however, when he looked up and realized that this time he was not in fact alone. A figure stood with his back to Alec, facing out the sprawling windows, but even without seeing his face, the broad frame was easily recognizable as Cyrus.

While they had never established specific boundaries, finding his brother in his room without him felt to Alec like a bit of an invasion. Alec glared at the back of his brother's head in disgust, and then cleared his throat to announce himself, even though he knew full well Cyrus had heard him enter. When Cyrus didn't turn to acknowledge him, Alec could feel his face growing red with anger, but he tried to remember what Nel had told him about keeping a cool head if he wanted to be taken seriously as a ruler.

Finally, Alec broke the silence, "Something I can do for you, Cy?"

Cyrus finally turned to face him, acting as though he hadn't noticed him before. "Alec," he said, but it wasn't a greeting so much as a cold, almost judgmental statement.

Alec hadn't been in a room alone with his brother in quite some time, and he felt somehow cornered by it. His temper flared for a second when he looked at Cyrus's right hand and saw him clutching one of the scepters in it. Alec thought for a wild moment that it was his own scepter that Cyrus had picked up, but a quick glance to the corner of the room showed his charred staff leaning untouched where he had left it. Cyrus was holding his own scepter, something he had seemed reluctant to do since they were named kings together. Despite Alec's past insistence that his brother should be carrying this *weapon of the king* with him at all times, seeing Cyrus with it now ignited a flurry of something akin to jealousy inside of him. Cyrus had shown no interest in ruling since they arrived here, and yet now here he stood, looking as effortlessly powerful as any ruler from history.

Alec again thought of what Nel had warned him about, how his brother was trying to bait him. This was an obvious ploy on Cyrus's part, and Alec decided not to get drawn in. "What is it, Cyrus?" Alec asked in what he was sure was a strong, level voice.

"We need to talk," Cyrus answered in a no-nonsense sort of way. "I've been having some unsettling conversations with Jack."

Alec rolled his eyes but caught himself before allowing the emotions he truly felt at that statement bubble to the surface. "Is that right?"

"Alec, I'm on your side, but I can't have you running around second-guessing me behind my back. If this is going to work, we need to be on the same page."

Alec's anger flashed again but this time he was less successful reeling it in. "On my side?" Alec practically laughed, although he didn't find anything remotely funny about this exchange. "First of all, I'm beginning to think you've never been on my side, and second, how dare you accuse *me* of talking behind *your* back."

Cyrus's eyes widened dangerously and he said, "I'm gonna need you to watch your tone. Don't forget who you're talking to."

"I know exactly who I'm talking to," Alec snapped, and his anger finally got the better of him. "I think it's time we said a few things that have gone unsaid for too long. You think I don't hear the whispers around the Temple, the talk behind my back? I can feel the sideways glances between you and Jack like ants over my skin! But like it or not the people chose me. You think you're a ruler of anything? Those people out there don't even know who you are. You maybe used to be a leader back in the old world, but you have no strength left. Enjoy your retirement, and stay out of my way."

Cyrus crossed the distance between them in seconds and grasped Alec roughly by the collar. Alec clawed at Cyrus's grip but was overpowered easily. He thought Cyrus was going to hit him at first, but he instead pulled him close, practically lifting Alec off his feet, and growled threateningly, "Do you feel strong right now?"

"Get the hell off me!" Alec shouted, lashing out wildly but unable to find a grip with his boots barely scraping the floor. Alec could feel his confidence deflating and was instantly disgusted that he didn't have the strength to defend himself. A swell of raw hatred burst forward and he thrashed violently. Any love he had held for his brother extinguished in that moment and he wanted to see him hurt. He wanted to see him dead. "The people won't stand for this!" Alec shouted, "You've just buried yourself! I'm the king! You can't…"

"The king?" Cyrus barked, "You can't even stand on your own two feet. You want to have an honest conversation? I've been standing up for you, giving you a chance, but you're unfit to rule. I can't imagine what would become of this Kingdom if it fell under the power of an immature, egotistical fanatic like you."

Alec glared into Cyrus's eyes but what stared back at him was not cruelty, but pity. It made Alec hate him even more.

"Listen to me very closely little brother," Cyrus began again, and a hint of a smirk betrayed how he was enjoying this power grab, "the world doesn't owe you anything. Your failures in life are entirely due to your own shortcomings."

Cyrus abruptly released Alec, who fell to his knees hard. "Although I'm sure it's easier for you to blame me," Cyrus finished, "that's always been your way after all."

Cyrus turned and strode towards the door, his heavy bootfalls echoing off the walls. Alec let him go, looking down at his own hands, which were shaking with anger. He tried to calm himself down, but he could feel his face contorting into a hideous mask of rage. He watched his hands clench into fists, yet he had no recollection of purposefully doing so. He stood up and bellowed out his brother's name, although Cyrus was apparently too far down the hall already to hear. Alec looked around the room wildly, acting more than ever like that captive lion who had just been provoked. His eyes landed on his scepter in the far corner of the room, which he snatched up and stormed down the hall with.

"Cyrus!" he bellowed again. He was furious with himself that he hadn't said more when Cyrus belittled him like that. He had been so caught off guard by the attack that he had said almost nothing. He continued down the passageway, eventually coming to the staircase that led downstairs. If Cyrus thought Alec would make less of a scene with other people around, he was sorely mistaken. Alec had no intention of being silenced or cowed into submission. He had earned his place as king.

Alec heard footsteps approaching up the stairs and readied himself for round two with his brother, but it turned out to be Nel.

"What are you yelling about?" Nel asked, looking concerned.

Alec blew past her, thinking the last thing he needed right now was a lecture from her. He had no intention of calming down, he intended to get even.

"Alec, what's wrong?" Nel asked, running down the stairs after him. "What happened?"

Alec paid her no attention and burst forth into the cavernous rooms of the main level. He scanned each room erratically, looking for any sign of his brother as he charged forward. He could hear voices coming from the entrance hall ahead and sure enough when he passed through the final doorway, there was Cyrus.

Alec stormed forward and shouted, "Who the hell do you think you are?!"

Cyrus turned to look at him and Alec could swear there was a sneer on his face. Jack was with him and looked thoroughly baffled. There was also a third man peering out from between the two, who also looked shocked at Alec's sudden entrance. Now Cyrus was looking stunned as well, as if he couldn't have imagined Alec would follow him after their confrontation.

"I asked you a question!" Alec roared again, still striding towards his brother, "who the hell do you think you are?! These are *my* people! This is *my* Kingdom!"

"Alec!" Cyrus yelled back, "calm down! We can talk about this later."

"We'll talk about it whenever I damn well please! You think you can strong arm me into bowing to you?"

"Alec!" Cyrus yelled again, "someone's here to see us."

Alec's eyes finally settled on the man standing behind Cyrus and Jack; a small, middle-aged man with greying hair and perpetually worried eyes.

"Who are you?" Alec barked at the man.

The man teetered on his toes in a sort of wobbly half-bow, raising his hands in surrender and fealty. "Begging your pardon, my King, I am actually here to see you."

After his experience with that horrible woman and her team the other day, Alec was taken aback by this man's respect, and if he were being honest, he liked the fact that this man referred to him as 'my King'.

"What's your name?" Alec asked in a far less confrontational tone.

"Heath, my King," the man responded. "I brought something for you, information for you, my King."

"I see," Alec responded, now regretting that he had stormed in here in such dramatic fashion moments earlier.

"He refused to tell anyone but you," Cyrus said with a hint of annoyance in his voice.

Alec ignored his brother and moved closer to Heath, who was still looking jumpy as though he might turn and flee at any moment.

"It's just," Heath began, looking around nervously with his busy eyes, "I want to make sure I'm protected. I thought maybe by telling you…"

"Why don't you tell me what the information is," Alec interrupted in a commanding voice, "then we can talk."

"Okay," Heath agreed softly, "I… it was me. I was the one who left you a note on your doorstep… months back… before you were king."

Alec studied the man intently. Of course he remembered what Heath was referring to; how could he forget the night Nel was taken from him by King Mora. He had been shouting his intentions to disobey the king's orders when a knock had come on the door. The hand-scrawled note outside had said "HE CAN HEAR YOU" in big block letters.

"That was you?" Nel asked in surprise. She, of course, had been with him when they received the letter, and it wasn't even an hour later that Mora and the Neodactyls had shown up to take Nel away.

"It was, Madam!" Heath said, nodding his head fervently.

"The note warning you of Mora listening in?" Jack asked, slowly filling in the blanks.

Heath nodded again, "I could hear you shouting, sir… I mean my King, and I knew others could hear you as well… others who were loyal to King Mora."

"Who?" Alec demanded. Remembering that night and how powerless he had felt when Nel was taken brought his anger boiling back to the surface.

"I just…" Heath stammered, still looking around nervously, "I thought if I brought this to you, arrangements could be reached… I'm a humble man and don't have much… perhaps in exchange for my words…"

"Who told Mora what we were discussing that night?" Alec demanded again.

"Alec," Cyrus warned from over his shoulder.

Alec caught himself before allowing his anger to get the best of him. This was one of his people, after all. He moved forward and put a comforting but firm hand on Heath's shoulder.

"Heath," Alec began gently, "you're not from here, are you?" He suspected as much after hearing him refer to Nel as 'Madam'. It didn't seem right for this place.

"I'm not," Heath admitted with a shake of his head, "been here a while now, but I'm originally from New York."

"I see," Alec said reassuringly. "So you know how this place works, what's at stake. I want to bring this Kingdom into the future, but I can't do that if there are Mora loyalists lurking behind my back. Who told Mora what Nel and I were talking about that night?"

His reassuring approach seemed to work because Heath nodded apprehensively and replied, "I can take you to him, if you like."

Alec nodded and said, "Right now, Heath."

## CHAPTER THIRTY-FOUR

# TRAITOR

Despite Cyrus and Jack's objections, Alec had several of his Temple guards scramble to ready his chariot while Alec himself coaxed the Neodactyls into the harnesses in front. After a chaotic few minutes, Heath led the way out of the Temple onto the main road leading towards town.

It was an odd journey with an exceptionally odd grouping of people. More than once Nel had glanced around from atop the chariot and wondered how the hell she had found herself as part of this bizarre quartet. Herself and Alec rode the chariot, lurching and bumping its way along the uneven path beneath the rising moon. The last remnants of the evening's light had receded into the shadows during their journey. Heath had led the way towards town with Cyrus and Jack flanking his sides, tossing the occasional question his way, then turning to Alec with pointed expressions as though Heath's every answer was further proof that this journey into town was a bad idea. Three Temple guards brought up the rear; rusted machetes in hand and blank expressions on their faces. Nel wasn't sure the guards were necessary, but she understood it was important for Alec to do things his way.

By the time they entered the town square, many of the doors and windows were closed up for the night, although there were still quite a few straggling vendors and workers busy gathering their belongings along the sides of the road. The villagers gave the chariot and the king's entourage a wide berth, but Nel caught many of them staring up at Alec with a mix of admiration and intimidation. She supposed that made sense, after all it was her understanding that King Mora would ride this very chariot through town on a whim and leave fear and death in his wake. The bystanders barely gave Cyrus a second glance, a thought that brought a smile to Nel's face as she realized they likely had no idea that he was also their king.

In what should have been no surprise to any of them, Heath ended up leading the group directly to their old living quarters in town. Nel herself had not been in their old rooms since the night she was taken by King Mora, and it felt strange to be returning atop the very chariot he once rode. Strange, yet powerful. She was no longer a tourist in this land, but among its leaders; and the fear she had felt that night was something she need never feel again.

As it turned out, there was a parallel set of housing that ran along the back of their own prior quarters, the entrances to which were on the next street down. Nel had never given the layout a second thought before, but they appeared to share the rear wall. The housing on the other side of the wall was more or less identical to their own housing, but the mirror image of it. The same beige stone walls with the same rust-colored stains dripping down the sides from years of streaming rainwater. The doors were all identical as well, one of which Heath pointed out as his own as he passed it. But onlookers were beginning to take notice of their entourage and wooden-slat windows were starting to be opened up by curious neighbors across the road. The quiet, indistinct murmuring of whispered theories being discussed between townsfolk had suddenly filled the air with a palpable, paranoid buzz, and Heath began to look around uneasily.

Heath turned to Alec aboard the chariot behind him and said, "Sir, my King, I just want to make sure I'm offered some kind of protection after this. I don't know which of these people is loyal to you and who is loyal to Mora. I can't just go back to…"

"Mora is long dead," Alec declared in a flat, almost dismissive voice.

"Yes my King," Heath started again, "but I just…"

"MORA IS DEAD!" Alec shouted out to the watching neighbors lurking in the shadows behind their windows. The announcement made Nel jump, but she grinned privately to herself all the same. "COME OUT IF YOU WANT, YOU ARE WELCOME OUT HERE."

A couple of the neighbors who had been peeking through cracks in their open doors stepped uncertainly out onto the road, but most stayed behind their windows under the perceived safety of their own roofs. Several even retreated further back into the deep shadows of their homes, as though they could hide the fact that they were watching.

The homes on their own side of the street were windowless, however several of the doors had begun to open, no doubt drawn by Alec's shouting. While most of these new faces looked openly curious or even shocked to see the king's chariot outside their front doors, one face wore a different expression altogether; dread. The man was small and hunched a bit with greasy hair and a greasy complexion, but eyes that were blue, piercing, and unblinking.

Alec had taken notice of the man as well because he looked to Heath, who gave him a small but distinct nod of affirmation. Jack and Cyrus both looked uncomfortable but did nothing. Jack put a reassuring hand on Heath's shoulder and encouraged him to back up and out of the center of the road where everyone's attention was now affixed.

Alec nodded to himself in a 'what are we gonna do about this' sort of way and worked his way passed Nel on the close quarters of the chariot platform. Nel was impressed to see that he wore an expression not of anger but of almost fatherly disappointment; an expression that Nel knew was not genuine, but it showed that he was finally weighing the situation before reacting. Alec stepped off the back of the chariot and down onto the stone street with a heavy crunch, the sound of tiny rock debris grinding beneath Alec's boot heels the only noise on the otherwise silent road. His ever-present scepter gripped in his right hand, Alec strode slowly and deliberately around the side of the chariot, running his fingers casually through the feathers of the nearest Neodactyl as he went without breaking his pace. The greasy man watched Alec's approach through little more than an eyeballs-width gap in the door, seemingly debating whether he should shut it or not. Alec stopped a few strides from the door and looked down at the charred and ancient-looking scepter in his hand, purposely drawing out the moment and allowing the silence on the street to reach a deafening pitch.

Finally, without looking up from his scepter, Alec said, "Why don't you come out here a sec." When the man did not move, Alec looked up to meet the man's eyes without ever raising his head. "That wasn't a question," Alec said softly.

The man opened the door slowly and shuffled out onto the main road, eyeing the Neodactyls warily. Nel heard Cyrus whisper to Alec, "We're just talking to him," but either Alec didn't hear him or chose to ignore him. The man stopped a good few paces from Alec, who smiled in amusement at the man's timid nature.

"What's your name?" Alec asked in a would-be-friendly tone that was nevertheless laced with menace.

The man responded with a mumbled word that sounded like 'Rock,' but Nel couldn't be sure.

Alec nodded his head again and, after a pause, said, "You know Heath, don't you?" He pointed in Heath's direction, who seemed to physically shrink further into himself as though he were trying to will himself to vanish from the street.

"He's a traitor," Rock spit out, with visible spittle flying off his lips.

Alec nodded once again with an expression of amused surprise on his face, and repeated, "A traitor you say? Hmm. Now that's an interesting word, isn't it?" Rock seemed to cower on the spot, even as Alec's tone was kept light. "Let me ask you a question then," Alec began again, now striding slowly towards Rock, who seemed to be on the verge of running for it. "You say Heath was a traitor. This of course would be in reference to him betraying the former king, is that right?" Alec had now reached Rock and put a heavy arm around his shoulders in a comforting manner that wasn't fooling anyone.

"Yes, yes exactly," Rock sputtered. He seemed somehow nervous and defiant all at the same time.

"Mmmhmm," Alec responded, "but now I'm your king, isn't that right? This puts you in a bit of an awkward spot, does it not?"

"I'm... I'm loyal," Rock responded, though he didn't specify who exactly he was saying he was loyal to.

Alec seemed to feel the same way. "From what I hear, you sold us out to Mora. Now my question is whether you are loyal to the crown or to the king."

Heath did not seem to take Alec's meaning because he furrowed his brow in a not-so-bright expression and looked to Alec questioningly. The audience of watchful neighbors had given up all pretense of being disinterested and were now openly gawking at the scene unfolding in the street.

Alec, his arm still draped around Rock's shoulders in a sort of captive embrace, continued, "What I mean is there is a difference between being loyal to the title of king, no matter who wears said title, and being loyal to one man, one specific ruler. Do you take my meaning now?"

Nel thought Alec was being purposefully unclear as a way of toying with Rock, but Rock didn't need the extra help to be confused. He was still furrowing his brow and seemingly trying to piece together Alec's point, or possibly trying to piece together what Alec wanted to hear. Alec smacked Rock on the back of the head hard with the palm of his hand and said, with the first trace of a raised voice, "Are you loyal to me or are you loyal to the rotting, festering corpse that is the remains of your previous king?"

Rock blinked rapidly in surprise at the blow and responded with another ambiguous answer, "I'm loyal to the king, of course. Always I am loyal to the king."

With that Alec grabbed Rock roughly by the back of the neck and walked him forward towards the chariot. He shoved Rock down into a kneeling position right in front of the waiting Neodactyls, both of which hissed and flashed their yellow eyes hungrily but did not strike. Rock tried to look away from the creature's greedy eyes but Alec pushed the back of his head forward, crouching down himself without any fear of the animals. Cyrus finally moved out from his spot beside Jack and Heath and began to approach Alec swiftly. Nel made her first move since stepping down off the chariot and walked forward to intercept Cyrus. While Nel was quite a bit smaller than Cyrus, the fact that he hadn't seen her coming was enough for her shoulder body-checking him in the chest to halt his approach. Alec saw the scuffle out of the corner of his eyes and one of the Neodactyls raised its head threateningly towards them. Cyrus seemed to think better of continuing his stride and stopped pushing against Nel, who nevertheless kept her body firmly between him and Alec.

Rock was still struggling against Alec's grip, trying desperately to move his face away from the sharp beak of the Neodactyl, which seemed to become more agitated the more Rock squirmed. "Which king are you loyal to?" Alec demanded, now having dropped the understanding tone of false benevolence. "Answer me now or join your beloved king in the afterlife."

"No sir!" Rock now yelled desperately, still fighting with everything he had against Alec's hand on the back of his head. "I'm loyal to you! I'm loyal to the king! I'm loyal to you!"

Alec did not remove his hand and the Neodactyl nearest to Rock was approaching a frenzy of excitement. "YOU'RE NOT LOYAL TO THE THRONE ANYMORE, YOU ARE LOYAL TO *ME*!" Alec roared. Rock was now physically digging his palms into the stone street, his feet kicking out wildly behind him trying desperately to find purchase.

"YES SIR!" Rock was yelling. "YES MY LORD! I SWEAR IT!"

The nearest Neodactyl's slit pupils seemed to be pulsating with overwhelmed stimulation as it started positively wheezing in short, loud huffs of excitement.

"ALEC!" Cyrus warned in a commanding voice from behind Nel as the second Neodactyl closely watched him.

"Do we believe him?" Alec asked, looking back to Nel. He then turned his head to the gathered crowd and addressed the collective group, "What do you all think? Do we believe him?"

Alec's momentary lapse in concentration seemed to be all it took, and the consequence was instantaneous. Nothing short of a geyser of crimson blood shot out of Rock's neck as the Neodactyl snapped down on his throat, severing arteries and tendons like they were made of string. Alec released Rock in an instant and his hands rose up in confusion as blood shot up into his face and chest. Alec stumbled on the spot, spinning and looking down as the brown cobblestone bricks turned to red around him. The Neodactyl that had struck only did so the once. It had lashed out and then instantly recoiled its neck back to a waiting position. The damage had been done to Rock of course, who's nearly headless body now lay slumped in a heap on the street.

There were gasps of horror now from the watching neighbors, some of whom had fully retreated back into their homes and re-shuttered their windows. Others seemed to be frozen in shock with their jaws hanging open in dumbfounded looks of terror and disgust. Cyrus and Jack seemed to be absolutely stunned into silence.

Alec was starting to compose himself again and had started looking around at the watching villagers in defiance. "This is what happens when you betray your king!" Alec shouted, still turning on the spot to address everyone at once. "Your loyalty is to me! It's the only time I'm going to remind you!" Standing there with his scepter; his face, chest, and arms covered in blood, he looked like Death incarnate. Nel even found herself disturbed by the image. But as the townsfolk began to fade away into their homes, cowed into silence by what they had witnessed, it occurred to Nel that this story would spread. No one would dare cross Alec now.

Once the final window had closed and they were alone on the dark street, Alec seemed to abandon his defiant pose once again and began wiping blood from his eyes and cheeks in clear discomfort. No longer an imposing figure of Death, he now looked disgusted and half in shock.

"What the hell, Alec," Cyrus breathed, still too alarmed himself to raise his voice beyond a hoarse whisper.

"It was an accident," Alec muttered, still rubbing blood off his face and out of his hair. "Not an accident, I… I didn't do that. I wasn't going to…" He trailed off, looking down at the unmoving mass that was Rock's body.

"He was professing his loyalty to you," Cyrus started again, regaining a little strength in his voice. "To us. He was one of our people."

"He wasn't one of our people," Nel spat bitterly, finally moving her body out of his way, confident Cyrus knew better than to make a move against Alec with the Neodactyls around. "He was one of Mora's spies."

"Mora's dead!" Cyrus shouted, causing the Neodactyls to bristle in alarm. "Mora's dead," he repeated more softly but no less forcefully, "he doesn't have spies anymore. That was one of our people."

"He almost got me killed," Nel responded, "or have you forgotten me being dragged away in the dead of night?"

"He was obeying orders from his king at the time," Cyrus argued, "isn't that exactly the type of loyalty you want, Alec? Unwavering loyalty to the crown…"

"Loyalty to the crown isn't loyalty to me," Alec snapped.

"Jesus, Alec," Cyrus said with open disgust, "wiping out people loyal to a previous leader is exactly how dictatorships are born."

"Don't you *dare* lecture me!" Alec hissed back, "not after our last conversation!"

"Heath had just walked in the doors when you came up to us," Cyrus insisted, "he had barely explained what he was there for when you…"

"Before that!" Alec practically yelled, but he kept his voice low to avoid unwanted attention. "In my chambers! When you were strutting around like you actually give a damn about ruling this place. Who the hell are you kidding walking around with your scepter and giving me orders! I'm the damn KING!"

"What the hell are you talking about?" Cyrus shouted back. "I haven't been in your quarters and I certainly haven't touched that damn scepter since you gave it to me."

Alec crossed the distance between himself and his brother in a second and actually looked like he was going to hit him. Instead, he stopped a foot from Cyrus's face, raised a shaking, blood covered finger and started to open his mouth, his lip quivering and his face contorting in anger. "I will fucking bury you for this," he said in a raspy sort of whisper. His eyes looked piercing white against the blood-soaked deep red of his face.

Nel put a hand on Alec's arm, feeling the blood beneath her fingers with an internal pang of disgust, and said, "C'mon Alec, it's over." She couldn't be sure what was going on. When she had come across Alec on the stairwell in the Temple, he had been out of his mind in anger and had stormed down to the main level to confront Cyrus about… something. But if what he had wanted to confront Cyrus about was an argument they had in his quarters, she had to admit to herself that was not possible. She had seen Cyrus down on the main level not three minutes before she ran into Alec. Not to mention Cyrus looked genuinely confused by the accusation just leveled at him.

"C'mon," Nel insisted again, this time succeeding in coaxing Alec to back away from his brother and walk with her around the side of the chariot. They stepped up onto the platform and the Neodactyls instantly pulled forward with a jolt, seemingly knowing it was time to go without being told.

"You *will* tell us how you're controlling those things," Cyrus called out as the chariot passed by him in the road. "You lost control of them tonight, didn't you?" he called after them, but he was already being absorbed in the billowing dust kicked up in their wake. He turned to Jack as the cloud obscured him from view and Nel could only make out one word of what that conversation was going to be about: 'Sanity.'

## CHAPTER THIRTY-FIVE

## SECRET MEETING

Even with Cyrus being king over these lands and of this Temple, and despite the fact that anything he did within his own Kingdom should, and likely would, go unquestioned, he still felt awkward and a bit nervous standing out in the cavernous open room of the entrance hall. Perhaps those paranoid nerves were to be expected by anyone who had agreed to a secret meeting in the dead of night, and that is exactly what he was doing. Jack had asked him to meet by the doorway leading down to the dungeons at midnight, and with three minutes left to go, Cyrus was already starting to get antsy. The Temple was a big place, and they were unlikely to be overheard in most of the less-traveled corners of the structure, but the dungeons had the distinct advantage of allowing them to see someone approaching before they were within earshot. This cloak-and-dagger nonsense of organizing secret meetings and sneaking about his own Temple would have seemed absurd a few days ago, but not after the scene on the street in town. Cyrus didn't know exactly what Jack had in mind to talk about, but he could guess, and he just hoped he had a solution to the mess they had found themselves in.

Cyrus checked his watch again, a strangely useless artifact from his previous life that he inexplicably still carried with him, and noted with annoyance that Jack was now two minutes late. As if hearing his thoughts, soft but echoing footsteps announced Jack's arrival from across the room.

"Sorry," Jack whispered hurriedly, "Nel was still prowling the hallways upstairs."

The two of them proceeded down the staircase to the lower level, following the corridors and the windy steps to the now familiar sight of the narrow hallway lined on one side with iron bars. It had been a long time since they were trapped down here with the Neodactyls, receiving advice on storming the Temple from Henry.

Cyrus started to say something but Jack put his finger up to his mouth in silence, looking down towards the opposite end of the hallway where, to Cyrus's surprise, he could see flickering torchlight radiating out of the open door to Henry's old writing room. The soft, almost imperceptible sound of paper being moved around told them without question that someone was in there. Cyrus moved forward quietly, slowly creeping down the hallway towards the room with Jack right on his heels. He slowly peered around the doorframe, dreading the possibility of coming face to face with his brother and having to find an excuse as to what they were doing down here. He breathed a sigh of relief when he recognized the small, hunched form of Henry rifling through the endless loose papers and journals that filled the table surfaces.

"Henry," Jack exclaimed so loudly that he caused the elderly historian to convulse in alarm. Henry grabbed the table for support as he turned to look at them, and for a moment Cyrus was worried he may actually collapse from the shock, but he composed himself and smiled warmly back at them.

"Didn't expect to have company at this time of night," Henry laughed, shaking his head.

Jack apologized for startling him, fairly pointing out that the room was technically Henry's old room.

Henry brushed it off, saying, "I can head off if you were wanting to talk in private."

"No no, we'll find elsewhere to chat," Cyrus insisted, trying to keep the curious fact that they were seeking out the farthest removed room of the Temple at midnight to talk as breezy as possible.

"We'll let you get back to your reading," Jack agreed, turning to leave back down the corridor.

"I had all these journals back then," Henry explained with a shake of his head, "and I haven't seen any of these letters and notebooks in years."

Jack looked impatient to leave with one foot already out the door, and said, "It's a long time you were down here. I'm sure it's quite an adjustment."

Henry laughed with a shrug of his shoulders and said, "I had such purpose back then."

Cyrus felt bad for the old man, who once again reminded him of himself in some strange way, but a future self. "You'll find your purpose again," Cyrus assured him, "it'll just take time."

Henry nodded but waved his hands dismissively, as though to say only a young man would be so naïve about their ability to rekindle their purpose. "I'm making no headway down here, the room is yours." He started ambling towards the door when he stopped and said, "I don't mean to pry, but I take it this is about your brother?"

Cyrus looked sideways to Jack with uncertainty and responded, "What makes you say that?"

"Because he's become a problem," Henry responded.

"This is what I'm saying," Jack said to Cyrus, nodding his head vigorously, "I'm really worried this has become a bigger problem than we've been admitting. I mean, that spectacle on the street…"

"Yeah, I know," Cyrus agreed, "I just can't believe…"

"…that we're at this point?" Jack finished his sentence incorrectly for him, "we are. He's become a real threat."

Cyrus couldn't disagree, and he wanted to verbalize his own concerns, but when he opened his mouth, all that came out was, "He's my brother."

Jack tilted his head in a noncommittal nod as though he had been anticipating this response. "He murdered someone, Cyrus. We all saw it. Dress it up however you want, that's what happened."

"I think he lost control," Cyrus said rather weakly.

"Now that's an understatement," Jack retorted. "Yeah I saw his face too after it happened, I don't think he meant to kill him, at least not consciously."

"And unconsciously?" Cyrus responded darkly.

Cyrus's question hung in the air for a moment before Jack broke the silence by asking what was on both of their minds. "Henry, you've been here a long time. What is Alec's bond with those creatures? How is he controlling them?"

Henry shook his head, "I wish I knew. You have to believe me, I would tell you if I knew. This is just how King Mora started out."

Jack shot Cyrus a meaningful glance.

"You were here when Mora took power from the past king?" Cyrus asked, perhaps subconsciously steering the conversation away from his concerns about his brother.

"King Irias," Henry confirmed with a nod and a funny look on his face. "Most of what I heard about King Mora's rise to power was from talking with the people." He gestured behind himself at all the piles of journals and papers. "At one point I suppose I thought this would all mean something."

"He's gotta be stopped, Cyrus," Jack announced, bringing the conversation squarely back to the issue at hand with jarring insistence.

"What do you mean by *stopped*?" Cyrus asked accusingly.

"I'm not suggesting we hurt him," Jack insisted, "but we have to start thinking of the long game here. He's gaining power exponentially. Ydoro was right, it's the people's perception of him that gives him strength. And right now…"

"…Right now the people are either terrified of him or in awe of him," Cyrus finished bleakly with a depressed nod of his head.

"Precisely," Jack agreed. "Nothing will be solved by confronting him directly. He's too volatile. What we have to do is outmaneuver him. Chip away at his authority without him realizing what we're doing."

Cyrus considered this for a long moment. "Henry, again you've been here a long time, you know these people, how they think," he gestured at the stacks of papers once again, "what are your thoughts?"

Henry seemed amused at being asked his opinion. "Well, the thing is, these people have always responded to strength above all else."

"Maybe, but I can't see a show of force working in this instance," Cyrus repeated, "I believe we need to approach this less like a fight and more like a chess match. Any thoughts on how we do that?"

Henry furrowed his brow, then smiled and shook his head, "You know, I never really followed sports other than baseball."

Now it was Jack's turn to furrow his brow. "Well, not sports Henry. Ya know, a chess match. The board game?"

Henry nodded sheepishly with a laugh, "Right, of course. I think maybe I'm more tired than I realized... and it's been a long time."

Cyrus nodded in understanding but Jack still looked confused.

"Perhaps I better leave you to it," Henry said, shaking his head in apparent embarrassment. "I will say this, you may want to take a firm stand against the King now while you have the chance. You have no idea how fast things can change in this Kingdom."

"Us being here is living proof of that," Cyrus agreed, "have a good night Henry."

As Henry ambled out the door at a painfully slow pace and started down the hallway, Cyrus turned back to Jack to continue their conversation. To his surprise, Jack was still wearing a look of worried confusion on his face.

"What is it, Jack?" Cyrus asked in alarm.

Jack only shook his head in way of response and put his finger to his lips. He looked entirely consumed by something, and Cyrus couldn't tell if he was thinking or straining to listen for something. Cyrus spent a long time just staring at Jack, who was gazing down at the floor as if he could see something there that no one else could.

"Jack?" Cyrus finally said again.

Jack again shook his head, but then leaned in close to Cyrus's ear and whispered, "We'll talk later."

With that, Jack turned and wrenched open the door on the opposite side of the room, began up the staircase, and closed the door behind him; a clear indication he had no desire to be followed. His footsteps sounded hurried as he ascended the staircase behind the now closed door, until at last Cyrus, standing in the middle of the historian's old workshop, was left in silence and confusion.

## CHAPTER THIRTY-SIX

# IN THE SHADOWS

Eating dinner in the dining room was one of those absurdly mundane routines that felt supremely strange in its banality. Jack had found that to be the case in several instances, where the least unusual tasks felt like the most foreign these days. Perhaps it was when this world and his own ran parallel, it accentuated how strange the rest of this world truly was. At any rate, Jack finished his dinner alone. He had been hoping to see Cyrus and talk further about the abrupt ending to their conversation the night before, but so far they hadn't found a moment alone. Maybe it was for the best they didn't talk before Jack had time to hammer down the rough edges of his 'theory'; could you even call it a theory if you had no idea what you were theorizing? Truth be told, Jack was starting to think he was just being paranoid. When he had left Cyrus last night, he had run up through the Temple to the living quarters ahead of Henry and waited in the shadows of one of the many unused rooms along the hallway leading to the king's chambers. He had the strangest suspicion that he was going to see Henry hobbling his way in to see Alec, and perhaps report everything that himself and Cyrus had been discussing. That had not been the case. He did eventually see Henry return, but he went to his own bedroom without speaking to anyone.

Jack got heavily to his feet and started towards the door when Nel rounded the corner, stopping awkwardly when she saw him. Things had been extremely tense between the two of them for months now. Gone were the days of light-natured banter between them, or the way Nel used to throw an arm around his shoulders and lean against him in her mildly flirtatious, overly friendly way. Ever since Jack had woken up in his room after their battle with Mora, and Nel had talked to him about 'picking a side', they had barely spoken one-on-one. Back then, Jack had not been certain there was a need to pick sides, now he realized it would be essential for everyone in the weeks to come.

"Jack," Nel nodded tersely at him.

"I was just leaving, don't worry," Jack responded dryly as he went to move past her.

Nel put an arm out in the doorframe, blocking his exit. "You don't have to avoid me, Jack. I can hear the oozing disdain in your voice, if there's something you wanna say, come out and say it."

"I've said my piece to you, Nel, I don't know what more there is to say."

"Oh I don't know," Nel said almost playfully, although not in a fun playful way but more the way a cat would play with a mouse. "Maybe you wanted to talk to me because you can see Cyrus losing his footing in this Kingdom. Maybe you've started to realize that you've hitched yourself to a sinking ship. *Maybe* you're starting to see the value in the way Alec does things."

Jack looked back at her with a stony expression and replied, "On the contrary, Nel, he's showing his true colors. You can't agree with what he did out there that night."

"Can't I?" Nel responded, "Maybe you don't know me as well as you think. And you certainly don't know Alec as well as you think."

"I've seen all I need to from him," Jack said blandly, "are we done here? I've got better things to do than chit chat with Alec's pawn."

Nel laughed, but it was a humorless, dangerous laugh. "Charming as ever, Jack," she said, finally moving her arm out of his way. "Just remember, we're not too proud to take you in, if you're not too proud to admit you picked the wrong side."

"It must be exhausting trying to be so witty all the time," Jack responded, "why don't you save it for your king." He started to leave before an idea occurred to him. "Hey, Nel?"

Nel seemed caught off-guard by the change in his tone. She raised her eyebrows questioningly in way of response.

"What do you know about Henry?" Jack asked.

"Henry?" Nel repeated in a manner suggesting she couldn't fathom why anyone would want to know more about the man. "I don't know, old guy. Lived in the dungeons for years. Wrote journals."

"You were in the cell next to him," Jack pressed, "did he talk about himself? Anything at all?"

"Hell, I don't know," Nel shrugged in obvious disinterest. "I know he had a son back in our world, Benton or Benjamin I think, something like that. Honestly, he had more to say about baseball than his kid. He said he used to go to games with his dad as a boy."

That was interesting, Jack thought to himself. Henry had brought up baseball the night before as well, in a rather awkward conversation. "Did he say which team?" Jack asked.

Nel rolled her eyes. "Why, thinking of catching a game together?" Nel smirked but it didn't survive long on her face when Jack didn't laugh with her. "Hell, you're dull," Nel finally said with an exasperated shake of her head, "It was the Boston Red Sox."

"The Boston Red Sox?" Jack questioned, "you're sure?"

"Yeah," Nel answered, visibly losing patience. "What's your interest?"

A piercing shriek echoed from the main hall causing both of them to jump.

Jack started towards the entrance hall but Nel didn't follow. "It's just the Neodactyls," Nel called out after him, "aren't you used to them yet?"

Jack was not used to them yet, and didn't think he ever would be, but he wanted to find out what they were doing roaming about the Temple. As he entered the entrance hall, he found that the creatures were not alone. Alec stood importantly atop his chariot by the main doors as a Temple guard busied himself with the harnesses of the Neodactyls. Jack had a passing thought of leaving before Alec saw him, but it was too late; Alec looked over his shoulder and they locked eyes for just a moment.

"Jack," Alec called out in a manner somewhere between friendly and condescending, "came to see me off?"

"Alec," Jack nodded as a way of greeting, now continuing his stride towards the doors so as not to look like he was trying to avoid him. "Another evening ride?" He meant the comment to sound conversational but he was pretty sure it came across as judgmental.

"That's where the people are, out there," Alec insisted with dripping superiority, "there's more to this Kingdom than these stone walls, you used to know that."

Jack nodded without responding. Nel was one thing, but Jack had no intention of getting drawn into a debate with Alec. Alec seemed to realize this because he gave a casual salute of his hand and turned back towards the door. Without so much as a whip of the reins, the Neodactyls sprinted forward in almost perfect unison and the chariot was carried off out the door and into the night. Jack walked forward and stopped just inside the frame of the doorway. He could see the bluish cloud of kicked up dust illuminated by the moonlight working its way fast down the road into the forest that led to town.

As the rattling of wooden wheels faded away, the sounds of the night took their place. Frogs chirped back and forth, crickets sang in their monotonous hum, and a Shrieking Bat in the distance screamed shrilly. Then came a crunch of gravel from off to his right and Jack turned with a start, squinting his eyes through the darkness to find movement. The crunching continued in the obvious pattern of footsteps, and not just any footsteps; there was definitely a *person* approaching. Through the miniscule amount of orange torchlight trickling out into the deep darkness of the night air, Jack could finally see a figure walking out of the shadows; someone with a short, small build and shoulder length hair.

"Annica?" Jack exclaimed in surprise as her face finally swam into view. She seemed to be alone, an unusual occurrence for her.

Annica smiled and hammered her fist and shoulder into his chest as a sort of affectionate half-hug. "Good to see you Jack," she said softly, in a voice far less fiery than usual.

"What's going on?" Jack asked, still thrown off by her unexpected emergence from the shadows of the trees.

"He's a problem," Annica stated bluntly, "your king."

Jack nodded in understanding but responded, "Not here. I know what you're saying, but not here, not now."

"Jack, you know we don't get involved in this sort of thing," Annica continued with a persistence that was difficult to ignore, "but seeing as we know each other…" Jack shifted uncomfortably on the spot but Annica seemed to misread his discomfort as passivity. "Jack, this is serious, you will lose control of this Kingdom."

"I know it's serious," Jack responded in a harsh whisper, "believe me, I'm not disagreeing. We're working on it."

"Well work faster. The people are settling in for the next Mora," Annica continued, finally taking Jack's cue and lowering her voice, "they'll become passive. If you want to make real change, you have to take the opportunity while you have it."

"We're weighing options," Jack promised, "but it's complicated. What would you have me do?"

"Bring Easttown and Westtown together *now*," she insisted, "build more through-roads, bring resources to the East for once; build, repair, expand. But show strength while you can, Jack. The people out there don't even know who Cyrus is, but they sure as hell know who Alec is, and believe it or not he has allies."

"So, what then?" Jack asked in mild frustration. It seemed that Annica was presenting plenty of issues but no real solutions.

"Cyrus has allies too," Annica said with an ever-so-slight twinkle in her eyes. "I've met both kings, but I'm one of the few who has. I've been spreading the word in Easttown that we finally have a king who's on our side, but all they ever see is Alec."

Jack nodded in understanding, and while he didn't want to tip his hand too much at this time, he felt an internal swell of gratitude towards Annica for her ambition in turning public opinion in Cyrus's favor.

"I'll leave you with this," Annica said, likely noting how uncomfortable Jack seemed about having this conversation out in the open, "you and Cyrus can make a grab for power here, but it's gotta be soon. And Alec has the upper hand right now."

With that, Annica started backing up the way she had come and said, "Good seeing you, Jack." She turned, walked several more paces and was swallowed up by the night.

Jack stood in the doorway for a moment more, contemplating their conversation, before stepping back into the golden glow of the room. He considered heading to bed but didn't think he would be able to sleep. His mind was spinning. He started wandering aimlessly through the quiet Temple and found his feet carried him back to Henry's old writing room. He shouldn't have been surprised; Henry was definitely one of the things weighing heavily on his mind.

Jack started rifling through the many papers and journals strewn about the tabletops, not knowing what he was looking for. He remembered reading that letter Henry had written to his son, Benjamin, but couldn't seem to find it now. That was not surprising considering, later that same night, the Neodactyls had been locked in this very room with a Shrieking Bat. What he did find were countless other journals filled cover to cover with notes and sketches about the Kingdom, about the locals, about the customs, and about life. Jack picked up one of the nearest notebooks from the tabletop; this one a worn, sun-damaged leather cover with badly dried out binding. He started leafing through it, pausing here and there to study a sketch of a local, a drawing from town, or a note of interest. He stopped at a page with an impressive portrait of two men; one older and one potentially in his teens. It was the older of the two that had caught Jack's eye, as he had remarkable similarities to Ydoro, albeit with a stronger jaw and a heavier brow. As he analyzed the page, it occurred to him that this man must have been Ydoro's father, who had come to the Kingdom with him when he was young. Jack's eyes drifted to the younger man in the sketch, who must have been Ydoro himself as a young man. Indeed, he displayed Ydoro's high cheekbones and gentle eyes. The two looked stoic yet passive, leading Jack to believe they had likely posed for the portrait. Jack could imagine Henry walking amongst the locals in town and asking people if he could sketch them, and potentially write a bit about their story.

There was no writing or label attached to this particular drawing, just their complacent faces to convey their story. Jack continued to flip through the journal, pausing again a few seconds later as he encountered a second face he recognized. King Mora had a full page dedicated to his portrait, and unlike the rough, although highly detailed, sketches of the town locals, Mora presented as a figure of significance. His chin stuck out importantly, he held his head high with his shoulders squared and his face a statue of resolute authority and strength. He wore the same robes, or at least similar ones, that the group had first encountered him in, a pendant hung from his neck that looked like a metal claw holding an eye, and each hand clutched a scepter, framing his physique impressively. It looked every bit a portrait of a king, and even reminded Jack a bit of the statues of emperors' past from the more ancient parts of the world. Below the sketch, outlined in a shaded border that looked like a plaque, were the words, 'King Mora, 1923'.

Jack closed the book and tossed it unceremoniously back onto the tabletop and the piles of other journals and papers that covered it. It was difficult to find such things all that interesting when he was still trapped here. He spent a bit more time sifting for clues, but when he found himself re-reading the same sentence describing the layout of the Kingdom three times and still not comprehending it, he decided he was finally ready to sleep.

His feet carried him back through the dark and incredibly silent Temple on their own. He had finally gotten used to the layout and it no longer felt like the maze it once did. As he entered the upper-level corridor that connected to their rooms and culminated in the king's chambers, he noticed flickering torchlight coming from within, and he wondered absently whether Alec had returned from his ride.

No sooner had the thought crossed his mind than Alec peered around the door opening and down the hall at him.

"Jack," Alec exclaimed brightly.

Jack was taken aback by the cordial greeting and tried, but probably failed, to hide his surprise. "Good ride, Alec?" Jack asked rather dismissively.

"Absolutely," Alec answered, "I was thinking I was the only one awake by now. Come on in."

Jack considered declining, given how tired he was, but approached Alec's quarters instead, acting more casual than he felt. As he entered the room, he realized with a jolt that the Neodactyls were both sitting off to the right, although they seemed fairly calm at the moment. One was sitting on the ground preening its feathers while the other was casually busying itself with what looked like a loose piece of wood flooring. Neither gave much notice to Jack as he entered the room.

"Don't worry about them," Alec reassured him, seeing Jack's wary eyes. "Well, I wish I could offer you a drink, but I have yet to find Mora's liquor stash," Alec joked in an uncharacteristically light-natured way. At least it was uncharacteristic of him recently. "Have a seat."

Alec gestured to a few chairs that Jack was sure had not been there when Mora resided in this room. There were three in total, and they bordered one side of the glowing altar that held Alec's scepter as though it were a campfire. Jack took a seat while Alec himself settled in on the circular bench-cushions that surrounded the opposite side of the altar in a half-circle. Alec put one foot up on the bench and leaned back casually, still smiling warmly at Jack.

"We just need Nel and Dalton here and it would be just like that first night on the ship," Alec mused. "What was that brown crap that Nel had us drinking?"

"Uh, I think it was whiskey," Jack answered, still taken off guard by Alec's pleasant demeanor.

"That was a fun night," Alec nodded to himself with a reflective smile on his face. "Different times, of course. Who would've known what was in store for us."

Jack nodded in agreement as Alec looked at him for a response. "How is it you're so comfortable in this place?" Jack asked before he could help himself.

Jack had been worried that Alec might take the question as an accusation, but to his pleasant surprise, Alec smiled and responded, "I don't know, actually. I *feel* this place, though, if you know what I mean. I never had much going for me in the outside world. I don't miss much, to be honest."

Jack raised his eyebrows in surprise at the candid reply. "What are you talking about? You were a prestigious professor, you had..." Jack trailed off as he realized how little he actually knew about Alec's life in the real world. He must not have had a wife, unlike Cyrus who was always talking about Cynthia back home. He never spoke of friends, or even family apart from his brother.

"Exactly," Alec replied, finishing Jack's thought for him. "What is there to go back to? But this place... I tell you, I can feel the life in this place coursing through my veins like raw energy. I've never before felt the way I feel here."

It was a very honest answer, Jack felt, but he thought maybe Alec was misunderstanding what that feeling was. In Jack's opinion, *power* was the feeling Alec had never felt before.

"I don't know," Alec continued with a shrug of his shoulders and a far off look in his eyes, "but that night on the ship, watching the stars and the ocean pass by, and talking about life with you and Nel and Dalton, it felt like the first time something *real* had happened in a long time. Like, that's the day that woke me up."

Jack just nodded, not knowing how to respond. It was a side of Alec he hadn't witnessed in a long time, and it was refreshing and hopeful to see again.

"Do you ever think of moments like that in your life?" Alec asked finally.

Jack shrugged, surprised at being asked, and replied, "Not in a long time I suppose. My life had become fairly routine, although that's always the way I liked it. Structure and discipline were my way of life. I was working my way towards becoming captain, that was really my focus."

"You didn't have anyone back home?" Alec asked.

"Not in a long time," Jack repeated again. Silence hung in the air after he spoke.

At long last, Alec said, "Well, I'll let you get to bed, Jack. It was really good talking to you."

"Yeah you too," Jack responded as he stood up, surprised at how true that statement was.

"Hey I'm thinking next time we find something to drink around here, what do you say?" Alec asked jovially, "I know Ydoro had some sort of booze, I'm sure we could scrounge something up."

"Yeah that sounds good," Jack replied with a laugh as he made his way to the door.

"Oh and Jack, just one more thing," Alec called out from the bench behind the altar, still with his foot casually resting on the cushion next to him. As Jack turned to face him, he saw that the good-natured smile had left Alec's face entirely. "If Annica ever shows her face here again uninvited, I'll feed it to the Neodactyls."

Jack stared into Alec's eyes, the glow from the frozen fire dancing ominously within them, and a shiver ran down his spine as he saw nothing but cold calculation reflected back at him. One of the Neodactyls hissed quietly from the corner. Jack had no quick-witted retort as he did with Nel. There was nothing to be said at all. He looked into Alec's eyes a moment longer before turning and exiting the room. A feeling of intense dread overtook him, and he couldn't help thinking, somewhere deep in his subconscious, that this was the beginning of the end.

**CHAPTER THIRTY-SEVEN**

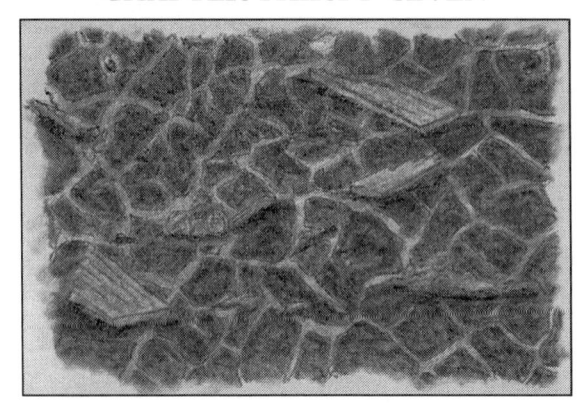

## AMONG THE PEOPLE

Through the trees ahead, Cyrus could see the faint, pulsating shimmer of the Fire Fields coming into view. He had not been out this way since their arrival to the Kingdom, and truth be told, he was not thrilled about journeying back alone. Jack had seemed strangely preoccupied over the last few days, and even an invitation to Henry had been declined. Henry's exact words were 'that's a long way for such an old man to walk,' so Cyrus had resigned to making the trip by himself. He felt shame at not having come out this way sooner to inspect their original 'landing site', but it was incredible how quickly one could get wrapped up in the day-to-day and forget to find a path forward. And having exhausted all theories that made any sense at all, Cyrus decided revisiting the site of their arrival offered the best possibility for a path forward.

He emerged from the treeline and out into the overcast afternoon light. There were swaths of harsh, white sunlight dappling the field ahead, but the clouds beyond were an ominous, bruised blue that seemed to warn of a coming storm. It made the glowing orange beneath the cracked earth of the Fire Fields look all the more bright and eerie by contrast.

Cyrus walked out a ways, trying his hardest to get his bearings and figure out exactly where they had landed all those many months ago. There were absolutely no identifying markers to use as a guide. He arrived at what he thought was roughly the center of the field and scanned the trees around the perimeter, searching for anything he would recognize. He finally spotted something that jogged his memory; a large stone. It did not stand out in the least, and Cyrus would never have recognized it except for the fact that he had helped roll it out of the woods with Jack, Nel, and Alec to use as a headstone for Dalton Sydney. That was where they had buried him after he was murdered by King Mora. That really felt like a lifetime ago when Cyrus stopped to think about it.

Having found a marker to work off of, Cyrus began walking at an angle, trying to remember the trajectory they had travelled to bury Dalton. Even after narrowing his search area considerably, it was several minutes before he was able to pinpoint exactly where they had arrived. It was marked by a ten-foot area of scattered debris that presumably had come with them when they were *pulled* from the Atlantic Ocean. The scattered remnants were nearly impossible to see from a distance because they had become pale and bleached by the sun, but once close enough, they were unmistakable. Cyrus kicked over a dried-out piece of wood with his boot revealing its darker underside. Surrounding it were various other artifacts of similar unimportance; more wood, metal screws, bolts, a few scraps of fabric, and a pair of eyeglasses. Cyrus crouched down and scooped up a few of the metal bolts, half-heartedly examining them. He didn't know what he had expected to find out here, but there truly was nothing to see. He tossed the bolts aside and put his hand, palm-down, against the burnt, cracked earth. He still found it strange how the ground looked as though it should be hot to the touch, but it wasn't. Only when it came in close contact to the scepters did it become volatile. Cyrus picked at one of the large cracks with his fingernail and it eroded into dust not unlike dried-out mud. He stuck his finger down between the fissures and picked at the glowing particles that looked like fire. They were just particles, or some sort of dust, and they clung to his fingertips as any dust-like substance would.

They continued to glow faintly on his fingertips, but when he blew on them, they flew off into the air and turned grey and ashy.

Cyrus shook his head in disappointment at the lack of clues in the field. He had been sure at least something would be found to help explain how they ended up here. Ydoro had insisted from the very beginning that the fields were not the key, and it was looking more and more like he was right. He stood up, shaking the last remnants of the dust off his hands, and began doing a final sweep of the area.

He stopped, suddenly with the intense feeling that he was being watched. Cyrus raised his head slowly, looking at the opposite treeline from where he had entered the field, leading towards Easttown. There were villagers there, several of them, watching him from the shadows of the trees. Cyrus initially felt a surge of unease, realizing he was out here by himself and entirely unprotected, but as he looked into the villagers' eyes, and they looked back at him, he saw nothing more than curiosity. They craned their necks and squinted their eyes, clearly wondering what he was doing out in the middle of the field.

Cyrus raised his hand and waved at the onlookers uncertainly. A few of them looked to each other questioningly, and one waved cautiously back. They weren't hiding their curiosity and made no move to continue about their business once Cyrus had noticed them. They just kept staring at him with unabashed interest. As Cyrus looked back at them, he realized there were far more of them beyond the trees than he had originally noticed. Finally, he started walking towards them, which caused the first movement from the group as they started to retreat uncertainly. Cyrus waved his hand again and signaled them to come out into the field. A few turned and disappeared into the forest, but others seemed more receptive to the invitation and slowly started emerging into the open air.

"Hi there," Cyrus called out, still walking forward to meet the curious group.

One member of the onlookers suddenly turned to the woman next to him and whispered something in her ear, and at once the group was alive with panicked chatter. Almost in unison, the entire group dropped to their knees and bowed their heads low, evidently just realizing that they were in the presence of their king.

Cyrus shook his head quickly and said, "No, no, please, that's not necessary."

When no one from the group moved out of their respectful bow, Cyrus approached the woman near the front and reached out to touch her arm. She looked up into his eyes timidly, and Cyrus smiled back at her. "Please," Cyrus said again, "stand up. All of you, stand up."

The woman rose to a standing position again and, after some whispered murmurings, the rest of the group followed suit.

"I'm Cyrus," he announced to the group. "I *am* one of your kings, but I assure you, that's unnecessary. I'm just here looking for something."

After a moment of uncomfortable silence, during which time all of the villagers seemed uncertain if they should make eye contact with Cyrus or not, the woman who he had encouraged to stand up finally spoke, "What are you looking for?"

Cyrus gave a hollow laugh. "I'm not sure, actually. Clues."

A few of the villagers nodded but Cyrus had the distinct impression they did not know what he was referring to and simply did not want to question the king. "You see," Cyrus continued, intentionally looking to each of the faces around him to encourage conversation, "I'm not from here. Maybe you know that already. Myself and my team, we came here through some sort of… well I don't know what. But our own world is very different from this one."

Now the nodding from the group seemed more genuine, and there were more mumblings back and forth.

"Is every one of you from this world?"

Most of the people nodded their heads, but there were a couple who didn't.

"You're not from here?" Cyrus asked one of the villagers, a late-middle-aged man who had shaken his head 'no'.

"No sir," the man responded, "from a town just outside of London."

"And you?" Cyrus asked an older woman who had not answered one way or another.

"I'm from here, but my father wasn't," she responded in a matter-of-fact way. There was no regret or pain in the way she stated it, unlike Ydoro who seemed to be perpetually trying to keep that part of his past buried. "He was from a place called Virginia. Ended up here as a young man, met my mother, started a family."

Cyrus could not seem to reconcile the casual nature in which she talked about her father coming to this world, as though he were an immigrant migrating to a new country to start a life.

"But he... surely he didn't come here willingly?" Cyrus asked before he could stop himself, although he realized immediately after he said it that it was a silly question.

"No no," she answered politely, "from what he told me, he had gone into town to pick up more grain. He had a small farm, see. He didn't know exactly what happened to him. Said he got a blinding headache, became disoriented, and found himself walking through our town here instead of his own."

"He had been in town?" Cyrus asked in barely contained bafflement. Until now he had assumed everyone had been out on the ocean when they were *pulled*.

"In town," the woman confirmed with a nod. "I guess he had a wife back home, but he didn't talk about her much. He moved on, started a new life. He must've hoped she did the same."

Cyrus was having trouble wrapping his mind around that. Given this woman's age, her father would have come to the island in the 1860's or 70's. It made Cyrus wonder if anyone on this island were truly local or whether enough generations had passed that their ancestral homes had simply been forgotten.

"Have you never tried to leave?" Cyrus asked the group as a whole, though his question was clearly more directed at the man from London.

"I worried for my family for a while," the man agreed, "but life in England wasn't the easiest back then, with the war and all."

"The Great War," Cyrus reflected with an understanding nod. He doubted there was a person on the planet who wasn't affected during the war years.

The man, however, shook his head in mild confusion. "Haven't heard it called that, but sure. Comparatively, the Kingdom hasn't been so bad. Although it's changed over the years. Easttown didn't used to be so isolated."

"How did that happen?" Cyrus asked. It was a subject that kept coming up again and again.

"It was King Irias's doing," another local from the group said. "He turned the towns against each other. Made us the laborers while the West consumed our resources."

Another local from the group spoke up, "We had thought things would go back to the way they had been once King Irias was overthrown. After all, these were once our neighbors, our friends. But apparently the West had grown accustomed to us supporting them, so when the time came, none spoke up for us, and the rift only grew under King Mora."

"I assure you, we're working on a solution," Cyrus promised them, recognizing a pattern that apparently was inherent in many civilizations, regardless of how foreign the world seemed. "We're working on ways to bridge the two towns together, share resources."

As he looked around, he saw glimmers of hope begin to twinkle in many of the onlooker's eyes, and he was reminded once again that this was a real society, and their actions had real consequences. Feeling inspired to speak further given the group's rapt attention, Cyrus continued, "I met with Annica the other day about this very thing." He declined to mention how badly those talks had crumbled once Alec had entered the discussion. "Ydoro has been serving as an advisor to us as we learn more about the Kingdom. And there's Henry, the historian, who comes with a wealth of knowledge from all of his years documenting."

At the mention of Henry's name, the group began to buzz with excitement.

"Henry's alive?" one woman called out. "He was taken so long ago, we thought for sure he had been killed!"

"You knew Henry?" Cyrus asked, eager to see such enthusiasm for one of their own.

"Everyone knew Henry," the man from London said with a smile, "He spent years walking between the two towns with his endless journals. He'd ask you to pose for a sketch, or request that you talk about your life. Even if you weren't from here, he wanted to know. Wrote it all down like he had big plans."

Cyrus smiled, realizing now what a valuable resource Henry would be in uniting the two towns. It sounded as though he had been someone truly loved by the people. "We found him locked up in the dungeons," Cyrus confirmed, "he'd been in there a long time. And his journals are still there as well."

The group was alive with chatter and smiling faces. "He really was something special," a woman exclaimed. "When he arrived, and had such interest in us and our ways, it united people. And it made everyone feel heard, feel stronger."

It was no wonder Mora didn't like him, Cyrus thought to himself. He had been giving the people a voice.

"He's alive and well, and we will be enlisting his expertise in uniting the towns," Cyrus promised. It was difficult not to promise such things when being faced with the hope in the eyes of the gathered crowd. "We can make this place better, bring these communities together. Just give us some time, we are listening to you."

Cyrus stayed a while longer talking to the people from Easttown before finally heading back the way he had come. When he had left the crowd, they were excitedly talking and smiling, a far cry from the apprehensive distrust they showed upon initially seeing him in the field. It was not what Cyrus had come to the Fire Fields to accomplish, quite the opposite in fact. But he was perhaps starting to understand what Alec was referring to when he insisted that there were 'real people' out in the towns. Cyrus was overcome with the realization that this was not a made-up world with made-up people. What was happening with the transfer of power from King Mora to Alec and himself had real consequences for these people.

Cyrus also found himself disagreeing with something Ydoro had told them on their very first night in town; he did not get the sense that these were a 'passive people' uninterested in who was leading them.

**CHAPTER THIRTY-EIGHT**

# PAST LIVES

J ack had to find Cyrus. They needed to have a talk as soon as possible. Jack didn't have any further proof of his suspicions about Henry, but he couldn't live with this nagging feeling in his gut that something was very wrong with Henry's story. Jack had walked out of his room only moments before and looked apprehensively down the hall towards the king's quarters, remembering with wary unease the conversation between himself and Alec two nights prior. To his surprise, Alec was standing in the center of his room conversing quietly with Henry, who looked as hunched and benign as ever. They both looked down the hall and locked eyes with Jack; Henry offering a warm smile but Alec wearing a calculating smirk.

Jack did not like the way Henry seemed to be close with everyone. He didn't know what he and Alec were talking about specifically, and for all he knew it was just friendly chit-chat, but it struck him as odd that Henry would be so friendly to Alec's face, and then privately tell Cyrus and himself how dangerous Alec was as a ruler. It was only feeding into Jack's paranoia about Henry. It had started days earlier with Henry's apparent confusion when Cyrus had made a reference to the game of chess. It was certainly possible Jack was reading too much into things, but it seemed to him at the time that Henry had absolutely no awareness of the game at all; indeed, as though he had never even heard of it. Chess was one of the oldest games in the world, the idea that an adult would have never heard of it was nearly impossible to imagine. Henry had backtracked, however, and blamed the late hour on his confusion. Perhaps that was the truth and Jack was judging too harshly, but he was having trouble getting it out of his mind. Furthermore, there was Henry's apparent obsession with baseball and the Boston Red Sox, which seemed commonplace on the surface, but Jack was convinced there was something off about his timeline. He needed to talk it over with Cyrus.

Jack arrived on the main level and made his way towards the entrance hall, making a quick scan of the room before hurrying into the dining area. Still no Cyrus. Jack was trying not to appear too urgent as he walked about the Temple, concerned how it would look if Nel were to see him. As he turned back around, ready to check the historian's room in the dungeons, he finally saw Cyrus approaching from the far side of the cavernous entryway.

"Cyrus," Jack whispered in a hurried grunt, "I need to talk to you."

Jack, not waiting for Cyrus's reply, escorted him towards the door leading to the dungeons, the same place they had met at midnight several days earlier. He pulled Cyrus down onto the first stair, just out of the light of the entryway, and looked back the way they had come for anyone who could potentially be listening in.

"What's up?" Cyrus asked in mild alarm at Jack's clear distress.

Jack took a few hurried breaths and tried to think of a way to present his questions to Cyrus without them seeming random and confusing. Failing instantly at this, Jack bluntly asked, "What do you think of Henry?"

"Of Henry?" Cyrus blinked in surprise. "I actually just had a conversation with the people from Easttown about him."

"And?" Jack asked, his impatience getting the better of him.

"And I think he will be a critical asset in uniting the towns," Cyrus finished. "The people really seemed to love him, outsider or not. And I think he was a crucial voice against King Mora."

"Okay," Jack nodded his head thoughtfully, trying to decide how best to proceed. "Let me ask you this; how old would you peg Henry?"

Cyrus raised his eyebrows in clear bewilderment, but responded, "I don't know, seventy-five, eighty."

"My thoughts too," Jack said, glad for the affirmation, "but let's give him the benefit of the doubt. Maybe the harsh life here has had its toll. Say he's sixty."

Cyrus laughed at the absurdity of the idea, given Henry's feeble appearance, but nodded.

Jack continued without so much as a smile, "So that would mean he was born in 1875 at the absolute latest…"

He looked to Cyrus for agreement, who nodded slowly, clearly trying to predict where Jack was going with this.

"Henry says he grew up watching the Boston Red Sox with his dad as a kid, that's what he told Nel…" Jack stated as though this explained everything, but Cyrus's brow was still furrowed.

"Yeah, so?" Cyrus responded, his confusion slowly giving way to visible concern at Jack's mental wellbeing.

"So the Boston Red Sox weren't founded until 1901, and weren't even called the Boston Red Sox until 1908," Jack said, "That's only twenty-seven years ago. There's *no way* he watched them as a boy."

Cyrus's eyes were working back and forth as he finally understood the meaning of Jack's strange questions. "Maybe Nel misunderstood…"

"Maybe," Jack replied, unconvinced. "I want to talk to Ydoro about it. We know Henry's story; he was a history teacher, had a wife and kid, Benjamin. Mora imprisoned him for writing an unflattering account of his rule… Ydoro's been here a long time, knows people. Maybe he knows if the story's true."

"Okay," Cyrus agreed with a tone of understanding but not without a hint of skepticism. When Jack started nodding fervently, Cyrus responded, "What, now? Is it really that urgent?"

"I'm worried it might be," Jack answered grimly.

\*\*\*\*\*

Jack and Cyrus's walk into town started out quiet and awkward. Jack kept feeling as though he should elaborate on his theories about

Henry, but lacking anything new to say on the subject, he was just thinking in circles. He debated back and forth about telling Cyrus about his conversation with Alec two nights prior before finally deciding to do so. Cyrus was predictably baffled by Alec's deliberate threat towards Annica, but he also didn't seem to know how to reconcile Alec's more recent behavior with the brother he knew. Jack himself felt the most disturbing part of his conversation with Alec was not the threat against Annica but rather the realization that Alec's friendly, reflective demeanor beforehand had all been an act. Cyrus, for his part, didn't seem to have much to say on the subject, but Jack suspected he was having trouble processing it.

As they arrived on the familiar bustling main street that served as the town square, only a few people seemed to know who they were at first. Most of the people brushed past them without ever looking up and one local nearly ran them over with a rickshaw that was overloaded to the point of tipping. Slowly, however, whispering began to spread throughout the street and people started looking up at them apprehensively as they passed by. Jack was having a hard time reading the atmosphere in town and couldn't be sure whether the locals were being respectful or mistrusting. It wasn't a moment too soon, as far as Jack was concerned, that they arrived at Ydoro's heavy wooden door with the serpent knocker.

Ydoro greeted them excitedly and stepped out into the sunlight rather than inviting them into his dark, cramped home. The moment he was outside, people in town started nodding to him as they passed or called out his name as way of greeting. He seemed to know everyone in town, and he smiled back at each of them as if they were old friends.

"How are things in the Temple?" Ydoro asked, still smiling at passing townsfolk as they walked down the main road at a casual stroll.

"Hard to say," Cyrus responded darkly.

Ydoro looked sideways at the vague response and said, "Trouble in the Dorn Kingdom?"

"We have some concerns about Alec," Cyrus admitted, "He's become emboldened somehow, more aggressive, more…"

"Unstable," Jack finished the sentence for him, and Cyrus gave him a disapproving look, but didn't disagree.

"I'm not sure I'm best suited to advise you on such things," Ydoro said in a sympathetic but somehow passive tone. "I'm here to serve you both, and Alec's way of doing things isn't without its benefits. He rides through the streets, meets the people…"

"Murders the people," Jack again finished the sentence.

Ydoro nodded his head in understanding, but then pointed out, "That's not different than what people in the Kingdom are used to, though. Yes, it's harsh and brutal, and may seem barbaric in many ways, but raw power of that sort can be effective."

Cyrus shook his head and responded, "There's a better way. I've seen it with my own eyes. The people of Easttown recognized and respected me as their leader without a show of strength."

"That may very well be a better way," Ydoro agreed, "but who do you think the people will follow if it comes to that? Fear is a powerful incentive to recognize your brother as the true king."

"You don't think they respect me as a true king, the same as Alec?"

"They do now," Ydoro clarified, "but right now they don't have to choose. Be careful of distancing yourself from Alec."

Ydoro wasn't wrong, and Jack knew that, but he still responded by saying, "We actually didn't come here to talk about Alec. We wanted to ask you about Henry."

Ydoro looked entirely unprepared for the mention of Henry's name and even seemed to take a moment to understand who they were referring to. "Henry Fine?" he finally asked in confusion.

Cyrus opened his mouth to clarify but Jack put up a finger to stop him. "What can you tell us about Henry Fine?" he asked.

Ydoro shrugged and said, "What do you want to know? I knew him well. He came here from our world, really bright guy. Reminded me of you a bit, actually," he said pointing to Cyrus. "But he didn't have any trouble adjusting. At least not for a while. He wanted to learn about everyone here, every custom, every festival, every rule. He'd draw people's portraits, sketch the houses. It's like he thought this place couldn't touch him. Like it was all an immersive research venture. Of course,

King Mora didn't like what he was writing and started leaning on him to present the Kingdom in a different light. Mora wanted to be remembered as a powerful ruler, not a ruthless dictator. When Henry's usefulness ran out, Mora killed him."

Cyrus again started to respond, but Jack stopped him and asked Ydoro, "What can you tell us about Henry's past? His time before coming to the Kingdom?"

"Well, I know he left behind a wife and kid. He definitely cared for them, and certainly began to reflect more on the life he lost towards the end. I think his wife was, umm, Elizabeth maybe. I know Ben was his son, Benjamin."

"And did he talk about baseball at all?" Jack asked.

Ydoro smiled broadly and responded, "Oh sure, he loved talking about his Boston Red Sox. Of course most of the people here had never heard of baseball so he had trouble finding an audience."

"He said he used to watch them?" Jack asked, finally breathing a small sigh of relief.

"Oh yeah," Ydoro announced, still with a reflective smile on his face, "he used to go all the time with his dad, from what I remember."

Cyrus looked sideways to Jack with a shrug of his shoulders and a nod of his head.

Jack's relief was short lived and quickly turning to confusion. Ydoro was confirming everything they knew about Henry, but something still felt wrong to Jack.

"Why are you so curious about Henry?" Ydoro finally asked. "He was long before your time."

After a moment of thought, Jack nodded to Cyrus to finally say what he had clearly been itching to reveal from the start.

"He's alive," Cyrus announced happily. "Probably older than you remember him, but we found him locked away in the dungeons when we took the Temple."

Ydoro furrowed his brow and shook his head in concern. "He's not alive, Cyrus. I buried Henry Fine myself."

A cold shiver ran down Jack's spine. His mind instantly started tracing all the conversations he had had with Henry.

"What do you mean?" Cyrus asked in alarm. "He's… we have him in the Temple right now… he said… he told us…"

"You have someone in the Temple right now who says his name is Henry Fine?" Ydoro asked in visible concern. They had stopped mid-stride on their way up the street, causing the locals to weave around them.

"Well, I don't know that he ever said his last name," Cyrus sputtered, "but he said all the journals belonged to him… he said he was the historian."

Ydoro shook his head in a disturbed, almost pitying way, "No, that's not possible, Cyrus."

"He's an older guy," Cyrus continued, "much older, actually. He seemed kind…"

"What does he look like?" Ydoro asked, rather more urgently than was usually his way.

"Umm, I don't know," Cyrus answered, "small and frail, grey-brown eyes. He has a sort of birthmark high on his forehead."

Ydoro straightened up and his brow unfurrowed from a thick knot of confusion to a look of deep concern.

"What? Who is it?" Jack asked desperately. "Do you know who it is?"

Ydoro looked back at him with puzzling, almost uncomprehending eyes. "I've only ever known one person with a mark like that."

## CHAPTER THIRTY-NINE

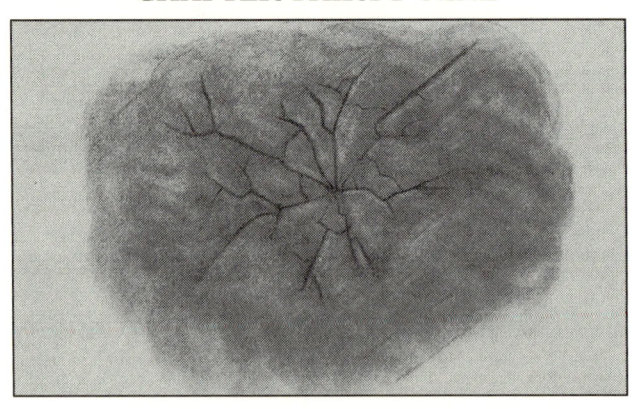

# FRACTURE

Alec was feeling invincible. He had just returned from another chariot ride, this time reaching some of the smaller pockets of town. He wasn't greeted with quite the same excited cheering in recent days as he had enjoyed on his first ride, but he clearly commanded a deep respect from the people as he passed them. Many would bow as he approached, some would bring their fists to their chests in a show of fealty, and he still noticed plenty of smiling, awe-struck faces from the public.

He ascended the staircase not just with confidence, but with authority. The guards stood up a little straighter as he passed them; their sole purpose to follow his direct orders. He had left the Neodactyls with a guard on the main level, tasking him with untethering them from the chariot and getting them settled in their room. As he emerged in the corridor leading towards the king's quarters, he caught movement out of the corner of his eye and briefly hoped it would be Nel. To his mild disappointment, it ended up being Henry, ambling out of one of the rooms.

"Good ride, my King?" Henry announced with a smile.

"Absolutely," Alec boomed jovially. "You should make your way into town yourself one of these days. Get some fresh air."

Henry smiled warmly and replied, "For now I'm just content being out of my cell. But I think the time will soon come when you'll have use for me out there."

Alec hadn't broken his stride down the hallway and Henry was struggling slightly to keep up. Alec nodded and responded, "I'm sure you're right."

"For now, you have Cyrus and Jack to talk to the people for you," Henry said, "and having them consult with Ydoro today was a smart move."

Alec stopped mid-stride and turned to face the clearly winded old man. "Cyrus and Jack were consulting Ydoro today?"

"That's what I heard," Henry replied with visible confusion at Alec's question. "I had assumed you had sent them."

Alec's eyes darted back and forth as he contemplated why they would be seeking Ydoro's counsel behind his back. He could feel white hot anger beginning to bubble up, but he was able to push it aside, something he was getting better at every day. He finally replied simply, "I did not."

"In that case, my King, you should be careful," Henry said heavily, "I know he's your brother, but he is not above corrupting the people of this Kingdom against you."

Alec's heart was beating faster and faster, but he forced himself to respond rationally. "He doesn't have that sort of support. The people out there don't even know who he is."

"Not yet," Henry warned, "but give him the opportunity to keep holding secret meetings in town… it could become a problem for you."

Alec shook his head with more certainty than he was feeling and replied, "No, I have control of the Neodactyls, thanks to you. Without that, Cyrus is just one man."

"Just be on your guard, my King," Henry said with a small bow of his head, "I only want what's best for you, and I fear your brother will try to force you into a conflict with him. Public opinion can be a powerful weapon to wield."

Alec turned and walked down the hallway and into his quarters, leaving Henry to continue about his business. Where Alec would usually be feeling anger, he was instead experiencing a sense of deep unease. He wished he could talk to Nel, but he hadn't seen her since his return to the Temple. He stabbed his scepter roughly into the glowing altar and walked past it to look out the expansive windows filtering in the mid-afternoon light. The surrounding forest seemed to drift like waves in the breeze, and beyond it, the yellow-gold stone houses of town shined brightly in the sun. It was impossible to see from the Temple, but Alec knew from his earlier ride that the streets below were bustling with activity. Was his brother down there right now trying to sway the support of the locals?

Alec shook his head in disgust and turned on his heel, nearly colliding with someone in the process. He blinked in surprise and realized it was Cyrus, who looked equally as alarmed. Cyrus backed up a step, but as he took in Alec's face, his expression turned instantly dark.

"What the hell are you doing?" Cyrus practically shouted.

Alec scoffed at the audacity of being questioned in his own chambers, but before he could react further, Cyrus punched him across the face causing stars to erupt behind his eyes.

Alec's surprise and confusion quickly turned to fury, but unlike last time, he had no intention of being intimidated into submission. Perhaps it was simply the adrenaline, but rather than feeling incapacitated by the pain in his cheekbone, he felt more powerful than ever. He shook his head to clear it, then lashed out at Cyrus, striking him squarely in the jaw. His fist exploded with pain, he had never hit someone before, but it felt good. Cyrus, who clearly wasn't expecting a counterattack, staggered backwards and almost looked like he would fall onto his back. Alec used the opportunity and punched him again, causing blood to spray from Cyrus's nose. Alec swung again, but this time Cyrus ducked his head out of the way and lunged towards Alec, ramming his body backwards with his shoulder. Alec stumbled sideways and Cyrus charged headlong into him, smashing Alec's entire body against the enormous windowpanes. Alec scrambled to get his hands up to defend himself, but Cyrus grasped a large handful of his hair and smashed Alec's head into the glass of the window with a loud crunch.

Everything went momentarily dim for Alec, and he blinked rapidly, struggling to stay lucid. Cyrus kept his hand firmly against Alec's head, which was still pinned against the window, and turned it sideways, giving Alec a look at the Kingdom below... and the steep drop-off from the wall if the window were to shatter. Alec could see a spiderwebbed crack in the glass where his head had hit and a small amount of blood that had rubbed off from his scalp.

"You have no business here anymore," Cyrus growled at him, his eyes looking half-mad with hatred. "You're either leaving through the main door, or straight down right here, right now. This is the one and only time I'm giving you the choice."

Once again, Alec felt the sense of helplessness at his brother's superior strength, but this time it gave him power. Alec felt a burning, dormant strength well up in his chest and begin surging through his veins like fire. It was almost painful the way he felt it take over his body, like an army spreading to the borders of a country to defend the city. It was poison and it was in total control of him now. Alec erupted with a roar of fury he had never heard come from another human in all his life and smashed at Cyrus, somehow loosening his hold on him. Alec's inhuman war-cry didn't stop as he punched Cyrus across the face once, twice, three times, and then kicked him squarely in the chest. Cyrus careened backwards past the altar, looking like he would finally fall. Alec strode forward, surprising even himself with his newfound strength, and kicked Cyrus again. This time Cyrus staggered farther into the living space, finally leaving Alec enough clearance to arm himself with the one thing he had been craving since Cyrus first hit him; the weapon of a true king.

Alec turned and grasped his scepter firmly, wrenching it free from its fiery altar and sending glowing embers across the floor. If he had felt powerful a moment ago, now he felt like a god. He looked up and Cyrus was still on his feet, moving towards him once again. Quick as lightning, Alec swept out with his scepter, nearly taking Cyrus's head off had his brother not anticipated the attack and backed out of the way.

"Woah!" Cyrus yelled out in alarm, holding up his hands in surrender.

Not this time, Alec thought to himself. He allowed the raging fire in his soul to take control of him once again and he swung out with the scepter, this time smashing it into the side of Cyrus's face and causing him to buckle onto one knee. His face twisted with hatred, Alec smashed the scepter into Cyrus's head again, finally causing him to pitch backwards and land on his back, sprawled out on the wooden floor. Like a panther moving in for the killing blow, Alec sprung forward on top of Cyrus, twirling the scepter in his hand to expose the sharp, spear-like tip at the bottom. He stabbed the point down hard, stopping within half an inch of Cyrus's neck. Cyrus winced in anticipation, his face a mess of sweat and blood.

A shout from the doorway alerted Alec to approaching danger and he looked up to see Jack barreling into the room towards the fray, ready to tackle Alec to the ground. Alec didn't even have the chance to raise the scepter in defense before an otherworldly shriek reverberated off the stone walls and a giant feathery object collided with Jack from behind, causing him to spill out onto the ground violently. Jack turned, and the approaching Neodactyl snapped at him with a threatening hiss. Jack crab-crawled backwards but the creature descended on him like some sort of nightmare vulture over a fresh kill. Jack continued to scramble until the Neodactyl trapped his leg beneath one of its giant, scaly feet and pierced his calf with its enormous black talons. The creature screeched again and planted its other foot on Jack's chest, forcing him down to his back.

Alec began to turn his attention back to his brother, still struggling at the tip of his scepter, when another shout from the doorway announced Nel and Ydoro entering the room. They both looked shocked at the chaos unfolding and Nel appeared to make a move towards Alec, but the second Neodactyl rounded her from the hallway and, raking its talons across the wooden floor to control its slide, came to rest directly between her and Alec. She stopped her approach abruptly with wide eyes and yelled to Alec, "What the hell is this?" Ydoro had backed up to the wall with his hands raised.

"Stay out of this!" Alec shouted, turning his gaze back to Cyrus, who was taking deep, rasping breaths.

"What the hell are you doing?" Nel yelled from behind the Neodactyl, which was still snarling at her threateningly.

"He attacked me!" Alec yelled, once again turning his attention back to Cyrus.

"Who did?" Cyrus grunted from the floor, a bit of blood starting to form where the tip of the scepter had been touching his throat.

"Don't play games with me," Alec hissed menacingly.

"I don't know what you're talking about," Cyrus insisted, "we just returned from town…"

"I know you were in town," Alec growled.

"But we just got back," Cyrus said, finally tilting his head enough to look Alec in the eyes. "I walked into the room and you hit me."

Alec was startled when he looked back into his brother's eyes and saw no lie there. Cyrus looked shocked, and confused, and scared, but that look of animalistic hatred he had worn before was no longer present. Alec shook his head, willing himself to not lose his nerve, and dug the scepter tip further into Cyrus's neck.

"Alec!" Jack shouted from beneath the Neodactyl, which was holding him prone.

"You don't know him," Alec said in response, "he's been playing his part well, but he'll kill me the moment my guard is down."

"I was with him!" Jack yelled, "he just walked into the room right before I did!"

"Then explain that!" Alec screamed, gesturing to the broken window behind him. But the confused expressions on Jack and Nel's faces gave him pause.

Alec turned his head apprehensively towards the windows and saw with horror that the glass was entirely intact. No spiderwebbed shatter mark from his head hitting it, and no blood. And yet his head was still throbbing from the impact, and he could certainly feel the trickle of blood streaming down his forehead from beneath his hairline.

The toxic, burning fire in his veins was beginning to ebb away as he began to lose his conviction. Looking around at the team watching him, every single one of them wore an expression of shock and concern. He looked down at Cyrus again, who was shaking his head slightly and looking into Alec's eyes with utter disbelief. Cyrus had attacked him, of that much Alec was certain. But he had to admit, he could not explain why the window wasn't shattered, or why Cyrus seemed genuinely confused by the accusation.

At long last, Alec relaxed his grip on the scepter and removed it from Cyrus's neck, stepping aside to allow him to stand. He gave a short whistle and both Neodactyls released their captives and slunk to his side. Alec stroked one of their necks soothingly, but his mind was elsewhere. He could still feel the wounds from the beating he had just taken at Cyrus's hands, but the more he surveyed the room, the more details weren't adding up. Cyrus, who eased himself off the floor, had a bruise forming where Alec had struck him with the scepter, but his nose wasn't bleeding where he had punched him.

"What the hell, Alec," Cyrus murmured, watching him apprehensively. Jack was shaking his head and gingerly prodding at the small puncture wounds in his calf from the Neodactyl's talons. Even Nel looked concerned.

"Something happened," Alec attempted rather lamely. "I can't explain it, but I was attacked." Perhaps the reason Alec wasn't willing to fully explain the incident from his point of view was because he didn't feel he should, as the king, need to explain his actions. He also did not want to give his brother further reason to question his sanity. "I can't explain what happened, but..."

When Alec trailed off, Cyrus finally said, "Okay I don't know what's going on with you, but here's the deal; those birds are going to be put down."

"The hell they are," Alec snapped.

"He's right," Jack said, "they're a danger. And you've already proven you can't control them."

"This isn't a debate," Alec snarled, "they're my right as the king."

"You're not the only king," Cyrus retorted aggressively, "we share that responsibility. And I also have a responsibility to keep this team safe." He ignored Alec's snort of humorless laughter and continued, "those animals are being put down."

"Make a move then," Alec threatened, "see what happens."

"Might I suggest we cool the temperature a bit here," Ydoro said in a much more level tone than everyone else.

"This Kingdom is mine," Alec hissed, "and the next word I hear against me I'll consider an act of treason. You're either with me or you're not part of this Kingdom."

As Jack and Cyrus stared at Alec in disbelief, a soft voice from the doorway said, "Might I be of any assistance, my King?"

It was Henry, who was slowly shuffling his way into the room. Alec didn't know that there was anything he could do, but was grateful when he walked past the group and took his place behind Alec, a clear symbol of his support.

Ydoro, who had been standing in the shadows near the wall, leaned forward with his mouth open, gaping at Henry. "It's not possible," he uttered with wide eyes. He looked as though he were seeing a ghost.

Henry, seemingly just noticing Ydoro in the room, was wearing an odd expression as well. His usual good-natured half smile had fallen from his face.

Ydoro shook his head, his mouth still hanging slightly open, and looked around to each person in the room before saying in quiet disbelief, "That's King Irias."

Alec turned to look at the old man standing next to him, small and frail as ever. Of course, he had heard the stories of Irias, the former king who Mora had overthrown. But the man beside him didn't look dangerous at all. Henry looked back at him with a slightly sheepish expression on his face; clearly not a denial.

"He's a ruthless madman, Alec," Jack insisted. "Why do you think he hasn't wanted to leave the Temple?"

Henry was shaking his head and glancing from one person to the next as though assessing the danger.

"Deny it," Cyrus challenged.

Instead, Henry turned to Alec. "I've given you my loyalty. Haven't I proven myself to you? I'm sorry I lied, but think back to our first conversation. My counsel won you this Kingdom."

Alec considered a moment what this revelation meant, but also realized he currently had very few allies on his side. Henry had proven loyal time and again, and had even warned Alec that Cyrus would try to make a move soon.

Alec turned back to the group and said, "I don't care who he is. He's under my protection."

"Alec, you don't understand," Ydoro said quickly, "You can't believe anything that man says, trust me, I know. The Henry he's been masquerading as was a young man, a good man. Irias was a tyrant."

"He's under my protection!" Alec bellowed again, "and if you want the same courtesy, then you will show your loyalty to me now!"

Nel seemed uncomfortable, but slowly stepped forward and walked towards Alec. She brushed her hand against his shoulder as she took a place at his side. Jack and Cyrus were both shaking their heads slowly in disgust.

"We share this Kingdom," Cyrus said, "*that* was the agreement."

"Don't make me laugh," Alec said with a smirk, "the people don't even know who you are. You think you have power because you were closest when Mora lost his footing on that ladder? Have you heard the stories their telling in town about our assault on the Temple? Oh wait, of course you haven't, because you didn't think it was worth meeting the people. You thought you could hide behind these walls and rule from a distance."

"The people of Easttown tell a different story," Cyrus responded boldly, "but you haven't bothered meeting them."

"To hell with the people of Easttown," Alec said with a laugh, "you can have 'em. Have you seen Easttown?"

"Have you?" Cyrus asked back. "They're your laborers, without them you have nothing."

"They're all yours," Alec said tauntingly, "I have plenty of labor in the West. I don't think you'll get very far with a bunch of poor, country farmers."

"Alec we can work this out," Cyrus insisted, although his voice was still confrontational, "but we can't as long as those damn birds are here."

"The birds are a part of me," Alec said, "they're not going anywhere."

Cyrus was shaking his head in disappointment. "Then we can't stay."

If Cyrus had been thinking this declaration would somehow sway Alec, he was mistaken. "Then Easttown is waiting for you," Alec said with a small grin.

Ydoro, who had remained silent throughout the exchange, finally said, "I believe it is important to be clear what we are talking about here."

"Oh Ydoro," Henry, or Irias apparently, said with a laugh, "squirrely as ever. I believe the King has been quite clear. You are welcome to remain here, under his *protection*, or you are welcome to make it on your own."

Alec smirked at the support from Irias and was grateful for him pointing out that his brother had nothing to bargain with.

"Actually," Ydoro said pointedly, "I believe what we are talking about is Easttown seceding from the Kingdom."

"Easttown?" Irias laughed in disbelief, "you want Easttown?"

Cyrus turned to Ydoro and started mumbling something about that not being his intention. Alec laughed coldly at their floundering as they realized they had negotiated themselves into a corner. Ydoro started whispering back frantically.

"Look at this," Alec said mockingly, "the all-powerful King Cyrus, realizing he's the king of nothing. If you want to beg for a town of peasants, I'm all ears."

Cyrus was still whispering in concern, but Ydoro turned back to Alec and said, "We want to be clear. This Kingdom currently recognizes two kings. If your brother is no longer welcome here, what's being proposed is that Cyrus becomes the king of Easttown, and you remain king in the West." When the room remained silent, Ydoro finished, "It would mean effectively splitting the Kingdom in half."

Alec again laughed at Cyrus, who was shaking his head. "This is what you want, brother?" Alec asked in amusement. "You want your peasants in Easttown?"

Cyrus looked at Alec apprehensively, as though he were scanning him for weaknesses, but he stopped shaking his head in disagreement.

It seemed Alec's taunting had changed his tune slightly. "Those peasants are building *your* houses, maintaining *your* roads, supplying *your* food."

"We have crop fields in the West," Alec said, shaking his head. "And labor's cheap around here."

"Again, allow us to clarify," Ydoro interjected, "if we separate from the West, you will have no authority over our people. They will immediately cease working for you and will no longer fall under your rule. If you want something from us, you propose a trade line, but we owe you nothing."

Alec smirked again, "The Temple is in the West, you would be giving up all claim to it."

"He would," Ydoro answered for Cyrus, "But the Fire Fields would be neutral territory. That's the dividing line."

The room went silent, and Alec looked to Irias and Nel at his side for guidance. Irias was chuckling and shrugging his shoulders as if to say, 'if that's what they want, it's of no concern to you.' Nel wasn't reacting at all but instead looking into his eyes, giving him strength.

"This would be it," Cyrus said, stepping forward a pace. The Neodactyls hissed threateningly. "You're my brother, Alec. I can't pretend to understand what's been going on with you, but I've always tried to be there to support you." Alec hadn't raised his head to look at his brother, instead he continued to stare into Nel's eyes. Cyrus continued, "If this is the path you're choosing, I can't support you anymore. We'd be agreeing to go our separate ways."

Alec finally tore his eyes away from Nel's gaze and looked at his brother, standing in the center of the room in his worn-down trekking clothes, his hair having grown down well past his ears, the patchy burn still covering part of his face before being lost beneath his stubbly beard. Alec didn't know the man standing before him anymore. The confident, jovial person who Alec would meet for drinks at their favorite pub down the street from their university seemed long gone. Alec now found himself wondering if that person ever existed. After all, that was the man who had stolen Cynthia from him, given him breaks throughout his schooling and subsequent career just to have a hold over his life, and forced him to come on this expedition just so he could lord over his little brother and make himself feel important. Cyrus had always wanted to keep Alec in his shadow.

"You can keep your support," Alec finally responded, "I don't need it. I've never really realized it until now, but everything you've ever done for me you really did for yourself."

"It's not true," Cyrus said morosely with a shake of his head, but he seemed unwilling to argue further.

"Separate ways, then," Alec confirmed. "I accept your proposal... and recognize the secession of Easttown."

Jack looked to Cyrus apprehensively, who nodded his head slowly.

"I think we're done here, then," Alec said in contempt.

"Not quite," Ydoro said, "I think it's important you shake on it. A formality it may be, but this agreement is going to affect the lives of every person on this island."

Alec smirked and held out his hand, betting that Cyrus would have a harder time feigning the pleasantries. Cyrus did indeed pause, looking to Jack and then to Ydoro before stepping forward and grasping his brother's hand firmly.

"This is goodbye then," Cyrus said somberly.

"You chose this," Alec insisted confidently, "once you've crossed the borders of my lands... don't come back."

He released Cyrus's hand and turned away from him towards the window. He felt strangely alone for the first time in his life, and yet simultaneously free. It felt like a piece of him had died off, and he could feel the hole where it used to be, but he also knew he didn't need that piece of himself anymore. Nel's hand ran up his arm and came to rest on his shoulder.

"You did well, my King," Henry said from his other side, and Alec realized with a strange drop in his stomach that Henry would only be speaking that way if the confrontation was over.

Alec turned back around and saw with the slightest twinge of loss that Cyrus, Jack, and Ydoro had left.

Alec Dorn was finally on his own.

**CHAPTER FORTY**

# TIMES OF CHANGE

The next several weeks passed in a strange haze for Cyrus. It was one of those situations where he was surprised at how quickly new circumstances came to feel like the new normal, and before long it felt like ages since they were in the Temple with Alec.

After that fateful encounter with his brother, Cyrus, Jack, and Ydoro had left the king's quarters in a fog of confusion and disbelief. Cyrus couldn't believe how fast things had changed, however Jack was quick to point out that this confrontation was a long time coming. Alec had been growing more and more withdrawn from the rest of the group, embracing his newfound power with a desperate hunger Cyrus had never seen before. It was easiest, or perhaps the most comfortable, to blame Nel and her influence over Alec for his descent into unchecked delusion, but Cyrus suspected the truth wasn't quite that simple. It seemed likely that Alec's newfound resentment towards the world, and Cyrus specifically, was a long time brewing, and he just needed a push to let it out. In the weeks since, Cyrus had begun to blame himself for not trying harder to make amends with his brother that day, but the truth was, as he had looked into Alec's eyes, searching for that bond they once shared, it had seemed devastatingly hopeless. The power that

Alec now wielded was more important to him than anything, even familial ties.

As soon as they had left the negotiation with Alec, Cyrus had turned on Ydoro, demanding that he explain why he had pushed the confrontation in this direction. To his surprise, Ydoro did not deny the accusation but insisted that, when he saw the opportunity, he seized it for the good of the entire group. He had not felt comfortable choosing sides before, but it was Alec's complete dismissal of Ydoro's warning about Irias that had changed his mind. Ydoro conceded that when they had entered that room, they were in a hopeless situation. He explained how the Kingdom would have slowly continued to slip under Alec's complete control, until there was nothing left for Cyrus to do but step aside. It was the perception of the people, he had insisted, that gave Alec that power. Cyrus had made a critical error in not engaging with the locals from town. By not showing his face and demonstrating no interest in ruling, he had effectively given up his claim to the 'crown', at least in the eyes of the public. Alec had control of the two Neodactyls, a scepter that he wasn't afraid to wield, the chariot of his predecessor, and complete authority over the Temple and its guards. Cyrus was fast becoming a footnote in the history of his brother's meteoric rise to power. But that all changed in Ydoro's mind when he heard Cyrus talk about the support he had garnered in Easttown, because Alec had made a critical error as well. By entirely sidelining the Eastern half of the Kingdom, as his predecessor had done, he had failed to recognize the importance of their support. It left a void that Cyrus had unknowingly tapped into, and it came with a wealth of benefits.

The moment Ydoro had heard Alec and Irias talking so blasé about the importance of Easttown, he had realized there was a single path forward for Cyrus. He wasn't apologetic for proposing the idea of splitting the Kingdom, even as Jack suggested he had created an unnecessary and dangerous rift between the team. Rather, he insisted he had scored Cyrus a critical hit in the eleventh hour. Still, as they exited the Temple, their belongings slung over their backs and their heads held low, it felt suspiciously like defeat. Cyrus, after a short internal debate, had taken the second scepter with him. He hadn't touched the damn thing since

Alec had handed it to him during their first week in the Temple, but if he was committing himself to leading the people of Easttown now, he thought he might need it. It also gave him a hint of satisfaction knowing how Alec regarded the scepters as the 'weapons of the king'. With the weapon firmly in Cyrus's care, Alec would have trouble forgetting that he was in fact sharing the Kingdom.

Ydoro had led them into town so that he could gather his belongings from his home. He was a staple in the eyes of the townsfolk, and many peered inquisitively through the door as he packed, quietly murmuring to each other questioning where he was going. He bartered a wagon and two oxen, oxen that didn't look quite normal in Cyrus's eyes, from an older, weathered-looking woman in town. At first, he had proposed to rent the animals from her and leave them waiting in the Fire Fields after they had crossed into the East, but the woman was perplexed as to why he couldn't return them back to her in town, and Ydoro was reluctant to explain why they would no longer be welcome back once they had crossed Alec's lands. In the end, the woman had accepted a trade for Ydoro's living quarters.

Once the wagon was loaded up, Ydoro could no longer avoid addressing the fast-gathering crowd, so he had taken several minutes to explain the splitting of the Kingdom and the change in leadership. As the people reacted in confusion and expressed feelings of abandonment, Cyrus spoke up and insisted that any of them would always be welcome in Easttown, despite the border being drawn at the Fire Fields. Their disdain for Easttown was well noted and many of them openly scoffed at the idea. It seemed what they really regretted was seeing Ydoro go.

The oxen had trudged along through town and into the surrounding forest, dragging the heavy wagon carrying their few scant belongings and the three of them sitting atop it. Cyrus felt like they were in the old west and being banished to the wilderness from an established settlement. He imagined a family being tried and convicted of a crime, with the worst sentence back then being sent off to fend for themselves, losing the benefits and luxuries of being a part of a society. Of course, their trio wasn't quite being banished to the wilderness, but they would have to start from scratch in many ways. Easttown was foreign to Jack and Cyrus, even within this foreign world.

As it turned out, the people of Easttown were exceedingly welcoming, and showed nothing but unbridled excitement at the prospect of having their king living within their own town borders. Word seemed to have spread quickly about Cyrus's conversation with the people in the Fire Fields several days back. Some of the Easttowners bowed as their wagon trundled into town, but many simply smiled and some even reached out their hands for Cyrus to grasp as he passed. As a town, Easttown was not so different from its counterpart in the West, but undeniably more run-down and aged. Many of the buildings had fallen into disrepair, the roads were more uneven with large stones having been upturned from heavy use, and there was far less of a marketplace feel on the main street. In place of the vendors lining the roads in the West, there were cracked wooden barrels, forgotten piles of stone, a leaning, dried-out cart with a missing wheel. The town had plenty of people, but less *life* in it. That didn't mean the townsfolk weren't eager to impress, however, as they set Cyrus, Jack, and Ydoro up in the largest housing units they had to offer. As rundown as they were, Cyrus found the housing much less cold and utilitarian than their original stone quarters in the West. These homes were elevated wooden structures that creaked and moaned as you walked on them, but seemed sturdy enough. In place of walls, canvas-like tarps were strung between the heavy, tree trunk beams at each corner to create a dwelling not dissimilar to a research station in the field. The homes offered to them did indeed seem to be the largest in town, but not by much. The bigger difference seemed to be the state of disrepair, which was minimal compared to several of their neighbors. One structure a few doors down had its entire roof caved in and logs propping up one of its badly leaning outer walls.

Cyrus had addressed the gathering crowd that day, at the encouragement of Ydoro, not only explaining their new circumstances of being separate from the West, but also of how they would move forward as a community.

"I know that every one of you knows the meaning of a hard days' work," Cyrus had said from atop the oxen-drawn wagon, "and while that work will continue, from now on it will be working towards furthering our own comfort here in the East. There will be no more crossing the Fire Fields to work in the West, that Kingdom will no longer reap the benefits of your work. Instead, you will apply those trades toward rebuilding our own roads, fixing our own houses. I want teams established to gather and grow food, fishing and hunting expeditions as well, but this food will no longer be going to the other side of the island. It remains here to feed our own people. To make our own Kingdom strong."

Deafening, raucous applause had followed his speech and every single person looking up at him seemed to be beaming with delight.

"Inspiring words," Ydoro had said quietly to him, "be careful, you almost sounded like a real king there."

Cyrus had smiled and replied, "I'm only their king out of necessity right now. Our goal remains the same, we're finding a way back to our world."

Weeks had passed since that day, and as always, no further progress had been made towards leaving. It was the only area in which progress hadn't been made, however. The people of Easttown knew how to work and were good at what they did. Furthermore, the fact that the benefits of their work would finally be enjoyed within their own town seemed to spur on some healthy competition. Suddenly, structures were being erected at an alarming rate, and becoming more and more elaborate as they went. The roads were being repaired and expanding further up into the surrounding hills. Annica and her team were turning out to be invaluable, and her natural leadership skills were perfectly suited for splitting up and assigning tasks within the work pool. While food used to be nothing more than a necessity for survival, new wannabe chefs were suddenly cropping up all over town, trying their hands at more exciting cuisine. The bulk of their crops and meat used to be exported to the West, but no longer. Cyrus couldn't help himself; he was proud of how fast the town was able to turn itself around. Easttown was truly thriving.

On this particular day, Cyrus found himself squinting in the sunlight and watching the town get built up around him from his elevated deck off the front of his house, a new addition that several of the builders had enthusiastically insisted on creating for him. The sounds of hammering and chopping rang out from all around him, echoing off the hillsides, and plumes of dust at the various worksites scattered around town rose up and caught the afternoon sunlight in orange and yellow bursts.

As he watched, Ydoro came striding up the road, weaving between the people and greeting them as he passed. He had taken on much the same role as he had in the West, minus the fake accent and strange robes. The people trusted him, and he was integral in connecting the people into a real, cohesive society. He beamed up at Cyrus as he approached, and bounced up the stairs in a confident, carefree sort of way before taking a spot at Cyrus's side.

"My King," Ydoro said with a smile.

Cyrus chuckled and responded, "I've told you, you don't need to call me that."

"All due respect, but I'm not going to stop. I do believe you're the first person I've met who actually deserves the title."

Cyrus shook his head but smiled in spite of himself. "It's come a long ways in a few weeks," he admitted.

"You've done good work here," Ydoro said, still smiling and surveying the town. "You should be proud."

"I didn't do anything," Cyrus argued, "I just let the people do their thing."

"You gave them a chance," Ydoro insisted, "that's more than they've had in a long time."

"So no news to report?" Cyrus asked, eager to get off the subject.

"No bad news," Ydoro responded, "Annica's team want to establish several outposts on higher ground, and we're expanding our fishing docks to include a prep-station. In time, we may move the entire operation down to the coast, with your permission."

Cyrus laughed again and said, "That's your department, Ydoro, I trust whatever you say is best."

"Very good, my King," Ydoro replied with a nod of his head, though the formal address was said with a slightly playful, amused tone this time.

"So what do you think," Cyrus asked, "at what point can I start calling you Randall? Don't you think it's time to reclaim who you were?"

Ydoro shook his head with a good-natured smirk and said, "I've become perfectly accustomed to being Ydoro. In fact, it's Ydoro who has earned his place here, I think. It would seem wrong to change my identity now."

Cyrus shrugged but didn't push the topic.

"I actually do come with some interesting news," Ydoro said, "one of our cooks came to me today, apparently he has a couple friends across our Western border." When Cyrus looked surprised, Ydoro explained, "Many of our people do. They still have ties with people in your brother's Kingdom. Anyways, according to his friends across the border, they're having trouble growing the Balsat Roots that we do here. You know, those pinkish ones you'll see in stews sometimes? Anyways, they were asking about opening a trade route to share them."

Cyrus raised his eyebrows and nodded thoughtfully. "You know I have no problem helping the people, but I can't give them something for nothing. It's important that our Kingdoms remain on equal footing."

"Agreed," Ydoro said, "they have crops in the Western fields that we could use starts of, I would recommend we propose a bi-weekly trade."

"Perfect," Cyrus nodded, "do you have someone else you can entrust trade operations to? I'd rather it not be you, you have enough on your hands as is."

"I have someone in mind," Ydoro confirmed with a nod and a smile.

"Of course you do," Cyrus responded with a laugh. "Have you seen Jack around?"

"I think he was up in the hills with Annica," Ydoro said. "Speaking of, I'm supposed to meet with a merchant out by the foothills."

Ydoro gave a shallow bow and skipped down the stairs to the dusty road below. "It's a shame you're not staying," he called up to him, "you're a natural at this."

Cyrus waved the compliment away and asked, "You still stopping by tonight?"

"Wouldn't miss it," Ydoro called over his shoulder as he strode back down the road towards the bustling town.

Cyrus had been teaching Ydoro how to play chess during the evenings, a topic that had been born from imposter-Henry's confusion about the game, and one of their first clues that he was not from their world. Ydoro had of course heard of chess, but never learned to play as a kid. Cyrus supposed it was as good a way as any to pass the time here, and as he had explained the various pieces used in the game; the kings, queens, knights, and so on, Ydoro had felt it was quite applicable to their own circumstances in the Kingdom.

As Cyrus watched Ydoro bounce through the crowd and vanish up the stone street, he had the slightest feeling of satisfied contentment, a feeling that was incredibly rare these days. It didn't last, as a vision of Cynthia's face swam into his mind and a longing for home settled in once again. He had to be careful that he never became too complacent here; he had a life waiting for him back home after all. But seeing Easttown literally rising up around him, he couldn't help it; he felt pride at what had been done here.

# CHAPTER FORTY-ONE

# SOMETHING TO FIGHT FOR

Jack pulled heavily on the rope with his entire body, letting out a strained grunt, which was mirrored by a half-dozen additional voices behind him. As the tension released and the gigantic beam settled into place, Jack took a deep breath and released his grip.

"That should do it," Cain exclaimed from behind him, releasing his own hold on the rope along with the five other members of his team. They were erecting a pully system that would make it easier to distribute rocks from the higher hills down into the main part of town. Annica, as always, was serving as foreman, and grinning broadly as she surveyed the progress.

Jack jumped down from the boulder he was standing on and hopped sure-footedly from stone to stone before landing next to Annica. He turned to survey their work, which had only started to take shape within the last several days.

"Just couldn't resist working for me again, could you," Annica joked.

Jack shrugged and replied, "Outdoor work suits me well. It's what I've always known."

From this vantage point near the top of the hillside, the entirety of Easttown was visible in the valley below. The progress that had been made over the last few weeks was staggering, and the credit had to go to the people, who had never before had the chance to work for themselves and their own community, at least not in recent memory. Jack would be remiss if he didn't also credit Cyrus for his work making Easttown flourish. Jack briefly entertained the idea that he had misjudged Cyrus from the start, but the truth was that this was a new side of him. It sounded as though Cyrus had always been a natural leader in his old life, but he had lacked the introspection, or possibly self-awareness, to be an inspiration to others. People followed him before simply because of his gregarious nature, now they followed him because they truly respected him. Cyrus, for his part, still seemed uncomfortable with the idea of being king, a title the man Jack had first met on the expedition ship would have relished. It seemed to Jack that his near-death experience on the dinghies, followed by the death of Dalton, had broken Cyrus down to his core, and yet he had slowly but surely built himself back up, becoming a more grounded, level-headed person in the process, and someone Jack was actually proud to follow. It made Jack smile thinking of the chest-pounding animosity between the two when the expedition had first started.

"You've started something here, Jack," Annica said reflectively, now gazing down at Easttown, "you and the King I mean. I always stayed out of those sort of affairs in the Kingdom. I was content just to let whoever wanted to rule do so however they wanted to. Our life was better than most in Easttown, we were afforded certain luxuries that kept us happy. But you've given us something to fight for, Jack. All of us."

"Well I'm glad to hear that," Jack said mildly, "we don't belong here, though. Eventually we will find a way. Believe me, Cyrus will never stop looking for a way back to his wife."

"So that's Cyrus's reason," Annica said thoughtfully, "what's yours?" She had begun walking further up the hillside and Jack followed, not struggling to keep up as he had the first time they had met. "I mean, what are you running back to?"

Jack frowned for a second and it occurred to him that he had never actually considered the question. "I suppose it's just… it's my home. It's where I'm from."

"So?" Annica responded bluntly. "What's so important for you to get back to?"

After another moment of contemplative silence, Jack finally answered, "I honestly don't know."

Annica smiled, jumping over a gap between two large rocks. "People do make a life here, you know. Even outsiders." When Jack didn't respond, Annica finally asked, "So what was your world like? How was it different from ours?"

"Well," Jack started, wondering where to begin, "It's bigger, that's one thing. Or maybe it's the same size but we have the ability to move around more. We have shipping lines that connect all the oceans. There are so many different countries... er, Kingdoms I guess you could say, each with their own leaders and their own laws."

"Sounds complicated," Annica observed, "how do they all get along?"

Jack laughed and said, "They often don't. War and conquest have always been the way of my world. In my country we have a president, he's sort of the king. But it works differently than here."

They arrived at the peak of the rocky hillside and from the top, the western side of the Kingdom was visible on the horizon. The Fire Fields glowed serenely past the treeline, and beyond that, the forest sloped downwards towards the valley that nestled the town of the West, hidden from this vantage point. To the right, perched atop the tree-covered hillside, the deep black stone of the Temple was impossible to miss, standing in stark, ominous contrast to its natural surroundings.

"What is it Alec did in your world?" Annica asked, gazing west at the fortress.

"He was a teacher," Jack said with a shake of his head.

"A teacher?" Annica laughed, "I can't see that."

"And Mora, he was apparently from our army. A soldier at one point."

Annica laughed again. "Is that right? I'm noticing a pattern in your people. War and conquest, like you said... I'm not sure I like your world too much."

Jack shrugged but didn't argue. She made a fair point.

"Do you think this will last?" Annica finally asked, "this peace?"

Jack, continuing to stare at the distant Temple warily, answered, "For a time… hopefully. I think things are starting to change, and change can be hard to undo. I think the progress that Easttown has made will shape the future of the Kingdom for generations… but as far as peace goes… I don't know." He looked down at the rocky ledge beneath his feet and gently kicked a small stone over the precipice. "There's a lot of baggage that comes with our new kings."

Annica shook her head, evidently unfamiliar with the phrase.

"They have a history," Jack explained, "a complicated history. I don't understand it fully. But I think it's behind every decision the two of them make. I hope having them apart will allow them each to lead with clearer intentions, but I fear the consequences when they do meet again."

Annica nodded at the grim warning, and said, "Well this time you'll have us by your side."

Jack turned to her and asked, "So you're not sitting on the sidelines anymore?"

Annica winked at him and replied, "It's like I said; you've given us something to fight for. If a fight does come, we'll be there."

Jack nodded but didn't respond. He hoped it wouldn't come to that, but a feeling in his gut warned him that the newly brokered peace would be put to the test sooner than they would like.

## CHAPTER FORTY-TWO

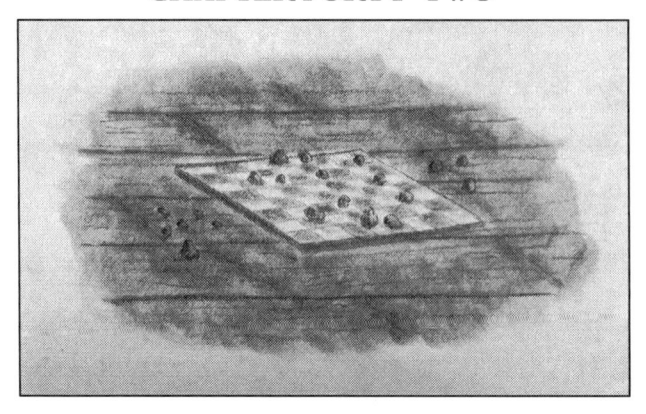

# FUTURE AND PAST

Cyrus Dorn was laughing, and it was a genuine laugh, the laugh of someone who was content in their present life. Of course, Cyrus wasn't content, how could he be while Cynthia waited for him out there somewhere, but he felt genuinely happy for the first time in a long time.

Cyrus was sitting casually on the floor of his wooden deck, the warm glow of the surrounding torches creating flickering orange dashes of color to cut through the cool, steady light of the full moon above. Their makeshift chessboard sat on the ground in front of him and Ydoro sat on the opposite side, also laughing and seemingly forgetting it was his turn. Jack was perched on the railing overhanging the stone street below, a drink in his hand and a smile on his face.

It had been nearly two months now since they had left the Temple and everything they had come to know in the West. Two months since they had given power back to the people of Easttown, and the town was thriving. The restoration of the roads and buildings had been completed at an incredible rate and now all focus was on expansion. New property was being built up closer to the coast, tradesmen were opening up new shops, food was in abundance, and the people were working together like a well-oiled machine. That was in no small part due to Annica, who Cyrus had officially named Easttown's Commander of Development.

SOMEWHERE

She was incredibly adept at assigning and guiding work throughout the town, and had consistently innovative ideas for improving workflows and generally making a better life for the people. She brought the larger ideas to Cyrus for approval, but most of her communication ran through Jack, whom she clearly had a bond with and spent a lot of her time, to the point that Cyrus wondered if they were an *item*. Jack had been named Advisor to the King, despite the fact that Cyrus didn't initially see the benefit of such titles. Ydoro, however, had convinced him that creating such a hierarchy would not only solidify Cyrus's role in the Kingdom, but encourage a sustainable model for years and decades to come, should Cyrus no longer be around to lead. In an appointment that Cyrus felt was long overdue considering the invaluable role he had served under several different monarchs, Ydoro was named Ambassador of the People. In this position, he represented the voice of the people of Easttown and the ears of the King. It was a job he had done for years, of course, but Ydoro had beamed with pride when Cyrus had made it official.

Despite Cyrus's resistance, they had fallen into a bit of a routine in recent weeks, but it didn't scare him like it used to. He still had every intention of finding his way home, but the work he was doing felt important. In fact, it felt more important than anything he had done in his life prior.

Ydoro finally seemed to remember the game in front of them and cautiously moved a piece across the board. Of course, the pieces did not look like real chess pieces at all, rather they were differently sized stones with markings on them designating their status. Ydoro had caught on to the game quickly, and it provided an excellent way for their team to casually talk at the end of a day.

"You know," Cyrus began, "in its original form, this game is about the strategy of war. Kings would play it to size up their opponents, learn how they would view a military campaign… see what sacrifices their rival was willing to make to gain victory."

Ydoro nodded and responded, "So is that what you're doing, my King? Sizing me up?"

Cyrus chuckled and said, "I suppose it can also just serve to sharpen the mind." He picked up the stone that was meant to represent the king, with a crude crown etched in its surface, and continued, "I always just fancied it the game of kings. I liked to imagine Caesar playing this very game to focus his strategies for war."

"And now you're the king," Ydoro pointed out, somehow without a hint of insincerity.

Jack raised his drink from his place on the railing and announced, "May your reign be more successful than old Julius!"

Jack and Cyrus laughed jovially, but Ydoro's muted reaction made Cyrus wonder if he had gotten the joke.

"So let me ask you a question, Cyrus," Jack said, still with a warm smile on his face. "What is it you're going back to? Annica asked me this and I couldn't think of an honest answer. I mean, I know you have your wife back home, but was this your life? Playing chess and teaching at the university?"

The question wasn't asked in a judgmental way, rather it seemed Jack was genuinely looking for a real answer.

"Well, getting back to Cynthia is my only priority," Cyrus began, "but no, I didn't just teach and sit at home. We travelled. We had adventures. Cynthia and I had been all over the world; South America, Asia, Africa, you name it. We had a real life." Cyrus realized he hadn't thought of his own world in quite a while. Cynthia had certainly been on his mind almost constantly, but not his old life. It was a slightly sobering thought. He continued, "You know, we lived in this college town, the university was walking distance, I had colleagues, friends... I'd meet my brother for drinks after work." The thought of his brother hurt a bit, considering their current relationship. "He wasn't always like this, ya know. We were close, for a time. I guess I just never realized he wanted... more from the world."

"I think it goes beyond that," Jack said with a shrug. "He seems to think the world *owes* him more. That's what makes him dangerous."

Cyrus didn't like the insinuation, but it was hard to argue. "I really don't know where we go from here," he admitted. "I mean, say we do find a way out of here. Will he come with us? I do wonder about that."

"If he didn't go with you," Ydoro added, "you'd be leaving the future of the Kingdom in his charge."

"He'd come with us," Cyrus insisted with more certainty than he felt, "if it came to that. He'd wanna go home."

There was silence before Jack finally said, "If you say so," and took a swig of his drink.

Crunching footsteps announced a person walking up the street towards the deck. With the flickering torchlight pulsating in the foreground, it was impossible to see into the darkness beyond. The three of them looked expectantly towards the staircase for the mysterious visitor as they stepped heavily up the stairs.

"Hope I'm not interrupting," said a warm, albeit gravelly, voice as Cain's smiling face swam into view.

"Not at all," Cyrus assured him with a smile. "Care for a drink?"

"Not staying long, my King, but thank you," Cain said, leaning heavily against the tree-trunk support at the corner of the deck. "I come with news from the trade front."

Cain had been appointed Master of Trade, hand-picked by Ydoro based on an enthusiastic recommendation from Jack. He had done good work in the role so far, in fact better than Cyrus could have imagined. He lacked some of the finer touches for diplomacy, but it was exactly that blunt gruffness that seemed to work so well when dealing with the trade delegates of the West. Their trade lines had been opened for over a month now and had more or less progressed without a hitch. Cyrus had initially worried how Alec would handle the proposal, but it didn't seem like he took much part in it.

"So," Cain began, "it seems the West is having trouble with their fish supply. I know, I know, they have just as much ocean on their side of the island as we have. I think the problem is they're struggling to set up a long-term operation at the coast, but what do I know. Anyways, they're growing their own vegetables now, but they want fish. Now, we are set up with a booming operation at the coast, the problem is the West is running out of trade to offer us."

Jack laughed with a roll of his eyes and said mockingly, "Is that right?"

Cain shrugged and said, "I can turn them down, but it may cost us in the long run. Say we need something down the road…"

Cyrus thought a moment, then looked across the chess board at Ydoro, who was watching him expectantly. Finally, Cyrus said, "No, don't turn them down. If the people need help, we provide it."

Ydoro smiled and Cain nodded in halfhearted approval.

"Find something to trade for it, though," Cyrus clarified, "it's important we continue to establish guidelines. If it's not something of equal value, that's okay, just make sure it's done."

"You got it, my King," Cain said with a small bow of his head.

Cyrus looked down at the makeshift chess board and an idea occurred to him. "Actually, I have a trade to propose. It'll require the authorization from someone in the Temple, though."

Cain raised an eyebrow in curiosity and said, "Okay, and what's that?"

"I want Henry's research. All of it. All journals, notebooks, drawings, everything from that room in the dungeons."

Jack nodded his head thoughtfully, and Ydoro looked slightly puzzled.

"Do you think they'll agree to it?" Cyrus asked Cain.

Cain nodded thoughtfully and responded, "I think I can talk them into it."

"Good," Cyrus said, "then that's what we ask for in return."

Cain gave a casual salute of his hand and said, "Consider it done, my King." As he turned to leave, he gave Jack a smack on the shoulder before disappearing back into the night.

"Why do you want Henry's research?" Ydoro asked.

"He thinks he can find a way out of here," Jack answered for Cyrus, studying his face from his spot on the railing.

Cyrus nodded in confirmation and said, "He was here a long time. He met lots of people, saw a lot of the Kingdom. He never figured it out, but who knows, maybe he got closer than he realized. Besides, the history of this Kingdom shouldn't be left to Alec."

The silent night air was cut by an earth-shaking blast from off to the west. It wasn't exceptionally loud from such a distance, but it could be felt rattling in the ground below like a drawn-out tremor from a strike of lightning. All three of them jumped up and ran to the edge of the porch, leaning out into the night air and looking off to the west. The lower valleys that the Western town rested in could not be seen from this angle, but up in the hills beyond the Temple, a plume of dark smoke could be seen against the deep blue of the fading evening sky. Whatever had happened up there must have been significant to be felt and seen from so far away.

Cyrus looked to Ydoro and then to Jack. "What could that have been?"

Jack, who was still squinting in the direction of the smoke, replied, "I think that's the hillside I used to work on. Annica's old worksite."

"What could cause that?" Cyrus asked in concern.

Ydoro shook his head, looking off to the west in clear confusion.

Jack pulled his eyes away from the distant hillside and took another swig of his drink. "I wouldn't worry about it. It's really not our problem anymore."

"There must be people up there," Cyrus continued, "why though? What would people be doing up there at this time of night?"

Jack shook his head, "Those aren't our people, Cyrus. Not anymore. Just let it be."

Cyrus sat back down at the game and Ydoro took his place across from him. Ydoro looked deep in thought as well but when Cyrus looked at him, he smiled and said, "Jack's right. Besides, I'm sure we'll hear about it in the days to come."

Ydoro looked down at the board in front of him and thoughtfully moved a piece. Jack put his foot up on the railing and took another casual sip of his drink, but his eyes betrayed his curiosity as he glanced several times off to the west and the slowly dissipating smoke rising from the hillside.

**CHAPTER FORTY-THREE**

# BORDER SKIRMISH

When trade routes were first established between the two Kingdoms, it was decided that the meeting point should not be in the Fire Fields, despite it being the most obvious location due to its status as the only neutral territory on the island. Concerns were brought up, specifically from Jack and Cyrus, that trade occurring in the neutral zone could invite pirating that could risk complicating relations between the two trading parties. Admittedly, this was a concern born almost exclusively from their own world and the society they had left behind, but a safer solution was agreed upon to have the trade delegates meet in an area where the two Kingdoms physically touched. As a result, a dirt road was created early on, to the north of the Fire Fields, and a trade post was in the process of being erected. With Easttown's herculean expansion efforts, they already had dwellings cropping up on their side of the border almost up to the trade line, while their counterparts in the West had nothing but road and a single, unfinished stone hut leading back to their Kingdom. It was in this area, along the Kingdom border at the soon-to-be trade outpost, that Jack could hear the angry shouting of dozens of voices as some sort of conflict unfolded on the road ahead.

Jack picked up the pace and wheeled around the last bend in the road to find Cain shaking his head and yelling at a large group of people descending from the west with carts pulled behind them and bags slung over their shoulders. Cain's attention seemed to be split between the oncoming group and a large, bearded man standing directly in front of him, who looked remarkably like Cain himself.

"I'm not encouraging them," Cain was shouting at his lookalike standing along the Western border, "I'm telling them to turn around! We don't want this!"

"It's the King's orders," the Westerner said back, "these people are not to cross the border to the East."

"And what the hell do you expect me to do about it?" Cain yelled, "they're your people, you stop them." As the group continued to approach, Cain looked over the bearded man's shoulder and continued to shake his head. "Turn it around, people!" he shouted at them. "It's not my call, but we can't have you here!"

Jack finally skidded to a halt at Cain's side, his feet kicking up a plume of dust from the road. His arrival seemed to give the approaching crowd pause, but they continued shouting indecipherably in their direction.

"What's going on?" Jack asked.

"Oh thank god," Cain exclaimed when he saw Jack, "maybe you can sort this mess out."

"It's not my call, Cain, you know that," the bearded Westerner interjected.

"Yeah, yeah, I know, now shut up a sec," a visibly agitated Cain snapped. "It's like this, Jack, apparently there was some sort of explosion at our old dig site up in the hills last night. Some geniuses tried to weaponize frozen fire to make mining easier and it all went sideways."

"They paid with their lives, Cain!" the other man exclaimed, "show some respect! They didn't want to be up their working."

"Yeah, yeah," Cain waved his hand in annoyance. "Jack, this is Bohrman, my trade delegate in the West. We were meeting to discuss the trade for Henry's research materials like the King asked, but now this damn caravan showed up wanting to come East."

"So what's the problem with that?" Jack asked.

Cain threw up his hands theatrically and answered, "*I don't have a problem with it. Their king doesn't want them coming.*"

Bohrman interjected, "The King feels the borders should be respected and has requested that the East not allow Westerners to permanently relocate to your Kingdom."

Jack shook his head in confusion, "Alec said that? Why?"

Bohrman sighed and said, "It's the King's wishes."

"It's a crock of shit is what it is," Cain growled angrily to Bohrman, "are you gonna tell him the whole story or should I?" When Bohrman shrugged his shoulders uncomfortably, Cain continued, "Okay fine, damn coward. Here's the deal, Jack. The *Western* king had ordered them to be working up in those caves last night. Felt enough progress wasn't being made. So, with the pressure on, the workers decided to try a quicker way to get the job done and it ended with… well… boom. So now some of the other workers, and the families of the victims, they're wanting to leave, but the King's claiming disloyalty."

"Oh hell," Jack spat with a roll of his eyes.

"My thoughts exactly," Cain said, "but he's holding up trade over this."

"What does this have to do with trade?" Jack asked Bohrman directly.

"The King feels…" Bohrman began.

"Okay, okay," Jack cut him off. "Well, we can't take part in this. We respect your king's wishes within his own borders, but it's not our responsibility to keep those people out."

The crowd began to get more restless from behind Bohrman, with many of them still shouting and gesturing wildly.

"Listen," Jack shouted to the crowd, "this is not our call to make. We can't take you in if your king won't allow you to cross our border."

The crowd started to yell more loudly and as a few stepped forward, the rest followed suit. Soon the entire group was on the move again, with their carts rumbling behind them as they approached the border.

"No, please," Jack yelled, "we can't take you in."

Cain and Bohrman joined in yelling at the crowd to turn around, but with little effect. The truth was the three of them would not be able to stop the dozens of people from crossing the border. Jack was shaking his head vigorously as the nearest Westerner approached, but he had no idea what his next move was.

He never had to decide, as it turned out, because an echoing screech stopped the entire group in their tracks. The hairs on the back of Jack's neck stood up as he anticipated what was about to follow.

Sure enough, the first of the Neodactyls stalked out from off to the side, with Jack having no idea where it had come from, followed closely by the second. They strutted out deliberately and in unison, hissing threateningly but clearly in control of themselves. It almost seemed as though they knew what was expected of them; stopping the people from continuing down the road towards the East. It worked, of course; the people had stopped abruptly, with many of them shamelessly positioning themselves behind their cohorts for further protection.

Jack scanned the area but saw no sign of Alec or his chariot. The Neodactyls paced along the road, scanning the group as a whole with their yellow eyes and chittering softly.

"Go home, people," Jack yelled over the Neodactyls to the group. "This isn't the way, it's not worth it. Please."

The group seemed to finally be running out of steam. It seemed that no one in the crowd wanted to draw attention to themselves with the Neodactyls present, and as a result, the yelling and shuffling started to ebb away, with an eerie silence taking its place. Jack noted a distinct look of betrayal in many of their faces, but he knew there was nothing he could do for them, at least not at the moment.

A Shrieking Bat screamed in the distance and a bird chirped nearby, but the silence from the previously raucous crowd was painful. Finally, a man in front of the group shook his head with a look of crushing disappointment and said quietly, "They're no different than our king."

Muttering from the crowd picked up softly, drowning out the sounds of birds with the angry buzzing of voices. Most of the murmurings were indistinct, but Jack specifically heard the word 'lied' uttered several times. Slowly, the people started to turn away dejectedly, many readjusting their bags of belongings or struggling to turn their carts around in the crowd. It was a heartbreaking scene, and Jack had the intense urge to do something more for them, but he had no power in this situation.

"You've done the right thing," Bohrman insisted with a grunt. "It's not worth causing a disruption in our trade over something so trivial."

"You're a spineless shit, you know that?" Cain growled, but he was looking thoroughly relieved that the commotion was dying down. Indeed, the last of the people were turning and following their counterparts back down the road heading west, most still shaking their heads disappointedly. One of the Neodactyls followed after them slowly while the other paced near the treeline, almost like hounds herding sheep.

"This was really worth holding up trade over?" Jack snapped at Bohrman, who blinked somewhat stupidly and shook his head dismissively. "And if this is so trivial, then why not let them come? What does Alec… what does your king care if they come East?"

Bohrman shook his head again in a non-committal half shrug and repeated, "The King wishes for his people…"

"Okay got it," Jack cut him off, having lost his patience talking to a man who clearly had no intention of giving real thought to the situation.

Jack turned to leave in frustration but Cain put a hand on his arm to stop him. "Just to be clear," Cain said to Bohrman, "we expect our trade for Henry's journals to go through after this nonsense."

Bohrman puffed out his chest as though swelling to make himself look bigger and more intimidating, an amusing image considering he and Cain shared almost identical body types. "You expect? I will present your desires to the King, but I will not be strong-armed into…"

"No you will make this trade go through," Jack began venomously, but Cain put a hand on his arm again to stop him.

Jack paused, realizing this was Cain's arena after all, as the Master of Trade. He stepped back, but Cain himself stepped forward, bringing his face quite close to Bohrman's while still looking down the road where the last of the crowd had just disappeared around the corner, and the Neodactyls still lurked at a distance.

"Look at it this way, Bohrman," Cain began softly, "we wouldn't have minded allowing those people, *your* people, to join us in the East.

We have the resources to sustain them. The only reason we turned them away was because your king wished it. Now, *our* king wishes for something. I believe it would be counterproductive to cause a disruption in trade over something so trivial… as you stated."

Bohrman paused before answering, "I'll do my best."

"You do that," Cain responded, but he had become distracted. He was looking down the road that the Westerners had retreated on with a squinted, confused look in his eyes.

Jack followed his gaze and saw the Neodactyls still prowling the road, but they seemed to be retreating behind the unfinished trade outpost on the Western side. Jack watched as they disappeared from view, but he could still hear them cooing softly behind the dwelling. Jack sidestepped a few paces and lowered his head slightly to see through the exposed holes that would eventually become windows. He was able to see straight through to the other side through a foot-wide hole in the opposite wall. It was enough to confirm that there was a person standing behind the building, greeting the Neodactyls. The person had a frayed, gray traveling cloak with the hood pulled up, but Jack didn't need to see their face to guess who it was.

As though feeling Jack's watchful eyes, the figure vanished from view with crunching footsteps, the Neodactyls close behind. They seemed to be heading back west.

Bohrman and Cain were also looking in the direction of the trade outpost, both with furrowed brows.

"Was that him?" Jack asked Bohrman without ever taking his eyes off the building, even though there was no longer anything to see. Bohrman, however, looked as confused as he was, and didn't respond.

Had Alec been watching them from behind the building the whole time? It was well out of earshot of their conversation, but Jack still found it unsettling that Alec had potentially been lurking behind the trees as the chaos at the boarder had unfolded.

Cain shook his head and pointed a finger at Bohrman, "The King wants Henry's old journals, make that trade happen. We'll be in touch." He looked at Jack and gestured his head back to the east, indicating that they were done talking. Jack nodded to Bohrman and they turned and left him standing at the border.

"He's a decent guy, he'll get it done I'm sure," Cain reassured Jack. "Sometimes he just needs a little nudge to see things clearly."

*****

As it turned out, Cain was right. Within the week, a cart was brought to the border piled high with journals, papers, notebooks, and drawings; the contents of Henry's cell, and the culmination of his life's work.

**CHAPTER FORTY-FOUR**

# THE LIFE AND DEATH OF HENRY FINE

The next few weeks were a whirlwind of research, with timelines being plotted, the island being mapped, and theories being shaped. Cyrus's own house was now covered wall to wall with pages of Henry's journals. There was a method to the madness and a system for sorting the papers, but one would be forgiven for thinking they had simply thrown the pages up in the air and let them land where they would. It looked like chaos, but for Cyrus and Jack, who had hardly left the room in two weeks, they finally felt like they were building towards something.

They had yet to uncover a key that would truly unlock the mysteries of the new world and make sense of their sudden appearance in it, but they both had the distinct feeling that somewhere amongst the exhaustive notes that Henry took, there would be a clue. After all, Henry had spent nearly a decade in the Kingdom with the specific intent to observe and document. The real trouble was becoming abundantly clear, however; Henry had not been trying to find a way out. He had been totally enamored by the Kingdom and its inhabitants, to the extent that he only began to think of escape once he was already locked in his cell.

Dr. Henry Fine had been quite young when he died at the hands of King Mora. It was somewhat difficult to track his exact age as they had not found an instance where he wrote his specific date of birth, but based on the brief and scattered mentions of his life before the Kingdom, Cyrus had pegged him at about thirty-three years old. What was clear was that he had died twelve years ago, in 1924. No clues were given as to how it happened; it did not seem that he knew it was coming. The journal entries simply stopped after a certain point, seemingly without significance or finality.

Henry's arrival in the Kingdom was well documented, and seemed as sudden and random as everyone else's. He had been a consultant on an excavation in Sudan, and himself and a guide had been attempting to locate a rumored burial site. Their search had led them into a cave, which Henry described as feeling strange from the start. He documented how he had felt light-headed even before he had crossed the threshold, and began having blurred vision soon after. He became disoriented and found himself on the main road of the Western side of the Kingdom. It was nighttime when he arrived, and it took him quite a while to first make contact with another person. The guide had been with him when he arrived, but did not receive much mention throughout the journals. It made Cyrus wonder if something had happened to him, but if it had, it seemed Henry was too interested in the Kingdom to take much notice.

His journals started off organized like a typical expedition journal, with dates as headings and almost daily observations written down. As the years went by, however, it seemed he changed focus and the organization became much more confusing. In place of writing his own thoughts and observations, his style seemed to alter to more closely resemble research, with different notebooks being used for different purposes and endless loose papers having no obvious connection or place. It appeared to Cyrus like Henry had been starting to prepare for writing a book on the history and culture of the Kingdom. As such, and probably in no small part due to the destruction the Neodactyls caused when they had been briefly locked in the room, there was no rhyme or reason to many of the papers. One paper would have a portrait of a local and the next would have a breakdown of how the community caught fish. One would talk about dining customs and the next would be an experience Henry had with the King. It made for slow reading and while Jack and Cyrus would bounce ideas off each other as they came across new information, most of their new theories were very thin.

"I've maybe got something here," Jack said half-heartedly to Cyrus as they approached their third week of digging. The sun had set for the day and they were running on fumes, but they were determined to keep going as long as they could.

"What is it?" Cyrus asked, he himself reading a page comparing Easttown's homes to those in the West.

"It's not much," Jack admitted, looking down at a loose paper in his hand, "but here Henry had started a list of people's lineages, and noted whether their relatives were from this world or our world."

"Mmmhmm," Cyrus mumbled, unable to suppress his lack of enthusiasm. "Add it to the pile by the door." The pile by the door was where they had been stacking possible leads to circle back to, all of which were about as exciting as the one Jack had just found.

Cyrus placed the page in his own hand face down on a stack in front of him, denoting it was 'unhelpful' and glanced down at the next. It described the machetes used by the Temple guards, in excruciating detail. Cyrus added it to the 'unhelpful' pile and scanned the next; a biography of a local man named Gedman Olark, along with a small portrait. Cyrus added it to the 'unhelpful' pile. The next was a page about the scepters of the king. It included a rough sketch and a few details describing their look, but it seemed clear based on the brevity of the page that Henry had never been near enough to hold or examine one. Cyrus looked up into the corner of the room where his own scepter leaned forgotten against the wall, then added the sheet to the 'unhelpful' pile. Next was a breakdown of the importance of wagons and a thorough analysis of the varying qualities of their build.

A knock at the door caused Cyrus, blurry eyed from reading, to jump slightly. He looked up to see Ydoro standing there, glancing around the room in mild interest.

"Still at it?" Ydoro asked, but it wasn't really a question.

"Nothing of much interest just yet," Cyrus said before Ydoro could ask, "but who knows."

"You can take a break, you know," Ydoro said gently. "Resting your eyes might be a good thing."

"We're just finishing up for the night," Cyrus promised.

"You would have liked him. Henry, I mean," Ydoro said to Cyrus, looking around at the pages strewn about the floor with a far-off look in his eyes. "I mean, most people did, but you remind me of him a bit."

"Well let's hope I have better luck than he did," Cyrus said somewhat grumpily. He was beginning to become frustrated at Henry's apparent disinterest in getting back to his own world. So few of his endless pages of notes talked about leaving, or even about how strange it was that he had ended up in a different world.

"This page talks about Mora's rise to power, and how he seized it from Irias," Jack announced, somewhat victoriously, before frowning and looking up at Cyrus. "Do we care about that?"

Cyrus shrugged. "Is it anything new?"

Jack looked back down at the notebook and skimmed it over. "I suppose not. Although I can see why the townspeople don't have a problem with Alec ruling over them. Mora was pretty ruthless, and they respected him for it."

"Or feared him," Cyrus responded dismissively. "Things are different now."

Ydoro, who was still standing in the doorway awkwardly, finally said, "Alright, well, I guess I'll leave you to it. See you tomorrow."

Cyrus and Jack both grunted their goodbye's and Ydoro left.

"I don't know," Cyrus sighed heavily, "maybe there's nothing worth finding in these pages."

"There could still be something here," Jack insisted, though he sounded tired.

Cyrus looked down at the stack of loose papers in his lap and rolled his eyes, suddenly unconvinced. "Yeah but these are really useless," Cyrus complained. "I mean, these are each individual pages describing encounters Henry had with different people in town." Cyrus began reading the titles off as he rifled through the pages. "'*Morgan Yolz Outlines Upkeep in the Temple*'. '*Guard Duty with Cirian Mives*'. '*Wolman the Farmer Shares His Secrets*'. '*The Mystery of a Man Named…*'"

Cyrus's voice had caught in his throat.  Hair on the back of his neck was suddenly standing on end.  The title of the page before him didn't make any sense.  He looked blankly down at it, willing himself to see through the fog of exhaustion.

"What's that?" Jack asked blandly from across the room.

Cyrus rubbed his eyes, blinked hard and stared down at the title of the page again.  His heart started beating like he had just run a race.

"What is it?" Jack asked again, now realizing with alarm that Cyrus had trailed off for a reason.  "What does it say?"

Cyrus looked up at Jack with baffled, uncomprehending eyes.  He looked back down at the page and read the header aloud, "*'The Mystery of a Man Named Dalton Sydney'.*"

**CHAPTER FORTY-FIVE**

# THE MAN WHO SHOULD NOT BE

C yrus read aloud from the yellowed, dried out paper in his hands.

*The Mystery of a Man Named Dalton Sydney*

*Today I encountered a man who I do not believe had any worldly business being here. The argument could of course be made that many, if not all, people in this land have no worldly business being here, given how myself and many others were forcefully pulled from our own world to this one, but this man was different. He came sprinting into town from the direction of the Temple, causing quite a stir amongst the shop owners. In my interviews, I have more or less met with everyone in the Kingdom willing to talk to me, so can readily identify a newcomer. This man also had the disheveled, slightly mad look a person shows when they have just been 'transplanted'. I have seen it many times before at this point. The difference with this man was the way he talked. I am used to newcomers asking, 'where am I?', but this man's first question was, 'who is the king right now?' Doubly intriguing was his reaction to my answer. When I told him King Mora was the ruling monarch, he seemed perplexed, as though he were expecting someone else.*

*When I pressed him for information, he told me his name was Dalton Sydney and that he had made a mistake. When asked what sort of mistake he had made,*

*he replied, 'I am not supposed to be here.' Unfortunately, Mr. Sydney had apparently come from the Temple itself, and it was no time at all before King Mora's guards were rushing into town to find the intruder, who they said had shoved past them on his way out the doors many minutes earlier. Upon seeing the guards coming for him, Mr. Sydney hastily asked me if I had ever seen anyone in the king's quarters who was 'not supposed to be there'. I told him I had spent very little time in King Mora's chambers, but asked him for clarification of what he was referring to. The guards, sadly, could not be dissuaded from pursuing him, however, and Mr. Sydney left in a rush. Confoundingly, he ran back in the direction of the Temple, from where he had just come. I never saw the man again.*
*I asked at the Temple later that day about our unexpected visitor, but the King said he had no knowledge of the man. This likely means Mr. Sydney was killed, sadly, for reasons I will likely never know.*

The passage ended abruptly, with no further questions or theories presented. As was the case with many of Henry's journal entries, and especially his loose pages, it seemed as though he had simply started writing down his thoughts and encounters as he had them, not knowing what he was going to do with them later.

Jack looked at Cyrus from across the small, wooden room, watching the orange glow from the torchlight flicker on his face, enhancing the thin lines around the edges of his eyes. He looked tired, and suddenly far older than Jack had seen him before. But his expression itself showed nothing. His face was entirely blank as he finished reading the passage aloud, his shoulders slumped slightly as though reading Henry's words had drained him of his last vestiges of energy… or perhaps his last vestiges of hope. Jack felt it too. An inescapable hopelessness that came from reading about Henry's encounter, and it was swiftly transforming into a feeling of numbness. Jack supposed they should talk aloud about what Cyrus had just read, but he couldn't even bring himself to speak at the moment.

Suddenly, and without any warning, Cyrus violently crumpled the paper in his hand and threw it hard against the opposite wall with a furious yell.

"That doesn't make sense!" Cyrus roared, stabbing his pointer finger through the air at the fallen piece of balled up paper. He looked like he was ready to have a meltdown. He was shaking his head feverishly and his eyes were darting back and forth around the room. "How could he have been here? How could Henry have met him? That's impossible! This is all impossible!"

Jack crossed the room cautiously and picked up the crumpled piece of paper, unruffled it, and looked for himself. If there had been any doubt in Jack's mind about the validity of what Cyrus had read, it vanished when he saw at the bottom of the paper a small, rough sketch of a bespectacled, disheveled man standing on the streets of the Kingdom. It wasn't as precise a drawing as many of the others in Henry's journals, likely because it had been done by memory, but it was unmistakably a drawing of Dalton.

Cyrus was still pacing the room, now trampling right over their stacks of journals and loose papers without care. "That was at least twelve years ago," Cyrus said loudly, although Jack suspected, despite the volume of his voice, that he was mostly talking to himself. "Henry died twelve years ago, we've been here a number of months. And Dalton died! We buried him! Is this some kind of trick? Like Irias pretending to be Henry? But that's his picture! That's him! And how would anyone have known a man named Dalton Sydney would be coming here twelve years later?!"

"Cyrus," Jack finally said forcefully, speaking for the first time since Cyrus had finished reading. His tone was strong enough that it stopped Cyrus's pacing, but now he looked expectantly at him as though waiting for an answer.

"Explain that to me," Cyrus demanded, pointing at the paper in Jack's hand with a shaking finger. "Explain to me how that makes sense. Make me understand."

Jack shook his head calmly, far more calmly than he actually felt. "You know I can't do that, Cyrus," he responded softly, "it doesn't make sense. It's not possible. And yet, this journal entry is saying it happened."

"The journals," Cyrus finally said, as though this had suddenly triggered an epiphany in his mind. "They came from Alec. What if he doctored them? Maybe he's trying to get us to…"

Cyrus trailed off, possibly realizing that his theory didn't make a lot of sense.

Jack shook his head and responded, "It's the same handwriting. The sketch is the same style. I think it's safe to say it really was Henry."

Cyrus shook his head again and resumed his pacing over the strewn-about papers.

"We have to wrap our heads around this," Jack said firmly. "We have to see past what doesn't make sense and look at what that journal entry is really saying."

"It's saying we're screwed!" Cyrus snapped.

Jack nodded his head in understanding and raised his hands bracingly. "It's giving us more than that. It's giving us our first real clue." Jack looked back down at the wrinkled paper in his hands and skimmed Henry's description of the encounter. "See here," Jack said, pointing, "Dalton said *'I'm not supposed to be here'*, he knew! He knew he didn't belong there! And look at what he asked Henry. He asked him if he'd ever seen anyone in the king's quarters who wasn't supposed to be there. That's important!" Jack's heart was starting to beat incredibly fast. He felt like he was suddenly beginning to see this written encounter for what it was; not a soul-crushing defeat but at long last a trail to follow.

"What are we supposed to do with that?" Cyrus asked, throwing up his hands in frustration. He was clearly not capable of critical thinking in his present state of mind.

"Think about it, Cyrus," Jack implored him, "that's not the first time we've heard something strange about someone in the king's quarters. Think of the last time we saw your brother."

"I remember he aligned himself with that treacherous weasel Irias and split the Kingdom in half," Cyrus spat bitterly.

"No, before that," Jack said patiently, "don't you remember? Why did we fight with him in the first place?"

"He wouldn't put down the Neodactyls," Cyrus said, finally seeming to slow down enough to think rationally.

"Before that," Jack implored, and he could tell by the change in Cyrus's expression that he finally understood.

"He said I attacked him," Cyrus said quietly, finally looking into Jack's eyes.

"He said you attacked him," Jack agreed. "Why would he say that? Why would he think that? We had just arrived from town, but the moment you entered his chambers he was prepared to kill you. And he kept gesturing towards the window behind that altar."

"He saw something," Cyrus said breathlessly.

"He must have," Jack responded with a nod. "Now, I know people have appeared all over the Kingdom. Hell, we first appeared in the Fire Fields. But there's something happening behind that altar in the king's chambers, that's not a coincidence. It's Dalton's own words." He said the last sentence while brandishing the crumpled paper like a weapon.

Cyrus took a deep breath and said, "Okay," nodding and finally composing himself. "Okay, you're right. There's something here. There's just one problem."

Jack smiled humorlessly and nodded, "We no longer have access to the Temple."

"So do we parley with Alec?" Cyrus asked with naïve hope in his eyes. "Maybe if we explained to him what we're looking for…"

"Cyrus, he wouldn't even meet with us," Jack insisted. "Honestly, you should have seen things at the border. Think about it, why would he care if some of his people wanted to join us in the East? He won't offer any concessions to us, and he certainly doesn't want it to appear we're working together. It's important to him that the West is standing alone."

Cyrus sighed heavily. "How did we get to this point? I used to know him."

"You don't know him now," Jack insisted. "I'm certain that was him I saw at the border, lurking behind that trade outpost. He wouldn't even engage with us. He must have just been waiting back there to make sure we didn't let his people cross. And I don't know what he would have done if we had. He had his hood pulled up, I suppose to blend in with the crowd, but..."

Jack trailed off, a thought just occurring to him.

"Well, what then?" Cyrus asked, throwing up his hands in defeat. "If Alec won't let us in? It's not like we can sneak in. There's not even a back entrance to that place."

Jack smirked slightly and tilted his head, almost guiltily, as though he didn't quite want to say what he was about to say. "We don't need a back entrance, what if we walked in through the front door?"

Cyrus raised his eyebrows and said firmly, "I'm not challenging him like we did with Mora."

"No, no," Jack agreed, "nothing like that. But Alec goes everywhere with that scepter of his. And there's only two of those in the Kingdom, the second of which just so happens to be in your possession. I saw him at the border, he was wearing a dark grey traveling cloak and he had the hood pulled up. That's not hard to replicate."

Cyrus nodded slowly, but it was a resigned sort of nod. "You're suggesting we impersonate Alec to get into the Temple."

"Well, you specifically," Jack clarified, "I wouldn't be able to go in with you. But we can get into Westtown easily enough; what if I were to create some sort of distraction that would draw Alec out of the Temple? He comes out, rides into town. While he's out, you walk in through the front doors, scepter in hand, hood pulled up."

"But you said it yourself," Cyrus replied with a shake of his head, "Alec would *ride* into town. He doesn't go anywhere on foot. The guards would find it suspicious if Alec left on his chariot and came back without it."

"I don't think they talk to him," Jack persisted. "I've never heard one of the Temple guards so much as ask a question without prompting. And you remember how Alec storms around the Temple. If you marched in there with purpose, moving fast, acting agitated, I don't think there's any chance in the world the guards would stop you."

Jack could see Cyrus weighing his words. Jack himself hoped the logic was sound, and he wasn't being reckless in presenting this plan. The consequences could be dire if they were caught inside the Temple, but it could be their chance at escaping, and he thought that was likely worth the risk. Besides, despite all of Alec's posturing and declarations of power, Jack couldn't imagine Alec would actually hurt them. He was *pretty* sure he believed that.

Jack's doubts must not have shown on his face because Cyrus finally nodded in agreement, a look of steely resolve setting in behind his eyes. Jack suddenly didn't share Cyrus's confidence, and it was with a distinct, sickly feeling in his gut that he started to feel like the trajectory he himself had just set them on would lead to the end, one way or another.

## CHAPTER FORTY-SIX

# THE WEST

"Fire?" Cyrus balked, looking half-amused, half-concerned.

"Fire," Jack nodded before turning to look at Cyrus in the fading pale blue light. "No good?"

Cyrus shrugged and moved his head in a non-committal half-nod. "It'll probably work. Isn't there a cleaner way, though?"

It had been a little less than twenty-four hours since their discovery of Dalton Sydney's story within the depths of Henry Fine's extensive writings. They had eventually gotten some sleep that night, and had both woken up with fire in their eyes, ready to do something with the new information that would change their fortunes forever. Neither had any desire to wait, so they had spent the day strategizing how they would enter Westtown, how they would breach the Temple, and how they would sneak into the king's quarters unnoticed. Cyrus had the more dangerous part in the plan. He would be entering the Temple alone, dressed as his brother, and accessing Alec's chambers to inspect the fiery altar by the far windows. Jack himself worried about the possibility of Cyrus not finding anything of note around the altar, but he had to keep reminding himself that Dalton was pointing them towards that specific place. There had to be a clue there.

Ydoro had been brought in to discuss the plans during the day, but he obviously would not be able to join Cyrus and Jack on their quest into Westtown. Ydoro was possibly the most recognized face in the entire Kingdom and there was no chance he would be able to walk through town unnoticed. Jack, on the other hand, had spent very little time with the people of the West, having been shipped off to work the hills with Annica early on. Ydoro was able to offer much in the way of advice, not to mention lending Cyrus a grey traveling cloak that, according to Jack's memory at least, looked like a perfect match to the one Alec had been wearing at the border. Under the cover of darkness, with the hood pulled up, and the blackened scepter in his hand, he looked just like his brother.

Jack had wanted Cyrus to concentrate on his own mission of entering the Temple unrecognized, so had not yet shared with him the specifics of his plan to draw Alec into town; but once the sun had set behind purplish storm clouds on the horizon, and they found themselves walking side by side through the wilds towards the Western border, he didn't see the harm. He explained to Cyrus that the most certain way to draw Alec out of the Temple would be with fire in the streets of town. It could be seen from the Temple windows and would draw a crowd, which would be imperative for Jack to escape back across the Eastern border.

"What do you plan to burn?" Cyrus asked, with a skeptical smirk.

"Something near the edge of town," Jack answered, "I want to cause a scene without destroying the Westerner's homes. It's not their fault. I'm sure they live in fear of Alec riding into town."

"And for starting the fire?"

"It's early enough still the outdoor lanterns will still be lit," Jack reassured him, "I'll use one of those. Really, I don't want you worrying about my part of this. You have enough to think about already. I'll keep your brother occupied as long as I can, but be quick in the Temple."

"No no," Cyrus said firmly, turning and pointing a finger into Jack's chest. "Do not wait around to see the outcome of your diversion. Light the fire and go. Head straight back to the border and get to Easttown."

"I'm not leaving you over there," Jack scoffed.

"You're not leaving me," Cyrus insisted, "but we don't know how fast I'll need to be fleeing the Temple, it'll be much better if I know you are already long gone."

Jack considered this and finally nodded his head in agreement.

"Promise me," Cyrus pushed, "by the time I see Alec leave the Temple, you'll already be long gone."

"I promise," Jack said, struck once again by how far their relationship had come.

They were approaching the border between the East and the West. They had been travelling about twenty feet off the main trail, for obvious reasons, but through the gaps in the trees they were able to see that the border was unguarded. Even so, it was with a bit of apprehension when they finally stepped foot back into the West for the first time since splitting the Kingdom. They continued on after crossing the border in silence, confident that the raucous symphony of bugs chirping and the occasional Shrieking Bat call would drown out their footsteps to anyone who happened to be out this far.

At long last, they could see torchlight through the trees ahead, indicating Westtown drawing near. This is where they had decided they would split up, with Jack heading to town and Cyrus going around and up the hill towards the Temple.

As though reading his thoughts, Cyrus whispered, "Parting of ways, I guess."

Jack stopped walking and turned Cyrus to face him. He surveyed his new wardrobe, nodding in approval. He really did look like Alec, with the scepter in his hand and his hood pulled up.

"Slouch a bit," Jack instructed him. "Alec's shorter than you, and has worse posture."

Cyrus smiled slightly and did as he was told.

"Perfect," Jack said. "Be careful. I'll give you time to get up to the Temple before I start the fire, but don't dawdle. Get in, get out. And for god's sake find us something we can use."

Cyrus nodded and clapped Jack on the shoulder in a brotherly fashion. "Remember what you promised. Set the fire, and head straight back to Easttown."

"You got it," Jack assured him again, "good luck."

"You too," Cyrus grunted, and with a turn of his head and a swish of his cloak, he was stalking off into the night.

Jack watched him go until he was out of sight, then continued on his way towards the torchlight ahead. He was far more aware of the sound of his own footsteps now that he was alone, not to mention what seemed like his absurdly loud breathing. He knew it was all in his head, however, and that no one would have any cause to question him walking into town from the forest. People walked out this way all the time. The closer he got, the more sound he could hear from town; the clatter of wagons and tools, and the indistinct murmur of voices chatting in the streets.

Jack finally reached the far wall of the easternmost building at the edge of town. He ran his hand along the cool stone and walked towards the corner on his right. He could hear plenty of voices in the street, but none sounded like they were close enough to be bothered by his appearance. He took a deep, bracing breath and stepped out from behind the building and onto the road.

Flickering torchlight illuminated the cobbled stone street with a warm glow, but the torches were fewer this far removed from the center of town. A few people milled about the road, mostly packing up their carts for the night and talking to one another. They gave no notice to Jack at all. He would have to wait until the street cleared a bit more before lighting a fire, but that didn't seem like it would take long. His eyes scanned the sides of the buildings and came to rest on the nearest torch, leaning out in a sconce about twenty-five feet from him.

Was he imagining things, or had one of the cart vendors just noticed him eying the torch? The man now looked to be busy rolling up a tarp, but Jack could have sworn he saw the man's eyes narrow suspiciously when he had looked at Jack moments ago. It was beginning to occur to him that simply standing by the side of a building near the edge of town was likely not doing a particularly good job of blending in. He had to move, or at least look like he had a purpose.

Jack began sauntering in a would-be-casual way up the road, trying his best to look like he belonged. He accidentally locked eyes with one of the chatting women as he passed her, and his heart gave a sort of uncomfortable twitch, but she continued on with her conversation without pause. He turned a corner off the road at the first chance he got and found himself in a small alleyway that was, thankfully, unoccupied. He exhaled loudly, as though he had been holding his breath since arriving in town and tried to slow his heartrate. No one suspected anything, he told himself. No one had any reason to wonder about his presence in town.

Cyrus had probably made it up to the Temple by now, which meant he was currently hiding in the forest near the gates, waiting for Alec to ride out and his path to be clear. Jack couldn't make his move just yet, however, there were still too many people on the road.

So he waited. He waited for what felt like an eternity. Twice, a person walked past the mouth of the alley and Jack's heart skipped a beat, but neither person so much as looked in his direction. He thought he felt a drop of rain once or twice, and he looked apprehensively up at the dark, roiling clouds above, hoping the weather wouldn't affect his plan. At long last, it seemed quiet enough to chance a peek around the corner onto the road. He peered slowly around the stone wall, painfully aware that if someone did happen to see him leaning around the corner so cautiously, he would look incredibly suspicious. His stomach did an uncomfortable somersault at the thought, but he breathed a sigh of relief when he stuck his head out and found the street entirely empty.

Voices could still be heard drifting through the still night air from the main stretch of town, so Jack knew he had to be quick. From this vantage point, it was apparent that the building he had originally been hiding behind was unoccupied, and it had a scraggly thatch roof. Perfect kindling. He would grab the torch, walk back the way he had come in, and toss the torch onto the roof on his way back into the forest and back east. No one would have to know he had ever been here.

Jack took one last look around to make sure no one had entered the side street, and then began walking swiftly towards the torch in its sconce. He was only ten feet away from grabbing it when he heard the dull hum of voices along the main street start to kick up into a low rumble. People were suddenly jabbering excitedly, and the amount of voices seemed to be multiplying by the second. Jack had no intention of being sidetracked by whatever was causing the commotion and told himself it was of no concern to him. That was until he heard a man's voice rise above the din with a loud declaration.

"It's the King! The King's coming!"

Jack's hand was inches from grabbing the torch when he stopped dead. He wheeled around with wide eyes, surveying the still empty street. It didn't stay empty for long. Suddenly people were pouring out through their front doors and rushing off around the corner towards the center of town. Jack was surprised. He would have expected the people to be barricading themselves indoors at the announcement that the King was in town, but he didn't have time to dwell on it.

Trying to force himself to concentrate on the plan, he turned back to the torch before realized there was no need to proceed with the fire. If Alec was truly in town, then there was no need to draw him out of the Temple. Cyrus's path would be clear. But why would Alec have ridden into town at this hour? Jack paused a moment, considering fleeing back into the forest, but he had a nagging urge to peek around the corner onto the main street, just to see if Alec was truly there. Jack gave a few apprehensive looks around before giving in to his curiosity and joining the last few people on the road walking briskly towards the center of town.

It wasn't a long walk; only a turn left and a quick turn right, and he was emerging onto the main road. Jack stopped quickly before walking too far out into the open, although it hardly would have mattered. The throng of people was so dense that there was no way Alec would be able to spot him in the crowd. Being jostled and pushed this way and that, Jack found it exceedingly difficult to stay pressed up against the far buildings where he wanted to be, and the heads bobbing in and out of his field of vision were making it impossible to scan the street ahead for a glimpse of Alec.

Then finally, through a small opening between two people's craning necks, Jack saw him. King Alec Dorn rode slowly into focus, mounted impressively on his chariot, (had the chariot been given an upgrade?), pulled by the two slinking Neodactyls. Alec looked every inch a king from the ancient world; he still wore the grey traveling cloak, this time with the hood down, and he clutched the charred ruby scepter in his hand. His head was held high, his shoulders squared importantly, and he seemed to have a new hairdo. His long, dark hair had been pulled back into a knot at the crown of his head that cascaded down his neck; a look that the Alec of old would never have been able to pull off but the new Alec seemed to wear with ease. Upon further inspection, his chariot had indeed been upgraded. It seemed to be the same basic structure, but most of the chintzy, rickety wood pieces had been replaced with heavy, strong metals, much of it brushed in a gold color. Several decorative frills had been added as well giving the entire vessel a more ornate look.

The crowd of people stepped over each others toes to give the chariot a wide berth, especially trying to avoid being trapped too close to the Neodactyls, but none of them seemed to be fleeing. Indeed, no sooner had the chariot passed them than the crowd would close ranks again, seemingly wanting to be as near to the King as possible. The people were still babbling excitedly, some even shouting questions to Alec that Jack couldn't make out.

Alec finally put his hand in the air to silence the crowd, which only partially worked. "You've all been so patient," Alec began in a strong, authoritative, yet understanding, voice. "I'm doing everything I can for you but so far I have some unfortunate news: I have implored Easttown to share their good fortune and open their borders to us, but so far they have staunchly refused."

An angry ripple of murmuring swept through the crowd, and Jack himself felt his face flush with fury. The murmuring of the people was matched by a deep, low rumble in the sky as indistinct lightning briefly illuminated the ominous clouds above.

"I'm not giving up, though, I promise you," Alec continued. "Their king, off to the East, he thinks you are beneath his own people. He would have you starve and die to lift his own people up. Use you as steppingstones for his own vanity. I know times are tough right now, but we will get through this together."

As the crowed yelled and cheered, Jack was practically sick with disgust. The way Alec had twisted the story was absurd, but what really boiled Jack's blood was that the people were clearly buying into it. Listening to Alec rile up the crowd with such ease was incredible, all while giving them no actual facts or even solutions. But the crowd clearly didn't notice or care. Alec was giving them someone to blame for their hardships, and they were all too willing to accept that at face value. Even their purported hardships were ridiculous, from what Jack understood from Cain. They had many of the same or similar resources as the East, but they were used to the laborers coming in from the other side of the Kingdom. As Cain had aptly pointed out when they had complained about a fish shortage, it was the same ocean.

As Alec surveyed the raucous crowd with an amiable smile on his face, he extended his hands out as if embracing the entire town. He turned briefly to one of the guards behind him and whispered something in his ear, all while never dropping his smile. The guard nodded and left his side. The Neodactyls watched the townspeople nervously but seemed much better controlled than Jack had seen them in the past. The people were giving them plenty of space, however.

"What happened up in the caves?" a woman from the crowd shouted.

"It was an unfortunate accident," Alec assured her in a most understanding tone. "I don't know what the workers were thinking trying to work that late into the night. But I assure you, precautions are being taken to make sure everyone stays safe. You see, when the East abandoned us, they gave no thought to the safety of our people. Instead of passing on their expertise, they simply left, took their skills and resources, and closed the borders behind them."

As the crowd thundered angrily, Jack could hardly believe his ears. These people were somehow entirely unaware that it was in fact Alec who had ordered those workers to be laboring up in the hills after nightfall. It begged the question of what had happened to all the workers and their families who had shown up at the border a few weeks back.

"Steps are being taken to implore the East to see reason," Alec said, extending his hands bracingly.

Jack had heard enough, and had lingered far too long by now, but this was valuable insight into what was happening in the West. Jack turned to leave the way he had come, but the crowd had closed in so tightly around him it was nearly impossible to navigate through. He squeezed between several people and practically shoved another, who was paying no attention to him at all while clapping enthusiastically in the air to whatever Alec was saying. Jack hadn't strayed very far from the sidestreet he had come down, but the shuffling, boisterous throng of people had worked him slowly away from his planned exit.

As he forced his way passed a yelling, applauding group of women, he could hear Alec exclaiming, "The East wants to hammer us down, but I assure you I will not allow them to succeed."

Between several more bobbing heads, Jack could finally see the entrance to the sidestreet approaching, but with a sudden twinge in his stomach, he saw that a guard had been positioned directly in the narrow pathway. Jack quickly turned his head away from the guard, on the off chance that they would recognize him from the Temple. With his heart starting to race out of control, Jack started frantically looking for another way out of the crowd. He located another sidestreet maybe twenty feet down the wall on the opposite side of the building to his right, and it was miraculously unguarded. With a deep breath, Jack started pushing his way through the people, like trying to walk against the current of a river.

"The East wants to see us fail, make no mistake," Alec was shouting.

As he pressed around a particularly large and muscular townsman, Jack saw with a jolt that there was a guard in the crowd ahead, walking in his direction. The guard was making much easier headway through the excitable mob than Jack was, but it wasn't until the guard looked up and locked eyes with him that he realized he was in trouble. Jack turned back the way he had come, but with a sickly realization suddenly washing over him, he saw another guard slowly weaving his way towards him. This guard also locked eyes with Jack, though his face remained entirely passive.

"If anyone was looking for further proof of the East's treachery," Alec continued, "I'd like to turn your attention to a traitor within our own midst, walking amongst you like a rat gathering crumbs to hoard back in its burrow."

Jack stopped moving at once, and with a sinking sense of dread, looked up at Alec, who, to his horror, was looking straight back at him.

"Everyone," Alec exclaimed as the crowd fell into a deafening, eerie silence, "say hello to my old friend Jack Viana."

A hand grasped one of Jacks shoulders roughly and Jack knew it was the guards without having to turn around. He continued to stare up at Alec as the entire crowd turned their collective heads to Jack, each with something akin to hatred in their eyes. Alec, for his part, projected a different emotion as the subtle, barely perceptible hint of a smirk pulled at the corners of his mouth. It was triumph.

## CHAPTER FORTY-SEVEN

# THE WINDOW

Cyrus had been only halfway through his slow ascent to the Temple, still staying well off the road under the dark cover of the trees, when he had heard the distinct rumble of wheels followed by the unmistakable sight of Alec mounted atop his chariot careening down the path towards town. Despite the deep shadows of the forest under which he trekked, Cyrus still found himself ducking down as the chariot passed, and waited until the night air was completely silent again before standing back up. Cyrus was mildly surprised to see Alec already heading towards town. He had thought Jack would give him a little more time to get up to the Temple, but no matter, he was almost there.

After a few more minutes of hiking, the Temple finally loomed ahead, seeming to rise out of the mist from the forest like an imposing black monolith, a dread fortress from the old world. Cyrus didn't think the Temple itself had actually changed, but it looked somehow more foreboding... more real. Under Mora's rule, everything from the look of the Temple down to the uniforms worn by the guards looked strangely forced, as though they were trying to harken back to medieval designs but only succeeding at a pale imitation. But the Temple standing before him now, blocking out the moonlight and creating a gargantuan silhouette against the bruised purple and black sky, emanated doom.

Cyrus pulled his hood around his head a little tighter and looked up apprehensively at the battlements. He prayed this was going to work. Remembering what Jack had suggested, Cyrus hunched his shoulders and bent his knees slightly, trying to appear roughly Alec's height. The scepter in his hand felt unnatural and foreign, but he attempted to adjust his grip and think of it as an extension of his hand, as Alec seemed to. Any hope of getting through the front doors unnoticed hinged on him appearing agitated and unapproachable. If anyone stopped to question him, the plan would fail before it ever started.

The front doors appeared to be closed, which likely meant that guards stood directly inside, waiting to block entry to any intruder. But Cyrus wasn't an intruder, he told himself. He was Alec Dorn, their king, and he had no obligation to answer to anyone within those walls.

With that mentality firmly in mind, Cyrus took a deep breath and strode out onto the road and up towards the ominous black Temple. He thought it likely that guards from the battlements were watching him as he approached, but he dared not look up to confirm. He was finding it difficult to control the pace of his gait; too quick and he would look like he was rushing, but too slow and he could possibly be stopped by someone. As the entrance drew near, Cyrus shook his head forcefully to clear his mind, gripped the scepter tight in his hand, and threw the doors open powerfully without breaking his stride.

He barely observed the guards out of the corners of his eyes as he brushed past them into the shimmering golden light of the torches in the cavernous entrance hall, but he sensed their presence.

"My King," a guard greeted him from behind, but Cyrus didn't so much as grunt in response as he stalked off towards the door on the far wall. He was in. There were no footsteps following him as he passed through the second door and finally onto one of the many staircases that snaked up into the far reaches of the Temple.

Cyrus breathed a tentative sigh of relief but didn't dare count his blessings just yet. Getting through the front doors was certainly the biggest hurdle, but he didn't even want to think of the ramifications of meeting Nel in one of the corridors. He found himself practically running along the stretches where there was no one around, but he had to keep reminding himself to keep up the façade. He ascended one staircase, and then another, and then another, thankful that he had learned the layout before leaving. Ignoring a cramp in his side, Cyrus finally found himself in the hallway of living quarters leading towards the king's room. He had miraculously not passed a single guard since entering the Temple.

With a fresh surge of confidence, Cyrus walked towards Alec's chambers, at the very least assured that Alec himself would not be in there. He passed through the door into the familiar room; the room where the Kingdom had been split in half, and the last time he had seen his brother. It was unchanged from what Cyrus could remember. Alec's bed chamber stood off to the left along with the room of trinkets Mora had kept. Windows bowed out along the far wall of the main room and served as a backdrop to the semi-circle of stone bench that surrounded the odd fiery altar.

Cyrus paused in the doorway, observing the altar from a distance. He had paid it very little attention whenever he had been in this room previously, but Alec had certainly spent plenty of time near it. Henry did not mention the altar specifically in his account of meeting Dalton, but he had mentioned the king's chambers, and Alec had very clearly been looking over his shoulder after he had fought with Cyrus, as though expecting to see something back there. Cyrus's gut told him if there was something to be uncovered in the room, it would be around the altar.

Cyrus approached it slowly, struck for the first time by how ornate it was, but at the same time realizing it was not affixed to the floor. Somehow Cyrus had been remembering a stone structure built into the very Temple itself, but that was not the case. In fact, the word 'altar' did not really describe it particularly well because, apart from its unique craftsmanship and design, it was little more than a golden basin filled with fine, pebble-sized stones that he knew to be frozen fire. The basin was held aloft by four intricately detailed legs that ended in clawed feet, but it looked like the entire piece could be moved if one so desired. The frozen fire within the deep walls of the bowl was ashen and dark at the moment, a result of its distance from the scepter.

Cyrus stopped directly in front of the altar and lowered his scepter head slowly towards the grey contents of the basin. As he had witnessed in the Fire Fields with King Mora, the particles of dark stone began to glow a pulsating, vibrant orange and the topmost layer began to lift out of the bowl as though magnetically attracted to the scepter top. The scepter itself had started to glow as well, not on its blackened surface but from within the deep fissures that spiderwebbed across its ancient looking shell. Cyrus moved the scepter back and forth and the fiery embers trailed after it, moving in a sort of circular orbit around the staff top. This was how Mora had weaponized the usually benign particles. Cyrus absent-mindedly touched the leathery patch of skin under the drape of his bangs where he had been hit when they first arrived.

Seeing the presumably chemical reaction between the staff and the frozen fire was intriguing to be sure, and especially mesmerizing to witness up close, but Cyrus was having trouble seeing how this could possibly offer clues to their escape. Emulating what he had seen Mora do in the Fire Fields, Cyrus gave the scepter a swift flick with his wrist and a jet of burning ash propelled through the air and hit the far wall with a sizzling snap. He hadn't really expected this to offer much in the way of clues, and it didn't. The faint crackling on the stone wall slowly subsided and the embers died away, leaving a blackened scorch mark in its place.

Cyrus straightened up again and gave the gold basin a soft rap on the side with the end of the staff. He furrowed his brow and started scanning the area around the altar looking for anything to give his search direction. Remembering that Alec often had his own scepter stuck freestanding in the loose frozen fire particles, Cyrus stabbed down hard into the bowl, releasing a torrent of glowing ash all over the surrounding floor. The strewn about embers burned briefly and then fizzled out, leaving nothing more than dusty remnants in their place. The scepter stood straight, glowing lightly at its base where it was in close contact with the frozen fire. Nothing happened, however.

Cyrus left his scepter on its altar and backed away slowly, surveying the alcove in its entirety, which now had a warm, dancing glow to it. Still nothing of interest happened. He turned and began pacing the room, keeping his eyes on the scepter to see if anything changed as he moved around. It didn't. With a sinking realization, he was beginning to worry that the plan may have all been for nothing. Thinking of the plan suddenly made him notice something else as well. No fire could be seen coming from the town below. Cyrus should have been able to see Jack's fire from the windows, but there was nothing. Had it already been extinguished?

With a start, Cyrus noticed the sound of footsteps shuffling down the corridor behind him. He made a move towards the altar but realized it was too late to get out in time. He turned and walked briskly towards the trinket room on his left, careful to keep his face obscured beneath his hood.

"My King, you're back," said a wavering voice from the door. It was unmistakably Irias.

Cyrus stopped walking and tried to decide what to do next. He couldn't very well ignore Irias, now that he had clearly entered the room, but he couldn't turn around either. The best Cyrus could think to do was act agitated and dangerous, a mood Alec seemed to radiate often.

"Leave me be," Cyrus growled in a low voice, praying he sounded enough like Alec if he kept his speech to a nondescript grumble.

"Did something happen, my King?" Henry pushed, his voice dripping with insincere concern in Cyrus's mind. "Perhaps I can offer some counsel," He continued, sounding like he was walking further into the room.

"I said LEAVE ME BE!" commanded Cyrus, and in a stroke of brilliance that surprised even himself, he lashed out at the trinket-covered shelves and flung the objects crashing towards the floor in a sudden explosion of noise.

Cyrus couldn't be positive that Irias had been stopped dead in his tracks, but it wouldn't be a stretch of the imagination to picture it. Cyrus waited, faking heavy breathing to imply the danger of another outburst.

Finally, after what felt like an eternity, Irias said quietly, "As you wish, my King," and seemingly turned to leave. Cyrus tried to follow the dragging sound of the footfalls as best he could, and only dared turn around when he was positive they were far down the hallway. Sure enough, when he did apprehensively peek over his shoulder from beneath his hood, the room was empty once more.

Cyrus walked out quietly, surveyed the room, and then tiptoed to the doorway. He looked down the hall, trying to keep the hood as low around his head as possible, and verified that Irias had left. With any luck, he would tell anyone else approaching that their king was in no mood for being disturbed.

He turned back around to face the altar once again and, with a start, he realized the room wasn't empty after all. For one wild moment he was convinced it was Irias, and that his cover was blown. But it wasn't Irias. It wasn't a guard either. It was a man, standing calmly on the opposite side of the fiery altar, with his hands clasped together in front of him and a warm, gentle, but almost pitying, smile on his face. His hair was a little longer than Cyrus remembered it, but not by much, and he wore traveling robes that did little to hide his small build. The glasses he wore on his face, however, were exactly the same as the ones he had worn when they had first started the expedition together many months ago. Dalton Sidney was standing before him.

Cyrus was stunned into silence. He opened and closed his mouth several times, he assumed with the intention of speaking, but he had no idea what he was planning to say. A strange tingling sensation was running down his spine like warm liquid flowing through his bones. He wanted to move, do something, do anything, but instead he just continued to stare.

Dalton, or the imposter who looked like Dalton, continued to smile back at him, a look of serene patience on his face. When he finally spoke, it was in the same voice Cyrus remembered. "It's been a long time, Cyrus."

It couldn't be the real Dalton. Obviously. That was out of the question. But Cyrus didn't feel threatened by the *apparition*. He wanted to say something to it, but when he finally found his voice to speak, all he could manage was, "But… you died."

To his surprise, Dalton smiled mildly and responded, "Did I? Hmm. I hope you gave me a proper send off."

Everything about the person standing before him was exactly like the Dalton he remembered. His look, his speech patterns, his mannerisms. But how could it be him? Cyrus finally asked the question he had meant to ask right off the bat. "How are you here?"

"You haven't figured it out yet?" Dalton asked. It wasn't condescending, more like he was trying to gauge his audience.

"I… what's to understand?" Cyrus was at risk of babbling incoherently, so he tried with all his might to focus his mind. "You can't really be here. You can't be the real Dalton."

Dalton moved his head around in a non-committed sort of way. It was somewhere between a nod of affirmation and a shake of disagreement. "That's only partially true. I really am Dalton Sidney. But I may not be quite the Dalton Sidney you remember. Let me ask you, what's happening in your world right now? Who rules the Kingdom?"

The way Dalton said 'your world' concerned Cyrus more than he could say, but he answered the question. "The Kingdom has been split in half. I rule in the East, Alec rules here in the West."

Dalton nodded in understanding before Cyrus had even finished talking, as if this was no surprise to him. "The disagreement over the Neodactyls? Or Irias showing his true identity?"

"Umm… both," Cyrus responded, dumbfounded. "Jack created a diversion in town so I could sneak into the Temple."

"Really?" Dalton said, and this time he did seem mildly intrigued. "I haven't heard that one before, not quite like that at least."

"What do you mean?" Cyrus demanded.

"Look," Dalton said, still very patiently, "in this place, you and I are able to see each other, but we're not from the same world. Or maybe it's more accurate to say we started out from the same world, but have diverged. Now, we are only able to see each other through a small tear. Think of it as a window."

"A tear in *what*?" Cyrus asked.

"Reality," Dalton answered simply.

Cyrus shook his head in confusion. "That's... that's... that's... what the hell are you talking about?"

"C'mon Cyrus, you know what I'm talking about. If you've snuck into the Temple uninvited, we have limited time here. Think of this as a window you can look through. You can see my world, and I can see your world, but it's a mirage. A visual illusion almost. It's real but... out of reach."

Dalton's explanation was becoming absurd and it sounded like he was talking in riddles rather than being direct... and yet, something in Cyrus's gut told him there was truth in it.

"You said this place," Cyrus began, "you mean this room? What's so special about this room? The altar?"

"It's not the room," Dalton said with a shake of his head, "and it's not the altar. It's the scepter itself." When Cyrus looked skeptical, Dalton continued, "You must have at least realized the material that makes up that scepter is unfamiliar to us, in our world, right?"

Cyrus hadn't spent very much time examining the scepters at all, however he supposed that statement was true, and he also supposed he had noticed that at one point, before he had become complacent in the new world. In response, he nodded silently.

"Right," Dalton continued, "I don't have all of the answers, but whatever material that is, it reacts with the fabric of... time and space I suppose." He said this as if he were giving an impassioned lecture at a university. "The same way it reacts with the minerals in the Fire Fields. In order to appreciate what I'm saying, it is essential that you understand one fundamental truth; that all of this..." he waved his hands through the air in front of him, "is not just nothingness. It's not just empty space. There are infinite planes of existence, right here, right now, each passing by one another without ever coming in contact. You can't see them, but sure as the air we're breathing, they're there. I said *'right here, right now,'* but of course even that is relative. My *'here'* is different than yours. As near as I can tell, we are still in the same *'now'*."

Cyrus was gaping at Dalton, but finally, and in contrast with every emotion he was actually feeling, he started to laugh. "What sort of an idiot do you think I am? That doesn't exist, none of this exists."

"Then I wouldn't exist," Dalton said, as though they were having a discussion on theoretical physics over a cup of coffee, "not from your point of view at least. And you wouldn't exist from mine. But here we are. That scepter has pulled back the curtain, just a bit. I don't know how the specific realities are connected, because I can tell you there are countless numbers of them, but those scepters create windows."

"I've had this scepter for months now," Cyrus insisted, "I've never seen through any windows in my reality!"

"Actually I believe you probably have, in fact I'm sure of it. But from what I can tell, a window is created when the scepter is left stationary. And it's not instantaneous. So, if you lean it against a wall and step away, it gradually eats away at the fabric between our planes of existence, our realities, but it's only a small window that it creates. And that window is only showing you that exact spot, that space, but in a different… I suppose *alternate* world is the best way to put it. But if the scepter was left leaning against a wall, and that wall remains the same across multiple times, then you won't perceive that you are seeing into a different world. It still looks like the same wall you know. But in a space like this, in the king's chambers, around this altar, there are a lot of variables across time and space. Specifically the people."

Cyrus didn't really know how to process this strange theoretical knowledge dump, but the one thing that was clear to him was that this *was* theoretical. Dalton had been a smart man, but he was working off of some fairly wild assumptions to reach his conclusions. And yet, something about it was making sense to Cyrus.

Cyrus finally spoke, slowly at first, "So when you talk about variables, you're saying there's different worlds where you didn't die when we first arrived here, that sort of thing?"

"Absolutely," answered Dalton, holding out his arms as if to say, 'and here's the proof.'

Cyrus looked into Dalton's face, at first looking for signs of a deception of some sort, a reason why this might all be some trick, but instead he found himself simply gazing into his eyes and realizing with more certainty that this was in fact the same person he had met on the expedition ship. He was more sure than ever that the man was in fact the real

Dalton Sidney, or apparently a version of him, if his theories were to be believed.

"You're staring," Dalton said with an amused smile.

"I'm sorry," Cyrus said with a shake of his head, "it's just... it's like seeing a ghost."

Dalton smiled again, but this time it was a sad smile, "For me as well."

"I... what do you mean?" Cyrus asked.

"You didn't make it," Dalton admitted, "over here... where I come from."

"I... really?" Cyrus gaped at him, "How? How did it happen? Actually no, I don't think I want to know."

"It wouldn't matter either way," Dalton assured him, "it's an entirely separate reality. One doesn't affect the other, and we're connected only by this." He indicated the scepter, still twinkling softly in the fiery basin.

Cyrus was beginning to feel a bit light-headed, like his mind was slowing down in an attempt to process everything he was hearing. "Why does that make me feel so... defeated?"

To Cyrus's surprise, Dalton chuckled a bit at this admission. "What's funny?" Cyrus asked.

"Nothing," Dalton answered, "it's just, I've heard that exact sentence before."

"Have you?" Cyrus asked, "from who?"

Dalton had an almost guilty look on his face as he answered, as though he had hoped to avoid this specific question. "From you actually."

"I... what?" Cyrus was dumbfounded, but realization slowly washed over him. A truth occurred to him that was at once both comforting and horrifying. "How many times have you had this conversation with me?"

"With you?" Dalton said, "Maybe sixty times." Cyrus's jaw literally dropped open at this revelation. "With Nel too..." Dalton continued, "and Jack. Even Alec."

"Why?" Cyrus asked incredulously. "Why not just go live your life?"

Dalton's eyes dropped to the floor, "It's not just you who didn't make it, in my reality. It was all of you. I'm alone in my world."

Cyrus didn't have any idea how to respond to that. He ended up saying, "I'm sorry," rather lamely, and it occurred to him how odd it was to be apologizing to someone else for his own death.

Dalton shrugged as though it wasn't a big deal, but Cyrus could tell that it was. "So I've sort of devoted my time to finding you guys, out there in your own worlds, and helping you where I can." Dalton laughed and continued, "Ya know, it's incredible how much the smallest of details can alter the course of our lives. I've seen worlds where you're king, where Alec's king, where Nel is queen. And you'd be shocked to hear how identical those timelines were, up until a point. And one tiny alteration, one seemingly insignificant decision, can have world-changing consequences. But you'd never know it, while in your own world. We never have the benefit of hindsight, the ability to see the whole picture of what our choices truly mean."

There was one question burning in Cyrus's mind, and he finally asked it. "Have you ever seen a world where Alec and I successfully rule together? Coexist?"

Dalton solemnly shook his head, "That I've never seen. I've found myself wondering if certain things are just meant to be. For instance, why have I never come across a stranger in the king's quarters? It's always someone from our team. I've never found a world where Mora is still the king, or some other outsider came to this world instead of us. Why is that? It's almost as if deviations can occur, but we're stuck on this path, like how a train has to stay on its tracks."

Cyrus was still haunted by the idea of Dalton in a world by himself. "Isn't there a way to, you know... I mean, we're connected now, can't you somehow..."

Dalton seemed to pick up where Cyrus was going with his rambling question because he smiled and shook his head. "It's a window, nothing more. The scepter has created a small tear to peer through, that's it."

That didn't ring entirely true for Cyrus, however. "Actually, I came here looking for answers specifically because *you* had crossed into this world, and a man named Henry Fine had talked to you."

"That was a mistake," Dalton said darkly, "and it nearly cost me my life." When Cyrus continued to stare at him, awaiting further explanation, he begrudgingly continued, "Okay, I've told you how this is a window that has been created... well, there *is* a way to a create door."

Cyrus's face must have lit up because Dalton quickly put up his hands to stop him.

"It doesn't work the same, though," Dalton insisted, "the doors are unpredictable and dangerous. I won't tell you what to do, but my heartfelt advice is to try to live the life you have, whatever it may be. You could get lost trying to change it."

Ignoring everything Dalton had just said to him, Cyrus pressed, "How do you open a door?"

Dalton seemed to hesitate explaining anything further, but he eventually answered, "A break in the scepter. When a fragment is broken off from the staff, it creates a sort of vacuum between your world and another. I'm certain that's how we got here. The vacuum seems to initially pull from both worlds, allowing you to cross either way, but once it... equalizes I guess, the door is only open one direction; from that other world *towards* the scepter. But there's no telling what that other world will be, or even *when* it will be. Unlike this window here, a fracture in the scepter causes a fracture in time as well. And that resulting doorway will not necessarily be on a parallel plane of time."

Cyrus was already leagues ahead of him and thinking of ways he could return to his own world, and Cynthia.

"Cyrus, I implore you," Dalton cautioned, "be careful with this. I know how tempting it must be to force your way back to where you came from, but I worry that that life is long lost already. And you could find yourself entirely adrift from your own time."

"I'm already adrift from my own time," Cyrus insisted, perhaps a little harsher than he had intended.

"You're not," Dalton said, "not yet. You still have your people, your team. That's not nothing. You don't realize it until you've lost it all."

Cyrus was shaking his head. As far as he was concerned, any risk in experimenting with these so-called *doors* was well worth it. Things couldn't get worse than they were now.

# SOMEWHERE

A yell from the staircase in the hall brought Cyrus back to reality with a start. He turned and heard voices yelling to one another, and they were drawing nearer.

"Cyrus!" Dalton said forcefully, "Please listen to me. Don't take my warning lightly."

Cyrus turned back to Dalton and could see grave concern in his eyes, but he was realizing how little time they had left. This was likely the last time he would see Dalton Sidney.

"I'm sorry we couldn't save you," Cyrus said, and he could hear footsteps behind him rushing down the hall towards the king's chambers.

"Cyrus! Wait wait wait, this is important!" Dalton practically yelled, "*If* you open a door, make sure to keep a piece of the scepter on you when you go through!"

"Here!" A voice from behind Cyrus screamed, and he turned to see two guards stampeding into the room with machetes in hand. Cyrus turned frantically to the only weapon he had available to him.

Dalton was still yelling from behind him, "It's important Cyrus! If you don't, you will become unte…"

With an almighty wrench, Cyrus pulled the scepter from the basin and instantaneously Dalton stopped speaking. He knew without looking that Dalton had vanished. The window only stayed open as long as the scepter stayed immobile. But the guards were bearing down on him; apparently the charade of posing as Alec was over.

Cyrus rushed to the side of the altar and kicked it hard with his boot, knocking it crashing over the floor and releasing a storm of hissing, spitting embers. The guards split and each ran towards him from alternate corners of the room, hoping to flank him. Cyrus, going off of some sort of animalistic instinct more than anything else, raked his scepter across the flickering ashes on the floor and launched a firestorm of burning debris at the nearest guard. The guard bellowed in pain as the blast caught him in the chest and slammed him into the far wall. To Cyrus's horror, the fire had ignited the guard's shirt and he was soon batting violently at himself to try to stop from being consumed in flames.

The second guard had used the opening to launch his own attack on Cyrus from the opposite side, swinging his machete violently towards his neck. Cyrus was able to block the attack with the scepter, which hissed angrily with a burst of glowing sparks. The guard pulled his face back from the flash and Cyrus capitalized on his distraction by stabbing the spear-pointed bottom of the scepter down into guard's foot. It pierced straight through to the floor beneath and the guard screamed in pain. With his opponent off-balance, Cyrus shoved him backwards and he toppled to the floor. With no intention of lingering, Cyrus careened around the remnants of the spilled metal basin and ran from the room, noting out of the corner of his eye that the first guard was now entirely engulfed in flames.

Cyrus sprinted full tilt down the hallway and practically flew down the staircases, taking them four at a time. He was back to the ground floor before he had time to think and careening towards the front doors. Unfortunately, the entire Temple seemed to have been alerted to his break-in, and while they were clearly still scrambling their response, a group of six frazzled-looking guards now stood blocking the exit. The door was open behind them, framing what appeared to be a violent rainstorm beyond.

With alarmed shouts, the guards spotted Cyrus running towards them, but it was too late to slow his momentum. They raised their machetes anticipating a fight, but Cyrus held his scepter crosswise in front of himself, lowered his head, and barreled straight into them at full speed. The surprise was enough to knock the guards backwards, and with a bit of a spin and duck, Cyrus was able to launch himself out the door and into the rain. It wasn't perfect, by any means. Cyrus's foot caught on one of the guard's legs as he dove, and he found himself free-falling down the shallow slope and skidding on his hands in the mud.

His move may have surprised the guards enough to get him through the door, but none of them had actually lost their footing entirely, and they were all scrambling out into the storm after him within seconds. Cyrus, knowing he had no time to waste after his fall, dug into the ground with the toe of his boot and propelled himself forward, half-falling, half-running towards the treeline. He could hear the guards stomping after him, shouting indistinct commands to each other that were being lost in the roar of the hammering downpour.

Cyrus reached the woods and reserved some hope that he could lose the guards in the dark of the forest. It was then that he heard a shrill, earsplitting screech that cut through the howling gale like a knife through butter. The Neodactyls had joined the pursuit from the Temple. Their padded feet made unmistakable smacking noises in the mud as they deftly glided over the soupy terrain that was slowing the guards down. Cyrus chanced a glance over his shoulder and caught just a glimpse of one of the animals stalking lightly at the edge of the trees, head bowed low searching for his scent, like a hound of hell bearing down on its prey.

## CHAPTER FORTY-EIGHT

# FLIGHT FROM THE TEMPLE

Cyrus ran. He ran like he had never run before. He could barely see where he was going in the blackness of the woods, but he knew he had to get as far away from the Temple as possible, as fast as possible. He could hear the sopping wet leaves beneath his feet squelching with each stride and soaking vegetation smacked across his body as he tore deeper and deeper into the dark, endless abyss that was the forest. His eyes were practically forced shut from the water drenching his face, more from the wet leaves than the rain itself. He tried to be mindful of twisting his path every so often, so as not to run in a completely straight line, but he hoped he was still headed in the direction of Westtown. Becoming totally lost in the woods on the wrong side of the border would not help his situation.

After what felt like ages, Cyrus vaulted a fallen branch in his path and ducked behind a large tree; crouching down next to it and tilting his head to listen. The rain was deafening, but not quite loud enough to drown out the shouting of voices from back the way he had come. It was confirmation that he was still being pursued, and if he could hear them through the storm, they weren't far off. He sucked in a deep breath, choked slightly on the water droplets that entered his throat, and kicked off from the ground again, continuing his flight.

He wasn't sure if the guards knew who they were pursuing or not. Someone in the Temple clearly knew something, since the two guards had stormed the king's quarters ready for a fight. And the Neodactyls had been released to join the chase. With a sick twisting of his stomach, he realized that could only mean one thing; that Alec had ordered the hunt. That didn't necessarily mean he knew who he was hunting, however. It was certainly possible he only knew there had been an intruder.

Cutting through the misty haze of swirling water, blurry, ill-defined splotches of orange light began to swim out of the darkness ahead. It had to be street torches from Westtown. Cyrus put on a fresh burst of speed, nearly slipping on mud in the process, and forced himself onward. The voices behind him were still present, but he couldn't tell if they were actually chasing him or just on his trail.

Cyrus altered his course slightly now that he had marked where Westtown was, hoping to enter on a sidestreet and hide in one of the alleyways. But was that really the best course of action? Now that he considered it, he wondered if it would be safer to hide in the forest, or perhaps up a tree, until the search had been called off. He had no time to weigh his options, however, because a shout from off to his right announced that he had been spotted. As Cyrus turned his head, a lone guard careened in his direction, yelling, "He's here! He's here!" as he went. Cyrus briefly considered standing his ground and fighting, but sloshing footsteps from behind told him he would soon be outnumbered. Cyrus bolted towards town, not knowing where else he could go.

As the last of the sopping tree branches slapped at his front, Cyrus finally emerged onto the dimly lit cobbled stone street and found it entirely deserted. No surprise, given the torrential storm, but it meant he would not be able to blend into a crowd and disappear. He would have to find a place to hide. This proved to be impossible, however. The two pursuing guards had gained on him, and as Cyrus tore down street after street, they were able to keep pace. He found himself back in the center plaza, right outside Ydoro's old house with the metal knocker. He made a move to dart down a street to the right when he slipped on one of the rounded stones of the imperfect street and felt his ankle twinge horribly. That was it. A few limping paces further and he found he could run no more. He stopped, the rain hammering at him from all sides, and turned to face his attackers, raising his scepter in the process.

The guards stopped as well, apparently unsure if it was a trick or not. Their hesitation didn't last long, however, for they both reached down and unsheathed their machetes in unison. Cyrus couldn't tell if they recognized him or not, but he supposed it wouldn't matter once they brought him before Alec. He gripped the scepter tightly, painfully aware of how little experience he had wielding it, and winced when he put weight on his bad ankle. This was no fight he could win. As if his situation wasn't dire enough, splashing footsteps echoed off the surrounding buildings and four more figures appeared in the plaza, fifteen feet behind the first two guards.

One of the two nearest guards yelled over his shoulder, "Here!" rather unnecessarily, but refused to take his eyes off Cyrus. The four rear guards started to approach slowly out of the storm, mere silhouettes against the flickering torchlight on the far side of the plaza. Cyrus shook his head and decided his fight was done. After a last desperate scan of the surrounding roads, he lowered his scepter, letting it fall to the ground with a clatter, and raised his hands in surrender. The two guards in front relaxed their stance slightly, but the rear guard all began to raise their weapons for attack. Cyrus stretched his hands higher into the air in response, but the weapons his would-be assailants pointed were not machetes, and they were not aimed at him. Through the blinding rain, Cyrus could barely make out the shape of the weapons in the stranger's hands, something between a slingshot and a small crossbow, but a second later, he saw the damage they could do. With a hollow *thuk* noise, the weapons were discharged into the back of the two nearest guard's heads. Their bodies went instantly rigid and, while they both weakly grasped over their shoulders at the wounds, it was clear this was nothing more than a muscle response, and their arms soon fell limp to their sides. They stayed standing upright a few seconds longer, as if their bodies had not yet realized the trauma the brain had just sustained, but slowly their eyes unfocused, with one even drooping horrifically and turning over white. The guards didn't fall so much as just spill onto the pavement unceremoniously, with their legs buckling beneath them and dispensing their bodies into two strange heaps. It was from this position that Cyrus could finally see the large metal bolts that had been embedded deep in the guard's skulls.

Cyrus looked up at his rescuers in disbelief, and while they were still heavily backlit, he could now see that they did not wear the uniforms of the Temple guards. The two outermost members of the party appeared to be solidly built men flanking a third with a significantly heftier frame. The fourth person, standing a pace ahead of the rest, seemed to be a short, thin woman.

Footsteps from Cyrus's left announced another guard approaching fast from one of the connecting streets, but the woman had her weapon reloaded with a fresh bolt faster than he could react. With another *thuk*, the guard's head pitched back violently, and unlike his former brothers in arms, he crashed to the ground with a brief scream and a hard wet smack.

Silence fell over the plaza, apart from the steadily roaring downpour, and the woman rushed forward frantically, finally revealing her face.

"You okay, my King?" Annica shouted at him, her eyes wide yet focused. "Where's Jack?"

"Jack?" Cyrus yelled back, still in shock at Annica's sudden entrance and having practically forgotten that he had not started this mission alone. "Jack went back already! He should have been way ahead of me!"

Annica looked around the plaza briefly, then nodded her acceptance and said, "Okay, we have to get you outta here!"

She tried to tug at his arm to get him to run, but Cyrus grunted as a tremor of pain shot up his leg. "It's my ankle," Cyrus said in answer to her look of concern.

Annica nodded and shouted over her shoulder, "Cain, help me with him!"

Cyrus didn't even have time to look before Cain had put a beefy shoulder under the crook of his arm and lifted him practically off the ground.

"We make for the eastern edge of town," Annica commanded, "I don't think the guards will pursue us all the way to the border."

A screech ripped through the air of the plaza from one of the adjoining roads.

Annica's face looked stricken. She looked to Cyrus and asked softly, "The birds are out?"

Cyrus nodded silently and Annica's eyes began to dart from side to side, scanning every inch of their surroundings. "We're going, now, now, now!"

"Wait, the scepter!" Cyrus cried out, suddenly realizing it was still on the ground.

One of the other two men reached down and grabbed it without saying a word, and the group was off at a slow, awkward run. Annica led them down one of the many winding side streets, and then onto another. She seemed to be heading east, as she had said, but her frantic searching betrayed her true desperation; she was looking for a place to hide. Cyrus was beginning to realize that Annica's rescue plan had not anticipated the Neodactyl's involvement, and it scared her.

As she turned down another street, Annica peered into a small, narrow alleyway and started to proceed down it, but realizing it did not have an exit on the other side, she cursed and turned back around. "Won't do, keep moving," she ordered, pushing past the group to regain the lead. But as she stepped onto the main road once again, she jumped back into the alley suddenly, pressed herself against the wall of the building, and put a single finger up to her lips. When Cyrus locked eyes with her, she mouthed soundlessly, "It's here."

Cyrus suddenly seemed to be breathing far louder than he usually did, and he swore it could be heard over the storm. The group of five tried to press themselves against the stone wall as best they could, but there was no denying they were exposed. Cain leaned Cyrus carefully next to Annica and patted him reassuringly on the chest before crouching down in the center of the alleyway, like a sprinter awaiting a gunshot to start a race. Was he actually planning on rushing the Neodactyl when it inevitably appeared in the entrance? It seemed absurd, but it looked like that was exactly what Cain was intending. His eyes were fixed and ready, the toe of his boot anchored to launch himself forward.

A soft clicking noise carried around the corner followed by the unmistakable intake of the bird's rattling breath. Cyrus could hear the pads of its feet squelch against the wet stone as it approached, but it was impossible to gauge how close it was. Annica pulled out her small bolt shooter and loaded a new projectile into place. She did not look confident it would save them. As she raised her weapon above her head, apparently hoping to shoot down at the creature before it could force its way through her, a shiver ran up Cyrus's spine. He had just heard a low growl, and this time it was clearly right around the corner.

Annica took one deep, bracing breath, and then all hell broke loose. The Neodactyl sprung around the corner like some demonic jack-in-the-box and released an ear-splitting scream. The quills around its head vibrated aggressively and it gnashed its beak forward with a sharp snap. Annica was the only person close enough for it to reach, but she had been waiting. She fired a bolt down towards the creature's head, but its strike had thrown off her aim. The projectile embedded into the Neodactyl's shoulder, and it howled in pain, but didn't slow its attack. Instead, it launched a fresh assault on Annica, who managed to jam her crossbow into the monster's snapping mouth, but having already fired her bolt, this did little more than to stop its beak from closing around her arm. It forced its powerful head towards her, and she was lifted off the ground, being pressed upward against the building wall.

Cain launched himself forward and smashed full-bodied into the side of the bird, causing it to drop Annica and spill out onto the main road. Its talons caught easily on the cobbled stones, and it managed to regain control of its fall, but Cain wasn't so lucky. He stumbled forward and found himself sprawled out directly at the Neodactyl's feet.

The Neodactyl coiled its body, ready to pounce, when the man to Cyrus's right rushed out from the alley and fired another bolt, this one piercing the animal's muscular neck. It howled again and its yellow eyes flashed in the direction of its new aggressor. The man didn't attempt to reload. He dropped the weapon where he stood and ran as fast as he could back in the direction the Neodactyl had come from. The creature charged after him like a cat chasing after a mouse. They had both disappeared around the corner before Cyrus could process what the man had just done for them, but that didn't stop the sounds that echoed out from the next street down. It started with a shrill, rattling shriek followed by a horrifying scream of pain. The ensuing crunching of bone was mostly lost in the wind and rain.

"We have to get off the streets," Annica said breathlessly as she got to her feet from where she had fallen. "Cain, now!" Annica added as Cain, also lifting himself off the ground, looked off in the direction the Neodactyl had run. "The other one's got to be out here somewhere."

"What's the plan, boss?" Cain asked Annica in a tone that made it seem like he was asking for a miracle.

Annica squeezed her eyes shut briefly, as though willing an idea to come to her. "That strip of houses at the edge of town, to the south. They'd fallen into disrepair, no one was living in them."

"People may have moved in since we were last here," Cain warned, but he nodded his head anyways, like he knew they didn't have a better option.

Thankfully, after another few minutes of dodging down street after winding street, they came to the described buildings and found them to be mercifully still vacant. In fact, the dwellings were so dilapidated that they looked closer to collapsing in on themselves than welcoming new inhabitants. They were made of a stone composite that looked quite a bit older than some of the more sound-looking structures in town, and large areas had eroded away near the base of many of the outer walls creating black, gaping holes. The roofs themselves were entirely gone, having collapsed in on themselves long ago.

"Around the other side," Annica exclaimed in a hoarse whisper as she sidestepped a large mound of fallen rubble. She was caught dead in her tracks, however, when an unmistakable hiss sounded from around the corner, blocking their way. She brought a finger up to her mouth to silence the group, wearing a wide-eyed, petrified stare on her face. Her eyes did a quick scan of the street and landed on the crumbled holes in the base of the walls beside them. She stabbed a finger aggressively towards the openings and everyone began to scramble towards them. The gaps were plenty wide, about six feet along the wall, but only offered a foot or so of clearance from the sopping wet earth. Luckily, draining water seemed to have eaten away at the once level ground, so large pools of rain and mud now sloshed beneath them offering additional height for anyone willing to get wet. Annica was first through, showing them the way. She splashed down into the puddle of gathered water beneath the rotting stone and slid easily into the vacant house, disappearing entirely into blackness beyond. As Cyrus, using Cain for support, lowered himself to the ground, the man holding Cyrus's scepter fed himself through the opening awkwardly and vanished from view. As the soft splashing of the Neodactyl's footsteps grew nearer, Cyrus looked at Cain and wondered if a man of his size was going to fit. As though Cain himself were thinking the same thing, he looked to Cyrus with a smile and a shrug of his shoulders, then shoved his legs through the hole and started to worm his way deeper in. Cyrus followed suit beside him, having a slightly easier time of it, but not by much. His lower half immediately sunk into the cold, muddy water and he tried to use his arms as best he could to force his torso under the wall. The thick mud oozed around him, threatening to trap his limbs in the suction. Annica's smaller body had made it look so much easier. Knowing that the hunting Neodactyl could only be seconds away from turning the corner onto their street, Cyrus forced his shoulder down into the puddle and halfway submerged his head, finally retracting his face into the shadow of the building and disappearing from view. On his left, Cain had managed to heave himself through the hole with considerable effort and was likewise hidden from the main road.

 Cyrus continued to work his way backwards through the water with the thought of putting as much distance between himself and the opening as possible, but Cain started shushing frantically and Cyrus froze. The slopping water around him leveled out and, with his mouth and nose only inches from the surface, tiny ripples were forming as he tried to control his breathing. The incessant downpour beyond the hole in the building was creating an echo effect, especially with his face so close to the ground, so it sounded unnaturally clear when he heard the first footfall on the street outside. Cyrus held his breath, although he couldn't imagine it would make a difference with the hammering rain, and waited for the animal to pass. It was walking slowly, he could tell, as though it were tracking them, but he hoped to God that was not the case. Even if it could track them through scent, the rain would surely mask their path, right? Cain, laying half-submerged in the puddle beside him, looked pale as a ghost as he watched for the creature outside. The other two members of their group were presumably further inside the wreckage of the partially collapsed building, although Cyrus dared not turn his head to look.

The light but distinct footsteps continued to grow closer, and with them came a bone-chilling rattle; an intake of breath somewhere between a hiss and a snarl. Cyrus couldn't see the animal yet, but it couldn't be more than a few feet from the opening. From this angle, he would only be able to see its feet when it appeared... unless of course it decided to duck its head to inspect beneath the wall. The thought chilled his blood and a shiver ran down his spine... a shiver that continued long past when it should have ended. A shiver that seemed to have settled in the crook of his back. It was with a start that Cyrus realized it wasn't a shiver at all, something was tickling at his waterlogged shirt. In a move that caused a painfully loud echo of sloshing water, Cyrus turned to see a small, rodent-like creature, similar to a rat, perched on his back, evidently using him to stay out of the water. With a creepy scratching noise, the rat began to dig at the threads of his shirt with its tiny claws. Cyrus bucked his body, almost involuntarily, and caused a noisy ripple in the puddle to glide out through the opening and splash gently onto the stone road. He could no longer hear the Neodactyls footsteps and he knew that must mean it had stopped walking.

Cyrus clenched his fists to regain control of his body, willing himself to ignore the increasingly voracious scratching in the small of his back. Cain was looking sideways at him, giving him a look that screamed 'don't you dare move'. And he wouldn't move, he told himself. He couldn't. Their lives depended on it. Unfortunately, as the rat moved a few inches up Cyrus's back, his body gave a reactionary shutter and the resulting splash from the puddle slopped out onto the street like a pot boiling over. Cyrus winced at the noise, but the rat had lost its footing and slid into the water. It busied itself trying to scramble for solid ground, first attempting to reclimb Cyrus's clothes, then wading towards the hole in the side of the building. Its claws clicked against the rock as it wiggled itself out of the puddle and into the rain. It zigzagged this way and that, as though it were trying to avoid the individual raindrops, when...

*Wham!*

With a wet smack and a crunch, the Neodactyl's scaly foot came stomping into view, crushing the rat between its toes and using its black, steely talons as pincers to puncture the animal's body. The bird's head came into view next, bending swiftly and ripping off half of its prey with a jerk of its neck. Cyrus lowered his eyes, as if the creature would feel him looking out of the darkness at it. It was incredibly close, only a few feet. The only thing protecting Cyrus, Cain, and the rest of their party were the shadows they hid under. The Neodactyl snapped up the second half of the rat hungrily and raised its head again, releasing a guttural growl as it did so. But it wasn't moving on. Its feet stayed planted outside the hole in the side of the building, and Cyrus thought he could hear it sniffing.

Crackling thunder cut through the air above causing tiny ripples in the water beneath Cyrus's face, and when the last of the reverberations had rolled themselves out, heavy bootfalls could be heard rounding the opposite corner from where the Neodactyl had come.

A man's voice, presumably a guard, uttered a swear upon coming across the creature in the road.

"Shit, one of the birds is down this way," the voice said.

"Woah, easy now, easy," said a second voice, evidently talking to the Neodactyl, which Cyrus imagined was looking their way and assessing whether the newcomers were a threat.

"Turn around," the first voice insisted, "I'm not getting closer to that thing than I have to."

The Neodactyl made a low hissing noise, and while Cyrus couldn't tell whether it was a threat display or not, it seemed the guards had no intention of finding out and shuffled back the way they had come. As they went, one of them could be heard inquiring if anyone in town was known to be loyal to the East and could possibly be sheltering their quarry.

The Neodactyl, to Cyrus's relief, began to stalk after the guards, and it was only once its footsteps were well out of earshot that he finally released a long, shaking breath.

"We have to go," Annica whispered from somewhere in the dark behind Cyrus. "They're gonna start knocking on doors soon looking for you, and once the town's awake, we'll be trapped."

Cyrus made a move to stick his head out and make sure the coast was clear, but Cain put a hand out to stop him.

"I'll do that," Cain growled, and he shimmied his way back out the hole they had climbed in through. Once on the road, he stood up, cocked his head listening, then waved for Cyrus and the others to follow him.

Once back in the street, Annica whispered, "We're at the eastern edge of town, straight through those woods should bring us to the Fire Fields."

Cyrus followed the group closely as they rushed back into the forest again, Annica and Cain in the lead, Cyrus limping behind them, and the man carrying Cyrus's scepter bringing up the rear. It felt like ages that they were running through the forest, and Cyrus kept jumping at every shadow or swaying branch he saw, certain that his brother's nightmare creatures would come leaping out of the dark at them. But a pale, fiery glow began to emerge through the trees ahead, and even with it appearing cloudy and indistinct through the haze, it could only be the Fire Fields, which meant they were almost out of the Western Kingdom.

As they grew closer, the field grew more vibrant, and once they finally stepped out into the open of the *Neutral Territory*, the orange light from within the fissures of cracked earth was electrifying. In the dark, and possibly compounded by the still hammering rain, the burning glow illuminated them from the ground up, throwing strange and abstract shadows across their features. Annica looked over her shoulder several times as they crossed the fields, making sure they weren't being pursued, and even though Cyrus knew she would call out if anything was approaching, he couldn't help but glance over his own shoulder all the same. But nothing ever jumped out of the shadows at them, and they made it to the other side undisturbed. It was with an enormous sigh of relief that Cyrus finally stepped over the border after what seemed like ages and found himself within Easttown's limits once again.

They made the rest of their way using the road; they figured it was safe to be out in the open within their own territory. They walked in silence, even this side of the border, still thoroughly shaken from their narrow escape. Cyrus, for his part, was starting to think about how he could possibly explain to Jack everything he had heard from Dalton. It seemed like an eternity ago that Jack and himself were walking towards the Temple. So much had happened since then.

As it turned out, more had happened since their walk than even Cyrus realized, for when they finally stepped into the town proper, Ydoro was waiting for them out in the rain, an anxious look on his face.

"Where's Jack?" Ydoro asked in alarm.

After everything Cyrus had been through that evening, he had not been remotely prepared for the possibility that Jack had not made it back ahead of him.

"What do you mean?" Cyrus demanded, "didn't he come back?"

Ydoro shook his head apprehensively and opened his mouth as if he wanted to offer a plausible explanation, but the words caught in his throat. Ydoro knew as well as Cyrus did; if Jack hadn't come back by now, then something had gone terribly wrong.

## CHAPTER FORTY-NINE

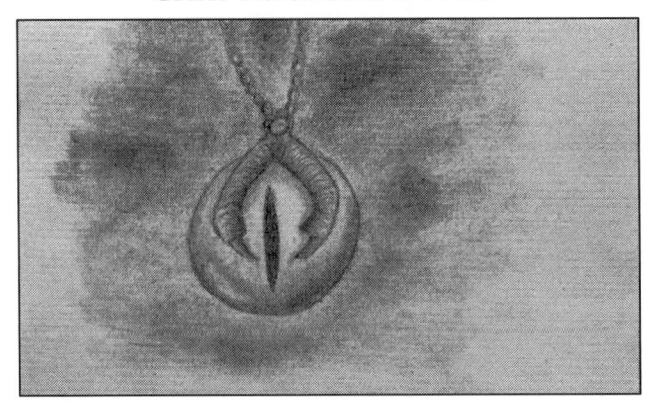

# THE PRISONER

Swift footsteps snapped along the wood floor behind him, echoing off the damp stone walls of the corridor in staccato beats. Something about the faltering, hesitant walking pattern made him sure it was bad news he was about to receive.

The footsteps came to a halt and a wavering voice said, "My King, they were unable to obtain the second intruder."

Alec Dorn turned around to face the guard standing in his doorway; a wide-eyed young man whose head was slightly bowed in a sign of respect.

Alec's eyes narrowed and he could feel sickly anger uncoiling in his chest like a giant serpent. He took a deep breath and leveled himself out.

"You searched the town?" Alec asked icily.

"We did, my King. The birds too. We couldn't find any witnesses who saw them, but... umm... they killed three of our men."

This last piece shocked Alec, but as he remembered the violently torn up room around him, he realized it shouldn't.

"We did also find a fourth body in town," the guard continued, "it seems they were killed by one of your... one of the birds. We don't know who he was, or whether he was from the East or West."

"No matter," Alec said dismissively, "bring our guard's bodies back to the Temple, put them in the dungeons for now until we can burn them… leave the fourth out there to rot."

"Yes my King," the guard responded quickly with a brisk nod of his head. "And we will continue to ask in town if anyone saw who the intruder was."

Alec shook his head and began to stride around the guard and out the door, "I know who it was."

As he headed towards the staircase, he passed the room housing the Neodactyls, who both looked up from preening their wet feathers as they smelled him coming. Without breaking his pace, Alec gave a short whistle and both creatures sprung forward and fell into step at his side. They were well trained, not that he could take credit for that. In fact, Irias was the one to thank for truly taming the animals. They were smart in their own right, but wild nonetheless. Many animals, specifically birds, would imprint on the first living being they came in contact with, trusting it as they would a mother. Alec was well aware of this phenomenon, all biologists were, but the bond with the Neodactyls was something different. He supposed it *was* a form of imprinting, just one that was unknown in modern birds… or perhaps just untested. Irias didn't discover imprinting, of course, he probably didn't even know the term, but he and his men long ago had unlocked the secret to harnessing that power over nature. Once it was discovered what exactly the creatures imprinted *on*, they were able to control it, manufacture it. A false imprint. Of course, that had come back to bite Irias, and he lost his Kingdom for it. Mora discovered his secret and was able to use Irias's own weapon against him.

As Alec arrived on the ground floor, he walked importantly through the enormous halls, the Neodactyls chittering at his sides. Nel stepped out from the dining hall on his left and smiled as she saw him.

"Have you talked to him yet?" Alec asked her without stopping, sounding accusatory without intending to.

"No," Nel insisted, "I wasn't even sure I wanted to."

"Come on," Alec said with a beckoning wave of his hand, and they continued on towards the door on the far right wall that lead down into the dungeons.

With heavy, echoing footsteps, they descended the turning staircase and found themselves in the familiar hallway lined on one side with walls of iron bars. Alec couldn't quite identify the emotion that was flowing through his veins at the moment; he thought it was somewhere between anger and betrayal. But he had learned to control, and even direct, his reactions, and Nel seemed quite impressed with his progress.

As Alec rounded the last cell wall, revealing the occupant within, he had to admit that a tiny fraction of his anger ebbed away. Jack sat against the right wall of the cell, and while he wore a stoic, unbroken expression, he looked afraid. This man had been his friend once, or so he had thought. That was the part that hurt most of all; Jack was a physical representation of everyone, the entire world in fact, choosing Alec's brother over him.

"Impressive entrance," Jack muttered in a gravelly voice, indicating Alec's admittedly strange entourage, but it didn't sound sincere.

Alec felt his anger tick up just a bit. "You made a grave mistake coming here," Alec growled.

"I don't disagree," Jack answered in a failed attempt to sound unconcerned. When Jack finally turned his eyes up to Alec and took in his full appearance, Alec was pleased to see there was no smirk on his face, no indication of superiority, no sense of privilege. He was scared of Alec.

Alec lowered himself to one knee in a would-be cordial act and said softly, "I know my brother was here. What was he doing in my Kingdom?"

Jack just shook his head in way of response, still gazing into Alec's eyes with a strange expression.

"He was in this Temple," Alec continued, "I know it was him. But after everything that happened, everything he did to make certain he ruled in the East, why come back?" When Jack still didn't respond, Alec carried on, "I have to admit an error in my judgement; what he's done with Easttown is beyond anything I could have imagined, and it was a misstep to concede half of the Kingdom so freely."

"You lack imagination then," Jack shot back in a low rasp, "that was your mistake, underestimating the people in the East, but let's not rewrite history here; you didn't concede half the Kingdom for *free*. Cyrus was king, and you only became a king yourself because he willed it so."

Alec's anger ticked up another notch.

Nel stepped forward towards the bars and said, "Alec is king this side of the border. You'll be hard pressed to find anyone in town who says otherwise."

"Because they're being lied to," Jack spat, "do you know about all that, Nel?" His eyes were searching hers as if looking for a crack in her resolve. "His rally in town square was despicable. Convincing all of his people that the East is responsible for their misery."

Alec slammed a hand against the bars of the cell violently, causing the Neodactyls to hiss in alarm, and said venomously, "My brother is the reason their Kingdom was split. There are consequences when a ruler takes half the resources and abandons the people."

Jack nodded his head with raised eyebrows, "Ah, I see. So you actually believe it, the shit you're spewing to them. Here I thought it was an act."

"None of this is an act," Alec snarled, "that's always been my brother's problem. He doesn't see this as a real place. He thinks it's all some fantasy world."

"Oh he knows it's real enough," Jack said softly, looking straight into Alec's eyes. "Are you intentionally avoiding saying his name?"

Alec's anger ticked up a few more notches. His heart was starting to beat faster. "He means nothing to me anymore."

"You still won't say it," Jack smarmily pointed out.

Alec put both hands aggressively against the bars and leaned in closer to the cell. "*Cyrus*," he growled, "*Cyrus* split their Kingdom. *Cyrus* betrayed me. *Cyrus* abandoned me. And now *Cyrus* delivered you to me, abandoning you as well."

Jack smiled. "He made it back. If he found what he was looking for, it will be worth it."

"What is it that inspires such loyalty from you," Alec hissed, having a harder time containing his anger now.

Jack stared back at him briefly before responding. "Well, he's not you."

Alec's blood churned to a boil and his eyes flashed dangerously.

Jack spoke again. "You know what really shows me how lost you truly are? You didn't even ask me what your brother was looking for. Your question was about my loyalty. About *him*."

Alec's lip curled in disgust and he stood up from his crouch. "All trade stops," he announced to Nel. "The borders are closed. We're sending someone back with a clear message to the king in the East." Alec began stalking away from Jack's cell and lowered his voice to Nel. "I need you to find someone from Easttown, anyone will do. You're going to give them something to be delivered *directly* to my brother."

"What did you have in mind?" Nel inquired with a faint smile.

"A warning," Alec answered. They had reached the staircase and Alec stopped, turning to Nel and lowering his voice further. "I need you to go into town on my behalf. Ask the guards to point you in the right direction, they usually know who's coming and going in town. Check the taverns, you'll find someone from the East. *Make them fear you.* I want them *shaking* when they return to my brother."

"Why me?" Nel asked. It wasn't a lack of enthusiasm for the assignment, but a genuine question.

"Because this isn't a message from me," Alec explained, "this is a message from the West."

They ascended the remainder of the stairs and arrived in the entrance hall, warmly lit and casting long, spidery shadows.

"How do you want me to scare them?" Nel asked. "They don't know me like they know you."

"My friends are going with you," Alec said, nodding his head to the Neodactyls, which had busied themselves snapping aggressively at each other.

Nel's eyes widened and she shook her head insistently. "Absolutely not, I have no control over…"

Alec reached into the folds of cloak around his neck and drew out his necklace; a bronze clawed foot clutching a small orb. Nel stared at it.

"I trust you," Alec said quietly, "and no one else."

"That was Mora's necklace," Nel whispered.

Alec nodded his head. "This is how the Neodactyls know me. This is how Mora took control of Irias's Kingdom. They can smell it, it's a pheromone that's being given off. They were trained long ago, and they imprinted on that trainer. But they don't recognize their trainer by sight. They identify them by smell. With this."

Nel was still staring at the dangling pendant in his hand. "How did you get it?"

"Irias… Henry back then… he told me of its power, and where I could find it."

"Around Mora's neck," Nel answered.

"Exactly. He also told me how important it was for seizing power in the Kingdom."

"You took it when Mora fell," Nel said, with understanding seeming to wash over her. "When we were on the ladder, you took the necklace for yourself."

"You'd prefer my brother had claimed it?" Alec said with a snort of laughter.

"That's how you knew the Neodactyls wouldn't kill you," Nel said softly, as pieces slowly fell into place. "In the dungeons, when you released them… I thought you were crazy."

"I told you I knew what I was doing," Alec said with a slightly guilty grin.

"You didn't tell anyone," Nel said, "you didn't even tell me."

Alec shook his head. He understood she felt let down, like he had broken her confidence, but all he could do now was explain. "I couldn't tell you. We had just won a major victory, but we didn't understand this place yet. If I'd let him, my brother would have seized this entire Kingdom for himself, and damned all of us in the process. Taking this was my insurance policy. So I couldn't be left behind."

"You still could have told me," Nel insisted.

"At that very moment you were pushing my brother to take up the king's mantle," Alec pointed out, "as I recall he didn't even want it at first, but you pushed him to take it."

"*I* didn't want the crown to fall to the locals," Nel snapped back, "Cyrus was the best we could do at the time. Get over it." Nel took the pendant in her hands and leaned in close, examining it. She then looked up into Alec's eyes and said quietly, "Trust me next time."

Alec bent slightly and kissed her, and she allowed it this time. She had a habit of flirting with him just to the point that he wanted to kiss her, and then stopping him at the last second. It was maddening. But usually if she was impressed with what he was doing or the way he was handling himself, she would kiss him back. She must have been happy with his necklace deception, even while being annoyed that he hadn't included her in the secret.

Alec slipped the necklace off of his own neck and placed it gently on Nel's.

"Be careful with this," Alec cautioned her. "And be careful with them," he said, indicating the birds. "This pendant will give you their loyalty, but they're emotional creatures. When you're calm, they're calm. When you're anxious…"

"I get the idea," Nel said with a nod of her head. "So what is it that I'm delivering?"

Alec lowered his head slightly. "You're not gonna like it, but we have to send a clear message to the East. Bring me one of the guard's blades, and meet me in the dungeons."

## CHAPTER FIFTY

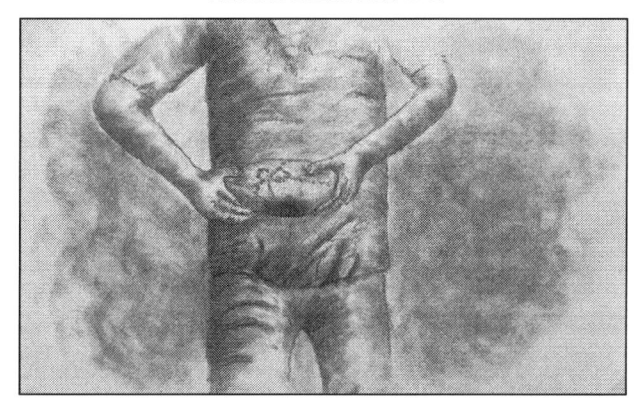

## MOVES AND COUNTERMOVES

A deep, low ripple of distant thunder rolled across the sky, but as the first faint, pale-yellow vestiges of morning light began to penetrate the purple and black clouds, the storm had mostly blown itself out. A cacophony of multiple raised voices filled the small, torch-lit room of Cyrus's home as Cain, Annica, and Ydoro all argued about ways to find Jack. Tam, which Cyrus learned was the name of the man who had carried his scepter back east, stood off to the side, contributing little but listening intently. They had made shockingly little progress. The longer the night had worn on, the more devastated and hopeless Cyrus had felt. He couldn't help but think that, of the original research expedition that he had been responsible for, he himself was the only one left.

"Be smart, Annica," Cain scoffed in a raised voice, "we can't just charge over there and get him. Hell, we don't even know what happened to him."

He was right, of course. Cyrus had told them everything he knew about Jack's plan for the night, which was actually embarrassingly little. But one thing was clear; Jack never lit the fire in town that he had intended. Cyrus remembered looking out the windows from the king's quarters and noting that he didn't see any burning buildings, and there was no sign of damage when Annica and her team had rescued him. Thanks had to be given to Ydoro for implementing that rescue mission. Apparently when Cyrus and Jack didn't return to the East, he had summoned Annica and Cain from their sleep, confident they were the best people for the job. They had been, and Cyrus was grateful, but he couldn't shake the feeling that he had abandoned Jack in the West, even though he hadn't known it at the time.

"Is there a trade scenario do you think?" Ydoro asked Cain, hopefully.

"What, give us back our *Advisor to the King* and you can have this bucket of fish?" Cain said gruffly, "I don't see it happening."

"We must be able to reason with him," Ydoro insisted, "he is still your brother, Cyrus."

It was strange hearing Ydoro call him *Cyrus*. He was usually the first one to push the formalities. Cyrus had been quiet for a good ten minutes now, but when he finally spoke, even softly, everyone stopped arguing and listened. "I thought that, before. But after seeing those birds, the Neodactyls, and the way they came after us... they would have killed us if they had caught us. Hell, they *did* kill one of us. Me being his brother wouldn't have changed that. And those creatures are under his control, so if they were involved in the hunt, that's because Alec sent them." He paused for a second, and took a deep breath. "No, Ydoro," he finally said, "I don't think he can be reasoned with."

The dull roar of arguing rose up once again. Cain was stabbing his finger commandingly at Ydoro, Annica had her hands in the air bracingly, and Tam was nodding along with one of their points. Cyrus felt lost without Jack. It was a strange feeling. He hadn't fully realized just how much he had come to rely on his counsel in this world, but without him to bounce ideas off of, he felt incredibly alone.

Through the swell of impassioned voices, Cyrus heard a faint clearing of a throat, and some soft words he couldn't make out.

"Excuse me," the voice said again.

Cyrus turned towards the door and found the source of the voice. It was a rain-soaked man in his early thirties, with a face as white as a sheet and a dripping canvas package in his hands. The rest of the group had finally noticed the intrusion and fell silent upon seeing the newcomer. It was with a significant drop in his stomach that Cyrus noticed the canvas package in the man's hands, which was tied with a rope-made bow, had a red substance saturating through the bottom of the fabric that looked suspiciously like blood.

"What the hell is this," Cain demanded in a tone of unchecked disgust.

Cyrus stepped forward and said gently, "Who are you?"

"I'm sorry to intrude," the man said, "my name is Garen, I'm one of yours, from the East."

Cyrus felt a minor pang of guilt for not knowing the man. The way he said 'one of yours' implied such loyalty, and Cyrus wasn't sure just now that he deserved it.

"I was in Westtown, having a drink with a few people I know over there…"

"Having a drink in Westtown?" Cyrus questioned with confusion.

"It's quite common," Ydoro chimed in. "And Westerners come here. There weren't always borders."

"No, of course not," Cyrus said somewhat sheepishly, "I just… it's easy to forget that not everyone in the East and West is at odds with each other. Please, Garen, go on."

"Well, I was having a drink, and a woman came into the tavern… and she had the King's birds with her." Cyrus felt a chill run through his body. "She questioned me and my friends. She kept saying it was okay that I was there, and that I was welcome in the West, but… she still made it sound like a threat."

"I see," Cyrus said gently, as the rest of the group listened intently, "and what did she want from you?"

Garen raised the drenched and seeping package up and said, "She wanted me to give you this. She said it had to go directly to the King."

"I see," Cyrus said again, this time with a darker expression falling over his face. "I'll take that, thank you Garen. I know this couldn't have been easy."

As Cyrus took the package carefully and placed it gently on the small table in the corner of the room, he said, "Feel free to stay, Garen, if you'd like."

"Is that what I think it is?" Cain asked, peering over Cyrus's shoulder.

"We'll find out soon enough," Cyrus mumbled, feeling like he was slipping into a bad dream. His words barely seemed to want to come out, and his fingers felt stiff and unmoving as he worked the knot in the bow. As the rope fell away, Cyrus looped a finger into the fold of wet fabric and opened the bundle to reveal its contents. The sight couldn't have been a surprise to anyone given the size and shape of the package, but the entire group gasped and groaned all the same. Lying in the indistinct wad of waterlogged canvas was a severed hand, cleaved neatly at the wrist by a large blade. The cut looked fresh, but the long walk through the rain had washed away a good deal of the blood, and it now looked strangely clean, and pale.

Cyrus's stomach gave a sudden lurch but he regained control of himself. "Did the woman say anything else?" he asked.

"Just that it was a message," Garen said, now standing along the farthest wall as though he expected the hand to jump up and grab him. "He said you had sent a traitor into his Kingdom."

"He's sick," Cain said, shaking his head. "I knew he was unhinged, but this..."

"Alec wouldn't do this," Cyrus said softly, although he didn't really believe his statement. The honest truth was that the brother he knew was long gone. He had become twisted by this place, by his newfound power.

"We have to find him, we have to get him back," Annica said, but her voice wasn't as strong as it usually was. When Cyrus turned to her, he saw that she had tears in her eyes. With a quick wipe of her face, she cleared her throat and stated more firmly, "I'm going back for him. I'll go myself if I have to."

"Wait wait, Annica," Cyrus pleaded, "let's not do anything rash."

"Like going over there to rescue you?" Annica snapped, "because that's what we did. That's what we do for the people we care about."

"I'm not saying we do nothing," Cyrus responded as rationally as he could manage, "but I need you to understand what this is. Think of it as Alec playing a game with us. This isn't a message, it's a *move*. Now we have to counter him."

Annica shook her head vigorously and spat, "This is real life. This isn't your game of chess."

Ydoro spoke up thoughtfully, "But it is. It's the game of kings for a reason."

"I leave the politics to you," Annica said, "but I'm not leaving Jack over there to die."

"You won't be able to enter the Temple," Cain urged, in a deviation from his usual lockstep agreement with Annica, "especially not now. They'll have the place locked down since our breach."

"There's something else," Garen spoke up again, still in his soft, mildly shocked voice. "When I was reentering Easttown, there were Temple guards assembling at the border."

"What?" Cyrus snapped. "How do you mean?"

"I… I don't know what they were doing," Garen stammered, "I was just following my usual road back and I saw them gathering there. They hadn't been there when I went west."

Annica seemed spurred into action. The tears had dried on her face and she now wore a look of hardened defiance. "Cain, gather our men and meet me at the border right now."

"Wait a minute," Cyrus began, "we don't want to force a confrontation…"

"*He's* forcing a confrontation," Annica said quickly, while Cain paused in the doorway, "and we're responding. Moves and countermoves, right?"

Cyrus thought a moment, and his eyes traveled back to the severed hand on the table. "Right," he agreed.

Annica smiled just slightly and nodded her head, "My King."

She turned and headed out the door, patting Cain on the shoulder as she passed him. "And Cain," she said authoritatively, "be sure the men are armed."

Cain gave a curt nod of his head and both of them descended the stairs outside and ran off in opposite directions.

Cyrus was left reeling from the sudden end to their discussions, but he was quickly regaining clarity. "Ydoro, with me. I want to see what's happening at the border. Garen, go home, get some sleep. It's been a long night."

But Garen didn't go home. He seemed to want to know the situation at the border as much as any of them. Perhaps he felt *involved* now, but Cyrus didn't stop him. The three of them proceeded down the road leading west as the sun peeked over the horizon behind them, finally bringing the start of a new day.

As they approached the border, they found Annica standing alone on the Eastern side. She didn't appear to have any weapons that Cyrus could see, and she was saying nothing, but her defiant stance spoke volumes, and seemed to be unnerving the garrison of guards in the West.

*Garrison* was perhaps too strong of a word for the military presence amassed on the Western side of the border, but it was unsettling nonetheless. Six guards, armed with machetes, stood in a neat line in the road just shy of the Eastern marker, forming a sort of blockade. They glanced at Cyrus, Ydoro, and Garen as they approached, but quickly refocused their eyes onto the horizon.

As Cyrus came to a stop along Annica's right side, he asked softly, "What's happened?"

"Nothing yet," Annica answered, still assessing the guards before her. "I asked them what they were doing here, and they ignored me."

Cyrus studied the guards carefully, scanning each one's passive, expressionless face. Finally, he stepped forward a pace and announced, "I am the King of the East, and you will tell me what you are doing at our border." One guard's eyes flicked briefly to meet his, but quickly looked away again. Apart from that, the guards gave no answer. Cyrus continued, "A military presence at our border will be viewed as an act of hostility. If you don't have the authority to start a war, you *will* answer me."

One guard's eyes lowered to meet Cyrus's again, and he looked briefly as if he were about to speak, but at that moment, a raucous band of

Eastern townfolk, led by a scowling Cain holding what looked to be a massive chunk of fallen branch, rounded the corner from behind them and started yelling insults and threats to their Western counterparts. When Annica had told Cain to 'gather their men', Cyrus had no idea the extent of her allies. Cain had arrived with somewhere close to thirty angry-looking men and women, each jeering at the guards along the border like a barely contained mob. They each held something mildly threatening in their hands, but they were mostly very poor excuses for weapons. Many held kitchen knives or wooden club-like objects (though none as impressively enormous as Cain's), and some had little more than rocks. But the boisterous, aggressive energy coming from the group was intimidating, and the guards were finding it extremely difficult to hold their passive stance.

"So what is this?" Cain shouted out towards the West as a whole. "This is a trade route, you'd be well advised to go back the way you came."

The guards exchanged apprehensive glances but did nothing to respond.

Cain shook his head in annoyance and said, "Alright, we'll play it that way." He then passed close to Annica and lowered his voice, "Have you checked the road to the south? Or the Neutral Territory, Fire Fields area?"

Annica's eyes widened just a bit, "That's a good point."

Cain nodded and turned to his men. "Our entire border, walk it."

Annica raised her voice and instructed further, "If you find *any* Western guards along our border, I want two of our men for every one of theirs."

The group, practically pulsating with excitement and fury, began to dissipate, quickly assigning ten of their ranks to stay on the trade road.

"Now this isn't really necessary, is it?" came a gravelly voice from behind the five-person Western blockade.

The guards parted slightly to allow the substantially-built Bohrman to approach.

"Bohrman!" Cain shouted upon seeing him, "What the hell are these men doing? This is a trade route!"

Bohrman shook his head with a defeated sort of expression and said, "No more trade. I'm sorry Cain, it's the King's orders."

Cain guffawed loudly, but Cyrus was having trouble seeing the humor in the situation. Cyrus stepped forward and said, "What are you talking about? What did Alec say?"

Bohrman looked supremely uncomfortable speaking directly to the King of the Eastern Kingdom, but he cleared his throat and said carefully, "With respect, I'm not authorized to discuss the specifics. Suffice it to say the King feels we are unable to move forward with our current arrangement."

Cain laughed again and responded, with much less respect than Bohrman was striving for, "That's your plan? You think we need what the East has to offer us? This trade agreement is practically charity as is."

"Cain," Cyrus warned. He was beyond caring about exacerbating the situation, but he didn't think it wise to discuss their trade strategies so openly.

Bohrman continued, "The King would also like it made clear that our border is closed. No person, civilian or otherwise, will be permitted to enter the West under any circumstances. Any breach of this understanding will not be met kindly."

"Is that a threat?" Cain snarled, "You see all these men I just brought here today? That's just who I could wake at the crack of dawn with five minutes notice. You have no idea what we're capable of."

"Cain," Cyrus warned again.

"Yes, yes," Bohrman said with a wave of his hand, "I saw your impressive men... and their rocks."

"Keep pushing," Cain growled, but Cyrus was quickly realizing it was pointless to argue with this man.

"It's fine, Cain," Cyrus insisted, "let it be."

Cain put up his hands in frustrated surrender and nodded his head in understanding, but he quickly added, "Fine, but I want *our* men stationed here too. And I suspect it's the same near the Fire Fields."

"It's just a precaution to ensure the King's wishes are being respected," Bohrman assured him, but his voice was dripping with superiority.

Cyrus put a bracing hand on Cain's shoulder before he could react, and repeated, "It's fine, we're done here."

As Cyrus, Cain, and an extremely uncomfortable-looking Garen turned to walk away, Annica pointed to the group of ten Easttowners and directed them towards the border line. They approached with unbridled enthusiasm, and to Cyrus's slight disapproval, they planted themselves directly in front of their Western counterparts, practically nose to nose. It created an extremely tense-looking standoff, which Cyrus supposed was the point, but he did nothing to stop it.

With a last wary glance over his shoulder, Cyrus began walking back east. The fact that he hadn't slept since the previous night was suddenly occurring to him, and he felt exhausted.

With an angry grumble, Cain said, "I guess that ends our peace with the West."

"The peace was never real," Cyrus lamented, "at least now they've made their stance known."

"And we've made our stance known," Annica said pointedly, "we have to be extremely careful how we proceed now. I worry that any weakness they perceive will be exploited."

"They won't see any weakness from us," Cain said brusquely.

Except it wasn't just weakness from the men that they would be looking for, Cyrus thought to himself. He would have to be exceedingly intentional with every action he took moving forward.

**CHAPTER FIFTY-ONE**

# WESTERN DOMINION

Nel felt wrong. She felt off. Dirty, somehow. Those feelings had been trying to creep into her mind for about a week, ever since she had taken the Neodactyls into town and delivered the severed hand to that Easttowner. But Nel was unique, as far as she could tell. She had a superpower that set her apart from everyone else. She could turn that sick feeling in her stomach off. It was something she had discovered about herself when her mother had died all those years ago, and ever since then, she had embraced it like a suit of armor. She had been called 'cold' and 'remorseless' and every other word in the dictionary, and people thought they were hurting her by saying it, but Nel wore it as a badge of honor. Other people felt things so deeply that they would end up crippled by grief or pain or regret. Nel wondered why. When Nel's mother had passed, she had been inconsolable. The weight in her chest felt like it would crush her very soul into nothingness. But she found a switch within herself, an off button for her pain. And once it had been turned off, she discovered it was difficult to turn it back on. Her siblings ostracized her for it. They couldn't understand why she didn't fall apart like the rest of them. The older ones began caring for the younger ones, and they bonded over their shared loss, but Nel was left behind because she wasn't showing her grief in the 'right way'. She left home after that, and discovered that switch within herself was easy to keep 'off'.

The experience in town, however, was threatening to flip the switch back 'on', and she didn't like it. It wasn't so much the task that Alec had entrusted to her. The delivery had gone smoothly, and to her amazement, she had no trouble controlling the Neodactyls. There was also a certain power that she felt when she strode into town, and she found it strangely electrifying. However, it was the look in the local's eyes that had been haunting her since that day. Alec had instructed her to make them fear her, and she had done just that. It had been fun, almost intoxicating at first. But the way the woman in the tavern had looked at her, or refused to look at her, was awful. It was real terror, and Nel was responsible for it. She understood Alec's reasoning, of course, and sending a warning to the East was absolutely the right choice, but it had felt just a little too real in that moment.

No matter, Nel flipped the switch back 'off' again and buried those thoughts in the past where they belonged. Yet she still found herself walking towards the dungeons, as though drawn there by some feeling she didn't understand. She had nothing to say to Jack, but felt the need to talk to him anyways.

As she walked through the entrance hall, Irias walked out of the dining area and smiled at her approach. It was a slightly creepy smile in Nel's eyes. Not because of the intention, which she had to assume was pleasant enough, but because of the way it stretched and contorted his waxy skin around his mouth. It ended up as more of a jagged grimace than a grin.

"Nelida," Irias exclaimed in his gravelly voice. He always addressed her by her full name for some reason, and it bothered her just slightly.

Nel forced a smile back and asked, "How are you?"

"Fine, fine," Irias said with a nod of his head. "I'm just on my way up to see the King."

Nel found Irias to be a very strange man. Perhaps it was simply the fact that she had known him as Henry for so long, and it was difficult to reconcile the two different personas in her head. He had lied to them all from the very start, but when the truth finally came out about who he really was, it seemed nobody cared. Nel, for her part, didn't appreciate being conned, but could understand his reasoning. From what he had told them since, Irias was not a welcome name in the Kingdom any longer. He had ruled for a long time, and had real strength back in the day. But Mora had been younger and had capitalized on Irias's waning power. The way he told it, Mora had turned the Kingdom against him with lies and rumors. Nel wasn't sure she bought that completely, and was at the very least certain that Irias's rule had made him quite a few enemies; but she couldn't fault him for that. She could tell he missed his power, and probably found his role as an advisor to Alec a pale but suitable substitute. It allowed him to feel strong and important once again even though he was clearly well past his prime. Lately, however, he had been pushing to reenter the public eye, convinced it was time the locals saw and understood his influence in the Kingdom. Nel wasn't surprised. Power was like a drug in that way.

Nel nodded her head to Irias and said, "Tell Alec I'll be coming up in a bit."

Irias gave her a disapproving look and responded, "I shall let *the King* know."

He shuffled on past her and Nel smirked slightly with a roll of her eyes before continuing towards the stairway leading down to the dungeons. She passed a guard on the stairs, who she nodded to curtly, and made her way to the lower level. The guards still made her mildly uncomfortable given her experiences with them during her attempted escape, but she reminded herself they were only following orders.

Nel walked briskly down the hallway of cells until she finally came upon Jack's. He was one of her oldest acquaintances, but she would not have necessarily considered him a friend. They had a certain bond at one point, a trust that comes from working and relying on each other out at sea, but it seemed the sun had set on that relationship. The Jack she knew had been strong and opinionated, but unmoving. Like a tree which weathered the storms that had swept all others away. But that wasn't the man in this cell. The Jack of this Kingdom was weak, and it disgusted Nel to see it.

Jack was leaning against one of the stone side walls and looked up as she came into view. She hadn't come to see him since her conversation with Alec and the delivery of the hand, and he looked worse for wear. He was dirty and run down, and it looked like some of the fire had left his eyes, but it didn't stop him from glaring at her when their gaze met.

"I have nothing to say to you," Jack growled before she had even opened her mouth to speak. "Whatever your master wants, he can come say it himself."

Nel came to see him of her own accord, but his words struck a nerve with her. "Bold words, Jack. But play your cards carefully, Alec is a dangerous man."

"Don't I know it," Jack responded darkly. When Nel just stared back at him, he raised both hands in mock-surrender and said in a falsely apologetic voice, "Begging your pardon, oh great one. Please don't hurt me… or pretend to hurt me."

This statement did surprise Nel, and despite her best efforts, she must have shown it on her face.

"Oh what?" Jack continued, "you didn't think I'd catch on to what they were doing in the next cell over? Yeah, I get it. They dragged one of the bodies in from town, chopped off his hand, passed it off as mine, and sent it east to scare Cyrus. Did I get all that right?"

Nel glowered at him, but composed herself quickly. "Cockiness doesn't suit you, Jack. Why don't you leave that to your king."

"What is it he's hoping to achieve, though?" Jack asked, with a bit of that old fire returning to his eyes. "I mean, at the very least Alec must know that a trade freeze will hurt the West more than the East. Is he just that desperate to prove his power?"

Nel was losing her patience with the conversation. "Despite what you may think, Alec has made the West strong. I believe you'll appreciate that soon enough… if you ever see the outside of this cell."

"Oh good," Jack replied, "because I was starting to worry Alec was throwing an entire civilization of people into chaos over a spat with his older brother."

Nel shook her head and smirked slightly, but the smirk was for show. In reality, she was saddened by what she was seeing. When she finally replied, she said softly, "Jack, what happened to you? I used to know you."

Jack smirked back and answered, "I used to know you."

There was something in Jack's eyes that she still recognized; something of her old crewmate still in there. "Remember years ago, Jack, when we went out on that big shipping vessel together. It had that young new captain, couldn't have been more than twenty-five. He came on board and started posturing and barking orders and practically pissing on the deck to claim his territory. No business being captain at all. Do you remember?"

Jack nodded slightly, "Wilmot, wasn't that his name?"

"Wilmot, yes!" Nel exclaimed with a smile, "*Captain* Wilmot. What a piece of work. You remember he was constantly telling us how his father was a great captain, as if that somehow made him owed our respect. And you remember what you and I did after we'd spent a few days at sea with him?"

Jack had the shadow of a smile on his face, but it was only fleeting. "Of course I remember. We locked him in his cabin during the night."

Nel laughed remembering the day, but Jack only slightly broadened his reluctant smile. "He spent the entire day trying to get out," she continued, "yelling to crew members through the door, who kept acting like they couldn't understand what he was saying. When we finally unlocked the door during the night, he didn't even notice. The next morning, he came storming out ready to fight, and everyone said they didn't know what he was talking about." She chuckled again, but Jack never joined in as she had expected him to. "As I recall, Jack, that was your idea."

Jack held his slight smile and nodded his head with cocked eyebrows. "It was."

"And now you follow Cyrus Dorn," Nel pointed out, "another captain who takes himself way too seriously. What happened to the Jack I used to know?"

Jack stayed silent for a moment, seeming contemplative, before responding, "I grew up."

Nel's expression darkened. "Hmm," she replied, "well I certainly hope he was worth the devotion."

Jack nodded slowly while looking back at her, the smile having entirely left his face. "I'm comfortable with the decisions I've made. I hope you can say the same."

With that, Jack turned away from Nel and resumed staring at the wall, the way she had first found him. Nel nodded her head but could think of no response to his comment. She lingered for another moment before turning and walking back down the hall. She knew that Jack's unbroken resolve was nothing more than a mask, and that behind it he was afraid, but his bold, arrogant demeanor still bothered her. He acted like he couldn't be touched while being held captive. Unfortunately, Nel knew that not to be true. Jack was wrongfully deducing that because Alec had elected to cut off a dead guard's hand in place of Jack's, that Alec was unwilling to cause him real harm. The truth was, Nel feared for Jack. Alec was only beginning to test the limits of his royal power, and so far, he had found them to be essentially boundless.

Nel made her way back through the Temple and up towards Alec's living quarters. She had somewhat hoped that Irias would be done talking with him by then, but as she entered, she found him still chattering away in his gravelly yet somehow silky voice.

"Nel!" Alec exclaimed happily as she walked in.

"I'm sure Nelida would agree with me," Irias said with a vigorous nod of his head.

"What's that?" Nel asked skeptically.

"Irias is concerned about skirmishes along the borders," Alec explained. "My guards tell me the Easttowners are beginning to test our resolve along the trade routes. Possibly trying to push us into a conflict. I'm of a mind to ignore it for now… but…"

He looked at Nel and she could tell he was searching her expression for clues of her thoughts on the matter. Alec was getting increasingly better at trusting his own instincts, but she also knew her own approval was of great importance to him. This meant that what she said in response to this moment would likely have great effect on his decision. She initially thought it the more level-headed and mature response to ignore the border skirmishes, as Alec had suggested, but Jack's cocky, demeaning retorts in the dungeons stung at the back of her mind.

"They're testing you," Nel finally said. "A stronger response might be appropriate."

Alec seemed initially surprised by her statement, but eventually broke into a grin. "I like your spirit."

"Easttown is nothing more than a band of rebels," Irias insisted, "If we cut the head off the snake, they'll be in ruin faster than you can blink."

"The head of the snake meaning my brother?" Alec asked, "I'm not doing that. Deal with his people first."

"From what I hear, Easttowners have been pushing past our borders, starting conflicts with our guards. Even planting sentries in the forest to the west," Irias continued.

Alec looked distressed by these revelations and barked back, "Well then *we* push past *their* borders. Remind them that we have significant power to stop them."

Irias cleared his throat and said, "I wondered, my King, whether you would consider allowing me to lead a group to the border? My fighting days are long gone, of course, but the East will remember me. They stayed in line during my reign. Showing that you and I are aligned, it could have an impact."

Alec looked skeptical, and Nel thought he had every reason to be. In Irias's own words, he was well past his prime; could he really have any impact at all in the East?

Alec finally answered, "Irias, I don't want to count you out. You've been crucial in helping me secure the Kingdom. But I want to make sure I'm using you where you're strongest. Up until now, that has been by my side. I'm asking you; do you truly believe your presence will cause a stir in my brother's Kingdom?"

Nel was suddenly struck by how calculated Alec's response was. It wasn't emotional, it was strategic.

"These people feared me," Irias hissed with more ferocity than Nel had yet seen in him. She could sense the shadow of the ruler he once was. "Seeing me will get a reaction, I can guarantee that."

Alec considered this, eying Irias as though assessing for weaknesses. He finally answered, "I can't give you the Neodactyls. They stay with me."

Nel thought this preemptive declaration was wise, considering Mora took control from Irias in exactly that way. If Irias were planning a double-cross, that would be the way to do it. Nel half expected him to argue with Alec's statement, but he surprised her.

"The Neodactyls are yours," Irias agreed with a fervent nod of his head, "they belong to the king and I respect that. All I ask is for a handful of guards."

Alec contemplated again, finally turning to look out the window to the sprawling Kingdom below. Without turning back, he spoke again, "You're asking me to essentially announce to the public that you are alive and well after all these years. Let's not mince words, these are a people that you bullied and beat into submission over a decade of abuse from what I hear." Irias looked like he wanted to interject but Alec finally turned away from the window and continued, "I don't judge, but I do have to wonder how your public resurgence would help me. The West trusts my leadership, I'm not seeing how the return of their old enemy would be beneficial."

To Nel's surprise, Irias smiled at this and responded adamantly, "I wasn't an enemy to the West. The East vilified me because I turned them into the laborers. They blamed me for causing a rift between the two sides, but the West never complained… and the East learned their place."

Alec seemed to like this idea as the hint of a smile twitched at the very corner of his lips. "Perhaps it is time to expand the public face of the Temple. I can't be dealing with all of these minor disputes personally."

Nel secretly wondered whether this was the real reason he was softening to Irias's offer. While it was true that an effective ruler would delegate such responsibilities, Nel had an inkling that what was really keeping Alec away from the border was a subconscious fear of a confrontation with Cyrus. Alec hadn't seen him since the Kingdom was split, and Jack had called it right when he pointed out Alec's refusal to say his brother's name. Nel kept this thought to herself.

"I would be an emissary of the king," Irias agreed, "enforcing your will, nothing more."

Alec nodded his head, thinking everything over. After a long silence, he finally said, "Okay, go. Take ten men with you. Make an impression at the border, I don't care how you do it. Remind them that no matter how many houses they build or how many fish they catch in the East, the real power is from the Temple. The fighting strength is here, and they only have their own Kingdom because *I* allow it."

Irias bowed his head slightly and responded, "I can do that, my King."

"And one more thing," Alec said, "I want you to bring Nel with you."

Irias caught his disappointed reaction quickly, but it had been hard to miss. Nel herself was taken aback by the order, and not at all sure she wanted to accompany Irias on his venture.

Alec held up his hand before either of them could object and said, "I don't want to hear it, this is important. Irias, this is your chance. Show me that you have a public role to play. Put an end to this back and forth with the East, show them our strength, and lock down our damn borders. Make it count, and we can rule this Kingdom together."

Nel of course knew that Alec meant this metaphorically, but Irias's greedy eyes lit up all the same.

Alec pointed at Irias and said with a note of finality, "Don't let me down."

Irias bowed low and said hastily, "Absolutely, my King." He turned and shuffled out of the room quickly, as though worried Alec would change his mind if he lingered too long. Nel stayed behind a moment longer, and once Irias's footsteps were far enough down the hall, she approached Alec slowly.

Alec smiled at her. "What do you think? Not bad, huh?"

Nel offered him a smile back and said, "You're getting better at this. It's what I could see in you all along."

Alec bent his head slightly and Nel kissed him. It was a strange relationship they had. They certainly weren't a couple, she would never allow that, but there was a chemistry between them that she found extraordinarily useful. She had told him long ago, back when they first met, that she saw a fire within him, buried deep down. With careful stoking, that spark had become a roaring inferno, and it had helped him attain incredible power in just a few months time. But she still sensed a fragility that he kept hidden away, something that could undermine his stranglehold on this Kingdom if allowed to show its face. Of course, it was that very fragility that allowed Nel to have so much sway over how Alec ran the Kingdom. He was uncertain, still testing the strength of the newfound power he was standing on. She had to remind herself that this was a man who never had the chance to find his own footing, up until now. She found that she had to achieve just the right balance when interacting with him; when she gave too much, he became drunk on his own power and lost the ability to hear the logic of her advice, but when she gave too little, his spark faded and he would give way to uncertainty and doubt. He was doing well right now, and the kiss was his reward.

When they parted, Nel wasted no time speaking what was on her mind. "Why do you want me to go with the old man to the border?"

Alec nodded his head in understanding, "It's important, Nel. I want to give Irias some freedom, and if used well he could be a real asset, but I don't trust him. He's not one of us."

"One of us?" Nel asked. She found this an odd statement, considering Alec was not currently speaking to half of their group.

"You and me," Alec responded, and his eyes burned brightly with ambition as he said it. "We make this world the way we want it to be… and damn the rest."

Nel smirked slightly and repeated, "Damn the rest. We'll prepare to leave right away."

"Just be careful out there," Alec insisted, "Irias can think he's in charge, but you'll be watching him. Whatever happens, don't allow him to make me look weak."

Nel smiled and responded with a nod of her head, "My King." It was a playful statement, she never actually addressed him as such, but his reaction to her words was a broad grin as his internal fire burned high.

**CHAPTER FIFTY-TWO**

# THE DOOR

Cyrus let out a deep, heavy sigh as he walked briskly through town, Cain marching alongside him.

"I know it's not the news you wanted," Cain said, "but we've made very little headway at the borders. Our people are dedicated, but there's just no getting around the fact that your brother has more men at his disposal. The blockades are manned day and night. At last count, I believe three of our men have made it over the border unnoticed but haven't reported back yet."

Cyrus nodded in understanding. "And Bohrman won't discuss what's happened to Jack?"

"Bohrman won't even come to meet me anymore," Cain snarled bitterly, "damn coward."

"Alright," Cyrus said as his home came into view, "we have to figure this out, we can't leave Jack over there."

"I'm open to ideas," Cain responded, throwing out his hands in frustration.

"Yeah I know," Cyrus assured him. He was exhausted, they all were. It had been a hard few days since Garen had arrived from the West with the package. Cyrus walked up the stairs to his deck, leaving Cain below. He finally turned and said, "We *will* figure it out."

Cain nodded up at him and replied, "I believe you," but Cyrus could hear the skepticism in his words.

Cyrus ducked into his dimly lit living quarters and stood in the center of the room for a moment, allowing the merciful silence to wash over him. He raised his hands and massaged his temples aggressively. He had gotten very little sleep over the past few days, unsurprisingly so considering he had no idea where Jack even was at the moment. The guilt that accompanied that hard truth was haunting and inescapable, constantly eating away at him and cutting into his every thought. It was so all-consuming that it felt wrong to even think of anything else. And yet any hope of rescuing him had stalled completely. Cyrus felt entirely helpless, unable to cross the border, unable to even talk with anyone from the West. Annica wanted to send a small party over the border at night and mount a rescue mission, but even she had to admit that path was likely foolish considering the plan had already been used once to rescue himself. Cain wanted a show of force. He insisted the Easttowners were angry and ready for a conflict, but per his own admission, Alec had the stronger numbers, not to mention the bulk of the trained fighters and sharpened steel. They looked to Cyrus to make a decision, but so far he had come up with no way forward.

As Cyrus opened his eyes again, they flashed briefly to the end of his room where the lone scepter stood leaning against the corner in the shadows, small strips of brilliant sunlight dancing across it from seams in the fabric walls. Another pang of guilt shot through Cyrus's mind. If it didn't involve rescuing Jack, he felt like he had no business thinking about it... and yet there was something major weighing on his mind. Dalton Sidney had appeared to him in Alec's chambers, and had told him that the reason they ended up in this world was the very scepter leaning against the wall before him. It hadn't made any sense, but of course nothing made any sense these days. He had spent considerable energy racking his brain to remember everything Dalton had said to him. It was all fuzzy and distant, probably because of everything that had followed as a result of his border crossing, not to mention his lack of sleep.

He finally gave into his mind's persistence, pushed his guilt aside, and grabbed the scepter off the wall. It was heavy, but well-balanced. He held the gnarled, twisted top close to his face and examined the blackened bark. He dug a fingernail into the surface but was surprised when none of the charred-looking substance crumbled off. It looked very much like burnt wood, the way trees looked after being consumed by a forest fire or a strike of lightning. But this material, unlike wood, was extremely hard. When he held the scepter up to the light, some of those deep ribbons of ruby red shone out from the cracks beneath the surface. It was just sunlight illuminating a transparent material, and nothing compared to the glow it emanated when placed near frozen fire. But still, it almost seemed as though there were a second material, buried deep within the burnt-looking shell.

Physically, the scepter was certainly odd when inspected up close, but rather unremarkable considering what power it held, if Dalton were to be believed. According to him, the artifact that Cyrus held in his hand had the ability to open windows to alternate worlds. That's how Dalton had described it, windows and doors. Windows when the scepter was left stationary for an extended period of time, and doors when a fragment was broken from the scepter. He had warned that the doors were unreliable and dangerous, but the windows had seemed fairly safe. How could Cyrus test Dalton's claims? The trouble was, as Dalton had astutely pointed out, the windows only reflected the space immediately surrounding the scepter. That made it difficult to perceive a change if the reflected space was consistent from one reality to the next. The way to test it, then, would have to require altering something. Creating a change around the scepter that uniquely reflected this specific moment in this specific world. An idea came to him.

"You're starting to look like your brother," said a voice from the doorway.

Cyrus nearly dropped the scepter to the ground in surprise. He had been so engrossed in his examination of the strange object he had not heard Ydoro's approach up the stairs.

"Sorry to startle you," Ydoro exclaimed in concern. Upon seeing the searching, slightly wild expression on Cyrus's face, he entered the room cautiously. "Are you alright?"

"Umm, yeah," Cyrus responded with a shake of his head, trying unsuccessfully to clear it. "Come in a sec, I'm going to test something out." When Ydoro looked concerned for his sanity, Cyrus continued, "Look, I found something, when I was in the Temple. I don't know what to do with it yet, or how to explain without sounding crazy. Just, have a seat, and keep an open mind."

Ydoro looked positively baffled, but to his credit, he did as he was told and eased himself into a chair in the corner of the room without saying a word.

Cyrus turned away from him, not wanting to get distracted, and began rummaging on the surface of his table until he found what he was looking for; a medium sized, sharp knife. He turned again to face the center of the room, kicking a few objects aside until a large area of weathered, wooden floor was exposed. He thought a moment longer, deciding on what symbol to carve, but he supposed it didn't really matter. Finally, he bent to the ground, pointed the knife downward, and dug it hard into the aged wood. As he ran the blade in a diagonal line, it etched a clear, bright track as it revealed the lighter inside of the boards. He carved a line roughly six feet long, and then did the same in the opposite direction; intersecting the two to create a large X. Ydoro stayed quiet in the corner. Cyrus looked down on his handywork for a moment, then grabbed the scepter and placed it in the center of the carved X. He then stepped away.

He took a spot along the canvas wall of the room and stared at the floor. Poor Ydoro likely thought he was attempting to conjure some sort of spirit with the display, but Cyrus did not want to attempt explaining until he saw it for himself.

The seconds dragged by, then became minutes. And still Cyrus did not stop staring at the floor. He barely even blinked.

Around the two-minute mark, Ydoro cleared his throat slightly and readjusted in his creaky chair. He seemed as though his patience had finally run out and he was just about to ask for an explanation… when something happened.

It was subtle, almost imperceivable at first. It started in the center of the X, right where the scepter had been laid across the intersection of lines; the carved tracks began to vanish. It wasn't that the wood was healing itself, more that the carving was disappearing as if it had never been. Slowly radiating out from beneath the scepter, the wood floor became unmarked once again. Cyrus's eyes followed the no-longer-connected lines that had once formed an X as they slowly receded away from the scepter; erasing themselves from the inside out. Cyrus blinked a final time and the carved X was gone entirely, revealing a completely unmarked, although still dingy floor. A floor from another reality.

Cyrus looked sideways at Ydoro and saw that his mouth was hanging open. It was only then that Cyrus realized his own mouth was doing the same.

Ydoro stood up from his chair, slightly wobbly, and asked in a soft croak, "What just happened?"

Cyrus grinned, in spite of his shock. "We opened a window."

\*\*\*\*\*

Cyrus spent the next ten minutes explaining to Ydoro everything that had happened inside the king's chambers in the Temple. Ydoro hadn't known Dalton, but his surprise was no less for it. He asked infinite questions to which Cyrus knew embarrassingly few answers. He was reminded of all the questions he should have asked Dalton when he had the chance. When it came time for Cyrus to finally explain his little science experiment on the floor in front of them, Ydoro was already nodding in understanding.

"So those lines I carved in the floor," Cyrus was saying, as much for his own clarification as for Ydoro's, "they're still there, but the floor we're seeing is this same floor from a different… plane of existence I guess. A different reality. One where I did not just carve an X into the floor. And the radius must not be very large, in fact…" Cyrus scanned the outer borders of where he had cut and found what he was looking for; a single line only a couple inches long, the very end of one of his carved lines that was just far enough away from the scepter that it hadn't been 'erased'. "There," Cyrus said pointing, "that's the range of the window."

"And it only stays open as long as the scepter stays still?" Ydoro asked, his tone somewhere between excitement and bewilderment.

"I think so," Cyrus answered. "That's what Dalton seemed to think. I suppose we can test it."

Cyrus walked forward in the direction of the scepter. He looked down, half expecting his feet to have disappeared entirely, but they were still there. He reached out with the tip of his boot and gave the scepter a soft tap. The result was instantaneous. The carved X reappeared as though it had never vanished in the first place. It wasn't a slow progression like the way it disappeared, it was simply back in the blink of an eye like it had always been there. Cyrus bent down and picked up the scepter, suddenly having a much greater appreciation for the 'weapon of the king' he had been so carelessly tossing aside for months.

Ydoro was positively gaping at the scepter. "So can we… your friend Dalton, I mean… he said we can't pass through one of these windows?"

"That's right," Cyrus answered contemplatively. He was feeling strangely more like his old self, reminded of his work at the university. This had absolutely nothing to do with his field of work, but the experimentation felt warmly familiar. "Dalton said that windows were just a reflection of another plane of existence. He told me that infinite realities were playing out right now, in this very space, but that we couldn't see or feel them. They exist simultaneously without ever affecting one another. These scepters allow you to pull back the curtains on just one."

Ydoro was looking at the air around him as though attempting to see past the veil of space and time and peek into one of these alternate realities.

Cyrus continued, "But we're pulling back the curtain on one of many. And Dalton didn't know of a way to control which world we see." Thinking of the way the X had receded away from the scepter, Cyrus posited aloud, "it's almost as if the material that makes up the scepter somehow eats away at the space and time around it, erodes that invisible shroud just a bit."

"But you said Dalton mentioned doors?" Ydoro asked eagerly.

Cyrus nodded his head hesitantly, "He did. But he said they were dangerous… and unpredictable. He kept cautioning that we could become… I forget how he put it exactly. Lost, I guess. Lost in time, maybe? I don't know, we were interrupted soon after that. But it was clear the doorways don't just lead to the same space in a different reality, it seemed like there was a connection between our world and this one. Dalton said that's how we got here; someone unintentionally opened a door."

"By breaking a piece from the scepter?" Ydoro asked.

Cyrus looked down at the staff in his hand. Drawing an X in the floor was one thing, but he found himself suddenly nervous about experimenting further. Dalton's panicked warnings right before the guards came running were suddenly ringing in his ears, not that he could remember half of what he had said. Cyrus shook his head in a way that said 'I must be crazy' before crouching down and grabbing the knife up off the floor where he had discarded it.

"Wait," Ydoro said, "should we really be rushing into this?"

Cyrus, who was still crouched on the floor, holding the knife near the base of the staff, considered this carefully. Was he rushing into this? But if he didn't try something, how would they ever have any hope of getting home? An image of Cynthia suddenly flashed into his mind, and his resolve was restored. He raised the knife to shoulder length and brought it down hard against the side of the scepter.

Nothing happened.

Cyrus leaned closer to the rough bark and could not find any noticeable damage. Apparently breaking a piece off the scepter was harder than it looked, which would of course explain why doorways weren't opening very often. Cyrus readjusted his grip on the scepter and angled it against the floor, then took the knife in his other hand and held it crosswise near the bottom, as a sculptor would prepare to shave a scraping off a wood piece. With the right amount of leverage, he could see that the material was beginning to cut. He teased the blade back and forth, working it in just enough to find a bite in the burnt-looking surface. He kept expecting something to happen as he worked, but nothing did. When he was finally satisfied that he had worked the knife under enough of an edge, he took a final deep breath, then pushed down hard towards the ground, feeling the shard break loose as he did.

This time the result was immediate. Cyrus instantly felt the familiar horrible sensation of having all of his muscles contract as though his every tendon and ligament were tightening. Cyrus jumped away from the fallen shard fast, pulling the scepter away as he did so. The knife, however, he was not so careful with, and he let it go when he stood up. It fell to the floor, gave a quick spin, and was gone entirely. Cyrus backed to the very edge of the room and could feel his sinuses exploding from the pressure. But it was less, so much less, than what he had felt out on the ocean. His head throbbed, but not blindingly so. And yet, it was clearly the same sensation that he had felt when he first fell out of his own world and into this one. He had opened a door.

Ydoro was standing in the far corner of the room looking exceedingly uncomfortable. "Did you see it take the knife?" he asked as if there were any way Cyrus had missed it.

"Where do you think it leads?" Cyrus asked.

Ydoro finally pulled his eyes away from the now slightly vibrating shard and looked at Cyrus with a pleading expression. "We can't. Not like this."

Cyrus, however, couldn't shake one wild thought from his head; that could be his own world waiting for him. Cynthia could be on the other side. He turned to Ydoro, who shook his head vigorously in response.

"Dalton said the door stays open from the other side," Cyrus assured him, "I'm just going to look."

"You're the king," Ydoro pleaded, "you can't abandon your people like this."

"I'm not, I promise," Cyrus responded, and he meant it. "I just want to take a look."

With that, Cyrus began to walk towards the small shard of ruby scepter on the ground. The closer he got to it, the more shockingly painful his headache became. The blinding sensation started when he was a few feet away from the fragment, and at two feet his muscles began to contort again. At about one foot away, his hands clenched into immovable fists and his limbs began to squeeze inwards like he was a sponge being wrung out. He lost all control of his body and his eyes forced themselves shut from the blinding pressure.

Suddenly he was hit in the face with what felt like a battering ram, and he attempted to take a deep breath, only to choke on an excessive amount of water. Another enormous hit to the face knocked him backwards and he realized they were in fact waves crashing around him. He reached out his hands and found that he could extend his arms again, but he still couldn't see from the stinging salt water. He turned his head away as a third wave smashed into him, and he forced his eyes open. It was dark, extremely dark. A glance up at the sky told him it wasn't his vision that was failing him, as an absolute symphony of stars illuminated the cloudless night.

But Cyrus's panic was setting in quick. He turned several times in the water and realized there were no identifying landmarks of any kind, and in fact he had no idea which direction the door had just deposited him through. In every direction, there was nothing but endless, dark ocean. He started breathing extremely fast, to the point of risking hyperventilating. He swam one direction a couple strokes, then another for a couple strokes.

"YDORO!" Cyrus yelled, although he knew that was pointless.

He had to calm down. He eased onto his back and forced himself to look up at the stars. He breathed. In and out. In and out. It worked. He could feel the panic receding and his sense returning. The door couldn't be very far. In fact, the waves and current were clearly taking him in one direction, which meant the door had to be the opposite way, back the way he had drifted from.

He rotated himself back onto his stomach and began swift, intentional strokes against the current. One stroke. Two strokes. Three strokes. And then he felt it. That familiar clenching of his jaw and contorting of his muscles. From this side of the door, it was absolutely excruciating. He tried with all his might to continue swimming forward, but it became impossible once his joints seized up and he lost his vision once again. Luckily, it seemed the door had already grabbed ahold of him, and in another instant he felt himself fall hard against the wood floor of his home in Easttown.

Cyrus gagged and spit a significant amount of ocean water onto the ground, choking and shaking his head as he attempted to open his eyes.

"My King!" came Ydoro's panicked voice. "I thought I was going to have to follow you! Are you okay?"

Cyrus opened his eyes and blinked away the saltwater tears before looking around the room. He had made it back. "I was in the ocean," Cyrus coughed.

"I wondered that," Ydoro exclaimed, "water started dribbling around the fragment on the ground, like it was leaking almost."

Cyrus looked down at it, but of course water was pooled all around it now from his sudden, wet return. He also realized he was no longer feeling any effects from the shard. He reached out his hand and held it an inch away from the tiny piece, but nothing happened. It seemed the door had closed from this world, just as Dalton said it would. He gave it a small flick with his finger, sending it to the other end of the room, and to his surprise, the piece began vibrating again and he could instantly feel the pressure from the door return. When the shard came to rest near the far wall, it began spewing out tiny little bits of debris; dirt and grass, along with some leaves.

Cyrus arched his eyebrows, thinking of the implications of what he was seeing. The debris being strewn about the floor around the shard was dry, suggesting the door in the connected world had moved... and moved significantly. Cyrus had the sudden impulse to test his theory one more time. He looked at Ydoro, who apparently recognized his intention and immediately began shaking his head again. But Cyrus's adrenaline was running high and he had already made up his mind.

Cyrus strode purposefully towards the shard, feeling the pressure in his head intensify and his muscles seize up once again. With his eyes squeezed shut from the pain, he stumbled forward blindly and tripped over his own feet, slamming down hard on his hands. Through his clenched fists, he could feel grass in place of the wood floor of his house. He crawled on his hands and knees, awkwardly so with his muscles still contracting painfully, until the pressure in his sinuses began to lessen. Slowly, he opened his eyes and looked up to observe his surroundings.

The first thing he noticed was that it was dark, again. But he was on solid ground this time. A quick scan of the area told Cyrus he was somewhere on a hillside, away from any cities or landmarks. Few trees dotted the landscape, leading Cyrus to believe he was possibly at a higher elevation. Otherwise, there was very little to see in the moonlight, but his theory was confirmed. By him flicking the scepter fragment a few feet back in the Kingdom, the corresponding door in this alternate world moved drastically, possibly dozens or even hundreds of miles.

Cyrus nodded his head in grim satisfaction before turning back the way he had come, wanting to be mindful of Ydoro's free-running panic back in the Kingdom. The familiar blinding headache and constricting muscles accompanied each step forward until he heard his footfalls echo off the wood floor. It was a few more steps until he could open his eyes again and see he was back in his living quarters in the Kingdom, Ydoro by his side.

A few moments silence followed his return. Ydoro kept shooting glances at him as though worried he would suddenly travel through a third time. But Cyrus had no intention of leaving again at the moment. He was satisfied with the results of his experiment.

"It moved," Cyrus grunted simply, guessing Ydoro would need no further explanation than that.

Finally, Ydoro spoke. "So that's how we got here. We were unfortunate enough to happen across one of these doors, unknowingly left open."

"Exactly," Cyrus exclaimed in a far more excitable fashion than Ydoro seemed to be feeling. "For you and your dad, it was happenstance, but not for our team. Dalton said when a piece is broken off, it initially creates a vacuum in both directions, pulling towards both worlds simultaneously. Once it 'equalizes', the door from *this* world closes... but the door in the outside world stays open. Indefinitely I guess."

"And that's why we can't feel that pull anymore from where we're standing," Ydoro said softly.

"Right, from this side at least," Cyrus answered.

He walked over to the small fragment, sitting along the far wall, tentatively bent down and touched it with his finger. Nothing happened. Slowly, he prodded it, and it rolled over once. Unlike the previous time, it did not start sputtering and vibrating when moved. It seemed the door had finally closed. Cyrus closed his hand around the shard and lifted it up, examining the rich, ruby stone in the light. His initial excitement was beginning to wane. A disheartening thought was starting to occur to him.

"Months back," Cyrus began slowly, "when the door that brought us here first opened, it created the vacuum that Dalton described, and that was strong enough to violently pull a cargo ship off its bearings. But it got stuck, lodged itself on some rocks, and that bought it just enough time for the vacuum to level out. It stopped pulling so forcefully... but the door was still there." Cyrus took a deep, bracing breath before finishing his thought to its crushing conclusion. "And the door would have stayed there, unnoticed, except that I had to rush out onto the ocean to investigate." He gave a humorless laugh as he remembered the disappearing seagulls they witnessed from the ship and how important they had seemed at the time. Cyrus continued on softly, allowing the revelations to come out in an almost monotone dribble, talking more to himself now than Ydoro. "We were brought to the Fire Fields, which means a shard of the scepters was broken off in the Fire Fields. Could have been a tiny piece, something that would pass out of all notice and care. And when we arrived, all it would have taken was one of us moving that little shard, kicking it by accident, who knows. That's why the other dinghy didn't come through after us. The door never closed, it just moved. Possibly hundreds of miles. To another speck of ocean probably, where another unlucky father and son will one day happen across it."

Once Cyrus had talked himself into silence, Ydoro said quietly, "You can't blame yourself. You didn't know. None of us knew."

Cyrus shook his head to clear the thoughts from his mind. Ydoro was right, there was no point dwelling on what-ifs.

"But I think you've figured it out," Ydoro continued supportively, "a while back, you had asked me what happened in the Kingdom three days prior to your arrival here, do you remember?"

Cyrus thought a moment before answering. He did remember. "You said there was a man who had challenged Mora."

"That's right," Ydoro said with a nod of his head, "and the challenger had confronted King Mora in the Fire Fields… and fought him with a spear."

Everything suddenly clicked into place for Cyrus. "A fragment was broken off during their fight, it must have been. In this world they didn't even notice, but in our world it created an anomaly… opened a door for us to fall through."

Ydoro looked extremely hesitant to ask his next question, as though afraid to hear the answer. "Does this mean you're leaving? Going home?"

Cyrus sighed deeply as an excited yell echoed from somewhere outside. He looked down at the small ruby fragment in his hand and turned it over. "I wish I could. But that's not my world we saw. That's just one of many simultaneously existing worlds. We have no way of knowing where or even when that is. I worry my own world is probably entirely lost."

"You don't know that," Ydoro insisted, "you've just made a major stride in understanding this place. Who knows what the future will bring."

Cyrus nodded his head appreciatively but was becoming distracted by the continuing yells outside. With a sudden drop in his stomach, he realized the yells weren't *excited* at all, they were panicked. Ydoro seemed to be coming to the same conclusion because his brow began to furrow in concern. Cyrus absent-mindedly put the shard into the pocket of his pants and began to move cautiously towards the front door. There were now unmistakable sounds of people running and screaming in the streets outside. As they listened, the shouting began to swell to a deafening level as though a wave of fear and chaos were descending on the little canvas-covered dwelling they were in. Something was coming.

**CHAPTER FIFTY-THREE**

# THE KING OF THE PAST

The situation had spiraled out of Nel's control, and she felt powerlessly swept along with it, like a branch caught in the current of a river. It was true that Alec had given explicit instructions to Irias to present a show of strength to the East, but this seemed like a bridge too far. Not only was Nel unsure that Alec would approve of Irias's improvisation, she worried he would find himself bound on a certain path if things played out wrong. As Nel looked sideways at Irias's ancient, crinkled face marching forward with a hungry resolve etched in its features, she knew he wasn't doing this for Alec. He had gotten a small taste of his long-lost power, that which had been so precious to him in his prime, and it had consumed him without mercy. He would now look to prove his worth at all costs.

The trouble started once they reached the border of their Western Kingdom and came face to face with a rowdy blockade of Easttowners. The journey to the border had been uneventful, if slightly awkward. Irias and Nel had walked side by side in silence with their ten-person brigade marching behind them. Nel had nothing of importance to say to Irias and still slightly resented being sent on the mission in the first place. This was Irias's moment to show his merit to Alec, but Nel had nothing to prove. As it would turn out, the silent journey would be vastly preferable to what was coming.

The raucous band of Easterners spotted them coming down the trade road and immediately began jeering and slinging insults at them. They appeared to delight in the fact that the West was needing to send reinforcements and, rather than being intimidated by their approach, it seemed they took it as a sign of unease from the Temple. Five Western guards had already been stationed at the border, and with the addition of Irias's garrison, they outnumbered the East. Still, it quickly became apparent that Irias had expected a different reaction. Someone from the crowd called out, "Better go back the way you came, old man!", while another cried, "Are you supposed to scare us?" It was clear that not a one of them recognized their old dictator.

The Western blockade parted respectfully, allowing Irias to stride forward and come to a halt in front of the eight or so Easttowners. He squared himself up importantly and announced in the strongest voice he could manage, "In the name of the King…"

But he was cut off by a loud "Oooo," from someone in the crowd.

"The Western king has something to say," laughed another.

Irias's face twisted in fury. "You will respect the authority of…"

He was cut off again by someone shouting, "Your authority ends on that side of the border."

"Are you lost?" someone cackled in mock-concern.

"You will remember your place," Irias announced in a dangerous growl. "I am King Iri…"

"I think we know our place just fine!" someone yelled in unashamed glee. "It's right here, between you and *our* Kingdom."

Irias looked like he had just been slapped. The fact that no one from the East seemed to recognize him at all must have been gnawing at him, but then to be cut off just as he attempted to reveal himself appeared to be more than he could handle. Shaking with indignation, he drew himself up to his full, but still unsubstantial, height and stepped forward with bulging, dangerous eyes. "Do you have any idea…"

But Irias had stepped over the dividing line between the two Kingdoms and the reaction was instantaneous. The three Easterners closest to the front shoved Irias hard in the chest and, taken off-guard, he stumbled backwards and tripped on the hem of his robes. It caused him to fall sideways awkwardly, and he ended up clutching onto one of his infantrymen's arms to stop himself from going to the ground. The Easterners did not pursue him across the border, but they all guffawed loudly at his ungraceful stumble. Once he had regained his footing, Irias looked beside himself with rage.

"How dare you touch me!" Irias screamed, his usually gravelly voice producing a sound almost akin to a tearing noise. Turning to the men behind him, he exclaimed, "Seize them!"

But the men did not obey his orders at once. They looked sideways at each other as though questioning whether they were in fact permitted to cross the Kingdom border. This drew loud laughs from the Eastern company who released another onslaught of fresh jeers. Irias's eyes were practically popping out of his skull as his face turned a deep shade of red. "Seize them!" he screamed again.

Nel knew that the guards had been instructed to obey any of Irias's commands and it seemed their initial hesitation had passed. Two of the garrison stepped forward, evidently with the intention of grabbing the three men who had pushed Irias, but the entire Eastern company stepped forward in unison, no longer laughing.

The nearest Easttowner spoke up, "You take one more step and you will be in the Eastern Kingdom... and subject to our laws. You've already exhausted your one warning, the next one won't be so gentle."

The two guards looked to Irias for instruction, who beckoned them forward impatiently, hate etched in every line on his face. The forwardmost guard nodded, unsheathed his machete, and stepped forward. His boot had barely touched the ground when the Easttown man in the front of the group pulled a small kitchen knife from his sleeve and stabbed it upwards into the fleshy area under the guard's chin. There was a soft crunching sound as the blade penetrated cartilage, tissue, and bone, leaving the guard staring dumbfounded as blood, a shockingly small amount, trickled down his neck. His eyes slowly unfocused and, as the Easttown man wrenched the knife free, he slumped forward into a shapeless heap on the ground.

It seemed to take a moment for Irias to register what had happened, but as he stared down at the motionless mass in front of him, his fury finally broke.

"Kill them!" Irias barked, all pretense of collected resolve gone.

This time, the guards did not need a second telling. They had spurred into action upon seeing their fallen comrade, unsheathing their own blades and preparing for combat. It was barely the blink of an eye before the road had become a frenzied melee, with blades flashing and blood spraying in every direction. It wasn't an evenly matched fight, with the Western garrison outnumbering the East almost two to one and their weapons being far superior. Within a matter of seconds, the Western guards had cut down five of the eight Easttowners, leaving the final three scattering into the trees on either side of the road.

As the three sets of running footsteps faded away, Irias looked around himself, surveying the carnage and breathing heavily as though he himself had been fighting. His eyes still had that wide, slightly mad look, but he appeared to be regaining his composure.

With his face settling into a disgusted grimace, Irias finally said to his fighters, "We're following the road into Easttown."

Several of the guards opened their mouths as if to object, but it was Nel who spoke up. "Your orders were to give a show of strength at the border. Alec didn't say anything about storming the town."

"What do you think those three that escaped will do?" Irias snapped. "They're making their way into town to spin their version of what happened here. So, we can allow that, turn around and report back to the King that there was a confrontation but we have no idea the outcome, *or* we can follow through on the King's wishes and make a statement, here and now. Remind Easttown that they are still well within the reach of the Temple."

Nel hesitated. She knew this was not what Alec had intended of the mission.

Irias continued, "The King said to make an impression at the border, I plan to see that through."

"You don't think this made an impression?" Nel shot back at him, waving her hands over the bloodied bodies strewn about the road.

"We won't let the East claim this was simply a murder. They'll use that to say the King, *our* king, broke the agreement. Is that what you want? For *Alec* to have to answer for this?"

"Marching to Easttown will only make things messier," Nel insisted.

"We can't be afraid to get our hands dirty," Irias hissed, and Nel thought this was ironic considering he was doing none of the actual fighting, "when they see me in town, when they recognize me..."

"But they *don't* recognize you," Nel cut him off, "none of them. They don't remember you."

Nel had expected this to wound Irias's pride, but to her surprise, he smiled. "They will. I promise you that."

Irias turned to the garrison and ordered, "To Easttown, now."

Nel thought of arguing further, but she didn't necessarily disagree with Irias's logic. It also occurred to her that this was Irias's mission to succeed or fail at, and it was perfectly okay with her if he wanted to gamble on a bold move.

So she found herself marching down the road towards Easttown, looking sideways at Irias through the corner of her eyes and trying to deduce exactly what he was planning. He didn't speak their entire way to town, but his expression seemed to ignite with feverish ambition with each step. She didn't know what sort of display he was planning to make, but he was clearly looking for a public audience to make his *statement*. It did occur to her, and she assumed it had occurred to Irias as well, that the further into Easttown they walked, the more outnumbered they would become, but the band of 'guards' at the border had proven what they suspected all along of the East; they had no real weapons and no real fighters.

As they turned a bend in the road, the main town square came into view through a pair of enormous, lush trees. Nel had not visited Easttown when it was under Mora's rule, but it was immediately clear that things had changed drastically from those days. She had been told of a dilapidated, run-down shadow of their Western town, with laborers and farmers practically living in the streets, but what she saw before her now was an entirely different story. The village was bustling and vibrant, with people laughing and talking, working and resting. From all that she could tell as an outsider, it was thriving.

Two men pulling a large, wooden cart saw their approach and halted their progress immediately. They were clearly unarmed, laborers by the looks of them, and Nel would not have anticipated any trouble from them. Afterall, why would a down-on-his-luck worker care what happened to the town as a whole? She was therefore quite surprised when one of them spoke up and started approaching them.

"Hey! What the hell is this?"

Irias seemed to have lost his desire to verbally spar with those he clearly regarded as his inferiors, because rather than engage with the Easttown man, he simply turned to the guard on his left and gave a swift horizontal wave of his hand. The guard took his meaning and unsheathed his machete. The man barely had time to react before the guard ran his blade down the length of the Easterner's body, from shoulder to hip, as though chopping through a patch of dense underbrush. The man collapsed, sputtering and gargling blood as he died, while his friend turned tail and ran towards the town square yelling.

The streets entered a state of panic almost instantly, with people jumping over wagons and work equipment, shouting to their cohorts, and running for cover through doorways or behind buildings. No one stood to fight, just as Nel had suspected. This was a town that may be thriving on the surface but was woefully unprepared.

Irias was grinning as the chaos unfolded, the smile twisting his lined features into an abstract contortion of what a human face should look like. His eyes were wide and ravenous as he surveyed the destruction, the same way he would a feast he was about to consume. This was the King Irias of town legend. This was the King Irias of the past.

"Spread out," Irias ordered, "and I want whoever's in that house." He pointed to a centrally located home raised off the ground with a new-looking deck installed on the front of it.

The guards obeyed, with some running right, some running left, a few going around the back of the house and a few approaching the front staircase. But they had not started their ascent before the door burst open and Cyrus Dorn came charging out followed closely by a shocked-looking Ydoro. Nel had not seen Cyrus in several months and leadership clearly suited him. He wore a beard and his hair, while unkempt, framed his square-jawed features well. He looked rugged, but the Kingdom had not sapped his good looks; in fact, she recognized a bit of his old spark back in those eyes that had looked so broken down and defeated last time she saw him. Nel's first thought was that he looked powerful, without really trying to.

"You are trespassing in Easttown," Cyrus roared impressively, taking the stairs down two at a time to reach the dusty road below. "Our borders are closed to you."

But Cyrus faltered as his eyes ran across the butchered body in the street beyond, and the distraction cost him. One of Irias's guards had rounded the back of the house and managed to walk up behind Cyrus unnoticed. With a swift jab using the handle of the machete, the guard knocked into the back of Cyrus's head, causing him to pitch forward and land hard on his hands and knees. Ydoro gave a shout, but another guard seized him by the robes and pushed him towards the center of town square. Blood ran down the side of Cyrus's scalp and he shook his head dizzily, but the guard had grabbed him by the hair and was now dragging him mercilessly forward, causing him to crawl awkwardly to stop from falling.

"Cyrus Dorn," Irias announced victoriously, a wide grin still distorting his face, "the King of Easttown."

Cyrus was deposited roughly to the ground some ten feet from Irias, looking like a sacrificial lamb being offered to a predator. The remaining guards spread out, creating a sort of circular perimeter around the scene, which Nel appreciated because the Easttown residents were beginning to reappear. After their initial panic, it seemed many were electing to return and see the action for themselves, trickling back out of their homes in wide-eyed curiosity. Some seemed to be carrying stones of varying sizes as protection, causing Nel to smirk.

Cyrus blinked up at Irias through blood seeping into the side of his eye, then his gaze fell onto Nel standing beside him. His expression changed slightly as he observed her, almost with a hint of betrayal in his eyes. He scowled at her before turning his attention back to Irias and saying, "You have no authority in Easttown, and no protection. This is a breach of…"

"There seems to be a great deal of confusion," Irias cut him off, "about what this Kingdom is. You have been allowed to operate in the East undisturbed, but it seems to have given you the impression that you are self-ruling."

"Bring Alec to me!" Cyrus spat, "this is not our agreement!"

"You are a vassal of the Western Kingdom!" Irias bellowed, and murmurs from the crowd seemed to remind him that he was also addressing the town as a whole. "Did he tell you that?" he asked the gathered townsfolk. "Yes, I thought not. Perhaps he's had all of you living under the delusion that you are *his* subjects. That is not the case. Your true king resides in the Temple in the East."

"That was not the agreement!" Ydoro burst out, mimicking Cyrus's declaration. "I was there!"

The guard standing over Ydoro hit him hard in the side of the head, drawing gasps from the swelling crowd of onlookers.

"This is worse than I could have imagined," Irias said silkily, "I can't imagine the King allowing Easttown to continue operating in this manner. In fact," he looked to Nel briefly before continuing, "I think an example will have to be made."

Nel looked to Cyrus and saw realization dawning on his face. This was no longer a warning Irias had planned, it was an execution. There was an uncomfortable twinge in her own gut, and it was telling her this was a step too far. She turned to Irias with the intention of telling him so, but noticed he was not looking at Cyrus, but at Ydoro.

"Ydoro, you've served the Kingdom faithfully for many years, but you've chosen the wrong side on this one."

He gave a flick of his wrist and the guard holding Ydoro forced him down to the ground, his hands slamming onto the dirt in front of him.

"You can't!" Cyrus roared, and to everyone's surprise, he managed to wrench free of his would-be captor and throw an elbow hard into the man's jaw. His freedom was short lived, however, as three additional guards grabbed hold of him from behind and forced him back to his knees.

"I can do whatever I want," Irias responded icily in a dangerous, quiet voice, "and this is a long time coming. You've been allowed far too much latitude up until now. Must be our king's compassionate heart." He straightened himself up and grinned around at the still-growing crowd.

A voice from somewhere within the throng of onlookers suddenly rang out in disbelief, "That's King Irias."

Irias grinned more broadly, the papery skin around his mouth threatening to tear in the process. This was the moment he had been waiting for. The people finally recognized him.

Gasps from the crowd drifted around town square like a wave, and the fear from the people was instantly palpable. Mutterings of *'King Irias'* were heard sporadically, and many were shaking their heads in shock and confusion.

"I thought you might remember me," Irias said with his horrifically wide smile. He spread his arms wide as though embracing the entire village and continued, "you all have been led astray. I don't blame you, and the King does not blame you. The fault lies here, with the pretender king and of course the ever-faithful Ydoro."

He turned his merciless gaze back to Ydoro and shook his head. "It's a shame really. We could have used loyalty like yours." He looked to the guard holding Ydoro to the ground and raised his hand to give the order. "After this," he shouted to the now enormous crowd surrounding them, "put your allegiance back where it belongs and all will be forgiven. With the true king. And with me."

There was silence for a moment before a single voice finally rang out from the circle of onlookers in a strong declaration, *"My King."* It was a clear statement of fealty. Irias closed his eyes with a smile, savoring the moment. *"My King,"* echoed more voices, with many raising their fists to their chests in a way Nel thought reminiscent of a Roman salute. Irias's smile stretched broadly once again, a look of utter victory plastered across his face. Seeing the loyalty Irias was able to inspire so suddenly, Nel finally realized how dangerous the man before her truly was. Alec had made a vast miscalculation in underestimating him, and it looked as though he would now pay the consequences.

As the swell of *"My King"* swept its way around the gathered crowd, and more and more people raised their fists to their chests, Nel looked around apprehensively, suddenly feeling as though she were surrounded by people not loyal to Alec, but loyal to Irias.

Irias's hand remained poised, the chant seeming to have granted Ydoro a brief reprieve from his execution. The king of the past raised his smiling face, tilting it back as though listening to a symphony play a favorite piece of classical music. Except something was wrong. Nel noticed it before he did. The crowd was not saluting Irias. Its eyes were turned entirely to Cyrus, still held on his knees by the three guards. Cyrus was beginning to notice as well. He looked around in wonder from beneath his curtain of hanging, bloodied hair; clearly as surprised by their response as Nel was.

"My King," someone from the crowd called out, "We await your orders."

Irias continued to grin up at the sky, clearly still unaware that they were not speaking to him.

"You heard them," Cyrus said, and the smile on Irias's face finally faltered. He lowered his head slowly and began to scan the faces around him, noticing for the first time that they all wore expressions not of fear, but of hate. Of loathing. At long last, his eyes landed on Cyrus, who had the slightest hint of his own smile playing at the corner of his mouth. Irias's face no longer looked remotely human. The muscles in his hollowed cheeks hung slack, drawing his features downward into a practically demonic scowl as he bore into Cyrus's eyes.

Cyrus stared back for a long moment before he finally spoke, "You have one last chance. Go back the way you came and never return."

Irias's eye twitched compulsively but he seemed to be lost for words.

Then Cyrus spoke again. "Actually, I take that back. You came into our home, killed our people. No more second chances for you." Cyrus turned his head slightly to address the crowd, "Easttown! You remember your old king!" His eyes flicked back to Irias for just a moment before he said, "Do what you want with him."

Irias returned Cyrus's stare in disbelief, but as he looked around the crowd and saw the rocks in their hands, he smiled. "Is this supposed to scare me? A band of rebels brandishing rocks? This is exactly…"

But what exactly it was never became clear. A stone the size of an apple smashed into Irias's jaw, breaking it with a damp cracking noise. His eyes blazed with uncomprehending fury as blood slowly dripped from the side of his lips, but when he tried talking again, it appeared that he could not get his mouth to reopen. King Irias had spoken his final word.

Irias spun to give his guards non-verbal orders, but the Easttown audience had begun to swarm forward like bees protecting their hive. The guards holding Cyrus and Ydoro prone gave futile swings with their machetes, but the Easterners rocks found their targets first.

Nel dropped to the ground as the street erupted in violence. The people were taking no notice of her as they descended on the guards, disarming them easily and beating them down onto the road. Irias still stood, spinning dumbfounded in a circle as though looking for a weakness he could exploit. He was making muffled, angry gurgling noises like he was still trying to speak. His eyes were looking more and more desperate, almost as though he thought he could still correct the situation, if only he could talk. And then another rock, hurled from off to his right, crashed into the side of his head and he seemed to lose the ability to hold his arms upright. His eyes were starting to glaze and he was standing at an awkward angle, still stumbling in an odd circle. A final rock, this one much larger and brandished by a woman with arms the size of small trees, was brought down on his head from above, and it was over for him. His skull caved in, and his ancient skin became slack and shapeless as his lifeless body crumpled onto the dirt.

Nel stayed on her hands and knees and attempted to crawl away through the mob. She took countless knees to the head as people ran over her unnoticed. Stars erupted in her eyes several times and she worried she would lose consciousness, but she had to keep moving. If she could only get to the edge of town square, she could run for the border. Once she was back west, she would be safe, and Alec would reign fire down on Easttown for this outrage. But she had to get back to tell him.

Through the wild, pulsating sea of angry voices, shouts began to sound out over the rest. "Where's the girl?" "She was right there?" "Find her!"

Nel's heart dropped and she continued her scramble forward. The crowd was so dense that no one was feeling her push past them on the ground. She had to be nearing the edge of the mob. And then someone finally screamed the words she had been dreading.

"She's here! She's here!"

The voice was close, right above her, and she immediately felt hands grasping at her and boots kicking and stomping. She threw her arms up to her head to cover it, waiting for a rock to come crashing down and end her life.

"Stop!" called out a strong, authoritative voice. "Don't touch her!"

The mob around her did as they were told, pushing her into the dirt to hold her in place, but they stopped their attack.

The voice, closer this time, said, "Get her up, stand her up."

The Easttowners were not gentle as they scraped her from the ground. She was pulled roughly to her knees, and then to her feet, but infinite hands held onto her unnecessarily, as if she could possibly run through the dense crowd.

Through dust and dirt in her eyes, she blinked painfully to see Cyrus standing before her, blood still dampening his hair and the side of his forehead, but his eyes burning with anger. He was looking at her with an expression of utmost disgust.

He surveyed her for what felt like an eternity, and several times Nel thought he was going to say something, but he didn't. When he finally did speak, it was with a disappointed shake of his head. "I wish I could say I expected better from you."

Staring into Cyrus's pompous, disapproving eyes, Nel's temper boiled violently in her chest. Anger, even retaliation from him would be understood, but how dare he look down on her. How dare he judge her. She felt something within her uncoiling, hot and sickly and volatile. She erupted at him, lashing out with every bit of strength she had. She managed to sink one blow to the face before she was restrained once again, but it didn't stop her from raging forward with her entire body: screaming and spitting and baring her teeth like a wild animal.

"He'll destroy you for this!" Nel shrieked, "every single one of you! You think he'll let this stand? Easttown is finished! There will be nowhere left to hide from him!"

To Nel's fury, Cyrus remained calm, and his voice never raised above a conversational pitch. He looked around briefly at his mob and replied, "Does it look like we need to hide from him?"

Nel screamed and released another attempted onslaught, but she was held back by dozens of hands that were starting to pull her deeper into the crowd, away from Cyrus.

Cyrus turned and spoke loudly to the group, "Annica and Cain are manning the border near the Fire Fields. I need one of you to run to them now."

A young man stepped forward at once and announced, "I can go, my King."

Cyrus nodded and said, "Tell them what happened here, and give a message to the Temple guards at the border to be carried west to the King. The message is this: Nelida Yore is being held in Easttown. The King is to send an emissary to the Fire Fields by midday tomorrow with Jack Viana. This is not negotiable. If he does not meet my terms, he will never see her again."

"Yes, my King," the young man said with a swift nod of his head. He turned, cut through the crowd and was off.

"You think he'll trade you Jack?" Nel sneered, "you don't know him very well!"

Cyrus turned back to look at her. "Lock her up. Feed her, but keep a guard on her every second, day and night." He walked closer to her and spoke more softly, "And Nel, I *know* he'll trade me Jack."

With that, Cyrus spun on his heel and walked back through the crowd, which parted respectfully to let him pass.

**CHAPTER FIFTY-FOUR**

# THE NEUTRAL TERRITORY

The day ended as fittingly as one would expect; with a blood-red sunset bathing the earth in scarlet brilliance for several minutes before receding into the deep maroons of twilight. It had been a red day, a day of loss, but also a day of hope, in the strangest of ways. Cyrus walked the streets of Easttown with a renewed sense of vigor and purpose, but he found himself feeling almost guilty for having received such a show of what he considered unearned loyalty. He didn't know what he had done to inspire such devotion from the Easttown residents, but he certainly now felt a significant weight on his shoulders to lead them through these turbulent times.

Following the death of Irias, the atmosphere in town had changed dramatically. The main street always had a certain hustle and bustle about it, but now it seemed to have taken on a more militant energy. These people weren't fighters, or at least they had no combat training like their Western brethren, but they were incredible workers and, as Irias had discovered, a force to be reckoned with. Annica and Cain had returned from the Fire Fields not long after the violence in town square had ended, furious at having missed out on the action. Annica insisted that, had she been in town at the time, the situation would never have gotten as far as it had. Cyrus didn't kid himself into thinking she was referring to finding a diplomatic solution. She appeared angry that the crowd had even allowed Cyrus to be dragged from his home in the first place, but he had trouble feeling anything but grateful. The town had risen up when he needed them most, and while he appreciated Annica's enthusiastic commitment to seeing him protected, he felt the people had more than demonstrated their loyalty.

Ydoro had wanted to have the bodies of their fallen enemies buried, or at the very least burned, but he was overruled by the majority of the townsfolk, who seemed to feel they did not deserve such a send-off. In the end, and against Cyrus's gentle suggestions to the contrary, the bodies had been gathered up, carted to the Fire Fields, and dumped unceremoniously into the middle of the neutral territory. "Let the animals take 'em," Cain had said gruffly, and Cyrus wasn't sure if he had been referring to the local wildlife or the Westtown guards.

Cyrus's warnings to keep Nel heavily guarded did not fall on deaf ears. She had been tied up against a post outside one of the larger homes along the main thoroughfare, the thought being that there would be constant eyes on her in such a public space. That of course did not preclude the necessity for guards, and two person shifts had been organized. She had been fed and well cared for, just as Cyrus had insisted, but the people of Easttown were not hiding their disgust with her. It would only be for one night, and then, with a little luck, she would be swapped for Jack and no longer the East's problem. Cyrus remained convinced that Alec would agree to the trade. By this time, he would have received his brother's message, and Cyrus could only imagine him, wild with rage, pacing his quarters and weighing his options. But he no longer had either of his advisors, and Cyrus knew full well his feelings for Nel. Alec was nothing if not emotional; he wouldn't do anything that would put Nel at further risk, and Jack was of no more use to him.

Cyrus prowled the darkening street, watching as the shadows grew long and the sky grew dim. He didn't know exactly where he was going or what he was intending, only that he felt the people needed to see him at the moment. He felt a strong desire to be doing something, *anything*, for the Easttowners, and while it was limited what he could actually do in the here and now, with the sun going down, he was sure that hiding in his house was not an option. Besides, there was something in the air, a tension of sorts. While one might expect there to be a level of tension following a traumatic afternoon, this was not that sort of tension. This was more of a taught, brittle tension; like a branch under immense pressure, about to crack. People walking by Cyrus in the streets now greeted him every time with their newly adopted salute; a fist thumped to their chest and a swift dip of their head. *"My King,"* always accompanied the gesture. It was nothing new for passersby to acknowledge him by title, but it now felt like a bit more than simply a sign of respect. It now felt militarized somehow, and Cyrus wasn't sure how comfortable it made him.

His wandering feet carried him to one of the newly developed roads extending up into the foothills, and several figures came into view ahead of him, slumped in the shadows of their front door and bent low, working on something. As he approached, Annica looked up and grinned. *"My King,"* she exclaimed with a quick salute, and her team all followed suit. Cain's bulky frame was missing from her usual band and Cyrus suspected he was manning the border near the Fire Fields again.

"What are we working on?" Cyrus asked with a wry smile. For some reason, it felt especially odd having someone as indomitable as Annica addressing him as *My King*.

She held up a knife and a long, smooth branch, the tip of which had been whittled into a wickedly sharp point. "Weapons," she answered simply.

Cyrus raised his eyebrows and nodded his head but didn't respond.

"We're going to be needing them in the days to come," Annica continued, "mark my words."

"You think so?" Cyrus asked, but in his gut he knew she was right. Even if the trade the following day were to go smoothly and things were to return to their recent normal, he had a sense that things had been put into motion that could not be undone. It felt like they were on a train that had reached critical speed, and nothing and no one could stop it now.

Annica was nodding her head as she watched Cyrus's face, as though she knew the conclusion he was arriving at and wanted him to know he was right. "Our time of peace is over," Annica said softly, almost comfortingly. "We weren't ready today, but now we will be. They have no idea what strength the East has. They will, though."

"Annica," Cyrus said bracingly, "we're not starting a war with the West."

Annica smiled gently and looked down at her spear tip again. "I mean no disrespect, my King, but this is beyond you. And it's so very important that you understand that. You are our king, and you've earned that place. You gave us a chance that we hadn't been given in a long time. But know that some of these cuts run too deep for you to heal."

Cyrus contemplated what she had said and thoughtfully nodded his head. He didn't want to encourage further violence, but she was right. This went beyond him. Looking around, he noticed that they were not just making spears. They also appeared to be carving up stones into various brutal shapes, many ending up hewn into jagged, angry blades. He also recognized a small pile of the handheld bolt-firing weapons they had used during his rescue from the West.

"Just promise me these are only precautionary," Cyrus said, eying the growing stacks of weapons with unease.

"Precautionary," Annica repeated, "but today, they thought our doors were open to them. These will make them reconsider the type of welcome they'll receive the next time they march into town unannounced."

Cyrus nodded, not entirely convinced by her words. "I want you with me tomorrow," he said, and Annica looked up from her carving. "You care for Jack, as I do. I need help making sure things go according to plan. He can't end up as collateral damage if things go sideways."

Annica assessed him for a long moment before finally nodding her head. "I won't let anything happen to him. That's my priority."

Cyrus searched her eyes and believed her. He didn't quite know what her relationship was with Jack, but he could tell how much she cared for him. That was all Cyrus needed to know.

He left the group shortly after, wandering back through the now dark town and squinting whenever he passed the occasional blazing torch along one of the buildings. He caught Nel, still tied to her post, leering at him ominously from the shadows behind her two guards. She wore an expression of stony resolve, still punctuated by a trace of her ever-present smirk. Cyrus considered trying to talk to her, now that the action was long over and the crowd wasn't surrounding them, but he decided better of it. He honestly could not think of a single thing to say to her.

When he finally made his way back to his home, he found himself lying awake in bed, staring up at the canvas ceiling with his mind reeling. It seemed like ages ago that he and Ydoro were opening *windows* and *doors* in this very room, but it was only hours earlier. And tomorrow was shaping up to be just as eventful. He thought it extremely unlikely he would be able to quiet his anxiety enough to actually sleep, but his exhaustion was finally catching up to him, and he drifted off almost instantly. He slept all the way through the night.

*****

The new day rose bright and shining, but the darkness from the previous afternoon's events had certainly carried over, and Cyrus could still feel it in the town, like a stain on its very soul. He toiled the morning away pacing along the streets, running over scenarios of the prisoner swap in his head, and consulting with Ydoro. It was decided that Annica and Ydoro would accompany Cyrus and Nel to the neutral territory, while Cain and a handful of his best fighters would already be stationed at the exchange point. Cyrus did not expect Alec to come personally, but he could not help dreading the thought of coming face to face with his brother again. He had not seen him since the day the Kingdom was split, and that had been months ago, exactly how many he wasn't sure. In his absence, the Alec he had known had come to be replaced in his mind with a figure of dread; an obscured, shadowy phantom haunting him from the past. It felt like another life that he and his brother worked together, met for drinks together, visited each other's houses, and participated in each other's lives. Reflecting on their relationship now, it was hard to imagine a time when they had been close. He didn't want to see

Alec, especially after what had happened the day prior, but there was a small part of him that longed for that confrontation. He was beyond wanting to reason with his brother, but his feelings had been bottling up and brewing since their last exchange. What he really wanted to do was scream at him; shake him back to reality, but in his heart he knew that was futile. When their paths did inevitably cross again, he doubted whether their meeting would be even that civil.

As the morning groaned slowly forward and midday finally approached, Cyrus and Ydoro met outside his house and exchanged brief looks of apprehension before striding across the main square towards the post where Nel was still tied. Cyrus, in a first for him, was clutching the scepter firmly in one hand. He had of course carried it once before when he was impersonating Alec, but this was the first time he carried it for himself. It was partly out of caution for the safety of the artifact, which he was only beginning to understand the importance of, but it was also to make a statement. As ridiculous as he thought Alec was when he strode around with his scepter and billowing robes, it made a statement to the people. Cyrus was learning to respect the significance of perception, and after the previous day, he felt strongly that he needed to present a counter to Alec's *'King of the West'*. Annica was already on guard duty, standing with one of her freshly made spears in hand and a machete hanging from her belt. As their boots crunched over the loose dirt of the road and kicked up little clouds of yellowish dust, Nel looked up from her knees wearing a look of unbridled hatred.

"The *King* has arrived," Nel hissed sarcastically, although some of her spirit seemed to have burnt out over the course of the night. While the decision to have her tied to an outdoor post appeared crude and unnecessarily hostile in some people's eyes, namely Ydoro's, it had been a mild evening and she had been made as comfortable as one could be under such conditions. And the truth was, Cyrus did not trust her in anyone's home.

"It's time to go," Cyrus said to her simply.

Nel looked at the scepter in his hand and smiled broadly. "Wow, never thought I'd see the day. The great Cyrus Dorn trying to emulate his baby brother."

Annica stepped forward and placed her newly sharpened spear tip against Nel's throat. "Take care how you speak to the King," she growled menacingly.

"It's okay Annica," Cyrus insisted, softly but firmly. "She's not going to be our problem anymore. Get her untied."

It was a bit of a production loosening the many knots holding Nel in place, but once she was freed, she stood, slightly shakily, still with a wrapping of rope around her chest, binding her hands, and trailing behind her as a tether. Annica held the end of the lead, a scowl of determination on her face.

"Don't try anything," Cyrus warned Nel, "we're taking you back to where you came from. It's a better deal than you could have hoped for after the destruction you caused yesterday."

"You don't scare me," Nel sneered.

"Letting this exchange go smoothly is in your own self-interest," Cyrus said, "and seeing after your own interests is what you're best at. It's a no brainer, even for you."

Nel never dropped her smirk, but she didn't respond. Perhaps she recognized the truth in his words, or more likely she had simply exhausted her clever retorts. Either way, the group began the trek towards the Fire Fields in relative silence, making for an awkward, yet peaceful, journey. It didn't last long, however, for just as Cyrus's mind began running over potential scenarios again, Nel spoke up as though reading his thoughts.

"He's not coming, ya know," she said, picking up her pace just slightly to match his stride. Annica readjusted her grip on the tether but didn't stop her.

"I'm not expecting him to," Cyrus responded flatly. "I don't care about him, I'm only here to trade for Jack."

"I actually believe that," Nel said with a grin, "which is funny because you think you're the noble one. You think you're so much better than Alec, yet you can forget him like nothing. Your own brother."

"I'm not getting into this, Nel," Cyrus replied, "or perhaps you've forgotten the military brigade he sent to my people yesterday."

"Your people," Nel laughed, "coming from the man who didn't want any part of this. You just can't stand being in your brother's shadow. You'll do anything you can to stop him."

Cyrus came to a halt and turned to face Nel, "I didn't ask for this. Alec has forced my hand by letting this power go to his head and now he's consumed by it. What your angle in all of this is I may never know... but you're damn right I'll do anything I can to stop him."

Nel looked momentarily taken aback by Cyrus's sudden outburst, but her face split into a broad smile once he'd finished and she nodded her head in apparent satisfaction. "There's a little of that Dorn fire coming out. It should make for an interesting day when the two of you finally meet again."

Cyrus blinked, surprising even himself to hear the words spoken out loud that he had been feeling for the last few months. Ydoro was watching him apprehensively, but not without a look of mild pride on his face. He didn't like that Nel had managed to rile him up, however he didn't regret what he had said. It felt almost relieving to say it out loud.

Cyrus turned away from her and began walking again, more anxious than ever to get Nel out of the East. The remainder of the journey passed in silence, and with a final turn of the road, they entered the Fire Fields, glowing mutely in the harsh afternoon sun. Cain and a force of some ten fighters paced along the eastern edge of the field, and an opposing group of similar size prowled the west. But there was no sign of Jack. Cyrus's heart dropped uncomfortably as he scanned the area in vain.

Cain nodded at their approach and gave Cyrus the new fist-to-chest salute. The rest of the company followed suit.

"No sign of Jack?" Cyrus asked.

"Nothing yet," Cain reported.

Unlike the trade road where there was a clear dividing line between the two Kingdoms, the entirety of the Fire Fields was designated neutral territory. That meant Eastern and Western delegates could roam the open space freely. Even so, rather than form up nose to nose as had been done on the road, the legions seemed content patrolling the outer perimeters of their respective sides in ominous fashion, shooting the occasional hostile glance at the opposing party.  The East, for its part, was better armed than the West; an unusual first.  The West carried their usual machetes, but the East now bore an assortment of Annica's freshly made spears, a few bolt-firing weapons, stone-carved daggers, and more.

Upon seeing Cyrus, Nel, and their company arrive, the Western guards seemed to tense up a bit from across the field, and a few of them even moved their hands to the blades on their belts, but Cain put a quick stop to further escalation by casually adjusting his grip on the bolt launcher hanging from his belt.

Cyrus sidled over to Cain and muttered quietly, "If they were to rush us…"

"I'd love it if they tried," Cain growled in an almost longing voice.

"Is this them?" Annica called out, and Cyrus looked up.

From across the clearing, emerging slowly from the treeline, came a small brigade of about eight individuals.  The majority seemed to be guards with their trademark machetes swinging from their belts, but the bulky, lumbering leader appeared to be Bohrman, and to his right, tied in a manner not dissimilar to Nel, was Jack.

He looked to be okay, apart from being tied up.  Cyrus had worried what condition he would be in, but as he strode forward, he looked strong.  In fact, the closer he approached, the more Cyrus felt he looked *too* strong considering what he had been through.  That was when Cyrus noticed his hands, *both of them*, tied out in front of him around the wrists.  His heart leapt momentarily, but his mouth quickly melted into a grimace as he realized what must have happened.  It had all been a ploy.  Alec had sent Cyrus the hand hoping for a reaction, knowing full well that he would assume it belonged to Jack.  It meant that Alec was trying to push a conflict.

As Bohrman labored forward, the guards already in the field formed up behind him, and they marched closer and closer.  They were about ten feet away when Cain stopped them.

"That's far enough," Cain commanded, and the entire company halted.  Cyrus looked at Jack, who gave him a quick wink and a weak smile.

"What is this?" Bohrman asked in annoyance, assessing Nel. "Where's the rest of our men?"

"After the stunt they pulled?" Cain barked, "you must be joking. The deal was for the girl."

Bohrman looked around at the Eastern militants as though sizing them up. "We were told we were escorting a company of twelve back to the Temple. Where are they?"

Cain glanced sideways at Cyrus, looking for guidance on how best to answer. Cyrus decided to step forward and speak himself.

"They're dead," he announced in a tone of simplistic finality. "They crossed our borders in violation of our agreement. The King of the West is lucky to be getting one back." He somehow couldn't bring himself to say his brother's name at the moment.

"Dead?" Bohrman repeated, looking appalled. "The King won't stand for…"

"As I said," Cyrus cut him off, "you're lucky to be getting one back. But it comes with a warning. If a Western militant is ever caught this side of the border again, they will be killed on sight."

Bohrman opened and shut his mouth several times, seemingly unable to form his thoughts into a sentence. Cyrus was happy to see him squirm. "This is… you can't… how dare you."

"We'll be taking Jack now," Cyrus announced in a clear, authoritative voice. He wasn't always comfortable giving orders as king, but this was one he had no intention of having questioned.

Bohrman's eyes widened, seemingly gaping at being talked to in such a manner. "The King will not stand for this," he finally said, his moustache quivering. "This is not what was agreed upon."

"The deal is non-negotiable," Cyrus said firmly.

Bohrman shook his head and began to turn away, "The King will take it under advisement. But I can't agree to this." He began to motion to the guards holding Jack, indicating that they escort him back the way they had come.

Cyrus's heart dropped and he stepped forward. "Stop," he bellowed.

Bohrman glanced briefly over his shoulder, "If you have nothing further to offer..." But it was the subtle hint of a smirk playing at the edge of his lips that set Cyrus off.

Cyrus turned to Cain and his men. "Jack is not to move from this field," he commanded, "under no circumstances are you to allow him taken from here, that's an order."

Bohrman's jaw fell slack in surprise, but Cain grinned and nodded his head. He slowly drew the bolt-launcher from his belt. "You heard him," he said to his brigade, all of whom readied their various weapons.

"This is not what I want," Cyrus said to Bohrman, who was still turned half-sideways, stopped midway through leaving. "But Jack is coming with us. Don't force a conflict here."

Cyrus's piercing eyes were burning into Bohrman's bulging, watery ones. He could not think what else to do to control the situation, but Jack was here now, and he would not let him be taken again.

"It's you forcing a conflict, *my King*," Bohrman finally said, having turned a sickly pink color. Cyrus didn't know if the title was meant to appease him or as a slight, but he found he didn't much care. "And I *know* you don't want this. The King of the West will not forgive further escalation. And allow me to remind you of the considerable forces he commands."

"Irias said something similar just yesterday," Cyrus responded calmly, "and he's not here today, is he? Be smarter than him."

Bohrman continued to stare. Cyrus had the distinct impression that the man was trying to decide whether to call his bluff or not. But Cyrus was not bluffing. He would not allow Jack to be taken again, and if that meant further bloodshed, then so be it. Cain remained poised with his projectile aimed carefully at the head of one of Jack's guards, and the rest of his company appeared balanced on a knifes edge, prepared to attack if the order were given. A trickle of sweat slowly dripped down Bohrman's now beet-red forehead as his mouth twitched slightly, still staring into Cyrus's unblinking eyes.

"Guards," Bohrman finally announced without taking his eyes off Cyrus's. The silence as the entire group awaited his command was so complete that Cyrus could hear the blackened particles of frozen fire beneath his boots settling further into the ground. He swallowed dryly, still without blinking. Bohrman narrowed his eyes slightly and opened his mouth to speak. "Escort the prisoner back west."

*Thuk.*

Cain had fired the bolt from his weapon and it embedded two inches into the skull of one of Jack's guards. The man's head pitched backwards dramatically, and his entire body collapsed to the ground with a crunch of sand and stone.

The standoff was over and both sides exploded into action. The militants collided with each other; clanging metal and bellowing yells rang out across the fields as the prior silence of a moment before was shattered. Cyrus whipped his head back just in time as a machete raked through the air, intercepted quickly by one of the Easttown men. Bohrman had thrown his hands up over his head and began tripping over himself as he fled the melee. Cain was attempting to fire more bolts at the assailants, but one of the Western guards had grabbed hold of his wrist and was trying to wrestle the weapon free of his grip.

Cyrus could see Jack, from the opposite side of the fighting, trying to wrench himself free of his bonds amidst the chaos, but a guard held him tight from behind. Cyrus sprung forward, sidestepping several battling duos, and raced towards Jack's captor. The man saw him approaching too late, and Cyrus barreled through him like a fireman breaking down a door. The guard flew off his feet and skidded across the gravelly ground, his machete ricocheting away from his hand. He had lost his grip on the rope holding Jack as well, which now hung slack behind him. Cyrus seized Jack's shoulder and shoved him roughly towards the East, away from the combat, but Jack gave a shout, and Cyrus looked up. Nel had managed to obtain a machete, cut her bonds, and was now assaulting Annica with such ferocity that the latter could not regain her footing. She was stumbling backwards as Nel's blade sliced through the air again and again and again, each time just missing her by inches. Nel looked deranged as she seethed forward, her sword singing as it cut the empty space between them. Annica's foot finally caught, and she crashed backwards across the charred earth, spraying dust and ash into the air. Nel seized the opportunity and raised the blade over her head, but Cyrus was faster. As he had done in Alec's chambers, and seen King Mora do, Cyrus raked the twisted knot of his scepter across the now glowing ground and sprayed a torrent of blazing embers towards Nel. She was able to dodge the blast just in time, but it had forced her backwards and onto the defensive. Annica wasted no time in regaining her footing, and she stood up fast, drawing her own machete from her belt.

"Leave her!" Cyrus yelled, but Annica seemed to have taken Nel's attack as a personal offense.

She let out a guttural howl and charged Nel, locking blades with her several times with ear-splitting clangs. As metal scraped against metal, Nel managed to grip Annica's wrist and began forcing her weapon down towards the ground. Annica freed her other hand and punched Nel across the face hard, causing her to stagger back into one of the Western guards.

The fighting was beginning to break up as the Eastern company drove the West back the way they had come. Of the seventeen Westerners in the party, only five remained standing. Bohrman had long since fled and could now be seen in the distance approaching the opposite treeline. The final three guards were finally relinquishing their attack and beginning to scatter, and Nel, seeming to wise up to the circumstances, gave a final icy glance at Cyrus and Jack before turning and running after Bohrman.

The Eastern party, which was still almost entirely intact, began pursuing the fleeing Westerners across the open field, a bloodied Cain leading the charge. Cyrus shouted to let them go, but his voice was lost over the open air. Nel was fast, but the Eastern party was quickly closing the distance between them, and it was looking doubtful that she would reach the Western border in time.

Suddenly, an eruption of leaves and branches blew out of the treeline ahead of Nel and the two Neodactyls sprinted forward, dragging the King's chariot behind them. From the distance, Cyrus could not make out any features, but the chariot bore a hooded rider, and it was no mystery who it was. The creatures cut a wide circle, weaving between Nel and her pursuers, the chariot skidding precariously along the sand and billowing ash and soot in every direction. The birds came to a halt with a horrible screech that echoed across the neutral territory and the chariot swayed to a stop behind them. Cain and his brigade stopped abruptly, leaving plenty of room between themselves and the new arrivals.

Cyrus's stomach squirmed and his heart lurched painfully as he observed the hooded rider from across the field. While he couldn't see the rider's face, he could sense his gaze burning out from beneath the shadows, boring into him from across the glowing expanse. The figure stepped down from the chariot, silhouetted in the acrid yellowish-orange cloud of dust, and slowly walked several paces forward. The scepter was clutched in one of his hands and he dragged it threateningly over the ground, creating a glowing trail behind himself. The Easttowners collectively took several steps backwards, but Cyrus could tell the rider was not looking at them. The figure stopped, standing perfectly still, and continued to stare out at Cyrus, who stared back, seemingly unable to move. His heart had started beating rapidly in his chest and that uncoiling sensation in his gut was more pronounced than ever. Several hundred feet separated them, but Cyrus could feel his brother's anger like a hot, radiating force pulsating out of his soul.

The silence was crushing as the two brothers stared across the vast gulf at each other. To Cyrus, it felt like the entire world had disappeared around him and all he could see was Alec. But it wasn't the Alec he knew. Hidden unseen beneath the shadow of his hood, peering out from somewhere in the gaping maw of his cloak, Cyrus could sense something truly monstrous; a feral creature consumed by rage and hatred. He couldn't be sure how he knew these things, but he felt certain they were true.

At long last, Alec finally turned away from Cyrus and strode slowly around the back of the chariot. He greeted Nel there, or at least Cyrus could assume, it was impossible to tell what they were doing from such a distance, and led her onto the back of the chariot. He put a protective arm around her and shot one last glance across the field before the Neodactyls spurred into action, pulling forward with a jerk. They cut a wide circle, the wheels of the chariot tottering over the uneven terrain, before finding the road leading into the forest and disappearing back west. The Easttowners turned around and started back the way they had come, the three Western guards having long since disappeared into the forests to the north and south.

Cyrus found that his heart was still hammering uncomfortably in his chest. He had not expected to see Alec, and the experience felt like a punch to the gut. His head felt heavy as he slowly turned to Jack, Ydoro, and Annica, standing at his side.

Jack looked him up and down, taking in the scepter grasped in his hand. "This is a new look for you," he said with a smile.

Cyrus supposed it would seem strange to Jack, seeing him as though he were still impersonating Alec, like the last time they saw each other. It was also just occurring to him that Jack still didn't know about his talk with Dalton, not to mention that he was holding an artifact that could open doors to another reality. Cyrus sighed deeply and returned the smile. "Jack, you wouldn't believe how much we have to catch up on."

**CHAPTER FIFTY–FIVE**

# THIS IS HISTORY

J ack was smiling and shaking his head. The smile wasn't because he found any of this even remotely humorous, but the sort of unintentional, unwelcome smile that came from extreme mental discomfort. Jack remembered as a kid, attending the funeral of one of his friend's grandparents, and the most unfortunate smile spreading across his face during the services. He had no control over it, and he had not been amused in the slightest, but it seemed to be born from awkwardness; a flood of emotions potentially too complex for a nine-year old to fully understand. That was the sort of smile Jack wore now, and it felt just as inappropriate now as it had then.

He was sitting on Cyrus's front deck, listening to the tale of everything that had happened since the fateful night that Jack had been captured. Cyrus talked of how he had seen Dalton Sidney in Alec's chambers, how they had conversed about wormholes, or 'doors' as he called them, and how he had narrowly escaped the West with his life. His mouth had hung open for the entire recounting of the Dalton conversation and he eventually had to force himself to stop interrupting with questions, because there were simply too many. But as Cyrus described opening a 'door' in his very living quarters and stepping through into another reality, that's when Jack started his awkward smile. It just didn't make sense. And yet it made perfect sense, in a strange way. It fit with what they knew, but seemed so… impossible.

"But, that has to be our world you were seeing, doesn't it?" Jack asked when Cyrus recalled standing on the dark hillside the day prior.

"Not necessarily," Cyrus answered. He was calm, and extremely deliberate with his explanations, and Jack thought it was likely for his own benefit as much as for Jack's. "In order for this theory to hold true, there are infinite realities. Some where Dalton dies, some where he doesn't. Some where I'm king, some where you're king. You get the idea, the possibilities are endless. Dalton said there seemed to be patterns, like a trajectory that all different realities took. He pointed out that he's never come across a reality where we don't come to this place. But the odds that the world I saw yesterday was the very same world we came from are astronomical."

Jack felt like the air had been let out of his lungs. "So we're still trapped here?"

Cyrus nodded his head somberly. "It won't help us with getting home."

Something in the way Cyrus said this gave Jack pause, but he shook it off. "I wonder if your brother's discovered this."

"Even if he has, he won't use it," Cyrus insisted, a slightly haunted look in his eyes. "He doesn't want to get back. Not anymore."

Jack stayed silent for a long time before finally speaking his mind. "He's got to be taken care of."

Cyrus barely reacted to this statement, as though he knew it was coming. With that hollow look still in his eyes, Cyrus said, "I can't kill him. He may be lost, but he's my brother." His voice had cracked and his thoughts seemed to drift; trailing off to a time long past. "I'm supposed to protect him, you know? He was my baby brother, we did everything together growing up. Even as adults, we've spent so little time apart. But this place, it's changed him. The truth is I don't recognize him anymore, and regardless of whatever feelings I have about him, we can't allow him to continue."

"I wholeheartedly agree," Jack responded, with perhaps more exuberance than Cyrus's morose statement warranted. But seeing the pain in his eyes, Jack felt compelled to say more. "You're not responsible for what Alec's done here, you know that, right?"

Cyrus smiled slightly. "Kind of you to say, but not entirely true. I certainly didn't mean to, but somewhere along the way, I did create a monster."

"Blame yourself all you want," Jack responded, "but you couldn't have known. Not everyone was built to attain power. Your brother is someone who, for whatever reason, has felt he was due more from the world than he was ever given. It's not that he strives for better things, we all do that, but he thinks he is owed more, and that's different. When someone like that comes to a place like this, and suddenly finds himself in possession of enormous power, it can break them."

Cyrus gave a single snort of laughter. "He doesn't seem overly broken to me."

Jack nodded his head in understanding, "There is more than one way to break."

Cyrus acknowledged this with a far off look in his eyes. "We can cross that bridge when we get to it," he replied, and the second time since their conversation started, Jack felt like he was not being told something. That a thought was on Cyrus's mind that he could not yet bring himself to share.

Jack leaned back and looked out over the winding road below. People were walking around town, but something felt different, just a little off.

"It's quiet," Jack finally said.

"I feel it too," Cyrus said grimly. "There's something in the air. Ever since we were attacked yesterday, there's an energy in town that's not quite right. I worry what it means."

Jack looked at Cyrus and asked, "Have you talked to Ydoro? He knows the people better than anyone."

"He's always been the voice of reason," Cyrus growled, "but even he seems changed after yesterday's development."

Jack stood up and studied the people as they walked below, going about their business as they did every day. Yet there *was* something different. "Do you think they would plan something without your approval?"

Cyrus stood up as well. "Annica told me yesterday that this was beyond me. And I think she may be right. Seeing the way they attacked Irias... I mean, they've been living this, Jack. This has been their lives for decades now."

"You gave them something to fight for," Jack pointed out.

"I helped them build up their town, but they've moved beyond what I can offer. And I can't fault them for wanting to defend what they've built."

"I'm going to Ydoro," Jack said abruptly.

He strode down the steps and cut across the small plaza to one of the side roads, Cyrus trailing behind him.

"It's best to leave it be, Jack," Cyrus insisted.

But Jack carried on, and after turning a corner, found himself surprised to see exactly the man he was looking for, sitting outside of his house working on something small in his hands.

Ydoro looked up as they approached and smiled broadly.

"Good to see you out and about again Jack!" Ydoro exclaimed. "And my King," he said with a fist-to-chest salute.

"That's new," Jack observed apprehensively. Cyrus merely gave a half-shrug. "What's happening around here?" Jack asked Ydoro, who had gone back to the project in his hands, which seemed to involve carving a small piece of stone with a blade.

Ydoro looked up and gave a weak attempt at an innocuous smile before dropping the façade. He shrugged almost guiltily and replied, "The East is ready to hit back."

"Hit back?" Cyrus repeated in alarm.

"Is something being planned?" Jack questioned.

"I'm not the one to ask," Ydoro insisted. "I wouldn't do anything without your approval."

"But others are?" Cyrus asked sharply.

Ydoro went back to his carving, "I'm not the one to ask."

Cyrus paused, either rethinking his approach or recognizing the futility of the conversation. "At least tell me you're not working on weapons like Annica and her team."

"No, no," Ydoro assured him, "I'm no fighter, as you know. These..." he held up the small stone in his hand, which Jack could now recognize as a miniature figure, "are chess pieces."

Cyrus furrowed his brow, then smiled. "The town is ready to blow and you're making chess pieces? I'm not sure how many more games we'll be playing."

Ydoro smirked to himself, as though in on a joke that no one else knew. He continued carving. "You once told me that chess was the game of kings. A sounding board for the strategies of war. I know you have trouble accepting this place, even now. You see it as somehow artificial, or temporary. But what's happening here, it's our history. No different than the classes from our own world about Egypt, the Roman Empire... this is real to us. And worthy of memorialization."

Ydoro blew the loose dust from his carving and held it out, this time allowing a closer look at the figure. It was rough, and intentionally a bit abstract in its style, but undoubtedly beautiful. The figure wore a long robe, had one hand clutched around a staff of some sort, and a rough patch around one side of the face and forehead shown partially obscured behind a curtain of long hair. The figure's head was uncovered, but a marking on the base beneath the feet showed a crown, denoting the piece as a king.

Cyrus seemed at a loss for words staring at his own likeness chiseled into the stone, and Jack for his part had no idea Ydoro could do such work.

"It's the game of kings indeed," Ydoro continued, "and you've earned your place in our history."

Jack's eyes traveled to a small pile next to Ydoro, which seemed to be comprised of several more stone figures. When Ydoro saw him looking, he picked them up and handed them to Jack. There was another king, this one looking less powerful and significantly more sinister, with a hood up and a heavier, angled brow. There was a queen, with shoulder-length hair and a short, petite frame, a carving of a Neodactyl captured in a frozen run with its beak open, a burly, bearded man holding some type of blade, and a muscular, short-haired man with a chiseled jaw and a piercing stare. Jack brought this last one close to his face and smiled.

"You've all earned your place in our history," Ydoro said, watching Jack studying his figure. Jack looked to the base and saw a small bishop's cap inscribed in the rounded surface. The bearded figure was also a bishop, and the Neodactyl was a knight. Jack handed the pieces to Cyrus, an odd sensation welling in his chest.

"What about yourself?" Jack asked Ydoro, "where's your piece?"

Ydoro shook his head sheepishly.

"These are beautiful," Cyrus said, handing the pieces back to Ydoro. "I don't know that I've earned your devotion, but I certainly don't take it for granted."

"Things have been set into motion that will reshape this Kingdom forever," Ydoro said, "and I very much hope you do not take it as a slight that things are moving forward without your approval. These people have lived in the shadows too long. You showed them their strength, but this is their future they fight for."

Cyrus nodded his head, recalling Annica's words from the night prior. "Bigger than me," he mumbled to himself.

"The assault on Easttown yesterday changed things, it changed me," Ydoro continued. "Because as much progress as we have made this side of the border, the West thought they could snatch it all away when they wanted. Yesterday, we showed them it won't be easy. But now, we have to show them we're a stronghold, a power equal to their own."

After his ordeal being captured, and hearing about Cyrus's harrowing rescue, Jack found it hard to argue the point. The West was relentless and brutal, they would likely try again to ensnare the East, unless given a compelling reason not to.

"Ydoro, these are your people far more than they are mine," Cyrus said, "I may be their king, but you have a loyalty that you've earned over the many years you've been here. When we first met, you served as our guide, and that's exactly what you remain. The people trust you to guide their way, guide them through life, guide them to brighter futures. There will come a time when I am no longer the King of the East, but I know the people will be in good hands."

Jack thought he could see the faintest shadow of a tear in the corner of Ydoro's eyes, but he simply smiled and nodded his head in understanding.

"Make a piece for yourself," Cyrus insisted forcefully, referring to the pile of chess figures, "I think the kingside castle would be quite fitting."

Ydoro smiled at him, a look of pride shining brightly through. "My King," he agreed with a bow of his head.

Cyrus and Jack walked on soon after, not entirely reassured about the quiet tension they could feel simmering throughout the town. Around several more bends in the road, they came across Annica, Cain, and two other members of their team, sitting out in front of her house and carving weapons. A decent sized stack of spears and blades already peeked out from behind them. When Annica saw Jack approaching, she raised her eyebrows somewhat accusatorially, but looked back down at her work after a short moment.

Cyrus patted Jack on the back and said, "I'm gonna keep walking," evidentially sensing that Jack intended to stop.

As Cyrus continued on, Jack came to a halt in front of Annica, who still didn't look up from sharpening a spear.

"Good to have you back, Jack," Annica said through loud scrapes with a blade.

"I heard you came west looking for us after I was captured," Jack said.

"Well, I didn't know you had been captured at the time," Annica responded casually.

"Cyrus also tells me you were ready to storm the Temple after you thought they had taken my hand," Jack continued.

"Don't be ridiculous," Annica said, still concentrating hard on her sharpening, "I'm not stupid enough to storm the Temple."

Cain cleared his throat awkwardly. "Actually boss, I had to talk you out of that plan. Had to get kinda forceful about it, truth be told."

Annica shot Cain a dangerous look, but Jack smiled to himself.

"Well either way," Jack said, "I'm glad I had someone looking out for me." When Annica didn't reply, he continued, "And I was thinking, now that I'm back, I wondered if maybe you'd like to…"

Annica looked up at him with raised eyebrows, and with everyone else from the group now staring at him, Jack hesitated.

Annica finally smirked. "How 'bout this, Jack; I'm gonna concentrate on the hostility from the West at the moment. We make it through this, you can take me for drinks. Thank me for the rescue attempt."

Jack nodded his head, somewhat disappointed by the lack of clarity in her response.

After a few moments of silence, Cain chimed in, "Ya know, I was there for the rescue attempt as well, and I do get pretty thirsty…"

"Shut it, Cain," Annica said, and then smiled sheepishly after a moment, in spite of herself.

Jack smiled to himself as well. Perhaps it was a date after all.

## CHAPTER FIFTY-SIX

# STREETS OF RED

Jack's dreams led him back home, to the crowded docks of New York and the heavy salt air of the sea, but it didn't last. His subconscious soon turned dark, and he began experiencing visions of everyone he had come to know since arriving in the Kingdom lying dead in the streets. People called out in pain as Jack walked amongst the bodies strewn about the cobblestone roads weaving through town. He recognized Cyrus first, then Cain, Ydoro, and finally Annica. There was a strange, detached sensation as he looked into their lifeless eyes, as though he were experiencing it from someone else's point of view. He looked down at his hands and realized with a start that he was carrying one of the scepters. It was glowing, and as he watched it, it seemed to grow more vibrant, pulsating with ribbons of light from deep within its core. Soon it had become too bright to look at, and yet he couldn't seem to look away. It was like a chasm he was falling into, and he was powerless to stop himself.

He stirred awake suddenly and found himself hanging half off his cot, sweat beading on his forehead. A quick scan of the room told him it was still dark out, but he could see the very first dull greys of dawn beginning to gently penetrate his surroundings and soften the blackness of the air. He shook his head to clear it and walked over to a water basin perched on his table. A quick splash on his face did wonders for emptying the strange dreams from his mind. And yet he still had an odd feeling, like something had happened while he had slept. It was a subtle feeling, but persistent, and quite unyielding.

    He dressed, pulled on his boots, and walked to the door, stepping outside and cocking his head to listen for... anything. It was dead quiet, as one would expect for the very early dawn, but it still somehow felt *too* quiet. There was a stillness in the air that hung heavy, like a blanket smothering the day before it had a chance to begin. Was this just the residual effects of his dreams? He somehow didn't think so. He stepped out into town square and spun in a few slow circles, taking in his surroundings with a strange sense of building dread. A glance at Cyrus's home showed that it was still dark and he was, presumably, fast asleep inside. Jack began hiking up the same side road they had taken the day before, passing Ydoro's dark hut along with countless others. Everyone seemed to still be asleep... or not home. He picked up his pace, still unable to explain this intrusive sense of urgency. He rounded a corner and found himself on Annica's street, approaching her door. He paused. He couldn't just go barging into her home at the crack of dawn. Even a knock on her door would require an explanation. But as he scanned her front stoop, something occurred to him; the piles of weapons they had been making the night before were gone. It was possible, of course, that she had brought them in for the night, but why? The stoop seemed like the most logical place to keep them, in particular the long, unwieldy spears.

    Jack's concern got the better of him and he made the final few steps up to Annica's door and knocked softly. When he heard no stirring from within, he rapped louder.

    "Annica?" he called in a hushed bark. Still nothing.

    It was possible she was on patrol at the border. Why was he so worked up about this feeling? He walked further down the road, still without coming across a single other person, then veered off towards the trade road, and the Western border. He was being paranoid, and he knew it. Even as his feet carried him to the border, he wondered how he was possibly going to explain why he had felt compelled to check on the patrol party before the sun had even fully risen. The awkwardness would of course only be compounded if Annica were there, given their conversation the night prior. He had half-convinced himself to turn back when he caught sight of the border ahead. He didn't know what he had expected to find; possibly a large, surging group brandishing their newly forged weapons at the Western guards, or maybe just the usual border patrol turning around and piercing him with inquisitive stares. What he had not expected was to find the border entirely vacated. There was no one manning the crossing, not on either side. For the first time since the Kingdom was split, the trade road was entirely unguarded.

A knot squirmed to life in his stomach. This seemed to confirm his inexplicable sense of dread; something was most definitely not right. He approached apprehensively, still squinting through the shadows of the pre-dawn light. On the ground just west of the border, Jack could make out a couple dark pools that looked suspiciously like blood. It was possible it was from two days prior, when Irias had stormed through the barricade, but he somehow doubted it. After a few more cautious steps, Jack apprehensively entered the Western territory, half-expecting militants to jump out of the trees and seize him, but nothing happened. He surveyed the forest around him and finally saw something of note. Some ten feet off the road, partially concealed in shrubbery from the forest, there lay a body. In fact, there were several, all seemingly dragged from the road, but not purposely hidden, at least not very well. Jack sprung into the thicket and ran towards the bodies, thoughts of a Western ambush racing through his head. But the closer he got, the more it became clear that the bodies did not belong to his Eastern kin. Every one of them was a Western guard.

Jack backed out of the forest with his heart now hammering unpleasantly. Uncomfortable questions were beginning to form in his mind as well. Had something happened here that had triggered a response from Annica and the Eastern guards? Or had her team made a conscious decision to breach the border? Recalling the amount of weapons he had witnessed them making, he was beginning to suspect the latter.

After a brief internal debate, Jack began walking slowly down the trade road, heading further west into enemy territory. He didn't know what he hoped to find, or what he would say if he did come across Eastern fighters this side of the border, but he felt certain that Annica was leading them, and her small group of loyalists were likely to get themselves killed.

But five minutes down the road and he still had yet to come across a single person. Each step he took west made him increasingly nervous, and a very small part of him considered the possibility that his instincts about the entire situation were wrong, and he was walking back into the arms of the captors he had just been released from. It was also suddenly occurring to him that he did not have a weapon, and he cursed himself for not thinking to grab something beforehand. A Shrieking Bat called out overhead and Jack looked up apprehensively, wondering whether it was reacting to his own passing or something else in the forest. The sky was finally beginning to slowly lighten, becoming a nondescript pale-beige color that promised an imminent sunrise.

As he watched, the sky suddenly became alight in a flash, as though the sun had abruptly decided to race forward several hours. It lasted only a couple seconds before fizzling back out, and was accompanied by a deep, igniting pulse of sound from the west. Something had erupted up ahead, and not terribly far. Shouts and screams began to fill the air and Jack realized it must be coming from the main thoroughfare through town. He broke into a run and sprinted around the remaining twists and turns in the road. Another flash burned across the dawn sky, and then a third.

Jack rounded the final bend, slipping on some loose gravel as he did so, and nearly barreled over a group of six people facing away from him, towards town square. They all turned in unison and raised their various weapons, but stopped abruptly when they laid eyes on his face. Annica and Cain both stared at him in confusion as Jack registered the scene behind them. The entirety of the road ahead, buildings, roofs, wagons and all, seemed to be steadily engulfing in flames. This was the outermost edge of Westtown and people were beginning to stream out of their homes and flee from the burning inferno. Jack's mouth hung open as he took in the destruction.

"What are you doing here, Jack?" Annica questioned. It wasn't accusatory, more regretful, as though she wished he hadn't seen this.

"What are you doing?" Jack demanded back. "You're going to get yourselves killed. And Cyrus didn't…"

"The King was kept out of this to spare him the guilt over what needs to be done," Annica insisted. "Two days in a row we've been attacked, our people murdered. This is not a move against our king. This is *for* our king."

"It's time to move," Cain growled.

"Jack, I'm sorry," Annica said, and he could tell in her eyes that she meant it, "but please understand this is our lives we fight for. We take a stand now, or accept another lifetime of oppression."

When Jack just stared at her, unable to find the right words, Annica leaned in swiftly and kissed him briefly on the lips. "I've gotta go."

Annica turned back towards the burning street and gave a hand signal above her head. It was only then that Jack noticed there were people on the unburnt roofs, apparently more of her Eastern company, who nodded at her and began traveling further into the city.

Cain turned to Jack and said gruffly, "Either head back or stay close."

With that, the company of six proceeded down the burning street and deeper into town. Jack hesitated only briefly and then followed. The occupants of the houses appeared to have all run further west, but once they reached the center of town, where would they have left to go? Up to the Temple?

"These are innocent people," Jack exclaimed, unable to bite his tongue. "What's your plan here?"

Annica never broke her stride, or even looked back at him, but did respond. "These are not innocent people. They've trampled over us for generations now, taking our resources, using our labor, and never once speaking up for us. But they're not our targets today. This assault will draw the cavalry."

"You want the attention of the King and his men?" Jack asked.

"We're counting on it," Annica answered, and this time she did briefly glance over her shoulder and wink at him.

As they turned a corner and the Temple came into view, looming high above the town like a watchful sentinel, Jack glanced up uneasily. He felt like he could feel the eyes of the lookouts on the battlements, of the militants, of Nel and of Alec. There was no doubt they would be coming, and they would be bringing the entire wrath of the West with them.

"When's the next one going off?" Annica asked Cain.

"Any minute now," Cain said.

As though on cue, a fresh barrage of explosions ripped through the air ahead and flashed into the sky, throwing the entire town into an orange and red glow. Behind them, flaming roofs had started to collapse into the streets while up ahead, renewed screams of panic rang out. And then a new sound pierced through the dawn like a blade. It was coming from the distant hill where the Temple sat, and Jack had never heard anything quite like it. It was something akin to an alarm bell, but so much more haunting. A deep, moaning siren of sorts that blared in repeating five second bursts. He didn't know how the noise was being made, but he didn't have to question what it was for. It reminded him of the air-raid sirens during the war. A cruder version, but nonetheless effective. This would bring every fighter under the West to this spot.

Annica turned a final corner and came to a halt in the middle of the street. At first, Jack thought she had seen something to make her freeze, but it soon became apparent that she had chosen the spot to stop. The remainder of her company spread out into a 'V' pattern flanking her sides, similar to a flock of geese following their leader. After a moment's jostling for position, Jack forced himself into the spot directly to Annica's right. Annica looked up at one of the roofs a hundred feet ahead and gave a hand signal, which was answered by the man atop it with a brisk nod of his head. He quickly vanished from view.

"Have you really thought this through," Jack whispered to Annica, warily eying the burning street ahead. "You're challenging the entire might of the West with, what, ten fighters?"

Annica turned to him briefly and simply smiled. She did not answer his question.

Before he could hear it, he could feel it in the ground; the stomping of countless bootfalls announcing the approach of the Western guards. If Jack had felt a sense of impending doom earlier in the morning, now he felt crippled by the sensation. He had a sudden thought that he shouldn't be a part of whatever this was. Not out of self-preservation, but because this was an act of aggression by the East against the West, and didn't involve himself or Cyrus. Of course, upon further inspection, this was an absurd notion. Cyrus was King of the East, and Jack was inescapably a part of it, whether they had sanctioned the aggression or not. Alec would not separate the two, so Jack shouldn't either.

The deep red plumes of smoke drifting lazily across the street ahead began to change direction slightly as the air behind it was disturbed. Silhouettes began to appear through the haze, indistinct at first then becoming more pronounced, and revealing dozens of men. As they breached the edge of the smoke, Jack could see that each of them held a machete and wore a scowl of determined resolve. And *dozens* was an understatement. As the full company became visible, there must have been close to fifty fighters that Jack could see. The only advantage that the East seemed to have was their vastly superior arsenal. A quick scan of the approaching *army* showed they held nothing that could fire from a distance, or even be thrown; they were armed with rusted machetes only. Even so, their numbers alone made a favorable outcome for the East impossible.

Jack looked sideways at Annica and was surprised to see no faltering in her determination. The entire band of Easttowners seemed ready and willing to take on the entirety of the Western forces.

"Last chance to leave, Jack," Annica said, as though sensing his hesitation.

Jack did take an unconscious step backwards, but found himself unable to turn and leave. He should leave. This was not his fight, and the East was going to be slaughtered. But he couldn't leave Annica. He looked sideways at her again, waiting for her to change her mind, willing her to come to her senses.

As the West drew ever closer, Annica said, "I'd guess you have about ten seconds, Jack. Leave now, or you're one of us."

"I *am* one of you," Jack replied in a cracking voice, although he didn't know himself whether his statement was him agreeing to stay or simply saying what he felt.

Annica seemed to take it as the former because she turned to him briefly and smiled. "You sure are," she said. "Are you ready?" She unsheathed her bolt-launcher and raised it towards the Western company.

Jack tore his eyes off Annica and looked to the fighters ahead.

With her weapon still raised, Annica spoke again. "Three… two… one…"

Her timing wasn't exact, but it was damn close. Several of the Western guards fell suddenly to the ground as bolts struck them from off to their sides. An onslaught of rocks and spears rained down on the company from seemingly every direction, to the point that Jack couldn't initially tell where they were coming from. As it turned out, they were coming from everywhere. Eastern fighters had appeared on the flanking rooftops, the winding side-streets, and even from within the homes that were not burning. The Western company devolved into panic and confusion. The once orderly ranks fractured and then broke completely, with members diving and ducking and running for cover. Knowing that retreat was not an option, and likely impossible anyways given the assault from all directions, the Western guards rallied quickly and began engaging with the Eastern attackers. Steel clashed against steel and screams and blood filled the streets, but all pretense of organized combat had given way to madness. This was war, and it was dirty and brutal.

Annica and her team had begun firing bolts from their position, but it wasn't long before the fighting started to spill towards them, and they had to seek cover. Cain and several others sprinted towards a home on the left of the street while Jack followed Annica and another behind a wall to the right. The sheer number of combatants that Annica had been able to raise was astonishing to Jack. The East were hard workers, to be sure, but he never would have considered them fighters. Based on the melee that was unfolding before him, it looked as though the East just about matched the West's numbers.

Annica kept reloading her bolt-launcher and ducking out from behind the wall to fire, but she was running low, and after several more shots, she ran out. Far from being concerned by this, Annica tossed the weapon to the ground and pulled a stone-carved hatchet from her belt with an absurdly exaggerated top that could double as a knife.

Jack gaped at her and she turned briefly to look at him.

"What?" she asked, almost innocently.

She gave him a quick smile, then peeled out from behind the wall. The fighting had worked its way down the street towards them and she sunk her weapon violently into the neck of one of the Western fighters. As the man collapsed, Annica bent and swiped up his fallen machete, tossing it to Jack. Jack was embarrassed to fumble and nearly drop it, but he held on. Annica gave a laugh as though she found the lack of grace endearing, then turned and clashed with another Western guard.

Jack wanted to follow her but was immediately attacked by another Westerner. Jack initially hesitated as the man slashed at him, parrying his swings and backing up as though by not engaging, his assailant would move on. But the man's eyes looked wild, and something finally clicked in Jack's mind that perhaps he had not fully appreciated before; this was all too real, and life or death for these people. With all preamble over, it was kill or be killed. Jack might not be trained in combat, but he could fight. With that realization arming him, Jack let out a roar of a war cry and stomped his boot down hard on the man's knee, shattering it and causing his legs to buckle beneath him. Jack slashed the machete across the man's throat, releasing a spray of crimson onto the dirt below.

The chaos around him had become absolute insanity. People were leaping over their fallen comrades, dueling each other in the streets by any means necessary. People hammered machete against machete, spears were whipping through the air and flames continued to consume many of the surrounding houses. The fighters were spreading out. The battle had started to bleed up the side roads and into the rest of town. Jack clashed with two other Westerners, dispatching them after brief struggles, and then began looking around wildly for Annica and Cain.

There was no sign of either, though still plenty of combatants on the road. Jack dodged a flying spear and barreled forward, slashing down another Westerner as he did so. It was then that a monstrous shriek rent the air.

Jack looked up in horror, as did many of the militants still fighting. For a brief couple seconds, it seemed everyone forgot their individual duels and began wildly scanning their surroundings for the imminent arrival of the Neodactyls. They did not have to wait long. First came the sound of rattling wheels, and the crunch of swift, sure-footed steps on stone and gravel. And suddenly the battle changed. The chariot of the King erupted from the end of the street, pulled deftly by the two Neodactyls and ridden by a wild-looking Alec. His long hair, still knotted in back, billowed out behind him as he leaned over the front of the chariot, like a jockey willing his horse into a race. He looked half-mad as he charged, his scepter held aloft beside him, ready to strike.

The first people the chariot reached had no chance. The Neodactyls sprinted down the street, running people down as they did so. One of the creatures snatched a man by the throat as they ran him over, dragging him ten feet before his legs got caught beneath the chariot wheels and he was sucked under and disappeared in a cloud of dust. Jack was fairly certain it had been a Western guard, but it seemed Alec did not much care. The man was far from the only person to be run down by the chariot. Every time the wheels bounced and the vehicle jumped a foot in the air, it meant another person had been run over.

Combatants further up the road had more time and were diving out of the way as the Neodactyls chittered and snarled. Alec began swinging his scepter out the side of the chariot, smashing through anyone he could reach. Jack dove for cover behind a building wall, afraid of the consequences if Alec were to see him, but the chariot roared past without Alec giving him a second glance. The destruction left in his wake was shocking, but it didn't slow the fighting for long. The Neodactyls ripped around a corner and out of view, spreading terror and panic up the next street.

Jack stared after the chariot a moment too long and nearly paid with his life. A machete swung through the air and he dodged his face out of the way just in time. Raising his own blade, Jack hammered forward and traded blows with his new opponent. This particular guard was better matched to Jack's fighting abilities and was able to meet Jack's attack swing for swing. Jack stabbed forward, blocked. He swung from the shoulder, blocked. He swiped for the legs, blocked. The man was working Jack backwards, keeping him on the defensive. One wrong step and it would all be over. Jack ducked another swing so close he could feel the blade brush the top of his hair. In desperation, Jack lashed out with his fist and sunk a blow along the man's cheek. It was enough to unbalance him, and Jack used the much-needed opportunity. He sliced right, sliced left, and forced the man backwards and further into the street.

In a sudden blaze of red spray, the man vanished entirely from the spot he had been standing and Alec's chariot catapulted past. Jack whipped around in shock and saw the man's ruined body flop unceremoniously into the side of a building. The chariot, which was now speeding further down the road and tearing through people as it went, seemed to have a new weapon. Protruding from the center of the wheel spokes on the left side of the chariot, a wicked, curved blade had been installed that, as the wheel spun, sliced through the air like a rotating dicer, hooking onto anything it passed. It was a sickening, incredibly effective instrument of war.

Jack used the lull in fighting caused by the passing chariot to race across the street and weave up one of the side roads. He was aiming to cut through and run to town square, where he had an idea he would find Annica and Cain. Along the side roads, he passed two pairs of fighters locked in combat, but it seemed the main action was still taking place along the main thoroughfare.

Jack turned a corner and staggered sideways as the burning awning of a house collapsed in front of him, pelting him with bits of burning ash. He shielded his eyes and looked around, realizing he had arrived in town square. The generally bustling area had become a combat arena. Everywhere he looked, people smashed through each other with various degrees of weaponry, almost everyone bleeding profusely from one wound or another. This was well over the fifty or so fighters Jack had originally seen walk into town. It must mean more Western fighters had come when they heard the alarm blare. But the East still seemed able to match their numbers. Every able-bodied person from Easttown must have shown up to fight.

An inferno roared to life down one of the side roads across the plaza, and at first Jack couldn't account for what had caused it. But a moment later, Alec's chariot rumbled out through the flames and Jack got his first look at another upgrade to the mount. While the curved blade still rotated through the air on the chariot's left side, the right had been outfitted with some sort of a crude flame-propelling unit. Seemingly at Alec's beckoning, a roaring jet of fire would launch out from a small port beneath the carriage and consume anything within a ten-foot span. Jack watched as the device wiped out five people in the blink of an eye. He suddenly felt sick thinking of the countless dead from the morning alone.

Alec thundered diagonally through the plaza, igniting several people who weren't fast enough to jump out of the way, and disappeared again down a road heading back east.

"Jack!" came a loud voice from off to his left.

Jack started at the sound of his name and wheeled around to see Cain, beckoning him from the doorway of one of the homes. Jack ran to meet him and breathed a heavy sigh when he was no longer out in the open.

"You alright?" Cain grumbled. He looked like hell. Blood covered half his body in such quantities that Jack had to assume it was not his own. A large cut along his forehead was leaking into his right eye and a shallow but nonetheless horrific-looking stab wound was coloring his shoulder.

"Fine," Jack answered, still surveying Cain's battered body apprehensively.

Cain chuckled briefly, "You should see the other guy."

Jack didn't laugh. There was nothing funny about any of this.

"Where's Annica?" Jack asked.

"North of here, last I saw her." When he noticed the worry in Jack's eyes, he said more gently, "she's the toughest person I've ever known. She'll be fine."

Jack nodded in appreciation but quickly changed the subject. "Have you seen the King's new toy?"

"Oh yeah," Cain growled, "He's gonna burn half the Kingdom down before long."

"So what do you think?" Jack asked, "Can we take it down?"

Cain grinned at him, and Jack didn't know how he could possibly manage a smile at a time like this, but he found it mildly comforting all the same. "I haven't gotten a good look at the mechanism controlling it, but it looks extremely unstable to me."

Jack nodded his head in agreement. "Alright, let's get a closer look, but keep your head down, if he sees either of us, we'll be the first in his crosshairs."

Cocking his head to listen, Cain said, "I think we're about to get our chance."

Sure enough, Jack started to hear the telltale rumble of the chariot lurching down a nearby street. The two men ducked out from their cover and ran along the exterior walls of the adjoining homes, stopping just short of the road. The chariot rattled past and into the plaza again, this time with Jack watching the flames carefully as they erupted violently from its side. He couldn't make out exactly how Alec was activating the jet, but he could see a sickly yellow-green substance leaking out from a large canister that had been installed on the undercarriage. Whatever the substance was, it seemed to be responsible for the ignition, and Cain was right; the mechanism looked precarious and unstable.

When the chariot had rolled by, Jack ran into the street and scooped up the residue that had leaked from the canister. It was a sandy powder, and Jack had seen it before. It was the same substance that Mora had thrown into his face when they assaulted the Temple. Remembering the way the powder had rendered him unconscious for such a long time, he kept his hand far away from his nose and brushed it off his hands quickly. Evidently the stuff was flammable, and extremely volatile.

"That's Powdered Dreamwood," Cain said, looking over his shoulder. "I had no idea it was so combustible."

"He must have some sort of chamber housing fire beneath the chariot," Jack posited, "and when it's blown over the powder, it erupts."

"But that thing's leaking all over the place," Cain said, "if it's really that combustible, he would have secured it better."

Jack turned and swiped a burning piece of fallen thatched roof from the ground and held the flame to the green substance on the ground. It flashed violently into a small fireball and burnt out almost immediately. "Alec's always been reckless," Jack said with a shake of his head. "He'll be hard to knock off while he's on the move, but that canister is exposed, if we can get a flame to penetrate it… it's not a small target."

Cain started scanning the area around them and then ran to a nearby fallen body. Still clutched in the dead man's hand was one of Annica's newly minted spears. Cain wrenched it free of their grip and brought it to Jack. "If we can get the tip of a spear to burn, we could try to hit the canister with it."

Without much thought, Jack reached up and tore the sleeve off his own already-battered shirt. It shredded away easily, apparently the elements had taken their toll on the fabric over the months. He wrapped the sleeve tightly around the blade at the top of the spear and handed it back to Cain.

"It won't burn long, but it doesn't have to," Jack said, "just light it and throw it."

Cain nodded briskly. Jack glanced around but found no sign of Alec. There was no doubt he would be back soon, however. He seemed to be making circles between the main road where the fighting had begun and the town square.

"Watch it!" Cain bellowed, and Jack was able to duck his head just in time as a blade sliced through the air from behind him, nearly clipping his ear.

Jack spun and raised his own blade, trading blows with his attacker in an attempt to keep him away from Cain, who shielded the fabric-tipped spear and backed further away along the wall. The man swung his machete from the shoulder, but as Jack lifted his own weapon to block, his assailant adjusted and swiped low, cutting a deep gash along Jack's stomach. He howled in pain and moved to clutch the wound, but the man slashed again, and Jack only just stopped the blade by grasping the man's wrist, at the cost of dropping his own machete. It became a battle of strength as they both wrestled over the weapon, but luckily, Jack was the stronger. He bent the man's hand backwards until his grip loosened, then wrenched the blade free and stabbed forward, putting his entire body weight behind the motion. It crunched straight through the Westerner until the hilt stopped against the man's ribs. The man blinked at him in surprise, and opened his mouth as though to say something, but only a soft exhale of air came out. His eyes closed and his body crumpled onto the sand.

Jack left the blade embedded in the victim and picked up his own weapon off the ground. Across the plaza, terrified screams preceded the arrival of Alec's chariot, which came hurtling into view from a side road on the opposite side and sliced two people down in the process. It completed a wide, unsteady turn and launched a jet of fire into several of the combatants. Jack turned wildly to look for Cain, who was a ways down the outer wall of the burning houses. Cain had noted Alec's arrival as well, but was occupied keeping another Westerner at bay while trying to keep the tip of the spear firmly wrapped in fabric. Jack moved to help, but a tingling along his spine made him look back at the chariot. Alec had spotted him. He looked like an apex predator that had just identified its next meal. There was a wild hunger in his eyes, and Jack recognized nothing of the professor he had sat with on the ship months ago. Jack raised his machete and gave it a brief twirl, hoping this would project some confidence that he in truth did not currently possess. Jack had half-expected a smirk from Alec at this display, but his face remained stony. In fact, his expression looked downright monstrous as he stared into Jack's eyes and began rolling forward.

The Neodactyls screeched in unison as they sprinted forward from across the plaza. Alec bent low over the reins and raised his scepter out to the side. Jack couldn't be sure whether Alec meant to bludgeon him, let the Neodactyls shred him, or just run him down completely, but his lone machete was going to be of little use regardless.

## SOMEWHERE

The chariot was fifteen feet away and closing fast. Jack quickly realized he was going to have to run to save himself, and was about to do exactly that when he looked to his left. Further down the wall, Cain stood ready, and he had managed to light the tip of the spear. He looked like a Greek god with his burly frame, wild hair, and the flaming spear held aloft. Alec was only ten feet away from Jack when Cain launched the weapon. It spiraled through the air, streaking fire and embers from the burning cloth in its wake. Alec never saw it coming, but Cain's aim was true. It struck the chariot right above the canister of leaking green powder and flashed vibrantly. This Alec did notice, and he looked down to see the source. With an almighty explosion, a second flash tore through the undercarriage of the chariot as the canister of Powdered Dreamwood ignited. The chariot careened sideways as the one wheel was blown off its axle and bounced away across the sand. The mount crashed downwards and splintered along the ground, bending metal and launching shrapnel in all directions. The Neodactyls snarled as their harnesses became entangled in the shattering vehicle, and Alec was able to jump clear just before it flipped entirely and came to rest in a twisted heap.

Jack stared at the wreckage with his mouth hanging slightly open, but Cain was far more prepared. With an air of authority, he kicked a machete out of the sand and stooped to pick it up, then marched briskly forward with the weapon held high. The ensnared Neodactyls hissed menacingly, and the nearest snapped out with its beak, but was held back by the entangled harness still looped under the ruined chariot. Cain brought the blade down swiftly and the creature's head was cleaved clean off its neck. The body dropped with a thud and twitched briefly before going still.

The other Neodactyl shrieked wildly and dug its talons into the dirt, attempting in vain to charge forward. Cain made to step around the decapitated bird and take out the second, but Alec was beginning to regain his footing. He staggered forward, pulled a blade from his belt and hammered down on the twisted leather reins restraining the creature. The straps snapped and the bird launched itself at Cain, flying through the air with a demonic scream. Cain stepped backwards but the animal was on him before he could turn. He stumbled away, flailing wildly at the attacking creature, and while he was able to put distance between himself and the chariot, he hadn't been able to find sure footing since he was set upon. He lashed out a final time with his machete, causing the Neodactyl to bellow, but his perpetual backwards fall had finally unbalanced him, and he smashed to the ground hard. With his blade still clutched tight in his hand, he stabbed repeatedly at the bird's plumage, but it was already on top of him, its jaws snapping inches from his face. He was able to keep the creature's head at bay, but its tearing, slashing talons finally found their target. With a violent slice of its curved, black claws, it raked into Cain's chest, and Jack saw a spray of blood explode from his mouth.

Jack yelled out and started to run towards the creature but suddenly felt cold steel against his throat. He froze. Other Easttowners had started charging forward to help Cain, and the Neodactyl stepped off his chest, hissing. Jack turned apprehensively to see who had a knife to his neck, but he could have guessed. Nel sneered at him over his shoulder. Alec was finally getting unsteadily to his feet, looking much worse for wear. His cloak was torn and scorched in several places and covered in yellowish sand and dirt. He had a cut along his cheek from the fall and appeared to be in mild shock. He looked down at the dead Neodactyl, and in that split-second, the situation changed again. Nel gave a surprised gasp from behind Jack, who turned to see Annica with a knife to Nel's throat. Jack was at Nel's mercy, and Nel was at Annica's.

Alec raised his head, still looking stricken by the events of the last thirty seconds, and yelled out, "Stop!"

The plaza went silent. Spread out around the shattered chariot, Easterners and Westerners had weapons raised against each other in defense, waiting to see how the standoff would unfold. The remaining Neodactyl had its quills up and its neck coiled, looking feverishly from one Easttowner to the next as they formed a half-circle around the creature. Flames continued to consume the surrounding buildings, not to mention the scattered corpses throughout the square.

Alec let the silence draw out. He scanned the area slowly, likely trying to assess the situation, possibly even trying to determine which side had the greater numbers. From Jack's point of view, it was a draw. Alec's look of shock was beginning to recede, slowly being replaced with an expression of murderous rage. His eyes finally fell onto Jack.

"Where is he?" Alec demanded in a tone of unbridled contempt.

"He's not here," Jack answered. He thought of explaining that Cyrus had not been a part of the assault, but it wouldn't make a difference. And it would bring his leadership into question for the other Westerners.

Alec smirked, but Jack could tell it was forced. "I wouldn't want to be here either, if I were him."

Alec began to slowly walk forward, and Annica tightened her grip on Nel, "One more step and the girl dies."

Nel responded in a hiss, "And with my last breath I will tear Jack's windpipe from ear to ear."

Alec did stop. He was still unwilling to risk Nel's life, and Jack breathed a silent sigh of relief for that. Alec began to pace sideways instead, once again surveying the crowd around him. If he gave the order, the battle would continue, and the West may very well win, but both Jack and Nel would die, and his remaining Neodactyl would almost certainly be butchered by the Easttowners surrounding it. The East may not have a clear path to victory, but Alec had nothing to gain by continuing the fighting, and he knew it.

"My brother invades my Kingdom," Alec said, "slaughters my people, and he can't even face me himself."

"Cut the crap Alec, "Jack snarled, "you cast the first stone. It's the rules of war."

"War," Alec repeated, "now that's interesting. And here I thought all the East ever wanted was peace."

Jack glanced briefly over at Cain, lying on the ground. He wasn't moving. "You can't win here today, Alec. Not without sacrificing everything."

"I've sacrificed," Alec responded, "and my people have sacrificed. They're willing to put their lives down for the greater good."

"And what about Nel?" Jack asked, and he felt her knife tighten along his throat. "Are you willing to sacrifice her? Because that's what'll be necessary to win the day."

"Meanwhile my brother is willing to sacrifice everyone, including you," Alec retorted. "All this bloodshed, just to avoid facing me personally."

"Be careful what you wish for, Alec," Jack replied, "you still can't even say his name. If I were to bet, I'd say you're afraid of him."

This had exactly the effect Jack had hoped for. Alec's jaw clenched and his nostrils flared. His knuckles turned white from squeezing his scepter so hard. But he couldn't make a move against Jack, not at the moment.

"You think you're clever," Alec said with a curl of his lip. It wasn't a question. "If my brother... if *Cyrus* wants to see me, he knows exactly where to find me. But he'd rather send his people to the slaughter."

"The neutral territory," Jack said, "today at sundown. You wanna see your brother? He'll be waiting for you."

Jack didn't know why he said it, all he knew was that he needed to offer Alec an out. He had goaded him easily enough, and that historically had made him emotional. And with emotion came poor judgement. But if Alec felt trapped, then he became unpredictable.

Alec looked as though he had just swallowed a beaker of acid. It was like his every feature were desperate to react, to burst forth in anger, bubbling just below the surface of the skin. He kept it hidden, for the most part, likely for the sake of his public audience.

"And I suppose you want your people to be allowed to leave here unharmed," Alec responded.

"Now that's up to you," Jack answered, "it depends what you're willing to sacrifice."

Jack stared unblinking into Alec's eyes. He was betting everything on Alec's feelings for Nel. When Alec finally did speak, it was not what Jack was expecting.

"Sundown tonight," Alec said, "the Fire Fields."

Alec took a step backwards, and the surrounding militants seemed to collectively exhale just slightly. He whistled softly and the remaining

Neodactyl padded back towards him, still surveying the crowd menacingly.

Annica kept her blade at Nel's throat, but surveyed the scene carefully before finally calling out, "Easttown, fall back!"

The Eastern fighters relaxed their weapons just a bit and began slowly shuffling towards the edges of the plaza. Several of them stopped beside Cain and bent over his bloodied form, and Jack's heart lurched a bit when he saw their somber faces.

Jack felt the knife ease off his throat, and he pulled away from Nel quickly, turning to make sure Annica did the same. Annica took her time with it, but finally dropped the blade away and gave Nel a rough shove back towards Alec and the ruined chariot. Annica started towards Cain, but several of the Easterners stopped her and shook their heads.

"He's gone, Annica," one of them said, which only made Annica struggle towards him all the harder.

She pushed her way through the crowd and bent over him, placing a hand on his cheek and bowing her head low. Jack walked slowly behind her and peered over her shoulder at Cain's body. His eyes were closed, and he almost looked peaceful, apart from the blood. Jack glanced up at Alec, half expecting him to be smirking, but he was already beginning to walk away, followed by his fighters.

*****

The walk back to Easttown was a grim, silent affair. Many of their company were limping, and every one of them was bleeding from one wound or another. Some were being supported by others, and some were carrying or dragging the bodies of their fallen friends. Annica had tears resting under her eyes but wore a stoic expression of deepest resolve. Jack's abdomen was beginning to burn painfully, now that he had the time to think about it, and he kept reflecting about Cain and how he had given his life to bring Alec low. Without his actions, they very well may not have seized the upper hand in the battle.

The staggering, shuffling band of fighters turned a bend in the road and found two men standing ahead of them. One of them was Ydoro, staring carefully at the ground. The other was Cyrus, and he wore an expression of deepest sorrow. Jack didn't know how much Cyrus knew of the morning, but judging by his face, he knew enough, and he was in mourning for where the actions would now lead.

## CHAPTER FIFTY–SEVEN

# ALEC

Every step Alec took back to the Temple had caused his blood to boil and churn all the more. His people formed up behind him along the road in a show of respect, but it was humiliating to be walking back when he had ridden into battle on a chariot. His surviving Neodactyl prowled along beside him, and Nel walked on his right, but his anguish over the defeat made him want to scream. The injustice was almost crippling to him; that battle should have been his to win. Truth be told, he was ecstatic when his guards reported Easttown had invaded the Kingdom. It was his chance to finally crush the illusion of peace with the pretender King in the East, but it had all been taken away from him in a matter of seconds.

It was all okay, however. He kept reminding himself of that. His brother had finally overreached, and it would end up being a dire miscalculation on his part. Jack had been trying to make Alec look weak when he suggested a meeting in the neutral territory, he knew that. But Jack had miscalculated too. He didn't know Alec had been training to use the scepter in combat, ever since his brother's break-in. The Fire Fields were the absolute worst place Jack could have suggested for making Alec look weak. This would be the end of the East, and that's what he had to keep reminding himself of. Rather than stomping out insurrections as they cropped up, this would present a much cleaner way of bringing the East back under his rule. It would be cutting the head off the serpent, so to speak.

Not that Alec intended to kill his brother, he didn't think he could go through with that. But to knock him down, knock the crown off his head, that he could do. What wasn't as clean was the history that would be brought to the Fire Fields. Cyrus Dorn was no longer his brother, and had not been for some time. The important thing would be to remind himself that this was simply an opposing ruler, an enemy of the Kingdom looking to steal his land and enslave his people, nothing more. Any bond they once shared had long since been severed. His brother had stolen his life when he took Cynthia from him, and Alec's entire existence since had been a shadow of his true potential. But Cyrus had made sure to keep him low, to make him *grateful* for all the chances he was given. *Given*, as though he didn't spend every moment of his life trying to scratch and claw his way to the kind of success that Cyrus always found so easily. But no, that wasn't true, Cyrus never *found* his success, he took it from others; climbed over everyone else to reach that high-hanging fruit.

Alec clenched his jaw so tightly he felt at risk of shattering his own teeth. His grip became a stranglehold around the shaft of his scepter and his eyes darkened. Maybe he would kill his brother after all.

## CHAPTER FIFTY-EIGHT

# CYRUS

C yrus had started and stopped several times when addressing Jack and Annica back in Easttown. Many of his diatribes included various iterations of *'what were you thinking,' 'you've started a war,' 'you could have been killed,'* but none of his thoughts ever formed into rational arguments because at the end of the day, he didn't feel he had any right to tell the people of Easttown how to deal with the West's oppression.

There was no getting around it anymore, Alec was dangerous; a malignancy on the Kingdom that would eventually corrupt and darken an entire civilization of people. Aside from retaining his power, he seemed to care for nothing at this point. Cyrus would argue that even his feelings for Nel were little more than a sense of possession for him.

"I had to say something to get us out of there," Jack was saying, "you don't have to face him."

"You're damn right I'm going to face him," Cyrus spat, "this has to end. I wish I could put it off indefinitely, but I think the train has run out of track."

"I'm sorry, Cyrus," Jack said, "I didn't mean to put you in this position…"

"It's not your fault," Cyrus admitted, trying to set his frustration aside, "this was inevitable. Besides, he may just want to talk. Alec is no fighter."

Jack tilted his head in disagreement. "He wasn't. But this isn't the brother you grew up with. I think it's quite possible he'll be looking for a fight."

Cyrus nodded grimly. It wasn't unexpected to him, but unfortunate just the same. He didn't want to hurt his brother, but that was maybe the point they had come to, at long last. He did have a plan, however.

"Any advice?" Cyrus asked.

Jack shrugged and studied Cyrus. "You're bigger than he is, he may back down when it comes to it. Don't let the Neodactyl anywhere near you."

Cyrus shook his head, "This is a personal vendetta, he wants it to be about me and him. He won't bring his creatures."

"Creature," Jack corrected him, "thanks to Cain."

Cyrus nodded. It would be a long afternoon, dusk was still many hours away. His stomach squirmed into knots at the thought of seeing Alec again after all this time. Cyrus wasn't afraid of a confrontation with his brother, but *was* afraid of what he would see when he looked into his eyes. He wondered whether he would even recognize the person he had become. It was a strange sensation, contemplating whether someone you had loved your whole life truly meant to do you harm.

He looked out over Easttown, gleaming yellow and gold in the afternoon light, and wondered whether this could possibly be the last day he would spend in the Kingdom.

## CHAPTER FIFTY-NINE

# SUNDOWN

The cool blues of the day were beginning to fade into a warm amber, the shadows elongating like spindly fingers across the grounds of Easttown. Along with the setting sun, the time had finally come for Cyrus to face his brother. The moment was a long time coming, and yet he felt entirely unprepared for it. This would not only have far-reaching consequences between the two of them, but the day would likely find its place in the annals of the Kingdom's history as well. Ydoro had been quick to point that out, examining his carved chess pieces as he did so. If talk dissolved, and the day was to end in combat, the victor would very likely become the new ruler of the two Kingdoms, either uniting them as one or carving them up further. It was important to keep in mind that this conflict was far bigger than their personal feud. Perhaps that would help with doing what needed to be done.

The entire town had spent the afternoon bandaging themselves up as best they could, leaving very little time or energy for remorse or sorrow over their fallen brethren of the morning. The consensus seemed to be that they would have time for their grief later, after the confrontation at sundown. This of course implied they thought Cyrus would be the victor and Easttown would be allowed to continue on and thrive. Cyrus wasn't so certain. If things didn't go his way today, Alec would dismantle Easttown brick for brick, all the way down to the foundation. He further worried that he may put the population to the sword, or at the very least the leadership.

Cyrus had spent some time hidden away in his house, trying to get a better feel for the scepter. It was unwieldy as far as weapons go, top-heavy and rough in hand. The key would be keeping his distance from Alec. The staff was of course capable of launching frozen fire, although at what distance he wasn't certain. He gently ran his fingers along the rough patch of skin on his temple where King Mora had wounded him. He knew of no way of blocking those jets of fire, so agility would be his best option. After swinging the scepter around a bit, parrying with an invisible foe, and mock stabbing with the sharpened end, he had to admit he felt more ill-prepared than ever. He did make sure to practice blocking potential blows, attacks from the sides, from straight on, and most importantly from overhead.

Now he was out of time. Prepared or not, sundown had arrived, and the time had come to walk west and meet whatever fate was in store. By all rights it should have felt like a lonely journey, but when he stepped out through his doorway, it seemed the entirety of Easttown was gathered in the streets below his porch, looking up at him with something close to awe on their faces. Annica was right near the front of the crowd, bloodied from the morning but smiling supportively nonetheless. Ydoro stood near her, gazing at him with unabashed wonder in his eyes, as though he really were looking upon Julius Caesar himself. And then there was Jack, standing apart from the crowd at the base of Cyrus's steps, leaning against the railing and looking at his feet, a strange half-smile on his face. Looking down at the scepter in his hands, and then out at the gathered townsfolk, it was the first time that Cyrus did not feel like an imposter in the role. Whether he had earned their devotion or not, these people looked up to him, and this night was for them.

Cyrus put his hands on the railing of his porch and gazed around at the people, *his* people. He cleared his throat and started to speak, slowly and very deliberately. "You know, I was once told you were a complacent people. When I look around, I don't see a complacent people. I see an oppressed people. I think you had been kept in the dark for so long you had forgotten what it meant to see sunlight. I think you had forgotten your strength. The strength of the people. But when I look around now, I don't see an oppressed people anymore. I see warriors. The enemy came into our lands and you refused them. You pushed back. You hit back. And no matter what happens tonight, I know you will fight for what's yours. Because you're the victims no more, and you've remembered your strength. If it comes to fighting tonight, I fight for you!"

Applause rang out across the plaza. It wasn't the sort of applause that followed a rallying cry, but the type that accompanied a performer's final act. A standing ovation as a beloved artist took their final bow. Or perhaps that was simply Cyrus's subconscious projection of how he thought the night would go. Either way, it warmed him in a way he could not have imagined, and it gave him strength. He walked down the steps slowly, with Jack finally meeting his eyes when he came level.

"We're with you," Jack said, putting a hand on Cyrus's shoulder. He didn't say more, and he didn't need to.

Cyrus began to pass through the crowd, and the people started raising their fists to their chests in salute. No one said *'my King'* this time, the streets remained entirely silent, but the power it gave Cyrus was immeasurable. As he reached the edge of the town square, he realized that Jack, Ydoro, and Annica had all formed up behind him, and the entire rest of the population had formed up behind them. It seemed all of Easttown were to accompany him to his confrontation. It made Cyrus smile to himself.

The procession was fairly slow-moving, but Cyrus still found himself nearing the Fire Fields all too soon. He supposed it had something to do with his growing dread for what was to come. The sun was just about to dip below the horizon when he saw the familiar orange glow of the neutral territory peeking through the trees. There was still plenty of greyish-pink light in the sky, but the brilliant flame blaze from the ground ahead drowned it out.

Cyrus ducked under a low-hanging branch and emerged from the treeline into the vast expanse of glowing embers and charred-looking earth. Across the gulf, there stood a grouping of people, with more spread out along the sides of the field. Similar to Easttown, it seemed the entirety of the West had also shown up to watch the fireworks. Even though the group of people were little more than shapes from this distance, Cyrus could still make out Bohrman's hefty frame, and Nel to his left. At the center of it all was a figure that could only be his brother. He held his scepter in hand and his remaining Neodactyl stood beside him. Cyrus could feel Alec's gaze upon him like a spot of light from a magnifying glass. He tightened his grip on his own scepter, willing it to make him feel stronger.

Cyrus turned to Jack on his right and asked quietly, "Thoughts?" It was an intentionally generic question, but Cyrus felt like he needed some guidance. It probably wouldn't be wise to simply charge across the field to his brother.

"Well you'll certainly have an audience," Jack replied, scanning the people along the sides of the field. "But you can take comfort in the fact that your brother's inner circle has significantly dwindled."

'Significantly dwindled' may have been an overstatement, in Cyrus's opinion, but it was hard to not observe the absence of Irias, the other Neodactyl, and Alec's beloved chariot. Cyrus did feel a swell of strength feeling the presence of Jack, Ydoro, and Annica around him.

"Be careful please," Ydoro whispered. "The consequences would be devastating if you were to fall."

A figure from across the field began to walk forward, but it wasn't Alec. It appeared to be Nel, striding out confidently with no obvious weapons in hand.

Cyrus began to step forward, but Jack put out his hand to stop him. "It's a parley," he said quietly, "a discussion of terms. If Alec's not going, neither should you. I'll see what she wants."

Jack walked west without further discussion, and Cyrus hoped he was right. What if it was an ambush and Nel attacked him?

Jack walked more than a hundred feet before finally meeting Nel in the center of the field. They were far out of hearing distance, but Cyrus strained to decipher what was being said nonetheless. The two parties kept about ten feet between them as they talked, which gave Cyrus some comfort. There was no gesturing or movement of any kind, the sort of thing you don't notice but come to expect from civilized conversation. This was clearly not that. Even from a distance, it was obvious that the exchange was terse, formal, and rigid. This was a discussion between two people who no longer had any desire to interact with one another, representing two opposing sides between which a chasm had ruptured.

Abruptly, at least from Cyrus's point of view, Jack turned and began walking back east, and Nel did the same heading west. Jack's face looked grim, his expression contemplative and dark.

After what felt like an eternity, Jack finally rejoined their group and again took his spot on Cyrus's right, turning back to face west.

"He wants to fight," Jack growled, "Nel says he wants this duel to put an end to the conflict. He's claiming it's so that no more innocent people die, of course, but it's a power play."

"He sounds confident," Cyrus said warily.

"Yeah," Jack breathed slowly, "he does. I don't think he plans to kill you. He wants to best you in combat. Show the Kingdom that he's earned his right as king."

"What else did Nel say?" Cyrus asked.

"Nothing important. She had a script she was following. I asked her if she thought this was right. She didn't respond."

Cyrus nodded his head silently as movement began to stir on the opposite side of the field. This was it, they had arrived at the end of the line. The figure holding the scepter began to walk forward alone.

"You still don't have to do this," Jack said.

"Yes I do," Cyrus replied, "it would be the same as defeat if I don't. And I can't leave Alec to destroy everything that's been created here."

"You are a true king," Ydoro said.

Cyrus nodded but said nothing. He felt queasy, and strangely detached, as though he were looking through someone else's eyes. He felt like he should be saying goodbye to people, or thanking people for what they had done for him. But the words just caught in his throat and he stayed silent. The best he managed was to put a hand on Jack's shoulder and smile.

Jack gave a half-smile back and said with a slight shrug, "Give him hell."

Cyrus turned, faced west, took a long, bracing breath, and began to walk forward. His footsteps seemed to practically echo as they crunched across the glowing earth. The sound of gravel and sand beneath his boots was the only sound in the universe as he strode, violating the silent evening air with each footfall. Ahead of him, his brother's face was finally beginning to swim into focus after all these months, and he was almost surprised to find that he recognized it. It wasn't the monstrous, twisted visage that he had come to know in his nightmares, but a version of the face he had known his whole life. He felt a pang of guilt at the recognition, and suddenly wanted to find a solution that didn't end in bloodshed. But the closer he came, the more he realized that the familiarity in Alec's face did not extend to his eyes. There was a darkness behind them that was undeniable and alarming, like a disease that had been allowed to fester and mutate. Alec was about ten feet away from Cyrus when he came to a halt, stabbing his scepter firmly into the ashen ground and planting his feet authoritatively. Cyrus did the same, though with far less pomp.

There was biting silence between them for a long time. The wind whistled through the trees gently, but the Kingdom as a whole seemed to be waiting with bated breath, not daring to exhale. There was unrestrained hate in Alec's eyes as he surveyed his brother, and his gaze fell to the scepter clutched in his hand.

As though in defiance of the very laws of nature, Alec finally broke the brittle silence and spoke. "The *King* of the East."

Cyrus extended his arms out and looked around. "Who's the façade for, Alec?"

"I'm simply using your newly embraced title," Alec sneered. "I take it that's why you're finally carrying the scepter. This mantle that you refused for so long."

Alec's eyes continued to flick to the scepter. It seemed to bother him a great deal that Cyrus was now carrying it.

"This is the real world, Alec," Cyrus began again, "These are people's lives, this actually matters. Look around you, this isn't a fantasy world of yours."

# SOMEWHERE

Alec smirked and shook his head. "Why don't you look around yourself. Is this a world you recognize? Do you see your stuffy campus? Do you see your throng of prickly teachers? Do you see any of your pompous administrators to suck up to? No, you're right, this isn't a fantasy world of mine. I couldn't have concocted something like this." Alec gazed up at the sky, then down at the glowing earth, its light casting deep, cavernous shadows along his face that made him look terrifyingly warped. "But it is reality," he said, looking back up at Cyrus. "You haven't been able to accept this place because you're still holding onto what you lost. I'm embracing what we found."

Cyrus just gazed at his brother, unsure of how to even speak to him anymore.

"Let me ask you a question," Alec said, "what are you doing here? You didn't care to rule. You had no interest in it. So why now? Is it truly just that you hate to see me succeed without your *'help'*? You just have to stand in my way?"

It wasn't an honest question; it was accusatory and dripping with disdain. But it didn't change the fact that Alec genuinely believed it.

Cyrus began talking, but slowly, as though any sudden move would set Alec off. "The thing is, you created me. You're right, I didn't care to rule." Alec adopted a self-satisfied smile at hearing this, as though it vindicated him. But Cyrus continued, "And if you had remained the man you *were*, then I would never have stood in your way." Alec's smile faltered. "You could've had it all," Cyrus said with a shake of his head, "but you chose this instead. In the end, I guess we create our own worst nightmares."

Alec looked deranged at hearing Cyrus's words, as though his smirk had become caught as it slid from his face.

"You think I'm afraid of you?" Alec hissed. "You think you mean ANYTHING to me?!" He screamed the end of the sentence, his voice echoing around the clearing and causing several Shrieking Bats to screech and take flight from the nearby trees.

Despite his original attempt at tiptoeing around his brother, Cyrus suddenly felt like he wanted to push Alec, to prod at him and see what happened. To hurt him. "I do think you're afraid of me," Cyrus answered, "and I think you've realized you're running out of people to blame for your own shortcomings. You know why you were so easily corrupted by this place? Because you're weak. You're a weak man who's always thought the quickest path to success was to tear others down. But the truth is that's always been a mask to distract the eyes of the world from seeing your own insecurities, your own flaws... your own incompetence."

Alec looked murderous. About halfway through Cyrus's speech, Alec had upended his scepter and lowered the gnarled top towards the frozen fire beneath them. The glowing particles had begun their ominous orbit and Alec held it there threateningly. But he didn't move. It almost looked as though he were too enraged and stunned to react.

"Now let me ask you something," Cyrus said, "if we were to find a way out of here, would you come with me?"

Alec barked humorlessly in an attempt to force a laugh. "You wouldn't leave this place either, don't kid yourself."

"No that's where you're wrong," Cyrus insisted, and there was a calm strength in his voice that confirmed to himself that his words were true. "I would be right behind you. We don't belong here, either of us."

Alec's hand whipped the scepter head forward faster than Cyrus would have imagined him capable of, and a jet of fiery ash blazed over Cyrus's shoulder.

It was a single attack, and Cyrus couldn't be certain that it was even meant to hit him, but he was shocked nonetheless. It was also interesting that of all the insults Cyrus had thrown his way, saying he didn't belong was what got a reaction.

Cyrus decided to lean into it. "Can't you feel it, Alec? You invaded the East and were denied, you tried to change the rules at the prisoner swap and lost your brigade, and you tried to stomp us out at the Battle of Westtown Plaza and were defeated. You're a virus, a cancer on this place. The Kingdom is shaking you off."

The next jet of frozen fire from Alec was definitely meant to hit its mark, and it was only with a swift duck and sidestep that Cyrus was able to avoid it. Both brothers were now on the move, circling each other slowly like two predators trying to protect a fresh kill.

"That scepter is mine," Alec snarled, pointing with his own weapon to the one in Cyrus's hand, "and the last thing you're going to do as king is bow down and hand it back to me."

Cyrus smiled, and it wasn't forced this time. "Then make a move."

Alec paused for just a second, and then his face contorted into a visage of rage as he released a battle cry and sprinted towards Cyrus. He launched himself into the air with a kick from the ground and stabbed out with the scepter as he crashed back down. Cyrus was able to parry the worst of the blow with his own staff, but the weapon still tore into his shoulder and sent him careening backwards. Alec did not let up his charge and vaulted after his brother, slashing out with every step he took. Cyrus blocked each attack, but just barely. Every time the scepters connected with one another, angry red sparks burst from beneath the charred bark and stung at his arms like tiny biting insects.

Alec adjusted his grip on his scepter and swung for Cyrus's head like a baseball player up to bat. Cyrus ducked and used the opportunity to spin away, trying to put some distance between himself and his brother. But Alec would not be deterred and turned on his heel, raking the head of the scepter across the ground as he did so. A violent glowing fireball exploded from the ground and blazed through the air, this time catching Cyrus in the thigh.

Cyrus screamed out in pain and fell to one knee, the fabric on his leg sizzling and melting into his flesh. Alec continued his pursuit and raked the head of the scepter along his opposite side, launching another storm of embers towards his opponent. Cyrus dug his good leg into the ground and somersaulted out of the way, landing awkwardly several feet to his right. Alec prowled forward and Cyrus managed to tilt onto his side and flick his own scepter towards him, sending a fairly weak spray of ashes at his brother. It bought him enough time to find his footing again and he stood back up.

Testing his wounded leg tenderly, Cyrus limped backwards a few paces and Alec stalked after him.

"This isn't what I want," Cyrus said, "is this really the person you want to be?"

Alec did not pause his pursuit. "You're damn right it is," he responded with a perceptible hunger in his eyes, "I've never felt better."

Alec sprinted forward again, hammering into Cyrus with his weapon, who stumbled backwards blocking the onslaught. Sparks rained all around them as the scepters clashed and Cyrus for the first time could hear gasps from the surrounding onlookers.

Cyrus continued to be pushed back on the defensive, barely managing to block Alec's swings, when he felt his ankle twist against a bit of uneven terrain and his injured leg gave out. He went down hard, his one knee buckling and crashing onto the hard earth. With Cyrus's head brought low, Alec swung again with his scepter, this time connecting squarely with the side of Cyrus's face. His head pitched sideways and blood sprayed from his mouth. Stars erupted behind his eyes and he suddenly felt like he was falling, slipping to the edge of consciousness. His hands hit the chalky, ash-covered surface of the field and he rolled himself onto his hip, away from the next blow that would no doubt be coming.

Cyrus scrambled along the ground and worked himself back onto one knee, raising his dizzy head just in time to see Alec charging towards him like a lion, his scepter raised above his head and his eyes wild with fury. Cyrus gripped his own scepter in both hands, held it crosswise and raised it over his head as Alec's attack came crashing down. Cyrus winced when the blow came but he could feel the scepter crack in half between his hands. Alec's weapon cleaved straight through the staff of Cyrus's, causing a violent fissure that exploded in a storm of red and gold sparks. Cyrus's head immediately erupted with pressure and he threw the bottom half of the scepter off to his right. It bounced along the glowing earth like a live wire, spitting embers and ash until it finally came to rest some fifteen feet away from them.

Cyrus was entirely unable to keep his head up anymore and he finally lurched forward, slamming his hands down onto the ground. He dropped the top half of his scepter in front of him where it rolled forward innocuously. Alec's boots squared up in front of Cyrus and he looked down at his bloodied brother, kicking the top half of the ruined scepter away from his hand as he did so.

Silence once again filled the air as Cyrus looked down blurrily at the glowing, cracked ground. He wondered whether his brother would actually kill him, but in his haze, found that he did not much care. Alec's voice, exceedingly calm and full of contempt, came from somewhere above him. "Some king you are." The duel was over and Alec had gotten his wish; to best his brother in single-combat before the eyes of the Kingdom.

Alec's boots turned and he strode off confidently towards the thrown bottom half of the scepter. Cyrus raised his head slightly and turned to watch.

Alec closed the distance authoritatively, paused before the shattered piece, and bent forward to grasp it... but he couldn't.

His hand began to contort into a fist. His muscles seized and his arms bent and warped, closing in on themselves like rigor mortis setting in. Alec realized what was happening too late and tried to step backwards, but his legs were buckling, and he was losing all control of his motor functions. He turned towards Cyrus with a twisted snarl on his face and began to yell out in pain and anger. The force of the newly created wormhole was mercilessly dragging him in, but he still raged against it with every ounce of strength he had. He began screaming incoherently as he fell to the glowing earth and tried to use his gnarled, useless hands to claw forward. The vacuum dragged him ever backwards as he locked eyes with Cyrus, his fists creating trenches in their wake as they were pulled along the ashy ground. For the briefest of moments, Cyrus glimpsed a disturbance in the air behind Alec, a sort of bending of the very molecules in the empty space, and he could swear it formed a tunnel. Alec's screams suddenly softened, as though they were being heard from underwater, and he gave one last withering look at Cyrus before his face slid out of focus, the disruption in the air closed in around him, and he was yanked out of the world and sent off to a new one.

Alec was gone. Within the span of a few seconds, Alec had been up and fighting, and now there was no trace of him. The bottom half of the shattered scepter lay ominously on the glowing field, offering no indication of the power it possessed.

Silence had fallen on the neutral territory. Almost everyone present would likely have no idea what had just happened to Alec. But everybody could clearly see that he was no longer here. People from the East and the West began to walk out onto the field, murmuring to one another and scanning around, as though Alec had pulled some magic trick and would be reappearing at a different spot.

As the people began to move closer, Cyrus warned, "Do not go near that," indicating the scepter piece. People did not need a second telling after seeing what happened to Alec and gave the artifact a wide berth. It occurred to Cyrus that they likely thought Alec was dead, a notion he did not plan to dispel them of just yet.

A hand on Cyrus's shoulder alerted him to Jack's arrival, and he turned to find him staring blankly at the air where Alec had been moments before.

"Was that planned?" Jack asked softly.

Cyrus nodded his head in confirmation. "I couldn't kill him. But I knew how much that scepter meant to him. Even damaged, I figured he would go straight for it."

Ydoro was grinning at him and Annica was nodding in approval. Cyrus surveyed the faces of the Westerners and found many of them in states of shock and confusion. They milled around the area as though aimless without their leader. It occurred to Cyrus that Alec had likely never established any sort of leadership structure, and in its absence, it was entirely unclear who his people were supposed to follow. He scanned the faces and finally identified Nel, looking just as lost as the rest, and blending away into the crowd almost guiltily. Cyrus smirked at this, then a thought suddenly occurred to him and he squinted towards the Western treeline. The Neodactyl was gone. Had it simply run off into the forest once Alec fell? Cyrus still didn't know how Alec managed to control the creatures, but without its master, would it obey anyone else? Either way, it was a question for different minds than his own.

"Do you have any idea where you sent him?" Jack asked Cyrus, still staring transfixed at the invisible wormhole around the scepter piece.

"There's no way of knowing," Cyrus answered, "it could be anywhere."

Jack grimaced at the thought. "I fully support you banishing that maniac to another world, but wow, he will have a hard time navigating that new reality alone."

"He won't be alone," Cyrus said blandly, "I'm following behind him."

It seemed to take Jack a moment to comprehend what Cyrus had said, but he finally turned to look at him and read it in his solemn eyes. "No," he said flatly. "You're not thinking this through."

"I have actually," Cyrus responded, "I've known it for a while now. I don't expect you to understand, but I can't send him alone. And I have no place here."

Ydoro was listening from the side and looking crestfallen. Annica was looking carefully at the ground.

"You're their king," Jack exclaimed in exasperation. "Hell, you're my king. You've become the person you were born to be."

"No I haven't," Cyrus said glumly, "I've just found a better version of myself. But this Kingdom doesn't need me, they would thrive on their own. And this isn't my world."

"It's not my world either," Jack retorted, "but I'm finding my place here." Annica looked up at him upon hearing this and smiled faintly.

"And I'm happy for you," Cyrus said, "really I am. But I can't stay."

Ydoro chimed in, "You said it yourself, though. It's not your world you would be going back to."

"What about Cynthia?" Jack asked, "Have you given up trying to find a way back to her?"

"It's not about giving up," Cyrus insisted, "it's about refocusing. I've been trying so hard to fit my life back together in the way it used to be, but there is no fitting it back together. It's shattered, the pieces are lost, and the world has changed."

Silence followed his words, it seemed no one had a valid response to his statement.

Jack shook his head, "I really can't talk you out of this?"

"It's been the plan for a time," Cyrus said softly, "It just didn't need to be said until now."

"And what about everything you've done here?" Ydoro demanded, "All the progress we've made? It'll all come apart."

"No it won't," Cyrus assured him, "it was built to last. If the progress couldn't stand a change in leadership, then it was no progress at all. And the Kingdom will still have good people to see it continue, and build it up better than ever."

Ydodo looked painfully distraught and seemed to be searching for reasons why Cyrus's words were untrue. "And what about your legacy?" he asked, "You built this. It will likely be the greatest thing you ever do in your life, but it'll fade. It'll be nothing more than a story in the Kingdom."

"That's no small thing," Cyrus said with a comforting smile, and he was almost surprised to find how sure of his decision he now felt. "We're people, stories are what we have. It's what separates us from every other creature on this planet. And it's what connects us to people from our time, from times long before, and times long after."

"It'll all just fade into legend," Ydoro persisted.

"And that's okay," Cyrus assured him, "it's what your chess pieces are for. For remembering."

Ydoro had tears in his eyes, and Cyrus hugged him. "Thank you for everything, you're a true friend. And I know the people of the Kingdom will be in good hands."

Ydoro smiled weakly and nodded.

"I've gotta go," Cyrus said to Jack, "that door will not stay open forever."

The crowd that had initially wandered out onto the field had mostly dispersed. Many had walked back the way they had come, though some still lingered along the edges of the forest. Only Cyrus, Jack, Ydoro, and Annica still remained. Cyrus glanced back west and saw no sign of Nel.

Finally, Cyrus turned to Jack, who gave him a smile and a shrug.

"It's been an adventure," Jack stated, trying halfheartedly to treat Cyrus's departure as no big deal.

"I wouldn't be here without you," Cyrus said seriously, and Jack dropped his smile and nodded in understanding. "You'll be okay?"

"Oh yeah," Jack said with a casual wave of his hand, "if I had a dollar for every time I had to reestablish my roots in an alternate reality…"

Cyrus smiled and extended his hand, which Jack grasped firmly, but then pulled him into a hug with his other arm.

"Be careful," Jack said, "please. I can't be looking after you out there."

"I will," Cyrus promised.

"And I've had an idea," Jack said, "that door will eventually close from this side, but will remain open from the other side, so long as that fragment isn't moved. You take good care to remember where you are when you come out the other side. I'll make sure that fragment is never touched again. So you'll always have an open door back if you need it." He thought a moment, then said, "Ydoro, think you can help me out with that?"

Ydoro's face lit up. "Absolutely. We can build something around it so no one can ever touch it. A monument even!"

Cyrus smiled and shook his head. "I'm sure you can do without a monument, but I get the idea."

"Hey, you're not king anymore," Jack teased. "You get no say in how many monuments we want to build."

Cyrus laughed. "Take care of yourselves." He turned to Annica, who had remained silent the entire time, and said, "And Annica, take care of them."

Annica smiled and winked at him. "You got it, my King."

Cyrus finally looked towards the piece of scepter on the glowing field and walked towards it. The pull had weakened dramatically, to the point he could no longer even feel it, but he knew to expect that. He approached slowly, not entirely sure how much warning he would have before being whisked away. With that thought in mind, he looked briefly over his shoulder at his three companions, all watching him somberly. He turned away quickly, not wanting to lose his conviction. He continued a few more paces until he was standing right over the weapon, still not being pulled through. Cyrus furrowed his brow, and then remembered something from his experimenting with Ydoro. He carefully extended the toe of his boot and tapped the scepter-half gently.

The result was instantaneous. Pressure filled his sinuses and a blinding pain behind his eyes clouded his vision. He could feel his fingers cramp, then his elbows and knees. His joints locked, then pressed themselves inward. Cyrus forced his eyes open as he felt a dragging sensation in the pit of his stomach, and looked back to his friends one more time, who were little more than blurry shapes at this point. It was the last look he got of the Kingdom before his eyes were pushed shut and he was carried onward and into another reality.

## CHAPTER SIXTY

# REBIRTH

D arkness, cold and merciless, pressed in on Cyrus. He tried to breathe but choked. He was suffocating. But the cold wasn't just from the darkness, he suddenly realized he was underwater. He thrashed out with his arms and legs and found them to, thankfully, be working again. His head broke the surface of the water, he took an enormous breath, and blinked the bitter salt water from his eyes. He was in the ocean again, and it was dusk. The sun no longer shown in the sky, but its light still dimly illuminated the surface of the water and outlined a coastline of rocky cliffs a short ways away. Cyrus's first thought was that the distance was swimmable, but it would take time, and no small amount of energy.

Cyrus turned and began scanning the horizon around him, searching for Alec. What if he had drowned being forced into the water so unexpectedly? He saw no people as he turned, but to his extreme surprise, silhouetted against the fading sky behind him with several decklights and a spotlight shining brightly, was a ship. It was similar in size to the one that had brought them to the anomaly all that time ago, but clearly a different ship. Without knowing the world he was in, Cyrus quickly debated whether to signal the boat from the water or try swimming to shore. He had no way of knowing who or what was onboard, but at some point he would have to make contact with the people who lived here. Suddenly the spotlight washed over him, bathing him with yellow light, and the decision was made for him.

Voices began yelling back and forth from the deck, looming high above the water, and the ship approached ever closer. Feeling it was now pointless to do anything but ask for aid, Cyrus began signaling over his head, waving his arms wildly and shouting out to his potential rescuers. He gave another scan of the water, but still no sign of his brother. Given the distance of the ship, there was no way Alec could have reached them in the time it took for Cyrus to follow through the wormhole.

The voices on deck were becoming louder and more excitable; he supposed it was not every day they came across a castaway at sea. But then he heard something he was not expecting.

"It's him!" called out an elated voice. It was a voice he knew. A woman's voice.

Cyrus pushed his wild hair out of his face and blinked up at the railings of the ship, squinting against the intensity of the spotlight. There were several people all leaning out over the metal railings, but it was a woman that drew his focus, and even in the dark, it was a face he would know anywhere. It was Cynthia.

"IT'S HIM!" she yelled again, "HE'S HERE!"

Someone shouted to throw down a ladder as people ran back and forth along the deck. Cyrus swam forward with every bit of strength he had, his head spinning with shock and elation. He didn't know how this was even possible, but at the moment he did not much care. The rescue ladder unfurled down the side of the hull and splashed into the water in front of him, and he reached out and grasped it. He was dizzy and disoriented as he climbed out of the water, one rung at a time, and felt the gentle breeze of the ocean air cool his face.

"I can't believe he's here!" Cynthia yelled from above, "Does Alec know?"

"I'm here," came another exuberant voice from the ship deck that was unmistakably his brothers.

Cyrus's chest tightened and he felt the air deflate from his lungs. How was Alec already onboard? That didn't make any sense.

As he reached the final few rungs, multiple hands leaned out and grasped him by the arms, hoisting him up and over the railings. He splashed down onto the metal grating of the ship floor and everyone backed away, apparently in an effort to give him air. Cyrus wheeled on the spot, not caring about any of them but Cynthia. And there she was, pushing her way towards him from between two of the deckhands and beaming at him.

"Cynthia!" Cyrus practically yelled and wrapped his soggy arms around her in an enormous, wet hug. She hugged him back and he felt *right* for the first time in forever. Being locked in this embrace, Cyrus didn't want to ever let her go. Glancing over her shoulder, he saw the crew all smiling and wearing expressions of shock and amazement, and to his surprise, Alec was amongst them, beaming happily from ear to ear.

Cyrus worked his way out of the hug, grasped the back of Cynthia's head, and leaned in to kiss her. But her eyes widened, and she pulled back.

"Woah!" Cynthia exclaimed, further untangling herself from his arms and patting him genially on the shoulder. "I'm happy to see you too, Cyrus."

Something was wrong. She was withdrawing from him, like he had overstepped somehow. Cyrus looked around, his brow furrowed in confusion, and Alec approached him, still wearing that warm, welcoming smile.

"Cyrus!" he exclaimed and he pulled Cyrus into an enormous bearhug.

Cyrus let it happen, still baffled into silence. When Alec released him, Cyrus was standing stiff as a board, a blank expression on his face. And he took a good look at Alec for the first time. He was dry, apart from the damp patches where he had hugged Cyrus. But his clothes were dry, and *modern*. Gone was his black, fraying traveling cloak, his expedition boots, even his scruffy start at a beard. Come to think of it, the topknot in his hair was gone because his long locks were gone too.

He had short, stylish hair, even shorter than he used to wear it at the university. And he was happy to see Cyrus. It occurred to him all at once, like a wave crashing over his very soul. This was *not* the Alec he knew. This was not the brother he had travelled to the Kingdom with, dueled with, and sent through the wormhole. This was the Alec of *this* world.

Cyrus's brain suddenly fogged over, like a cloud overtaking a sunny day. He felt dizzy all over again, and nauseous.

"Welcome back," Alec exclaimed jovially, and to Cyrus's horror, he fed his arm around Cynthia's waist and pulled her close to his side. They were together. Not only that but a quick glance at their fingers revealed they were married.

Cyrus retched. This was all wrong. Something had gone horribly wrong. The dizziness was becoming more than just a fog, he felt like he would lose consciousness. Of all the realities to come to, how could this be the one?

"Hey, you alright?" Alec asked in concern.

"Give him air," Cynthia insisted in an exceedingly worried voice.

"What's happened?" Cyrus demanded, swaying on the spot. Several pairs of hands lunged out to steady him. "Where am I?"

"You're safe," Cynthia tried to assure him, like she was talking to a frightened child. "You're with us now, and you're safe. I can't even imagine what you've been through."

"What I've been through?" Cyrus asked weakly.

"Well yeah," Cynthia said. "Where have you been? You've been gone for months."

Cyrus willed himself to steady out. He had to get a grip. He stayed silent for a long while, gathering his thoughts, before responding. "What happened?"

"You don't remember?" Alec asked in concern. "The shipwreck? That shipping vessel that was pulled off course? We were called out there to investigate. We were out on the dinghies; Lieutenant Allen, Cynthia, and I were in one, but you were ahead of us with Jack, Nel, and Dalton. And then you just vanished, all of you, along with your boat."

"No, no, no," Cyrus stammered, "that's not right. None of this is right."

"It's okay," Cynthia insisted gently, "of course you're disoriented. Alec, let's get him inside."

"Yeah of course," Alec responded, and fed an arm under Cyrus's shoulder. "You okay? Think you can walk?" he asked in concern.

Cyrus mumbled something that was probably incoherent to everyone around him and Alec helped him stagger forward and through the crowd of onlookers.

"You gave us quite a scare," Alec was saying as they walked further into the ship.

"I can't believe we found you," Cynthia said with one hand on his arm in case he were to fall. "I mean, the odds!"

"You must have quite a story to tell," Alec said, but their words were all starting to become background noise to Cyrus. "How 'bout this, we'll get you to your cabin, you can get dried up, a fresh set of clothes, then we can get some warm food in you. And then you can tell us what happened. Where you've been for five months."

Cyrus just nodded vaguely. He was barely listening anymore. And when they showed him to his cabin, they said something that just sounded like gibberish, and fixed him with concerned stares before he closed the door and was finally alone. He exhaled deeply and planted his palms firmly against a bolted-down table. He had to get out of here. Out of this world. He had made his peace with starting over in a new reality, but not this. He stood there, dripping water all over the floor, and squeezed his eyes shut, thinking. What had happened? He must have ended up in an alternate reality where Alec married Cynthia instead of him. That much seemed clear. But the timeline of events that led Cyrus to the Kingdom was still more or less intact. But with subtle changes. Alec boarded the wrong dinghy, and that made all the difference. In this reality, he didn't join Cyrus and the team on the island. He stayed behind and... what? Searched for him apparently.

"Are you alright?" came Alec's voice from the door. He was using gentle, soothing tones like he was talking to someone in the middle of a psychotic episode, which was not far off from how Cyrus was feeling.

"Fine," Cyrus called, but his voice cracked. He stood up from the table and hurried around the room, drying himself off and pulling on a new set of clothes. As he balled up his soaked pants and shirt, he felt something in one of the pockets and reached inside to see what it was. It was a fragment of the scepter. The first tiny shard that he had broken off when he was experimenting in his Easttown home. He had entirely forgotten he had been carrying that around. He pushed it down into the pocket of his new pants and tossed the waterlogged ones aside.

Cyrus opened the door again, and before he knew it, he was whisked further into the ship and found himself sitting in the mess hall, slumped against a dining table with Cynthia eying him apprehensively from the other side. Alec joined a moment later with a steaming cup of coffee and placed it in front of Cyrus.

Cyrus looked down at it and said dryly, "I might need something stronger than this."

Alec and Cynthia both smiled, as if this minor joke confirmed to them that he was still his old self. But he wasn't his old self. Not to them. He wasn't the Cyrus they knew, and never would be. He was a stranger to them.

"I'm sure I can find something in a bit," Alec responded, "but let's get some food in you first. The cook's firing up the ovens back there." He looked older somehow, but also healthier. It was a strange sensation for Cyrus as the eldest sibling to be cared for by his younger brother.

Cyrus nodded and sipped his coffee. He could feel both pairs of eyes boring into him, like he was some specimen on display at a museum. They let him finish half his mug before they spoke again.

"So where have you been?" Cynthia asked cautiously. Alec glanced sideways at her as though questioning if it was a good idea to be so direct with their infirmed guest.

Cyrus waited a long while before responding, contemplating where to begin, and how much to say. "I was on an island," he finally began softly. "An island ruled by a mad king. It was different than our world. There were creatures I'd never seen before, people who had never seen the outside world."

Alec and Cynthia exchanged a worried glance.

"I know it's hard to accept," Cyrus answered their unasked question, "but I promise you every word is true. And not everyone made it. We were set upon instantly when we landed, and the King, he…" Cyrus trailed off, not entirely sure how to explain his journey without revealing that there was an alternate version of Alec with them. "Not everyone survived that first encounter, but those of us who did were put to work. You have to understand, no one leaves this place. Some of the people who lived in town, all of them maybe, they ended up there from different… places." He had almost said *'different worlds'* but that would invite uncomfortable questions. "But we stormed the Temple, the sort of fortress where the King lived, and overthrew him. And then we began to rule in his stead."

Alec was expressionless but Cynthia was gaping at him. Cyrus couldn't tell if this was out of shock or actual disbelief. He probably sounded crazy.

"Then how did you get back?" Cynthia asked tentatively.

Cyrus didn't know exactly how to answer this without explaining the battle for the Kingdom. "I made a discovery that allowed me to open… doors to the outside world. But I didn't know where it would lead me."

"Doors?" Alec repeated. "Can you get back through? I mean from this side?"

"I… I don't think so," Cyrus answered. He was remembering how Jack and Ydoro had promised to leave the scepter fragment undisturbed, in case he needed a way back, but he would never be able to find it out at sea.

"There were other survivors?" Cynthia pressed.

"There were," Cyrus confirmed, "but they didn't want to return."

Cynthia looked stunned by this, but Cyrus suddenly thought of how foolish he had been to follow the door without knowing where it led. He could have made a life in the Kingdom like Jack, if he had just tried. It would have been infinitely better than whatever hell he had now found himself in.

"We should still try," Alec said, "see if we can find a way."

"We can't," Cyrus said firmly. "The door's closed."

At that moment the cook set a bowl of soup down on the table in front of Cyrus and he jumped slightly, almost having forgotten where he was.

"Eat up," Alec insisted, "I'm gonna have a word with Cynthia, I'll be right back."

The two of them got up from the table and stepped out into the hall. Cyrus ladled several spoonfulls of the brown soup into his mouth. It had very little taste, or maybe he just didn't care. He glanced towards the doorway that Alec and Cynthia had disappeared through and wondered what they were saying about him. Probably trying to determine if he was out of his mind or not. Truth be told, Cyrus didn't care what they thought.

Cyrus finished the entire bowl of soup, realizing he must have been hungrier than he thought, and pushed the empty dishes away from him. He reached down absent-mindedly and felt the scepter shard in his pocket. It suddenly occurred to him that Dalton had warned him to always carry a piece of the scepter with whenever travelling through a door. What had he said? *'If you don't, you will become unte...'* That was it, he was pretty sure. *Untethered* maybe? Untethered from what? Maybe from his world? Maybe that was how he had miraculously come across Cynthia and Alec out at sea? Because otherwise, what were the chances he would open a door exactly where their ship was searching? And Alec didn't have a fragment with him when he went through the door, so maybe that explained why he was not here. He had an entire scepter with him, but perhaps that was different. Cyrus's head was beginning to spin.

The door from the hallway opened again and Alec walked back in, wearing a supportive but somewhat concerned smile on his face. It was so incredibly strange to look into the eyes of his brother-turned-former-enemy and see only worry looking back at him. Cynthia did not follow.

"How are you managing?" Alec asked as he eased himself back into the chair across from Cyrus. "I can't even imagine what this must be like, having to explain all of this."

Cyrus laughed humorlessly. Alec didn't know the half of it.

"We do believe you, though," Alec continued in a reassuring tone, "we want you to know that." As though reading Cyrus's thoughts about Cynthia's absence, Alec said gently, "I think it was a little much for Cynthia, but she's here for you. We both are."

Cyrus shook his head. It wasn't *his* Cynthia, and he had to keep reminding himself of that. The same way that this wasn't the Alec he knew, this Cynthia had not shared a life with Cyrus. It was incredibly important for his own sanity to keep that in mind.

"It really is good to see you," Alec said as though worried if he stopped saying reassuring words, Cyrus would lose it.

"It's just... this is all wrong," Cyrus began, "you have no idea what it was like in that Kingdom. And now that I'm back, everything feels different. I don't know how to just pick up the pieces, I've lost too much."

"You *just* made it back," Alec said softly, "don't push yourself, these things take time. You'll adjust back into our world."

Alec was talking about returning to life after experiencing a trauma, but he didn't understand the other aspect, the real problem. Alec seemed to recognize that his words were not offering the desired comfort. Attempting a different tactic, he finally said, "Hey, how 'bout that drink? And maybe some fresh air."

Alec stood from the table and helped himself around the back to the kitchen area, rummaging through cabinets and drawers. Cyrus thought he could probably use some fresh air, but it wouldn't help his spinning head. Neither would a drink for that matter. His thoughts floated to Jack, Annica, and Ydoro back in the Kingdom. They were getting back to their lives right now, and Cyrus could have joined them. He wondered briefly what would happen now that Alec was gone. Would the Easttown leadership move into the vacated Temple now? Would Nel ever be seen again? The way she had slunk off in the aftermath of the duel made him wonder. She had bet everything on Alec.

"Aha!" Alec exclaimed victoriously, walking back around the counter holding two glasses and a bottle of some sort of liquor. "C'mon Cy, the ocean air will do you good."

They walked out to the deck and up towards the bow of the ship. The sun had fully set by now and deep grey and blue streaks now painted the dark sky. White waves crashed below them soothingly as the ship plowed onward. The crew had mostly vacated the outer decks as well, leaving a quiet, peaceful air to the night. Alec poured two generous glasses of the amber liquid and handed one to Cyrus while raising his own.

"To your return," Alec declared, "the Dorn's are reunited again."

Cyrus nodded his head, unable to explain out loud why Alec's toast was tragic and crushing.

Cyrus responded with his own toast, "to the Kingdom."

Alec drank, but furrowed his brow and smiled a bit in confusion. "You miss the place?"

Cyrus wasn't sure how to answer that, and at first didn't plan to. But before he knew it, he was just talking, as though he had no control over the words softly dribbling out of his mouth. "It was incredible, truth be told. We made real change there. I honestly believe the most important things I'll ever do in my life were on that island. I became a person I never dreamed I could be, and found qualities in myself I didn't even know existed. We built a town... hell, we built a civilization, you should have seen it. I did things I never knew I could do."

Alec watched him quietly until he had stopped speaking. "It sounds like a magical place," he finally said softly.

"It wasn't all magical," Cyrus corrected himself, "it was also harsh and unforgiving. And who knows, maybe that's what made the victories so sweet, that they were hard fought for. But there was plenty of violence... and death." Cyrus paused, reflecting on his first days in the Kingdom. "When we first arrived, I was a different person entirely. And when the King came and tore us down, I thought we'd never get up again. I was so terrified of losing everything, and so certain it was my fault."

"And was it?" Alec asked carefully.

Cyrus thought for a long moment before answering. "I don't think so. The more I mull it over, the more I'm certain the King had picked one of us to kill from the start. To make his point."

Alec looked sick at the prospect. He raised his glass and said, "To Dalton, he was a good man."

Cyrus clinked his glass against Alec's, took a swig, and then paused. His heart started beating incredibly fast, and at first, he couldn't identify why.

"It sounds like you grew a hell of a lot while you were out there," Alec continued.

But Cyrus had stopped listening. Something was wrong. He looked sideways at his brother, waiting for him to look back. Alec was gazing down at the foaming surf as he talked, but when he finally seemed to sense Cyrus's gaze upon him, he turned and their eyes locked. And there it was. The question Cyrus had been tossing around in his head for the past few seconds was answered by one look. Cyrus had never said that Dalton was the person who had died.

Alec stared back at him benignly, but Cyrus had seen it when the realization clicked, and something behind his brothers' eyes changed. A part of himself that he had been trying to hide had bubbled forward for just a second, and both of them knew it. The only way Alec could have known that Dalton had died was if he had been there. And if he had been there for Dalton's death, he had been there when they stormed the Temple, took control of the Neodactyls, split the Kingdom in two, battled in Westtown Square, and dueled in the Fire Fields. This was not an Alec from another reality, it was the Alec he had always known... and the deranged King of the West.

Alec didn't react. But Cyrus had seen him register his misstep. Alec knew he had said something he shouldn't have. But he stayed quiet and took another sip of his drink.

How was this possible? How was *this* Alec, clean cut and successful, not to mention happily married to Cyrus's wife, also the Alec from the Kingdom? The very person he had dueled with no more than an hour ago.

*Untethered*. Dalton's word. Cyrus felt at the scepter fragment in his pocket and thought he understood. It wasn't untethered from his *world*. It was untethered from *time*. The fragment in his pocket had kept Cyrus tied to his own time, but not Alec.

"How long ago did you get back?" Cyrus finally asked quietly. He hoped Alec was done playing games and would answer honestly. What was the point of the charade at this point?

"Seven years," Alec answered simply.

Cyrus shook his head in disbelief. He felt numb, and somehow rooted to the spot. He wanted to do something, anything, but couldn't seem to find the strength. He thought of throwing himself over the railing and into the dark ocean, he thought of smashing the glass in his hand and burying the edge into Alec's throat, and he thought of simply running. But he did nothing. Alec had used his head start in this world to steal Cyrus's life. And by all accounts he had succeeded.

"Why the act?" Cyrus asked.

Alec finally turned to face him, and the familiar hunger had started to return to his eyes. "So I could see your face when you realized you were in *my* world now."

Cyrus turned his body to square up in front of his brother. His chest felt like it was on fire, seething with rage. He could reach out right now, close his hands around Alec's windpipe and squeeze the life out of him. As Alec stared him down, the desire became almost unbearable.

"You started the drinks without me?" came a voice from behind them, and Cyrus turned to see Cynthia approaching with a smile on her face. "Hang on a sec, I'll grab a glass."

She walked back into the ship, a slight skip in her step as she remained blissfully ignorant to the true situation, and the way her life had been hijacked. But she would no doubt be returning any moment. This was not the time to make a scene. Cyrus turned back to face the ocean. Alec did the same.

"So what happens now?" Cyrus asked.

"Make yourself comfortable," Alec answered, and there was a definite tone of venomous satisfaction in his voice, "you've got a long road of rediscovery ahead of you."

This wasn't done. This could not be the end. Something was painfully evident to Cyrus; the war between them was not over. Whether in this reality or in the next, Alec Dorn was his bitter rival. No longer brothers of any sort, Cyrus would fight Alec through every world they found themselves in until he clawed his way back home. Perhaps that was their destiny, who could say. There was a morbid comfort in that, as though it gave him purpose, and clarity of mind.

Cyrus took the final swig from his glass and gazed at the dark horizon. One thing was certain and vital to keep in his mind, no matter what Alec had done; Cyrus had changed in his time on the island. He was not the man he used to be. The man that had boarded the expedition vessel five months back had been a scholarly, gregarious yet self-centered family man, somebody who was perhaps deeply flawed but content, important in his own right but would be forgotten by time, respected yet unremarkable. The man who now stood shoulder to shoulder with his one-time brother turned hateful enemy would be remembered by history. He had summoned the power of an entire civilization when they were at their weakest, overthrown a tyrant, and manipulated the very fabric of reality. Alec would come to know the strength that Cyrus Dorn had conjured within himself. He was a leader. He was a warrior. He was a king.

# AUTHOR BIO

Photograph by Katie Stukel

A storyteller at heart from a young age, Ryan Freerksen grew up filming intricate (and absurdly long) Claymation movies on his old Hi-8 camcorder before attending college for filmmaking. Almost a decade would pass before he realized his love for film was not rooted in its technical aspects but rather the crafting of a captivating tale. The characters of *Somewhere* clawed their way out of his subconscious one day while he worked a particularly toxic desk job, and they were persistent enough that he found his narrative voice once again. He currently lives in Illinois with his wife Katie.

Made in the USA
Columbia, SC
29 June 2024

12cc8bc4-d934-4bcd-965b-451fdd4c423dR01